The WILDERLING

CLAIRE LORRIMER

BALLANTINE BOOKS • NEW YORK

Library of Congress Catalog Card Number: 82-90942

ISBN 0-345-30917-0

This edition published by arrangement with Arlington Books (Publishers) Ltd.

Manufactured in the United States of America

First Ballantine Books Edition: July 1983

For my father and my uncle,
who were part of it all.

The Wildering: Any plant growing wild, especially one escaped from culture.

From: *The 'King's English' Dictionary*

Acknowledgements

I would like to thank all the people who have so willingly volunteered their help during the research for this book. They are too numerous for their contributions to be mentioned individually, but I must thank the following:-

Miss Margaret Slade (Archivist at The British Red Cross Society); The Registrar (St Mary's Hospital, Roehampton); Mr. Jarman (The Imperial War Museum); The American Embassy; Mrs. Fry (Secretary to The Norland Nursery Training College); G. Clark (aeronautics); The staffs of: The British, East Grinstead, Croydon, Edenbridge and Sevenoaks libraries.

I particularly wish to thank Miss Alenka Lavrencic and Miss Mary Robinson who, despite their busy lives, found time to give advice and facts.

As always, I must acknowledge the invaluable contributions of my research assistant and secretary, Penrose Scott, and the hard work of Joy Tait and my team of assistants, Wendy Rose, Janice Wade and Florence Holden.

Finally, I offer my thanks once more to my family for their encouragement, patience and support.

Author's Note

The Wilderling is not a war story. It is a novel about the
Rochford family and the younger generation of Rochfords
who inevitably become involved in the First World War.

My father, who was wounded first at Ypres and then on
the Somme, did not talk very much about his life in the
trenches, although he left me with a lasting impression of
the horrors and the dangers and an awareness of the enormous sense of patriotism that sustained young men like
himself. He believed in England as other men believe in
God, and steadfastly maintained that there was no better
person in the world than an Englishman.

In writing this book I regret that he is no longer alive to
give me a better understanding of his war.

I regret also that I never knew my uncle who died aged
twenty-three. I have only a snapshot of him in Royal Flying
Corps uniform standing beside his Sopwith Camel, and his
citation from George V. On 30th March 1916, he was
awarded the Military Cross for conspicuous gallantry, having saved the lives of two of his men under heavy fire.

The characters I have created in this book are very real
to me and fiction has been apt to become inextricably confused with fact. I have found myself wondering whether
Oliver might have flown his airplane alongside my
uncle's? Could George have gone 'over the top' with my
father? I suppose it doesn't really matter but I am saddened
by the thought that many of today's children are unaware
why we sell replicas of the Flanders poppies. I would like
to think that the readers of this family saga will believe, as
I do, in the credibility of its characters, fictitious or otherwise, and that as Lawrence Binyon wrote:

"...*at the going down of the sun and in the morning
we will remember them.*"

Claire Lorrimer, 1982

PART ONE
1911–1912

When she sleeps, her soul, I know,
Goes a wanderer on the air,
Wings where I may never go,
Leaves her lying, still and fair,
Waiting, empty, laid aside,
Like a dress upon a chair…
This I know, and yet I know
Doubts that will not be denied.

RUPERT BROOKE, *Doubts*

Prologue

⟨ ∼ ⟩

1911

ON 1ST FEBRUARY, 1911, LORD ROCHFORD OF ROCHFORD MANOR died. The family lawyer, Richard Bartholomew, dispatched telegrams to the four close relatives whose presence he judged most immediately necessary. He doubted if the news he was obliged to impart would cause any grief, although he anticipated that it would cause major repercussions in the family. But he could not foresee the far-reaching and momentous effect it would have upon all their lives.

The first of these telegrams was sent to Lady Rochford, to her home in San Francisco, California, United States of America.

"Deeply regret to advise you that Lord Rochford died this morning following a fall while hunting stop please arrange to travel to England immediately stop urgent matters require your attention stop Richard Bartholomew."

The second, identical in content, was sent to the late Lord Rochford's brother, Pelham, and addressed to his house in the Rue d'Artois, Paris, France.

The third was dispatched to the head mistress of the Norbury Establishment for Young Ladies.

"Please advise Lucienne Rochford that her father died last night stop a car will collect her at four this afternoon stop signed Bartholomew family lawyer."

The fourth telegram, containing a great deal more information, was sent to Lord Rochford's eldest brother, Tobias, and delivered to his bachelor establishment adjacent to the home of his sister-in-law in San Francisco. Following the formal announcement of Lord Rochford's death, the lawyer had added:

"Please prepare Lady Rochford for the presence of her daughter Lucienne known to her as Sophia stop the girl returned from France and was reunited with her late father

3

nine months ago stop therefore imperative Lady Rochford return immediately."

At six o'clock that same evening, Richard Bartholomew silently handed Lucienne Rochford the telegram he had just received announcing the imminent arrival of the mother she had never known.

Chapter 1

ᕙᕗ

February 1911

Rᴵᴄʜᴀʀᴅ Bᴀʀᴛʜᴏʟᴏᴍᴇᴡ ᴡᴀʟᴋᴇᴅ ᴏᴠᴇʀ ᴛᴏ ᴛʜᴇ ꜰɪʟɪɴɢ ᴄᴀʙɪɴᴇᴛ and drew out the largest of the many thick folders it contained. On its cover was written *The Rochford File*, in his father's beautiful copperplate hand.

He took the file over to his desk and sat down, wishing yet again that his father was still alive. Although he himself was a fully qualified lawyer, at twenty-six Richard did not have the confidence born of experience and the Rochfords were the firm's biggest clients. It was not only an honor to be their lawyer but an absolute necessity, for in the small village of Havorhurst, there was little enough legal business to keep the firm financially afloat.

Sighing, he turned the pages until he reached the year 1894. This was the year the late Lord Rochford's first child was born.

March 14th. Born to Lady Rochford, girl.

March 15th. Baby baptised Sophia Lucienne. Died during the night. Buried St. Stephens Church, Havorhurst.

Those terse notes were followed by several pages of entries relating to affairs of the estate. Nothing of importance occurred until 1899.

February 1st. Son born to Lady Rochford.

February 2nd. Lord Rochford called about his Will.

December 22nd. Child christened Oliver Cedric in St. Stephens.

There were no further major events until 1903, when Lady Rochford returned from France where she had given birth to a baby girl, Alice Silvie, which happy occasion was overshadowed by the disappearance of Rupert Rochford with Dr. Forbes' son, Adrian. The last record for 1903 was of the death and burial of old Lady Rochford, Lord Rochford's grandmother.

Richard Bartholomew turned over the page to the following year and now his interest quickened. Here was the second reference to the child, Sophia. Lady Rochford had made a confidential visit to his father expressing her doubts as to the death of the baby girl.

"No proof to back suspicions," his father had commented tersely. *"Lady Rochford obviously overwrought. Her doubts raised by unfortunate ramblings of her aunt, Mildred Rochford, presently suffering effects of a stroke. Explained I could not act on such vague suspicions."*

But early in the following year, 1905, Lord Rochford had instigated an enquiry and Richard's father had eventually attended a Consistory Court Hearing in Rochester. The request for an exhumation of the child's coffin had been granted and on March 14th his father's entry read:

"Exhumation took place at dawn. No body but a brick in place of corpse. Deeply shocked. Case now in the hands of the police."

On the next day was a single line announcing the death of Mildred Rochford, the one person his father had hoped might clear up the mystery.

A month later the youngest brother, Francis, had died as the result of an unfortunate accident at the Manor. Richard Bartholomew remembered the funeral clearly, although his father had not discussed the details of the accident with him.

Throughout the remainder of the year 1905, the file contained detailed notes of the various police enquiries, their suspicions endorsed by his father that the family doctor had been involved in the unfortunate disappearance of the Rochford child. Dr. Forbes, Lady Rochford and her sister-in-law, Mildred, were the only ones present on the night the baby had supposedly died. But by 1906, the law was forced to abandon any hope of finding the child.

"She has vanished without trace and I doubt the mystery will ever be solved," his father had written.

Richard reflected sadly that the old man had died without knowing that Sophia Lucienne Rochford had arrived home on 7th May, 1910. Was it only nine months ago, he asked himself, that he had been urgently summoned to Rochford Manor to be told the astonishing news?

Richard closed the file, relying now on his memory of that meeting to clarify his thoughts. His first impression that afternoon was that Lord Rochford was clearly very drunk. His client stood in the library, back to the fire, red-faced and only partly coherent as he rambled on for some time about his wife's infidelity and her desertion of him. Richard had heard before his jealous assertions of Lady Rochford's affair with his eldest brother, Tobias, who had followed her to America. Lord Rochford had wanted Richard to begin divorce proceedings against his wife but the lawyer had been forced to point out that there was not one shred of evidence of adultery. Nor, as Lord Rochford kept insisting, that either his son, Oliver, or his youngest daughter, Alice, were illegitimate.

It had been close on half an hour before his client had suddenly come out with the problem he wanted Richard to deal with—the amazing appearance of his missing daughter, Sophia.

The girl had not been present. For reasons Richard was later to understand, she had remained at home only two days before her father had found a boarding establishment to which she had been hastily dispatched. Bit by bit, he had managed to elicit the facts from his inebriated client. Apparently the child had grown up in a convent orphanage in France. How she got there remained a mystery. At the age of ten she had been put into domestic service with a hat-maker in Paris.

The thought of a Rochford performing the menial tasks of a maid was shocking enough, Richard had thought, but it was several minutes before he could bring himself to believe the end of Lord Rochford's garbled story. Sophia—Sophie as she was then called—had been persuaded to change her employment and went to work as a waitress in a brothel called *Le Ciel Rouge*. Inevitably she progressed (or should the word have been regressed, he wondered) into the oldest profession in the world, and had subsequently been earning her keep in this house of ill-repute.

Lord Rochford did not appear to be half as shocked as was Richard himself. He swept aside Richard's doubts, swearing that the girl had seemed shameless and told him quite openly what she had been about.

"She might well have spent the rest of her young life there but for that idiot Dr. Forbes. Took it into his head four years ago to go and find her, y'know," Lord Rochford informed him, helping himself to yet another whiskey.

So his father's suspicions had been well-founded, Richard thought now. Then, he had felt only concern lest the police might become reinvolved if Forbes proved to have been the child's abductor and his illustrious client were caught up in a most unsavory scandal.

But, as Lord Rochford pointed out with remarkable shrewdness for a man who had certainly consumed half a bottle of whiskey if not a great deal more, Forbes was dead and could not be questioned as to how he had known where to find Sophia Rochford.

"We shall have to try to solve the riddle ourselves—discreetly!" Lord Rochford had reiterated several times. His daughter had told him that three years ago Forbes had offered to buy her out of her terrible employment and according to Sophia, he had gone back to England to raise the money her employer was demanding. But he never returned.

Richard reopened the file and turned back to the entries made in that year. He felt a moment of triumph when he found a brief comment by his father stating that the old doctor had died in the same month as Sophia claimed to have seen him. Small wonder he had not returned for her, then! Forbes had given the girl no clue as to her real identity but had presented her with a gold locket. By a stroke of Fate, the locket had been broken and on the back of the photograph it contained, were the names Cedric and Alice Rochford and the date of their wedding at Havorhurst. With commendable courage, the sixteen-year-old girl had saved sufficient money and set out for England to see if she could trace her forbears.

"She arrived in Havorhurst three days ago," Lord Rochford had ended his story. "The vicar looked up the register and next day, she was on my doorstep—the very day her mother departed for America."

"You have proof the girl *is* your daughter?" Richard had asked anxiously.

But Lord Rochford was in no doubt—and for one main reason. It seemed Sophia was a walking image of her mother—the only difference being in the color of her eyes.

"And those could as well be my sister Dorothy's—or Rupert's," Lord Rochford stated. "I'm convinced she's my daughter, Bartholomew, and now I want you to prove it. There's one other clue that might help you—that Convent she went to was not very far from the country house in Épernay owned by my late aunt, Lucienne le Chevalier. My grandmother was French, you may remember, and Aunt Lucienne was her niece. I suspect my grandmother had a hand in all this and I mean to find out what really happened."

Richard had not understood at first why Lord Rochford had sent his daughter away so hurriedly. But then he was given a graphic description of the girl and understood his precipitateness.

"Not only was she dressed like a street-walker but she talked like one!" Lord Rochford had grunted. "Couldn't let the servants start gossiping; it would be all round the village in no time. I'm told this boarding establishment is renowned for its success in training girls to speak and behave like young ladies. They take a great many children of the nouveaux riches who are hoping to raise their social standing by marrying their girls off to gentlemen. My daughter can stay there until they've reeducated her. After all, she has the right breeding and I'll say this much, apart from her clothes and the paint on her face, she looks well-bred. Dainty little thing! Pretty, too. Once the school has finished with her she can run Rochford now m'wife's left me."

It had been Richard's opinion that Lord Rochford should have notified his wife at once of the reappearance of the child. But his client would not listen to the suggestions. Bitter and unforgiving, he was determined to keep Lady Rochford in ignorance and Richard had no legal justification for insisting otherwise.

The following day, Richard had been called to the house again and instructed to set about finding the missing pieces of the puzzle. He left at once for France, armed with a faded sepia photograph of the late Mildred Rochford and a miniature of Willow, Lady Rochford, as a young girl.

"Spittin' image of Sophia," Lord Rochford told him. "Like enough to get the girl identified."

It had not taken long to verify the girl's story. The Mother Superior of the Convent identified Aunt Mildred as the woman who had brought the child to her, although she referred to her as Miss Beresford—obviously a pseudonym.

But there the clues to the past ended and Richard had to return to his client without solving the riddle as to how or why the baby had been spirited away from her mother and sent to France.

It was a lucky afterthought that had prompted Richard Bartholomew to ask Lord Rochford to look once more through his grandmother's effects to ascertain that there were no further clues. Amongst the letters the old lady had kept from her soldier husband, they had found one from a French priest, called Father Mattieu, which at long last provided the vital missing piece of the puzzle.

Dated October 1896, it read:

"Your most generous contributions both to my Church and to our orphanage arrived safely together with your letter. I am sure I do not need to tell you, dear Lady Rochford, how anxious I am to assist you in this delicate matter. I can assure you a place will be found for the child in the Convent orphanage where she will be carefully looked after in total anonymity. I understand perfectly your desire to protect your illustrious family name from any possible rumor concerning the child's abnormality and your secret shall remain with me as if you had spoken in the Confessional. Not even the Mother Superior will be advised as to the child's true identity..."

There were further flowery phrases and expressions of gratitude and a receipt for a banker's draft of five hundred pounds sterling—a large enough sum to draw a whistle of surprise from Lord Rochford.

"Hell of a lot to pay out for hush money," he had said bluntly.

"But why, Sir?" Richard Bartholomew asked. "*Why* did your grandmother go to such trouble to hide the baby?"

Lord Rochford shrugged his shoulders.

"Had this bee in her bonnet about insanity," he explained. "My mother died of melancholia and before that, there had been two girls who died in infancy from what was then diagnosed as 'brain storms.' Her last child, my sister Dorothy, was malformed. Grandmère believed there was a hereditary strain running through the distaff side of the Rochfords. Doubtless she feared the next generation of girls would be abnormal in some way too. I seem to recall that the baby was premature and a bit unsightly." He frowned thoughtfully.

"Forbes must have helped Grandmère—but then he was always a weakling and did what my grandmother told him. In any event, my wife and I were told that the baby had died. Since those days, of course, my brother Toby has disproved the insanity fears, established that Dorothy had had poliomyelitis and that the infants had died of diphtheria. By the look of it, there's nothing wrong with this girl, either. Pretty little thing!"

Richard put the Rochford file back in the drawer thoughtfully. By 'nothing wrong with the girl,' Lord Rochford must have meant she had no physical deformities. But her way of life was surely a terrible and irreversible handicap! He could not understand how Lord Rochford could pay so little regard to it. Yet he had seemed concerned only with avoiding any scandal.

"Can't have the Rochford good name put at risk!" he kept reiterating. "That's why I decided to call the girl by her second name—Lucienne. Less chance of anyone ever connecting her in the future with Sophie Miller, as she was known in France. As for my grandmother—there's no point blackening her name by letting the truth be known."

He had concocted a wild story about the baby being abducted by the wet-nurse and how when she died, she had confessed the truth and Lucienne's whereabouts at last became known.

Much as Richard wished to please his most important client, he refused to have any part in this explanation Lord Rochford intended to give to his friends and neighbors. It was tantamount to being criminal slander, he had pointed out—putting the blame, which should be laid at his grandmother's door—onto the shoulders of an innocent woman who was not alive to defend herself.

But his protests were swept aside and he had been firmly instructed to mind his own business.

Not for the first time, Richard wished his father were still alive to advise him. He himself saw no way in which he could do more than warn Lord Rochford of his legal position. He could not forbid him to repeat such a palpable lie.

Now the man was dead and he, Richard, had taken it upon himself this morning to advise Lady Rochford of her child's existence, contrary to his client's orders. When she arrived in England, he would be obliged to tell her also of her daughter's past—a task he dreaded.

It occurred to him now, that he might be able to pass on this unsavory duty to Mrs. Silvie Rochford, Lady Rochford's sister-in-law. She would not be so affected as the girl's mother by such shocking revelations.

Richard glanced at his watch. It was almost four o'clock. Soon Lucienne Rochford would be arriving back from her boarding establishment and he must go up to Rochford Manor to meet her. Curiosity and anxiety gripped him alternately. He was uncertain, too, of her feelings toward the dead man laid out on his bed awaiting burial. He hoped the girl would not be too distressed at the sudden death of her father. Fortunately, he would not be obliged to tell her that the man had been hopelessly drunk when he had fallen from his horse. The family doctor, Peter Rose, had not deemed it necessary to put as cause of death anything more than the bare fact that Lord Rochford had broken his neck. Privately he had told Richard that his liver was so damaged by alcohol that the severe fall might have ruptured it and finished him off. The truth was, neither he, Rose, nor anyone else had ever liked Lord Rochford, and when his wife left him taking the two children with her to America, no one had blamed her; nor blamed the eldest of the brothers for going with her. Tobias Rochford was as well liked as his brother had been unpopular.

Richard reached for his black frock-coat and hat from the mahogany clothes-stand and picked up his kid gloves and malacca cane. Unless the Rochford chauffeur had lost his way, he should be back with his passenger at any moment, he thought. It would not do for Richard to arrive at the Manor late.

But he was in plenty of time. The parlor-maid conducted him to the library and left him with copies of *The Illustrated London News* and *Punch*. Within five minutes, she returned bearing a large silver tray. Miss Rochford had arrived, she told him, and would join him in the library for tea.

Although Lord Rochford had told Richard how like the daughter was to her mother, he was totally unprepared for the sight of the girl who now came into the room. Her bone structure was delicately aristocratic, her movements fluid and graceful. Dainty, perfectly proportioned, she looked every inch what he knew she was not—an innocent, fresh, sixteen-year-old child on the brink of womanhood. Her voice when she spoke, was melodious with a slight French accent. Her opening remark was even more of a surprise to him.

"You are Mr. Bartholomew, the lawyer, are you not? Tell me, please, is it true that the Will is not read until after the funeral?"

Richard managed with practised control to hide the brief sense of shock her words engendered. After all, he told himself, less than nine months ago Lucienne Rochford had not even known of her father's existence. Only convention required her to show some grief at his death.

Avoiding a direct reply to the girl's question, he said:

"I have taken the liberty of making tentative arrangements for your father's funeral for the day after tomorrow, Miss

Rochford. Your uncle and aunt in Paris have telegraphed to say they will be here tomorrow. Your Uncle Tobias will be accompanying your mother from America."

The girl's large, violet-blue eyes which had been wide with curiosity, now flashed brilliantly as she leant forward in her chair, frowning.

"What has my mother to do with this? You may not be aware, Mr. Bartholomew, that my father made it quite clear to me that her name was not to be mentioned in this house. I do not want her here."

Richard coughed uneasily.

"Forgive me for interrupting you, Miss Rochford, but I must comply with the law, even if it should contravene your father's...er...his private feelings. Your parents were not divorced. Lady Rochford retains her legal status as his wife and is now your legal guardian."

Lucienne Rochford's eyes narrowed as she digested this information. The man sitting opposite her felt a moment of astonishment at the look of calculation openly apparent on the girl's delicate young face. He had momentarily forgotten the past events of her life and had been entirely captivated by the youthful innocence of her outward appearance. In her prim, high-necked, blue serge school dress, she looked even younger than her sixteen years.

"Your mother is a charming and gracious lady," he added quietly. "I am sure you will very quickly come to admire and love her."

Lucienne's small mouth pursed into a sulky pout. She tossed her head slightly, loosening a coil of ash-blonde hair.

"I do not want to meet this woman who deserted my father," she said coldly. "Moreover, I can never feel affection for her—nor, it would seem, does she have any affection for me. Since my return home, she has made no effort to come to England to see me."

Despite himself, Richard smiled.

"Lady Rochford can hardly be blamed for that omission," he said gently, "since she was unaware until yesterday of your existence. Your father forbade me to advise her of your unexpected return to the family fold. In fact, no one was to be made aware of your presence until you had completed your year in Norbury."

Lucienne gave a quick, Gallic shrug of her shoulders.

"It makes no difference," she said, her tongue rolling on

the 'r' in a manner which betrayed her French upbringing. "But it is a waste of her time to come to England now. I shall obey my father's wishes and she shall not be allowed in my house."

This time, the young lawyer could not withhold the anxious gasp which escaped his lips.

"Miss Rochford, I am afraid you are under a considerable misapprehension if you believe that this will be...er, *your* house. Your young brother, Oliver, is of course the new Lord Rochford."

The look in the girl's eyes was one of total disbelief. She gave a light, pretty laugh of genuine amusement.

"It is you who are mistaken, Mr. Bartholomew. My father promised me that I would be his heir; that if I learned to behave like a real lady, he would give Rochford Manor to me to run as I pleased—the servants—everything. He *promised* me."

Richard looked away from her searching gaze, his cheeks coloring slightly with embarrassment.

"I am very sorry to have to disappoint you, Miss Rochford, but there has obviously been some misunderstanding. It was certainly your father's wish that when you had completed your schooling, you would return here to take control of the house and act as his hostess. In the absence of Lady Rochford, it was a natural and sensible plan. But the estate—it is not within Lord Rochford's control. It is entailed, you see—that is to say, it passes automatically to the eldest male heir. In this instance, that is Oliver. Were there no male offspring, the title and estate would pass to your father's eldest brother. Do you understand?"

The girl jumped to her feet, two red spots of anger burning in her pale cheeks, her eyes flashing and her veneer of demureness gone.

"Since you are a man of the law, Mr. Bartholomew, of necessity I must believe you. But it is intolerable, *intolérable*," she repeated in French. "My father tricked me...cheated me. He is like all men—not to be trusted. And to think that I, who should have known better, allowed myself to believe him..."

Suddenly she burst into tears. Richard sprang to his feet and the next moment the girl threw herself into his arms and was sobbing against his shoulder.

"Please, please try to calm yourself," he said awkwardly,

the more so as her proximity had begun to affect his emotions in ways that were very far from professional. Her perfume was clouding his senses and he was painfully aware of the gentle heaving of her breasts against his chest, and the sweet, silky softness of her hair against his chin. Gently he eased her back into her chair and with a sigh of relief, seated himself at a safe distance opposite her.

Lucienne Rochford blew her nose delicately into a tiny lace handkerchief and ventured a glance at her companion from beneath dark, damp lashes.

"You will help me, will you not?" she asked appealingly. "If what you tell me is true, I have nothing—nothing in the world that is mine. Not even my name..." she added with a hint of genuine bitterness.

"Of that at least, I can reassure you," the young man said eagerly. "You were baptized Sophia Lucienne Rochford and your name is in the church register. I have seen it myself. I think your father's decision that you should be called Lucienne was, in the circumstances, a wise one made entirely in your interest. It is far less likely that on some future occasion you would be associated with...with..."

He broke off floundering, and Lucienne's tears gave way to a mischievous smile he found totally enchanting.

"You do not have to pretend with me," she said with engaging honesty. "You know, Mr. Bartholomew, there have been times this past nine months when I have become quite *ennuyeé*...how do you say, bored...with pretense. I have longed to say to Miss Talbot and to the pupils, that my real name is Sophie and that I worked for four years in a brothel in Paris called *Le Ciel Rouge*, where I was known as Perle."

The young man coughed, wishing he could talk to her as a friend rather than as a lawyer. But his duty must, he was aware, come first. He leant forward earnestly and said:

"You must never, ever talk of such things, Miss Rochford. I am sure your father explained that the most important asset a girl of good family can have is her good name, her reputation. Whatever has happened in the past—for which you can in no way be blamed—you *are* a Rochford. It was your father's wish to launch you in Society as his daughter and ultimately to find you a worthy husband."

Lucienne shrugged, her finely curved brows drawn into a slight scowl.

"I do not know if I wish to be 'launched in Society.' Certainly I have no wish to be married. I will not be any man's slave. I agreed to my father's wishes for one reason only—because he promised to give me this big house and the servants and as many horses and carriages as I wanted. Even a motor car of my own. For this I have endured that dreadful Establishment for the training of young ladies. Now you are telling me none of these things will be mine."

"I would be failing in my duty if I told you otherwise," Richard Bartholomew said gently.

"And this Oliver who will be the new Lord—the owner. Is he not just a boy—a child?"

"He is twelve years old, Miss Rochford. Your sister Alice is younger."

Lucienne shrugged indifferently.

"My father said they were bastards."

The lawyer swallowed nervously.

"I must warn you that that statement is slanderous," he said. "You must never say such a thing again, Miss Rochford. Despite what your father may have told you, there is no proof that either child was born out of wedlock—in fact, to the contrary. Were you to say such a thing publicly, you could be sued in court for many thousands of pounds damages."

Lucienne shrugged once again.

"So! It makes little difference to me. What I wish to know, Mr. Bartholomew, is if my father has left me any money in his Will."

Her bluntness unnerved Richard still further. He said awkwardly:

"I fear I would be acting unprofessionally were I to advise you of the contents of your father's Will before it is read after the funeral."

Lucienne's head tilted to one side and she looked with soft appeal into the anxious gray eyes of the young lawyer, assessing his vulnerability. He was by no means immune to her—that she had sensed immediately when he had greeted her. She judged him to be in his mid-twenties, very correct and conventional in his manner and attire—and quite possibly still a virgin.

She held out both hands toward him and, instinctively, he grasped them in his own as she said:

"We can be friends, can we not, Mr. Bartholomew? It is my hope that we shall be so. I am very much alone. I need a good friend whom I can trust—to whom I can talk with honesty. You must see how badly I need your help in a time like this. I do not even have a father now to whom I can turn for advice."

"But of course, of *course*, Miss Rochford, I am honored to be your friend. I...I understand your disappointment and indeed, Lord Rochford should not have allowed you to believe that you could be his heir. I don't think I would be violating professional etiquette were I to tell you that it was his intention to change his Will—he told me so—but I fear he never instructed me to prepare a new one, in which I do not doubt he would have provided for you. But you must not think of yourself as destitute, I beg you. Your mother, your uncles, aunts—they will all take care of you. You must believe me."

"Even if you are right," Lucienne said wryly, "I have no wish to be dependent upon anyone. I do not ask for charity. It is security I seek, Mr. Bartholomew."

"Look here, Miss Rochford," Richard sought to reassure her. "Will you permit me to give you a little advice? Don't worry too much about the future. I know your mother and despite your present feelings about her, I am sure she will do everything in her power to make up to you for your unlucky start in life. She may not wish to remain at Rochford Manor, and who knows, she might take you back with her to America. Or your Aunt Silvie might take you to live with her in Paris. She, too, is a delightful person, as is your Aunt Dorothy. You have a whole family now. You must not think of yourself as alone and deserted."

"Then if I am not to be lonely now—before my family arrive—will you dine with me?" Lucienne asked charmingly.

"Nothing would have given me greater pleasure," the young lawyer said quickly, "but I fear I cannot stay."

His regret was genuine for he found the girl fascinating. Despite the terrible facts about her background which could not be ignored, he, in the brief space of one hour, was totally captivated by her. Nor in his heart could he think of her as capable of allowing her body to be bought by men for their passing pleasure. Her appearance was far too youthful, too pure and virginal.

"It would not be correct for me to dine here alone with you. In fact, it would be most improper..."

Lucienne's eyes sparkled with sudden amusement.

"This must be another of Miss Talbot's boring, English conventions, I suppose!" she said, adding with a sigh: "You cannot imagine how many 'do's' and 'don'ts' were on Miss Talbot's list! To be truthful, Mr. Bartholomew, I have often doubted during these past nine months, whether the advantages of being a so called 'lady' are worth all the tedious rules that have to be obeyed if one wishes to be accepted as a member of the upper class."

She gave a soft chuckle, her face suddenly becoming that of a mischievous child as she said:

"Poor Miss Talbot nearly had a fit of the vapors because I had no black dress to wear as a mark of respect for my father and there was no time to buy one. I really do not think black would suit me, and it seems to me quite hypocritical that I should wear mourning for the father I knew so briefly. I was not permitted to return home during the school holidays, you know."

Richard struggled to suppress his sympathy and to keep his tone professional as he replied:

"I am sure Lord Rochford felt that to be in your own interest, Miss Rochford. He believed you would need time to become acquainted with a way of life that was strange to you."

Lucienne's smile faded. The childish look gave way once more to that of a girl far older than sixteen.

"What you really mean but are too polite to say, Sir, is that my father was ashamed of me and did not wish to have further contact with me until I had been remolded and he could present me as the kind of daughter he could be proud of." She shrugged her slim shoulders. *"Tant pis!"* she added in French. "Who cares what that silly old man felt. I do not believe he had any natural affection for me, yet had he lived I would have given him much love. I had so often longed for parents."

The wistful tone of her voice was reflected in her eyes. Her companion said quickly:

"You will find your mother a warm and loving person, I do assure you."

"My father told me she was cold, cruel, without feeling. He must have known her better than you, Mr. Bartholomew. She treated my father cruelly, did she not?"

Once again, the young lawyer strove for a professional reply.

"You must ask Lady Rochford about the past," he said evasively. "I am here purely to discuss present events. Your uncle and aunt will be arriving from Paris tomorrow morning and I will arrange the details of your father's funeral with them."

The girl looked suddenly wistful again.

"Is it not strange that I should have had relatives living in Paris and did not know it! This uncle—Pelham, I think you called him—he is my father's eldest brother?"

"No, the eldest Rochford is Tobias. He is living in San Francisco not far from your mother. There is another brother— your Uncle Rupert. He lives in Europe and travels a great deal. Then there is your Aunt Dorothy—she is now Mrs. James McGill. They have a baby daughter and live in the West Country. Doubtless they will come to visit as soon as your mother arrives home."

"And that is in two weeks' time, you say?"

Richard Bartholomew nodded.

"Lady Rochford, your Uncle Tobias and the two children are traveling from New York on the *Carpathia*. You must be very curious to meet your brother and sister, Miss Rochford. They are pretty children and very well brought up."

Lucienne's laughter filled the room.

"Unlike me, you mean, Mr. Bartholomew. And do not deny it, for I have heard such criticism daily from Miss Talbot. Oh yes, it is easy to learn to talk with the right accent; to wear the right clothes; to have correct table manners and deportment. What is not easy for me is to subdue myself. Do you understand what I mean? I must not speak as I feel or laugh when I am amused or be angry when I am cross. I must all the time suppress my true instincts and pretend . . . always, always pretend. *C'est très ennuyant!* I do not enjoy being a lady."

Despite his resolve, Richard smiled.

"I suppose there *are* a great many restrictions—but it will soon all become a habit, Miss Rochford. You must not forget that you were born into a noble family—indeed, you have the title of Honorable as a right. And if I may say so, your appearance leaves little doubt as to your breeding."

Lucienne's face softened at the compliment.

"It is true that at *Le Ciel Rouge*, Madame and the girls often called me *la Duchesse* without knowing my true background. Nevertheless, Mr. Bartholomew, I have not found the process of transformation either easy or enjoyable. I have persevered only because it was the condition my father laid down if I was to take my place as his daughter here at Rochford. It is intolerable that I have endured so much boredom only to discover that a mere child is to inherit this big house and all my father's assets."

This time, Richard Bartholomew's professionalism deserted him as he said in a low voice:

"Miss Rochford, you cannot make me believe that you wish you had remained in...in your old way of life..." he broke off scarlet cheeked.

With a rapidity he was now beginning to expect, Lucienne's expression became once more childlike and mischievous.

"Oh, I don't know...in many ways I enjoyed my life. All the girls were my friends and Madame was like a mother to me. She always made certain we came to no harm and she was very fair about money..."

She broke off as she saw the horrified look that had now spread over her companion's face.

"But I do not expect you to understand," she said. "You have always lead a respectable, safe, conventional life. You cannot know what it is like to be poor, homeless and without security. And do not look so concerned for me...I would not talk of such things to others. To be truthful, it is quite a relief not to have to pretend with you, as I did at the school, that I have spent *all* my life in a convent!"

The lawyer was effectively silenced. It was not for him to try to explain to her that no young man she was likely to encounter, however attracted by her beauty, would be less than horrified to hear her speak so casually of the shocking life she had led for the past four years. The sooner her mother returned from America and took charge of the situation the better! He himself felt completely out of his depth.

"You must be tired after your journey?" he said nervously, "So I will leave you to rest. The servants will take care of you until your Aunt Silvie arrives in the morning. I will call again tomorrow after luncheon."

Only then, as he stood up to take his leave, did he realize that the tea had remained untouched between them, and shockingly, that Lord Rochford had been ignominiously forgotten as he had sat discussing the future with his late client's ravishingly pretty daughter.

With no similar feeling of guilt, Lucienne held out her hand in a charming gesture.

"I shall look forward to your return tomorrow, Mr. Bartholomew. After all, you are the only friend I have and I shall appreciate it very much indeed if you will do what you can to persuade my relatives that my father was quite wicked to break his promise to me. A rich man such as he should not leave his daughter destitute, and I will depend upon you to try to arrange an allowance for me." Her head lifted proudly. "You will understand that I have no wish to depend upon my relations' charity. Nor will I ever beg from any man."

Holding her small, soft hand in his own, Richard Bartholomew could not conceive that such a state of affairs could ever exist. It was far more likely that men would be begging a smile, a kiss or even just one kind word from the sensuously curved lips of little Lucienne.

Chapter 2

❧

March 1911

WITH THE DEEPEST AFFECTION, THE TWO WOMEN EMBRACED.
Over their heads, Pelham and Tobias Rochford grinned at one
another tolerantly.

"Silvie has been counting the hours!" Pelham said, his
handsome face crinkled in laughter as he shook his brother's
hand with genuine warmth. "Nice to see you, old chap. You're
looking well!"

"You too!" Toby replied, regarding his favorite brother over
the rim of his spectacles.

Pelham turned his attention to the tall, slender woman
standing beside his wife. Kissing her in French fashion on
both cheeks, he then held her at arms length.

"As beautiful as ever—if not more so!" he commented.

Willow smiled at him fondly.

"If I look well, it is because I am so happy," she said simply.
A shadow crossed her face briefly. "I know that sounds wrong
with poor Rowell so recently laid in his grave. But, Pelham,
I would be a hypocrite to pretend sadness when I am finally
on the point of meeting my little girl. Where is she? Is she
well? I cannot wait to see her!"

Pelham's eyes went briefly to his wife's face. Although only
Willow's sister-in-law, Silvie had been as close to her as if
they were true sisters and it had been agreed between them
that it would be Silvie who related Lucienne's unhappy past
to her mother.

"Let us go into the drawing room, *chérie*!" Silvie said
quickly. Her dark eyes were without their usual sparkle as
she looked at the two bright spots of color on Willow's cheeks.
"There is a great deal I must talk to you about and I have
sent Lucienne shopping with my maid in Tunbridge Wells so
that we have a little time to ourselves before you meet her."

Willow's brows drew together in an anxious frown. She

glanced briefly at the familiar face of the man beside her and seeing only incomprehension in Toby's eyes, looked more at the plump, friendly figure of her sister-in-law.

"Lucienne's not here to meet me? I don't understand. Is something wrong, Silvie? For pity's sake tell me what can possibly be so important that I must postpone seeing her? For two long weeks I have thought of little else."

Pelham took her arm and gently propelled her towards the drawing room door.

"Silvie will explain everything to you, dearest Willow. Try to be patient a few moments longer." His face broke into a grin. "And to reassure you on one count, I will tell you at once that your daughter is quite remarkably beautiful—in fact her resemblance to you when you were her age is uncanny. To look at her is to look at you when you first came to Rochford as Rowell's bride."

By now, they were in the large drawing room where Willow had spent so many hours of her married life. Nothing had been changed since she had left the marital home nearly ten months ago believing she would never return. Her eyes went to the high winged chair where once old Grandmère had sat, poor Aunt Mildred hovering nearby awaiting the autocratic old lady's next command. There, on the other side of the fireplace, was the armchair Rowell had favored.

For a moment, the room was full of ghosts, for it was here that one of the servants had struck a blow at Rowell's younger brother, Francis, causing his death as he hit his head on the marble fireplace. Here in this room, old Grandmère had berated poor, lonely Rupert for his unnatural friendship with Dr. Forbes' son and finally dispatched him to fight in the war in Egypt. Here, too, her young sister-in-law, Dodie, had sat so often in her invalid chair, uncomplaining, sweet-natured and untouched by the cruel taunts of her grandmother who had so abhorred her deformities.

Swiftly, Willow forced such memories from her mind. The past was over and finished; Francis, Grandmère, Aunt Mildred, Rowell were all dead. There was a new generation of Rochfords now of which the eldest was her long-lost daughter, Lucienne. It was strange how she still thought of her as Sophia, although there had never been an opportunity to call her by that name.

As if sensing Willow's confusion, Toby was suddenly at her side, helping her out of her warm, fur-lined traveling coat and sitting beside her on the big brocade sofa, her hand clasped tightly in his. She felt the familiar rush of love for him that was usually so overwhelming that any other thought paled into insignificance; but on this occasion it was only momentary. Not even Toby's reassuring proximity could keep her nervous excitement at bay.

"Please do not keep me longer in suspense, Silvie," she said urgently. "Tell me about my Lucienne!"

For a moment Silvie's courage failed her. She walked across to the window and stared out into the windswept garden with thoughtful eyes. Until her marriage to Pelham Rochford nearly four years ago, Silvie had been an independent young widow of private means, free thinking and to some extent, free living. Over the long years of Willow's far from happy marriage to Silvie's cousin, Rowell Rochford, the Frenchwoman had often preached the desirability of freedom, vowing she would never herself remarry. But she had finally succumbed to the endearing, elusive charms of Pelham Rochford who was as carefree and fun loving as herself.

But not even the liberal thinking Silvie had been able to conceal her sense of shock and dismay when the young lawyer had told Pelham and herself of the extraordinary life Willow's lost child had been leading. She knew that Willow would be horrified and unavoidably bitter that Rowell had concealed from her Lucienne's surprising appearance last May.

Knowing Willow so well, Silvie was certain that her love for her child would not be diminished because Fate had driven Lucienne into a house of ill repute. She would, Silvie guessed, feel only pity for her daughter and possibly guilt too, in that she had not found the girl before such a fate could overtake her.

But could her beloved, soft hearted friend bear the more immediate rejection she was about to face from her daughter? Silvie had done her utmost these past ten days before Willow's arrival to undo the damage Rowell had accomplished in the few hours he had spent with his young daughter. With sadistic cruelty, he had led the girl to believe not only that her mother was feckless, unfaithful and incapable of love, but that she would be far too engrossed with her other two children, Oliver and Alice, to be interested in hearing of Lucienne's existence; that she would never consider leaving America to return to England to visit the child she had long since forgotten. Silvie had failed to convince Lucienne that her father had lied; that since Willow and Toby were even then upon their way home, this accusation at least was proved false.

"If my mother is coming to England, it is because she wants to make sure that that boy, Oliver, will take my inheritance!" Lucienne had said coldly to her aunt. "Why cannot she leave me alone? I don't want her here!"

Silvie turned away from the window and looked across the room at Willow with a feeling of helplessness. Willow had been vulnerable since the day she had arrived at Rochford, her heart so clearly on her sleeve as she had gazed adoringly and innocently into Rowell's indifferent face. Her heart had been broken so many times, and yet again and again she had given her trust and love to those of the Rochford family who needed her; even to poor unhappy Aunt Mildred whom she suspected of having been involved in her baby's disappearance.

As gently as she could, Silvie began to relate the story of Lucienne's lost years and her miraculous reappearance.

"Both Aunt Milly and Dr. Forbes must have been forced into helping Grandmère carry out her evil plan," she said as she reached the point in the story where the little girl had been taken to the French convent. "It is more than probable that she was blackmailing the doctor. Grandmère knew that his son, Adrian, was having an illicit relationship with her grandson, Rupert, and I would not put it past her to have threatened to expose the boys to gain Forbes' cooperation."

"At least the old doctor tried to put matters right before he died. He went to France to try to find her," Pelham interposed. "But for him, Lucienne would not have had the locket he then gave her and would never have known that she had English relatives by the name of Rochford."

Willow gave an unhappy sigh.

"I will try to forgive him since my Lucienne is home at last!" she said. "But I will never think of him as other than a wicked, evil man."

Mustering her courage, Silvie continued the story she must tell, of Lucienne's days at the modiste working as a domestic and then the final horror—of her being coerced into the Parisian brothel as a waitress and finally how to sell her thirteen-year-old body for gain.

"They were kind to her and in her ignorance she was happy there," Silvie said quickly as she saw the color drain from Willow's cheeks. "She had no one to guide her, to advise her how ill-chosen and shocking was that way of life. Pelham and

I have talked to her a lot about those years, Willow, and you may find it hard to believe but she has no sense of guilt. Lacking moral guidance from anyone, she was innocent of wrong doing. It was no more than a means to earn her keep and a place in the only home she had ever known."

Willow's eyes were bright with unshed tears as she cried:

"You need not defend her, Silvie. I am not blaming her. I shall never blame her. I will make it up to her for those bad years. She shall have everything in the world she wants from now on."

"How ever much you may wish to give her her heart's desire, I don't think that will be possible," Silvie said quietly. She explained Lucienne's belief that Rochford Manor should be hers. "Rowell may not deliberately have misled her—we'll never know that—but she swears he told her she was to be his heir."

"The lawyer, Silvie and I have all told her there is no question but that Oliver is the new Lord Rochford," Pelham broke in. "That he will live here and manage the estate when he is old enough, just as it has always been the duty of the eldest son."

Willow nodded, glancing at Toby as she said:

"We discussed it before we left America. We had already decided to return to England and live here until Oliver marries. Of course, Lucienne will be part of our family and she will share everything with us. You told her this?"

Silvie reached out and laid her hand on Willow's arm.

"At the moment Lucienne does not feel very inclined to share anything with anyone," she said gently. "You must give her time, Willow. Do not expect her to feel towards you and her brother and sister as *you* feel towards *her*. You are a total stranger to her and she shows no inclination to be directed or disciplined as would normally be expected from a girl of her age. She is the strangest combination of child and woman— or perhaps it is not so strange when one takes her past into account."

"Even if I cannot give her Rochford, I can make her happy, I am sure of it," Willow cried. "Oh, Silvie, all this is too much to take in. I cannot bear to think of the child's suffering. It is a miracle that she has remained so untouched by the terrible life she has led. It is a miracle that she has found her way back to us. You will see, I shall find a hundred ways to make her happy. She shall live here with us and maybe it is not too late for her to enjoy those lost years of her childhood. As far as possible, she shall have everything in the world she wants!"

"You mean I can have Rochford Manor after all?"

From the doorway, the girl's voice rang out with startling clarity.

Lucy was wearing a brand new grey, tailor made coat and skirt. Aunt Silvie's maid had pointed out the aptness of the black velvet facings in deference to her state of mourning. A tiny black toque was perched on top of her head. She stared at her relatives with wary intentness, watching as the slim, golden-haired woman seated opposite her aunt jumped to her feet and held out her arms. This, she presumed, was Lady Rochford, her mother.

"Lucienne!" Willow cried. "My darling, *darling* child!"

Lucienne remained where she was, unmoved by the obvious emotion in her mother's voice.

"You did not reply to my question, Madame," she said coldly. "Did I understand you to say that I could have Rochford Manor for my own if I so desire?"

Willow's hands dropped to her sides. Toby stood up and put an arm protectively around her shoulders, painfully aware of her shock and distress.

"We will talk of Rochford presently," he said quietly but forcibly. "But first you will come and kiss your mother, Lucienne. She has been longing for this moment and I am certain that you, too, have been longing to meet her."

Lucienne hesitated, her keen mind working furiously as slowly she unbuttoned her black suede gloves. Both Richard Bartholomew and her aunt and uncle had stressed on frequent occasions these past ten days, how emotional a moment this reunion would be for her mother who was by English law now her legal Guardian.

"And will be so until you are twenty-one years of age," Richard Bartholomew had informed her. "I do beg you, Miss Rochford, to bear this in mind since your happiness must inevitably lie within her control."

Lucienne glanced again at the beautiful woman upon whose face she could see an agonized look of appeal. A warm feeling of pleasure spread over her. No one for as long as she could remember had wanted her affection so urgently. There had been many men who had as urgently required her body, but this was different . . . an emotion she could not recognize or understand. Somewhere deep within her, she longed to drop her coat, hat, gloves and run forward to be enfolded in that unknown embrace. But far more overwhelming was her sudden sense of power. It outweighed all other consideration. This woman needed her, wanted her love. It would be the simplest of matters to get exactly what *she* wanted in return for a small show of affection. That, she knew, was easy enough to simulate.

A small smile curved the corners of her mouth. From hours of careful practice before a looking glass, she knew exactly how to compose her features so that she looked very young, very innocent and appealing.

From beneath the sweep of dark lashes, she stared into her mother's eyes.

"Oh Mama!" she said softly, "I have been waiting so long to meet you. I think you are the most beautiful woman I have ever seen."

This last at least was true, Lucienne thought wryly, as she walked forward and was clasped in Willow's loving arms.

Chapter 3

May 1911

LUCIENNE LOOKED UP INTO THE SERIOUS FACE OF THE YOUNG, dark-eyed boy poling the rickety old punt towards the island on the lake. It was a perfect spring morning and the sunshine was reflecting off the mirrorlike surface of the water onto the boy's smooth, unlined cheeks.

"All right, Oliver, you can call me Lucy if you want," she replied to his question, "but only if you swear a sacred oath never to do so in front of the grown-ups!"

Oliver Rochford sighed in perplexity. After three whole months, he was no nearer understanding this astonishing sister who had suddenly appeared in the family circle. From his very first meeting with her on the day he had arrived home from America with Mama and Alice and Uncle Toby, he had been confused as to his feelings towards her. Sometimes he thought she was nearly as pretty as Mama and she looked very like her. Yet there the resemblance ended. His mother was gentle, sweet, adoring and totally predictable—whereas Lucienne was none of these. She had made no attempt to hide her scorn and contempt for him in those early days. It had been hard for a twelve-year-old chap to understand why she should dislike him when she barely knew him. Uncle Toby had explained that his sister had been expecting to inherit Rochford Manor and deeply resented the fact that he was the rightful heir—and for no better reason than that he was a boy.

He had tried not to take any notice of her snubs to his friendly advances; her refusal to be drawn into conversation with him. He had just reached the conclusion that he really did not like her at all when he came upon her down by the stables, her long skirts hitched up above her knees, trying to ride his old bicycle. Suddenly, the aloof, unfriendly girl had changed into a madcap laughing tomboy as the bicycle wob-

29

bled towards him, knocking him backwards and they fell in a heap on the muddy edge of the duck pond.

To his incredulity, Lucienne had neither been cross nor in the least put out by the mud clinging to her muslin frock and the untidy tangles in her hair. The more concerned he looked, the more *she* had laughed. It had been her idea to light a fire in the grate in the old tack room and his to bake potatoes and they'd become the very best of friends until...and there was the conundrum...until it was time to go back to the house. Like a flash, she had rounded on him, telling him she would never, ever speak to him again if he so much as mentioned one word of their adventure to any of the grown-ups. And so the pattern was established. In private, when they were quite alone, Lucienne was a child, not only willing to join in with him in any prank but often as not the instigator. Not even with his best friend, Henry Barratt, the youngest of the three brothers who lived nearby, did Oliver have more fun. But in the company of any adult, Lucienne was as cold and remote as on the day he had first met her.

He beached the punt inexpertly in a shallow inlet on the island and held out his hand to assist Lucienne onto dry land. Laughing, she ignored his offer of assistance and leapt gracefully onto the bank.

"All right, I swear!" he said as he landed beside her. "But Lucienne—I mean, Lucy—I simply don't see why it matters. I do wish you'd explain. Why *can't* they know we're friends!"

"Because I don't *want* them to know, that's why, my Lord Rochford!" Lucy replied, tweaking one of Oliver's dark curls but laughing as she did so. The boy's handsome mouth drew downwards as he scowled.

"You know I don't like you calling me Lord Rochford!" he said angrily. But Lucienne was not listening. Jumping to her feet, she ran toward an overhanging birch tree and hampered though she was by her long pleated tartan skirt, she was up in the highest branch before he had reached the lower one.

"You've torn your dress!" he called up to her. "Bet you wish you weren't a stupid girl and could wear knickerbockers like me!"

"That's easily remedied!" Lucienne called down and a moment later, her skirt went sailing past him and she sat swinging her legs in their knee-length frilly drawers, quite oblivious to whether or not he was shocked by such a sight.

Oliver grinned.

"I bet you wouldn't be sitting there so calmly if George or Howard came by!" he called up, enjoying the sound of her laughter as she called back:

"With four sisters of their own, all the Barratt boys must have seen a girl in her drawers before now."

She lowered herself onto the branch beside him and reaching out a hand, ruffled his hair.

"Don't you think they'd like to see me like this?" she asked mischievously.

Oliver blushed.

"How should I know! By the way, Henry heard them arguing the other night about which of them you like the best. Which do you like best, Lucy—George or Howard?"

Lucienne tilted her fair head to one side as she considered the question with apparent seriousness.

"Well, since you have asked me, Oliver, I'll think about it. George is older of course—twenty-four, he told me—and one day he'll inherit Sir John's estate, so if I married him, I'd be Lady Barratt, wouldn't I? But Howard is better looking and more fun in lots of ways." The serious expression on her face gave way to laughter as she added:

"But I haven't the slightest intention of marrying either one of them. I shall never get married—not unless it's to the richest man in the whole world."

Oliver looked into his sister's brilliant blue eyes. Her remark had made him uneasy—as happened so often.

"You're always talking about money and being rich," he said. "Uncle Toby said it's because you were very poor when you were at orphanage. Was it very awful at that Convent, Lucy?"

Lucienne shrugged her slim shoulders.

"We were always hungry," she said, her eyes thoughtful. "I think about it sometimes when we're at luncheon or dinner and half the good food served to us isn't even touched. I know Mama says the servants enjoy it but..." she paused. "I don't think Mama knows what it's like to be hungry. She always had everything!"

"But you have everything you want now, Lucy," Oliver said urgently. "Mama never refuses you anything. Uncle Toby says she is spoiling you. Lucy, why don't you love Mama? Everyone else does. I don't see how you can't *not* love her."

Once again, Lucienne ruffled his hair.

"I don't love anybody!" she said lightly. "Except you perhaps—just a tiny little bit!" The blue of her eyes deepened once again in thought. "I did once love someone I knew called Yvette. She was my friend. But she got married to a farmer and I don't have her address so I can't write to her."

"Cheer up, Lucy!" Oliver said. "You've got lots of new friends now. Absolutely everyone wants to meet you. You're quite pretty really and they all like you. Henry told me he had heard George and Howard grumbling that as soon as you have been presented next year, every young man for miles around will be calling—or getting their mamas to call on ours."

"Henry is just a silly boy like you and knows nothing!" Lucienne said, although she did not look displeased with Oliver's remarks. "Let's go and fish for tadpoles. You can take some home for Alice."

For once, Oliver kept his thoughts to himself as he preceded Lucy down the tree, rescuing her skirt on the way from the branch where she had flung it. Despite all her pretence, he was quite convinced that Lucy did love their little sister. Alice was a round, pink-cheeked, affectionate child with a nature as sweet as Mama's. She was always running to Lucy with a little posy of flowers or some other tiny gift and bore no grudge when Lucy received such tributes with seeming indifference. But Oliver had seen Lucy several times in the nursery, once giving Alice a ride on the old dappled, wooden rocking horse and on another occasion, playing the pianola for her while she danced. Patience, their Nanny, had been enjoying her day off and the nursery maid was getting tea so there were no grown-ups to see Lucy.

At eight years old, Alice was still too young to question the strangeness of Lucienne's dual personality but Oliver thought of little else and for once, he had found no satisfactory explanation in the story Mama and Uncle Toby told him about Lucy's strange past.

"What did they tell you about me?" Lucy had asked him when they had first become friends.

"Not much!" Oliver admitted, recounting his mother's brief explanation which, for some reason he did not quite believe to be the truth.

"Mama said you had been stolen by the wet-nurse who exchanged you for her own baby which had died. That was why the family all believed you were dead and why your name used to be on the headstone in the graveyard. Uncle Toby said the nurse went to work in France and then she died and you were an orphan and got sent to a Convent. Then Papa was sent an old letter from the nurse confessing who you really were—it had been lost for years—and so he finally found you at the Convent."

Lucy nodded, further dislodging the silky fair hair from its pins so that it hung in tendrils over her lichen-smeared cheeks. Still clad only in her pink blouse and drawers, she looked little older than her twelve-year-old brother but she was too deep in thought to be aware of it. The explanation of her past as given to Oliver was the story her mother and Uncle Toby had determined to tell the world; the same story she had been instructed to tell anyone who asked why she had never lived at Rochford as a child.

"It is not so much to protect the Rochford good name as yours, my darling," her mother had said, her eyes as always soft with appeal for Lucy's understanding and devotion. That particular look always made Lucy feel guilty, for the more sweetness and affection Mama lavished on her, the more tightened up her own heart became. Everyone from Alice, the youngest member of the family, to Uncle Toby who was the eldest, seemed to take it for granted that she would adore her newly discovered mother as much as *they* all adored her. Mama, it seemed, could do no wrong and everyone appeared to have forgotten that she had deserted her husband and removed his two children to the opposite side of the Atlantic where he could no longer see them. Her father had considered Mama's behavior had been ruthless and Lucy agreed with him.

She had spent but a short time with Rowell Rochford, yet in those memorable hours he had told her he was certain that he would be able to prove his youngest children were bastards and that Lucy was his only legitimate child, although Richard Bartholomew had denied the possibility.

Lucy's uppermost emotion was one of the resentment toward Willow, and although both children had found a way past her jealous antipathy, she was certainly not going to let her mother or uncle see how easily she had been won over. Oliver intrigued her. Along with his intelligence went a happy, mischievous nature which found a quick response within her.

The fact was, Lucy had had no childhood. Life within the forbidding walls of the Convent of the Bleeding Heart had been one of hunger and deprivation; of long hours of prayer in a bitterly cold church; of the backaching drudgery of scrubbing pots and pans in the kitchen, washing the mountains of greasy plates; looking after the sad, unhappy little ones who were caught in the same inescapable trap as herself. Her life as a maid in the private house of a modiste and his wife in Paris had been just as hard and a lot more lonely. She had been the age Oliver now was, she reflected, comparing the idyllic life he led with her own.

Sharing a tutor with young Eleanor Barratt, Oliver's schooling was carried out in a pleasant, sunny room in the nursery wing of the Barratts' huge country mansion. When lessons were over, the boy could amuse himself as he pleased.

He was the first member of the male sex whom Lucy had actually liked. Too young still to be interested (as were the men Lucy had known) in females as objects of satisfaction for their sexual appetites, Oliver's friendly gestures of goodwill could not be misconstrued as a means to get what he wanted from her. He liked her for herself, and for that alone, she found it easy to love him.

There were many times these past weeks when she had gone to bed thinking how perfect a world it would be if she really were Oliver's age and that neither of them need ever grow up. But Oliver did not share her wish. He could not wait to be a man and hardly a day passed when he did not ask her to look closely at his upper lip just in case he had begun to grow a moustache like those of the older Barratt boys. He often made her laugh by trying to speak in a gruff, manly voice. His heroes were threefold—his two uncles, Toby and Pelham, and the daredevil pilot, Gustav Hamel. He was totally obsessed with aviation in all its forms and was determined to learn to pilot both an airplane and a balloon as soon as he was old enough.

"I'll fly you through the skies, Lucy," he said. "Just imagine what it must be like up there in the clouds, looking down at the fields and trees so tiny and silent beneath us. Uncle Pelham has promised to take me and Mark to the new flying school at Eastchurch when he comes to visit in the summer. It's not far from Rochford. You can come, too, Lucy. You like Uncle Pelham, don't you?"

In many ways, Lucy preferred him to Uncle Toby. Her younger uncle's nature was much more akin to Oliver's—he was always laughing and ready for fun. His manner toward her was one of twinkling-eyed teasing. Lucy sensed that he alone of all the members of the family, did not feel her years at *Le Ciel Rouge* were a blight upon her life that could never be truly eliminated. But Mama and Uncle Toby had decided that those years must never again be mentioned by anyone, as if by silence they could be made to vanish.

But Lucy did not want to forget them. She was well aware after her months at the Establishment for Young Ladies and the last months with her newly discovered family, how disgraceful and unmentionably blackening for her reputation her life had been; how important virginity was for a girl of good family; how any man considering marriage would turn his back and disappear if ever he learned how she had once lived. But although reason accepted that these were the values of the world she now lived in, she could not forget how kind Madame Lou-Lou had been to her; how friendly and affectionate the other girls; how it had become the first and only home she had ever known and where she had been happy in her ignorance. But for that old English doctor coming to look for her, she might be there now, never knowing this incredible world of wealth and privilege and luxury. Now she was part of it and could never go back—but nevertheless, a little piece of her heart remained with those who had befriended her.

Lucy was immensely curious about her mother's relationship with Uncle Toby. A person would have to be blind not to see that they loved one another with totally uncritical devotion. Doubtless in time they would return to the United States to be married. But in the meanwhile, they lived side by side in the Manor without so much as a kiss exchanged between them. Lucy thought it quite unnatural that they should not exchange intimacies, at least in private. Her mother was still only in her thirties and an exceedingly attractive woman. Only too well aware of men's needs for physical outlets for their passions, Lucy considerd their regard for convention ridiculous. But then so many of the conventional forms of behavior she was required to learn were equally ridiculous in her opinion. The rules of behavior at *Le Ciel Rouge* were simple and obvious and, above all, few. Here in England at Rochford Manor, it appeared there were right and wrong ways for doing anything, from the positioning of cutlery to the complicated ways for the leaving of calling cards, and hundreds more besides. There was also a complicated social hierarchy, not only for titled friends and neighbors but even for servants!

It was obvious to Lucy that the Barratt family, whose dinner party she was attending this evening, were near the top of the social scale. Sir John and Lady Barratt owned an even larger estate than the Rochfords who owned all Havorhurst. Brought up in luxury, young Oliver paid little attention to the magnificence of the Barratt household. But Lucy had been impressed and considered it a feather in her cap that the two eldest Barratt boys were unashamedly fascinated by her. The youngest brother, Henry, who was only a year older than Oliver, was also Lucy's slave.

"It's because you're different from other girls," Oliver had tried to explain. "Most girls are soppy. They blush and giggle and all they can talk about are their clothes and the parties they've been to. It's always jolly being with you, Lucy. You enjoy everything and never seem to get bored."

Lucienne smiled to herself recalling how frequently she was bored, as for example, calling on Mama's many friends and sitting primly through dull tea parties, making even duller conversation. Conversation at luncheons and dinners at home was far more interesting when Uncle Toby would bring Mama up to date with the latest news from the morning papers. They would discuss the plans for the coming coronation of King George and his pretty wife, Mary, or even more fascinating, the trial of Edward Mylius who had libelled the King, claiming he had married an Admiral's daughter in Malta. Now the man had been sentenced to a year in prison, which Uncle Toby thought was not long enough, seeing how far-reaching the gossip had been about the King who was, in his opinion, a good, kindly man.

"This country needs the reforms Asquith wants," he told Lucy seriously. "Unfortunately the House of Lords keeps rejecting the Government's plans. They're trying of course to obtain Home Rule for the Irish; and better conditions for the working classes."

"You should not fill her head with such matters," Willow chided him mildly but Lucy begged to be informed and Uncle Toby supported her.

"After all, my love, times are changing very rapidly and I believe it will not be long now before women are given the vote. If that ever happens, they must know what they are voting for or against." He had smiled at Lucy over the top of his spectacles. "If you listen to young Annabel Barratt, you will begin to believe that women will soon be running the country!" he said grinning. "It's a matter of real distress to

Sir John and Lady Barratt that their daughter should be a Suffragette, let alone in cahoots with Christabel Pankhurst, one of the Movement's most militant leaders."

Lucy was only mildly interested in the growing demand for women's rights. There seemed to her to be little point, for example, in well-off ladies demanding the right to work as doctors or lawyers, when they had wealthy husbands who could afford to keep them in luxury. Her point of view, when expressed to George Barratt, won his approval.

"I would certainly not approve of my wife working," he said. "I've told Annabel once, if I have told her a dozen times, that she's queering her chances of remarriage by airing such views. She was divorced last year, you know, and that thoroughly upset both Mater and Pater. But all Annabel wants, so *she* says, is independence. Her marriage wasn't too happy, I'm afraid, and it turned her against men. As if women could manage in this life without them!"

Lucy longed to be able to tell him that she had once worked long dreary hours as a maid to support herself—and that she had no intention of returning to such drudgery. But she kept her promise to Mama never to speak of those days. Nevertheless, the remarks about Annabel had given her food for thought and tonight she would meet George's sister for the first time. The dinner party at the Barratts' house was being given expressly in her, Lucy's honor. With her own family mourning, convention dictated that her mother should not give the lavish entertainment at Rochford she had wished to provide for Lucienne.

"I long to give a really magnificent party to celebrate your return home, my darling, but I dare not," she had said regretfully. "As it is some people may consider it improper for you to attend the Barratts' dinner party but your Uncle Toby feels we should not refuse Lady Barratt's kindly suggestion. We will go up to London and choose something suitable for you to wear."

With an effort, Lucy brought her mind back to the present. Oliver had stopped at the edge of the lake and was absorbed in his task of fishing for tadpoles. They were always in abundance at this time of the year in the shallow water where he had landed the punt. Lucy unbuttoned her shoes, kicked them off, and pulling down her black lisle stockings, she allowed the cold wet mud to ooze slowly between her bare toes.

Oliver, she thought, must have enjoyed this delicious sensation a hundred times during his childhood, but such freedom had been unthinkable, unimagined in the confines of the Convent. He took it all quite for granted, while for her, such moments were new, delightful experiences, as sensual as they were novel. They were similar to the feelings evoked in her when she had first come to England over a year ago and had felt the soft, sweet smelling touch of Irish linen when she laid her cheek on her pillow; of the delicacy of silk against her skin; the feel of rich, lush velvets and thick piled carpets; the delight of eating with Georgian silver forks and spoons off fine china plates. Most of all, Lucy loved the bright glitter of the magnificent jewelry her mother wore each night at dinner, sparkling in the candlelight and gleaming against Mama's smooth white skin. She, too, was born to be rich, she mused on such occasions, and the beauty that money and title could buy were her birthright. She was the daughter of the late Lord Rochford and people like the Barratts accepted her as an equal. If he had left her little else, she thought, her father had left her this heritage.

"You must remember our father," she said now to Oliver as she scooped a tiny, legless tadpole into his stone jam jar. "Did you like him?"

Oliver's dark head remained bent over the water.

"I think I was a bit too scared of him to like him very much," he replied quietly. "Not that I saw much of him. I don't think he liked me, really."

Lucy was surprised.

"But why not? Because you were naughty?"

Now Oliver did look up, his eyes smiling as he said ruefully:

"Gosh, no! We were always on our best behavior with father. Mostly it was because I was frightened of horses—I was pretty ill once after a tumble from my pony and—well, I never did want to ride again. He tried to make me but Mama stopped him. Once I saw him..." he paused, his dark eyes suddenly even blacker with the unhappy memory "...once I saw him hitting Mama. I'd only say this to you, Lucy, because I know you'd never tell anyone but I'm glad he isn't here any more. It's much nicer at Rochford without him!"

"No one seems to mind much that he's dead!" Lucy said. "Whenever I start to ask questions about him, people change the subject. Not one of the servants will talk about him. They just say: 'It's not my place to comment, Miss Lucienne!' in that irritating, prim tone they always use."

"I don't want to talk about him either," Oliver said, startling Lucy as he jumped to his feet and reached for the punt pole. "We'd best go back now. It's nearly tea time and you've got to get ready for tonight's dinner party. I wish I was old enough to go with you."

"So do I!" Lucy said. "I'm sure I shall be dreadfully, dreadfully bored!"

Oliver helped her into the punt, grinning at Lucy's clever imitation of the way Louise Barratt talked. Louise was the second eldest of the Barratt sisters and had married Hilary Lennox, a Foreign Office official. Because he was considered exceptionally clever and was much respected by his superiors, both he and Louise had adopted an annoyingly blasé manner of speech, which seemed to be based on the theme that there was nothing left in life to amuse or excite them. Lucy had copied Louise's voice perfectly.

"Some of Hilary's friends will be there tonight," Oliver told her as he poled the punt toward the house. "And if they are half as dull as Hilary, you really will be bored, although you will have George and Howard to flirt with."

Lucy shrugged her shoulders indifferently. While it was quite amusing to be admired so extravagantly by the two young men, it was impossible for her to take either one seriously. They were both too gauche and inexperienced. George, who was old enough to go out in the world, seemed perfectly content to while away his time on his father's estate, hunting, shooting, entertaining and being entertained by his friends. He had no desire to travel to foreign countries; no spirit of adventure. Nice as he was, he was never anything but dull. And as for Howard, he was virtually still a schoolboy, although now nineteen years of age, he was soon to go to University to complete his education. Yes, Lucy decided, an evening spent in the Barratt boys' company was unlikely to be very stimulating.

But despite her apprehension, Lucy was to feel a swift surge of excitement as the motorcar transporting her and Mama and Uncle Toby drew up that evening outside the huge, imposing Queen Anne mansion where the Barratt family lived. The uniformed chauffeur ran round from the front seat to open the car door for them and at the same moment, the butler opened the heavy oak front door. Such perfect precision of service still impressed Lucienne. She had visited the house only once before on a formal call with Mama, and she liked the gray-haired Sir John and his plump, matronly wife. They were comfortable people, she had told Oliver, omitting to add that Lady Barratt reminded her of a genteel Madame Lou-Lou.

Sir John and his wife received their guests in the white and gold drawing room. This was the largest room, stretching as it did the complete length of the south side of the house. Its windows looked onto the terrace and steps leading to the sunken garden. Rich damask lined the walls and hung at the windows. Large mirrors faced each other across the room reflecting the gilt ornamentation into infinity. Some of the guests had already arrived and Lucy's quick glance scanned the smartly dressed groups of people in search of a familiar face.

Both George and Howard hastened to Lucy's side and George took her elbow in a proprietary manner as he led her toward his sisters, Annabel and Gillian. Neither of the two women had been present on Lucy's previous visit and George now performed the introductions. Only Gillian shared the same ginger red hair of the brothers; Annabel had blonde hair and hard blue eyes that seemed to Lucy to be summing her up in a most calculating manner. For what purpose, she could not imagine.

Howard then took her arm and led her toward a couple who were standing by the fireplace.

"Mrs. Rose, may I introduce Lucienne? Lucienne, this is Dr. and Mrs. Rose. I think you met the doctor at your father's funeral."

Before Lucy had a chance to reply, Hilary Lennox, Louise's husband, stepped forward.

"If I may drag you away presently, Miss Rochford, I want to introduce you to a friend of mine, Count Alexis Zemski," he said in his heavy drawling voice. "He's a fellow worker at the F.O., y'know!" He inclined his head in the direction of a tall, fair-haired man standing by the window in conversation with Lady Barratt.

But for the fact that he was a friend of the tiresome Hilary, Lucy thought, she might have been interested to meet this fellow guest. He had a broad, intelligent forehead and the high cheekbones which marked him out as different from his English counterparts. She supposed him to be in his thirties, for there was a certain maturity in his self-assured stance and the ease with which he seemed to be conversing with his hostess.

"Frightfully clever chap, don't you know!" Hilary continued. "Speaks numerous languages, including Serbo-Croat. His parents came from Croatia but Zemski was born in England and you'd never know he was a foreigner."

The doctor's wife, Stella Rose, appeared interested.

"I'd love to talk to him about the situation in the Balkans. One hopes Austria is going to be able to intervene successfully in the Italian-Turkish war."

"I'm sure Miss Rochford is not interested in such matters, my dear," the young doctor said gently with a smile in Lucy's direction. "My wife was once a teacher and her continued interest in political history takes second place only to her invaluable assistance in my practice."

Stella Rose smiled at Lucy.

"I was once a governess to the younger Barratt children," she said in her soft voice, "and to your young brother, Oliver, too. To be truthful, he was the brightest of all my pupils."

While paying polite attention to the conversation, Lucy was nevertheless aware that Hilary Lennox's foreign friend had turned his head in her direction and was staring at her. Even at this distance, she noticed the extraordinary green of his eyes as they steadily held her gaze. It was a look with which she was familiar—an expression of interest and admiration which, in the past, would have been instantly exploited by Madame Lou-Lou.

Lucy's mouth curved into a small, satisfied smile. It was reassuring to know that in the transforming process from one of Madame Lou-Lou's protégées to genteel young lady she had lost none of her powers to attract.

She turned to Hilary.

"This friend of yours, Mr. Lennox, is his family's estate near here?"

Hilary gave her a patronizing smile.

"My dear young lady, Alexis Zemski's parents were foreigners. They left their estate when they came to this country before he was born. He talks about it, though. He showed me a painting of the place hanging in the library of his London house. Spanking great castle surrounded by beautiful hunting country. I believe a second cousin lives there now. I know Zemski goes over there every once in a while."

"I suppose as he never lived abroad, he considers himself a Londoner," Stella Rose remarked.

"I suppose so," Hilary said vaguely. "Although Sir John says he's a damned fine horseman, and he should know, what? Loves the country life, I gather. Between you and me, I reckon m'father-in-law had his eye on Zemski for young Annabel before the silly girl married that E.N.T. surgeon. Zemski belongs to all the right clubs and has a penny or two, I believe. Quite an eligible bachelor! I dare say your Mama will have him on her list when you come out next year, eh, Miss Rochford?"

Lucy understood very well his meaning. Owing to her father's death, she could not be presented at Court this year while she was officially in mourning. She would not, therefore, be in the marriage market until her eighteenth birthday. It had been made quite clear to her by her mother that a 'good marriage' was desirable and in Lucy's best interests. Lucy kept her own counsel, for she had quickly realized that it was better not to defy her Mama openly. Nor was it necessary. She had but to plead with her soft-hearted mother to be allowed her own way in most things. But instinct had prevented her from trying to explain her own assessment as to what was in her best interests—and marriage was not included. To be married—even to a wealthy man—meant losing control of one's financial assets and although Lucy had none at the moment, she fully intended to be wealthy in her own right. Without money, she knew only too well, one was at the mercy of fate and she desired security above all.

She glanced once more at the man by the window and found he was still staring at her. Mama had been right, she thought, in the selection of her new gown. The pale gray chiffon dress had a high waistline and the floating material of the skirt was caught up with little ivory satin bows down the front. It was stunning in its simplicity and was far more striking than the colorful, flamboyant dinner gowns of the three Barratt girls. Lucy was satisfyingly aware of the admiring glances she was attracting. Both George and Howard were hovering attentively at her elbow and even the pompous Hilary had found it difficult to take his eyes off her. She was beginning to enjoy herself. It might be amusing, she thought, were she to be seated next to the Count. It would be quite interesting to see what he looked like when he smiled. So far she had only seen him staring with that searching intensity which reached across the room to where she was standing.

But when the gentlemen were invited to escort the ladies in to dinner in the paneled dining room, it was George who took her arm and sat down beside her at the long Regency dining table.

Candles glittered in the tall silver candelabra, sending dancing shivers of light off the elaborate crested plates set before the twenty guests. Footmen hovered behind the mahogany dining chairs unobtrusively serving the varied dishes, while the butler poured wine into the crystal goblets. Across the table, Lucy's eyes were drawn once more to the brooding gaze of the Count but they were too far apart for conversation to be possible; besides which, she was constantly being distracted by George's voice on her right and that of the doctor on her left. She began to flirt with George and looking surreptitiously across the table, was gratified to see that the foreigner's green eyes were still turning in her direction even while he made appropriate replies to his hostess on whose left he was seated.

Lucy was in no doubt that as soon as dinner was over and the gentlemen had rejoined the ladies in the drawing room, the Count would make his way to her side. Confidently, she redoubled her attention to George who blushed with increasing frequency at her compliments. She knew that if he had not been smitten before this evening, by the time the long dinner came to an end, George Barratt would be hopelessly in love with her. When he put his hand beneath her elbow to assist her up from her chair, she could feel the muscles of his arm jumping and his eyes, as they looked at her, were dark with desire.

Following the ladies to the powder room, her mother drew her to one side. Smiling, she said softly:

"I am so very proud of you, my darling. Everyone has remarked on your beauty and charm and, of course, young George is very obviously your slave." She put an arm around Lucy's shoulders. "You could do worse than consider George as a serious suitor," she said, unaware of Lucy's scowl. "Wouldn't it be marvelous, my love, if you were to become the future Lady Barratt and to live so close to Rochford? It would mean we would never be truly parted for long."

"I am glad you think I do you credit, Mama," Lucy said coldly. "But as you well know, I have no wish at present even to consider marriage, let alone to poor dull George!"

Willow sighed. She should have kept her thoughts to herself, she realized. Dear Toby had warned her that Lucy would be contrary and likely to resist any determined plan to marry her off quickly.

"I know you are afraid that her past might come to light," he had said sympathetically, "but Lucy is still at heart a child and has not yet come to terms with her family. Her new life with us and with so much to learn must be a strain. She will not want to complicate that life further by yet another change. And if George is intent upon marrying Lucy, I do not doubt the Barratts will consider it their duty to enquire more closely than they have so far done into the past seventeen years. You must admit that the story we have given out is somewhat suspect. For Lucy to have been stolen by a nurse and then to have found her way into a French orphanage is odd to say the least; not to mention the even odder coincidence that Rowell should have been advised of her identity so many years later."

Willow's fears for her young daughter overruled her common sense. Even if people believed the strange story, Lucienne could so easily betray herself. The girl had a way of looking at the opposite sex that caused Willow's heart to flutter nervously. It was both provocative and calculating. The demureness she had cultivated was but skin deep and Willow had observed the glances that were exchanged during dinner with Count Zemski! What must he be thinking, she asked herself. There were, too, less easily defined doubts about Lucienne's movements. No matter how young and virginal her attire, Lucienne's small, perfectly formed body moved with a sensual grace that, though Toby insisted it was natural, Willow feared was cultivated; a deliberate provocation to arouse men's passions.

"It is only because you know of her past that you imagine such things," Toby tried to reassure her. "Remember your cousin, Silvie, when first you met her? She is a French woman and Pelham put the matter in a nutshell when he said no man could ignore Silvie's femininity. All of us Rochford boys were aware of her."

Willow had sighed. It was true that Silvie had never lacked admirers and before her marriage to Pelham, had had a string of lovers, several of whom were younger than herself. But Willow did not want to think of her pretty little daughter leading what had been Silvie's life. She wanted to see her safely and happily married—secure in the protection of a good husband. Toby was right, of course, when he said it was far too soon to be considering such things. Lucienne must be permitted to enjoy herself before she settled down to matrimony.

She linked her arm through Lucy's, hurt as she so often was that there was no answering pressure of affection at this sign of intimacy. Together, they walked into the drawing room where their plump hostess awaited them. As Willow made her way over to Lady Barratt to compliment her upon the dinner, Annabel Barratt crossed the large room to Lucy's side.

"I scarcely had a chance to speak to you before dinner," she said, adding with a half smile: "I wanted to meet you because my brothers have never stopped talking about you since I arrived home from London."

Lucy glanced curiously at her companion. Although fair like herself, Annabel's hair was the deep, golden color of corn and her eyes forget-me-not blue. In her mid-twenties, her direct, forceful manner of speaking set her apart from her elder sisters, Louise and Gillian, who talked of little else but their wardrobes and domestic affairs. Lucy wondered idly if Annabel's forthrightness came as a result of her divorce.

The subject was taboo in the Barratt household, Lucy had been informed, so she was not a little surprised when Annabel referred to it.

"I suppose, like everyone else, you think that having made my bed, I should lie in it," the older girl said defensively. "I know the family disapproved dreadfully when I left my husband but I don't care. I like living by myself. I have my own flat in Montpelier Square, you know. I can do exactly as I please there, including my work for the Suffragettes—of which my parents heartily disapprove.

"I suppose you don't know much about the Movement," Annabel went on. "We want liberty for women, and of course, the vote. Christabel Pankhurst is a great friend of mine—she's our leader and she's suffered the indignities of imprisonment three times for our cause. One day, if you like, I will introduce you to her."

Lucy was impressed. To be willing to endure such horrors, as had been related to her, in aid of any cause, seemed to Lucy to be the epitome of martyrdom.

"I hope you won't let your family marry *you* off too young," Annabel said in warning tones. "They'll try, of course. Mat-

rimony is all that our parents' generation can envisage for
their daughters, whereas there is a whole new world awaiting
us if we've sense enough to demand it. It's terrible being
shackled to a man you don't even like, dominated by him and
having to lead *his* life instead of your own. We Suffragettes
think women who have brains should use them, don't you
agree?"

Lucy, who had been trained to use her body rather than
her brain, was uncertain of her reply. The Convent had in
fact given her a sound basic education but not with a view
to going to a University as Oliver would one day do. Work,
so far as her experience indicated, meant domestic drudgery
and no matter what, she would never return to that kind of
labor.

Annabel, she decided, was almost as boring as George. It
seemed so silly of her to live alone in a small flat when she
could have enjoyed the luxuries of the Barratts' household.
She talked ceaselessly, droning on about her friend, Christabel, and her mother, Mrs. Emmeline Pankhurst. The only
point in common they seemed to have was their determination
not to marry, Annabel for the second time and Lucy ever. For
totally different reasons, they disliked men—Annabel because
she resented their superiority; Lucy because she mistrusted
them. She had seen far too often how unfaithful they were
to their wives while professing to adore them; and she had
experienced at first hand the fickleness of their natures. Although it must be all of five years ago, and Lucy little more
than twelve years old at the time, she had given her unstinted
adoration to an artist by the name of Maurice Dubois. Three
times a week, she had been allowed out of *Le Ciel Rouge* to
go to his studio to model for him. She had believed sincerely
that he really cared for her, not just as a model but as a
person. But suddenly, without warning, or explanation that
she could understand, he had told her he never wished to
paint her again, casting her aside as if she were a worthless
object of which he had suddenly tired.

"I was watching you at dinner and I could see you were
intelligent," Annabel continued. "You're very pretty, too," she
added grudgingly. "I was the same at your age. Did you know
that Francis Rochford, the youngest of your uncles, wanted
to marry me? He was crazy about me but I preferred Pelham.
Poor Francis died, but I suppose you know that."

Lucy's interest was revived. She had not heard mention of

this dead uncle who, so Annabel now informed her, was a bit of a 'bad hat.' It seemed she knew the other Rochford too, called Rupert—between Pelham and Francis in age—who had left home in disgrace.

"An Oscar Wilde type!" Annabel said in a whisper. But her innuendo fell on deaf ears since Lucy had never heard of the playwright or of his disgrace. Even had she known of his crime, she would not have been particularly shocked since Madame had talked at length about the strange preferences men had for ways of satisfying their lusts.

The intimate conversation the two girls were enjoying had to stop as Lady Barratt approached.

"Lucienne, my dear child, I must compliment you upon your dress. Quite delightful!" She took Lucienne's arm and led her to one of the sofas. "Sit here beside me," she said in a conspiratorial tone. "I have something to tell you. You have made quite an impression on dear Alexis. He plied me with questions about you during dinner and has insisted I should introduce you to him when the men rejoin us. It's quite a feather in your cap, child. The girls—and their Mamas—have been after him for years but he has so far proved a confirmed bachelor. He comes from a most distinguished family, you know. His father was related to Prince Kinsky who was one of the Empress Elizabeth of Austria's attendant noblemen before she was assassinated, poor woman!"

Lucy was suitably impressed. It was the closest she had ever come to a genuine prince, albeit one of foreign birth. She awaited with interest her introduction to Count Zemski, but it was not destined to take place. As soon as the men rejoined them after their cigars and brandy, George hurried to his mother's side.

"Zemski has had a telephone message recalling him urgently to London," he told his mother. "Something to do with the war between Italy and Turkey. He rushed off in the most enormous hurry as if it were a matter of life and death. Odd chap, really. Nobody seems quite sure what he does. Even Hilary isn't in the secret."

Lady Barratt tapped Lucy's arm coyly with her fan.

"Now isn't that a shame, my dear," she said. "Never mind, I shall make sure there is another occasion for you to meet Alexis."

She stood up and moved away to prepare her guests for

the informal piano recital she had arranged for their entertainment.

George at once occupied his mother's place on the sofa. He looked down at Lucy.

"At least that is one less admirer to distract your attention from me," he said happily. "Would you think it dreadful cheek if I told you how pretty you look? You're the most stunning girl I've ever met, Miss Rochford."

Disappointed by the departure of the mysterious Alexis Zemski, Lucy decided even George's company was less boring than after dinner conversations in a lady's drawing room. She smiled at him from beneath her lashes.

"How could I be angry with so flattering a compliment," she said. "You may sit beside me at the recital if you wish, and you may call me Lucienne."

George's face turned a dull brick red.

"Jolly decent of you . . . er, Lucienne!" he stammered, longing with all the aching passion in his young body to plant a kiss on that softly smiling, inviting little mouth.

As soon as it was decent to do so, he would ask her to marry him, he decided. He'd never met a girl quite like her and had not had a good night's sleep since his first sight of her. She had had the same effect upon his brother, Howard, too. Hitherto they had been the very best of friends but now it was impossible for them not to be jealous of one another. He could see Howard making his way toward them, his brows drawn together in an angry scowl. Of course, he couldn't blame Lucienne for smiling so prettily at his brother since she was sweet to everyone but he wished she would not permit young Howard to let his hand rest in such a proprietary fashion upon her arm.

He could not know that Lucy was quite unaware of the contact. Her thoughts were elsewhere as her imagination conjured up the impression she would create were she to tell her former colleagues at *Le Ciel Rouge* that she had attracted the attention of a foreign count whose family connections included a real prince.

The next day, when young Oliver questioned her about the dinner party, Lucy mentioned Alexis Zemski, admitting that she had thought him a handsome man. Oliver studied her face curiously.

"It sounds as if you like him a lot more than George or

Howard," he commented shrewdly. "You haven't been ass enough to fall in love with him, Lucy?"

Lucy's face broke into a wide smile.

"Love!" she echoed. "What on earth has love got to do with anything, silly boy. I shall certainly never let myself fall in love. There's no fun in it—only pain." She looked at Oliver's uncomprehending stare and her face softened. "Don't look so bothered," she said gently, ruffling his dark curls. "If I've told you once, I've told you a dozen times, I shall never get married; and if I do, it certainly won't be to Count Zemski."

"That's all right then," Oliver said with a sigh of relief. "For one awful moment, I quite thought you were getting soppy about him, with all your chatter about his 'strange green eyes and curly fair hair!'" He mimicked Lucy with remarkable aptitude.

Lucy laughed and the tall, slim, fair girl with her leggy twelve-year-old companion forgot all about the dinner party as they climbed up to the clock tower overlooking the stable yard with a box of cigarettes, to indulge their mutual intention to learn how to smoke.

Chapter 4

May—June 1911

Reluctantly, Roberta Inman gently covered her lover's naked body with a sheet and then slipped her arms into the sleeves of his crimson, quilted silk dressing gown.

Still drowsy from the aftermath of passion, Alexis smiled at the tender concern on the pale face of the woman who had risen from his bed.

"You spoil me, Roberta!" he said, his voice warm with tenderness. "It is I who should be taking care of you!"

Roberta Inman smiled down at him, her raven black hair falling loose about her cheeks, her gray eyes gentle as she regarded the man she loved. The intense satisfaction his body had given her was, as always, yielding to a deep depression. It was a familiar emotion and one she now accepted as a matter of course. She understood why it overcame her: the reason lay quite simply in the fact that while she loved Alexis with all her heart, body and soul, he had never loved her.

She had been his mistress now for eight years, but knowing she could count upon his faithful devotion was only partial compensation for his failure to love her. Her need for his love was invariably heightened after their mutual desire was satisfied. She tried to tell herself that it was perhaps as well Alexis had never considered marriage to her, for she could never leave her husband. When she was still a very young girl, her parents had forced her into marriage with a man thirty years her senior—an elderly Scottish peer who was now bedridden. He had been impotent even on their honeymoon, and it was inevitable that sooner or later his young wife would be tempted to take a lover.

But there had been no one Roberta had really cared about enough until she met Alexis and then, for the first time in her life, she had fallen in love. He had been twenty-two years old and on the threshold of his career in the Foreign Office, after reading maths and physics at Oxford. Although he had a large circle of undergraduate friends, there was no woman in his life. His mother had died when he was only six years old and he had been brought up by his Croation father, a strict but kindly man whom Alexis greatly admired. But he, too, had died two years previously and Alexis lived alone in the huge house in Cadogan Gardens, looked after by a devoted elderly housekeeper.

Not only had Roberta been attracted to him physically, but her maternal instincts had been aroused and she had sensed his need for a feminine influence in his life. Five years his senior, she had no feeling of guilt when she had set out to seduce him. From the very first, Alexis had been honest with her. When he discovered she was genuinely in love with him, he had tried to end the affair but Roberta had persuaded him to continue their discreet rendezvous. Committed as she was to her invalid husband, there was no question of her relationship with Alexis ruining a happy marriage; nor was Lord Angus likely to die and leave her free to marry again. As it was, she and Alexis could trust each other to keep their affair a closely guarded secret and were hurting no one while giving each other comfort and pleasure.

The arrangement suited Alexis as well as Roberta. Entirely wrapped up in his work, he did not want the distractions of a wife and family. He traveled abroad frequently and the fewer the demands upon his time, the easier it was for him. As far as he was aware, Roberta had successfully rid herself of her girlish notions of love for him and he believed their relationship was one of comfortable, mutual affection.

A tall, statuesque woman, sophisticated and controlled, Roberta suited Alexis admirably. Moreover, he was genuinely fond of her, as well as grateful to her. He took her long, slender hand and pressed his lips to the cool, dry skin, drawing her down on the bed beside him.

"Don't hurry away from me, Roberta," he said. "Stay and talk to me for a while."

She smiled at him.

"If you would like me to," she agreed. "Tell me about that dreary party you had to attend last weekend. What a boring fellow Hilary Lennox is! I can't see why Louise married him— but she seems to admire him."

"Louise Barratt is not exactly intelligent herself," Alexis said smiling. "They are probably well enough matched. Besides, one should not forget that the Barratts had three girls to marry off and Hilary is well connected. As to the dinner party, Annabel and Gillian were home for Easter, as well as Louise—Gillian looking very pregnant and Macintyre the proud father-to-be!"

Roberta laughed.

"You must have been bored to tears!" she commiserated.

She was surprised as much by the expression that suddenly crossed Alexis' face as by the tone of his voice when he said hesitantly:

"As a matter of fact, I wasn't as bored as I expected to be. Lady Rochford and the eldest Rochford, Tobias, were there. He was the one who followed her to America, I gather. It's obvious to everyone they are very much in love and I suppose now her husband is dead, Lady Rochford will marry the fellow. He seemed a pleasant enough chap—and she's still very beautiful."

"*Can* they marry?" Roberta asked. "Isn't it against church ruling even for a widow to marry her husband's brother?"

Alexis shrugged his shoulders.

"I think it is in England but Lennox told me on the journey down that Lady Rochford had let slip to his mother-in-law that they might be able to get married in the United States."

"I hope they can if they really are in love," Roberta said. "Is it true that the late Lord Rochford's behavior was such that he more or less forced his wife to leave him?"

Alexis nodded.

"It's only gossip and one shouldn't rely on it. Lennox said the fellow had a string of mistresses and several illegitimate children, besides running through his wife's money to keep the family out of debt. To tell you the truth, Roberta, I have heard rumors that the daughter they so suddenly and mysteriously acquired was one of Rowell Rochford's by-blows. But the girl was at the Barratts' party and one thing is beyond doubt—she's her mother's child. I never saw anyone so like her parent. Only the eyes are different—blue instead of brown."

Familiar as she was with every cadence of her lover's voice, Roberta once again felt a moment of unease.

"Lucienne Rochford can hardly be a child if she was present at dinner!" she commented with assumed casualness.

Alexis nodded, unaware that his underlying excitement was obvious to Roberta.

"Lady Barratt told me she is seventeen although she has

not yet 'come out' officially. I did not actually talk to her—I had to leave directly after dinner as you know. But one could not fail to notice her. They say she has just emerged from a convent in France but...I don't know why I should have such an impression...I felt her manner was out of keeping with so sheltered and confined an upbringing. Maybe I was wrong. I don't really know."

But she intrigues you, Roberta thought unhappily, aware that for the first time in her relationship with Alexis she had cause to be jealous. As a rule, he was quite indifferent to the charms of the pretty young girls he was constantly meeting. Youth, he had so often told her, held little fascination for him. He preferred the sophisticated companionship of an older woman and, in any event, had no need of female companionship with Roberta around whenever he needed her.

Was that preference now changing, Roberta asked herself, aware suddenly of the tiny wrinkles that had begun to show themselves around her eyes; of the slackening of the skin beneath her chin; the loosening of the muscles of her full breasts. Alexis had said that the Rochford girl was like her mother and Lady Rochford was a renowned beauty.

"Perhaps you will solve the riddle when next you see the girl," she said lightly.

"I doubt if I'll be seeing her again in the near future," Alexis replied, his tone unconsciously regretful. "I have to go abroad for a month and anyway, as I've told you, she is not yet out and is still in mourning, so she won't be in London for the Season."

Roberta stood up with carefully feigned lethargy.

"It's time I went home," she said. "Angus will be wondering where I am." As she dressed, her thoughts were on Alexis and the Rochford girl. She realized that he must have been far more impressed than he admitted since he had worked out already his chances of meeting her again.

Slowly she pulled on her fine ribbed-silk stockings and fastened them to her beribboned suspenders. As a rule, Alexis loved to watch her dress, confessing that this insight into feminine behavior was a delightful intimacy he enjoyed. But when Roberta looked down at him again, she saw that he was fast asleep. His closed fists lay either side of his head on the pillow like a child's and, accompanying the pain of fear, Roberta felt a wave of tenderness. Her lover looked so young and vulnerable in sleep, the slightly damp hair curling on his high forehead, lashes dark on his flushed cheeks concealing the brilliant green of his eyes. His body, beneath the thin covering of the linen sheet was perfectly proportioned—firm, muscular, strong yet graceful. She knew every line and curve, and the particular smell of his body was so familiar to her that she could have identified him had she been blind simply by being near him.

Her love for him was an emotion so intense that, momentarily, tears stung her eyes. She bent her head and kissed him on his mouth. He did not wake but turned in his sleep so that his body curled sideways away from her. In her heightened state of emotion, the movement seemed to Roberta to be symbolic of his departure from her.

It will not be long before I lose him, she thought as she let herself quietly out of his house and walked away in search of a cab. Never before had Alexis failed to come downstairs with her and see her safely upon her way. And when I do have to relinquish him to someone else, it will be forever, she thought. Alexis himself had said so.

"I'll never leave you, my darling Roberta—not unless I marry, and that I don't intend to do."

But none knew better than Roberta that although he had attained the age of thirty, Alexis had not as yet fallen in love.

By the time she reached the house in Eaton Terrace, Roberta had managed successfully to calm her fears with reason. It was, she told herself, only she who had mentioned love in connection with the Rochford girl. Alexis himself had admitted no more than that he had been intrigued...and that was to be expected when she considered the sudden appearance of a girl who, so everyone believed, had died years ago. Perhaps she was Lady Rochford's child by another man! And yet as far as Roberta Inman was aware, no slur had ever been cast upon Lady Rochford's reputation. Roberta had met her once and thought her elegant, sweet and rather sad. She did not have the look of a woman who might, though unhappily married, find compensation with a lover. In any event, the late Lord Rochford would have been unlikely to recognize a child not his own.

As her manservant opened the door for her, Roberta smiled. What need had she to be wary of Alexis' curiosity when she herself found the girl's story so strange! With a sigh of relief, Roberta removed her hat and coat and, composing her features, went up the wide staircase to spend a companionable hour with the tetchy, ill-tempered old man who loved her as Alexis never would, and to whose bedside, pity chained her as surely as no other feeling could.

Roberta Inman was quite correct in assuming that Willow, while unhappily married to Rowell Rochford, had not had an affair with the man who loved her. Since the day Toby had left Rochford Manor and his beloved laboratory to follow her to America, he had asked no more of her than that he be permitted to look after her and the children. He had moved into a house in the same neighborhood as herself in San Francisco and insisted upon observing every propriety lest her reputation should suffer. By tacit agreement, they never spoke of the deep, passionate love they felt for one another and although those who knew them best could not fail to see through their careful friendliness, no one ever spoke of this deep-seated love.

In private, it was mentioned often between Nathaniel and Angela Corbett. Nathaniel had been not only the best friend of Willow's father but he was chairman of the huge Corporation, T.R.T.C. owned by the millionaire before his untimely death in the San Francisco earthquake. Now in his early sixties, Nathaniel still ran the Corporation in trust for Willow's two children, Oliver and Alice. It was this financial investment that made it possible for Willow to be independent of the man she had married and return to her homeland just over a year ago.

It had seemed tragic to Nathaniel and his wife that Willow and Toby could never marry. No couple were better suited and both admired Tobias Rochford in a degree comparable with their lack of respect for Rowell. His death at the comparatively young age of forty-five seemed to them like a miracle and it was Nathaniel who made the necessary legal inquiries that proved marriage was now possible for Willow and her brother-in-law. Had Nathaniel had his way, they would have been married in the United States before ever they returned to England. But his wife approved of their postponing such a ceremony until at least a year after Lord Rochford's death.

"They have waited so long, without hope, it is right that they should wait a little longer and observe the decencies," she said.

Somehow, Willow thought as she walked with Toby up to his laboratory, it seemed harder to keep the distance between them since they had come back home to this house where she had first discovered her love for him. It was in Toby's laboratory that they had for the one and only time in their lives, held each other in their arms and permitted themselves to admit their love and need for each other. Now that Rowell was buried in Havorhurst graveyard and his personal effects were disposed of, it was all too easy for her to forget him and the unhappy marriage they had shared. Despite the outward appearances of mourning, the house had begun to develop a new atmosphere in which children's laughter could be heard; the servants sang as they went about their duties; happiness was at last being allowed to flourish.

She herself, continued to wake each morning with a radiant joy in the knowledge that she had her beloved daughter beneath her roof once more. It still hurt her deeply, that after three months, Lucienne showed no desire for the intimacies of mother and daughter which Willow craved. She had adored her own quiet, loving, Quaker mother and Lucienne's reserve was hard for her to understand. She suffered each time her tentative attempts to get close to her child were rejected.

"I feel she blames me for her being lost all those years!" Willow said repeatedly to Toby. "But she refuses to let me talk about her birth and won't listen when I try to tell her how I suffered when they told me she was dead. Surely she must realize how much I love her when I can accept her into our family despite... despite the degradation of the life she was leading so short a while ago."

"I don't think Lucienne feels any guilt about those years," Toby said gently. "She is a very practical child. It was simply another way of life to her. I know it is hard for you to understand, my love, but Lucienne can see no evil in the Madame who took her into her house. Shocking as it must seem to you, the woman was like the mother she had never known; and the girls there befriended her and were like sisters. In a way, we should admire her for her loyalty. Silvie tells me she will not hear one word against any of them."

Willow sighed as Toby closed the laboratory door behind them. He had recently been to the newly opened Radium Institute in London and, as a result, had been inspired to renew his research.

"You're pleased to be home, aren't you, Toby?" she asked with a smile.

Toby paused, looking around his untidy domain with satisfaction.

"I suppose I have missed this place," he admitted, adding quickly, "although I never once regretted leaving it that dreadful day last year. It seems so much longer ago than twelve months. I could never have let you disappear across the Atlantic without me."

Willow reached out her hand and gently touched his cheek.

"As soon as it can be arranged, we will return to the States and be married. Be patient a little longer, my dearest."

Toby gave her his lopsided grin.

"I will, my sweet Willow—but it isn't always easy. I want you so very much."

Not daring to touch his cheek any longer, Willow withdrew her hand and stepped away from him.

"It cannot be more than I want you, Toby," she said huskily.

Their eyes met briefly, filled with tenderness and longing. Then the tension was suddenly gone. They smiled in perfect understanding and Willow turned and quietly left the room.

In June the new King was crowned George V; Mary, his Queen beside him. The Rochfords did not go to London but contributed generously to the Havorhurst village celebrations. Not one dwelling was without its gay bunting and the village shop did twice its normal trade selling souvenirs—Union Jacks, mugs decorated with the picture of the new King and posters of the King and Queen surrounded by heraldic signs.

Willow gave a small, informal dinner party for the Barratts, but of the two older boys only George was present as Howard had gone up to Cambridge to visit the college he would be joining in the Michaelmas term.

George took the opportunity to propose marriage to Lucienne.

"I know your mother would think you are far too young yet for us to get engaged," he told her in the privacy of the conservatory, his red, freckled face sweating with anxiety as he gazed into Lucienne's eyes, "but if you wanted to, Lucienne, we could be secretly engaged. You do care for me a little bit, don't you?"

Lucy was interested—not because she had any feelings for the large, dull George but because she was excited to think that he really did want to marry her. It was her first marriage proposal. How impressed Madame Lou-Lou would be! As for the girls, they would think her quite mad turning down a man who would one day be a baronet like his father.

"Of course I like you very much, George," she said. "But I certainly don't want to get married."

George took hope from her words.

"But I'll wait for you to grow up, Lucienne—however long you wish. No one need know we are promised to one another. I could give you a ring—my gold signet ring..." he added on a sudden inspiration. "You could wear it round your neck, Lucienne dearest, and it would make me the happiest man in the world."

Lucy gazed at his flushed face thoughtfully.

"Suppose I never wanted to marry you..." she said doubtfully.

"An engagement isn't unbreakable," George interrupted. "Most especially if it is not publicly announced. Not that *I* should ever want to break our engagement. Please, dear, dear Lucienne, say 'yes.'"

Gold, so Madame Lou-Lou vouchsafed, was the most valuable of commodities—worth far more than paper money, Lucy thought. It held its value in wars, in every country in the world, in any community. And George had offered to give her his gold ring. That it happened to be his signet ring meant nothing to her.

"How could I wear your ring around my neck without someone seeing it!" she temporized. "I would have to hide it somewhere, George!"

His face radiant, George informed her that she could hide it anywhere she pleased as long as she accepted it.

"And you will not tell anyone?" Lucy questioned, knowing instinctively that she was almost certainly contravening one of the hundreds of mysterious conventions she was still in the process of learning.

"I swear it on my honor!" George cried, pulling off the ring and pressing it into Lucy's cool palm.

"Thank you very much, George!" Lucy said politely. She was delighted by the gift and realizing how much it would please the donor, she stood on tiptoe and kissed him on the mouth.

George's reaction did not particularly surprise her. It was quite obvious how hotly he desired her. Perhaps, if he proved generous enough, she might allow him more than a kiss. But judging by the effect her brief embrace had upon him, she felt it unwise at this moment to encourage him further. At her suggestion, they rejoined the rest of the party and to George's chagrin, she ignored him for the remainder of the evening.

In July, the King's eldest son, David, was invested as Prince of Wales. Just eighteen years of age, the handsome young heir to the throne was already popular with the people who were delighting in the fact that his father seemed set to follow in the old King's shoes. There had been many who feared George V would make unwelcome changes, perhaps returning to the more severe, restricting edicts of his grandmother, Victoria. But he had already proved himself as keen a racegoer as Edward and, an excellent horseman, he went riding whenever he could. Seemingly tireless, he had carried out numerous visits to museums, institutes, even to the General Post Office, throughout the spring, and appeared to enjoy meeting people. He entertained the German Kaiser, inspected the troops at Aldershot and after the Coronation, attended the Spithead Review. Later in June, he presented himself before one hundred thousand children whom he had invited to the Crystal Palace.

Throughout the month of July England was enjoying a heat wave, the temperature rising to ninety-three degrees in the shade. Oliver and Lucy went secretly down to the lake to swim, Oliver in his underpants, Lucy quite naked. Her total lack of embarrassment gradually overrode Oliver's shock at this absence of modesty. He quickly became accustomed to the sight of his sister's pale, beautifully formed body flashing past him in the warm water lapping the shores of the island. He drew the line at this display of nudity only when his friend, Henry, begged to be allowed to join these escapades.

"It wouldn't be decent!" Oliver said in answer to Lucy's complaints that half the fun was gone if she couldn't feel the water on her bare skin. "Don't you understand anything, Lucy? He's a man—or almost!"

"Well, so are you!" Lucy laughed but Oliver only said crossly:

"That's different. You're my sister—and I'm not at all sure if it's all right for *me* to see you either!"

His feelings toward her were totally innocent but he nevertheless felt slightly guilty about the effect Lucy's nakedness had upon him. Until now, he had never thought much about the difference between men and women. Love, as expressed by the poets, had hitherto struck him as extremely soppy. The line *'Shall I compare thee to a summer's day?'* had until now meant no more to him than another boring Shakespeare sonnet to be memorized.

Looking at Lucy, he could appreciate, *'For here lies Juliet and her beauty makes this vault a feasting presence full of light.'* His sister was so pretty, he could understand why both Howard and George Barratt wanted to marry her. It was re-assuring to hear from her own lips that she had no intention of marrying either—or indeed, of marrying at all.

When his mother had informed him that he had inherited his father's peerage and with the title, the Rochford estate, the material advantages had not occurred to him. But now he knew of Lucy's desire not only to be rich but also to be mistress of Rochford Manor, he realized it was in his power to make both dreams possible.

"You can run my house for me, Lucy," he told her. "You can invite anyone you please and have as many parties and clothes and jewels as you want. I'll never ask you to do anything you don't want to do or see anybody you don't like. It will be your home as much as mine."

"And what of Mama?" Lucy inquired.

"We'll build a dower house for her." Oliver had already thought of how his plans for himself and Lucy would affect Willow. "Uncle Toby often said Grandmère should never have gone on living at Rochford once our parents married. He said she caused an awful lot of trouble and Papa should have built a dower house for her."

Lucy dried her naked body with her petticoat and pulling on her white camisole and frilly drawers, spread her wet garment on the bullrushes to dry. Then she lay down beside Oliver on the sun-browned grass and laced her hands behind her head.

"Tell me about this old grandmother," she said. "You knew her, didn't you, Oliver? Was she as wicked as Mama said?"

Oliver grinned.

"I quite liked Grandmère and I think she liked me. I was very young when she died, nearly five I think, so I didn't see much of her evil ways. I only knew what Mama and Uncle Toby told me. They said she was cruel to Aunt Dodie who lived here before she married Uncle James. Grandmère hated her because her leg and arm were deformed. And she tried to stop Aunt Dodie marrying Uncle James because he was only a schoolteacher and Grandmère thought that too lowly an occupation for anyone marrying a Rochford. She was an awful snob and only tolerated Mama's parents because our grandfather was a millionaire. Mama said she was intolerant with everyone except Uncle Francis whom she spoilt because he looked like Greatgrandfather; and especially unkind to Uncle Rupert because he was artistic and not manly enough to please her. But she was kind to me and played games with me and read me stories and sometimes she gave me one of the little violet-scented sweets she kept in a box by her bed."

Lucy tried to reconcile this image of an autocratic but sometimes kindly old woman with the wicked harridan Aunt Silvie had blamed for Lucy's abduction. Grandmère's portrait painted at Rochford by Millais, many years ago, hung in the gallery and each time Lucy passed it, she silently cursed the old lady who had tried to deny her her rightful heritage. But for her, Lucy would have grown up in this house enjoying the luxuries little Alice enjoyed and would not now be having to learn to think and talk and behave like a lady; she would have had no shameful past to hide—a past so terrible, she had been told, that it must never be mentioned to a living soul.

Aunt Silvie had called the old grandmother 'ruthless' and described her as having 'a will of iron.' Now, Lucy decided, it was her turn to be ruthless and pursue her own aims regardless of any opposition. As yet, she was unsure of the extent of the Rochford wealth. She knew that her mother's father had left his entire fortune to Oliver and Alice and that this included a vast business in America called the Tetford Rail Road and Transport Corporation. It seemed likely therefore, that young Oliver would be very rich when he came of age and that she might do a lot worse than follow his suggestion to run his home for him.

But glancing now at the boy's youthful body stretched out beside her own, she realized that this dream held no real security for her. With his dark curly hair and large, laughing brown eyes, Oliver was destined to become an extremely handsome young man. He greatly resembled their Uncle Pelham whose good looks, good humor and sense of fun made him instantly attractive to women. The likelihood was that Oliver would one day fall in love and marry. Then she would be cast aside.

Lucy's mouth hardened. Security lay in one area only—

in becoming financially independent. Upstairs in a locked jewel case she had already tucked away George's gold ring, a pearl necklace Uncle Toby had given her on her seventeenth birthday last March; and more valuable still, a real diamond and sapphire brooch Mama had given her on the same occasion. Only yesterday she had added to her growing hoard, the gold sovereign which each of the children had been given to commemorate the Coronation. Lastly, she still had in her possession the gold locket that the old doctor had given her when he had first come in search of her at *Le Ciel Rouge*.

Lucy had been permitted to look at her mother's jewelry and she was well aware that her own few possessions were of minute value in comparison. But she had plenty of time, she thought as she watched a dragonfly skimming across the lake toward them. Mama had promised her a real diamond tiara when she was presented next Season. Before then, there would be Christmas which Oliver had described as a time of year when they received the very best of presents—his bicycle; Alice, her big, three-story dolls' house complete with every last piece of furniture in perfect replica.

Lucy closed her eyes, allowing the tension to ease from her body. There was no doubt that Madame would say she had landed on her feet in no small way! Mama had forbidden her to write a letter to Madame. But, Lucy comforted herself, Aunt Silvie had said she would invite her to Paris and then she could go secretly one day on her own to visit them all at *Le Ciel Rouge*. What an impression she would create in her fine clothes and jewels! She might even pay a call on Maurice Dubois, the artist. What pleasure there would be in showing him how greatly he had misjudged her future!

"What are you thinking about, Lucy?" Oliver broke into her reverie. "You've got such a funny smile on your face."

Lucy opened her eyes and met Oliver's curious gaze. Her smile gave way to a laugh.

"I was thinking about how I might be revenged upon someone who once hurt me," she said happily.

"I don't believe it, Lucy," Oliver replied. "You would not be a bit like Mama if it were true. She forgives everybody. She has even forgiven Papa for making her so unhappy."

"Well, I have not forgiven him for making promises to me he could not keep," Lucy rejoined. "So you see, young Oliver, I do not have the dear, sweet, kindly nature you attribute to Mama! She is weak and I am strong."

"Strong willed, like Grandmère!" Oliver teased.

Lucy was not annoyed. She smiled as she said:

"Perhaps I am like her—ruthless."

"As if you could be!" Oliver cried. "Come on, Lucy, let's have another swim before it's too late. It will soon be tea time and George is bringing Henry over afterward so we can all play tennis. George says he'll teach you."

Apart from this new game, there was plenty to occupy Lucy during those long, hot summer days at Rochford. There were drives in the motorcar, sometimes to Tunbridge Wells with her mother and Alice to buy gloves or a hat or shoes; there were large picnics with the Barratts and Rochfords of all age groups; tennis parties, croquet matches and days at the seaside. And always for Lucy, there was George or Howard hovering around vying with one another to be first to fulfill her every whim.

At the beginning of August, there was a surprise visit from Alexis Zemski. He drove up to Rochford Manor in an open Lanchester—unaccompanied by a chauffeur. He presented himself to Willow and Toby, explaining that he had lunched with their neighbors, the Barratts, and being so close at hand, had decided upon the spur of the moment to pay them a call.

Willow hid her surprise as she invited her unexpected guest to join the family for tea on the lawn. Although she was aware of his long-standing friendship with Sir John and Lady Barratt, she and Toby had met him but once and that very brief occasion did not justify a visit of this nature without prior invitation.

But seeing how his eyes roved quickly over the family grouped in the shade of the big lime tree and came to rest on her pretty daughter, Willow suddenly made sense of the Count's visit. She was not displeased. Although Lucienne was not officially 'out,' she was seventeen years old and the handsome young man was an extremely eligible bachelor, much sought after, according to Lady Barratt, by mothers with daughters of marriageable age.

If Lucy was surprised to see the near stranger walking toward her, she showed no sign of it, nor appeared impressed by his attentive conversation during tea. She had planned secretly with Oliver to go swimming as soon as they could escape from the 'grown-ups' and the arrival of a guest meant a curtailment of their plan. She soon became aware of the extraordinary intensity of the Count's gaze and for the first time in her life, was made uncomfortable by a man's eyes. To arouse admiration was success in Madame's book and Lucy was well accustomed to such looks. But Alexis Zemski's strange green eyes did not express the kind of hungry desire she took for granted. His look, she thought, was calculating—as if he were trying to discover the person inside herself; as if he were trying to fathom what she was really thinking while she replied in pretty phrases to his polite conversation.

Alexis Zemski was unaware that the girl he had come especially from London to see again, felt threatened by him. His curiosity about her past was based purely on his interest in her as a person, for it had soon become clear to him that Miss Lucienne Rochford was quite different from all her contemporaries. Nor did she, in any respect, fit his idea of a young girl but recently released from the confines of a convent. She was far too self-possessed; too self-assured. Moreover, he soon realized, she was making no attempt to play the coquette with him, as was customary with all the silly young debutantes he encountered during the Season. He sensed that for some reason she did not like him, and her reaction to him became a challenge.

Alexis was not a particularly conceited man but with more than his share of good looks, his athletic frame and easy grace, since his early youth he had attracted the glances of women of all ages. Roberta had told him a dozen times that he had that special charm women found irresistible and she had assured him that the young Rochford girl would certainly not be indifferent. Now he was not only surprised but far more disappointed than he could have imagined. He had been unable to get the girl out of his thoughts.

Saying nothing to his mistress of his proposed visit to Havorhurst, Alexis had given way to his longings and using the Barratts as an excuse, called on the spur of the moment to see the fair-haired Lucienne.

But if his presence had failed to impress the daughter, Alexis certainly managed to engage the interest of the young Lord Rochford. When Oliver discovered that Alexis could not only fly but actually had an airplane of his own which he kept at Brooklands in Surrey, the boy was beside himself with excitement. His swimming expedition with Lucy was forgotten as he plied Alexis with questions.

Willow tried to quiet him.

"Oliver has always had his sights set on the heavens," she

said apologetically. "We once had a balloonist land in the garden when Oliver was a little boy. Since then he has been determined to become a pilot when he is old enough. Now please don't pester Count Zemski any longer, Oliver. He must be tired of all your questions."

But Alexis had taken a fancy to the boy, so different in looks from his elder sister but nonetheless handsome. He was aware of Lucy's blue eyes regarding him resentfully and wondered if she could possibly be jealous of his attentions to the child. But when he offered to take Oliver some time to see the airplanes at Brooklands, the boy at once turned to his sister and said:

"You would like to see them, too, wouldn't you, Lucienne? Could we all go, Sir? I mean, could we take my sister with us?"

Alexis smiled, staring into Lucienne's eyes as he said:

"I would be delighted if you would come along, Miss Rochford. I have a biplane made by the Short brothers."

Lucy's interest was aroused.

"Is it difficult to fly an airplane?"

Alexis smiled, strangely excited by the flash of fire in Lucy's eyes.

"No, not really, Miss Rochford."

"But dangerous!" Oliver said quickly. "Since that crash last December, the monoplanes have been called 'Man-killers.' Isn't that right, Sir?"

Alexis nodded.

"But improvements are being made all the time and now the War Office has seen the possibilities of using airplanes in war time. We have had an Air Battalion since April."

"I read all about it," Oliver cried. "As soon as I leave school, I am going to join it. I have to go to Eton first though. I start next month. My friend, Henry Barratt, goes there and in a way, I am quite looking forward to it. Henry says Ullathorne's is a good house to be in."

"I, too, went to Eton," Alexis said. "I enjoyed my time there although I had to work a little harder than the other boys since we spoke mostly Croat at home when I was a child."

"You have no accent at all, Sir," Oliver said. "Not like Lucienne. She still rolls all her 'r's' and uses lots of French words when she can't think of the English ones."

"Bearing in mind that Lucienne has only been learning

our language for little more than a year, she speaks very well," Willow broke into the conversation.

"And if I may say so, her accent is delightful to listen to," Alexis added. "I hope you won't become too perfect, Miss Rochford."

"I expect she will in time," Oliver said. "Lucienne's quite good at most things."

Willow gave an indulgent smile.

"Unfortunately, that does not include needlework."

Lucienne had shown no inclination or aptitude for tapestry or petitpoint—or indeed, for any of the usual feminine pastimes.

"You could do it if you wanted to, couldn't you, Lucienne?" Oliver insisted.

Lucienne shrugged indifferently although she was annoyed to see a slight smile hovering round the mouth of their visitor as he listened to the conversation.

"I'm sure this subject must be very tedious for Count Zemski," she said. "Can we not talk of something else?"

Alexis' interest deepened. He knew that he could not bring himself to return to London without at least some promise of seeing Lucienne again. He turned to Willow.

"The conductor, Thomas Beecham, has arranged for Diaghilev's Russian ballet to come from St. Petersburg to England, Lady Rochford. If you are interested in ballet, I understand that Pavlova, Fokine and Nijinsky will be dancing in *Le Spectre de la Rose*. I will obtain a box one evening if you and your family would care to join me?" Alexis noted the quick, interested glance Lucienne stole at her mother and added persuasively:

"I heard that the company was a great success during their season in Paris."

"I would love to go," Willow said warmly. "Lucienne, my dear child, you would enjoy it enormously and it's wonderful that your first introduction to ballet should include Pavlova. She is quite magnificent, I have been told."

"Then I will telephone you as soon as it can be arranged," Alexis said, satisfied now to say his farewells. He shook Oliver's hand man to man and promised not to forget the outing to Brooklands in the near future.

"A jolly decent chap!" Oliver exclaimed as soon as Alexis was out of earshot. "Didn't you think so, Lucy? He's what I call a real sport. Didn't you like him, Lucy? You never even smiled when he said goodbye."

"He's all right, I suppose," Lucy said shrugging.

"I thought you considered he was good-looking?" Oliver persisted.

To his disappointment, Lucy gave another indifferent shrug.

"I suppose he is but I'd like him better if he didn't stare so!"

Oliver's flushed, excited face broke into a grin.

"That's because he was admiring you, Lucy. He probably thinks you're pretty. Perhaps he's madly in love with you."

This time, Lucy laughed.

"Of course he isn't, silly!" she said. "And even if he was, I wouldn't care."

Oliver looked thoughtful.

"I wouldn't mind if you married him, Lucy. I'd like a brother-in-law who owned his own airplane. He could teach me to fly!"

"I don't care if he has twenty airplanes and a dozen airships, too," Lucy retorted. "I'd never marry a man like him, even if I wanted to get married and I don't, as well you know."

But to Oliver's inevitable *why* wouldn't she marry a man like Alexis Zemski, Lucy had no answer. Only later, in the privacy of her bedroom, did she come to the conclusion that it was a matter of instinct—a feeling that the Count might well, for all his charm, be every bit as ruthless as herself; that he would get what he wanted in life just as she meant to have what *she* wanted. And that, as far as she was concerned did not include the bondage of marriage.

She fell asleep and dreamed, not of those strange, compelling green eyes but of Monsieur Maurice, the artist. It was a familiar dream in which she relived the hateful, humiliating moment when he had told her he never wanted to paint her again. How she had hated him as she had flung his money aside and run out of his studio knowing he would never invite her there again. In her dream now, as in reality five years ago, she ran through the rain-drenched streets back to the comforting arms of the middle-aged Yvette.

"Forget your artist, *ma petite*," Yvette had said, holding her in her arms. "No man is worth a woman's tears!"

"But I loved him. Truly I did..."

And this night, as always when she dreamed, Lucy woke to find her pillow wet with the tears she had sworn never again to shed.

The following day a taxi cab drew up outside Rochford Manor. The driver was instructed to wait while the occupant rang the bell.

Lucy and Oliver were renewing their attempts to teach themselves to smoke in the clock tower. From their vantage point they looked down at the tall, thin young man waiting for Dutton, the elderly butler, to open the door.

"He's wearing naval uniform," Oliver whispered, although they could not be overheard from such a distance. "I wonder who it can be!"

"It's not one of the Barratts," Lucy commented, noting the deeper copper tones of the young man's hair, distinguishing him from their ginger-topped neighbors.

Willow recognized him instantly as he was shown into the library. Taller, more man now than boy, this was the eldest of her late husband's illegitimate children. They had last met three years ago and she had not expected to see Philip Grey again. He had called on that occasion to repay a loan she had made him after his mother's death, before making his way up to the north of England to live with an elderly great aunt.

Despite Philip's unorthodox relationship to Willow's own family, she had both liked and admired the boy. He had sunk his pride to ask her assistance only out of a sense of responsibility for his destitute young brother and sister. She had never blamed him for being his father's bastard—a child of Rowell's long association with a mistress he had flaunted and then abandoned in the cruelest fashion. She therefore greeted Philip warmly.

"You must be how old now—seventeen?" she inquired as she bade him be seated. "And in uniform, too."

"I'm a naval cadet, training at Dartmouth," Philip replied, his young face unsmiling, his eyes dark with worry. "Please forgive this intrusion, Lady Rochford—the second one, I'm afraid."

Willow smiled, surprised how pleased she was to see this pleasant boy again.

"You have heard of your father's death?" she asked.

Philip nodded.

"Yes, Lady Rochford. But it is not about *his* death I have

come to talk to you. It is about the death of my Great Aunt Augusta."

"Oh? I am sorry to hear of it," Willow said, for she was aware that the old lady had taken Rowell's three young children under her wing and educated them after their mother's death and their father's desertion.

"It was not altogether unexpected," Philip said, leaning forward anxiously. "My great aunt was eighty-one and had been failing in body and mind for some time. The difficulty is, I have discovered, that she was grossly taken advantage of and the money she had earmarked to see my brother and sister cared for after her death, no longer exists."

"Perhaps you had better tell me the whole story," Willow said. "I may then be in a better position to advise you."

The young man attempted a smile.

"My own life and career are in the Royal Navy now. But my brother and sister are still only children and my great aunt intended they should complete their schooling. She was a fairly wealthy woman, Lady Rochford, but all her money was tied up in her husband's chemical works in Northumbria. When he died, she took control and under the guidance of the general manager, John Griffeth, all went well. But just over a year ago, Griffeth died and the assistant manager, a fellow called Bertram, took his place."

Philip's hands were twisting his naval cap round and round as he attempted to keep his voice quiet and calm.

"I never liked Bertram—he was too subservient, too smarmy would be a better description. But my great aunt would not hear a word against him. The auditors could find nothing wrong with the books and so I had no reason to back my instinct that all was not well. Then, six months ago, there was a fire. The works were burnt out—a total loss. The shock killed poor Aunt Augusta. When matters were gone into by the executors regarding the claim for the insurance—and the fire was a genuine accident—it was discovered that Bertram had grossly devalued the works for insurance purposes. Whilst leaving them at their true value on the books, he had been pocketing the difference between the high premiums and the low. But as he died in the fire, he cannot be called to account."

Philip paused but only to draw breath before he continued:

"Anyway, Lady Rochford, everything was lost. There was

not even enough to give the servants pensions. I have asked
the executors to sell the house so that my great aunt's
companion—who was to have stayed on to look after Mark
and Jane—will be provided for. Beyond that, there is nothing
and my naval pay is minimal. The executors have suggested
I should put my brother and sister into an orphanage..."

As his voice trailed into silence, Willow's thoughts winged
back to the past. Even before her marriage to Rowell, her
husband had been obsessed by his mistress, Georgina Grey.
He had installed her and their children in a house in London
which had been more a home to him than Rochford Manor.
Yet Rowell had finally tired of her and disclaimed all responsibility for this second family. Now for the second time
in their lives, his children were destitute.

As if reading her thoughts, Philip said earnestly:

"For the second time, I am here to ask you for a loan,
Lady Rochford. But this time, I am even less sure that I
will ever be able to repay it."

"I'll lend you the money, Philip, of course I will..." She
broke off, her thoughts in a turmoil. "How old are the
children now?" she asked. She had never met either of them
and understandably, had put them out of her mind after
Philip had told her they were all going to live with their
elderly relative.

"Mark is nearly fifteen. Jane is just twelve," Philip replied.
"If they had been a few years older, it wouldn't have been
so difficult to arrange something for them. Mark could have
joined me in the Navy—although he has never wanted to
go to sea; Jane might have found a position as a governess.
She's very quiet and well mannered, but..."

He hesitated, his eyes miserable as he stared down at his
hands. Willow felt a strong maternal urge to put her arms
around the thin, unhappy boy and comfort him. But she
remained at a distance, unable to rid herself of the memory
that they were Georgina Grey's children. How boldly Rowell's
mistress had tried to humiliate her, his new young bride,
here in her own home! She had only to close her eyes to
see Georgina in her yellow silk ball gown with its startling
scarlet sleeves, standing in the doorway, beckoning to Rowell
as if he were her servant and calling him away from his
wife's side to take her a fan!

Yet the woman had come to a bitter end, Willow reminded
herself sharply. She had ended her days horribly ill and so

poor that this young son had had to come to *her* for help. Fate—not Willow—had wrought vengeance upon Georgina Grey. It was Rowell who had come out of it all without penalty or suffering.

The sins of the fathers...Willow thought now. But it could never be fair that children should suffer for their parents' misdeeds.

"I presume your great aunt had brought you all up to a certain high standard of living," she spoke her thoughts aloud. "Adapting to life in an orphanage would be a terrible hardship for children protected as they have been."

Philip nodded.

"I have thought the same thing, Lady Rochford—and rejected the idea except as a very last resort. I have written to my brother's and sister's schools and it seems that if I could afford the fees both could remain there during the holidays..."

"No!" Willow said sharply. "That, too, would be no life for a child." These two children were like her Lucienne had been, without a mother or father; without a family. There must be no more such suffering if it could be avoided.

She walked over to the window and stared down at the large bowl of scarlet roses. No wonder the poor boy was so unhappy, she thought. The very idea of his brother and sister in an orphanage must be even more distressing for him than for her. But what alternative was there? If the children were to continue their boarding school education; then there would only be the holidays to worry about...a few weeks at Christmas and Easter and a slightly longer spell in the summer. Perhaps, she thought, they could come to Rochford? Goodness only knew the house was big enough. Patience had only little Alice to care for—she could keep an eye on the girl, Jane. The boy might be a companion for Oliver—he was only two years older...

But could she tolerate having Georgina's children under her roof? They were certainly not hers, Willow's, responsibility! On the other hand, they *were* her late husband's.

She turned to look at Philip. He was sitting silently, lost in his own thoughts. The droop of his head touched at her heart strings. He looked so hopeless, so despairing.

"Philip!" she said sharply to cover the emotion she was feeling. "You are to bring your brother and sister here to me. They can continue to go to their boarding schools in term-time but their holidays will be spent here at Rochford. Your sister, Jane, will be company for Alice, and Mark is of an age to be company for Oliver."

Philip's pale face was now flushed a deep red.

"I could not possibly accept such a generous offer..." he was saying when Willow interrupted him.

"I know this was not your intention when you came to ask for a loan, Philip. But don't you see, it is the obvious solution and it will be no problem for me. Rochford Manor is large enough to house four times as many children. Besides, I feel obliged to shoulder some of your late father's responsibilities. He should have made provision for you all in his Will. As it is, I can well afford it. No member of my family will ever be in want in their life time. And remember, Philip, all three of you are Rochfords, even if you bear your mother's surname."

Willow could not mistake the look of incredulity on the boy's face. Perhaps it was understandable that he should look so stunned. He was quite old enough to appreciate the fact that wives were not in the habit of adopting their husband's illegitimate children. Maybe if she had loved Rowell, she herself would not have been able to be so charitable. She thought of Toby, the man she did love, upstairs in his laboratory ignorant of the encumbrances she had just added to their lives! But she need have no fear that he would think differently from herself. If it were what she wanted, then he would be happy to support her. Moreover, the two children she was about to adopt were his niece and nephew— as closely related to him as Oliver and Alice. They were all his brother's offspring.

"I want you to meet your uncle—or at least one of them— your Uncle Tobias. You will like him, Philip. He is a good man. He, too, lives here and I defer to his judgment in all things so he would be as much a guardian to Mark and Jane as I. It's only right you should make his acquaintance."

Willow could understand Philip's hesitation. He had despised his father, Toby's brother. He could not put his brother and sister in the hands of someone he neither liked nor respected.

But it was as Willow knew it must be—within the half hour that they talked alone together, Toby and Philip became the best of friends. They were both laughing and at ease with one another as they rejoined her in the drawing room.

Philip hurried forward to clasp Willow's hand.

"I can't begin to tell you how grateful I am," he said. "When I left home this morning, I could think of nothing else during that long train ride to London but what I would do if I had to go back to Mark and Jane with bad news. Now I have a very happy future to put before them. Uncle Toby..." he used the words awkwardly and with a shy smile "...has offered to drive to Northumbria to collect them both next week. I have been given compassionate leave but must return soon to Dartmouth. But may I call and see you again on one of my leaves?"

"Philip, this is now your home as well as Mark's and Jane's," Toby said quietly. "We shall be most put out if you treat it as less than yours."

Before Philip left, Willow saw Toby press some notes into his hand and her heart filled with gratitude to him for his thoughtfulness. They stood side by side as Philip's car drove him away. As Willow slipped her hand into his, Toby smiled down at her.

"Seems we are acquiring quite a family, eh?" he said. "First our little Lucienne—and now two if not three more youngsters. Let's go and tell the three we've got that we're about to double up!"

"Dear Toby, I love you so much," Willow whispered. "I need you so much, too. How shall we explain matters to them?"

"We shall tell them that we are adopting a family whose relations are now all dead," Toby said calmly. "The past is not their concern. As for our friends, Willow, I doubt if many will even remember poor Georgina Grey, let alone associate these children with her."

It was true, Willow thought, for even she now had difficulty in recalling the precise appearance of the woman who had once caused her so much pain.

Chapter 5

❦

November—December 1911

IT WAS A BITTERLY COLD NOVEMBER DAY. ALEXIS RANG FOR HIS manservant to bring more coal for the fire, although the large drawing room of his London house was relatively draught free. Since Roberta's arrival half an hour earlier, she had been aware of her companion's restlessness and half feared, half guessed its cause.

She waited patiently while the footman went about his duties, her eyes intent upon Alexis' back as he stood now by the window looking out onto the leafless trees of the square. As the servant left the room, he seemed to brace his shoulders as if finally resolute. Turning to face her, he said:

"I have something I must tell you, Roberta. It has been on my mind for several weeks. Perhaps I should have told you before..."

Roberta dropped her gaze so that she could no longer see the look of anxiety and embarrassment in Alexis' green eyes. Fear of what he was about to say wrenched at her heart; but she gave no sign of it as she forced herself to speak in a light, casual tone.

"I think I know what it is you are trying to tell me," she said. "You have fallen in love with Lucienne Rochford and being the honest person you are, you cannot bear to go on pretending that our relationship is unchanged."

Alexis took a step toward her, his sense of relief and gratitude so strong that he intended to take her in his arms. But there was something in the rigidity of Roberta's body that kept him from doing so.

"I am right, am I not?" she persisted in that same toneless voice. "You needn't be afraid to confess it, Alexis."

Yes, Alexis thought with renewed relief. Roberta was no lovesick girl who would throw a fit of hysterics. She had known from the first that theirs was a relationship based on mutual need, mutual respect and was limited, as far as he was concerned, to a deep affection. The word love had not been mentioned for many years.

"I want to marry Lucienne," he said. The confession was out at last. "I told you that I would be taking her and her mother and uncle to the ballet last week. I would have spoken to Lady Rochford that night but I wanted to tell you first. I know it must be hard for you to understand, Roberta. It has all happened so quickly that even I cannot really understand it myself. I had not expected to fall in love, especially not with a girl of Lucienne's age."

Roberta allowed him to talk, the words coming easily now he had begun. She was wearing a new, particularly smart, black tweed coat and skirt. The jacket was fastened with jet buttons and under it she wore a white blouse with a black silk tie at her throat. She had chosen it carefully in order to attract Alexis' admiration. His taste was always good and he approved her preference for clothes that were very simple and sophisticated. "Black suits you with your raven hair," he had once told her.

Now she could think only that she had chosen inadvertently—or was it with some sixth sense?—exactly the right color for the occasion. This was the death of their long affair, when it was right she should be wearing the color of mourning.

Her smile was tinged with irony as she said:

"You don't have to ask my permission, Alexis. But I appreciate your concern for me. I would not have wanted to hear of your engagement from anyone else."

Forgetting his intention, Alexis now went forward and sat down beside Roberta on the velvet upholstered sofa, taking her hand in his.

"There is no question of an engagement," he said earnestly. "Lucienne is still a child—only seventeen—and she has not yet come out. Besides which..." he added with a sigh "...I don't think she much likes me. All I want from Lady Rochford is her permission to call and see Lucienne from time to time so that I might have a chance of winning her regard."

Now Roberta was surprised out of her calm.

"I find it hard to believe that any girl or woman is immune to your charms, Alexis. Surely she must be flattered that London's most eligible bachelor is paying her court?"

Alexis gave a rueful smile.

"You don't know Miss Lucienne Rochford," he said. "For one thing, she is unaware that I am 'eligible' and she certainly isn't impressed by the fact that I have a title. After all, she *is* Lord Rochford's daughter. And you are forgetting that I was thirty on my last birthday and that must seem quite ancient to a girl still in her teens."

Roberta remained silent. Alexis' modesty was well known to her. He had never fully understood how fascinating he was with his high cheekbones and emerald green eyes. She loved more than anything in the world to lie beside him as he slept, ruffling his crisp fair curls, watching his face, waiting for his slow, tender smile.

Her love for him had now become a pain that was almost overwhelming. Tears choked in her throat but remained unshed as she said huskily:

"Alexis, you are not only handsome, but you are good, kind and thoughtful. Your precious Lucienne will come to love you even if she is too young yet to appreciate your worth. I wish you luck!"

Alexis took the hand he was holding and, opening Roberta's closed fist, pressed his mouth to her palm. In this moment when she had virtually released him from their unwritten bondage, he felt the deepest affection for her.

"I owe you for so many years of happiness, my lovely Roberta. I wish there were some way in which I could repay you."

Gently, Roberta withdrew her hand. Her body was now quite rigid with her attempt to keep control of herself.

"The debt is as much mine as yours," she said. "And in any event, Alexis, why are we speaking so solemnly. We don't have to end our friendship merely because we are calling an end to our affair. I for one, would like to keep you as my friend."

Alexis was frankly surprised. He had anticipated that Roberta would be deeply hurt by his confession and he would not have blamed her had she been resentful and desirous of ending their relationship entirely. Her offer of friendship was more than welcome for he saw it not only as a pleasurable companionship but perhaps more importantly, that Roberta's feelings had not been so deeply involved as he had feared. The last thing in the world he had wanted was to hurt her, and now he could believe he had overestimated her involvement.

"I'm glad you are taking this so well, my dear," he said truthfully. "I've been dreading the moment when I must tell you how I felt about Lucienne. I was afraid I might lose you entirely because of it. I can think of nothing I should like more than to keep you as my friend. We understand each other very well, don't we? And now more than ever I need a friend and a counselor. The fact is, I can't understand either my own emotions regarding this girl or hers regarding me. If you would meet her, Roberta, you might be able to judge her behavior toward me with a woman's eye."

Roberta stood up, forcing herself to move slowly, casually.

"We must arrange a meeting," she said lightly. "But now, regretfully, I cannot stay and talk, Alexis. There is a new specialist coming to see Angus this afternoon and I must not be late home."

Alexis accepted her excuse for her sudden departure without question. He saw her into a cab and then returned to the empty room. Next door in his study was a pile of papers that urgently demanded his scrutiny. He ought, he knew, to be working and giving all his attention to the various problems awaiting his specialized knowledge. But he was finding it almost impossible of late to concentrate upon his work. Love, he decided, was not the joyful, carefree pleasure he had imagined.

Lucienne's face haunted him. The memory of her small, warm slender body close against his in the crowded foyer during the interval at the ballet was tormenting his dreams as well as his daytime thoughts. Without knowing it, he decided, she was a hundred times more provocative than Roberta could ever be with all her experience. And yet in Lucienne there was an innocence that confused him. She had a habit of holding his gaze directly, not dropping her extraordinary blue eyes as most young girls did when confronted with a bold stare. A moment later, she would be smiling demurely at some teasing remark of her uncle's or clapping her small hands with a child's enthusiastic applause for the dancers on stage. He could not forget the rapt, almost hypnotic expression on her face when she confessed her total enchantment with the ballet.

"Lucienne had no opportunity for enjoying such entertainments at her Convent," Lady Rochford had remarked and almost at once, the girl's expression had changed once more

and the fire had gone from her eyes when next she turned
her head politely to speak to him.

Alexis smiled at his folly as he went into his study and sat
down at his desk. To feel jealous because a troupe of dancers
could light that fire in Lucienne's eyes when he could not
was ludicrous. The girl barely knew him and could not be
expected to fall head over heels in love with him just because
he had been swept off his feet by her. He needed time to win
her regard...and time was a precious commodity for him.
He was not his own master, for his work with the Foreign
Office was too vital to be set aside when the pressures were
on—as they were at this moment with Europe in such a
ferment.

His assignments abroad were conducted in complete secrecy and by their very nature, were both dangerous and
lonely. They required his total concentration and since first
setting eyes on Lucienne, he had been giving less than he
should. Perhaps it would not be a bad thing to forget her for
a while—if he could—and devote himself more fully to the
duties required of him. But first he must speak to Lucienne's
mother and declare himself.

With a self-deprecating smile, Alexis rang for his manservant and dispatched him to a florist in George Street to
buy two dozen roses. Tomorrow he would drive down to Havorhurst and deliver them to Lady Rochford in person.

If Willow was impressed by Alexis' declaration of his intentions, Lucienne was not. Although she had thought the young
Count both well mannered and attentive throughout their
evening in London at the ballet, she remained ill at ease in
his presence. She disliked the feeling he gave her that he was
trying to see into her mind. She infinitely preferred the attentions of the earnest but stupid George and, when he could
find an excuse to come up to the Manor, the shy, devoted
looks of the young lawyer, Richard Bartholomew. It amused
her to smile in the friendliest way when they encountered
one another and to watch the blush spread over his cheeks.
She thought it a pity that neither her mother nor Uncle Toby
felt it quite proper for Richard Bartholomew to be invited to
the house as a guest. It was not that they had any objections
to him, they both told her, but it was important they should
guard *her* reputation very carefully. In a small village like
Havorhurst, Mama said, gossip spread like wildfire and every-

one would soon know if Richard were calling as a friend rather than on business.

"It's very strange," Oliver commented shrewdly. "Both Mama and Uncle Toby have made no bones about the fact that they thought Grandmère cruel and snobbish to forbid Uncle James to call upon Aunt Dodie just because he was only a schoolmaster. Now they are just as determined to marry *you* to someone rich and titled—Count Zemski, probably!"

Lucy had laughed.

"Well, I'm no more likely to marry Count Zemski than I am to marry Richard. I've told you, Oliver, I shall never marry."

November gave way to December and preparations for the Christmas festivities began. Howard Barratt came down from Cambridge and Lucienne could not ignore his constant attentions. He rode over nearly every day on his big brown hunter and so timed his visits that he was frequently invited to stay on for luncheon or tea at the Manor. He was good company and went out of his way to amuse Oliver and little Alice and to be agreeable to the two newcomers, Jane and Mark Grey. They were both shy children, somewhat young for their years and old-fashioned in their manner.

"It's because they have been living with so elderly an aunt," Willow commented. "They will soon settle down. For the time being, everything is new and strange to them."

They were certainly little trouble to anyone. An extra nursemaid had been assigned to assist Patience, the Nanny, and Lucienne now shared a personal maid with Jane, the girl taking care of their clothes and hair and running their bathwater.

"It's a pity you're not so tidy as Miss Jane," the maid, Polly, told Lucy, whose habit it was to leave her clothes where they fell.

The newcomer, Jane, needed no such admonition and was little trouble to the maid whom she treated with unfailing politeness but never with familiarity.

"Knows her proper place!" Polly informed the downstairs servants. And it seemed that young Mark was equally well brought up.

With the arrival of the now fifteen-year-old boy, Lucienne saw less and less of Oliver who very quickly became Mark's shadow. Because Mark was young for his age, the difference in their ages was barely noticeable, more especially as Mark was as short in stature as Oliver was tall and leggy. By Christ-

mas, he, Mark and young Henry Barratt had become insep-
arable and had formed a secret union calling themselves
'The Three Musketeers' after the characters in Dumas' book.
Lucienne, therefore, had time to spare for Howard who took
it upon himself to teach her to ride.

Although always accompanied by a groom on such outings,
the servant rode behind them and Howard made good use of
the time alone with Lucy. He wanted more than anything in
the world to marry her, he told her. Not yet, of course, because
he would have to take his degree at Cambridge first. If Lucy
would wait for him...

Lucy would make no promises. She enjoyed Howard's company and found him an amusing companion. It amused her,
too, to see how much sharper he was than his brother, George,
never missing an opportunity to be physically close to her.
His young, strong arms were always waiting to lift her down
from her horse and if he were correcting the way in which
she held her reins, his ungloved hand would imprison hers
and retain it far longer than was necessary. Once in the privacy
of the stables, he had stolen a kiss and Lucy had not reproved
him. His boldness increased every day and he was hard put
to disguise the ferment of desire he felt whenever he touched
her.

He managed to obtain permission from Willow to take
Lucienne in his Sunbeam to Tunbridge Wells to do some
Christmas shopping—Lucy's maid, Polly, to act as chaperone.
The good-natured girl was willing to remain in the warm
interior of the car while the two young people went into the
shops. It was not long before Howard became aware that
Lucienne was far more interested in what took *her* fancy than
in the presents she had planned to buy for her family. In
particular, she coveted a porcelain trinket box which, she told
him sadly, was far too costly to be purchased, much as she
liked it.

Sweeping aside her objections, Howard drew out his wallet
and bought it for her.

"It is my Christmas present to you, Lucienne," he told her,
putting the valuable ornament into her hands. "I want you
to have it—I really do. I could see how much you liked it.
Please don't refuse it, Lucienne."

Lucy had no intention of refusing it. She stood on tiptoe
and kissed Howard with genuine gratitude. His face turned
scarlet and he hurried her out of the shop with a mixture of

delight and guilt. He knew very well that Lucy would not be allowed to keep so expensive a gift if her mother knew of it. If a girl received a present from a man, it could only be so harmless and uncompromising a gift as chocolates or flowers. But of course, he told himself, being brought up in France, Lucienne might not be aware of such things, especially coming as she had from Paris. Paris, according to all his friends, was a delightfully naughty city—where bewitching French-women like Mistinguett and Yvonne Printemps sang and danced at the Scala Theater, the Folies-Bergère and the Moulin-Rouge. Those who could afford it, so George said, took girls to one of the secret upstairs rooms at Maxim's for supper and showered them with flowers, diamonds, furs.

But this, alas, was England and on the journey home, Howard warned Lucienne not to mention his gift to her mother.

"She would almost certainly make you give it back," he said awkwardly. "I dare say it sounds very silly to you, Lucienne, but it would be against convention—you know, sort of putting yourself under obligation to me..."

Lucy regarded his flushed, embarrassed young face affectionately.

"I understand, Howard, and don't worry—I shall keep my beautiful box hidden away with my other treasures. I've never owned anything so lovely in my life and I don't care if it does put me under an obligation to you."

Howard looked even more embarrassed.

"Honestly, Lucienne, that wasn't my intention—truly it wasn't..."

"Nevertheless, I am indebted to you," Lucy broke in calmly. "As soon as I get an opportunity, I shall repay you in my own way."

The opportunity to balance the books—which was how Lucy saw the transaction—presented itself two days before Christmas. Her Aunt Silvie and Uncle Pelham had arrived from Paris and so, too, had Aunt Dodie and Uncle James with their nursemaid, Voilet, and their baby girl, now two years old. Philip Grey was on Christmas leave and the Manor House seemed suddenly full of people. Howard, George and Henry Barratt drove over in the family Bentley to assist with the decorating of the giant fir tree which had been brought in from the estate and placed in the great hall. The tinsel and wax candles kept for adorning the tree were still packed in boxes in one of the attic cupboards and Willow suggested

Lucienne should go in search of them. Howard at once offered to accompany her. George had been hurried away by Toby to give his opinion of a new gun he had bought Oliver for Christmas. Howard and Lucy were therefore quite alone as they climbed the uncarpeted wooden backstairs to the dry, dusty attics that adjoined the servants' bedrooms.

It was cold beneath the eaves and Lucy shivered as she stood on the bare boards surveying the paraphernalia of generations piled up around the walls. There were a great many items of army uniform dating back to the early 1800's when, Howard informed Lucy, her great grandfather, Cedric Rochford, had gained innumerable battle honors fighting abroad. There were several swords and rusty bayonets, a rifle, a tropical helmet and a padlocked tin trunk with her great grandfather's name painted on the lid. There were, too, huge glass domes containing stuffed birds, including an eagle on a wooden plinth. In another corner stood a pile of furniture which looked as if it had once been in the servants' rooms—a horsehair sofa with the contents spewing out onto the floor, an old marble washstand with a corner cracked off, an old iron bedspring.

"There seems to be mostly junk in this room," Howard remarked as he stared around him. "Let's try next door, Lucienne."

On the floor of the adjoining attic lay a huge polar bear skin.

Howard grinned.

"Shot by your grandfather, I don't doubt," he said as Lucy looked with misgivings at the lifelike head. "It's dead, you know. It won't bite you!"

Laughing, Lucy lay down on the moth-eaten rug, propping her head on the bear's neck.

"I'm not afraid of anything!" she boasted.

But Howard was not listening. He was staring down at her young, slim body lying so innocently abandoned before his gaze. How tiny her waist was; how pert and firm her small breasts pushing up against the soft silk of her white blouse. How delicate her ankles, peeping from beneath her skirt. How terribly tempting that laughing, rosebud mouth.

"Lucienne, Lucienne!" he cried hoarsely. "Do you have any idea quite how much I love you!"

Lucy's pose had indeed been innocent . . . love very far from her thoughts as she had flung herself down on the fur rug:

She had been thinking how exciting life had become all of a sudden. The big house was filled with a happy, breathless expectation as servants and masters alike were bustling around preparing in their separate ways for Christmas Day. It was the first such occasion she had ever spent in a real home where a large family had forgathered to enjoy themselves.

In the Convent, the day had merely meant extra long hours in church and a handful of nuts and raisins by the children's plates at lunch time. Lucy had been downstairs in the kitchens of Rochford Manor and seen the feast of good things which Cook and her minions were preparing for the family. At one end of the table a kitchen maid, with her sleeves rolled back, was busy pushing handfuls of stuffing into a huge turkey. At the other end Cook was putting the finishing touches to a game pie. On the dresser were a pile of mince pies, a dish of candied fruits and a baking tray with meringues just out of the oven and put there to cool.

How different it all was from the Convent. One day, she thought, when she was very rich, she would send food to the orphans—not money, for she was convinced, as were all the older children, that the Mother Superior did not always pass on the charitable gifts but hoarded them for her own use.

But those days were past, and now Lucy could not curb her excitement at the growing pile of brightly wrapped presents heaped beneath the Bechstein piano in the drawing room. Many of them bore her name on the labels, some small, some large—but all were without doubt of value. She had seen Mama's extravagant choice of gifts at Hamley's in London for the other children. The cost had not mattered and Lucienne had only just managed to withhold her gasps of amazement when she heard the toy shop assistant mentioning the prices almost as an afterthought. Everything had been charged to her mother's recently opened account—a system of payment new to Lucy and which on the train ride home, her mother explained.

Lucy's mood of euphoria, therefore, was due to happy anticipation and she turned her thoughts to Howard reluctantly. But she had not forgotten the beautiful trinket box he had given her which she brought out of its hiding place and admired every night after Polly had left her alone in her bedroom. With a sigh, she held out her arms.

"You may kiss me if you want," she said.

Howard needed no second bidding. In a flash, he was lying

beside her. With a boy's clumsy haste, he covered her face, neck and hands with kisses. He was breathing in deep gasps as he tried to control the ever growing force of his desire.

"Lucienne, my darling, my love!" he moaned, straining against her. "If you only knew how much I love you..."

It was not so much love as lust, Lucy thought as she guided his hands to her breasts. It seemed that all men preferred to call their bodily lusts by the name of love. Yvette had suggested that they felt less guilty about their passions if they could clothe them in romantic terms; that they did not like to think about themselves as animals, no better than the beasts in the fields on André's farm. Some did not care, of course, but simply took what they paid for in silence.

Lucienne wished very much that Howard belonged to the silent minority. Someone might come up to find them and without any doubt at all, they were breaking one of the all-important conventions.

Howard was now dripping with perspiration and panting heavily between kisses. With a sigh, Lucienne allowed her hand to stray down his thigh and rest between his legs. The effect upon the young man was almost instantaneous. He gave a violent gasp, relaxed heavily upon her and cried out:

"Lucienne, my darling, now we shall *have* to get married!"

Lucy managed to ease her way from beneath him. There was a look of complete astonishment on her face as she scrambled to her feet.

"Whatever do you mean, Howard? Of course I'm not going to marry you—or anyone else for that matter!"

Howard stood up, his young face pale and anxious.

"But Lucienne, I...you...don't you realize...?"

"I realize we shall be in trouble if we don't go back downstairs very soon!" Lucy said practically. Looking at Howard's unhappy face, her voice softened. "There's no need to look so miserable!" she exclaimed.

"But I love you!" Howard cried, helpless in the light of Lucy's obvious indifference to the momentous happenings of the past few minutes.

Lucy sighed. As far as she was concerned, her debt to him had been paid and she was now impatient to return to the others. But there was worse to come. There was a loud crashing on the wooden stairway and a moment later, George burst into the attic, his eyes taking in the motionless pair as he regarded them with jealous fury.

"What's going on up here?" he demanded. "You were supposed to be finding the decorations. Where are they? What have you been up to, Howard?"

"It's none of your business!" Howard retorted, glad of an excuse to give way to his feelings of frustration. "The way you go on, George, anyone would think Lucienne was your property."

George stiffened.

"As it so happens, Howard, Lucienne *is* my concern. It's still a secret, of course, but you might as well know that Lucienne and I are engaged to be married."

Lucy drew a deep breath. She was about to speak when Howard pushed past her and confronted his brother.

"That's a lie! You're no more engaged to Lucienne than I am!"

George rose to his full height, his face smug as he replied:

"In the contrary, Howard. Lucienne has my ring. If you were more observant, you'd have noticed I haven't been wearing it for the past five months."

Howard's glance went involuntarily to George's ring finger. His cheeks paled as he turned to Lucienne in appeal.

"It isn't true, is it, Lucienne? It can't be true..."

"It's only partly true," she said placatingly. "I mean, I do have George's ring but we're not engaged. I told George I would most likely never marry, didn't I, George?"

But Howard was no longer listening. Shocked beyond measure, he stumbled out of the room without a glance at his brother's triumphant face or at Lucy's indignant one.

She turned to George and said crossly:

"If I'd known there would be all this stupid fuss, I'd never have taken your ring, George Barratt. You'd better have it back since it's causing so much trouble. I don't want it anyway."

It was not the truth but despite George's protestations, Lucy returned his ring. As she explained to him, she had not fully understood the stupid convention that dictated the obligation that went with his gift. Had it been a necklace or bracelet, she said, she could have kept it.

That afternoon, George drove himself into Sevenoaks and bought Lucienne the most expensive gold necklace he could find. Meanwhile, his brother Howard, broken hearted, took one of the shotguns from the gun room in his house and without a word to anyone, went out into the beech woods surrounding the Barratt estate, determined to put an end to his brief, young life.

Chapter 6

January 1912

IT WAS ARRANGED THAT LUCY WOULD TRAVEL BACK TO FRANCE WITH Silvie and Pelham and spend January with them in Paris. Although both Sir John and Lady Barratt had exonerated Lucy entirely from any responsibility for the disruption of their family unit, the fact that she had been indirectly responsible was unarguable.

Howard, fortunately, had failed miserably in his suicide attempt. He had propped up his gun on a V-shaped branch stuck in the ground, attached a length of string to the trigger, intending to place himself at a reasonable distance before standing in line with the barrel and pulling on the string. As it was, he accidentally fired the gun while he was still only a few feet away, and the worst damage he inflicted on himself was to blow off his left ear. A gamekeeper in the vicinity heard the shot and believing he would find a poacher, found the dazed but not too seriously injured Howard instead.

George made up his mind to leave home to recover, at a distance, from his disappointment over Lucy and his shame regarding his quarrel with his brother. He joined the 9th Lancers, his father's old regiment, and went off to Sandhurst for officer training. Howard, with his head in a bandage, was sent away to an aunt in Bognor until the University term began and he could go back, chastened and somewhat relieved at his lucky escape, to Cambridge.

Willow was deeply disturbed.

"It is not so much Lucienne's behavior regarding the two boys," she said to Toby, "but that she seems to have no normal understanding of right and wrong. It is almost as if she is unaware of the difference and either cannot or will not understand when I attempt to explain matters to her. She accepted valuable presents from both Howard and George and it is that aspect of her behavior which worries me most."

"Perhaps we are apt to forget that it is a very short while since Lucienne came home," Toby replied comfortingly. "People like ourselves grow up in surroundings where unconsciously we absorb the values of our elders and teachers. Your daughter had no such training—not even in the Convent, as far as I can see. There it seems to have been a matter of survival and Lucienne has told me that any of the children would lie like troopers if it meant avoiding some of the horrible punishments inflicted on them. They would be shut up for twelve hours in a small cell with the window and the door locked on a hot summer day when the temperature was over ninety degrees. Lucienne says even the flies died of heat exhaustion and many of the less healthy children were unconscious when the door was eventually opened. They were given no food...and worse, no water. So much for Christianity, Willow. Let us at least try to show forbearance toward Lucienne now."

Willow tried to forget her elder daughter once Lucy had departed for France, and devoted her time to her other children. Oliver was returning to Eton and Mark to his boarding school in Yorkshire. Willow engaged a young governess to tutor Alice and Jane. Jane had not wanted to return to her boarding school and Philip had agreed with Willow that it would be less unsettling for her to remain at Rochford. She was Willow's shadow, following her everywhere with quiet, adoring eyes. The child was not only painfully shy but owing to her upbringing, old-fashioned and very timid. She had long since put the memory of her own mother out of her mind and Willow was the gentle, loving person she most needed now that her great aunt was dead and her adored elder brother, Philip, had gone away to sea.

Willow found it easy to love the young girl and often secretly wished that her own daughter could have been more like the pale, silent, little Jane. She failed completely to understand Lucienne and it was somewhat of a relief to put her in Silvie's care and not have to worry about her at Rochford Manor.

Lucy, too, was happy to be in the bright, amusing company of her French aunt. She deeply resented being held responsible even in the smallest degree for Howard's hushed-up attempt upon his life. After all, had she not but a few hours earlier been doing her utmost to keep him happy and content? Between George and Howard, Christmas had been quite spoiled for everyone; and not even the wonderful set of ballet music on flat records for playing on the new gramophone—the present from Alexis to the family—could compensate her for the loss of the gold necklace and the trinket box which Mama had made her return immediately.

Aunt Silvie's Paris house was elegant and very French. It was also a great deal smaller than Rochford Manor and there were fewer servants. However, Lucienne had been accompanied by Polly and it was pleasant to have her own personal maid and not have to share Aunt Silvie's.

The January weather was very cold and Pelham bought Lucy a Russian sable coat and hat which became her very well and pleased her enormously. This uncle and aunt were much to her liking and seemed to care less for the tiresome conventions than did her mother and Uncle Toby. Meals were served when they were hungry and as often as not, they would dine out. Lucy adored going to Maxim's, the Café de Paris, the Ritz, and other fashionable, expensive places. She often wondered whether Madame or the girls would recognize her if they saw her in such a milieu.

Aunt Silvie talked a great deal to Lucy about her mother, describing her as she was when she first went to live at Rochford as a seventeen-year-old bride.

"She looked so very like you do now, Lucienne," Silvie said, taking her niece into her bedroom to show her the portrait of a beautiful girl hanging over the mantelpiece. "Although the artist called this painting 'Juliet,' it is in fact a true likeness of your Mama."

Lucy stood on tiptoe, the better to see the scrawled signature in the bottom right hand corner of the portrait. Her heart was beating with nervous excitement and there were bright spots of color in both her cheeks.

"Juliet!" she murmured. "Painted by Maurice Dubois, 1905!"

Silvie nodded.

"According to an artist friend of mine, Dubois has become quite famous since then," she said, unaware of Lucy's thoughts. "He paints very much in the style of Henri de Toulouse-Lautrec whom he knew very well before the poor fellow died. Of course, Dubois' subject matter does not please everyone for, like Lautrec, he favors Montmartre types, characters from Parisian night clubs and the like."

"I would be interested to see his work," Lucienne said, but her aunt shook her head.

"If you wish to be educated in the best French art, *chérie*, I will take you to the Louvre tomorrow," she said.

But it was not art in which Lucy was interested. It was in Maurice Dubois...in the astonishing piece of information Aunt Silvie had unwittingly given her. She had not forgotten him showing her drawings and paintings of 'his Juliet'; nor how bitterly he had harangued her, Lucy, because somehow she had spoiled his memory of the woman he had loved. Now she understood. *He had loved Mama!* And it was because of her own likeness to her mother that he had been so eager, so inspired to paint her, Lucy. She, poor silly child, had supposed that he had been interested in her, a skinny little waitress from *Le Ciel Rouge*! How naïve and in retrospect, how humiliating! She could recall as if it were yesterday that the artist had always demanded she presented her face in profile so that he could not see her eyes. Mama had large brown eyes and Lucy's were blue...

Lucy was unusually quiet that evening during dinner, so much so that Pelham inquired if she were feeling ill. Lucy pretended a headache, and retired early to bed.

She had no intention of dismissing so admirable an excuse not to accompany her aunt and uncle to the race meeting at Auteuil, as had been planned. When she continued to pretend an indisposition next day, they offered to put off the engagement. Lucy would not hear of it.

"I shall be quite all right here with Polly to look after me," she said, lying back on her pillow. "I did not have a very good night and it will do me good to rest."

Neither Silvie nor Pelham had cause to suspect Lucy's eagerness to have them out of the way so that she could pursue her own plans. No sooner had their Delage driven away from the house than she rang for Polly to come and dress her.

"My new Poiret frock," she commanded, her eyes sparkling with excitement. "And pile my hair up high, Polly—the way that Mama says makes me look older. I want to look like her!"

Polly, a sensible girl in her early thirties, regarded her young mistress apprehensively. She sensed that Lucy was up to no good and yet Lucy refused for once to confide in her. When Lucy instructed her to go and call for a taxicab, Polly hesitated.

"Madame Rochford would not approve of you going out

without her!" she said. "Especially seeing as how you aren't
well and..."

"Nonsense!" Lucy interrupted, surveying herself in the tall
mirror with satisfaction. With her new sable coat draped around
her shoulders, she looked the epitome of sophistication. "I'm
as fit as a fiddle, Polly," she declared, pulling on her suede
gloves. "Now do as I say. And since you seem so afraid Madame
Rochford will find out I've been playing truant, you can tell
the taxicab to wait on the corner of the street. I'll walk there."

"I'd best come with you, Miss Lucienne," the maid cried.
"It won't do for you to go out alone—not a young girl of your
age."

"I'm going out alone and there's nothing you can do to
stop me," Lucy said sharply. But seeing Polly's expression,
her own face softened. "Don't be such a silly goose," she said.
"Remember that I once lived in France and I know this city
every bit as well as you know Havorhurst. Moreover I speak
the language like a native. Now go and call me a taxicab!"

A little of her self-assurance waned when at last she was
speeding through the Latin quarter of Paris to Maurice Dubois' studio. How well she knew the road! But supposing he
had moved elsewhere? Suppose he were simply not at home?
Away on holiday? It was five long years since she had last
walked from *Le Ciel Rouge* to the studio. It was almost too
much to expect that he would still be there—as she had left
him—surrounded by canvases, easels, turpentine, oil paints...

"Does Mademoiselle intend to alight?" the driver interrupted her thoughts.

Lucy stepped out of the cab, drawing her coat more closely
around her as the chill January wind whistled down the empty
cobbled street. She paid off the driver and began slowly to
climb the twisting, rickety staircase. A child was crying from
behind one of the closed doors. A woman shouted and a mangy
cat went scurrying past her, screeching as it made for the
street.

"Please God, let him be there!" Lucy prayed as once long
ago she had knelt on the hard stone floor in the Convent,
praying to a heedless God to find her Mama and Papa to take
her away from her cold prison.

Lucy was by no means certain what she would do or say
if the artist was in his studio. She had made no plans, knowing
only that she wanted him to suffer as once he had made her
suffer. As she lifted her gloved hand to knock on the door,

she was certain of only one thing—that she would not admit to being little Sophie Miller—the maid from the brothel he had once chosen to paint as a whore. He might think he recognized her but she would deny it.

The door opened and Lucy was face to face with the man she had never been able to forget. Maurice Dubois had changed very little. Now thirty-eight years old, he had only a sprinkling of gray in his dark hair. A moustache covered his upper lip and there was a daub of paint on his carelessly trimmed beard. His white smock was paint-covered and behind one ear was a sable brush dripping Prussian blue onto his shoulder.

"Aren't you going to invite me to come in?" Lucy inquired in English. "You do speak my language, do you not?"

The man nodded, his eyes wide apart as he stared curiously at the young girl standing in the open doorway.

"Yes, of course. I mean I do speak English and please, do come in!" The words came out in a rush. "Should I know your name, Mademoiselle? I feel certain we have met somewhere and yet..."

"No, we haven't met before," Lucy said sharply. "A friend told me you painted portraits and that you might be persuaded to paint me."

She walked past him into the studio, looking around her with a strange nostalgia. How many happy hours had she spent here—happy just to listen to her Monsieur Maurice talking; to watch his swift, skillful hands moving from palette to canvas and all the time talking to her in his soft, vague way, encouraging her to tell him her childish dreams...

"I am afraid you have been misinformed," he said as he came to stand beside her. "I don't do portraits now... although... are you *quite* certain, Mademoiselle, that we have not met? Could I have seen you somewhere? Do you live in Paris? If so, perhaps..."

"No, I live in England!" Lucy broke in. "Well, I must not waste your time, Monsieur Dubois. It's a pity you cannot oblige me. I had seen a painting of yours—'Juliet,' I think it was called—and I thought I would like one similar. I look a little like her, do you not agree?"

Color flared in Maurice's cheeks and he only just succeeded in withholding a gasp as he said:

"But of course, *that* is why your face is so familiar. You are indeed like her, Mademoiselle—very, very like. How can I not have seen it before? It is amazing—unbelievable! Moreover, it is not the first time this has happened. There was a child once who . . . but I must not bore you with such details. Please be seated. I have not said I will not paint you. In fact, I am already eager to do so. Have you time to remain a little while, Mademoiselle—?"

"Merton—Louise Merton," Lucy invented smoothly.

"I would like to make some quick sketches—just to familiarize myself with your features. Please, I beg you, do be seated."

He pulled forward a chair but Lucy remained standing.

"The fee!" she said. "I'm afraid I could not afford a great deal. The painting is to be a present for my mother and I have been saving my allowance so that I could surprise her. But . . ."

"Do not concern yourself about the fee!" Maurice broke in. "If I may explain, Mademoiselle Merton, art is not necessarily concerned with money. Every once in a while, one is forced to put something on canvas because one is inspired to do so. It is a force greater than oneself. Now that I have set eyes on you, I am impelled to paint you—it is as simple as that. I require no fee."

Waiting only for Lucy to be seated, he reached for a pencil and sketch pad and began rapidly to cover the paper with lines. He was totally absorbed and Lucy could stare at him unimpeded.

So he had believed her deception; believed she was the fictitious Louise Merton! The thought that she might be connected in any way with the gamine of five years ago had not crossed his mind. It had been a good idea to pretend she was English for that would certainly have directed his thoughts elsewhere.

The man worked feverishly, stopping only occasionally to smile briefly at his model before continuing. He was wrapped in his own world, unaware of Lucy as a person, she thought, her heart growing cold. Now, as before, he was drawing not her but his real love—his 'Juliet,' her mother.

When at last he paused and invited her to drink coffee with him, Lucy permitted her body to relax as she leant toward him provocatively.

"I am interested to hear about the woman you say I resemble," she murmured. "Will you not tell me about her?"

Maurice filled the kettle and placed it on the gas stove standing in one corner of the studio. He looked pensive.

"There is little to tell you, Mademoiselle. She was a very beautiful woman. Like yourself, she was English. She returned to her own country soon after I finished my first portrait of her and I have never seen her again."

"But you loved her, did you not?"

Maurice turned to look at the young girl sitting so poised and cool—much as his 'Juliet' had once sat.

"Yes, I suppose I did!" he said quietly. "But let us not talk about her. I would much rather hear about you, Mademoiselle. Are you on holiday here in Paris?"

Lucy nodded, allowing her fair hair to loosen from its pins so that it fell across one cheek.

"I am staying with my uncle and aunt. I find Paris quite exciting—more so than London where I live." The lie came easily. "There is little more to tell you. I lead a very ordinary life and next year I am to be married to a very ordinary young man. I suppose you could say that this is my last chance of freedom before I am chained forever by my marriage vows."

Maurice paused in the act of pouring the steaming coffee into two of his best china cups. He looked quite shocked as he said:

"You are not looking forward to your marriage?"

Lucy shrugged.

"No, I'm afraid not! But Mama and Papa want me to marry this man and I have agreed. It will mean a step up socially for my family and they are naturally very anxious I should make the most of such an offer."

Maurice carried the cups to the table and sat down on a chair opposite Lucy.

"I hope you will not think it impertinent if I inquire how old you are?"

"Twenty-two!" Lucy lied. "So you see, Monsieur Dubois, I shall soon be on the shelf. I suppose I shall never fall in love now," she added wistfully.

"You look so much younger—and you are so beautiful I cannot accept that you are nearly 'on the shelf,' as you put it. I know I have no right on so short an acquaintance to advise you, Mademoiselle, but it seems to me quite dreadful that you should be entertaining the idea of marriage without love just to please your parents."

"Is love so important, then?" Lucy inquired. "My friends tell me so, but I have never yet met a man I could love. I don't care for young men and the older ones I know are already married. I have had to abandon the thought of love, much as I longed to experience its joys."

Maurice was effectively silenced. The young woman's likeness to his 'Juliet' was confusing him, he decided. He was thinking and feeling just as he had done when he had first met *her*. Even knowing she was married and loved someone else had not prevented him losing his heart to her. He had possessed her for one night only...one night he had never forgotten. Now, before his unbelieving eyes, sat a young girl so like her he could not believe she was other than a figment of his dreams.

"Of course, if ever I were to meet someone who so took my fancy that I knew I *must* surrender myself to him or die, then I wouldn't worry about convention. I would sample the magic of true love," Lucy said softly. "But how could I realize such a dream, Monsieur Dubois? What man would dare kiss me, invite me to experience the delights of love with him? He would be afraid to ruin my reputation, would he not? He would feel guilty because I am young and unprotected. And *I* could not make such a suggestion without a man thinking me quite immoral. You see my predicament, Monsieur Dubois?"

"Please, please call me Maurice. I know we met only an hour ago but I swear to God it is as if we have known each other a long time. Does that make any kind of sense to you, Mademoiselle Merton?"

Lucy's look of surprise was cleverly feigned.

"It's strange that you should feel that, too. Here I am talking to you and telling you my closest secrets which I would not speak of even to a childhood friend or sister. And if I am to call you Maurice, you must call me Louise. That is only right, is it not?"

Maurice wanted Lucienne to lunch with him in a nearby restaurant but she dared not risk being away from the house when Silvie and Pelham returned. She would try, she promised him, to arrange to visit his studio again—one afternoon, perhaps, when she could escape the vigilant eye of her aunt.

Reluctantly, Maurice accompanied her downstairs and to the end of the road where he could call a taxicab for her. He asked for Lucy's address so that he could direct the driver but she evaded giving him this information, saying that she must first pick up a parcel awaiting collection at her aunt's dressmaker, Mlle. Chanel, in the *Rue Cambon*.

Maurice returned to his studio, his mind in a ferment. His unforgettable 'Juliet' had been every bit as elusive as this young English girl who so resembled her. He felt both uneasy and enormously excited. Was it possible, he wondered, that history could repeat itself in so incredible a fashion?

Lucy returned home well satisfied with her morning's outing. Maurice had never once associated her with the skinny, untidy child, Sophie Miller—or Perle as he and Madame Lou-Lou had called her. It was hardly surprising, seeing how enormously she had changed in the past five years. And she had spoken only French in those days. Today she had presented herself as a chic, modern young lady from England, well-to-do and well-bred.

That Maurice was greatly interested in her, Lucy was in no doubt. In the short space of an hour, she had convinced him of her vulnerability and her secret longing for love. She would be surprised if he was not even now envisaging himself as the one man who could reveal life's mysteries to her!

For several days, Lucy made no attempt to go back to the studio. Her aunt had suspected nothing and Polly had told no tales about her young mistress' little sortie. Lucy awaited an opportunity to escape once more from Silvie's chaperonage.

It was Silvie herself who provided the chance Lucy was awaiting. There had been a break in at her country home in Épernay and the visiting police detective had said it was imperative that Silvie and Pelham should travel to Épernay to assess the damage and evaluate the losses.

The weather was still bitterly cold and Lucy announced that she thought she might have a touch of *'la grippe.'* There had been an epidemic of influenza in Paris and Silvie at once rejected any idea that Lucy should accompany her and Pelham to Épernay.

"You must stay here in the house where you will be warm and quiet," she said firmly as Lucy made a feeble protest, "and if you feel at all feverish, you are to telephone for the doctor at once. I really do not like to leave you, *chérie.*"

"But of course you must go—and I shall be perfectly all right, Aunt Silvie, I promise you," Lucy insisted.

"Lucienne is really a remarkably easy child to have as a guest," Silvie said to Pelham as they caught their train from the *Gare de l'Est.* "I have been wondering if Willow has not put her on too high a pedestal and that is why her daughter seeks to avoid her company. In my opinion, she should not have Lucienne feel guilty just because she flirted a little with those two stupid Barratt boys. After all, it is natural for a young girl to want to attract attention and unreasonable of Willow to relate such behavior to poor Lucienne's past. I have seen no sign of any improper behavior since she has been with us.

Silvie might have been more inclined to share Willow's anxiety had she seen Lucy's expression at that selfsame moment as she once more climbed the stairs to Maurice's studio. Lucy had noticed him staring down into the street when her taxicab arrived and she guessed correctly that he had been standing there in the slim hope of seeing her. Her blue eyes were bright with triumph as he came hurrying down the stairs to greet her.

"I was afraid I might never see you again," he said fervently as he took her elbow and led her into the studio. "I cannot wait to begin your portrait."

"It is only four days since I was last here," Lucy said smiling as she drew off her coat and hat and sat down in the chair he had drawn forward by the gas fire.

Maurice went to put on the kettle for coffee, saying as he did so:

"I used my sketches to do a preliminary painting of you. I intended to show it to you but now that I see you again, I realize that it does not do justice to your beauty."

Lucy gave a long, elaborate sigh.

"You can have no idea, Monsieur Dubois, how delightful it is to be paid such compliments. My fiancé never says such charming things to me. But then he is English and it is well known that Frenchmen make much better lovers. I think Englishmen love only their horses and their dogs. Do you agree with me?"

Maurice looked pleased as he said eagerly:

"I have never understood the English. But then I am an artist and not interested in sport. It is people who interest me, and you in particular, Louise. But have you forgotten that on your last visit we had already agreed to use Christian names?"

Lucy smiled.

"No, I hadn't forgotten, Maurice, but I did not wish you to think me too familiar on so short an acquaintance. My aunt would not allow it. Indeed, if she knew where I was at this moment, she would be heavily disapproving—and fearful for my safety!"

"She need have no such fear, I assure you," Maurice broke in. "I would not dream of taking advantage of anyone as young and innocent as you. Your aunt may hold a poor opinion of artists but I shall behave with complete propriety."

"I don't share my aunt's opinion," Lucy said softly. "If you are to paint my portrait, Maurice, then it is only right that you should know that I am not *entirely* innocent in the ways of the world." She paused before adding: "I have suffered the greatest of misfortunes any girl can experience." As Lucy anticipated, she now had Maurice's fullest attention. He hastened to reassure her that any confidence she cared to make would be scrupulously honored by him.

Lucy lowered her voice and her eyes as she said hesitantly:

"A year ago, a friend of my father's took advantage of me. Does that shock you? I have never spoken of this terrible experience to a living soul."

Maurice was more surprised by the confession itself than by the fact contained in it. He had sensed from the first that this young girl was different. Until now, he had been unable to fathom the reason for her strangeness. Now it was explained. Moreover, he could understand why her parents were so anxious to see her safely married, why she herself was willing to give up all thought of love for the security of marriage.

He leaned forward and took one of her hands in his.

"I am a lot older than you," he said. "Therefore I can talk to you as a friend with some considerable experience of life. You must not brood over this terrible event, Louise. Young girls are taught to put great value on their virginity but you should not feel ashamed because of what was done to you. No one could blame you for what happened."

Lucy looked at him wide-eyed.

"You mean that there might be a man who could love me, despite what was done to me?"

Maurice now took Lucy's other hand, clasping both fiercely between his palms. Only with difficulty was he succeeding in hiding his excitement.

"Yes I do, my little Louise. It would be very, very easy for a man to love you—far too easy, as a matter of fact. Love is a distraction to a man as dedicated to his work as I am, so I try to avoid emotional involvements of any kind. But I will confess to you that I haven't been able to concentrate upon my work since last you were here. You have bewitched me with your beauty, Louise. It may be difficult for you to believe, but I have not left the studio for four days for fear I might miss seeing you."

Lucy allowed herself to be drawn nearer to him. She regarded him shyly from beneath her lashes. Madame Lou-Lou called it her expression *d'enfant.*

"I have been thinking a great deal about you, too, Maurice. Do you believe in love at first sight? People speak of it but..."

"I have known it to happen," Maurice declared, remembering only too well his first encounter with his 'Juliet.'

Gently, he raised Lucy to her feet. As he tilted her face upwards in preparation for his kiss, he hesitated, overcome suddenly by a sense of *déjà vue*. It was but momentary and the sight of Lucy's softly parted lips put all other thought from his mind.

Lucy did not greatly care for the practice of kissing and had in the past tried whenever possible to avoid this contact. It always seemed to her to involve an even greater degree of intimacy than the act of union itself. She was now very conscious of the crisp, scratchy bristles of Maurice's beard. But she gave no sign of her distaste as she molded her body against his and closed her eyes against his look of hungry desire.

Maurice went about his task of seduction slowly, gently and expertly, never doubting that Lucy was the inexperienced one of the two. He talked to her constantly in soothing, encouraging tones and for a short while, Lucy was able to let her mind wander. Time had stood still in this studio, she thought. Only the big pile of canvases in the corner had grown larger and the huge glass skylight dustier. The walls had not been repapered and there were still dark damp patches where the rain found its way in through the window frame. And looped over the back of an old wooden chair was the same Indian silk shawl Maurice had once draped around her shoulders...

The sight of it hardened Lucy's heart. She opened her eyes and looked at the rapt face of the man now lying above her. This much was different—there was no love in her heart for him now. All those years ago she had looked up to him as a kind of God: in those days she had nothing but her virginity to offer him and would have given herself to him willingly—

except that he had not wanted her. Now at long last their rôles were reversed.

Maurice was murmuring words of love in her ear and his hands were roving over her body. Lucy, moaning in simulated pleasure, decided that he had not heard her above the sound of his own voice and moaned louder.

"Don't be afraid, my adorable one!" Maurice cried. "I will be gentle with you."

Somewhere not far from the studio, a church clock chimed the midday hour. A smile flitted across Lucy's face as she tried to imagine her aunt's shocked disbelief were she to know that at this very moment, her niece was lying on a bed with the artist, Maurice Dubois! And how horrified her mother would be! but then *she* was in no position to criticize. She was far from being as saintly as everyone made out. There was little doubt from what Maurice had told her that he and Mama had been lovers. It proved her father's estimate of her mother to be true after all.

There was really no one in the whole world who could be trusted beyond doubt, Lucy thought. One must, as Yvette had so often advised her, rely only upon oneself. Even young Oliver had set her aside in favor of the newcomer, Mark Grey. For a short while he had wanted no other company but hers.

"Louise, my darling, was it not good for you, too?"

With a jolt, Lucy brought her thoughts back to the present. Maurice's words were opportune to say the least for now he had given her the perfect opening. The moment for which she had so carefully planned had now arrived.

Wordless, she edged her way from beneath him and began to rearrange her clothing. All the time the man lay on his back, watching her anxiously as she dressed slowly and in silence

"You are not going? What is wrong, *chérie*? Are you angry? Did I displease you?" His questions became more and more apprehensive.

Only when she was fully attired did Lucy turn to look down at him. In a cold, hard little voice, she said in French:

"Are you not going to pay me for my services, Monsieur Maurice? A few francs, perhaps, for old times sake? Or have you really forgotten your adoring little Perle from *Le Ciel Rouge*?"

Maurice's face turned a bright red and then whitened as suddenly he realized why this young girl had seemed so familiar to him. It was not his beloved 'Juliet' he should have likened her to but the unhappy little *femme de ménage* who had modeled so often for him. He had all but forgotten the child but now it seemed impossible that he had failed to recognize those large, violet-blue eyes; that white-gold hair so unexpectedly soft and silky for a child of the streets.

"Perle!" he muttered. "You...are...Perle?"

"Oh, no!" Lucy said sharply. "I am no longer that child, Monsieur Maurice. I am a lady of consequence now. I have been reunited with my family—a rich and titled one. Does that surprise you? No one will ever again treat me as you did—with scorn and derision. You, Maurice Dubois, threw me out like one of your unwanted canvases...not caring how I felt. But now everything is different. Now it is my turn to scorn you, for only a fool would believe, as you did, that a girl of my age would give herself so readily to a man as old as you. Why, I don't even like you...and you were vain enough to imagine I loved you! All the time you were trying to prove yourself the great lover, I was hating you. So now it is good-bye, Monsieur Maurice. I hope I shall never have the misfortune of meeting you again."

"Mon Dieu! Ce n'est pas possible!" Maurice said aloud, as without more ado, Lucy left the studio, slamming the door behind her. Too shocked and humiliated to move from the couch where but a few minutes earlier he had thought himself the very best of lovers, he lay perfectly still. How long had Perle waited for this moment of revenge, he asked himself? How right his friend Pierre had been when he had accused him all those years ago of being cruel to the child. But he had had no idea of her feelings; her suffering. Wrapped up in his own passionate desire to recreate his 'Juliet,' he had used the girl as long as it suited his purpose and then dismissed her. How apt even now were the words of Congreve, the 17th century English poet,—*'Heaven has no rage like love to hatred turned, nor hell a fury like a woman scorned.'* How satisfied the girl must now be, knowing that she had not only hurt but shamed him beyond his forgetting!

As Lucy hurried along the cobbled streets to find the nearby taxicab rank, she was glad that the first cold drops of rain had begun to fall. They stung like needles on her flushed face, cooling her fever. And those few pedestrians who passed her were unaware that it was not just the rain wetting her cheeks but the soft, unaccountable fall of her tears.

Chapter 7

❦

February—May 1912

I⊤ WAS 6TH FEBRUARY AND DESPITE ALL THE FIRES BLAZING IN THE hearths, it was bitterly cold in the drafty old manor house. Willow sat in the morning room reading a long letter from Nathaniel Corbett, partly concerning the business of T.R.T.C. but also announcing a proposed visit to England in the spring.

"We have booked a passage on Olympic *and will be arriving at the beginning of April.*

"I shall bring with me the details of our new method of central heating as Tobias requested. We have had it installed in our house in New York and greatly enjoy the benefits..."

"We could certainly do with more warmth here at Rochford on days like this," Willow said to Toby. He nodded, laying his *Times* down on his lap.

"The King and Queen will be feeling the change in temperature after their visit to India," he remarked. "The *Times* said the weather was quite terrible yesterday at Portsmouth when they landed. However, it seems their Coronation trip has been enormously successful."

But Willow's thoughts had strayed elsewhere—to the subject closest to her heart—her daughter, Lucienne. When Willow had met her and Polly at Dover as they came off the cross Channel steamer, she had realized at once that Lucy was far from well and insisted she go straight to bed as soon as she arrived home. Lucienne had argued that she was only suffering from seasickness but Willow thought she had lost weight while she was in Paris and looked pale and peaky.

"I shall send for the doctor if she is not better tomorrow. She seems so depressed!" she said to Toby, who smiled at her indulgently.

"You worry too much about her. According to the letter she brought home from Silvie, her stay in Paris was a great success, and she was no trouble," he said.

Willow attempted a smile.

"I dare say Silvie and Pelham spoiled her. Of course, Silvie being French, may understand Lucienne better than I do. There seems always to be a barrier between us. Even the kiss she gave me when we met was only dutiful."

"Give her time," Toby cautioned, a not infrequent rejoinder. "I am sure she is genuinely pleased to be back home with us."

Upstairs in her bedroom, Lucy was huddled beneath the bedclothes wishing with all her heart that she was back in Paris. She had missed her period and the terrible suspicion had crossed her mind that she might be pregnant. However unlikely it was that her brief moment of revenge upon Maurice could have led to such an appalling consequence to herself, the fact remained that she had taken the risk and it *could* have happened. Were she in Paris now, she could have gone to Madame Lou-Lou—the one person she knew in whom she could confide.

She had fully intended to slip away from her aunt's chaperonage and visit Madame and the girls, longing to display her fine clothes and impress them all with her new importance. But first there had been the excitement of shopping with Aunt Silvie and discovering the part of Paris which belonged to the rich and sophisticated. Then she had become obsessed with her desire to be revenged upon Maurice. But the expected feeling of triumph after she had succeeded in humiliating him had been strangely absent. She had felt miserable and depressed and in no mood to face Madame's searching eyes. Suddenly her holiday in Paris was over and there was no time left. In retrospect, it seemed unbelievably stupid of her not to have foreseen the possibility of pregnancy. Had she told Madame of the risk she had taken, Madame would have been shrewd enough and wise enough to suggest a remedy Lucy could use should it be needed.

The subject was one that had often been discussed at *Le Ciel Rouge*. All the girls feared this contingency and took quinine every month. If this failed, Madame would give them a herbal compound which was invariably effective. Unfortunately, Lucy could not now recall its name. Nicole had thought herself pregnant on one occasion and insisted that her own private remedy—sitting for hours in a boiling hot bath while drinking gin—was every bit as effective as Madame's cure and a lot more agreeable. But Yvette was of the opinion that Nicole had never been pregnant in the first place and both girls agreed that to miss a period was not unusual or necessarily indicative. As a consequence, Lucy set about convincing herself that it was simply the change of air or food that had affected her and that by mid-February, her monthly period would arrive as usual.

Lucy adamantly refused to see a doctor next day, professing herself entirely recovered from her sea journey. She went downstairs and managed somehow to sit through the lengthy meals, aided and abetted by the labradors who sat under the table eagerly awaiting the morsels of food she was able surreptitiously to pass to them.

She was still feeling far from well when, at the end of the month, Alexis Zemski called.

"I don't want to see him," Lucy told her mother. "You know I don't much like him, Mama. I would rather remain here in my room if you don't mind."

Willow stood in the doorway of Lucy's bedroom, her face revealing her surprise.

"But you have never said before that you disliked the Count, Lucienne. You never objected when I told you he had asked my permission to call on us. He is such a charming young man and obviously taken with you. He wants to marry you ... and that is a compliment you cannot ignore."

Lucy's pale face flushed. Her eyes were full of anger as she said:

"Well, I don't want to marry him ... and I don't agree he's young or particularly charming."

Willow hid her astonishment at the vehemence of Lucy's tone.

"I was not suggesting that you should marry him, Lucienne," she said mildly, "only that you should pay him the courtesy of coming downstairs since he has driven all the way from London especially to see you."

"Can't you say I'm ill? Please, Mama?"

"It is too late for that. I have already told him you have quite recovered from the slight indisposition you suffered on your return from Paris. Good manners demand you should come down and talk to him, Lucienne."

Suddenly, Lucy's anger cooled. She had no cause to fear Alexis Zemski. However much he stared, he could not see inside her. If only there were some way she could see inside herself and know whether there really was a child in her womb. If there were...

Hurriedly, she put such thoughts out of her mind and followed her mother downstairs.

It was only with difficulty that Alexis was curbing his impatience as he awaited Lady Rochford's return with her daughter. It was now nearly ten weeks since he had last seen Lucienne. Roberta's reassurance that it would be better for his cause if the girl did not know of his anxiety to see her had done little to allay it. As she came into the room with her mother, he knew even more certainly that he was hopelessly in love with her; that no matter what it cost in time and effort, he had to persuade her to marry him.

There was no outward sign of his turbulent emotions as he stood up and greeted her with a smile.

"I'd like to hear about your visit to Paris," he said formally. "It is a city I know quite well. Did you enjoy yourself there, Miss Rochford?"

Lucy's replies were equally formal as she looked at her visitor with indifference. He was, she decided impartially, undoubtedly a very elegant man. He wore a country suit with a pale camel waistcoat and sported a cameo pin in his striped silk tie. He had a mature self-confidence lacking in the young Barratt boys.

To Lucy's annoyance, her mother made an excuse to leave the room—an obvious ploy to leave her alone with the Count. But her companion continued to converse fluently and impersonally, as if unaware of her mother's absence. He told her that he had run into both Annabel Barratt and her idol, Christabel Pankhurst, in January while Lucy had been in Paris.

"It seems they are planning a campaign of vandalism in an attempt to force Lloyd George into a promise to include women in his Franchise Bill," Alexis recounted.

"Are you in sympathy with their campaign?" Lucy asked, her genuine curiosity momentarily aroused.

Alexis leaned forward in his chair, his eyes bright with interest.

"I do believe women should have the vote," he said, "but I do not agree with the violent methods people like Miss Pankhurst and her followers indulge in to acquire publicity for their cause."

Despite her intention to remain quite aloof during what

was to be the briefest of meetings, Lucy found herself interested in this discussion about women's rights. She would have liked to point out to Alexis one particular inequality of the sexes—that concerning the freedom permitted men to indulge their passions where they pleased, even those who were married. There were many husbands who frequented *Le Ciel Rouge*. Yet had their wives been unfaithful it would have meant divorce, disgrace and more often than not, poverty.

But now it seemed this was no longer the case. Women were beginning to demand a different state of affairs and, accc ;ding to Alexis Zemski, were on the way to winning recognition in several respects.

Alexis' own attitude to women had been formed to a great extent by his relationship with Roberta. She was highly intelligent and remarkably well educated for a female. He had been able to converse with her on many topics as an equal; and she had taught him a great deal about life as well as about women and their emotional and physical needs. Consequently, unlike many men, he respected women. He surmised now that Lucienne, too, possessed both intelligence and intellectual ability.

"It has been my experience that the prettier a girl, the less intelligence she shows," Alexis said thoughtfully, "but in your case, Miss Rochford, this does not seem to apply."

"I doubt if we know each other well enough for you to be a fair judge of my intelligence," Lucy replied without any attempt to disguise her sarcasm. It was ignored by Alexis.

"Perhaps not. But I would like to know more about you, for I am certain a lot more goes on inside your head than you care to reveal."

He was too near to the truth for comfort, Lucy thought. Suppose he were to discover that she was thinking about a crazy half hour she had spent on a bed with an artist in Paris; that she had been making Maurice suffer as once he had made her suffer! She imagined the horrified expression on Alexis' face and the thought made her smile.

Alexis was watching her changing expressions and was intrigued. What was passing through her head, he wondered. Was she laughing at him?

"Do you find my interest in you ridiculous?" he asked with a directness he had not intended. Lucy looked surprised. She said truthfully:

"No such thought crossed my mind. If I think of you at

all, it is because I cannot understand why a man like you should waste your time coming to see me when there must be a hundred more interesting things for you to do."

Alexis said quietly:

"I don't feel that time spent talking to you is wasted, Miss Rochford. It is my way of getting to know you better. Surprising though it may seem to you, I am hoping that one day our friendship will become as important to you as it already is to me. Your mother is aware of my intentions and she led me to believe that she had mentioned them to you."

Lucy was momentarily caught off guard. She had not expected such impetuosity from a man who seemed so controlled, so remote. At any other time, it might have amused her to have so eligible a suitor. But now his very presence seemed to threaten her. She decided to be rid of him.

"If my mother led you to suppose I was looking for a husband, she has deceived you," she said coldly. "I have no intention of getting married either to you or to anyone else now or in the near future. Nor do I have any special feelings for you."

Her rejoinder was not unexpected but Alexis was made uneasy by the forcefulness of her tone. Then he smiled.

"I expect you are familiar with that famous line in Shakespeare's *Hamlet*: '*The lady doth protest too much, methinks!*' I shall take reassurance from it."

Now it was Lucy's turn to be silent. She was unfamiliar with the quotation but while it was true that she felt no special regard for this man, it was not true that she was altogether indifferent to him. From their first meeting, she had feared him, without understanding the cause of her fear. She knew he could not harm her; that he had no hold upon her. And yet...

"I am asking only that we should be friends for the time being," Alexis broke in on her thoughts. "I realize that you have no affection for me as yet—but I hope that the future will bring a change of heart. Until then, I will not embarrass you with a proposal of marriage. Since I accept these limitations, can't we enjoy each other's company from time to time?"

Lucy shrugged. The matter was of little consequence to her although, she thought suddenly, she *could* do with a friend. She needed someone she could trust absolutely, someone who did not live at Rochford. If this man really did want her regard, there was a service he could do for her. She had been wondering whether Madame Lou-Lou would help her. Of all the people in the world, Madame was the one who could give her the advice she needed. But while a letter written to her would present no problem since she could post it unobserved, she could not receive a reply unnoticed here at Rochford.

Her mind made up, she took a step toward Alexis and laid a hand on his arm in appeal.

"If you truly want to be my friend, then there *is* a way you can assist me in a small matter," she said softly. "Will you promise that you will respect my confidence *with your very life*?"

Alexis hid a smile at her extravagant phrasing.

"But of course! You have my word on it."

Lucy lowered her voice still further.

"Then it is simply this. I want to write to an old acquaintance, but Mama doesn't approve of her. She does not wish me to keep in touch with her because she is not of the right class. But this woman was very kind to me once when I needed help and I would like to send her a little money by way of thanks. She is certain to acknowledge my gift but I cannot give this address because Mama would then know I had written to her. But if *you* would be willing to receive the reply and deliver it to me secretly, then I could repay my debt to an old friend."

Alexis was immediately uneasy. He had the greatest respect for Lady Rochford and he was surprised to hear of her snobbery. Nevertheless, Lucienne was her child and under age and it was a mother's decision as to who were suitable acquaintances for her daughter. Lucienne's plan would involve him in deceit—possibly in lies.

"Since Lady Rochford has refused permission for you to correspond with this woman, I would knowingly be acting against her wishes," he protested. "Is it really so important that you should write to her?"

Lucy's mouth tightened.

"You find it harder to go against Mama's wishes than to fulfill mine?" she asked bitterly. "A few minutes ago you were talking of marriage. It does not seem that you care for me very much."

Alexis accepted the rebuke although he felt it unfair. He said with unmistakable reluctance:

"I will oblige you this once, Miss Rochford, but only to prove that I do care for your happiness enough to risk the loss of your mother's regard. But please do not ask me to deceive her again because I would have to refuse."

Lucy's scowl was replaced with a bright smile. Genuinely grateful, she reached out her hand and touched his arm.

"I promise you that it is only this once I want to write," she said truthfully. "Once my debt is paid, I need not think any more about this poor woman. How kind you are, Count Zemski!"

Alexis covered her hand with his own, his pulses leaping uncontrollably at the contact. His inner misgivings were dulled by the immense pleasure of seeing Lucienne visibly soften toward him. There could be no harm in doing what she asked of him, he thought. It was not as if the girl was wanting to write secretly to a man of whom her parents disapproved. *Or was it?* Could she have spun him a false tale about the woman who had befriended her?

As if in answer to his thoughts, Lucy's next remark put his mind at rest.

"Can you stay here a little longer? I could hurry and write my letter to Madame Verdris now." She used the first fictitious name she could think of. "Then you could post it on your return to London," she said eagerly. "It would reach her more quickly than if I were to post it in Havorhurst. May I tell Mama you are staying for tea?"

Although reluctant to be without her company even for so short a while, Alexis agreed to wait until Lucy's letter was written.

Alone in her bedroom, Lucy locked her door and drew out a sheet of notepaper from her escritoir. Using her nail scissors, she carefully cut off the printed crest and her address. In its place, she put the number of Alexis' house, Cadogan Gardens, Mayfair, London.

The letter itself was not as easy to compose as she had anticipated. For one thing, she had left *Le Ciel Rouge* on the pretense of paying a brief visit to Yvette's family in Provence but had never returned. She had been frightened to tell Madame Lou-Lou that she was really going to England in search of her family since, being the favorite of all her girls, Madame Lou-Lou might well have dissuaded her from leaving. She would not have liked Lucy disappearing in such a fashion and without a word of explanation.

But her father had expressly forbidden her to write to anyone from her past. She had understood his reasons for secrecy and now she remembered the need for it.

Cautiously, she wrote:

"Dear Madame, You must have thought me very ungrateful leaving you without warning although Yvette promised to explain that should I not return to Le Ciel Rouge *after my holiday, it would mean that I had traced my family in England. I wish circumstances did not necessitate me writing to you under an assumed name, but my family are rich aristocrats and would punish me severely if I were to continue my association with* Le Ciel Rouge, *however indirectly. Now I have an opportunity to send you a token of my appreciation of your kindness..."*

Unfortunately, Lucy thought, she had no money of her own. But she was aware that her mother kept quite a large number of dollar notes in the top right-hand drawer of her dressing table. Lucy had few scruples in removing several of the largest denominations she could see. It was obvious to her that her mother put little value on these foreign notes since she could not even be bothered to lock them up for safety. Moreover, Lucy told herself, Willow had forced her to return the Barratt boys' presents and had not offered to reimburse her for their loss.

Hurriedly she wrote the remainder of her letter to Madame Lou-Lou, telling her of her predicament and asking for her advice, which, she thought wryly, would cost Madame no more than the price of a stamp. She signed the letter 'Perle'—Madame's pet name for her—and took it downstairs to give to her accomplice.

Alexis was drinking tea with her mother and Toby in the library. He had been watching for her arrival and went across the room to her where he was able surreptitiously to take the letter from her.

"I will bring the reply to you as soon as it arrives," he said gravely, in a voice too low for Toby or Willow to overhear.

As soon as tea was over, Alexis announced that he must return to London. He bade Lady Rochford good-bye with renewed doubts that he was justified in aiding Lucienne to deceive her. Her friendly smile and invitation to come down again whenever he wished only increased his feelings of disquiet. It was almost with relief that he posted the offending letter as soon as he reached London.

Two weeks later, Alexis drove down to Rochford again. There had been no reply to Lucy's letter and he was totally unprepared for the look of bitter disappointment with which she received this news. Lady Rochford had left them alone together in the drawing room. They were therefore able to discuss the secret letter openly.

Lucy regarded him with a look of disbelief.

"You would not withhold a reply? I mean, I am aware you did not approve of the secrecy of my correspondence..."

"I gave you my word I would bring a letter if there was one," Alexis broke in. Strangely disturbed by the look of anxiety in Lucy's eyes, he added: "Perhaps your friend realized that a correspondence could be embarrassing for you in the light of your new environment. She may have accepted your letter in the same light."

Lucy made no reply. Obviously Count Zemski had no idea of the seriousness of her situation. She had been depending absolutely upon Madame Lou-Lou's help. If only she had had the good sense to go to see her when she was in Paris! But she had never seriously believed herself pregnant. The possibility that she might conceive a child as a result of one brief, isolated moment of folly was so improbable as to make a visit to Madame ludicrous in the circumstances. It was only now with hindsight that she realized it would have been sensible to obtain whatever was necessary from Madame merely as a precaution.

Was it possible that Madame might still write, she asked herself? Or that her letter had been delayed in the post? But even as these remote possibilities came into her mind, she knew they were worthless. It must be all of eight weeks since her visit to Maurice's studio. Madame had made it clear to them all that if her remedy was to be effective, it must be taken very early on or would be extremely dangerous.

She became aware of Alexis' gaze and felt a sudden, totally irrational fear that he might be reading her thoughts.

"Will you excuse me for a moment?" she said abruptly. "I have left my handkerchief upstairs."

She managed somehow to reach the sanctuary of her bedroom. For the first time in her life, her courage failed as she realized that she was caught in the oldest trap in the world and as far as she could see, there was no escape. Two tears ran slowly down her cheeks. She brushed them angrily away and rang the bell for Polly.

"Please tell Mama and Count Zemski that I don't feel well," she said, "and that I shall not be going down for tea."

The Count's eyes were too penetrating, she thought as Polly hurried away to do her bidding. Her hopes might be dashed to pieces but her pride was still intact and she had no intention of letting Alexis Zemski see her tears.

Chapter 8

March 1912

By NOW LUCY WAS NO LONGER IN ANY DOUBT THAT SHE WAS PREG-
nant. It was only with the greatest difficulty that she hid from
Polly the telltale signs of her sickness every morning. She
looked pale and tired and Willow fretted about her health.
Moreover, Lucy was irritable and uncooperative and not knowing the reason, Willow was unable to understand her daughter's seething resentment at life's unfairness. Lucy was
trapped—and by her own folly. She could see no way out of
her predicament.

She went secretly into Havorhurst to see Richard Bartholomew at his office. Hopelessly lovesick, the young lawyer
hovered over her, only too anxious to assist her in any way
that he could. Lucy wanted him to find some legal loophole
whereby she could obtain a private income from her father's
estate. And this, he was forced to tell her regretfully, could
not be done.

"I am sorry but there are no legal grounds whatever for
disputing your father's Will," he explained. He looked at Lucy's
drawn, sullen face and longed to put a smile back into her
eyes.

"Aren't you happy at home, Miss Rochford?" he asked,
believing Lucy's sadness due to her having asked for but been
refused a pocket money allowance.

"I cannot stay at Rochford much longer," she murmured.
"I must get away."

Richard came round from behind his desk and stood beside
Lucy, his heart leaping painfully as a crazy idea crossed his
mind.

"Have you ever considered that marriage might be one way
of escape?" he inquired. "If you were to marry a man who
loved you, loved you deeply...with all his heart..." his voice

was throbbing with emotion, "there would be nothing in the world he would not do to make you happy."

Lucy realized quickly enough that this was in the nature of a proposal, however indirectly Richard might be wording it. She also realized that the young man was quite besotted enough to be duped by her. She need never tell him she was going to have Maurice's child and even if his doubts were aroused when the child was born, she could probably talk him into keeping it in order to keep her. It was a solution to her problem, Lucy realized, but she had no wish to be the wife of a struggling young lawyer. There would be no big house to live in; only one or two servants to wait on her and above all, very little money. Such an existence could never be anything but tedious. She had lived long enough as a member of the Rochford family to be acutely aware of the privileges of rank and wealth. On the other hand, Lucy thought despairingly, what alternative was there? If she only had money of her own!

Richard now knelt down on the threadbare carpet, gaining hope and confidence from the conviction that Lucy's long silence meant she was seriously contemplating his proposal. He could no longer restrain himself from speaking out.

"Dearest Miss Rochford...Lucienne!" he ventured, passion giving him a spurious courage. "Is it your mother's possible disapproval that is making you hesitate? Lady Rochford cannot doubt my love for you. I have loved you from the very first day I set eyes on you." He hesitated only for the fraction of a second before saying in a hushed voice:

"I don't care about anything that happened in your past. I have never blamed you for it and you need not be afraid I would ever raise the matter. Your reputation would be safeguarded if you married a lawyer. Miss Rochford...Lucienne ...I beg you to say 'yes' and thereby make me the happiest man in the world."

Gently but firmly, Lucy disentangled her hands from his hot, feverish grasp. She thought his emotionalism slightly ridiculous and in any other circumstances, she would have given him a definite and outright refusal. But now she was too worried about her future to turn down, without due consideration, the only solution that had so far presented itself.

"I will think it over, Richard!" she told him. "You must realize your proposal was quite unexpected. I do need time to think about it."

Richard rose to his feet, his cheeks pink with excitement. This was a situation he would not have dreamed possible when Lucy had called to see him less than an hour ago! As far as he had been aware, Lucienne Rochford had no greater interest in him than in any other occasional visitor to the Manor. Although she had always greeted him with a smile.

"I will come here again next week and give you my answer," Lucy told him now. "For the time being, I would rather that you did not call at the house in case my mother gets suspicious."

Only slightly deflated by her matter-of-factness, Richard showed his visitor to the door.

Fortunately for Lucy, Willow's attention was diverted from her by the return of Oliver and Mark from their schools for the Easter holidays. Their arrival prompted a visit from Alexis Zemski with an invitation to take anyone who wished to go, to see his biplane at Brooklands.

Lucy would have declined to accompany the party except that Oliver would not hear of it.

"Uncle Toby says Count Zemski is only going to all this trouble because *you* will be there, Lucy. You've got to go. You've just *got* to!"

Contrary to her expectations, Lucy enjoyed the outing, momentarily forgetting her own secret problem in the excitement and interest of the day. The party were nine in number and drove to Brooklands in two cars. Lucy and the boys, including young Henry Barratt, accompanied Alexis in his Lanchester; Willow, Toby and the two younger girls were chauffeur-driven in the family's Rolls Royce.

Alexis was very much the hero of the day. He not only looked impressive in his flying helmet and goggles and warm leather fur-lined jacket but he put on a magnificent display of aerobatics for his audience. He demonstrated the great speed of his machine, roaring over their heads at sixty miles an hour, finally skillfully landing it close enough for the three boys to smell the exhaust fumes. Each in turn was allowed to sit in the cockpit while Alexis patiently explained the controls. But his eyes were never far from Lucy's person and he succeeded in drawing her away from the family group for a few minutes before they returned to the cars for the journey home.

"It will not be long now before your presentation," he said. "I am looking forward to May when no doubt you will be moving to London and I shall be able then to see you more often."

Willow had decided against renting a London house for the Season. Until she and Toby could be married, she had no desire to reenter the ranks of Society; nor did she or Toby greatly enjoy the hectic round of parties and events that lasted from May until August. She had therefore arranged with Louise Lennox to present Lucienne at Court and to chaperone her throughout her Season as a débutante. Willow herself planned to give her daughter a large coming-out ball at Rochford in August when they could count upon fine weather. Lucy therefore was to reside with the Lennoxes.

But that particular plan, like her presentation and all the débutante parties, would have to be set aside, Lucy thought unhappily. She could not delay much longer the moment when she would be forced to confess to her mother that she was almost certainly pregnant—in fact, there was no longer any lingering doubt about it. She had come to the conclusion that confession might be the lesser evil than eloping with the penniless Richard. There was always the possibility that her Mama might take pity upon her, find excuses for her and be prepared to pay for her to go away somewhere in order to avoid the disgrace that otherwise would reflect upon the family.

Watching the unhappy expression clouding Lucy's pale face, Alexis wondered what possible cause there could be for her obvious distress. She had seemed happy enough throughout the day. She had the coming Season to look forward to and in the meanwhile a mother who doted upon her. She seemed to be on good terms with the two new arrivals at Rochford Manor, young Mark Grey and his sister, Jane. Was she quite simply bored with the uneventful country life she was presently leading at Havorhurst or was she merely bored with him?

He is staring at me again, Lucy thought with a swift rush of anger. His was not like other men's gaze—lustful and admiring. His eyes were searching, probing, watchful, inquisitive. He seemed, as he always did, to threaten her.

"You will have to ask Mama what plans have been made for me," she replied to his question, her tone cold, her eyes unfriendly. She was about to walk away from him but Alexis reached out and caught her arm.

"Don't go!" he said in a low, vibrant voice. "I have something I want to ask you, Lucienne. You must know how I feel about you. Will you think about marrying me—not yet, of course. You are very young and you won't want to commit yourself before your débutante Season. But I would feel a great deal happier if you would tell me that you don't entirely reject the idea."

Lucy's mouth tightened.

"Just because my mother let you know she approved of you, Count Zemski, you seem to take it for granted that I, too, hold you in some special regard. I hoped I had made it clear when last we met that I have no intention whatever of marrying you or anyone else!"

"Not even Richard Bartholomew?"

The color raced into Lucy's cheeks. Her blue eyes blazed with anger as she gasped furiously:

"Have you been spying on me, Sir?"

Alexis had meant only to tease her. He was shocked and not a little concerned by Lucy's reaction.

"That's unfair, Lucienne. I was only teasing you a little. Your young brother let slip that you had called at the lawyer's office without a chaperone." He watched Lucy's unrelenting face and added quietly: "Oliver was no more spying upon you than I was. He and his two friends had been down to the village shop to buy sweets and caught sight of you going into young Bartholomew's office."

"How dare he tell you what I do with my time!" Lucy cried.

"Possibly because he senses, young though he is, that I am very much in love with you, Lucienne. He is devoted to you and he happens to admire me. It is only natural therefore that he should want to assist me in my cause."

Lucy did not return his smile. Despite Alexis' defense of Oliver, she felt somehow that he had betrayed her. She also felt even further threatened by Alexis. If he were to tell her mother she had been calling secretly upon Richard . . .

As if aware of her thoughts, Alexis said quietly:

"You needn't be afraid that I would pass on to anyone anything that concerned you, Lucienne. Nevertheless I would be happy to hear from your lips that you have no affection for this lawyer and that your visits to him were on matters of business?"

"It is no concern of yours what I do or who I see!" Lucy cried in a low voice. "Please leave me in peace, Count Zemski.

What I do with my life is my own affair. Do I make myself clear?"

Alexis nodded, managing with a full measure of self-control to hide the dismay her words caused him. Oliver had described the lawyer as both young and personable. Was it possible that Lucienne—*his* Lucienne—had fallen in love with the fellow? It would explain her secret visits—and her indifference to him, Alexis.

On his return drive to London, Alexis managed successfully to talk himself out of the worst of his fears. Lady Rochford, he told himself, would not permit her daughter to marry an impecunious young laywer. The fellow's income was certainly not adequate to keep the girl in a suitable degree of comfort, if indeed he could afford to marry at all!

With such self-reassurance, Alexis decided he had no just cause to lose any sleep over the setback he felt certain was only temporary.

But at midnight, Lucy was very far from sleep. Her mind was twisting and turning, searching for a way to avoid telling her mother the truth. She knew there was no escape and it was a moment she was dreading. She had to face the possibility that Willow would turn her out of her home.

Lucy's pride rebelled at the thought that she must now seek her mother's help and tolerance. If there were any alternative other than marriage to the dullard, Richard, she would not consider so humbling herself.

Strangely, it was young Jane who unwittingly provided the opening Lucy needed. The two girls had had little to do with one another since Jane's arrival. Lucy was preoccupied with her own affairs and Jane clung to her brother until he went off to his boarding school after Christmas, since when she had attached herself to little Alice.

But on this night she went to Lucy, instinctively aware that whatever was happening to her was not a childish concern. Unwarned and unprepared for the sudden bleeding that overtook her, she ran crying in fear to Lucy's bedroom.

"Will I die, Lucienne? I feel so strange. It hurts, too. Am I very ill? Will I have to go to hospital? I'm so frightened."

Lucy dealt with the matter calmly, efficiently and with great practicality. She explained to the young girl simply and kindly that her 'affliction' was not serious but merely one of the more tiresome aspects of becoming a woman.

"You had best tell Mama," she told the tearful Jane as soon as she had calmed down.

"Oh, no, I couldn't!" Jane cried aghast. "I could not speak of such things. Oh, Lucienne, you are so sensible about everything. Can't you tell her for me?"

Lucy's face softened. The girl looked so terrified and helpless—very much as she had felt when she had been similarly taken unaware. Life could not have been altogether easy for Jane, she thought, spending her school holidays with a senile old aunt in her eighties and with only two brothers for companionship. Like herself, Jane had had no mother or sister to advise her.

"All right, I'll speak to Mama in the morning. Now off you go to bed—and don't worry. You don't know how lucky you are!" she added to the young girl's mystification.

As soon as Willow had completed her morning task of discussing the day's menus with Cook, Lucy requested a private talk in the morning room. Willow happily agreed, delighted that Lucy had for the first time sought her out for conversation—as Toby had forecast she would.

She listened while Lucy related the events of the previous night and nodded her approval of Lucy's handling of the situation.

"It was kind of you to be of such help to Jane, my love," she said when Lucy paused. She went to put an arm around Lucy's shoulders but before she could do so, Lucy took a step backward.

"I have something else to say to you, Mama—something which I'm afraid will come as a shock. Perhaps you'd better sit down," she said in a cold, emotionless voice.

Not seriously alarmed, Willow did as Lucy suggested. Toby had said only the previous afternoon that he was convinced Count Zemski had taken his opportunity at Brooklands to propose to Lucy. Willow's liking for Alexis had increased with every meeting and she would give her approval to a formal engagement if that was what Lucy wanted. She hoped her daughter was not about to tell her she wished to forgo her débutante Season. She looked anxiously at Lucy's inscrutable face.

"On the subject we have been discussing, Mama, I have to tell you that I have gone two months without a period. I am afraid that I am almost certainly pregnant."

Willow's cheeks turned ashen.

"No!" she gasped. "No, Lucienne! You cannot mean that. There must be some other cause. There *are* other causes you know—fatigue, even influenza can affect..." But Lucy could not allow her hope.

"No, Mama, the timing is too coincidental," she interrupted. "I read in a book that the missing of two consecutive periods after intercourse invariably implies pregnancy. Besides, I have also been suffering from morning sickness. I am afraid there is no doubt."

Lucy wished she could feel more pity for the woman struggling not to cry out in horror. But she was too concerned with her own fears.

"Who...when...but...?" Willow could only stammer her questions.

"I refuse to reveal who the man was!" Lucy said quietly but with unshakeable determination. "As to when...it was when I was in France. It was not Aunt Silvie's fault. She had to go away for a day with Uncle Pelham after her home at Épernay had been burgled. I went out of the house without her knowledge."

Willow covered her face with her hands as if she could shut out the pale, utterly innocent face of her guilty daughter. Lucy's guilt was self-confessed. Yet she showed no sign of remorse. Her tone was almost defiant.

"Did you not realize what could happen when you...you..."

"I never thought of it," Lucy interrupted truthfully. "I wanted to do it and I did."

"No!" Willow whispered. "Please say it isn't true, Lucienne? I don't understand it. *Why?* Was he someone you love very much?"

"On the contrary, I hate him!" Lucy said. "Does it matter, Mama?"

Willow leaned forward, her eyes suddenly hopeful and the color returning to her cheeks.

"But of course it matters, Lucienne. Don't you see, if you love this man and matters are explained to him, you could be married and then..."

"I would not marry him if he were the last man on earth!" Lucy broke in violently. "And it would be pointless for you to try to persuade me otherwise. I will never marry him. I will never tell you his name."

Willow sank back against the cushions, her legs trembling. This was quite beyond her understanding. She was wretchedly afraid that Lucy might have gone back to her old ways and actually 'sold herself'—but she dared not ask the question.

"What are we to do!" she cried unhappily.

The pronoun touched a chord in Lucy's heart. At least her mother had taken it upon herself to share the problem as if it were hers, too. In a way perhaps it was, Lucy thought. The disgrace would reflect upon everyone if her condition became known. She offered the only comfort she could.

"Richard Bartholomew wants to marry me!" she said in a matter-of-fact voice.

"Mr. Bartholomew!" Willow echoed. "The lawyer? But, Lucienne, he is not a suitable husband and..."

"Suitable or not, he wants to marry me!" Lucy said. "He's so much in love with me I don't think he would suspect anything if I suggested we eloped. If we went away immediately..."

This time it was Willow who interrupted.

"That is a shocking and immoral suggestion," she said. "To deceive a man who loves you into thinking you care for him is only little better than using his name to legitimize another man's child!"

"I do not see that I have any alternative, Mama," Lucienne said wearily, "unless you would prefer to see your favorite, Alexis Zemski, make an honest woman of me?" she added wryly.

For the first time during this nightmare conversation, Willow felt a ray of hope. The Count! She had been hoping that secretly Lucienne might be considering marriage to him. He was wealthy, eligible and well spoken of by everyone. Sir John thought the world of him and Hilary Lennox made no secret of his respect for his colleague at the Foreign Office.

But no sooner had this hope emerged than it had to be quelled.

"One could not expect such a man to accept another man's child!" she said emphatically. "No matter how genuine his regard for you, Lucienne, he would lose all respect and affection for you if he knew the truth."

Lucy's eyes regarded her mother with a look of bitterness.

"Men make violent promises of love but when that love is put to the test, it proves about as solid as a puff of smoke!"

"Has Alexis declared himself to you?" Willow asked.

"Twice! And twice I have told him I would never marry him."

Willow was finding it difficult to regain control of herself. She must talk to Toby. Of one thing she was certain—between them, they *must* rescue Lucienne from the terrible consequences of her behavior.

Toby was as shocked as Willow by the news of Lucy's condition.

"I suppose we should have foreseen such a possibility," he said uneasily, "but Lucienne seemed to have settled down so well to her new way of life. Are you certain she will not tell you anything more? There must be a logical explanation for her behavior. Why only once? With one man—and someone she hates? It makes no sense Willow."

Willow was close to tears.

"Maybe she will tell me the truth in time, Toby. But we cannot force it from her now. Besides, what good would it do? She meant it when she told me so adamantly she would never marry him. I dread the thought of having to tell Alexis."

Toby looked astonished.

"But why on earth should you involve him in all this?" he asked.

"Because he is already deeply involved," Willow reminded him. "He made it quite clear to me that he is genuinely in love with Lucienne and that he hoped he could persuade her in time to marry him. So we are going to have to tell him something, Toby. Even if we were to hide Lucienne away somewhere until after the baby was born, he would demand to know where she was. We would also have to give an explanation as to why we had canceled all our plans for Lucienne for her Season in London...*next month*, Toby. As if we would send her away or even take her abroad ourselves at such a time and at such short notice!"

Toby sighed.

"It's a grim state of affairs!" he said. "I agree we *are* going to have to tell Zemski some of the story—but I have the feeling we can trust him. I cannot believe a man of his caliber would reveal facts that were so confidential and potentially injurious to all of us."

Willow put her hand on Toby's arm and looking up into his eyes, said quietly:

"If I had been in Lucienne's place, you would have wanted to marry me, Toby."

He returned her gaze steadily.

"You *know* I would, Willow."

Willow's eyes filled with tears.

"Then perhaps Alexis will feel the same way and accept her child. If he loved her enough, then there could be hope for her future..."

Toby nodded.

"One thing is certain—he must be told of her condition. I will go and see him, Willow—do my best to explain. If, as is to be expected, he bows out of the picture, we shall have to think again what to do with Lucienne! I agree Bartholomew is not the answer."

He dried the tears now falling down Willow's cheeks. Mixed with his love for her was a sudden rush of hatred for his grandmother—the wicked, misguided old lady who had wrested the newborn baby from her mother's arms. Grandmère had not foreseen the possible consequences when she had shuffled the lives of human beings as if they were cards in a pack. By spoiling his youngest brother, Francis, she had been indirectly the cause of his death. By bullying poor Rupert so unmercifully as a child, she had edged him into a life of homosexuality. She had done her utmost to ruin his little sister, Dodie's, future. Now it was up to him and Willow to make sure that the lasting effects of Grandmère's unwarranted interference did not ruin Willow's daughter, too.

That night, utterly miserable and very frightened, Lucy lay on her bed in the darkened room wondering whether she dared resort to Nicole's remedy for getting rid of the baby. But in her heart, she believed there was very little hope.

Chapter 9

⤸

March—April 1912

ALEXIS ZEMSKI STOOD IN THE MORNING ROOM AT ROCHFORD Manor, staring pensively out into the garden. The long sweep of lawn down to the lake had been newly cut; the daffodils growing wild in great profusion around the trees and the water's edge were in full bloom. Spring had come and there was an air of expectation in the piercing songs of the birds which seemed to echo in his heart.

He was awaiting the arrival of Lucienne whom Lady Rochford had gone in person to fetch from her bedroom.

Alexis was filled with uncertainty. The facts Toby Rochford had related to him concerning Lucy's present condition had momentarily shocked him beyond speech. Nevertheless, it had been but a few moments before he had heard himself declaring to Tobias that he still wanted to marry Lucienne. A look of relief had crossed Toby's face to be replaced swiftly by an expression of profound concern. By the long silence that followed, Alexis guessed that his host was undergoing some inner conflict. Finally Toby had spoken out in a determined voice.

"Frankly, Zemski," he had said, "your chivalry obliges me now to be completely honest with you. I feel it would be unworthy of me were I to deceive you in any single respect, and if you will bear with me, I have a great deal more to tell you."

At first, after listening to the horrifying story of Lucy's abduction and then to Toby's brief account of her years at *Le Ciel Rouge*, Alexis had been too horrified to think in a logical manner. He found it almost impossible to believe that the girl he had thought so innocent and unworldly was the very opposite.

Yet, as Toby talked, Alexis began to see that much of the mystery of little Lucienne Rochford was now explained to him.

124

She had seemed unlike other girls of her age and it was this very difference that had first intrigued him.

Common sense demanded that he put the girl out of his thoughts and forget her as quickly as possible. But even before Tobias had finished his unhappy confession, Alexis found himself searching for ways to condone Lucienne's behavior. So much of it was not in truth her fault! She had been but a child—motherless, homeless and without resources or advice. Her very vulnerability aroused a man's natural desire to protect and defend her . . . Her very helplessness was a challenge to his chivalry. Moreover, he realized with intense unease, nothing Tobias had said had stopped him wanting Lucienne. Was it possible he could still love her—even now?

"I appreciate your telling me the truth and for trusting me." He had smiled wryly. "I suppose you and Lady Rochford guessed that my interest in Lucienne was no casual fancy and that I would never have allowed her to disappear from my life without a satisfactory explanation. Naturally enough, what you have just told me has come as a very severe shock. But in spite of all you have said, I can't dismiss Lucienne as easily as you might suppose. I would like time to think about it. As soon as I am more certain of my feelings, I will drive down to Rochford and talk to you again if you will allow me."

When Tobias left, Alexis wished he could invite Roberta to visit him so that he could talk over the whole shocking affair with her. But in the first place he had given Tobias his word never to reveal the facts to a living soul; secondly, his ex-mistress would undoubtedly tell him Lucienne was unfit to be his wife, a possible danger to his career and an unnecessary and impossible responsibility. Alexis did not need her to endorse what were after all his own opinions.

He spent a sleepless night going over and over in his mind the story Tobias had told him. In the early hours of dawn, he reached the conclusion that Lucienne's past life required his understanding and pity rather than his condemnation. But he could not reconcile himself to her recent profligacy. Tobias himself had been unable to explain it. Lucienne had seemingly refused to name the man who had fathered her unwanted child. *Was he somone she loved?* Alexis tormented himself with the question. If she did love the man, Alexis wanted no part in her future. Or had she quite simply sold herself? Alexis did not want to believe it. Besides, what need had Lucienne of money now that she was back in the family fold, he rationalized his convictions?

When morning came, Alexis decided that he could reach no decision until he saw Lucienne once more. He needed to hear from her own lips why she had risked everything she had so recently gained with so little thought of the consequences. For an innocent young girl to be 'caught' in a moment of folly was not unusual; but Lucienne had *not* been innocent. Nor was she unintelligent...Alexis was so deep in thought, he did not hear Lucienne enter the room until she spoke.

"Mama said you wished to speak to me, Count Zemski. I myself can see no purpose in it. However, Mama insisted."

She was standing with her head held proudly erect; her eyes not cast demurely down but ablaze with defiance.

Alexis felt a moment of admiration for her. The girl might justifiably have been close to tears; certainly humbled by her predicament and afraid for her future. Yet she seemed not to care. She was dressed very simply in a deep russet-colored morning dress, the color accentuating the pallor of her cheeks and the dark shadows beneath her eyes. She looked far younger than her eighteen years.

Alexis invited her to be seated, then sat down opposite her. He decided to speak in as matter-of-fact a tone as was possible.

"You are aware that your uncle came to see me in London yesterday?" he said. He saw her slight nod and continued. "You and I can therefore talk to each other now with complete honesty. I would be grateful if you would answer a question that your uncle could not explain, Lucienne. It concerns your feelings for the father of your coming child."

Lucy was momentarily taken aback. In the first place, she had been convinced she would never see the Count again. When Willow had informed her five minutes earlier that Alexis was waiting downstairs to talk to her, she assumed he had come to tell her that he was withdrawing his offer of marriage. Yet now he was asking her about Maurice....

"I really don't see what it has to do with you," she prevaricated sharply.

"A great deal, as it happens," Alexis replied. "I must know, Lucienne, are you in love with this Frenchman? Do you refuse to identify him because he is already married, perhaps, and cannot marry you?"

Lucy gave a short, bitter laugh.

"Oh, no, he's not married. But as you appear to be so curious, I will tell you this much—I hate him. He is like all men—concerned only with himself, his needs, his desires. I went to see him with one objective—to make him want me; and then, afterwards, I told him what I really thought of him. I don't regret it...even though..."

The angry flow of words ceased suddenly and she seemed close to tears. Alexis looked away from her downcast head, hiding the look of relief in his eyes. So it had been an act of revenge, he thought—a terribly costly one as it turned out. But in a way, even that was an indication that she had gone on impulse to the assignation, innocent of the need to protect herself. She had not stopped to consider the consequences as a more calculating person might have done.

Alexis was absurdly relieved to discover that Lucienne's behavior was neither born of passion, love, nor for personal gain. He still did not know why she should have wanted revenge so violently that she was prepared to go to such lengths to get it. He assumed she must have been hurt or cheated, but for the time being, it did not matter. There was something more important he needed to know.

"Although you may resent my interference in your private affairs, Lucienne," he said quietly, "I do have good reasons for asking these questions. May I continue?"

Lucy had regained her composure. She shrugged her shoulders helplessly.

"Words cannot harm me," she said, "and I promised my mother I would listen to anything you have to say."

Alexis leant forward in his chair, his eyes never leaving Lucienne's pale face as he spoke.

"Your uncle said that he had discussed your present predicament with your mother. They thought that it might be possible to send you away until after the child is born; that arrangements could then be made to foster the baby so that you could return home as if nothing had happened. Does that possibility appeal to you?"

He was quite unprepared for the violence with which Lucy jumped to her feet and confronted him. Her blue eyes flashed fire as she said in a low, violent tone:

"If my mother knew me better, she would be aware that I will never abandon my baby as she abandoned me. *Never!* Make no mistake, I do not want this child. I spent too many years of my own childhood looking after the little ones at the

Convent, wiping their dirty faces, washing the sheets they wet at night; spooning food into their mouths, dressing and undressing them, drying their tears. I don't want this child and if I could, I would have got rid of it. But since it seems I must give birth to it, then I will try to be a mother to it as best I can. Does that answer your question, Count Zemski? And now that you have satisfied your curiosity, perhaps you would leave. Or do you prefer to stay and gloat over my predicament?"

She has both pride and courage, Alexis thought as he rose to his feet. There had been no attempt to put the blame elsewhere; and above all, her sense of duty to her unborn child was selfless and paramount.

Impossible though it seemed in the circumstances, he found himself both admiring and respecting her.

"I will leave as soon as you give me one more answer, Lucienne," he said quietly. "Will you marry me?"

Lucy's eyes widened and her mouth opened in disbelief. Was it possible that despite all that had been told him, this man still wanted to marry her? Her mother had said that true love could overcome anything—but still she did not believe it. She regarded Alexis suspiciously.

"But why?" she asked frowning. "You know what I have been and you know that I am carrying another man's child. I don't understand. Why do you want to marry me?"

Alexis looked at her gravely.

"It is quite simple, Lucienne. I have never felt about any woman as I feel about you. Since I first saw you, you have haunted my dreams and even..." he smiled briefly "...distracted me from my work. You must know, Lucienne, the devastating effect you have upon men. I find myself not only able but anxious to forget altogether those unhappy years you spent before you came to Rochford. I want our life together to be an entirely new beginning for you. I can make you happy, I'm sure of it. I am offering you my name, a name for your child, a moderately good standard of living and a place in Society. Is that not enough to tempt you to say 'yes'?"

Lucienne continued to regard him warily.

"And what do you hope to get in return?"

Her unconscious cynicism cut at Alexis' heart. But he kept his voice casual as he replied:

"Your presence in my house; your willingness to play your part as my wife; perhaps, in time, your affection. I am aware you do not love me now. It is not a condition for our marriage that you do so."

Lucy allowed herself to relax, believing that at last she understood this strange man. He was prepared to pay any price to own the right to her body. Such an obsession had not been unknown at *Le Ciel Rouge* where one of the patrons had bought his favorite girl from Madame for a huge sum. He had set her up in a large house of her own in Paris where she lived in the utmost luxury. In return, she had only to be there when he felt the need for her body. No one else, Madame explained, could satisfy him as did that one particular girl.

Lucy glanced surreptitiously at Alexis. He was a good-looking man and at thirty, could not be called old. Was it possible, she asked herself, that her luck was changing at this eleventh hour and that her future could be so easily redeemed? There was no doubt whatever that she would be in a far better position married to Alexis Zemski than to Richard Bartholomew. Her mother, Uncle Toby—even Oliver—would all be delighted!

Alexis found himself on tenterhooks as he awaited her answer. He had come to Rochford without any positive idea of whether he would offer her marriage or inform her he never wished to see her again! Now, when it seemed possible that she was about to refuse him, he was even more certain that he had to have her.

There could be terrible disasters with his career, he thought. Were his superiors at the Foreign Office ever to discover the truth about Lucienne's past, he would be forced to leave the Service. He would be open to blackmail with all that implied. He was deliberately putting his whole career in jeopardy and yet, unbelievably, it did not seem to matter.

"Very well, I will marry you," Lucy said matter-of-factly. "But it must be understood that I shall keep the child!"

Alexis nodded. They would employ a nurse when the time came. He need not be involved with its upbringing. He himself would treat it impartially and fairly but it would be Lucienne's, not his.

Willow could not contain her happiness and relief when she was called back into the room and Alexis told her the news. Tears streamed down her face as she clasped Lucy in her arms.

"I'm sure you are both going to be very happy!" she cried. Her eyes were shining as she looked at Alexis. "Lucienne will

devote her whole life to your happiness, will you not, my
darling?" she added, oblivious to the bitter expression in her
daughter's eyes.

Alexis was as acutely aware of Lucienne's rigidity as Willow
was ignorant of the effect of her pronouncement. As far as
Lucienne was concerned, a bargain had been struck and she
owed Alexis nothing more than the right to her bed when it
pleased him.

Her silence went unremarked as Alexis began to outline
his plan for the immediate future. There would not be time
for a formal engagement. They must be married as soon as
possible. They could go abroad to avoid all the inevitable
curiosity so hasty a marriage would invite if they remained
in England. Willow could tell everyone they had 'eloped'; that
Lucienne had secretly objected to the coming Season her
mother had planned and the elopement was a way of avoiding
it. He, Alexis, could obtain leave from his job provided he
remained in Europe on call should he be needed in an emergency.

Lucy listened to these plans indifferently. She had long
since given up hope of enjoying her presentation and the gay
round of parties in London. It made little difference now
whether she remained at Rochford for the summer or went
abroad with Alexis. She still felt far from well and all she really
wanted to do was to go to bed and sleep.

Her spirits remained low and did not lift until two days
later when a jewel box arrived from Cartier in London containing a magnificent sapphire set in diamonds. The card
inside read:

*'An engagement ring to match your eyes. All my love,
Alexis.'*

Flowers, too, arrived almost daily, impressing Willow and
Jane far more than Lucy who paid little attention to the
romantic messages on the cards accompanying them.

A radiant Willow took Lucy to Harrods in Knightsbridge
to choose an extensive and extravagant trousseau. She was
far more excited than the bride-to-be. No mention was ever
made of Lucy's condition and when Lucy herself referred to
it, Willow quickly changed the subject. She insisted that Lucy
should buy for her future husband a gold ring as a wedding
gift. It was very costly and Lucy regretted that she would have
to part with it in three weeks' time.

Lucy's maid, Polly, was to go with her on her honeymoon.

The girl was agog with excitement and shocked by the calm manner in which her young mistress was preparing to be married. She alone of all the servants knew of the proposed elopement, the reason given to her being that Lucy wished to avoid the Season.

"To think that you could have gone to Buckingham Palace in a beautiful white gown and an ostrich feather and all and actually seen Royalty!" Polly exclaimed. But then her romantic nature came to the fore. "It's because you and the Count are so much in love you can't wait to be wed!" She exclaimed coyly as she packed Lucienne's trunks.

Lucienne allowed Polly's excited chatter to drift over her head. Her feelings had not changed in the past week. She felt even more trapped than before and she sensed that there was some dreadful penalty she would have to pay of which she was so far ignorant. She could not bring herself to trust fully Alexis' motives. Her Uncle Toby had said that this offer of marriage was an extraordinarily magnanimous gesture in the circumstances.

Alexis Zemski may have bought my body but not my soul, she thought defiantly.

Nathaniel and Angela Corbett arrived from America at the beginning of April. Now that Lucienne's future had been decided, Willow was overjoyed to see them. The elderly couple had known Willow's parents long before she was born and having no children of their own, looked upon her almost as a daughter. The Corbetts were gentle, kindly people and had the easy, friendly manner of so many of their countrymen. The Rochford family took to them at once and even Lucy found herself responding to their obvious interest in her. Her curiosity was aroused when she heard Nathaniel Corbett telling her mother about the expansion of the successful Tetford Railroad and Transport Corporation and how wisely Willoughby Tetford had invested his wealth for the future.

"I have news for you, too, Lucienne," he announced patting her knee paternally. "Your grandfather was quite specific regarding his estate, you know. He wished it to be divided equally between your mother's—and I quote—'*surviving children*.' This must include you, Lucienne, and since your mother wrote to tell me you had been brought back to the family fold, I have discussed with our lawyers the somewhat involved question of reallotment."

He regarded Lucy's intent face with surprise to find her so interested in dull business matters.

"When your grandfather died in the San Francisco earthquake, we were all unaware of the fact that mercifully you were still alive, my dear," he continued. "The shares in the Corporation were subsequently divided equally between young Oliver and Alice. It may take a year or two to put this right but you can be certain that it will be done. It is a matter of carrying out your grandfather's wishes exactly. I was devoted to him, you know, as was Mrs. Corbett."

Willow had said nothing to Lucy about this unexpected windfall and Lucy was both delighted and annoyed that her mother should have left her in ignorance of so important a matter. If her grandfather was a millionaire as Oliver had told her, then she must be rich—very rich.

"Why must I wait as long as a year or more to receive my inheritance?" she asked.

Nathaniel smiled.

"The legalities are a little more complicated than you may suppose, Lucienne. Your 'inheritance' as you put it so delightfully, is really a question of ownership of shares in the Corporation. If the business is making good profits, as indeed it is now doing, then the shareholders receive what are called dividends."

"Are you trying to tell me that I won't receive any money?" Lucienne asked flatly.

"No, indeed! That is to say you *will* receive a yearly dividend which means a division of the yearly profits of the Corporation. This may not be particularly large if it is thought necessary by the directors to use some of the profits on capital expenditure in order to increase the assets—but I feel this kind of talk must be very boring for a pretty young girl like you."

He was amused to see the stubborn lift to Lucy's chin.

"On the contrary, Sir, I find it very interesting. I consider all women should be educated in such matters if they are to receive the vote," she quoted Annabel Barratt.

"Good for you, my dear!" Angela Corbett applauded. "You should not be so patronizing, Nathaniel. The modern young woman is not content to remain as ignorant as girls were in *your* day!"

Nathaniel joined in the laughter at his expense and then sat down with Lucy to give her a half hour's instruction on the composition of the American Corporation of which she was soon to have a third ownership.

"Your daughter has a remarkably quick grasp of affairs," Nathaniel told Willow when their talk ended. "It is a great shame your father is not alive for he would have appreciated his granddaughter's business acumen."

There was no mention of Lucy's father, Rowell Rochford. As if by tacit agreement, no one spoke of him. Finally, Lucy cornered Mrs. Corbett and asked her outright if she had known her father. For once, the pleasant, smiling face of the American woman looked stern.

"No one likes to speak ill of the dead, Lucienne," she said gently. "The best I can say for your father is that he always put the financial welfare of the Rochford family before anything else. As head of the family, he shouldered those responsibilities as did his father and grandfather before him. It is a matter of personal opinion as to whether the fortunes of any great family such as the one you were born into, should take priority over the human beings who are part of it. I myself do not think that ruthlessness is ever excusable."

Was there no one who had thought well of her father, Lucy wondered, remembering how impressed she had been when she had sat opposite him at the dinner table the first night she had ever spent at Rochford Manor. In spite of the fact that he was far from sober, he had looked handsome and distinguished in his dinner jacket, and every inch the Lord of the Manor. He had too, behaved like it, ordering the servants about and returning to the kitchen elaborate dishes Lucy herself had thought magnificent, for no better reason than they lacked sufficient pepper or because the plate was not piping hot.

Uncle Toby never behaved in such a way, she quickly noted. He gave orders in a mild voice and more often sent his compliments to Cook than complained. Sir John did likewise and now Lucy wondered whether her father's behavior had really been as aristocratic as she had believed in her ignorance. Miss Talbot, at the Establishment for Young Ladies had directed that one should be firm but never rude to the staff and never in *any* circumstances familiar.

Alexis Zemski had told her that as soon as they returned from their honeymoon in Europe, she could engage what further staff were needed at his house in Cadogan Gardens. As a bachelor, he kept only a handful of servants. His house-

keeper, cook and the butler had been there in his parents'
time and they had ten junior servants under them to run the
large house. Alexis had further said that she might redecorate
and refurbish his house exactly as she wished—with the exception of his study which, he told her smiling, was sacrosanct
and the only room she could not treat as hers. He had arranged
for the banns to be read at St. Bride's, a beautiful little church
off Fleet Street, where they were to be married very quietly
early one afternoon with only Willow and Toby as witnesses.
Immediately following the ceremony, they were to take the
boat train to Dover and cross to Ostend for the start of their
honeymoon.

No one else knew of the wedding arrangements except
Roberta Inman. Alexis did not want her to hear the news of
his so-called 'elopement' from anyone else since she would
undoubtedly question such uncharacteristic behavior.

Understandably, Roberta was too astonished by news of his
impending marriage to hide her surprise.

"An elopement!" she echoed, looking at Alexis' excited face
in dismay. "But even if you and the girl are against a fashionable wedding, have you no regard for Lady Rochford's
feelings? Wasn't Lucienne to have been presented this Season?
Even though you might be quite a 'catch' for the girl, Alexis,
Lady Rochford is unlikely to forgive you for disrupting all her
plans in such a fashion. It sounds more dramatic than romantic!"

"I don't think Lady Rochford will object provided her
daughter is happy!" Alexis prevaricated awkwardly.

"But, Alexis, you hardly know the girl!" Roberta protested,
unable to withhold her inner misgivings. "Are you *quite* sure
you are doing the right thing?"

She was further dismayed by the finality in Alexis' voice
as he replied:

"Quite sure, Roberta! The fact is, I am hopelessly in love
with Lucienne and nothing else seems to matter—nothing!"

Not even that she was carrying another man's child, he
thought; not even that she had strayed, in her innocence,
into a house of ill-repute; that her youth and beauty had
inevitably been exploited by the shrewd owner and her innocence destroyed!

Strangely, what he found hardest to accept was Lucienne's
brief affair in Paris with the man she refused to name. On
her own admission, that action had been deliberate, yet he

knew that she had not been prompted by love; nor even by desire.

He had no need of Roberta's warnings about 'marrying in haste and repenting at leisure' for he had already realized that he had carved out a treacherous road for himself. In a way, he agreed with everything Roberta was saying and thought himself quite mad. But it made no difference. He went ahead with arrangements for the wedding, booking their passages to Venice and a honeymoon suite in one of the most beautiful hotels in that romantic city.

Whenever possible, Alexis drove down in his car to Rochford to see his future bride, returning from every visit newly disappointed, for while Lucienne showed no sign of wishing to change her mind about marrying him, equally she showed no sign of affection for him. She was entirely matter-of-fact about the wedding plans he discussed and indifferent to the arrangements he had made. The only time she showed any animation was when she told him about the beautiful trousseau her mother had bought for her.

"When I was at the Convent, I used to dream about wearing lovely dresses," she told him naïvely. "I never imagined that one day I would own so many pairs of shoes and do you know, Alexis, I have twenty different pairs of gloves, all in different colors?"

"You shall always have beautiful clothes to wear, Lucienne!" he promised her. "I will open accounts at the best shops and you can choose whatever you want if it makes you happy."

Perhaps marriage would not be so dreadful a bondage as she had feared, Lucy thought. Her future husband was obviously a generous man and prepared to be indulgent. It could be quite amusing doing up his house—their house—in London. The Corbetts, of course, knew nothing of the coming marriage but Angela Corbett went out of her way to discuss Alexis with Willow.

"I know he is quite a lot older than Lucienne but he would be a very good match," she remarked, for she had been much taken with the Count's faultless good manners and Continental charm. "They would make such a very handsome pair!"

The Corbetts' two-week holiday passed very quickly with visits to the Tate Gallery, the Tower of London and Kew Gardens. Unfamiliar as they were with such a horticultural rarity, they were particularly intrigued by the Maze and Hampton Court, where they spent a happy afternoon.

They had booked their return passage on 11th April, traveling from Southampton to New York on the maiden voyage of the White Star line, *Titanic*. Nathaniel and the Chairman of the White Star line, a man called J. Bruce Ismay, were old friends and he was to be a fellow passenger. Toby, Willow and Lucy drove with their departing guests to Southampton to see them aboard the magnificent eight-hundred-foot-long liner—the largest in the world.

They were invited to take drinks in the Chairman's stateroom, superbly decorated in the style of the Italian Renaissance. Afterwards, they were conducted round the huge vessel and shown the first-class lounge which was equipped like the Palace of Versailles, all in gold and white. The dining room was decorated in replica to Hatfield House and in the adjoining annex, the walls were covered with magnificent Aubusson tapestries.

While listening with half an ear to her mother's conversation with Uncle Toby, Lucy was far more interested in the conversational exchange she had overheard between Mr. Corbett and Mr. Ismay. They had wagered five hundred pounds on the length of time it would take the *Titanic* to reach New York. Lucy considered once again this enormous bet made so casually by two businessmen who thought little of it. Polly's wages for ten years! Perhaps even more shocking was the thought that many of Madame's girls worked long, exhausting hours trying to save such a sum for their dowries so that they could at last get married. But why should she concern herself any more with those poor unfortunates who did not belong to the wealthy upper classes? She herself would never be poor again.

When the farewells were finally made, the Rochfords drove home, excited by all they had seen and yet saddened at the parting from the Corbetts.

On the morning of Monday, April 15th, Toby, Willow, Lucy and Polly drove up to London, the luggage rack on the back of the Rolls piled high with Lucienne's trunks and Polly's basket. Lucy was quite calm but Willow sounded nervous and distressed.

"I do hope you will be happy, my dearest," she said over and over again as if she suddenly doubted it. "Alexis will take good care of you, I know. I only wish you were not going to be so far away."

"It is only for three weeks, Mama," Lucy replied coolly. "And Venice is not the end of the world."

"She's a lucky girl," Toby said, trying to calm Willow. "I've never been to Venice but I believe it is a magical city."

"I suppose I *am* being stupid," Willow said after a moment's silence. "Of course Lucienne will be perfectly all right. It's just that . . . that I have this uncomfortable premonition, Toby. I can't explain it but . . . I just feel something awful is going to happen!"

"Perhaps the bridegroom will not be at the church!" Lucy said mischievously, to be quietened instantly by Toby.

There were few people about when they reached St. Bride's—those who normally thronged Fleet Street in their lunch hour already back at work. Alexis was standing with the Vicar outside the church awaiting their arrival. He looked pale and until he saw them there had been a look of anxiety on his face. The sight of Lucy put all other thoughts from his mind. Dressed entirely in violet-blue to match her eyes, she looked amazingly beautiful. A large satin and tulle hat was perched on her crown of fair hair; the Medici collar of her matching jacket was frilled beneath her small chin. As Alexis smiled down at her, she stared back at him gravely. She looked very composed and remained so as the Vicar took them all into the beautiful old church and directed them to their places.

The simple ceremony was quickly over. At Alexis' request, there was no sermon following the marriage—only a blessing. A quarter of an hour after the service had begun, they were in the vestry signing the register.

So simple, so easy, so quick, Lucy thought! One minute she was the Hon. Lucienne Rochford; a moment later, Countess Zemski. Legally, she was now Alexis' wife and yet she felt no different. Her main feeling was one of relief that she had neither been sick nor fainted. She had enjoyed much better health of late and was almost able to forget that somewhere deep inside her, Maurice Dubois' child was growing inexorably.

Outside St. Bride's, the spring sunshine was bright after the dark interior of the church. Tearfully, Willow clasped her daughter in her arms.

"Alexis has promised me he will bring you to stay at Rochford as many weekends as possible," she said. "I seem to have had you with me so short a while, my darling. If only..."

Alexis took Lucy's arm and said gently to Willow:

"I will take care of her, I promise!"

They had but a few steps to walk to Alexis' waiting car in which his chauffeur was to drive them and their two servants to Victoria Station. Willow, her eyes full of tears, allowed herself to be led to their own car by Toby.

"Come now, my love, all is going to be well," he said. "You worry about Lucienne far too much. We can trust Zemski. He's a remarkably decent chap."

As they drove along Fleet Street the cry of a news vendor caught Willow's attention, making her forget Lucy and Alexis.

"*Titanic* sinking. *Titanic* hits iceberg!"

"Toby, did you hear? Stop, please, and get a paper. It can't be true. I don't believe it! Everyone knows she is unsinkable!"

There were few details in the paper to explain the headlines and those there were, were hopelessly conflicting. On the following morning, the *Times* announced that the *Olympic* had gone to the rescue of the floundering ship and that all passengers had been saved. The *Titanic* was being taken in tow by the steamer, *Virginian*.

"So your worst fears have proved foundless," Toby said reassuringly as he laid down the newspaper. "Nathaniel and Angela are alive, however dreadful their experience. We will telegraph New York for news of them tomorrow."

But for once the *Times* proved incorrect in its reporting. When the true facts were known, it was learned that *Carpathia* had picked up the pathetically small number of survivors from their lifeboats. Only seven hundred and eleven were got off the liner before it tipped up on end. She remained like that— a gigantic tower reaching out of the sea, before she sank suddenly beneath the waves. One thousand, four hundred and ninety people were missing, presumed drowned.

Although Willow and Toby were not to know it for several agonizing days, Nathaniel and Angela Corbett were among those who had gone down with the so-called 'unsinkable' ship.

Chapter 10

ᚼᚾᚮ

April 1912

THE HOTEL ALEXIS HAD SELECTED FOR THEIR HONEYMOON HAD
once been the private palazzo of a wealthy Venetian family. Lucy
surveyed with interest the huge entrance hall with its high ceilings and marbled floors, while Alexis spoke in fluent Italian to the
obsequious little manager who hurried forward to greet them.

Huge stone pots containing palms stood like sentinels on
either side of the glass doors. The pillars and walls surrounding the hall were heavily carved and high above Lucy's head,
the multihued ceiling was divided with intricate carvings of
grapes and vine leaves.

"Take a bit of dusting, that would!" Polly whispered as she
waited respectfully a pace behind her young mistress.

The two servants, Polly and Alexis' valet, Simpson, were
left to walk upstairs as the manager personally escorted the
English Count and Countess to the ornate lift. This, too, was
beautifully carved and gilded and Lucy was interested to see
her reflection on all three mirrored sides as the creaking iron-
grilled door was closed and the lift ascended to the first floor.

Alexis had commanded a suite of rooms. They were conducted first into the sitting room—almost as large as the library
at Rochford, Lucy thought. Here, too, the floors were of marble,
covered by the occasional rug. The glass of the window panes
was decorated with a coat of arms, presumably that of the former owner, Lucy decided. Over the white marble fireplace was
a huge oil painting of a sea battle but apart from this and one
or two smaller pictures of Venice on the other walls, the room
was bare of decoration and her eyes were drawn upwards to the
ceiling which had been painted a beautiful sky blue. There were
several marble-topped tables and a comfortable sofa and two
armchairs upholstered in a soft yellow damask.

Following Alexis and the manager into the larger of the

139

two bedrooms, Lucy was pleased to see the same blue ceiling—only here, delicately carved cherubs smiled down on the huge oak double bed. The bed cover, like the curtains, was yellow damask and the coloring had been carried through to what Alexis called his dressing room. Completing the suite was a vast, ornate bathroom, where the gilded taps were shaped like dolphins and obediently gushed hot and cold water as the manager demonstrated their efficiency.

All the rooms had tall casement windows with slatted shutters opening onto a balcony under granite arches. The balcony overhung a narrow strip of water, across which was another huge stone palazzo. The manager pointed to his right where, he said in rapid Italian, the slow moving water of the canal beneath joined up with the Grand Canal down which they had traveled a short while earlier in their gondola to reach the hotel.

"We have one hundred and seventy-seven canals spanned by more than four hundred bridges," he boasted proudly.

It was by now midmorning. They had spent the first night on the train in separate sleeping compartments—a novelty Lucy had enjoyed although it had proved very noisy and she had slept little. She was, however, now quite refreshed and gave an eager assent when Alexis suggested they might take a gondola after luncheon and do a little sightseeing. They would go on their own, he said, while Polly and Simpson did the unpacking.

Over luncheon in the big dining room downstairs, Alexis told Lucy about the *Ponte dei Sospiri*.

"In England we call it The Bridge of Sighs," he said with a smile. "It connects the Doge's Palace where the prisoners were sentenced, to the cells in the Venetian prison on the other side. The 'sighs' of course, came from the guilty about to pay for their crimes!"

"Is that really true, Alexis?" Lucy asked, certain that he was teasing her. He nodded.

"Really true!" he said. "We can go from the Palace to look at the mosaics in St. Mark's Church and by then, I expect we shall be ready for an aperitif in St. Mark's Square."

"I don't like churches!" Lucy said flatly. "I'd like to see the Palace, though!"

"Some of the churches in Italy are the most beautiful in the world!" Alexis said, looking mildly surprised.

"Well, I don't want to go in any of them," Lucy replied in

the same determined voice. "I spent far too many hours in them when I was a child, and when I left the Convent, I swore I'd never go in another—and I never will!"

"You went into St. Bride's!" Alexis reminded her smiling.

Lucy tossed her head.

"Only because I had to get married."

Alexis decided to let the matter drop. In time he would doubtless learn a great deal more about Lucienne's childhood. For the present, he could not take his eyes from her. There was some indefinable facet of her beauty which caught at his heart and filled him so full of love that it was closer to pain than joy. No matter what warnings Roberta had given him, he had no regrets. Lucienne belonged now to him. She was his wife—for better and for worse.

"Alexis, I do wish you wouldn't keep staring at me!" Lucy said, uncomfortable as always beneath the penetrating gaze of his green eyes. "You make me feel there must be something wrong with my clothes or my hair!"

Alexis laughed.

"On the contrary, my dear. I was staring because you are so very beautiful. Everyone is looking at you, men and women alike. The men are wishing themselves in my place and the women are wishing they looked like you."

Lucy's face relaxed.

"I suppose I should be pleased, then," she said amiably. "What else is there to see in Venice—other than the churches," she added smiling.

"There is a little island called Torcello where you can watch the lace-makers at work in their factory. I will buy you a lace mantilla. It would suit you, Lucienne."

"You seem to know an awful lot about every place we visit!" Lucy commented as the waiter put a huge basket of fresh fruit on their table. "Do you know all the cities in Europe?"

Alexis nodded.

"Most of them. Sometimes my work takes me to the big cities; sometimes I traveled just for pleasure."

"How many languages do you speak?" Lucy asked, for she had noted how fluently Alexis spoke her own native language, French, and now he had shown himself equally fluent in Italian.

"Fourteen, I think. But that is no real credit to me—I don't find them hard to learn. I think Russian was the most difficult—then Polish. German, French, Portuguese and

Spanish were far easier. Now, if you have finished eating, shall we be on our way? I am longing to show you this beautiful city."

Lucy decided that she might after all enjoy not only her honeymoon but her marriage. Alexis was a very agreeable companion, intent upon pleasing her. He was also very generous and bought her on the spot a cabochon jade ring set in diamonds which she admired in one of the little shops near The Bridge of Sighs.

When finally they returned to the hotel, Alexis retired to his dressing room to change for dinner. Polly was awaiting Lucienne with a bright, excited face. She had already run a bath for her young mistress and now laid out on the bed one of her new evening gowns.

"There's hardly a crease in any of the frocks," she chattered as she helped Lucy to undress. "And Simpson said he could borrow an iron from the management if I wanted. He's ever so nice, Miss—I mean, Ma'am..." she giggled. "I keep forgetting you're a married lady now! He says the Count is a good master—firm but fair. And Miss Lucienne—have you heard them gondoliers singing something fit to burst. Cheeky lot though but ever so romantic. One threw me a rose up to the balcony when he saw me watching him! Did you have a nice afternoon, Miss Lucy?"

Lucy nodded. She was tired now and content to listen to Polly's chatter while she luxuriated in the hot bath water liberally sprinkled with Essence of Roses. She was hungry too, somewhat surprisingly after so large a luncheon.

When she joined Alexis in their sitting room, her fatigue had gone and she looked happy and excited.

"Do you like it?" she asked childishly, showing off her new turquoise watered silk evening gown.

"Very much, my dear!" Alexis replied. "I shall be the proudest man in the dining room tonight when I take you in on my arm."

All heads did indeed turn toward the handsome couple as they went in to dinner. There were candles and flowers on their table and at one end of the large dining room, a small orchestra was playing light operatic arias, all of which Alexis appeared to know and was able to identify for Lucy.

It was after ten o'clock before the meal ended and Lucy stifled a yawn only with difficulty. When Alexis suggested they should retire, she readily agreed. In her big bedroom, Polly was waiting. The huge four-poster bed had had its covers turned down and Lucy's new crêpe de Chine nightdress lay spread across the quilt. It had tiny frills of lace and was the prettiest nightgown Lucy had ever seen, let alone worn. When Polly slipped it over her head, she felt the soft, silky material against her body and sighed contentedly as she climbed in between the sheets.

Polly was kept busy tidying up the clothes Lucienne had just discarded.

"Don't want a right old mess in here when the Master arrives," she said. "He'll be here presently." She looked at the pale face of the young girl in the big bed and her good nature prompted her to say: "I don't know as if your Mama spoke about what honeymoons are for!" She hesitated before adding: "But there's nothing to be afeared of, Miss Lucienne. My sister, Edna—she's married and so she knows what's what—*she* says it isn't half so bad as our Mam warned her it would be. In fact she once said as how it was one of the few of life's pleasures you could have for free. If you know what I'm meaning, Miss Lucienne."

"Have *you* never been with a man, Polly?" Lucy asked and was surprised to see the hot color flooding her maid's face in a bright blush.

"Lawksamercy, no, Miss Lucienne! Me Dad would thrash the daylights out of me if ever I let a man take liberties. I wouldn't do no such thing. The likes of me can't afford to lose their good name. I'll go pure to me marriage bed and if I don't never marry, then to my death bed and that's a fact." She looked at her young mistress almost with reproach. "Just because us lot are working-class it doesn't mean we're not decent, Miss Lucienne."

Lucy made no reply, her thoughts busy with her maid's moral attitudes. Whatever would Polly think if she guessed her mistress was even now with child! It would seem Polly would be even more shocked than Mama.

The arrival of Alexis from the adjoining bedroom put an end to Lucy's thoughts. Polly bobbed a quick curtsey and left the room. Alexis walked over to the side of the big four-poster. He was wearing white silk pyjamas with a black piping round the collar and cuffs. Over his shoulders was a Paisley silk dressing gown.

He sat down on the edge of the bed and reaching out one hand, ran his palm softly over Lucy's hair which Polly had brushed and then loosely plaited into one long silky rope hanging down her back. His eyes were unsmiling.

"How beautiful you are, my lovely Lucienne!" he murmured. "I love you very much, you know. Do you love me a little? Be honest with me."

Lucy sighed.

"If you hadn't asked me to be honest I *would* have said I loved you. I can't now, can I?" she said matter-of-factly. "The truth is, I'm not at all sure what love is. But I am very grateful to you, Alexis, and I do mean to keep my side of the bargain."

She saw a sudden look of dismay on Alexis' face and was surprised by it.

"I don't want you to think of our marriage as a 'bargain,'" he said urgently. "I married you because I want you for my wife."

Lucy brightened.

"Well, that's all right then. I don't mind at all how often you want me. You can do it whenever you want," she added generously.

Alexis withdrew his hand and stared down into her pale, questioning face.

"But do you want me to stay with you, Lucienne? Now? Tonight?"

"I don't mind, honestly, Alexis. You've been very nice to me all day and it's the least I can do to repay you, isn't it?"

Alexis turned his face away so that the girl he had married could not see his expression of despair.

Oh, God, he thought. What have I done? How can I make her understand that I am not bargaining for her body.

"Let us see if we can reach an understanding," he said softly. "Would you be disappointed if I kissed you good night and went back to my own room?"

Lucy was staring at him uncomprehendingly.

"You mean you don't want to?"

"I didn't say that. I'm trying to find out how *you* feel. It is very important to me."

"Well, I am a bit tired but truthfully, Alexis, I'd much prefer you did it than that you kissed me. I don't much like kissing. It always seems to me so messy and anyway, what's the point of it?"

For the first time, a brief smile crossed Alexis' face.

"I suppose it is just another expression of love," he said.

Lucy nodded.

"Maybe, but it's a bit of a waste of time all the same."

"That thought had not occurred to me," Alexis said. "But I will remember that you don't like kissing and we won't indulge in the practice." He stood up and pulled his dressing-gown more tightly around him.

"I'm going to let you sleep," he said. "It has been a long day and we are both tired. I'll come and have breakfast with you in the morning. Tell Polly to let Simpson know when you are awake."

He took one of her hands and held it briefly. On one finger was the large jade ring he had bought for her that afternoon.

"You might crush your finger if you lay on that during the night," he said. "Shall I remove it for you?"

Lucy snatched her hand away.

"No, I like it. I want to wear it," she said. "I might lose it if I took it off."

Surprised at her vehemence, Alexis said:

"But it's not of any great value."

Lucy shrugged.

"It is real jade, isn't it?"

Alexis nodded. Was it possible Lucienne put special value on the ring because it was the first present he had given her since their marriage? Or was it merely acquisitiveness?

She was snuggling down amongst the bed clothes like a small child preparing for sleep. She looked relaxed and content. For a moment, Alexis' heart filled with bitterness. This was his wedding night—a night he had been longing for with a deep, aching hunger. He had imagined the two of them in one of the most romantic settings in the world, naked, entwined, caught up in a vortex of passion and love. With Roberta he had known instinctively that love was the one vital element always missing—diminishing their relationship. Since their affair had ended, his dreams had been haunted by Lucy's delicate white body, her arms reaching out for him, her small beautifully-pointed breasts pressed against his heart. How wildly she had responded to his embraces! How sweet were her kisses! How eagerly she had received him, her lovely sapphire eyes closing in ecstasy as their bodies moved together in perfect unison!

Quietly, Alexis closed the communicating door between his bedroom and Lucienne's and, removing his dressing gown, he climbed into his single bed. The smooth sheets were cold against his body which felt hot and feverish. He turned out the light, trying to still his mind so that he could attain a much needed night's sleep. The last few days before the wedding, he had burnt the midnight oil in an attempt to clear his desk of all outstanding work before he departed on his three-week honeymoon. There had been one particular report which had required every ounce of his concentration. There had, too, been the meetings with the Vicar of St. Bride's, confrontation with his most senior superior, Fanshaw—the only person whom he was obliged, as a matter of duty, to inform about his impending marriage.

Fanshaw had not been pleased.

"You are aware that your bachelor status was one we considered of extreme importance when we gave you your job, Zemski?" he had said coldly. "You must be aware we would not have considered a married man."

"I know that, Sir. But if it comes to a choice between my job and the girl I want to marry, I've made up my mind I will have to resign if you refuse permission," he had replied.

Fanshaw looked shocked.

"You can't possibly do that, Zemski. You know we are depending upon you in several vital fields. Surely you can put off this marriage until Europe has settled down." He gave a deep sigh and said in a more temperate tone: "You say this girl is still in her teens. Can't you wait a while, Zemski?"

"No, I can't, Sir. She's going to have a child!"

Fanshaw's jaw dropped open.

"Great Scott, Zemski, I should have thought . . . well, that's none of my business. I do see that you've no choice under the circumstances but to do the decent thing. All the same . . ." He took off his spectacles and polished them thoughtfully. "You realize I can't change the system. You will continue to be away from home for weeks at a time. Your wife will ask you to explain your absences and you won't be able to give truthful answers. If she is like most females, she'll suspect another woman and will not let the matter rest. And you'll have to be doubly careful about security at home."

"I understand, Sir. I don't minimize the possible difficulties but I give you my word I won't let the Department suffer. You should know me better than that."

Fanshaw had not liked it but he knew Alexis well enough to be certain that he would not have threatened to resign without being prepared to do so. Even with Fanshaw's reluctant permission to marry granted, Alexis had still not felt entirely at ease. The Department were certain to look into Lucienne's background during the three weeks before their wedding and if they probed too deeply...

But there had been no urgent call from Fanshaw subsequent to their meeting and now he was reasonably certain that the Rochford family had passed the test. But this only went to prove even more adamantly what he had already suspected—that this particular branch of British security was far from fool-proof. It made Alexis more than a little uneasy since often his own life depended upon the work of the Department behind him. Nevertheless, he was for once grateful that their investigations were inadequate. It now seemed safe to assume that Lady Rochford's story that Lucienne had spent her childhood in a French convent had not been doubted and that if it passed Security, it would not be challenged by Society. Once Lucienne became Countess Zemski her past would not be questioned and could be well and truly buried.

Yet it was not so easily buried, he thought unhappily, as he twisted and turned in his bed. It was not after all possible to eradicate the harm those years had done to Lucienne. He remembered the small, puzzled frown on her face and the exact tone of her voice when she had said to him but an hour since: *"I'm not at all sure what love is."* And even more shocking to him was her assumption that he had married her in order to be able to bed her when he pleased—her part of the bargain, she had considered it.

That bargain would have been fair enough, he thought, had he not loved her. Many marriages had been contracted on those terms and even been successful. But he wanted more—much, much more. He wanted a happy, laughing, loving Lucienne—above all loving. And that had not been part of the bargain. It was only something he could wait for with as much patience as he could for as long as was necessary.

Still Alexis could not sleep as thoughts raced through his mind in an attempt to alleviate his disappointment. He found one small hope to cling to—that Lucienne was not as immune to feelings of love as she believed. Young Oliver had told him that when no one else was about, she showed him as much affection as any brother could be expected to tolerate.

"But she takes jolly good care that no one else knows she likes me—and Alice!" the boy had added thoughtfully. "I don't know why!"

Because life had taught her to mistrust love, Alexis had

thought then, and now he added silently, because she has never learned how to love. He pondered the question that thought raised. Were people 'taught' to love? Was it something a young child experienced in the warm, sweet-scented embrace of its mother's arms; in the soft touch of lips when the moment came for good-night kisses; in the tender, caring expression of eyes comforting, encouraging, forgiving? Lucienne had been denied these joys and love was new and unrecognizable to her. He had seen for himself how coolly she always responded to Lady Rochford's efffusive displays of affection.

"I must be patient!" he told himself, for he knew only too well that love could never be forced. Had he not tried himself to match Roberta's depths of feeling and had been unable to respond on the emotional level he knew she wanted?

His thoughts returned to his young wife, asleep now no doubt, in the big bed next door. Still restless and unable to settle, Alexis got out of his own bed and went to the communicating door, opening it very softly. A shaft of moonlight pierced the room from a gap in the damask curtains, touching Lucienne's head and turning her gold hair to silver.

She was not after all asleep for she said drowsily:

"Is that you, Alexis?"

His heart leapt, thudding with renewed hope as he walked over to her.

"Yes, my darling!"

Her eyes, quite visible in the moonlight, looked up into his.

"I was thinking," she said. "It does not seem right, somehow, that I have not shown you how grateful I am ... for you marrying me, I mean, and for the ring and everything. So I wanted to say you can call me Lucy if you like. I don't let anyone else but Oliver call me Lucy. But *you* can too—if you want!"

Alexis stood perfectly still. Had he loved her less, he might have laughed at such nonsense, felt bitter that on this, his wedding night, all his young wife could offer him was the use of a foreshortened name. But as he stared down at her pale, serious little face, he realized that this was the first indication she had ever given him that she felt some affection for him. Her offering might be childlike in its simplicity but it was no less an offering.

"Thank you, Lucy!" he said gently. And not trusting himself

to remain at this safe distance from her, he went quietly back to his own room.

The following evening, Alexis took Lucy to the opera where they watched a magnificent production of Puccini's *Madame Butterfly* in glittering surroundings. Lucy was enchanted by it and Alexis was newly enchanted by her as he gazed at her rapt face and excited eyes. When the moment came for him to go to her bedroom to bid her good night, she could talk of little else but the magic of the music. Her only disappointment in what had been a fairy tale evening was that the part of the American naval officer had been taken by a somewhat stout tenor.

"He did not look in the least like Pinkerton," she bemoaned. "He should have been tall and slim and handsome like you, Alexis!"

Smiling, but with his pulses racing at her compliment, Alexis moved over to the bed and sat down on the edge near her. She at once moved sideways to make room for him to get beside her.

"Are you going to stay with me tonight?" she asked curiously. "I'm not in the least tired, Alexis."

She held out her arms invitingly and Alexis' breath caught in his throat. From the very first moment he had seen her in Lady Barratt's drawing room, she had set his blood on fire and he'd known that he wanted her. Now she belonged to him and seemed as anxious as he that he should share her bed this night.

He removed his dressing gown and climbed into bed beside her. Her body through the thin pink silk of her nightgown felt warm and soft as she snuggled against him. He longed to kiss her mouth but remembering her aversion to kissing, he pressed his lips to her cheek. Lucy smiled happily as she wound her arms around his neck. Too full of emotion to speak, Alexis reached out and turned off the bedside lamp. Beside him, Lucy gave a little sigh of contentment.

"You've been so nice to me all day, Alexis," she murmured. "I can't remember when I was last so happy."

"Nor I, my darling!" Alexis said. He was glad now that he had waited this further day before claiming Lucy for his own. It seemed to him that all her cool indifference to him had vanished and that now she was as anxious as he that she should belong to him.

"I love you!" he said. "With my body, I thee worship. I meant those words, Lucy. I want you—only you."

Lucy made no protest as he lifted the nightgown over her head and let it drop to the floor. Her skin shone mysteriously in the moonlight, her small rounded breasts clearly definable as his hands covered them. He could feel the steady beat of her heart and his desire for her was so intense that it all but overcame his determination to be gentle with her. He was aware that Lucy was encouraging him. He could feel the soft touch of her hands as without haste, she removed his clothing. For the fraction of a moment, he thought of Roberta and knew that in all the years they had enjoyed their lovemaking, he had never before felt as he did now. This girl, his Lucy, was his woman—the one woman in the world destined for him. The curve of her waist and hips, the silky texture of her skin, the beauty of her breasts were both strange and yet astonishingly familiar. It was as if some half-remembered dream had suddenly become a reality.

His longing for her now almost a torment, he raised himself above her and felt her arms encircle his waist as she drew him down on top of her. Her face was in shadow and he could not read her expression although her eyes were open and seemed to be inviting him. Her lips were parted and forgetting her aversion, he kissed her passionately with a desperate hunger as her legs parted and her body arched to receive him. But as he was about to lower himself into her, he felt her face twist aside as she freed her mouth. Unimportant though the gesture was, Alexis felt it momentarily as a rejection.

"I love you, Lucy!" he murmured. "Don't turn away from me—ever. Look at me, my darling. You do love me a little, don't you?"

He felt a slight stiffening of Lucy's body beneath his own.

"I'm trying to be what you want, Alexis. I mean to be a good wife to you, I really do." She reached out her hand and touched his cheek. "I want you to be as happy as I am. I'll do anything you want."

Somewhere deep down inside him, Alexis knew that he had no right to ask for more. Lucy was offering him everything she had to give—and freely with the desire to make him happy. It was not her fault that she could not love him. In time she would. He would make her love him. He would make her understand that it was not just her body he wanted so desperately but Lucy herself.

As if sensing his uneasiness, Lucy said encouragingly:

"You've only got to ask me, Alexis. I promise I'll do my very best to please you..."

Outside the window, Alexis heard the sound of a man's voice singing 'Santa Lucia'—a gondolier, he thought, as he heard the gentle lap of the canal water against the stone walls of the Palazzo. 'Lucia,' Lucy! It was as if there were nothing—no one else in the world but her. His nerves jumped as her fingertips ran lightly over the taut muscles of his thighs. His nostrils seemed filled with the delicate scent of her hair; with the heady erotic scent of her healthy young body. It was a body made for love, he thought as still he remained poised above her, his blood pounding in his head, throbbing in his loins. This tantalizing, beautiful girl was his, his love, his wife, awaiting his pleasure. With one swift movement, he could claim that body and find release and satisfaction beyond imagining. Yet still he denied himself, his will stronger even than the immense force of his desire. For it was not Lucy's body he wanted so much as her—her very self, her spirit, her love...

"Oh, Lucy!" he cried out, biting his lips as the agonized words were wrung from him. "If only... if only you could..." But he would not beg for her love and the words 'love me' remained unspoken. He was conscious of Lucy's eyes regarding him, their expression puzzled as she waited for him to continue. She did not understand the true reason for his hesitation. His behavior struck her as extraordinary. She had not supposed that he was different from ordinary men but now she wondered if he had a problem—by no means an unusual state of affairs in her experience.

"If only what?" she prompted sympathetically. And when he still did not speak, she added helpfully: "I don't mind if there's a special way you want to do it. It's all the same to me, really it is, Alexis!"

Alexis closed his eyes as if by doing so he could close out the sound of Lucy's voice. He lifted himself up from her and stood beside the bed. Reaching for his dressing gown, he hurriedly donned it, covering his body as if to conceal from Lucy's bemused eyes the now total absence of his desire. Lucy sat up, frowning anxiously as she watched him. He knew that somehow he must find words to explain his actions to her and yet he could not bring himself to do so. In that confusing way she had of combining innocence with depravity; she might as well have told him outright that she was an experienced whore who was accustomed to men's sexual deviations; that the act of love itself could not have been further from her thoughts.

For a moment, he was so angry that he longed to strike her; to hurt her as she had hurt him. But her voice when she spoke was that of a bewildered child as she said:

"Please tell me what is wrong, Alexis? I know you wanted to. Was it something I did? Something I said?"

A deep sadness replaced Alexis' anger and became confused with renewed love and tenderness as he tried to keep a grasp on sanity; on the one single fact that Lucy had been trying to please him; to make him happy. For the moment, that must suffice. At least all physical desire for her was gone and he longed now for the privacy of his own room. He had no right to stand here in judgment on her. He had known the truth about her and accepted it. It was not Lucy's fault if the ugly face of truth had surfaced now, here, on his honeymoon where he had been naïve enough to suppose his love for her would be strong enough to overcome any obstacle!

He took her hand and kissed it, trying to smile at her.

"Don't worry, Lucy. I simply had not realized how tired I was. It *is* very late and you must be tired, too. I'm pleased you enjoyed the opera. We'll go again. Now get some sleep. I'll see you at breakfast."

He was aware that Lucy's eyes followed him as he left the room. Bitterly, he reflected that she was too experienced to believe his lame excuse of fatigue. But equally he realized that it would be a hopeless task to try to explain to her now. He was not even certain that he could explain to himself his own conflicting emotions. Certainly he no longer wanted to make love to her. All vestige of desire was gone. But alas, love had not gone with it! With total dispassion, he could consider his folly in refusing the comfort his beautiful young wife had offered him, knowing it was ridiculously idealistic and yet equally well aware he would have been false to himself had he given way to his body's need for her. Love, he decided, was a kind of madness for never yet in his life had he wanted a woman more than he wanted her. It had been all too easy to imagine himself teaching her the true heights of passion that could be reached by lovers when each wanted only to please the other. For all her past experience, his Lucy was ignorant of the kind of relationship he wanted to share with her.

When at last Alexis slept it was only to dream of Lucy, naked in his arms, her mouth melting beneath his kisses, her body twisting and turning in restless desire. He could see the fire in her eyes mirroring the fire in his blood, hear her voice crying out for release, feel them merging into one another to become one single being as that release came.

But in the morning when he woke, although the fever in his body had cooled, he felt lonelier than ever as he realized that Lucy had remained outside his dream and knew no part of it.

Lucy, however, was far from indifferent to Alexis' continued absence from her bed. There was no doubt about it, she thought disconsolately, Madame would consider it a failure. It was for her to attract Alexis and if she did not, then she must try harder to make herself irresistible.

She chose for dinner that night her new Paul Poiret dress. It was cut low over the bosom and bared her white shoulders.

"I want you to alter it, Polly," she told her maid. "Take out the lace fill in—and tighten the waist!"

Polly blushed.

"You'll like as not slip right out of it, Miss Lucienne, if I do!" she said. But she obeyed Lucy's instructions and when her young mistress dressed for dinner, she was round-eyed.

"The Master won't be able to keep his eyes off you, Miss Lucienne!" she giggled. "It looks ever so smart though."

Alexis could indeed not keep his eyes off his wife. Taking her out to dinner, he thought, was a mixed pleasure and torment. His pride in her ability to attract all men's glances was tempered by his own renewed desire for her. She had enchanted him all day long with her childlike enthusiasm for everything she saw and for any little gift he gave her—a picture from an art gallery; a bunch of Palma violets; a chiffon scarf she admired in a shop window. She was totally unspoilt and an eager pupil as she listened attentively to his knowledgeable explanations about painters, architects, history, geography.

"You know just about everything, don't you, Alexis!" she said admiringly. But he didn't. Least of all did he know about her. The moment he tried to discuss emotions with her, she retreated into her shell, her mouth setting into a stubborn line, her eyes remote and disinterested. Her manner cooled and the childlike innocence was gone. Would he ever find a way through that self-protective shell? Or was there nothing warm, loving, responsive to be found? He resolved not to go near her bed again until Lucy openly expressed some modicum of affection for him. Her compliments, her gratitude and her admiration were not enough. They were, he knew only too well, entirely impersonal. She gave voice to her opinions but never to her heart.

Lucy's anxiety increased when for the third night, Alexis slept alone. Then it occurred to her that she had been extraordinarily stupid. She was—and she had all but forgotten it—three months' pregnant and like it or not she was carrying another man's child. Small wonder her husband did not want to claim his rights! She was amazed that the obvious answer had not struck her before. From then on, she ceased inviting Alexis to stay the night with her, holding out her hand for his perfunctory kiss before summoning Polly to undress her.

By the end of their first week, Alexis felt a change of venue might help to quell his increasing restlessness. The days he was spending with his beautiful young bride were made totally rewarding by her radiant happiness and obvious enjoyment in everything he planned for her. But the nights were so far from being the honeymoon he had anticipated that he invariably awoke moody, frustrated and depressed. He was the more frustrated for realizing that the remedy was so easily attainable and he could satisfy his craving to possess Lucy's provocative little body with no more than a change of mind. Again and again he told himself that he was asking too much of life to expect her to love him; even to be capable of love; that the principle of 'all or nothing' was too high an aim. He could not be even moderately certain that his policy of waiting for Lucy to change her attitudes would realize that ideal.

There were moments when he wondered if he were entirely sane to allow that remote possibility to stand between him and what he so ardently desired. Lucy was his wife, he thought with angry frustration. He had every right to enjoy the delights she offered him. At such moments of self-doubt, his romantic, impossible ideals seemed utterly ridiculous and he would be determined not to allow another night to pass in aching solitude. But when the moment came for him to enter her room, his conviction waned and his decision was undermined by confusion. He would turn away, bitter, and with a feeling partly of despair and partly of contempt for his quixotic romanticism.

Since awareness of his stupidity was no help in solving the problem of the nights, he decided to fill their waking hours even more completely, especially since Lucy seemed quite tireless.

He took her to Rome, Sienna, Florence and finally to the

Lakes. It was at one of the big hotels on the edge of Lake Maggiore that Alexis had further cause to doubt his own sanity in marrying Lucy. It was nearing the end of April and the weather was becoming increasingly warm. They were consequently dining out on the big terrace when Alexis became aware of a middle-aged man at a nearby table staring intently at his wife. He was used to the admiring glances of any man in Lucy's vicinity, but on this occasion, it was no casual look but a concentrated stare.

He pointed the stranger out to Lucy.

"Do you know him?" he asked. Lucy shook her head.

Was she telling the truth, Alexis wondered. Could this be some man from her past—maybe someone who remembered her but whom she had forgotten among so many? The thought twisted in his heart like a knife. He had sworn to himself that he would never think of those terrible years of her life; never refer to them in any circumstances. Yet now, staring into Lucy's large, innocent eyes, he was already doubting her.

"Take another look," he said curtly. "You may have forgotten him."

Unaware of Alexis' fears, Lucy turned her head and looked directly at the stranger. As if in response, the man rose from his chair, said something briefly to his dinner companion, and came over to Alexis' table.

"Forgive me, Sir, for intruding in what must seem a very ill-mannered way. Would you consider it very impertinent if I were to inquire your name?"

The man was of medium height, fair-haired, blue-eyed. He had a small goatee beard concealing a rather weak, effeminate chin. His Italian accent was far from good and Alexis guessed at once that he was English.

He stood up and bowed stiffly.

"I must assume you have good reason for asking, Sir," he said coldly and in English. "My name is Zemski—Count Zemski."

There was an awkward pause while the stranger seemed to debate whether or not to return to his table without further comment. He glanced at Lucy and appeared to make up his mind.

"Your wife...My name is Rochford, Sir," he said awkwardly. "Rupert Rochford. You must think me unpardonably rude, but your wife bears such an amazing likeness to my sister-in-law, that I feel there must be some family connection."

Alexis felt the tension leave his body. A smile flitted across his face as he said with relief:

"Do sit down, Sir. And allow me to introduce my wife, Lucienne. I think you must be one of her uncles. Her mother is Willow, Lady Rochford."

"I knew there must be a relationship of one kind or another," Rupert Rochford said, smiling at Lucy as he seated himself beside her. "But I am still a little confused. I did not think my sister-in-law had a daughter old enough to be married. I had thought the child to be nine or so years of age."

Alexis summoned the waiter to bring a bottle of champagne. While they waited for it to arrive, he explained that Lucy was Lady Rochford's missing child. He further told Rupert of Rowell Rochford's death of which he had been unaware.

"I have been traveling extensively—it is a way of life I enjoy," Rupert Rochford explained, "but sometimes letters do not reach me for months after they have been posted. I was therefore ignorant on both counts."

He looked at Lucy and smiled.

"You are every bit as pretty as your mother was at your age," he said. "And quite astonishingly like her. I wish I could feel genuine sorrow at my brother's death but he and I had nothing in common, and frankly, my dear, we never did like each other. I left home some nine years ago, as you may know, and I have never been back. Now that Rowell is dead, I might pay the family a visit."

While Lucy and her uncle discussed the Rochfords' family affairs, Alexis studied this unexpected brother-in-law. Instinct told him that Rupert Rochford was a very different kettle of fish from his brother, Tobias. There was something delicate, almost effeminate in the fellow's manner which at first puzzled Alexis; then, when he suggested Rupert invite his friend to join them, Alexis suddenly understood the difference. There was a note of deep possessiveness in Rupert's voice as he introduced his friend.

"Count Maximillian von Kruege!"

It took but a further ten minutes for Alexis to discover that the two men had been close companions for the past seven years, traveling around Europe collecting rare books, and occasionally remaining a short while in their shared home in Brussels.

Maximillian von Kruege was physically Rochford's opposite. He was tall, dark and immensely self-assured. He was obviously the dominant partner and Rupert's manner toward the older man was openly respectful and deeply affectionate.

Alexis was interested in von Kruege's background. He had a French mother although his father was half German, half Austro-Hungarian.

"I find it easier to describe myself as a European," he told Alexis smiling. "Fortunately I have no interest in politics or my loyalties might be somewhat divided!"

To Lucy's surprise, Alexis readily accepted an invitation to go and stay with this unorthodox couple whenever he should happen to be in Belgium.

They stayed talking for an hour—Lucy giving Rupert news of all the members of the family while Alexis and Count von Kruege talked rapidly to one another in Hungarian.

When she and Alexis finally reached the privacy of their bedroom, Lucy said:

"I liked Uncle Rupert but I thought his companion a bit strange." She did not add that Count von Kruege was the first man she had met who had seemed totally indifferent to her charms.

Alexis sat down in the armchair as Lucy seated herself by her dressing table and began to unpin her hair.

"Now you are a married woman, it's perhaps as well you should know about such things," he said as he began to explain to her the problem of homosexuality. But long before he had said what he intended, Lucy broke in:

"I know already about such people, Alexis. Madame Lou-Lou told us men like that existed but, of course, they did not come to *Le Ciel Rouge*."

Seeing the taut expression on her husband's face, Lucy blushed. Her remark had been voiced impulsively, without forethought. Now she realized that this was the first time that she and Alexis had ever discussed her years at *Le Ciel Rouge*.

"I'm sorry!" she murmured. "I forgot..."

Alexis stood up, his eyes clouded.

"It's perfectly all right, Lucy. As a general rule, I do not want us to have secrets from one another, but at the same time..." He broke off unhappily.

Lucy put down her hairbrush and went across the room to him. She stood before him, her hands behind her back like a small, repentant schoolgirl.

"Really, I do understand," she said. "I promised Mama I would never talk about those days and it...it just slipped out. I hope you don't mind too much, Alexis?"

Mind, Alexis thought! Does she mean mind about her past or mind about her speaking of it? How easy and simple it would all be if only she had had no past. He was trying so hard to forget it. As for the child she was carrying, he had not given it a single thought. Looking now at Lucy's tiny waist and flat stomach, it seemed inconceivable that she was with child.

He managed somehow to smile; then told her to call Polly to put her to bed. Excusing himself, he went quickly to his own room. Standing at his window overlooking the magic of a full moon flooding the surface of the lake water, he covered his face with his hands.

"Oh, God!" he muttered. "What am I doing? What have I done? If only I did not love her!"

Perhaps the hardest thing of all to bear, he thought wretchedly, was her complete unawareness of his feelings. 'I hope you don't mind...' she had said, those big, innocent eyes of hers staring up at him, when his very heart and soul were in torment.

'Green eyes are supposed to be jealous eyes,' Roberta had once teased him. 'I wish you were just the smallest bit jealous of Angus, my darling!' He had felt no such emotion then but now...now he *was* jealous, he realized. He was jealous of every man who had ever known Lucy's perfect little body. Most of all, he was jealous of the man who had given her his child.

I'll take her home tomorrow, he thought. This honeymoon is a parody. It would be easier in London where he would have his work to divert him. Perhaps once the child was born, he could think again about establishing a real relationship with his wife. For the time being, it would be better for them both were he to forget the very word 'love.' Living with Lucy was like living with an unspoilt child—but a child with a woman's beautiful, irresistible body.

He went out onto the terrace and leant his head against the cool stone pillar of the balustrade. He was a man in torment, in hell, but a hell of his own making. He closed his eyes, shutting out the cold, indifferent beauty of the moon.

PART TWO
1912–1916

For if the soul be not in place,
What has laid trouble in her face?
And, sits there nothing ware and wise
Behind the curtains of her eyes,
What is it, in the self's eclipse,
Shadows, soft and passingly,
About the corners of her lips,
The smile that is essential she?

RUPERT BROOKE, *Doubts*

Chapter 11

❧

May—December 1912

ALEXIS REGARDED HIS WIFE ACROSS THE BREAKFAST TABLE. HER fair head was bent slightly forward as she read aloud from the letter she had just received from her mother.

Lady Rochford and Tobias were in New York where they had attended a memorial service for the Corbetts . . . a sad and moving occasion, Willow had described it.

"Toby and I cannot believe we will never see these old friends again," she wrote. *"Every employee of the Corporation who lived near enough to get to the Chapel was present, some openly in tears.*

"Your Uncle Toby and I are likely to be caught up for several weeks while the business is reorganized. As you may realize, Nathaniel was the keystone and his death totally unexpected. Provisions had not been made for so sudden and tragic an eventuality.

"Although it is of only the most minor concern, dearest Lucienne, the plans to have you included as a shareholder will be delayed. Nathaniel was carrying with him copies of your birth certificate, the exhumation papers and the sworn statements concerning your claim to be my daughter . . ."

Lucy looked up at Alexis questioningly.

"Does that mean all those important documents went down with the *Titanic*?"

"Don't look so woebegone, my dear. New copies can be acquired when your mother and Toby return to England. Your inclusion in your grandfather's Will will merely be delayed."

"So as far as T.R.T.C. is concerned, I still do not exist!" Lucy replied with an edge to her voice.

Alexis looked disturbed.

"At least you *do* exist, my dear. Sadly the Corbetts do not. In any event, you need not worry about your legacy, Lucy.

161

You do not need money of your own now that you are my wife. Or isn't the allowance I give you enough?"

Lucy's smooth forehead creased into a small frown.

"You have been very generous, Alexis, but I still want my rightful inheritance."

Alexis stood up, glancing at his watch. He must hurry if he were not to be late for the morning meeting. He walked round the table and kissed his wife's cheek.

"Will the man from Liberty's be coming again today?" he inquired, changing the subject.

Lucy's face brightened as she nodded. The head of the interior decorating department of one of London's biggest furniture stores was coming for the third day running to assist her in planning the renovation of Alexis' house. Yesterday they had chosen wallpapers and fabrics for the drawing room and dining room; the day before, she had chosen an entirely new suite of furniture to go with the new color scheme for her bedroom, bathroom and Alexis' dressing room. Today, she had insisted the man bring an experienced female assistant with him to advise her about the nurseries on the top floor. She had no particular interest in them but she intended that each of the twenty rooms in the house would be modernized and perfect so that her home was the envy of every visitor.

Alexis had agreed that they need not receive any callers for the time being.

"I want it all quite perfect first," Lucy had pleaded. Alexis had made no changes or alterations since he had inherited the big, four-story house in Cadogan Gardens. Lucy considered the furniture and furnishings old-fashioned, dark and dreary.

"I like everything bright and modern!" she told Alexis who was happy enough to indulge her in such a harmless, if expensive, feminine pursuit.

"You have a free hand to do as you please," he said indulgently. "But my study is not to be touched," he added with a note of seriousness.

Lucy was enjoying herself enormously. For the first time in her life she was able to select anything which took her fancy regardless of cost. Alexis had told her that everything would be charged to his account and she was to consider the renovations as part of his wedding present to her. He seemed happy just to see *her* happy; and reflecting on the first month of marriage, Lucy decided that she need not after all have feared such bondage. She had gained far more freedom than she had had at Rochford, for Alexis was away at work most of the day and she was able to do exactly as she pleased.

Busy with the task of selecting fine silks, chintzes and velvets for curtains and coverings, looking through huge books containing samples of wallpapers and leafing through catalogs of furniture, Lucy happily whiled away the hours. Only very occasionally did she feel the sudden slight movement of the child within her and her mood became apprehensive. Soon, she realized, she would lose her slim figure and be obliged to wear dull, shapeless maternity clothes—also obtainable at Liberty's, Mama had told her!

Willow had been their only visitor, traveling to London to see Lucy before she and Toby left for America. After they had attended the memorial service for the Corbetts in New York, she and Toby were to be married quietly and enjoy a brief honeymoon before returning to England.

The afternoon mother and daughter had spent alone together had not been a great success. Willow wanted to talk about the coming baby, Lucy's plans for engaging a nanny and to decide upon a name for her first grandchild. The more her mother enthused, the more reticent Lucy became. She felt it hypocritical for Willow to show such excitement now over an event that only six weeks ago, she had seen as a major disaster. Lucy's marriage did not alter the fact that her child was a bastard and would be born seven months after the wedding, she told Willow caustically. Willow swept such comments aside. No one would know the truth. People would accept that Lucy's baby was premature. A seven-month baby was not unusual.

"We will wait until June to announce that you are having a child," she stated. "Do you want a boy or a girl, my darling?"

Lucy did not want either, she told her mother truthfully, and now that she could actually feel its existence, she was even more certain that she could never love it. Fortunately, for Willow's plans for concealment of the truth, there were few outward signs of the coming child, although Lucy had put on a little weight and her breasts were certainly fuller. Surveying her darkened nipples in the mirror, Lucy smiled to think of Madame Lou-Lou's approving eyes. She had always maintained that Lucy lacked sufficient by way of "*poitrine*" to be really desirable. She did not mind her condition so much if it improved her looks.

The interior decorator and his assistant decided upon a

pale primrose yellow for the nursery suite—a color that would be equally good for boy or girl and which, he suggested, was more original than the pale blues or pinks usually favored.

Would the Countess prefer to discuss the choice of color first with the proud father-to-be before making a decision, he inquired ingratiatingly. Lucy grinned wickedly. The Count, she told her blushing companion, would only concern himself with their bedroom.

But after the man had left, Lucy's humor deserted her. Alexis was not in the least concerned with their bedroom. The fact that he never made any attempt whatsoever to pursue his rights left her uneasy. She tried once again to convince herself that it was only because she was carrying another man's child that he did not desire her body. But in her heart, she did not believe it.

It was now close on six weeks since she and Alexis had returned from their honeymoon and their domestic life had settled into a pattern. Alexis was away all day at work while she planned her renovations; and in the evenings, after they had dined together, he would go into his study for an hour or two while Lucy either read a novel—Louise Lennox had lent her *Three Weeks* by Elinor Glyn, supposed to be very *risqué* but which Lucy found rather silly—or wrote letters on Alexis' beautiful, thick-crested notepaper. She wrote to Oliver at Eton and to Jane at Rochford; to Philip who was away at Dartmouth; to her Aunt Dodie whom she had met briefly at Rochford last Christmas. This display of industry was not born of any love of putting pen to paper but because she obtained an inordinate amount of pleasure from receiving letters in reply. When Polly brought in the morning post on a silver tray with her early morning tea, it was invariably a thrill which Lucy found difficult to explain to Alexis when he remarked upon her excitement.

"Perhaps it's because I did not know who I was for so long!" she told him thoughtfully. "I never got a letter from anyone before I married you! Now, when I get a letter, I know I'm really me!"

She was unaware of the pathos of her remark or how it affected Alexis. It was one of those occasions, he told himself, when he no longer doubted that he was right to have married this child-woman. There were too many times when he did doubt it; when he asked himself if her porcelain beauty did not conceal a human being without a heart; without a soul.

Once as a very young child, he had been holding in his hands the pretty figurine of a shepherdess, admiring its perfect beauty, when it slipped from his grasp and fell to the floor. The head had snapped from the body and when Alexis bent to pick up the pieces, he had been childishly shocked to find that it was hollow. The gentle scolding he had received for handling so valuable an ornament, had been as nothing compared to his inexplicable disappointment. He had wanted the beautiful shepherdess to be as warm and living as she looked. So now, he searched for Lucy's heart.

Roberta, of course, was aware that Alexis had returned to London. She telephoned him at his office to inquire why he and Lucy would not receive her at Cadogan Gardens, despite the fact that she had twice left calling cards and flowers, too.

"I am not the only one of your friends agog to meet your new bride, Alexis," she told him. "You can't believe I would say anything to upset your Lucienne? New to London as she is, I would have thought she could do with a friend to guide her."

Alexis hastened to reassure Roberta that there was no ulterior motive behind their isolation from Society. Lucy, he explained, wanted to have the house perfect before she received guests.

"You shall be our first visitor, after Lucy's mother!" he promised her.

In due course, they must give a reception for all his friends, he thought. His boss, Fanshaw, was keen to meet Lucy and naturally enough, all his acquaintances were curious to see the girl he had eloped with in so uncharacteristic a manner. Lucy informed him that Liberty's expected to have the house finished by the end of June. He therefore told her to write out invitations to everyone whose name was on the long list he made for her.

"Don't worry about the domestic details," he said. "We will call in caterers on this occasion. Once the new staff have settled down, they should be able to manage future parties quite adequately."

The 'new staff' referred to by Alexis had been obtained from an excellent London domestic agency recommended by Willow. The servants were well trained with first-class references and Lucy found she had little to be bothered with in the running of her home, other than to discuss with Cook the day's menus each morning.

Except for the upheaval caused by the painters and decorators, life in Cadogan Gardens ran smoothly and the weeks sped by from spring to early summer. By the middle of June the house was finished and the Zemskis' long-awaited reception took place without domestic mishap.

Willow and Toby returned from the United States in good time for the occasion. They were now legally man and wife and although there had been no public announcement of their marriage, all the family friends and relatives were aware of it and genuine in their congratulations. Silvie and Pelham traveled over from Paris, partly for the Zemskis' reception but also to see Willow and Toby.

"Of the two pairs of newlyweds, our dearest Willow and Toby appear to be the more devoted!" Silvie observed to Pelham as they moved among the milling throng of people in the large drawing room.

"They waited long enough for this moment in their lives!" Pelham replied as he glanced across the room to where his brother was standing with his arm linked closely in Willow's.

"So many wasted years!" Silvie murmured sighing. "And Rowell never deserved that sacrifice. I could weep for thinking about the misery he caused Willow."

"You'll do no such thing!" Pelham said grinning. "This is a very special and happy occasion and not the time for tears. What do you think of our new nephew? Alexis seems a nice enough chap to me."

"And *very* good looking," Silvie replied, cheering up at once at this new topic. "If I were younger or he were older . . ."

"And that's quite enough of that, my love!" Pelham interrupted firmly. Silvie laughed.

"Don't worry, *chéri*. I am a happily married woman now." But her smile faded as Lucy passed by them to greet a newly arrived guest. Willow had informed her that the girl was already *enceinte*. Although Willow had sounded excited and joyful about the coming baby—"my very first grandchild," she had said—there was a note of anxiety in her tone which had not escaped Silvie who knew her so well.

"Do you think Lucienne's pregnancy was the real explanation for that extraordinary 'elopement,' Pelham?" she asked now. "And it was 'extraordinary' insofar as Willow's reactions were concerned. She sounded so unsurprised when she telephoned the news to us, one might almost have thought she knew in advance what they were planning."

Pelham shrugged his broad shoulders.

"I would not have thought Zemski was the kind of fellow to take advantage of a young girl. But if he did...well, good luck to them both. One must hope it was not a 'forced' marriage and that they really do love each other."

But Silvie, with her strongly developed woman's instinct, was far from confident that the relationship of the newlyweds was one born of mutual passion. Such couples had a way of looking at one another, even in public, that betrayed their need to be close; to exchange a touch however brief; to catch one another's eye and hold the glance a little longer than customary.

Ignorant of her aunt's private speculation, Lucy was deep in conversation with Roberta Inman. For some reason Lucy could not explain, the older woman was undermining the self-confidence with which she had approached this large reception. Lucy was wearing a pink and blue gown which had been made in Paris, the bill for which she had not yet dared to show Alexis. She had thought it the very height of fashion, but the Countess Inman was far more strikingly attired in a watered silk dress in brilliant emerald green. The skirt was long and narrow, the bodice, with its deep plunging V-neck, was draped over her full breasts, the cleavage concealed by a lace chemisette. She looked elegant and sophisticated—a tall, statuesque figure, graceful and poised as she offered Lucy her congratulations.

"I have known your husband a good many years, my dear," Roberta was saying. "I would therefore like you to consider me an old friend, especially as I understand you have not lived very long in England and never before now in London."

She drew out a tortoise-shell case from her pearl evening bag and put a cigarette in an amber holder.

"Alexis doesn't like to see women smoking," Roberta said smiling. "He will be pleased that you have not acquired the habit!"

Lucy felt a second's irritation that this stranger should know more about her husband's preferences than she did. But it was quickly forgotten as Roberta began to compliment her upon the alterations she had made to the house.

"It's vastly improved!" she told Lucy. "The rooms look so much larger and sunnier."

Lucy felt herself relaxing. Maybe after all she was going to like this woman friend of Alexis'.

"I wasn't allowed to touch Alexis' study," she said smiling. "I'm not even allowed to go in there. It reminds me of the

Confessional at my Convent. As a Protestant, I was never permitted to go to confession although I longed more than anything to be able to go inside that little cubbyhole and unburden myself of my sins."

Roberta smiled.

"Alexis told me you had been educated in France. How useful that you can speak the language so fluently. As you know, Alexis has many contacts in diplomatic circles and you will be a great help when he has to entertain foreign visitors."

Lucy had no idea what Alexis' work entailed and was quite ignorant regarding the functions of the Foreign Office. She knew nothing whatever about diplomats, although she knew there were several invited to the reception. Her ignorance left her with a feeling of vulnerability. She clearly had a great deal to learn and she decided that Roberta Inman could be of assistance to her.

"Will you come and lunch with me next week?" she asked. "You were quite right when you said I need someone to advise me. I want to be as useful a wife to Alexis as I can!"

Perhaps she really does love him, Roberta thought as Lucy moved away to speak to her aunt and uncle. But somehow, she had not had the impression of a starry-eyed bride. The girl seemed to her almost as if she were adopting the rôle of a wife in the way that an actress might play the part on stage. Roberta sighed. She would lunch with Lucienne next week and maybe then she would find out a great deal more about her and her feelings for Alexis.

Roberta herself needed to be certain that Alexis was happy. She thought he looked tired and as if he had lost weight. He certainly did not look as if he had recently returned from a delirious three-week honeymoon in Italy.

It's no longer any of my business, Roberta chided herself; but his marriage had made no difference to her feelings toward him. She still loved him and his happiness was of paramount importance to her. It was not proving easy to hand him over to another woman to cherish. That could only be done if she truly believed Lucienne was giving him the love and the care that had once been her prerogative.

Despite the undeniable beauty of Alexis' bride, Lucienne seemed to Roberta to be far too young; the difference in her age and Alexis' far too disparate; the marriage too hasty and ill-conceived. She sensed disaster.

Alexis himself was not unhappy. The reception was successfully accomplished and Lucy had proved an excellent hostess. She had undoubtedly charmed every man in the room and that included the testy Fanshaw! Although proud of her success in one way, in another, the ease with which she could strike just the right note with any man she spoke to, made him uneasy. With his younger colleagues, she had played the round-eyed little girl to perfection. With the more serious-minded Fanshaw, she had presented herself as a thoughtful, knowledgeable young woman intelligently interested in politics. She quoted phrases which Alexis was certain were her Uncle Toby's, as if they were her own views. She had discovered with remarkable speed that the hobby of one boring old politician was music and had immediately entranced him with her eager enthusiasm for the operas she had been to in Italy.

Lucy's perspicacity combined with her physical beauty made her irresistible, Alexis thought, although he accepted that she herself might be aware that the combination was a weapon she could use for good or evil purposes. Alexis saw the danger and feared it. He tried not to think about the ways in which Lucy had learned to be so discerning, or that she could be twisting *him* round her little finger with such practiced ease.

Following the reception, the invitations poured in. Alexis was too busy to accept most of them but he was delighted that Lucy was asked everywhere and was willing to go with her new friends without him to escort her.

There were days spent at the races at Ascot and Newmarket where she proved very lucky with her bets. Like most of the crowd at Newmarket, she backed the King's horse, Le Lac, and watched it win. She went to the Trooping the Color with Roberta who had also bought tickets for the Wimbledon Lawn Tennis championships.

But by mid-July, Alexis was required to go abroad on a mission that he anticipated would keep him away for a month, if not longer. Lucy, he said, must go down to Rochford as he did not care to leave her alone in London.

Lucy was bitterly disappointed and not a little angry.

"I don't see why I have to go away just because you are leaving England, Alexis," she argued hotly. "You said if we got married I could do as I pleased. I'm having a great deal of fun and now you want to spoil it!"

She looked and sounded so like a child whose birthday treat had been canceled, that Alexis spoke gently to her.

"I know you don't want to think about it, Lucy, but you *are* going to have a child and however skillfully you may dress to hide the fact, you cannot conceal it. So in any event you would have to withdraw from Society very soon. Besides, the weather is beautiful and the country air will do you good."

Lucy continued to argue and then to plead, but to no avail. Alexis announced that he was closing the house and sending most of the servants on holiday. One or two would be retained to caretake and Polly was to accompany her mistress.

"I'll drive you down to Rochford myself at the weekend," he told her. "And don't sniff, Lucy. I shan't be moved by your crocodile tears."

Although she had not wanted to leave London, once back in the beautiful surroundings of her home, Lucy found herself delighted to be there. Oliver and Mark were home for the summer holidays and the faithful Henry was again a frequent visitor, more often at Rochford than at Glenfield Hall.

The summer days passed pleasantly and at a leisurely pace. The two Grey children, Mark and Jane, seemed to be very much a part of the family now, Lucy thought with a tinge of envy. Her mother treated them as if they were in fact her own children and if there was anyone on the outside it was herself.

Willow's constant allusions to her granchild-to-be, irritated Lucy beyond measure. There were moments when she was tempted to cry out: "It's Maurice Dubois' baby—your lover's baby, Mama. How can you expect me to love it?" Perhaps, she thought, if she had not hated Maurice so deeply, she might have been able to feel more affection for it. If it had been Alexis' baby—but that was never a possibility, she thought wryly. A woman did not beget a child by a man who never went near her!

Lying in the hammock in the shade of the big lime, watching the younger children playing French cricket on the lawn, Lucy thought more and more frequently about the strangeness of Alexis' behavior. She was reasonably certain that Roberta Inman had once been his mistress. There had been many, barely definable reasons for such suspicion—a possessiveness in Roberta's tone when she spoke Alexis' name: a familiarity with the rooms on the first floor of the house; glances the servants sometimes gave her. Lucy had even asked Polly if she had heard any gossip downstairs about the Countess Inman but Polly was either too discreet to repeat it or the servants were too loyal to Alexis to gossip about his bachelor days. Not that Lucy would have objected to such a relationship if it had existed, she thought, but she did not want to believe that it was continuing now—although it *would* explain Alexis' indifference to her own attractions.

It was not a matter Lucy meant to ignore indefinitely. But until the child was born, she accepted the status quo. Afterwards, she fully intended that her husband should share her bedroom—and her bed. She would prove herself every bit as accomplished as the suave Roberta, she told herself, for despite Roberta's seniority, she was unlikely to be as experienced as herself in giving a man pleasure.

It was essentially a matter of pride. Lucy did not care to think herself less desirable than her husband's mistress, if such Roberta proved to be.

It was at Toby's insistence that George and Howard were once more made welcome at Rochford and the two families were able to make frequent informal visits to each other as in the past.

"With Lucienne safely married—and obviously pregnant, the boys are hardly likely to fight over her," Toby told Willow.

Of the two boys, Howard was the less frequent visitor to Rochford, mainly because he had a new passion in his life—motor racing. He all but lived at the motor track at Brooklands and when he was not there, he was tinkering with his Bugatti. Willow had forbidden Oliver and Mark to drive with him, much to their disgust.

"You let us go flying with Alexis—and that's far more dangerous," Oliver argued. But Willow did not think so. To compensate them, she allowed Toby to take them for the day to Ranelagh to watch the balloonists.

When Alexis returned at the end of August, Willow urged him to allow Lucy to remain at Rochford until the baby's birth. But Alexis, seeing Lucy's stormy eyes, gently refused the invitation. Arrangements were already made for Lucy's confinement in London, he told his mother-in-law. An excellent doctor would be in attendance and a first-class Norland Nanny had been engaged.

Sadly, Willow watched her daughter depart for London.

"I seem to have had her to myself so short a while!" she said wistfully to Toby.

Toby put his arm around her waist, drawing her closer to him. "It leaves you more time to concentrate on me," he said affectionately. "Aren't I enough for you to love, my dearest?"

Oliver, happening to enter the room as they embraced, decided they were unbearably soppy now that they were married and with an embarrassed smile, departed as quickly as he could. But he was happy to see his mother so obviously content and promptly forgot her as he realized this was a perfect opportunity for him and Mark to ride the Scott motor cycle. If his mother or Toby knew of this latest pastime, they would certainly forbid it, Oliver was well aware. They had had to bribe the chauffeur, Bill Longhurst, with copious supplies of cigarettes for him to let them borrow his second-hand machine. In the interests of secrecy, they had to wheel it down to the gravel path beyond the gardeners' cottages where they could then run the engine unheard by anyone in the house. They had devised a reasonable race track, circling the cottages, then the greenhouses and back along the cinder-path to the clock tower and the harness room. It was agreed between the boys that should they be discovered with the motor cycle, Longhurst would say they had borrowed it without his knowledge. But so far they had remained undetected, except by Jane. She had been coerced into the conspiracy by promises of an occasional ride on the pillion.

As far as Oliver was concerned, the two Grey children had proved a welcome addition to the family. Although Mark was two and a half years older, he did not appear so for he was slow-thinking and overinclined to caution. Oliver's influence was the dominant one and after only a few weeks of the holiday, Mark was proving himself almost as daredevil as the two younger boys.

As for the thirteen-year-old Jane, Oliver thought, although she was only a girl, she could be relied upon never to sneak and he quite enjoyed the feeling of superiority she gave him for all they were the same age. Whatever argument took place between the boys, he could usually count on Jane to add her vote to his, or at least, since her first loyalty was to her brother, not to vote against him.

He was sad to see Lucy leave but she and Alexis had promised he might go and stay for a night in London during the Christmas holidays and, if he got a good report, to take him to see his first music hall.

Lucy however, was not sorry to leave Rochford and to return to her own home. At Rochford, her mother gave all the orders but in Cadogan Gardens she, Lucy, was in command. Only occasionally was she obliged to defer to Mrs.

Taylor, the housekeeper, who knew so much more than Lucy about running a London house. Lucy was satisfied that Alexis considered she managed the staff most efficiently and he never interfered—except on one occasion when she had sent a house parlor maid into his study. For the first time she had seen him quietly but dangerously angry—his green eyes narrowed, his mouth hard and unyielding.

"I don't care what the girl was trying to find for you, Lucy! Understand this once and for all, any servant who goes into my study without my permission is dismissed on the spot. No one, *not even you*, my dear, is allowed in there. You should know by now that my papers are too important for me to risk their being disturbed."

With only six weeks to go before the baby was born, Lucy began to feel tired and impatient. She hated having to pretend that she was not expecting the birth for another fourteen weeks and longed to be able to tell the truth to Roberta when, at a quiet luncheon together, Roberta suggested she might be carrying twins she was so large.

But Lucy had given both Alexis and her mother her solemn oath that she would tell no one when the child was due— and that included Polly. She doubted if her maid was deceived, for Polly was endlessly curious. She had seen her married sister through four pregnancies and she suspected privately that Lucy and Alexis had preempted their marriage. She was, therefore, not in the least surprised when Lucy went into labor in mid-October. Nor was she surprised when the so-called seven-month baby showed little signs of being premature but was a lusty eight-pound girl in perfect health.

Although Lucy had a comparatively easy labor and, so Polly said, was well enough to have been up on her feet and at work like her sister two days after the birth, Lucy's spirits were low and she obeyed the doctor's orders to remain in bed convalescing. The Nanny she had engaged through the Norland training college, a middle-aged woman of long experience, took complete charge of the infant. She discouraged Lucy from any inclination to nurse it, insisting that the baby would do better on the bottle and be less tiring for Lucy.

The child was remarkably beautiful. The redness of birth quickly faded and she looked like a little china doll. She had Lucy's white-gold hair and blue eyes and Alexis, despite all his previous misgivings, was enchanted.

"She's even more like you than you are like your mother,

Lucy," he said as he sat in the chair by his wife's bed. He had just returned from Asprey's where he had bought a diamond bracelet for Lucy and a tiny gold one for the baby.

Lucy's attention was centered on his gift and she merely nodded her head as Alexis insisted the baby was quite exceptionally pretty. He was shocked by her unnatural disinterest.

"Nanny said you had asked her not to leave the baby with you this afternoon, Lucy," he said. "Aren't you feeling very well?"

Lucy looked up, her expression anything but maternal.

"I don't see why I have to be feeling ill just because I don't want the baby screaming its head off in here and disturbing me. As it happens I'm feeling very well, thank you." Her face softened. She held up her arm around which she had fastened the bracelet.

"Thank you very much, Alexis," she said, her tone suddenly warm and appreciative. "It's a lovely present!"

Alexis took her hand and raised it to his lips.

"You deserve it, Lucy. The doctor said you were very brave. We must now think of a name for this new arrival. We can't go on calling her 'it!'"

Lucy withdrew her hand.

"You think of one. I really don't care what we call her. You can choose, Alexis, since you seem so taken with the child."

Alexis was nonplussed. He had fully anticipated that once the baby was born, Lucy's former indifference would vanish and she would be like any young mother—adoring and possessive. Was it possible she lacked *all* capacity for love—even for her own child, he asked himself unhappily?

By mid-December, Alexis had still not succeeded in getting Lucy to decide upon a name. The baby was to be christened in St. Stephens on Boxing Day and a decision had to be made before then.

His own reactions to the infant astonished him even more than they surprised Lucy. He visited the nursery morning and evening and every day the baby girl seemed to him to become more beautiful—and more like Lucy. He had expected to feel only revulsion for this child—another man's offspring. He had intended to do no more than his bare duty toward it— for Lucy's sake. But their rôles had become inexplicably reversed. It was he who worried about the baby—its name, its weight increase, the possibility that it might have contracted a cold. It was he who listened to Nanny Meredith's proud chatter and complimented her upon her care.

"Teodora," he suggested one day, "after my mother. I've always thought that a charming name. And we could shorten it to Teo. Does that appeal to you, Lucy?"

"If that's what you want," Lucy said vaguely. She seemed more interested in the presents brought by visitors like Roberta.

Alexis became increasingly concerned over Lucy's attitude to her child until one evening, he returned home earlier than expected from a hard day at the Foreign Office. Lucy was not to be seen downstairs or in her room. Polly was laying out Lucy's clothes for dinner. Alexis inquired where his wife might be.

"It's Nanny's day off," Polly said matter-of-factly. "That'll mean the Mistress is in the nursery with the baby."

Alexis tried to hide his surprise.

"But I thought the nursemaid took care of the child when Nanny went out," he said.

Polly grinned.

"Rosie's willing enough, Sir, but mostly the Mistress sends her off downstairs. Rosie says..."

Alexis did not stay to listen to Polly's gossip but hurried upstairs to the second floor. Outside the day nursery, he paused. He could hear quite clearly through the closed door the sound of Lucy's voice. She was singing softly. He was unfamiliar with the tune or the words but they sounded like a lullaby.

> *"I sowed the seeds of love,*
> *I sowed them in the spring.*
> *I gathered them up in the morning so soon*
> *While small birds did sweetly sing...*
> *While small birds did sweetly sing..."*

So Lucy was no different from other mothers. She had the same capacity for love, Alexis thought. There was a whole wealth of tenderness in her voice—unmistakably so. He was overcome by the longing to go through the door and take Lucy in his arms. He wanted to tell her how desperately he loved her. But instinct halted him at the last moment. For some reason he had yet to fathom, Lucy did not want anyone to know she was at last taking an interest in the baby girl. If he startled her now, it might have the very opposite effect to the one he longed for and she could turn against the child.

Quietly, he made his way downstairs to the drawing room. He rang the bell and ordered the servant to bring him a whiskey and soda. His voice was steady but his heart was racing. It was madness, he knew, to set so much hope upon that moment of eavesdropping and yet now he could be certain that Lucy, his Lucy, had finally shown herself capable of love. If she could love her child, then the time might come when she could love him…

It was not many minutes before Lucy came into the room.

"Polly said you were home, Alexis. You are early, aren't you?"

Alexis nodded. His voice deliberately casual, he asked:

"And what have you been doing with yourself, my dear?"

Lucy walked across the room and sat down opposite him. Looking directly into his eyes, she said lightly:

"Nothing very exciting! I was writing a letter to Oliver when Polly told me you were back, so I came straight down. I'll finish it later."

On any other day, Alexis thought, he would have believed her. The lie was superbly told and utterly convincing. But this time he knew the truth.

"I think we'll dine out tonight, shall we, Lucy?" he said. "We haven't really celebrated Teo's arrival, have we, and next week we'll be off to Rochford for Christmas. Where would you like to go? Quaglino's? The Savoy?"

Lucy's face broke into a delighted smile.

"The Savoy, please, Alexis. What a lovely idea! I can wear my Poiret dress. All his new designs have a Russian look about them and mine is perfectly gorgeous. I can wear my diamond bracelet and the waiters will stare when they serve me and try to guess how rich I am."

Now she *is* telling the truth, Alexis thought. Her avidity never ceased to surprise him, and yet he knew and understood the reasons for it.

"Of course, I'll be wearing the bracelet to please you too, Alexis," Lucy continued smiling. "I want you to be proud of me, just as I'm always proud to be seen on your arm. Everyone says you're handsome and I agree. I think you are very kind to me, too."

For the time being, Alexis thought wryly, although I may doubt its sincerity, with that fulsome compliment, I must be content.

Chapter 12

❦

December 1912—August 1913

"It will be the most wonderful Christmas Rochford Manor has ever known!" Willow said to Toby as the house began to hum with the seasonal preparations. "Not only is it our first Christmas together as husband and wife but everyone we love will be here, too."

Lovingly, Toby put his arms around her and kissed the top of her head.

"I was thinking when I woke up this morning what a very happy man I am. Do you know, Willow, it is exactly sixteen years ago that I first realized I was in love with you?" he asked.

Willow laughed.

"And I woke up thinking it is exactly six months ago that we were married," she replied. "I must be the happiest woman in the whole world. I am still not quite accustomed yet to the fact that I am now really Mrs. Tobias Rochford at long last."

"And you are not the only one," Toby remarked with a cheerful grin. "I notice all the servants are still calling you 'Lady Rochford'—and some of our friends, too."

Willow looked up at him.

"You don't mind, Toby?" she asked anxiously.

"No, of course not, my love. The only thing I care about is that you are really and truly mine!"

"That you cannot doubt," Willow replied, color stealing into her cheeks as she recalled the depths of love they had shared since their marriage. Toby had proved himself an adoring and passionate lover.

For answer, he drew her closer against him and kissed her tenderly. She returned his kiss warmly before sending him off to his laboratory while she went happily about her tasks, Jane a silent but radiant assistant at her side. It surprised

Willow how remarkably sweet-natured and adaptable Jane was. She seemed not to have inherited either of her parents' less admirable qualities. Unlike her father, the girl was warm-hearted and affectionate and both she and her brother, Mark, lacked any sign of their mother's brash vulgarity.

Jane's world, too, was complete for even her older brother, Philip, had home leave for Christmas and would be able to share in the enjoyment. Mark and Oliver were already back from school.

Pelham and Silvie arrived from Paris on December 20th and the McGill family settled into Dodie's old suite of rooms in the west tower on the 22nd. Their little daughter, Alexandra, was immediately taken over by Patience who was beaming with pleasure at the prospect of having two babies back in her nursery. Alexis' and Lucy's new baby was due to arrive with her parents and Nanny on Christmas Eve.

Dodie's little girl, now three years old, was a lively, intelligent, happy child, described by Patience as a "proper little chatterbox." On first being able to speak, she had tried unsuccessfully to pronounce her long name, but could only manage to say "Zandra." To the little girl's great satisfaction, the family had immediately adopted this name for her.

Fiercely independent, Zandra wanted to do everything for herself.

"It is as if she is trying instinctively to make up for the extra work I cause with my handicap," Dodie said proudly to Willow, adding with a tender look at her husband, "and I think James has always encouraged her to help me as much as she can."

"In any event, she is a great credit to you both," Willow said smiling, as they watched the toddler shadowing her nine-year-old cousin, Alice, who was delighted for once not to be the baby of the family and went out of her way to mother the little girl.

There were, in all, twelve members of the family already installed with their servants when Alexis and Lucy arrived for tea on the 24th of December. The house was ablaze with lights, and candles flickered on the big Christmas tree in the hall. A faint flurry of snow lay on the drive and Nanny Meredith hastily brushed a white flake from the shawl covering the baby's fair hair as she followed Alexis and Lucy indoors. The family came hurrying out of the drawing room to meet them. Nanny, in her neat brown uniform, stood proudly holding her charge as everyone tried to get a glimpse of the new baby. Oliver and Mark grinned shyly at Lucy.

"Happy Christmas, Lucy. I've put you and Alexis in the guest suite," Willow said happily. "Patience is waiting upstairs to show Nanny Meredith where to take the baby. Polly, you can go to your old room though you will have to share it with Madame Rochford's maid, Bettine and Mrs. McGill's maid, Violet. Violet will help Patience and Nanny Meredith in the nursery. Alexis, your valet Simpson, will have to double up with Betts."

"Rochford Manor is bursting at the seams!" Alexis said, smiling at his mother-in-law. "It's my first family Christmas for years and years, I think I am even more excited than the children!"

Lucy gave no indication that the atmosphere of excitement was affecting her, too. She followed Alexis upstairs and began to unpack the Christmas gifts they had bought and lay them out on the big four-poster bed. Young Philip Grey had apparently appropriated the adjoining dressing room. A thoughtful smile appeared on Lucy's face as she realized that Alexis would be obliged to share her bed, there being no room available where he could sleep alone.

Alexis gave no indication whether he too, had noticed the fact. When Polly arrived to begin Lucy's unpacking, he gathered up an armful of parcels and took them downstairs to place under the tree.

They played party games with the children until dinner time, Lucy joining wholeheartedly in the younger children's activities. They played Blind Man's Buff and then Forfeits but when it came to Lucy's turn to surrender her forfeit she refused to part with her bracelet. "Then you will have to give Alexis a kiss instead," the children shouted. Between them they dragged Alexis and Lucy under the big bunch of mistletoe in the hall. Smiling, Lucy raised her face. Alexis' hesitation was only momentary as he recalled Lucy's aversion to kissing. Then he bent his head and put his lips on hers. The kiss lasted but a second or two and Lucy's eyes were still full of laughter as he drew back.

"Forfeits is a silly game," she cried but her tone belied her mood.

Alexis smiled down at her, determined that she should stay as happy as she was now during the whole week of their visit.

Lucy's mood was one of restrained excitement. She fidgeted like a child while Polly dressed her for dinner and then mischievously unfastened Alexis' bow tie when Simpson had at last arranged it to his satisfaction. Amused rather than angry, Alexis complained that if Lucy didn't stop her nonsense they would be late down for dinner.

It was nearly ten o'clock before the eight-course meal ended. The men agreed to forgo their cigars and take their brandy into the drawing room with the ladies. Silvie sat down at the piano and began to play carols. Before long, everyone was standing around the Bechstein singing.

Pelham slipped out unnoticed into the hall and climbed the stairs to the gallery. There, crouched behind the tapestry curtains which hung at one end, were the reasons for his departure from the family party—four of them in their night-clothes and warm woollen dressing gowns.

"Gosh, Uncle Pelham, you gave us a fright!" Oliver gasped. "We thought it might be Mater or Patience!"

"Well, it's me!" Pelham grinned, squatting down beside the four children. Alice climbed onto his lap and put her arms round his neck.

"How did you know we were here?" she demanded.

"Because lots of Rochford children have hidden here," Pelham replied. "It's *the* best hiding place for spying on grown-ups. I've hidden here lots of times when I was a youngster. Your Mama hid up here too, the night your Uncle Toby was having his twenty-first birthday party. He and I came up to the gallery to share some of the party food with her."

Oliver sighed.

"Wish we had something to eat. We only had dull old boiled eggs and creamed rice for our supper. What did you have downstairs, Uncle Pelham?"

"Roast grouse, Cook's special apricot meringue, tangerines..."

"You're saying it on purpose to make our mouths water!" Mark protested. "It's jolly well not fair, Sir!"

"Perhaps not!" Pelham agreed, his eyes twinkling. "Especially as I happen to know there were quite a lot of good things left over. They're probably lying in the larder this very minute waiting in case anyone happens to go down and find them..."

"You will, you will, won't you, because you love us!" Alice cried.

Pelham lifted her off his knee and stood up.

"No, I won't!" he said with mock sternness. "Just think what Mama would say if a grown-up went to her kitchen to steal a midnight feast. But..." he paused significantly as he looked into four expectant faces, "I daresay if I dropped a word in Philip's ear, it might do the trick. He may be eighteen but that's not quite grown-up, is it!"

Alice hugged him round his waist, her blue eyes shining. "I really do love you. You're my favoritist uncle!" she declared. "And when I'm old enough I'm going to marry you."

"Not if your Aunt Silvie has anything to say about it, young lady," Pelham laughed. "Now let me go back downstairs or your Mama will guess where I am!"

As he went down to the hall, Pelham paused. He had heard the sound of a violin coming from the drawing room—a sound he had not heard since Rupert had left home. Pelham walked slowly into the room. Alexis was playing the final bars of Listz' *Hungarian Rhapsody*, and the applause covered Pelham's return. Alexis smiled as he acknowledged the appreciation.

"It's a beautiful instrument," he said, fondling the Guarnieri.

"Rupert left it behind when he went abroad," Willow said. "When Lady Barratt told me how talented you were, I brought it down from the attic to surprise you."

Lucy was filled with admiration for Alexis' accomplishment. He had played fluently and with great feeling and the music had stirred her as most music did, filling her with the desire to dance. It seemed suddenly as if there were a special magic in the air, drawing everyone, herself too, into the mood and spirit of Christmas. There had been a lot of wine consumed during dinner and she realized suddenly that she was happy—*really happy*—for the first time in her life. There was no discord in this house. Her mother and Uncle Toby, Uncle Pelham and Aunt Silvie, Aunt Dodie and Uncle James, Philip, Alexis, were all smiling as they began to wish each other goodnight and discuss the hour at which they would leave for church next morning. It was the first small cloud on her horizon.

"I don't want to go to church!" she said to Alexis as they reached the landing to their room. "Need I go, Alexis? I don't have to, do I?"

She looked suddenly so young and wistful, Alexis knew he could not resist her appeal. He could not bear to be the one to wipe the radiance from her face.

"I suppose I could say you were not feeling too well," he offered. "After all, Lucy, it is less than three months since you had little Teo and we could pretend you have not fully recovered your strength."

Lucy laughed delightedly. Catching Alexis' hand in hers, she said:

"You *are* good to me. I do love you, Alexis. I'm having a lovely time and do you know, I really wasn't looking forward to coming home for Christmas. Isn't it strange that I should find myself so happy?"

But Alexis was not listening. His thoughts were centered on her words: *'I do love you . . .'* If it were true, then he would be as happy as she declared herself to be.

"Shall we let Polly and Simpson have an early night?" he suggested. "I can undress myself if you can, Lucy."

Lucy laughed.

"You forget I've only just learned to let my maid undress me. I do it much quicker than Polly anyway!"

Alexis followed his wife into their bedroom. He dismissed the two servants and sat down in the armchair while Lucy sat at the dressing table and began to remove the pins from her hair. It fell to her waist in a white-gold cloud.

"You look no older than Alice!" he remarked smiling.

Lucy stood up and went over to him.

"You'll have to unbutton me, Alexis," she said. "I'd forgotten they all fastened at the back!"

Alexis' hands trembled as he lifted the sweep of hair away from her shoulders and began inexpertly to undo the tiny pearl buttons of her dress.

"For someone whose fingers are so nimble on the violin, you're not very good as a lady's maid!" Lucy teased him when finally she stepped out of her dress. Her lace frilled petticoat floated as she moved.

"I could dance in this!" she cried, beginning to hum the strains of the *Hungarian Rhapsody* he had played. "I can dance very well, Alexis, even if I can't play the piano or the violin. Shall I dance for you one day? Now, if you like!"

Alexis drew a deep breath. His voice was husky as he said:

"Not now, Lucy. It's too late. Let's get to bed."

Without daring to look at her as she completed her undressing, Alexis hurried out of his own clothes. It seemed an eternity before she climbed into bed beside him with a long, contented sigh.

"I'm glad you haven't got a dressing room to sleep in," she said. "It's much nicer being together, isn't it?"

"Much, much nicer!" Alexis murmured as he reached out to turn off the light. The coal fire was still burning, the golden glow of the embers lighting up the room, the flickering flames casting shadows over Lucy's naked shoulders and arms. He could see the diamond bracelet glittering on her wrist and he smiled.

"You really cannot go on wearing that day and night," he said gently. "I know you are afraid of losing it but..."

"But it's the most precious thing I have!" she protested. "Please Alexis, don't take it off!"

Alexis sat up and reached over to the bedside table. On it, ready for the morning, he had carefully placed a small be-ribboned parcel.

"Your Christmas present," he said, handing it to Lucy. "I think you might prefer to open it now without everyone else around. Besides, it's after midnight so it is really already Christmas Day."

As Lucy sat up with a child's eagerness to open her present, the white linen sheet fell away revealing her breasts, rounded, golden in the firelight, the nipples dark and beautiful to Alexis' eyes. He could feel the warmth of her thigh against his body and his need for her became almost unbearable. He lay rigid watching her face as she withdrew the diamond necklace from its velvet box.

He was not disappointed by her look of delight.

"Alexis! It matches my bracelet. Oh, it's beautiful, it's per-fect, it's the most wonderful, perfect present!"

She held it out to him.

"Put it on for me, Alexis. Quickly. I want to wear it..."

She held it round her neck as he fastened the clasp. The cluster of diamonds dropped gracefully to her breasts, nestling in the shadow between them as if made for the purpose. Lucy stared down at herself, speechless with pleasure.

"Now you really cannot sleep in *that*!" Alexis said smiling. "It might break, Lucy, and then you couldn't wear it tomor-row."

Reluctantly, Lucy allowed him to unfasten it and then threw herself into his arms.

"You're the most wonderful husband in the whole world!" she cried. "And I'm the luckiest wife and I'll love you forever, Alexis. I promise I will."

Alexis' arms encircled her.

"If you love me just for now, my darling, I shall be happy enough," he whispered.

It did not seem to matter that Lucy turned her face away when he tried to kiss her. She raised no objection as his lips wandered over her body. She smiled at him happily as she responded willingly to his hungry demands. It seemed to Alexis as if she were melting into him or he into her. He could feel her hands drawing him closer and closer, her lips moist against his cheek, her legs entwined about his waist.

"Lucy! My Lucy!" he cried. "I've waited so long, so very long, for this..."

But now that the moment had come, he could not prolong its joy. The force of his desire for her was overwhelming and he could not control it. Lucy seemed contented as she smoothed the damp hair from his forehead and smiled into his eyes.

"I'm glad, *glad*!" she said softly. "I wanted you to want me, Alexis. I hated it when you left me alone night after night."

He caught her hand and pressed his lips to her palm.

"Oh, Lucy, never think that I did not want to be with you. How could you even imagine such a thing! Don't you understand, my darling? I wanted you on my terms. I wanted you to love me."

Lucy gave a happy laugh.

"So everything is all right now. Now we'll make love again, shall we?"

It was Alexis' turn to smile.

"That would be impossible, my dearest love. I gave you everything I have to give, body, heart and soul!"

Lucy leaned on one elbow, a small smile touching the corners of her mouth.

"But this time, *I* shall give *you* everything," she said as she began to kiss his body. Alexis lay quietly, unwilling to put a stop to Lucy's wish to please him yet afraid lest his lack of response might discourage her. But Lucy had no such doubts and soon Alexis felt his heart begin to pound once more and the hot blood raced once again through his veins.

She lay atop him now, her face a white mysterious mask as she began to ride with him. Pleasure, excitement and a renewed desire greater even than before, wiped all thought from Alexis' mind. He had so often dreamed of loving her, being loved by her but never, ever so completely.

Only when it was over and they were lying spent and

exhausted side by side, did coherent thought return. Alexis kissed Lucy's white shoulder as he lay looking into the blue depth of her eyes.

"I want you to be as happy as I am, Lucy. Tell me that you are!" he said softly.

Lucy's eyes widened.

"Of course I am, Alexis. Everything's perfect now, isn't it, between us, I mean. It wouldn't have been right to go on the way we were, would it?"

Alexis smiled.

"It was certainly very unnatural . . . and quite a strain!" he admitted.

Lucy sighed.

"I never really understood why, Alexis. You knew I was willing and yet . . ."

"Willing was not enough, Lucy. I had to know you loved me. You do, don't you. Tell me now that you do!"

"But of course I do, Alexis!" Lucy sounded surprised. "How could I not when you've given me such a beautiful present. Now I can wear it, can't I, without feeling bad about it, I mean? I never really did feel I earned my bracelet. It's not as if I'd had Teo to please you, although you seem to love her more than I do . . ."

She broke off as she became aware that Alexis had taken his arm from across her body and was now lying stiffly away from her.

"Alexis?" she questioned. "Did I say something wrong?"

"No!" Alexis replied quietly. "It is never wrong to be honest, Lucy, although the truth can hurt very badly sometimes. You spoke of 'earning' your bracelet. Tell me honestly—and I will not be angry whatever you say—was what happened between us tonight because you really wanted to do it or because you felt you owed it to me?"

"Well, of course I owed it!" Lucy said matter-of-factly, a small frown creasing her forehead as she tried to follow Alexis' reasoning. "When you said you'd marry me, we agreed I would be a proper wife to you and willing to let you have me whenever you wanted. I don't see why you mind whether *I* want it. You must know how I feel about that sort of thing."

"No, I don't know, Lucy. *Tell me!*"

Lucy gave a long sigh.

"Well, it's just something men want, isn't it? They need to do it because it's their nature and they like it. Most of them are quite happy to pay for their pleasure. But once they are married, they don't have to pay because their wives let them do it for nothing."

She paused, lost for a moment in thought before she continued:

"I suppose in a way, it's not really for nothing. I mean, wives get houses and clothes and if their husbands are generous, they get presents, too. Of course, some wives won't *let* their husbands do it even though they get given things and that's wrong—at least, I think so. Then the husbands have to pay some other girl to do it and that's not fair. That's why I'm glad *we* did. Now I don't feel it's unfair for you any more. So you see, I did want to do it every bit as much as you wanted to. Do you understand now, Alexis?"

Alexis nodded. Lucy's relentless logic was all too clear. He had invited her to be honest and now he must take the consequences. Lucy had earned her keep. Love was still incomprehensible to her.

"You're not cross, are you, Alexis?"

Her voice, wistful, childish, tore at his heart. He said with difficulty:

"No, I'm not cross, Lucy. But I want *you* now to try to understand *me*. It may not be easy for you but you must try. I don't see marriage as you see it. When I decided to make you my wife, it was because I wanted to share my life with you; because I could never want to marry any other woman but you. I was not intending to make a bargain with you, a kind of contract to which we must both adhere. It was—and still is—my intention to build a relationship with you that is based on mutual affection, trust, understanding. Whatever I may give you—house, car, gifts—I am giving you because I want to make you happy and not because I am expecting you to give me your body in return. I do not need—or want you on those terms, Lucy. I will not buy your love, or your loving."

He paused briefly and then added:

"If it makes things clearer for you, think of me as different from the other men you have known. I shall not make love to you again—not until you can convince me that you are offering yourself to me because it is what *you* want, *you* need, *you* desire. I shall not consider it unfair, mean, cheating, if you cannot feel as I want. You need have no conscience about it, Lucy. There are no conditions to our marriage other than that you should not be unfaithful to me. That is something

I could not tolerate, nor, thank God, do I believe you want or need to be so."

For a long time, Lucy was silent. She really did not understand what Alexis was talking about. She knew from his tone that when he used the word "love," it was important to him. But for her, it remained only a word. One could love or hate with a wealth of degree between the two. Good or bad, nice or nasty...they were all only words. Hate was easier to understand. She hated Maurice. Alexis was worth a hundred of Maurice and she not only admired but respected him. She wished very much that she could say she loved him. She did not want him to be unhappy. He had been kind to her and generous to a fault.

"We'll do whatever you want, Alexis," she said finally. "And I will try to love you, I promise."

In the darkness, Alexis bit his lip, not sure whether the tears that stung his eyes were for himself or for the child who lay beside him. He was certain of only one thing—that he must never take her again unless it were on his terms and she could give herself to him not from gratitude but from love.

For the first two months of the new year, Lucy amused herself playing the part of a London hostess. She gave several small, select dinner parties for some of Alexis' business associates and their wives, and they themselves were invited out a great deal. Her days were largely spent choosing a new wardrobe to replace the gowns she had discarded when she had been forced into maternity dresses. They were, she now told Alexis, hopelessly out of fashion. With different hats, gloves, scarves and shoes required for all the new outfits, her time passed contentedly enough on these shopping sprees.

Nanny Meredith had complete charge of baby Teo. Her references to Lucy concerning a change of diet or routine were perfunctory and always ended in Lucy deferring to Nanny's wishes. There was no disputing the fact that the infant was thriving in Nanny's care. Now almost five months old, the little girl was healthy, happy and adored not only by Nanny but by all the servants. Perhaps not least of all her slaves was Alexis. It was on his lap the child chose to sit when Nanny brought her down to the drawing room for a brief visit to her parents after Alexis arrived home from work—a daily routine that was seldom broken.

"How could I fail to love her when she looks exactly as you must have looked at her age!" Alexis once said when Lucy accused him of spoiling the child.

He could not have explained to Lucy that to him, the golden-haired, blue-eyed infant had become so precious simply because she was a part of Lucy—the only part of her that he could kiss and hold in his arms.

Lucy was not jealous. She was no less the baby's slave than Alexis although she gave no indication of her own love for Teo. As far as Lucy was aware, no one knew the power her child had to pull on her heart strings; how she longed each week for Nanny's afternoon off so that she could become the focal point in the top-floor nursery. Then, unseen, she would sit and play with the baby, sing to her and cuddle her. She wanted her to have a perfect life, unclouded by tears or unhappiness. If it was her Papa that Teo wanted, then Lucy was glad that Alexis always found time for her.

But Nanny's days off were too infrequent and by the end of the first three months of the year, Lucy was growing bored and restless. The Lennoxes, the Inmans, Mr. and Mrs. Fanshaw, were all a good deal older than herself. So too were Alexis' Austrian friends, the Count and Countess Kalnoky and a Croatian cousin called Ladislav Bartski. Lucy wanted younger company. She wanted Alexis to take her to the Picture Palace to see the silent films; she wanted to see Ivy Close acting in *The Lady of Shalott*, to dance the new Tango, the Bunny Hug, the Chicken Scramble. She had little interest in the dinner table talk which seemed so often to center around politics.

Europe, so the talk went, was a tinderbox. During their weekend visit to Rochford Manor, Toby suggested that the situation was worrying. Although Turkey had been forced into an armistice with the Balkan League, her statesmen were in London trying to bargain over the new territory claimed by Bulgaria. It seemed that it would not be long before war broke out in the Balkans, he forecast.

"Tobias was quite right," Alexis said not long after. "All the Balkan states are turning against one another. There is to be a conference in London presided over by the Foreign Minister, Sir Edward Grey, and watched over by the Great Powers, Austria, Hungary and Russia."

Alexis himself expected he would be involved and working very late hours. The delimitations of the frontiers between Russian-backed Servia and the new state of Albania, backed by Austria, Italy and Germany, had to be decided upon as a matter of urgency, he did his best to explain to Lucy.

"The elderly Field-Marshal, Lord Roberts, is demanding National Service as a precautionary measure," he said. "But I doubt very much the Government will support him. The nation is certainly against it although I, personally, think he is right."

Since Oliver was far too young to be called up for National Service, there was no one Lucy cared about who might be called upon to strengthen the country's defensive power.

"Must we always talk of war?" she asked. "It's so depressing a subject, Alexis."

It was at one of the rather dreary dinner parties Lucy dreaded at the Lennoxes' house, that she met again Gillian's younger sister, Annabel Barratt. At first, Lucy did not recognize her for she had had her long corn-colored hair shorn and now sported what she called 'an Eton crop.'

"Long hair is dreadfully old-fashioned," she told Lucy in her clipped, self-confident voice. "Christabel Pankhurst still has hers long, of course, but I think this style is more modern. You know Christabel had to flee to France last March. She's in Paris now."

Lucy became interested. When Annabel invited her around to her Montpelier Square flat to tea next day, she accepted the invitation almost with excitement. At least this was something new, she thought, wondering why the Suffragette leader had to escape to Paris.

Annabel was clearly greatly influenced by her famous friend, Lucy decided, as they sat drinking tea in the older girl's rather untidy, inelegant flat. The drawing room was littered with papers and pamphlets and the sofa had been pushed back against the wall to make room for a huge desk on which a large typewriter had pride of place.

"All our Suffragette leaders are in prison," Annabel proudly told the astonished Lucy. "Christabel was fortunate to escape."

"Why are they treated like criminals?" Lucy asked curiously.

Annabel's pale face turned a deep pink and her eyes became wide with excitement.

"Christabel is determined to make the people who matter notice the Suffragettes—so that attention is paid to our aims," she declared. "She plans strikes and the burning of buildings, the blowing-up of railways, defacing works of art—she's overflowing with ripping ideas! Did you read about Christabel's mother and the magnificent speech she made last month at the Old Bailey? It was on the subject of morality. Of course, Christabel too, campaigns against the double standards that exist in sexual morality."

It was a matter on which Lucy herself held strong opinions and now she began to pay more attention to Annabel's propaganda. It seemed that the tireless Christabel was concerning herself even with the problems of venereal disease—which Annabel discussed with as much candour as had Madame Lou-Lou. Lucy was deeply surprised. She had learned since her arrival in England, that such subjects were *never* mentioned by 'ladies' and should they ever be raised, a well-brought-up girl must appear ignorant of the meaning of such conversations. Yet here was Annabel, the daughter of a baronet, being as open as if they were discussing the new fashions!

It was after six o'clock before Lucy bade Annabel a reluctant farewell and the chauffeur who had been waiting patiently for two and a half hours, drove her back to Cadogan Gardens. Despite Polly's efforts to speed Lucy's change of clothes, she was late down to dinner and Alexis was far from pleased when he learned the reason.

"I don't want to pour cold water on your plans, Lucy," he said having seen the bright spots of color in her cheeks and heard her animated voice. "But I cannot recommend you should become involved with the Suffragettes. Although I do understand and appreciate what Christabel Pankhurst hopes to achieve—and indeed, is in some cases already achieving by way of recognition—many of her ways of getting what she wants are illegal, and *very* dangerous."

Lucy regarded him across the dinner table defiantly.

"I hope you are not suggesting I withdraw my friendship from Annabel. It's all very well for you, Alexis. You have your work to keep you entertained during the day. You don't seem to realize how bored I get. Annabel is interesting anyway. I have no intention of becoming too involved but they *are* fighting against evil. Annabel said they had received letters from clergymen praising them for their courage!"

From then on there was rarely a day when Lucy did not see Annabel, mostly at the Montpelier Square flat. Luckily Alexis was unaware of these daily visits for he seemed to be increasingly busy at work.

In June, Sir John and Lady Barratt opened their London

house for the Season and Lady Barratt saw Lucy through her
Court presentation—an occasion of such importance to Lucy
that even Annabel's Suffragettes dimmed to insignificance.
Willow insisted that Lucy should have her portrait painted in
her white satin Court dress. It was covered with white and
silver embroidery and, as she was a married woman, she had
worn three rather than two white ostrich feathers in her hair.
The artist, John Lavery, was impressed by Lucy's beauty and
demanded more sittings than usual. As a consequence she
ceased to be able to spend so many afternoons at Montpelier
Square.

In July, however, Lucy was once more in close association
with Annabel, for the scandal had broken concerning the
Piccadilly Flat case. It had a special significance for Lucy
because it involved a brothel keeper, Queenie Gerald. According to Annabel, who had had the facts from Christabel
who was writing a long article about it, the Government and
police had covered up the truth when Queenie Gerald was
tried. It seemed that many prominent men had made use of
the brothel at which all kinds of vice had been made available—flagellation, the procuring of virgins for rich gentlemen
and so forth. Queenie Gerald had been sentenced to three
months' imprisonment and Christabel was comparing this
inadequate penalty with the three years that her Suffragettes
had been given.

For the first time, Lucy was no longer sure that she was
in sympathy with the Suffragette movement—or Annabel. It
seemed logical to her that Queenie Gerald was only catering
to the demands of the men who used her Piccadilly flat. Like
Madame Lou-Lou, she was providing a service. Was it not
hypocritical, she thought, to send her to prison and not the
men who paid for the upkeep of her establishment? Did Christabel Pankhurst not know that the world was full of men who
went to such places simply because they could not enjoy the
same pleasures at home?

But Annabel had no inkling of Lucy's past and Lucy herself
had no intention of revealing it. She would have liked to
discuss the case with Alexis but he was unusually reticent
when the topic was raised and she guessed that he, too, was
remembering her past.

The weather had become very hot and London dusty and
stifling. Alexis suggested Lucy take Teo and Nanny down to
Rochford for a few weeks during the boys' holiday. He was

working very long hours and quite often was too late back to take her out to a theater or opera. Lucy decided that it might be quite nice to be in the country for a while. She looked forward to the thought of swimming and picnicking with the younger children.

Oliver, Mark and Henry were delighted to see her. With Sir John and Lady Barratt removed to London for the Season, their two youngest children, Eleanor and Henry, had been absorbed into the Rochford household. Peace reigned in the nursery and the children, including Lucy, were free to spend their days as they pleased. With the help of the gardener, Purkiss, the boys had repaired the old punt and mock sea battles were now enacted on the lake: Lucy, Eleanor, Oliver and Jane in the new punt; Alice, Mark and Henry in the other.

Philip was not home on leave but Mark was enjoying his last few weeks of freedom before leaving for the United States. He had completed his schooling and Willow had managed to obtain work for him in one of her late father's American companies, part of his T.R.T.C. empire. Mark had shown a considerable aptitude for mathematics and was a quiet, good-looking young man. Willow believed he would be a useful asset to the Corporation and at the same time, would be able to acquire the independence he, like his brother Philip, craved.

The entire family went down to Southampton in two cars to see Mark off. Willow was almost in tears as she hugged him. He looked suddenly so very young and lonely. But Mark himself was full of confidence.

Oliver and Henry pummelled him on the chest, hiding the emotion of the moment in typical schoolboy ragging. Jane looked white and miserable as she kissed her brother good-bye, but sensitive to her feelings, the two boys soon managed to make her laugh again as they drove slowly back to the Manor.

That night at dinner when the children were safely tucked up in their beds, Willow turned to Lucy.

"I wish you were not returning to London tomorrow, my darling," she said. "I shall miss you as well as Mark and goodness knows how Patience will survive without Nanny Meredith's company and your adorable little Teo to spoil. It seems to have been such a happy summer holiday, I can't bear to see it end."

"There'll be others," Toby comforted her. "Before you know where you are, it will be 1914 and summer once again."

Willow sighed.

"I suppose I'm silly, but every once in a while, I have the strangest feelings...forebodings, I suppose you would call them. I had that same feeling just before you were born, Lucienne, and then..."

"Now stop being morbid!" Toby broke in smiling as he reproved her. "You'd think the world was coming to an end the way you are talking."

Nevertheless, he felt a sudden shiver go down his spine. He would not speak of it to Willow or to Lucy but there was little doubt the war clouds were gathering in Europe and that if one read between the lines, one could no longer deny the dangerous threat of war.

Chapter 13

❦

February 1914–April 1914

To ALEXIS' DELIGHT, LUCY DROPPED ANNABEL BARRATT FROM HER visiting list and acquired a new set of friends of her own age. She had met by chance at the glove counter in Harrods one day the daughter of one of the Barratts' neighbors, Sam Sharples, a man considered very *nouveau riche* by Society, having recently made a fortune out of canning vegetables. The two girls immediately struck up a friendship.

Although Hilda was à plump, rather plain girl, as far as Lucy was concerned she had certain unmistakable assets. She was young, amusing and because of the generosity of her enormously wealthy father, she was independent. She had her own flat in London, a huge dress allowance, a Bugatti of her own. She even discussed with Alexis the possibility of buying her own airplane and learning to fly. With her lively sense of humor she made Lucy laugh, and her daredevil nature led both girls on a search for constant amusement and activity. Hilda was very, very modern and totally self-assured.

It was not until after Christmas that Alexis realized the undesirable influence Lucy's new friend was having upon his young wife. He was uncertain what to do about it. Hilda Sharples had no inbuilt sense of what was socially acceptable and what was not. She moved amongst the "fast" set and before long, she and Lucy had a group of two dozen or so friends with whom they indulged in all the latest pleasures. When they were not racing about in their expensive cars, usually exceeding the fifty miles per hour speed limit, they were drinking cocktails, talking in loud voices, going to the moving pictures at the bioscope, where they sat giggling in the semidarkness as they watched the latest "Keystone Cops" films. They went to the West End to watch the ragtime revues, singing the music and noisily repeating the saucy

195

sketches and exuberant dances, regardless of the places they happened to be where more sedate and restrained behavior was *de rigeur*. They took fancies which lasted for weeks on end to a particular variety performer. It became the rage, for instance, to wear osprey feathers in their hair and black stockings and bracelets round their ankles like the American, Ethel Levey, who had taken the Hippodrome by storm. There was not a theatrical performance they had not seen, even last year's productions of Strauss' *The Chocolate Soldier* and Lehar's *The Count of Luxembourg* in out-of-town theaters.

Most of their pastimes kept them out of Cadogan Gardens but when they had nothing better to do, they went back to Lucy's home to dance. Quite often when Alexis returned from work, the house would be alive with strangers clasped dramatically together as they danced a Tango or whirled dangerously to the ragtime beat pounded out on Lucy's gramophone. Half empty cocktail glasses littered the table tops and the air was dense with the smoke of the Turkish cigarettes they favored.

Alexis reminded himself that Lucy was still only twenty years old and that at her age, he had enjoyed a similar if quieter adolescence at Oxford. Late nights, dancing, drinking, talking—he too had tasted the grown-up world with the same heady excitement. But somehow these new friends of Lucy's were different from the norm—or seemed so to him. Perhaps he was too tired and too much older than they, he thought, to be able to 'join in the fun,' as Lucy put it. As often as not, he retired to his study and left his wife and her friends to enjoy themselves in their loud, extrovert fashion.

It was Roberta who pointed out to Alexis that he was treating Lucy more like a daughter than a wife. Roberta had called in one evening by chance when Lucy had gone to the theater. It had been her innocent intention to leave a selection of *Queen* magazines which Lucy had asked if she might borrow. Finding Alexis alone, she accepted his invitation to stay for a predinner drink.

Alexis had seen very little of Roberta since his marriage. She had been to the house on several occasions, mainly to offer any assistance she could to Lucy and to try to establish a friendship with her. Lucy seemed disinclined to develop an intimate relationship and of late, Roberta had called less and less often.

Alexis was surprised how pleased he was to see her. She

looked cool and quiet and restful, and he could relax in her company in a way he never could with Lucy or her friends.

"If I treat Lucy like a daughter, it is because she is still so young that I very often feel like her father!" he replied with a smile to Roberta's remark. "She is thirteen years younger than I am, Roberta, so naturally enough, she enjoys young company."

Roberta was silent for a moment.

"But is the company she is keeping altogether wise, Alexis?" she asked tentatively. "That man in her set they call 'The Baron'—he's a real lounge lizard and hangs around the Sharples girl and Lucy because they pick up all the bills he can't pay. And there is young Lord Montfervier-Ffoulkes. I hear he is running up a number of shocking debts everywhere he goes. Next thing he'll be thrown out of the Marlborough Club, so Angus told me. He had a letter which he happened to show me from a friend who is a member. I thought I ought to warn you."

Alexis passed a hand wearily through his hair.

"I *have* to let Lucy grow up," he said quietly. "I tried to warn her about Montfervier-Ffoulkes, but she won't listen."

Roberta looked away from his tired, strained face. It was perfectly clear to her that Alexis was not happy, despite his attempted smile. She knew too well that look of tension and it was only with an effort that she did not go over to his chair to put her cool hands on his forehead. So often in the past she had been able to soothe away his worries.

"You are not regretting your marriage, Alexis?" she asked quietly.

"No!" The word came too instantaneously for Roberta to be in any doubt as to its truth. But equally, she was in no doubt that something was very wrong with the relationship. But she could not help if she did not know the cause of the trouble.

"Alexis, I know how loyal you are as a person and how loathe you must be to speak of your Lucy in anything less than glowing terms. But sometimes an outsider can help and you should know by now that you can trust *me* absolutely. Won't you tell me what is wrong? Maybe there is something I could do."

Roberta had always been sensitive to his moods and feelings, but Alexis could not talk to her of Lucy's past or of her attitude to love and to lovemaking. That aspect of his life was between him and Lucy only.

"Lucy had a difficult childhood," he said vaguely. "All those years in a strict, repressive convent, and then the sudden transition to our world, our life..."

Roberta noticed the way in which Alexis had begun to twist his hands together as he did sometimes under stress. She thought she knew the reason.

"It's bed, isn't it, Alexis? It would be understandable if a girl brought up in a convent were averse to lovemaking, even frigid. Such institutions frequently emphasize the evils of sex and its delights. The fact that Lucy is so extraordinarily attractive does not guarantee that she wishes to attract. If that is so, it must be very hard for you, Alexis. Am I right?"

Right, but for the wrong reasons, Alexis thought bitterly. Roberta, with her customary sensitivity, had guessed his inner torment. He smiled at her ruefully.

"You will understand, Roberta, that I cannot force Lucy as some husbands might. I love her too much. I want her to come to me voluntarily. So you see, I have made my own bed of nails to lie on."

"Oh, Alexis!" Roberta said softly. "I wish there were more men like you in the world. But you've been married nearly two years now—and that's far too long. Would you like me to talk to Lucy? Perhaps I could explain such matters to her and rid her of some of her fears. An older woman..."

"No, Roberta, thank you." Alexis interrupted quickly. "I must handle this in my own way. I know you mean well, and in the circumstances..."

He broke off, coloring slightly with embarrassment. But Roberta said bluntly:

"Don't let's pretend with one another, Alexis. You were going to say it would not be right for your ex-mistress to instruct your wife on matters of sex. And you may be right. But there is something I want you to know, and I intend to speak very plainly so that you and I have no misunderstandings. I have missed you—terribly. I have found no one else to replace you in my life and like you, I am often very lonely and very hungry for love. I know that you love Lucy and that maybe one day soon, that side of your marriage will come right for you both. But in the meanwhile, Alexis, must we waste that part of our lives that used to be so satisfactory for us both?"

Alexis looked down at his hands, avoiding Roberta's searching gaze.

"Don't think I am unappreciative of your offer or of your honesty, Roberta. But it wouldn't work. It never was simply a matter of using one another as you have just implied. I couldn't do that to you!"

Roberta was far too shrewd to speak the words that sprang to her lips—that she wanted Alexis at any price. Her love for him had not so much diminished as increased during the past two years, and now she experienced a swift rush of joy at the thought that their love affair might be renewed, despite his marriage.

"I don't think you and I should talk in terms of 'using' one another, Alexis," she said softly. "Isn't it more a case of needing each other?"

She rose to her feet and went to stand behind his chair. Bending over him, she laid her cheek against the top of his head, her arms reaching down over his shoulders to fold across his chest.

"*I* need *you* very much, my dear!" she murmured.

Alexis let his head fall backwards so that he was gazing up into Roberta's pale face. How cool she looked! How calm and serene! He wanted nothing more than to rest against her and feel her soft hands stroking his forehead. He was so tired! And there were many times lately when he had despaired that he and Lucy would ever grow close. Lucy's pleasures in life seemed to exclude him utterly and they shared nothing but their love for little Teo. Even that Lucy did not really share with him, for she never showed affection for the little girl in front of him.

Roberta's voice was husky as she broke into his thoughts.

"Alexis, I have a friend, a close friend of mine who owns a flat in Mount Street. She is leaving for Canada next week to spend six months with her married son. If I asked to borrow her flat, I know she would allow it and she would ask no questions. Will you come there if I can arrange it? If nothing else, we could enjoy the occasional quiet dinner together."

Remembering how often his own house was invaded with the raucous laughter and noisy music of Lucy's friends, Alexis was tempted by this oasis of peace Roberta was describing to him. Perhaps it would mean that they ended up in bed together, but for the moment he did not wish to make decisions.

Roberta had suggested an occasional quiet dinner party and to that suggestion he could say yes without commitment.

Lucy never inquired where her husband went or what he had been doing. Alexis did not discuss his work with her and she saw no reason to be curious. She only shrugged her shoulders therefore, when in the following week he informed her he would not be back to dinner.

"I'll tell Cook we are both eating out," she replied. "We are all going to see the revue *Everybody's Doing It* and afterward we'll probably have supper at the Savoy."

Alexis paused in the doorway, staring down into Lucy's eyes. He felt strangely guilty that she should harbor no suspicions.

"I wish you wouldn't stare at me like that, Alexis," she said frowning. "You often do it and it always makes me feel self-conscious. It's as if you are expecting me to say something and I don't."

A smile touched Alexis' eyes as he bent and kissed her cheek.

"Have a good time, my darling!" he said and was rewarded with Lucy's engaging smile.

"It's going to be absolutely deevie!" she told him, using her friends' slang term for 'devine.' It would have irritated Alexis coming from anyone else but he had noticed Lucy trying very hard to adopt the mannerisms of her set without quite managing to do so naturally. She was like a little girl playacting.

He kissed her again, this time on the forehead, and watched her run lightly up the wide staircase, calling for Polly to come and help her change her clothes.

Roberta had discreetly brought no servants to her friend's flat.

"I'm quite capable of cooking a meal for you, Alexis," she told him as she assisted him out of his coat and put his hat and gloves on the hall stand. "We don't want any tittle-tattle. We would be bound to invite it were we known to be here alone, no matter how innocently we behaved!"

Alexis was no longer so certain that he wished to behave so innocently. Roberta was in demi-toilette, a black, lace-inserted blouse over a tight black directoire skirt. Her dark hair was caught back from her face in a loose chignon, the whole effect somehow Eastern and mysterious. She appeared perfectly at ease as she led the way into the small drawing room and poured him a drink from the cocktail shaker on the side table.

"Do smoke if you want, Alexis," she told him.

He took the glass and lit a cigarette.

"I feel like one of Lucy's friends when I drink a cocktail," he said smiling. "What's it supposed to be?"

"A Satan's Whisker!" she told him and laughed as she filled her own glass. "Go on, try it, Alexis. Tell me if you like it! It's two parts each of Italian vermouth, French vermouth, gin and orange juice; one part Grand Marnier and orange bitters."

Alexis relaxed against the cushions. He gazed round the room, but without real interest in his surroundings. His mind was elsewhere as he considered how unfortunate it was that sex had to complicate life. Yet celibacy was totally unnatural to him and he knew that there were far too many occasions of late when he had almost broken his own rules and gone into Lucy's bedroom. At such moments when he was alone, in the dark, his resolves had seemed absurdly idealistic and irrational. Of all the temptations that beset him, the worst was the knowledge that Lucy would not object; that it would make little difference to her whether he drowned in her beauty or not. What sane man would deny himself the pleasures of his own wife's willing body?

And now he was denying himself his mistress' willing body, too!

"Good God, Roberta, I am only a man!" he said suddenly. "I'm no monk or saint. But I don't want to hurt you. Don't you see, if Lucy at any time..."

Roberta moved swiftly around from behind his chair and knelt at his feet, her hand covering his lips.

"I understand!" she said. "I accept the possibility that one day, one evening, Lucy might come to her senses and you might fail to keep an assignation with me. Can't you see, Alexis, I don't care! It is *now* that matters."

Closing his eyes, Alexis drew her up between his knees and his mouth closed hungrily on her parted lips. It was a long time, he thought, since he had kissed a woman's soft lips.

"I need you!" he murmured. "God, how much I need you!"

Roberta led him through a doorway into a large bedroom where the coverlet of a big double bed had been turned down as if in readiness for the night. Had Roberta been so sure of herself, Alexis wondered as he undressed with a boy's clumsy haste? Did this woman know him so well that she had realized he was at the end of his ability to control his natural desires?

Her naked body was instantly familiar to his touch. She molded herself against him as she had done so many, many times in the past. There was no need for Roberta to seduce him—he was so hungry for her that his desire was equal to her own. With practiced ease, they reached their mutual release.

Outside the window the darkness of a soft spring night had fallen, and only the glow of the street lamps lit the room. Turning on his side to face Roberta, Alexis saw that she was smiling. He felt a moment of anxiety lest she had misjudged his true feelings. He did not want her to love him. He could never love her, not as he loved Lucy. He could feel gratitude, affection, but above all gratitude.

As if aware of his thoughts, Roberta said:

"We'll have to get up, Alexis. I put a beefgulyas in the oven and it will be uneatable if we don't dine soon!"

Alexis smiled, happy once again to be with her.

Roberta had prepared the beefgulyas in the Vienna style and they enjoyed it in a leisurely manner. When Alexis finished his brandy and after-dinner cigar, it was Roberta who suggested they must both go home. It was nearly ten o'clock, she said, and Angus would be worrying about her. Lucy too, might be home.

They kissed affectionately as they tidied the flat and then went their separate ways. Lucy had not yet returned and Alexis went to bed in his dressing room. He expected to fall asleep at once but discovered himself wide awake. He could never settle until Lucy was safely home, however late it was. And no matter how quiet she and Polly might be with her undressing, he always waited to hear the soft murmur of their voices next door to be certain she was back.

He did not think of Roberta as he lay in the darkness. His thoughts were entirely on Lucy. Outside the house he heard the noise of car engines followed by the sound of laughter and the slamming of car doors. There was a chorus of good nights, more laughter, a male voice raised in song: *Everybody's Doing It, Doing It, Doing It . . .*

And I am no better than any of them, Alexis thought as he waited for the sound of Lucy's footfall on the stairs.

The springtime was always beautiful at Rochford Manor, Willow thought, as she prepared for Oliver's return from school for the Easter holidays. The lawns were bright with clumps of wild daffodils, the borders filled with colorful polyanthus and the pussy willows white with pollen-laden buds. Down on the farms the wheat had turned the brown fields green. There was scarcely a farmhouse where Willow called that did not have its orphan lamb gavotting round the flagstone kitchen. There were signs of new birth everywhere.

There was to be a new birth in the family too, she thought contentedly. Dodie had announced that she was to have another child in November.

"Keep this a secret for a moment, dearest Willow," she had written, *"until I am quite sure. I know you will worry about my health but Dr. Mather says I should be able to carry another full-term baby although he would like me to come to stay with you for the birth. This is so that I do not have the cares of our house and little Zandra to sap my strength..."*

Willow was delighted and worried by turn, causing Toby to laugh at her changing moods.

"They are as variable as the spring weather!" he teased her. Her spirits soared again when Lucy and Alexis arrived at Rochford for a holiday covering the long weekend from Good Friday to Easter Monday. Oliver and Henry were still as interested as ever in airplanes and Alexis took them for a joy ride at Brooklands race track in Surrey. The airfield was in the center of the oval racing circuit round which the cars raced, and there were always crowds of onlookers eager to watch the cars trying to break their own speed records or the monoplanes and biplanes taking off and landing—sometimes accidentally in the sewage works beyond the race track boundary. They were very much in the mood for adventure, Oliver explained gravely, as he and the other boys at school had been inspired by the brave deeds of Captain Scott. He was shocked to learn that Lucy and Alexis had not gone to St. Paul's in February to the Memorial Service held there for the explorer and his party.

"If the King could find the time to attend, surely you could have done so," he said reproachfully to Lucy.

Lucy admitted shamelessly that she had not the slightest idea who Captain Scott was.

"Don't you read the newspapers?" Oliver said, horrified by her ignorance of so momentous an event. "Captain Scott was the explorer who led the British Expedition to the South Pole. He actually got there in January last year and then he and his party were overcome by a terrible blizzard on the way back. They died of exposure, in March, I think it was, but no one discovered their bodies until November last year."

"The sad part about it," Henry added, "was that a Norwegian called Roald Amundsen beat Captain Scott to the Pole, so really, he died for nothing, poor chap."

Their conversation turned once more to flying.

Oliver told Alexis that he and Henry had seen the air ace, Gustav Hamel, looping the loop in his airplane over Windsor Castle, watched by the King. The Eton boys and the residents of Windsor had greatly enjoyed the spectacle.

The highlight of the Easter holiday was an unexpected visit from Rupert Rochford and his friend, Maximillian von Kruege.

The family was in the drawing room taking afternoon tea when the butler announced that there were visitors. Before he could give their names, two men came into the room. The shorter of the two was smiling as he walked across to Willow and kissed her on both cheeks.

Oliver had not seen this particular uncle since he had left home when Oliver was only four. No one had ever told him the reason for his uncle's disappearance but he had guessed vaguely that Uncle Rupert had left under a cloud since Grandmère had forbidden his name to be mentioned.

He recalled a rather quiet, withdrawn man who, though never unkind, had shown little interest in him. Oliver noted now his dissimilarity to either of his other two uncles. He was noticeably shorter, with blue eyes, light brown hair and a small neat beard. But what interested Oliver most was the immaculate cut of his single-breasted reefer jacket and tweed trousers, giving him an almost dapper appearance.

Judging by his mother's demonstrative welcome and Uncle Toby's smiling face, they were pleased to see him. Wide-eyed, Oliver watched as Lucy went forward and kissed the newcomer.

Now the second stranger stepped forward and was introduced by Rupert to Willow and Toby. It seemed he already knew Lucy and Alexis. Oliver's curiosity deepened as he heard the name 'Maximillian von Kruege.' They did not see many foreigners at Rochford. As the man bowed in Continental fashion over Willow's hand, Oliver took note of his appearance. In a pale gray suit, a pink rosebud in his buttonhole and a pink silk handkerchief in his pocket, the visitor struck Oliver as being the very height of fashionable elegance. He was as tall and as dark as his uncle was short and fair.

Both men smiled pleasantly at Oliver, Henry and Jane, and Willow beckoned Oliver to her side.

"Rupert, you probably don't recognize your nephew, he's so grown up now," she said, "and you certainly won't recognize Alice. Jane, be a good girl and run up to the nursery and tell Patience to send Alice downstairs. Explain that Alice can have tea with us today as her Uncle Rupert has come to visit us."

It was obvious to Oliver that his mother was genuinely pleased to see this particular brother-in-law.

Willow's pleasure was in no way feigned. Moreover, she was charmed by the elegance and interesting conversation of his friend, Maximillian. The two men began telling Willow and Toby about their house in Brussels and how their hobby of collecting rare books had led to meetings with several great men of importance whom they might otherwise never have known.

"Although most of the collectors are of a literary bent," Rupert said, "it is quite surprising how many share this love of old and beautiful books, even military men such as General Baron von Bissing and Eric von Ludendorff. He travels from Dusseldorf whenever we have something special to show him."

Maximillian gave his slow smile.

"Sometimes we will exchange or sell a book but for the most part we find it difficult to part with any of them," he said in his accented English. "We keep silent when we have found something very special!" He turned to Alexis. "Rupert and I have been hoping that your work would bring you to our city as you suggested when we last met in Italy. We have been disappointed not to meet with you again."

Losing interest in the conversation, Oliver turned to Henry and remarked in a low voice upon the Count's elegance. At fifteen, he was old enough to be conscious of his own appearance and had recently become quite fastidious about the way he wore his Eton "tails" and the angle at which he wore his topper.

He was not renowned at school for his hard work, having a natural aptitude for most subjects which enabled him to achieve good enough marks to satisfy his tutors. He was, however, immensely popular, being good-natured and in particular, a good sportsman. He excelled both at Eton's peculiar form of football known as the Field Game and as a batsman. Other boys, even those older than himself, tended to copy his mannerisms and fads, and as far as Henry was concerned, if Oliver wanted to wear clothes like Count von Kruege, he was happy enough to do the same.

During Rupert's short visit to his old home, Willow found time to talk alone with him. They strolled to the lake together and Rupert took the opportunity to thank her for her past kindnesses.

"One can hardly believe that it is only seven years ago that I left home. So much water under the bridge since then for both of us, Willow!"

She nodded.

"It's good to see you well and happy now, Rupert," she said. "Maximillian is charming and I can well understand why you find him such a delightful companion. I used to worry in case you ended up as unhappily as the poor, unfortunate Oscar Wilde. Remember how we both loved his poems?"

"Max and I went to see his grave at Bagneux," Rupert told her. "His body was removed there five years ago, nine years after his death. Do you know, Willow, there are ten people who go to see his grave, as we did, for every one who goes to see the graves of Chopin, Balzac, de Musset."

"So he is honored in death," Willow commented. "Perhaps that is some small measure of compensation for the disgrace he suffered in his lifetime. Were he alive, he would doubtless be amused and proud that the great Epstein carved his tombstone."

Their conversation turned to family affairs, to Lucy's little daughter, Teo, and Dodie's expected second child. Rupert was naturally interested to hear from Willow the true story of Lucy's disappearance from home.

"Grandmère was an evil, cruel old woman," he said bitterly.

Willow did not argue the point. She said gently:

"We must try to forgive her, Rupert. She was after all a true product of her generation. The early Victorians were slaves to the values they had been taught. Grandmère believed the family should come first and that the ends always justified the means."

They were almost relieved when the moment came for them to return to the house and put away the unhappy memories they shared. As was customary, the family changed into evening clothes for dinner and Willow surveyed the large table with a feeling of contentment. Her beloved Toby sat at the head, Lucy on his right-hand side.

How pretty Lucy looks, she thought. I'm glad Alexis is here. He works too hard during the week! Her eyes turned to Oliver and Henry, both looking handsome and manly in their dinner jackets. The red-haired Henry was so frequent a visitor at Rochford that he was almost one of the family. Oliver was talking animatedly to Jane. Dear little Jane, always so good-natured, Willow reflected.

Rupert looked happy and proud of his friend, Maximillian. Judging by the ease with which the Count was conversing with everyone, he already seemed like an old friend.

I am at peace with my world, Willow thought, as her well-trained staff served the meal with their usual quiet efficiency. At this moment in my life, I am perfectly, absolutely happy.

Wishing everyone present to be as content as herself, she said to her guest:

"You must visit us more often, Count von Kruege."

"We were discussing the possibility before dinner, Mrs. Rochford," the man replied with his charming smile. "Perhaps in the summer around August, I think, we will be able to return."

"You will be more than welcome!" Willow murmured. But she had spoken automatically, for the Count's words had evoked a now familiar shiver of apprehension—a feeling she had only been able to describe to Toby in the past as a premonition. Now, as before, there seemed no logical reason for it. Summer was only three months away and there was nowhere in the world more peaceful than Rochford Manor and its gardens on a hot day when the sun turned the red bricks to gold and the willow trees to silver. The flower borders would be ablaze with color, the bright blood red of peonies, the blue of forget-me-nots, the orange of tiger lilies, the pink and white of carnations. The lavender border would be in full bloom, the heady perfume vying with the scent of roses in the sunshine. The roofs of the stables would shimmer with the movement of the swallows as they hurried to and from their nests. The children would be swimming once more in the lake...

Unaware of Willow's thoughts but as if to compound them, Toby's voice drifted down to her across the table, halting her reverie.

"Even if there *were* a minor war in the Balkans, I doubt

very much that there is any way in which England would become involved, Oliver. So I should think of some other occupation rather than joining the Royal Flying Corps."

"Alexis has promised to teach me to fly next holidays," Oliver's voice was excited and happy. "So if there *was* a war, Uncle Toby, Henry and I could shoot up the enemy from the sky. Wouldn't that be ripping?"

"Not if there were enemy planes shooting at you!" Alexis remarked with a grin. "Anyway, as your uncle said, if there was a war, young man, England wouldn't be involved, so that's that."

Willow felt the tension leave her body. Alexis, she thought, was in the Foreign Office and he should know, if anyone did, whether there was a genuine threat or not.

How silly I'm being! she chided herself silently as her eyes rested momentarily on her son's flushed, excited face. In a week's time, Oliver would be back at school, a boy again in his school uniform, with his trunk and tuck box. Whatever happened in Europe, he was far too young to be affected.

Nevertheless, the residue of fear remained. Despite all logical reasoning, that fear increased slowly until she could bear it no longer. She turned to look at the son whose safety seemed suddenly menaced.

"You are talking too much, Oliver," she reproved him sharply. "Grown-ups are not interested in your opinions. You forget that you are not yet a man, you know. You are only an ignorant boy for all your fine clothes!"

Oliver's face turned a fiery red. His dark eyes were bright with astonishment, for never before in his life had he known his mother to speak to him in such a tone or to use words so humiliating and cruel.

Chapter 14

❦

May—August 1914

ON HER RETURN TO LONDON AFTER THE EASTER HOLIDAY, LUCY did not at once rejoin the Montfervier-Ffoulkes set. Alexis had obtained tickets for the opera at Covent Garden and Lucy had only a week in which to find a new dress. It was to be a Gala Performance, with excerpts from *La Tosca*, *La Bohème* and *Aïda*, and was in honor of the King and Queen of Denmark who were in England on a State visit. Gillian Lennox informed Lucy that it was an occasion when the Opera House would be so illuminated by the diamond tiaras that lights would scarcely be needed.

"Absolutely everyone of importance will be there," Lucy told Alexis breathlessly. "King George, Queen Mary, the Prince of Wales, Princess Mary and also perhaps Queen Alexandra, the Queen Mother—although she is so deaf, she'd be unlikely to hear the lovely music. So I must look my very best. I've seen just the dress I would like to wear, Alexis, but it will cost seventy-five guineas." She paused, watching Alexis' face as she named such an enormous sum, before adding hurriedly: "It's really lovely, Alexis—it's made of pale blue floral-patterned silk, brocaded in gold thread. The bodice is embroidered in pearls and has cream and silvered beads and white paste stones embroidered onto a chiffon yoke." Her eyes sparkled with excitement as she continued: "The skirt is very fashionable, hobbled, so that I'll need new shoes, too, as my ankles will show. I thought silver glacé kid would be just right. Don't you think that would suit me, Alexis?"

Perhaps this was not the moment, Alexis thought, to raise the subject of the ever increasing bills Lucy had been running up recently. He had told her at the start of their marriage that she could charge anything she wanted to the accounts he opened for her at the various big stores. At first, these bills had been moderate but of late she seemed to be spending money indiscriminately.

"It *is* a Gala Performance, Alexis," Lucy went on. "We're bound to run into lots of people we know and so I do need something quite new that no one has seen before."

Alexis nodded. He would discuss finances with Lucy on some other occasion, he thought. At any moment Nanny would be bringing little Teo down to the drawing room for her evening visit to her parents before she was put to bed.

The little girl was now just over eighteen months old and had taken her first steps. Her vocabulary was increasing daily and she loved to sit on Alexis' knee and identify his eyes, nose, hair and 'mouff' as she referred to his lips, touching them with a dimpled finger. Lucy still tried to appear indifferent to the little girl's advances but Alexis noted that she was unable to resist returning the child's goodnight kiss when Nanny Meredith called to collect her.

But Lucy's moments of weakness were nearly always followed by a critical remark. "She's hopelessly spoilt" or "You really should not let her climb all over you, Alexis!" she would say. But Alexis was well aware of her true feelings, as indeed was Teo herself, for she showed no fear of a rebuff when she proffered her little face for her mother to kiss. Before long, Alexis thought, the child would have sufficient vocabulary to refer to her mother's visits to the nursery. It would be interesting to see if Lucy then continued to conduct them in such secrecy!

Having been told she could buy the chosen evening dress, Lucy was now happily looking through the latest fashion magazines to see what accessories she would need, and Alexis turned his thoughts to Roberta whom he had not seen since their meeting at her friend's flat. He realized that it was up to him to suggest a further assignation and after four days at Rochford sharing a bedroom with Lucy, he was tempted to make one. He needed the emotional outlet Roberta offered him, yet he was reluctant to make use of her in so blatant a fashion. No matter how much Roberta protested that she was more than willing to receive him on such terms, he still felt guilty. He felt guilty too, about his unfaithfulness to Lucy. He did not have the excuse that his wife was refusing him the intimacies of her bed. Lucy had indicated her willingness at Rochford and he had chosen to lie on the edge of the bed as far away from temptation as possible. At such moments when his body was on fire for her, he believed himself insane, or some kind of masochist that he should voluntarily put himself through these nightly ordeals. But in saner moments he knew that if he were ever to possess his wife's love, he must not now possess her body.

If only he had less respect and affection for Roberta, or less love for his wife, he thought wearily, how much easier life would be!

But Alexis could not avoid an encounter with Roberta sooner or later in the London social round. Inevitably he and Lucy came face to face with her at the opera when, in the interval, they joined the crowd of people stretching their legs in the foyer.

Lucy, radiant and beautiful in her new silk gown, greeted Roberta warmly.

"Isn't it all wonderful?" she asked. "Do you like my new dress, Roberta? Did you notice the dress the Queen of Denmark is wearing...?" She chattered on happily while Roberta's eyes met those of Alexis.

"I really must call in to see you soon, Lucy," Roberta said, and to Alexis: "I hope to see you, too, Alexis. You should come and visit Angus one day if you can find the time. It's far too long since he last saw you."

Alexis realized that this was the nearest Roberta would come to telling him that she would like to meet him again soon. He telephoned her from his office the following day and explained why he was avoiding her.

"Please try to understand, Roberta," he said. "It's just that I don't think our arrangement is fair to you. It isn't that I don't want to see you, I do. Will you come to dinner with Lucy and me one evening? I would like us to remain friends if it is possible."

If Roberta was disappointed she gave no indication of it but agreed to dine the following week at Cadogan Gardens.

Lucy meanwhile was reclaimed by her former set of friends. Now the house was either filled with their loud voices, music and laughter or it was so quiet when Alexis returned home from his office that he felt he was back in his bachelor days. He was unsure which state of affairs was the least disagreeable. He was determined not to let Lucy know how much he disliked her friends or their ill-mannered assumption that his house was theirs. Quite often he would be passed by one of them in the hall without even an exchange of names. But gradually he began to resent Lucy's continued absences in the evenings. He finally lost patience when she completely forgot that Roberta was dining with them and failed to return home. To make matters worse Cook had prepared dinner only for himself because, so Bulford informed him, the Countess had made no mention of a guest. As a consequence he and Roberta had to wait nearly an hour while a meal was being cooked.

Furious with Lucy, Alexis reflected that it could well be the early hours of the morning before she returned.

"It is the height of bad manners," he said angrily to Roberta. "I can do no more than apologize."

Roberta smiled.

"Lucy's forgetfulness may have upset you, Alexis, but surely we need not allow it to ruin our evening. Personally, I am quite content to have you all to myself!"

His anger evaporating, Alexis smiled ruefully. He was beginning to regret that he had not met Roberta at the flat after all. But it was too late now, he reflected. Nor was he really in the mood. His irritation with Lucy superseded any other emotion and that included the desire to make love to Roberta.

"You are more tolerant of Lucy than I am, Roberta," he said as Bulford brought in the drinks. "But then you do not have to suffer her friends as I do. They are a useless, good-for-nothing crowd of pleasure-seekers and I am not in the least happy about the influence they have on her. I try to make allowances since she is so much younger than I am. I do not want to spoil her amusement but I do wish her companions were less frivolous."

They talked with the ease of old friends, far into the night. His anger with Lucy now cooled, Alexis told Roberta some of the Rochford family history he had learned since his marriage. She was particularly curious about Rupert. One of her brothers had been with Kitchener in Sudan in 1894 when Rupert Rochford was sent home in a state of collapse. Roberta's brother had referred to him scathingly as 'a weak cowardly fellow, better fitted to be a woman than a soldier.' It was about the time of the Oscar Wilde trial and Roberta had wondered at the time if the Rochford boy was a homosexual. Angus believed he had been involved briefly with Lord Alfred Douglas. The incident had remained in her memory half-forgotten until she learned Alexis was marrying into the family. Now Alexis was able to enlighten her as to Rupert's real character.

"If you are broad minded enough to overlook his propensities, you'd find him an agreeable, interesting chap," Alexis said. "I liked his 'friend,' too; comes from an old family."

It was past one o'clock when finally Roberta rose to her feet and told Alexis that her departure was long overdue. Reluctantly, Alexis stood up and put his arm around her shoulders.

"Time always passes swiftly in good company!" he said as he led her to the door. He had sent Bulford off to bed some time ago and there were no servants about.

Roberta lifted her arms and put them round Alexis' neck.

"Goodnight, my dear!" she said, "and thank you for a lovely evening. Let's not leave it too long before we next meet. I'm really very fond of you, you know, Alexis."

"And I of you, Roberta!" Alexis said. There was more affection than passion between them as he bent his head and kissed her softly parted lips.

Through the closed door into the hall neither heard Lucy's key turn in the lock nor the creak as the heavy front door swung open. For once she was not accompanied by her group of friends but had traveled home alone in a cab. Her return therefore was unusually silent.

Lucy was in an angry mood. The man they all called 'The Baron' had tried to step beyond the accepted limits of friendship. He had stopped his car and attempted first to kiss her and then to lift her skirt. Lucy had slapped his face.

"Don't be such a prude, Lucy!" he had whined. "We all know you aren't in love with your husband. So what's wrong with a kiss or two, eh?"

"You've no right to say I don't love Alexis," Lucy had flared, her eyes flashing dangerously. "And in any event, what have my feelings for my husband got to do with my letting you treat me like a...a whore!"

The Baron had looked genuinely shocked.

"Great Scott, Lucy, there was no such thought in my mind. Look here, old girl, you *were* flirting with me at the dance, you can't deny it. You can't blame a chap for trying, now can you? I truly thought you wouldn't mind."

"Well, I do!" Lucy said fiercely. "And since it appears to be of interest to you, I don't like that sort of thing anyway. So I wouldn't kiss you even if I was willing to be unfaithful to Alexis—which I'm not. So leave me alone!"

Stupidly, the man tried to soften her mood. But when he put his arm tentatively around Lucy's shoulders she pulled away, opened the car door and ran off down the street. Before he could start the engine, she had hailed a passing taxicab and demanded to be driven to Cadogan Gardens.

Lucy was still too angry to notice that all the lights were blazing in the downstairs rooms. Now, as she opened the door into the drawing room and saw Roberta in Alexis' arms, she was too astonished to speak. Then as they stepped apart, their faces turning toward her, one thought dominated her mind—that her former suspicions were justified—Roberta Inman had once been Alexis' mistress and seemingly still was.

"Roberta is just leaving, Lucy," Alexis said calmly. "It would appear that you forgot she was our guest for dinner tonight!"

"Very conveniently, so far as I can see!" Lucy replied sarcastically. "Except that I seem to have returned home just a little too early."

"Lucy, Alexis and I were only saying good night," Roberta interposed quietly. "I'll leave now, if you will both excuse me."

She walked past Lucy, and Alexis went to open the front door for her. Lucy's taxicab had turned at the end of the road and was coming back along the street. Alexis hailed it and assisted Roberta into the back.

"It won't hurt Lucy to be a little jealous!" she said with a smile. "Keep her guessing, Alexis, that's my advice."

Lucy, however, was in no mood for guessing games. She wanted the question resolved once and for all. She was standing with her back to the fireplace, a look of determination on her face, as Alexis came into the room.

"You owe me an explanation, Alexis," she said, two angry spots of color burning in her cheeks.

Alexis went slowly to the table and poured himself a glass of brandy. He sat down and regarded Lucy with every outward appearance of coolness.

"I think perhaps *you* owe *me* an explanation," he said. "You had the exceedingly bad manners to forget to tell Cook that Roberta was coming to dinner. You yourself ignore the fact and return home at this late hour...Yet you have the effrontery to ask me to account for my behavior!"

"It's no use trying to make me feel guilty," Lucy cried. "I *did* forget Roberta was coming and it was rude and I'm sorry. As for where I was, I am surprised to hear you are interested, Alexis. But if you want to know, I went with my friends to the Empire Theater to see *The Dancing Doll*. Afterwards we dined at the Savoy and were on our way to Jerry Montfervier-

Ffoulkes' house to play some of his new gramophone records when a man you don't know tried to make love to me. I slapped his face, called a taxi and was driven home. Now would you care to account for *your* evening?"

Alexis was momentarily taken aback. He had tried not to ask himself if Lucy's madcap behavior ever included any sexual indiscretions. In his heart he did not think so. Nevertheless, he was glad to hear that she obviously did not encourage other men's advances.

Lucy took a step toward him. Her eyes were blazing.

"I suppose you are ashamed to admit that Roberta is still your mistress despite your marriage to me. I think it would have shown a lot more courage if you had told me from the first that you had an arrangement with her and that you would not require such services from me. At least then I would have understood why you did not want me!"

Alexis jumped to his feet and confronted her.

"That's simply not true, Lucy. I did want you . . . I still do."

"Then why don't you have me?" Lucy flashed back at him. "I've never once objected. What has that woman got that I don't have? That's what I want to know. I'm younger, prettier and there's nothing to show I ever had a child. Why should you prefer her body to mine?"

"I don't, Lucy!" Alexis' voice was very quiet as he sat down again in his chair, a look of hopelessness in his eyes. How could he ever explain to his wife that it was not the comparative attractions of their bodies that was important to him.

Lucy was regarding him furiously. It was not her feelings that were hurt, it was her pride, she thought. She would not have minded if Alexis had chosen to have a mistress had she herself denied him. That she could have understood. But that he preferred Roberta to her was unacceptable.

Slowly, methodically, she began to take off her clothes, ignoring Alexis' muttered protests. Dress, petticoat, chemise, drawers, stockings . . . each garment lay where it fell. When she was quite naked, she turned to confront him.

"Aren't you going to look at me, Alexis?" she asked, her voice no longer angry but low and inviting. "Are you really so enthralled by that old woman, Roberta Inman, that you don't want me?"

Alexis bent down and picked up the first piece of clothing that came to hand. It was her petticoat.

"Put that on," he ordered. "At once, Lucy—I mean it!"

"So my nudity offends you!" Lucy said, shrugging her shoulders. She pulled the thin crêpe de chine petticoat over her head. It clung provocatively to the points of her breasts and to the gentle curve of her hip bones. Her hair had fallen from its pins and she shook it loose as with a little laugh, she began to pirouette in front of Alexis.

"You have never seen me dance, have you?" she said. "I can dance the Cancan, you know. It used to be all the rage in Paris when I lived there. It drives men wild." Humming softly she twirled one of her bare feet and then kicked her leg high in the air. She was about to do the same with the other when Alexis once more jumped up from his chair. This time he caught hold of her and gripped her arms roughly.

"Stop it, Lucy!" he commanded in a low, hard voice. "For God's sake, stop it!"

Well aware of the effect she was having upon him, Lucy gazed up at his white face, her eyes smiling softly, invitingly. Alexis felt a brief moment of despair as he realized that his will was not strong enough to resist Lucy's calculated intent to arouse him. Her body was unbearably warm and sweet as she pressed herself against him, her mouth temptingly close.

With a small cry, he buried his face in her hair and his arms tightened around her. He felt her hands unbuttoning his shirt and then the light touch of her fingers against his bare chest. Her voice was a low murmur, her words indistinguishable, as he lifted her up in his arms and carried her to the sofa.

But as he bent over her and she drew him fiercely down upon her, he saw her eyes and the unmistakable look of determination in them. This time he could hear her quite clearly as she said:

"Now we will see who is better at this—Roberta or me. After we've done it, Alexis, you'll wonder why you ever bothered with her."

Slowly Alexis stood up, his arms falling to his sides. He looked down at his wife's perfect little body as she awaited his pleasure.

"We aren't going 'to do it,' as you put it, Lucy. If it makes you feel any happier, we do not need 'to do it' for me to know that your body would give me far more pleasure than Roberta's ever could. I love you, you see. I don't expect you to understand but I know you are not acting at this moment out of love for me but only to prove yourself to me. You are my wife, Lucy, and I will not treat you as a whore who must prove her worth."

He knew from Lucy's mystified expression that his explanation made no sense to her. She looked bewildered, angry, disappointed and—Alexis almost smiled at the irony—insulted.

All desire now gone, he felt only sadness and a deep pity not only for himself but for Lucy, too. The gulf between them had widened, he thought wearily. They had been married for two years and it seemed that they had even less in common than on their honeymoon. Lucy had her own friends, her own way of life. He had his work, his friendship with Roberta. The only thing they shared was little Teo and their house and servants.

"Go to bed, Lucy," he said wearily. "It's very late and you must be as tired as I am."

Lucy watched in silence as Alexis walked slowly out of the room. She felt bitter and humiliated. She was also confused. It was not fair of Alexis to refuse to accept *her* contribution to their marriage. By refusing to do so he left her hopelessly in his debt. It left her also with a feeling of insecurity. If Alexis did not need her, then he might one day tire of her as Maurice had done. Alexis might leave her as Mama had left her husband. If the sickly old Angus Inman were to die, Alexis might choose to replace her with Roberta.

The clock on the mantelshelf chimed the hour. The noise seemed to echo round the big, empty room. Slowly Lucy got up from the sofa and began to pick up her discarded clothes.

It had been altogther a horrible day, she thought. People, when you got to know them, were always disappointing. Roberta, whom she had thought her friend, had betrayed her in a way Yvette would never have done. Now Alexis had made her feel as if she were not fit to be his wife but should have remained in *Le Ciel Rouge* where she belonged. He had been unkind, cruel to reject her.

It did not occur to Lucy as she made her way up to bed that it was not Alexis who had made her feel so degraded but that she had been taught to degrade herself. Love had had no place at *Le Ciel Rouge*. A woman's worth was judged by her ability to give a man the bodily satisfaction he demanded. Love, Madame advised them, was a sentimental folly that brought only poverty or tears.

Alexis had no right to make her feel inadequate just because she could not give him the kind of love he felt for her. She would have done so long since if she had understood what this emotion was that so tormented him. She liked him, respected him, admired him. She was grateful to him. She was happy to be his wife and happy to please him. What more could she give him if he chose to reject her body?

Her indignation at the injustice of life was rapidly giving way to a sense of despair. Lucy opened her bedroom door, and told the weary little maid that she would put herself to bed, for her pride was still intact and she would not allow even Polly to see her tears.

Willow laid down the letter from James McGill and looked across the breakfast table at Toby.

"James is worried that Dodie might lose the baby. Their doctor seems in some doubt that she will after all be able to carry it full time."

"When is it due?" Toby asked, laying down his *Times*.

"Not until November. I would like to write and suggest she come to us at once," Willow said thoughtfully. "She can bring Zandra and Violet. James can join us at the end of the term. Patience can take care of Zandra for the time being— in fact, she will enjoy doing so."

"Just as you wish, my dear," Toby said, his mind still engrossed in the news item he had been reading. He decided not to add to his wife's concerns, especially as there was no real need to do so according to the way in which the news had been presented. The Archduke Francis Ferdinand and his morganatic wife, the Duchess of Hohenberg, had been assassinated at Sarajevo, the capital of Bosnia, on 28th June. The Heir to the Imperial throne of Austro-Hungaria had been murdered by a Slav fanatic and now, so the paper said, Austria was accusing Serbia of complicity in the crime.

Toby sighed. There had been a great deal of trouble recently in the Balkan states with crises over Bosnia and Herzogovina as well as the Agadir affair. It was to be hoped that this latest situation would also resolve itself, but on his last visit to Rochford, Alexis had expressed a degree of anxiety. Although he had told Toby nothing about the work he was engaged in at the Foreign Office, Toby was aware that Alexis must be involved in the Balkan situation. Coming as he did from a distinguished Croatian family, not only did he speak Serbo-

Croat, German and Hungarian as a native, but he undoubtedly still had family contacts in the Balkan states.

Alexis had told him on one occasion that his mother had been born Countess Zrinski whose family were known for their resistance to the Hapsburgs. The Slavs, he had explained, were both anti-German and anti-Hungarian; and it was as a result of a conspiracy in 1880 to unseat the pro-Hungarian government in Croatia that his parents, the Count and Countess Zemski, had decided to bring up their family in the more settled environment of England.

Alexis had led Toby to understand the situation could become very serious, and Toby respected his views. He continued to watch the Balkan situation with interest, and when Alexis and Lucy came to stay during the hot summer weekends, had long, private discussions with his stepson-in-law.

"I am afraid the repercussions are widening," Alexis admitted when, on 25th July, Vienna sent an ultimatum to Belgrade demanding, in effect, that Serbia should surrender her freedom. "Now Russia is mobilizing to defend Serbia and the Slav minorities in the Austro-Hungarian Empire. Germany, I suspect, will warn Russia and her ally, France, to keep out of their affairs."

Alexis' forecast became fact. Serbia was determined to resist and Austria declared war. On 30th July, they bombed Belgrade, the capital of Serbia.

There was no longer any question of keeping the fear of war from Willow and at the Bank Holiday weekend when Alexis arrived with Lucy on Saturday, August 1st, it was inevitable that talk should turn to war. They were having dinner that night when Alexis was called to the telephone. When he returned, his face grave, he told them that Germany had declared war on Russia.

"I'm sorry, but I shall have to drive back to London," he told Willow and Toby. "Parliament is meeting on Monday and I shall have a lot of work to do before then."

Oliver's eyes were bright with excitement.

"Do you think there's a chance *we'll* be drawn into it?" he asked.

Aware of Willow's anxious gaze, Alexis tried to speak lightly.

"We must hope not. Everyone is against war, Oliver—the people, the politicians, the King."

But on the following day, the British Fleet was mobilized and Winston Churchill, the first Sea Lord, reported to the

King that they were at readiness for war. On Bank Holiday Monday, Germany demanded free passage for her troops through neutral Belgium and the mood of the British people changed. On Tuesday, August 3rd, German troops crossed the frontier near Liège, violating Belgium's neutrality. Britain delivered an ultimatum to Germany stating that she would declare war upon her if she did not withdraw all her troops from Belgian soil. Both Lloyd George and Asquith sat up until midnight awaiting the reply, but no answer came and on August 4th, Britain was at war.

Alexis telephoned the news to Rochford, obliging a sleepy-eyed Dutton to wake Toby and bring him to the telephone.

"No need to tell anyone else until the morning," Alexis said, "but I thought you should know. The crowds are already gathering in vast numbers outside the Palace, waving and cheering almost as if it were good news to be celebrated. Tell Lucy she is to remain at Rochford with Teo and Nanny until I decide if they are to return to London."

When Toby opened his *Times* the following morning, the news therefore, came as no surprise to him. In huge black type the banner headlines declared that Britain was now at war.

He looked at Willow's white face and offered the only comfort he could.

"Don't worry, my love," he said consolingly. "It will all be over long before Oliver is old enough to be involved."

At the time, Toby genuinely believed, as did the rest of the world, that this ill-conceived, irrational war would not last for long.

Chapter 15

⌒⌒

August—December 1914

AT FIRST, IT SEEMED AS IF THE WAR WAS GOING WELL. LIÈGE AND Meuse were successfully defended against the German onslaught and the Belgian people were optimistic; moreover, the French and British armies were expected to arrive at any day. But by 17th August, the Belgian army was falling back and it seemed that the Germans would soon be entering Brussels. Rumors filtered through of German atrocities: villages being burnt, men and women shot down, churches desecrated, massacres, with drunken soldiers raping, looting and mutilating their victims.

The Belgian King who was in Antwerp, declared Brussels an undefended city in order to avoid useless bloodshed. Flags were taken down, shutters put up as the wounded joined the crowds of refugees fleeing into the city before the advancing enemy.

On 20th August, twenty thousand Germans marched into Brussels to be followed next day by ever increasing numbers of weary soldiers bringing their wounded with them.

In the meantime, the British Expeditionay Force were fighting side by side with the French in the neighborhood of Mons and Charleroi on the Franco-Belgium border. Throughout the night of Sunday, 23rd August and Monday morning, the Allied armies attempted to stop the lines of advancing German infantry. But although they fought bravely, their losses were appalling. Among the casualties was George Barratt of the 9th Lancers. As the army was forced into retreat, he lay unconscious and unnoticed in a deep shell hole on the battlefield.

Those who survived began their fight back to the River Marne—exhausted remnants of the 9th Lancers, the 18th Hussars, the 4th Dragoons, the Royal Munster Fusiliers, the Middlesex, the 2nd Worcestershire and Scottish Borderers, and the West Kents. They were harried continually by the Germans who aimed at their feet and legs with rapid fire in an attempt to obtain prisoners and halt a retreat.

It was thirteen days after the battle when the weary Allied army finally crossed the river and made a stand. If the city of Paris was to be saved, the British and French had to hold this new line. As it was, the Germans were far too close to the city.

In Paris, Pelham Rochford tried to persuade Silvie to go to England out of harm's way. Like all their compatriots, they were appalled when the Germans swept forward like a tidal wave across France toward Paris, apparently immune to the Allied attempts to stop them. Pelham announced his intention to offer his services to the Army. Silvie was outraged.

"Nothing will induce me to leave France when she is in danger," she said, adding, "nor would I leave you, Pelham. As to your joining the Army, you are far too old at forty-three. Leave the fighting to the younger men. You and I will find other ways to help our countries."

They both realized that the Château d'Orbais, their country house in Épernay, had almost certainly been overrun.

In Brussels, Maximillian von Kruege was equally determined to remain where he was. His sympathies lay with his mother's people, the French.

"How could they be otherwise?" he said to Rupert. "You know already my aversion to my Prussian father—and that goes for all his relatives too." He sympathized with Rupert who firmly rejected the idea of escaping to the safety of England. They believed like many others that the war would be over quickly and that the Germans would not concern themselves with noncombatants residing harmlessly in what had been declared a neutral city.

"Besides," Rupert commented, "I would feel cowardly were I to run away when a little, middle-aged English woman chooses to remain here, apparently without the least concern for the German army's advance across Belgium."

He was referring to a fragile, gray-haired lady who had visited them several times to look through their collection of books, and had on one occasion bought an old medical reference book. Her name was Edith Cavell and, a nurse herself, she ran a nurses training school in Brussels.

It was Miss Cavell who had managed to get hold of an English newspaper from which they had learned for the first time of the British and French retreat. Not that this depressing news had altered her decision to remain in Brussels where she was nursing the wounded of all nationalities.

"I shall not go home until I am forced to do so," she said firmly.

"When *she* leaves, we will!" Rupert said to Max with a glint of humor. "If she comes in again, Max, I must ask her if she knows of any way I could get a letter to England. I would like to let Willow and Toby know that we are alive and well."

At Rochford Manor the atmosphere was one of anxiety as news of the Allied army reverses filled the newspapers. Toby had bought a packet of flags and a map of Europe which he had pinned to the schoolroom blackboard, placing it in the hall where both family and servants could note the movement of the front line. Its proximity to Paris was unnerving and it was now apparent to them all that the Union Jack would not be flying in Berlin by Christmas.

A large poster appeared in the village shop, 'THERE'S ROOM FOR YOU, ENLIST TODAY' the words said above and below a picture of British Tommies leaving for France by train. The chauffeur, Bill Longhurst had already succumbed to this call to arms. He had enlisted in the Royal Engineers where he hoped his knowledge of mechanics might be of use in the Signals.

"Mr. Howard has done the same as me," he informed them. "He'll be a dispatch rider like as not, though he won't find them army motor bikes as fast as his Bugatti!"

Toby and Willow could do no less than give their approval to the chauffeur's intention to do his patriotic duty but Dodie's maid, Violet, when she heard the news, burst into tears. She and Bill had 'an understandin',' she told Willow. Although there had been no engagement, with Bill leaving for the front, they now wanted to marry as soon as possible. Dodie and James gave their consent and a short wedding ceremony was held for the couple at St. Stephen's a few days before Bill departed to do his training.

Sir John Barratt, Sam Sharples and now Willow and Toby responded to the Government's request for horses for war service. They were needed not only for the cavalry but for pulling gun carriages, supply carts and ambulances. Two of the hunters had left the Rochford stables already and two of the four carriage greys were to be collected next week.

At least Oliver was safely back at school, Toby tried to

cheer Willow as September gave way to October and yet another month went by. The Allies had halted the German advance toward the coast and were now dug in at Ypres where they had made a final stand. But the casualties had been astronomical, the Allies being outnumbered by never less than eight to one. In the infantry alone, only forty-four officers remained of the four hundred who had embarked from Britain, and not more than two thousand three hundred and thirty-six out of twelve thousand men survived the heroic repulse of the German advance.

"Such terrible loss of life!" Sir John said sadly to Willow. He had still received no news of his son, George, whom he steadfastly refused to believe dead. Now Howard too, was at the front, having joined the Royal Engineers soon after George had been posted as 'Missing.'

Lady Barratt managed somehow to conceal her fears in public, although privately she expressed to Willow her dread of the postman's knock lest it should herald a telegram announcing George's death—or Howard's. She had shown Willow a letter from one of her godsons serving with the British Expeditionary Force describing his miraculous survival when his battalion had been all but wiped out in Belgium.

"When we went into battle on 30th October, we had twenty-nine officers and nine hundred men," the young man had written. *"Now I am one of only five and I have lost all but one hundred and fifty of my men..."*

Lady Barratt opened the big ballroom at Glenfield Hall each Wednesday to encourage women to knit comforts for the soldiers. Not only her friends but her servants and other local women sat in an equitable circle knitting mufflers, balaclava helmets, mittens and socks for the troops. Her daughter, Eleanor, now twelve, young Jane and even the eleven-year-old Alice joined the group, together with as many of the Rochford female servants as could be spared.

Lucy had insisted on returning to London with Teo. Willow had been sad to see them go, but she was overjoyed when on 30th November Dodie gave birth to a baby son. The little boy was christened Jamie and although Peter Rose, the family doctor, was a trifle concerned about his small birth weight, the baby soon started to thrive under the devoted care of both Patience and Violet. Willow was delighted at the addition to her household and so, temporarily at least, her thoughts were diverted from the war.

* * *

London was no longer a city ablaze with lights. Fear of possible attacks from the air by German zeppelins had prompted the Government to order a partial blackout. But other than a strong anti-German feeling amongst the people—even to the extent of attacking shopkeepers with German-sounding names—life continued much as usual. There was always the comedian, Harry Tate, to give the apprehensive Londoner the relief of laughter. In the revue, *Business as Usual* at the Hippodrome, he mocked wartime absurdities in his sketch 'Fortifying the Home,' and people flocked to the Saturday matinées in their hundreds.

Two people among the many who saw this revue had other reasons besides Harry Tate's skits for having enjoyed his performance one rainy November day. They sat now at a small table in a Lyons tea shop not far from the Hippodrome, smiling tentatively at one another with the caution of strangers. They had met but half an hour previously when the middle-aged gentleman who was now ordering tea for them both, upset his box of chocolates over his lady companion's lap.

Madeleine Villier eyed her host surreptitiously across the tea table. She judged him to be, like herself, in the mid-forties. He was clean-shaven, not particularly handsome but pleasant looking with friendly blue eyes and a ready smile. Immaculately dressed in a dark suit, he had both the appearance and manners of a gentleman.

"I really do feel I must introduce myself, dear lady," he said as the uniformed waitress deposited tea and cakes on the marble-topped table in front of them. "My name is Anthony Black. Will you now do me the honor of telling me your name?"

He was undoubtedly polite, charming and flatteringly interested in her, the woman thought as he informed her that he was an author. When she revealed that she was a trained secretary, he joked that he could not have picked a better person over whom to empty his box of chocolates.

"Who knows but that I shall soon need an efficient secretary to type my manuscripts, Miss Villier!" he said as he passed the plate of cakes for the second time.

Before the little tea party had ended, he was inviting Madeleine, whose spinster status he had established, to accompany him one evening to the music hall. A bachelor such as himself, he told her, was often lonely and she would be doing him a great favor were she to accept his invitation.

With the sufficient degree of hesitation required in order not to appear too eager, Madeleine Villier agreed to the proposed meeting. She herself was unbearably lonely, she thought bitterly. Life had been cruel to her and there had of late seemed very little hope for the future. At forty-three, she did not expect to attract a husband. Her former blond prettiness had disappeared and her fair complexion had faded to an unprepossessing sallow color that even the use of rouge could not improve.

It was all the harder to accept the advance of the years, she thought, when you had once been as pretty as she had. At the age of twenty-one she had had the Honorable Francis Rochford at her feet, prepared to do practically anything to gain her favor. She could have married him; but she believed, mistakenly as it turned out, that she could do even better for herself despite the fact that she was a New Zealand girl without wealth or title and only an aging aunt to launch her in London society.

But Madeleine had not received another proposal and when her aunt had died, leaving her only the smallest of legacies, she had been forced to use the money to pay for a secretarial training in order to support herself in the future.

In her early thirties, Madeleine Villier had still had her looks. The Member of Parliament with whom she had managed to obtain a job took a fancy to her and, since he was already married, she had agreed to become his mistress. It was to have been only a temporary state of affairs, he had told her, for he intended eventually to divorce his wife. Several years later, under pressure from Madeleine, he finally admitted that he was afraid of the resultant scandal his wife had threatened if he divorced her. It might disrupt his career in politics. Realizing that there was no future in the relationship, Madeleine left him. By the time she was nearing forty, she was prepared to marry the first man who asked her. This turned out to be an impoverished army major who, being considerably older than Madeleine, was tempted by what remained of her 'chocolate box' prettiness. He proposed. Madeleine accepted, believing that even life on an army officer's pay would be preferable to earning her own living indefinitely.

But the Major soon tired of her. When war broke out in

August, he was posted overseas and promptly terminated their engagement.

Madeleine was furious and a little frightened. She had left the employ of her M.P. and was now typing dreary legal documents for a solicitor. Her pay was minimal and it was all she could do to maintain her aunt's little house in St. John's Wood. Mr. Anthony Black, author and therefore self-supporting, could well turn out to be the solution to her problems, she decided.

Before their second meeting was over Madeleine was even more convinced that her Saturday afternoon at the Hippodrome had been her lucky day. Anthony, as he now insisted she call him, had heard that a titled gentleman by the name of Count Zemski was in need of a personal secretary. Anthony could not recall how he had come by the information, but he strongly advised Madeleine to apply for the position.

"Your working conditions would be far more congenial," he said kindly, "since you would almost certainly be employed at the Count's large house in Cadogan Gardens."

Madeleine was delighted, not only by her new friend's thoughtfulness but by the prospect of a better job. Two days later, on a Saturday morning, she reported to Cadogan Gardens.

Alexis was surprised to see Madeleine. He had not advertised the post with an agency and he was curious to know how she had heard that he needed secretarial help. Anthony Black had instructed Madeleine to make no mention of his knowledge of the vacancy.

"It could get me into a spot of bother," he had said vaguely. "I'm repeating something I was not supposed to overhear."

She therefore told Alexis that she had heard of his requirements through friends of the Lennoxes. Hilary Lennox, so Anthony had told her, worked in the Foreign Office with Alexis, and Madeleine could claim a vague connection with Lennox's wife, Louise. Alexis did not question her further as he intended to take up her references in due course.

"Not that it really matters very much how you came to know of the vacancy," Alexis said with his pleasant smile. "Provided you can do the work and that you have good references, I shall be delighted to be so quickly accommodated."

Madeleine Villier seemed to him to fit exactly the picture he had in mind of the kind of woman he required—middle-aged, well trained and, since she had worked for both an M.P.

and a solicitor, he presumed she was discreet. Her typing was quick and accurate during the short test he gave her.

On Monday morning he took up her references, which were impeccable. The firm of solicitors said that they were sorry to lose her; the Member of Parliament, afraid lest Madeleine should ever betray him, gave her the highest praise. Alexis had asked Hilary if he would check with his wife if she knew Madeleine Villier personally and she'd confirmed that the woman had once been a visitor at Glenfield although she couldn't recall meeting her recently. Alexis, reassured by Madeleine's connection with the Barratts, asked no further questions. When Madeleine called two days later at his request, Alexis told her that the job was hers.

"And I have you to thank, Anthony," Madeleine told her companion that evening. "I am really most grateful. It was kind of you to think of me."

It was almost too good to be true, Madeleine thought a few weeks later. She had not expected to become emotionally involved with Anthony Black but she was finding somewhat to her surprise, that she was responding more and more readily to his flattery. He treated her with utmost respect and an almost old-fashioned courtesy which she found a pleasant change after the Major. He had been given to calling her 'old girl' and patting her on the bottom as if she were a horse or dog. Moreover, he had had a partiality to pickled onions and suffered from halitosis—or rather Madeleine had suffered from it. Their brief engagement had been singularly unromantic, whereas this new friend went out of his way to court her.

Madeleine was no longer in doubt that he found her attractive. If all went well it might not be long before he began to think of marriage. It seemed the obvious ultimate solution for two middle-aged people who were lonely and shared so much in common, she told herself. Madeleine began to pay increasing attention to her appearance.

Count Zemski said that she might begin her employment after Christmas.

"We shall be going down to my wife's family in Kent for the holiday," he had told her. "I expect to be at Rochford Manor until the New Year unless my work prevents it. So shall we decide upon 1st January for you to commence work?"

Madeleine gave no outward sign of the shock that his mention of Rochford Manor gave her. It was twenty years since she herself had last set foot in Rochford Manor. Momentarily, she was unsure whether to tell her new employer of her previous association with his in-laws. Lady Rochford's daughter, the Countess Zemski, was still unknown to her but it would not be unlikely for one of the older generation of Rochfords to appear at Cadogan Gardens and recognize her; or the Count might mention her by name at the Manor.

She decided to admit to a casual acquaintance with the family in the past without referring to her stormy affair with Francis. When Anthony heard she had been on friendly terms with the Rochfords, he was clearly impressed by her connection.

"You're really far too superior a person to be going out with a chap like me," he said modestly. "You deserve someone more interesting."

"I'm perfectly happy with what I have, thank you," Madeleine replied with a coy smile. She was rewarded when Anthony took her hand and with a romantic gesture that might have been made by her matinée idol, Gerald du Maurier, raised it to his lips.

Down at Rochford Manor, Willow was doing her best to prepare once more for Christmas. But her heart was not really in it.

"I shall miss Pelham and Silvie," she said sadly to Toby. "Philip will not be home either, and I hate to think of Mark all alone in America!"

Toby put his arm around her and hugged her.

"This isn't like you, my love," he said gently. "You must stop counting your misfortunes and count your blessings instead. We have Dodie and James, Zandra and Jamie—none of whom were with us last year. And Oliver will be back tomorrow and Lucy, Alexis and Teo will be here by Christmas Eve."

Willow attempted a smile.

"You're quite right, of course. I'm nothing but an old misery!"

She went upstairs to the nurseries. Violet was putting little Jamie to bed while Patience sat watching the three little girls in the schoolroom. Alice, Eleanor Barratt and little Zandra were planning a nativity play to entertain the grown-ups and Patience had been persuaded to sew their costumes.

The children surrounded Willow with glad cries.

"We need a crib, Mama," Alice told her. "Patience says we

can't borrow the wooden cradle because Jamie's using it, but can't he be put somewhere else just for as long as our play lasts?"

"Put him in the manger, I say!" remarked little Zandra with a wicked grin. Willow smiled. This child of Dodie's was developing into quite a personality. Only yesterday afternoon she had requested that Willow should read her a story. When they were comfortably seated side by side on the sofa, Zandra had proceeded to read to Willow a tale from the Bible which she had memorized and now repeated in an adult tone of voice. Every once in a while, she would stop and inquire:

"Now you do understand what I'm saying, don't you, Aunt Willow?" Or: "You know who Jesus was, don't you? There's a good girl!"

Willow had been hard put not to let the child see her amusement. Zandra was a perfect little mimic and a bundle of energy. Dodie could easily have spoiled her, Willow thought. There had been a stage in her life when with her deformities it seemed she had no chance of marrying, far less of bearing a healthy child. Watching Zandra grow up must for her mother be like reliving her own invalid childhood without the handicaps she had suffered, she reflected.

Lucy's little Teo, now two years old, was a far more docile child and inevitably, because her devoted Nanny did everything for her, she lacked inventiveness or independence although she was good-natured and only too happy to respond when someone engaged her attention.

Willow left the schoolroom and opened the door of the night nursery. Teo was enjoying her afternoon nap in her cot. Dodie's Jamie was asleep in the cradle beside her. Willow sighed as she closed the door. She did hope so much that Lucy and Alexis would have another child. Alexis surely must want a son, she thought. She wished she could feel more confident about Lucy's marriage. On the surface all seemed to be well. Alexis was always kind and attentive to his wife. Yet Willow sensed that their relationship lacked the intimacy of Dodie's and James'—or her own and Toby's. But she and Lucy had never become close as she had once hoped. Willow tried to mask her disappointment and only Toby was aware of it.

"Let's be grateful Lucy has adapted so well to her new life," he said comfortingly. "Her return to us so nearly proved disastrous and we should thank God that no one has ever suspected her past life and that Teo is accepted everywhere as Alexis' child."

"We should perhaps thank Alexis rather than God!" Willow replied with a touch of irony.

Christmas Day passed uneventfully with the traditional service at St. Stephens followed by a huge lunch with crackers for the children to pull—an innovation which Grandmère in her day had greatly disapproved of but which Willow had introduced. Alexis took Pelham's place as the red-robed Father Christmas and dispensed presents from beneath the Christmas tree. After tea they enjoyed the usual party games and the little girls' nativity play which the servants were invited upstairs to watch.

On Boxing Day Oliver went shooting with Alexis and Toby on Sir John's estate. Henry informed him that a German airplane had dropped a bomb on Dover and on Christmas Day, a seaplane had bombed the Thames.

"I must tell Alexis," Oliver said excitedly. "Now he can join the Royal Flying Corps and bomb the Germans. I bet they haven't a pilot to match him."

As soon as he got home he rushed off to tell Lucy the news.

"I do wish I were old enough to do the same," he said to her. "With a bit of luck the war will last long enough for Mark and Henry and me to join up. Don't you wish you were a young man, Lucy, instead of a girl?"

No, she did not, Lucy told him sharply. For the first time in her life, she felt really angry with Oliver and totally alienated from his way of thinking. She could not understand why people talked of war as something noble, glorious, inevitable; why people couldn't simply talk over their differences and resolve them without killing each other. She did not want the war to last long enough for him to be involved, to go 'missing' like poor George Barratt. But the real source of her anger was the thought he had put into her head—that Alexis was a trained pilot and might all too easily be called upon to face the terrible dangers of war...to fight battles that she imagined could be none the less dangerous for being in the air.

Chapter 16

January—March 1915

A GERMAN BY THE NAME OF VON KRAEVAL HAD BECOME GOVERNOR of Brussels which was no longer under Belgian control. Rupert and Maximillian's old acquaintance, General von Bissing, had been appointed Governor of the whole country.

"A piece of good fortune for us," Max said. "We can always appeal to him if we encounter any trouble."

An edict had been promulgated to the effect that all foreigners whose countries were at war with Germany must report to the *École Militaire*, to be registered and given an identity card with their photograph on it. Moreover, every householder was required to notify the authorities if there was an addition to their numbers. This was a vain attempt by the Germans to outwit the numerous people who were hiding Allied soldiers in their homes.

Until now, Rupert and Max had resisted the occasional demand for help from Belgian citizens who, knowing that Rupert was an Englishman, brought soldiers to them to hide. They had redirected the fugitives to the English nurse, Edith Cavell, who they knew was hiding a large number of Allied wounded in her clinic in the *Rue de la Culture*. This woman had failed to obey the German order issued the previous September to all English nurses demanding that they should return home at once. Ignoring the edict, she and the few nurses who remained in Brussels with her had continued to tend Allied and enemy soldiers as well as Belgian civilians. Seemingly fearless, she had devised a means of escape for her Allied wounded by obtaining false identity cards for them and employing guides to conduct them to the Dutch border.

Rupert and Max were filled with admiration for the woman's courage and soon after Christmas, they decided to offer limited assistance. Max had a Kodak camera and a large supply of film which he was prepared to use to take the necessary photographs required for the false identity cards.

Nurse Cavell had welcomed the offer. Max and Rupert were known to have regular visitors to their home on account of their rare books business. If the Germans should see the 'civilian' attired soldiers entering or leaving the premises where they were photographed, they were unlikely to be suspicious.

Nevertheless, the work was dangerous and became increasingly so as Nurse Cavell's escape route became more widely known and more and more Allied soldiers found their way to Brussels. Men who had been hidden by peasants in attics and barns were brought in from the countryside. Doctors, priests, nuns, dentists, a Princess and even an Abbé were all sending their concealed soldiers to Brussels in the hope that Nurse Cavell could assist them to safety.

Rupert stood now regarding Max at work in his darkroom and said thoughtfully:

"You know, Max, Miss Cavell was right when she said the other night that it is pointless doing such work half-heartedly. Her words when I spoke of the danger of being arrested were: *'Whether we have done much or little, we shall be punished in any case, so let us save as many of these unhappy men as possible.'* We have room to hide several men in our attic. I think we should offer to do so."

"It is as you wish, Rupert," Max said as he placed a number of negatives in a container of developing fluid. "If you are not afraid, then I am not."

"I am more than frightened!" Rupert replied, smiling ruefully. "In fact, I'm a terrible coward about most things. As a child I was frightened of the dark, frightened of my grandmother, frightened of being bullied at school—I lived in fear. I suppose in a way I should be well accustomed to the feeling."

"We don't *have* to become involved," Max said quietly. "And if things went wrong it might be worse for you, being an Englishman, than for me."

Rupert shrugged.

"Miss Cavell was right—we must save as many as possible," he said firmly.

All five Belgian servants employed by Max and Rupert were unquestionably loyal and could be trusted absolutely. The main difficulty in adopting the fugitive soldiers was that of obtaining extra food for them. Belgium normally imported four-fifths of her grain and now, with Antwerp in German hands, the sea routes were closed. Uncut crops from last year's harvest had rotted in the fields; refugees from the fighting zones who had poured into Brussels had swollen the city's population and increased the growing shortages alarmingly. It was far easier to obtain civilian clothing for the escapers than sustenance for them while they were in hiding.

There was a public kitchen where the poor and unemployed were given soup and a little bread, but it was mainly due to the generosity of the Americans that the population were still able to obtain the necessities of life. Max and Rupert were forced more and more often to delve into their dwindling resources of money. Rupert no longer received from England the regular payments arising from interest on the capital left to him on his thirtieth birthday by his grandfather. They began, therefore, to sell some of their books to the German officers. This entailed taking extra precautions to ensure that one of their German customers did not coincide with the arrival of a fugitive to be photographed.

It was certainly a dangerous path they were treading, but Rupert was determined to help his country against the Germans. After all, he often thought, his own family might one day need help and he would not care to think of an Englishman in enemy territory refusing them aid.

Much to Silvie's dismay, Pelham had carried out his intentions to offer his services in the Army. But the Colonel he had seen in Paris had been unable to guarantee him service in the field. Pelham had no taste for desk work, his nature demanding action of a physical kind.

He and Silvie had fretted throughout the months of September and October, accurate news of the fighting being extremely hard to obtain. Pelham suspected that most of the official communiqués were far from factual. However, by November there was no longer any doubt that the Germans had been pushed back to the east of Rheims. Although it was difficult to ascertain the exact amount of damage the enemy bombardment had done to the great Cathedral, the whole of Paris was shocked by such a gross act of vandalism.

Silvie suggested they should drive down to Épernay, for she was concerned for the many beautiful antiques in the Château d'Orbais. Pelham might not have agreed had he been able to visualize the scene that would meet their eyes when, after a long difficult journey due to the congestion of troop movements, they finally turned into the drive of the Château.

Although the building itself was not a ruin, the stonework had been pitted by shelling. There was not one window intact and the lawns had been churned up by the movement of horse-drawn and mechanical vehicles. But the interior of the Château was indeed ruined. The debris of a departing army lay everywhere—dust, dirt, broken furniture, glass, field tele-phone wires, damaged equipment. The beautiful carpets were littered with empty champagne bottles and were mud-encrusted. The valuable paintings and objets d'arts were gone.

Upstairs, the scene was almost more heart breaking. The delicate satins and brocades were torn and stained and soldiers had obviously slept in the beds in their filthy blood-stained uniforms.

But after the first shock had worn off, Pelham and Silvie were united in their determination not to return to Paris. Several of Silvie's old servants, including her elderly cook, Marie, appeared from one of the farms where they had hidden during the German invasion.

For the next few weeks, with the help of Marie and the old gardener, Pelham and Silvie set about restoring some order out of the chaos. Leaving most of the Château empty, they made a small suite of rooms as comfortable as possible for themselves, and Marie managed to salvage sufficient pots and pans to reopen the kitchen. For a little while, Pelham's energies were diverted by these unaccustomed activities, but before long, his thoughts turned once again to ways and means of involving himself directly in the war. He knew the fighting continued to the northeast along the River Aisne and discussing the battles one evening with the local priest, he was told of a Curé behind the lines who was hiding several Allied soldiers. Pelham at once hit upon the idea of crossing through the German lines in his car.

"I shall become a second Scarlet Pimpernel!" he announced to his shocked wife. "I always did enjoy the Baroness Orczy stories. I know most of that battle area as well as I know Havorhurst."

On many occasions he had shot pheasant and partridge over that countryside with a French Vicomte who had a hunt-ing lodge, near the *Fôret de la Montagne*.

Despite Silvie's protests, he made an experimental sortie, twice passing through the enemy lines without detection. But his subsequent sorties in search of Allied soldiers were of necessity infrequent. He dared not travel in bright moonlight lest his car, now painted black, should be a visible target for the German guns. Nor could he drive after a heavy rainfall when his wheels might become bogged down in the thick mud of the farm tracks. He had nonetheless so far brought over a dozen wounded back to safety.

Silvie dared not write of Pelham's exploits to Willow. She was afraid lest her letter might somehow fall into enemy hands and Pelham's life be put at risk. On his own admission he would be hopelessly vulnerable to a prepared ambush. His greatest advantage lay in the fact that he was unexpected. The most dangerous aspect of these journeys lay in crossing the river itself. The bridges were heavily guarded and Pelham's only access lay in the use of a heavy wooden raft he had persuaded two local farmers to build for him. Old though they were, the farmers turned out in any weather to ferry him across.

Silvie was far from certain if her letter would ever reach Willow. Nevertheless, she described in detail the ransacking of her once beautiful home and the strange life she and Pelham now lived in the few rooms they had partially restored.

But of Pelham's involvement in the war, she gave only a faint inkling saying that he had lost none of his patriotic fervor which he was expressing in his own inimitable way.

Willow was puzzled over this phraseology.

"I am convinced Pelham is up to something," she said to Toby. "I'll ask Alexis to call in to see them when he is next in Paris. Maybe he can find out more for us."

Alexis had been abroad twice since Christmas, but never for longer than a week. Lucy asked his new secretary, Miss Villier, if she knew where he had gone. But Madeleine professed herself as ignorant as Lucy.

"I only type your husband's routine letters and documents," she explained. "He has a secretary at the Foreign Office who attends to his other work."

Lucy was not displeased at having Madeleine working at home. The woman typed on a table in the morning room, Alexis' study remaining sacrosanct. There had been no further airplane bombings in London but in January a zeppelin had dropped bombs on the Norfolk coast and Alexis was convinced there would be further attacks on the capital. He had wanted

Lucy to remain at Rochford but with Oliver back at school, Lucy insisted upon returning to London. At Rochford she would have only the young girls and her mother and Uncle Toby for company. Here in London she had Hilda Sharples and their many friends to entertain her and with Alexis away so often, she had plenty of time for her own amusement. But she could not always be out, and now she could while away an hour gossiping with Alexis' secretary.

Madeleine refused to talk about the period of her life when she had been engaged to Francis, although Lucy longed to know about Rochford in those days and in particular about her great-grandmother. But Madeleine would not be drawn and preferred to talk of her 'boy friend' as she described the middle-aged man who called for her every evening after work to drive her home in his car.

It amused Lucy to see the gray-haired woman behaving like a coy girl as gradually she dropped her prim secretarial pose in Lucy's presence and started to confide in her. Mr. Black had sent her a beautiful bouquet of red roses for her birthday; he had held her hand in the picture palace; he had even written her a poem. There seemed little doubt that Madeleine expected a proposal before long and vaguely sorry for her, Lucy hoped she would get her Mr. Black if the dapper little man was what she wanted.

But Madeleine's hopes were not to be fulfilled so soon. After an intimate little dinner together in an Italian restaurant in Chelsea, Anthony Black informed her that he had had distressing news.

"It's my book!" he told her sorrowfully. "I have just had my manuscript returned by my publisher. The war seems to have produced a change of policy and the publisher says the subject matter is no longer very suitable..."

With a little cry, Madeleine was later to describe to Lucy as 'wrung from his heart,' he swept aside her attempt to sympathize. It was not so much his failure as an author, he told her, although his pride naturally was suffering. It was the far more unpleasant matter of money.

"Perhaps I should have confessed to you before now, dear girl," he had said in a deep, passionate voice, "but I am not a man of means. I had hoped that this book...that the money would enable me...that you and I..." His voice had faltered as he had looked at her with a despairing gaze. "I do not earn enough for us both to live on," he said finally.

Madeleine's heart sank. This was a possibility that had never crossed her mind. She had always supposed Anthony to be of independent means. Had she known before...But it was too late now. She loved him. For the first time in her life she was in love and money was of secondary importance.

She leaned across the table and caught his hand in hers.

"We could manage somehow," she said. "As you know, I own my aunt's house. I could keep on my job while you write another book. We..."

"No, my sweet, generous girl!" His voice was a mixture of tenderness and regret. "You must know how I feel about you, Madeleine. I have no right to say it but I cannot hide my heart. Think how I would feel, unable to support my own wife; living in her house; perhaps, God forbid, having to spend her money. No, no, Madeleine. It would be too demoralizing! I must first prove myself. I can and will write another book. With your encouragement, I know I can do it. It means we shall have to wait a little while longer but we have no acceptable alternative. You must see that!"

Madeleine was silenced. Bitter though the pill was to swallow, all was by no means lost. If he wrote another book...

She agreed wholeheartedly to give him her moral support. As she told Lucy next day, it was a comfort in a way to have it all out in the open and to have reached an understanding.

"And of course it means your husband won't have to find a new secretary for a while yet," Madeleine said smiling.

Alexis was home for Lucy's twenty-first birthday on 14th March. There had been talk of giving a big party to celebrate her coming of age but with so many of the men they might have invited now in uniform and far from home, the idea had been set aside in favor of a small family party. Alexis had got tickets for the ballet which he knew Lucy loved and Toby and Willow came up from Rochford for the night.

Willow told Lucy that Mark had written to her from America.

"He is coming home," she announced, biting her lip. "I suppose it is wrong of me to be cross with him for leaving his new job just when he has settled into it so well. He is eighteen years old and it is only natural he should want to join up. But how can I possibly be happy about it, Lucy, even though I *shall* be happy to see him home."

Lucy looked at her mother curiously.

"You're really fond of him, aren't you, Mama!" she said.

"He and Philip and Jane are almost as much your children as Oliver and Alice and I."

Willow's face relaxed into a smile.

"Perhaps it is because love begets love. I believe those three children look on me as a mother and I cannot help but respond."

She had never once regretted adopting them so impulsively that summer's day nearly four years ago. Once in a while, the sight of Jane's or Philip's red-gold hair reminded her of Georgina Grey but strangely, this memory no longer had the power to hurt her.

"I love them very much, Lucy," she said truthfully.

Lucy's thoughts turned to that word, love; it was a word both Alexis and Mama used very often. Both of them professed to love her yet she was convinced that Oliver had always had first claim to her mother's affections. As for Alexis, she was no longer certain that she came first in his. She was sure that he met Roberta regularly and although she had no way of proving it, she was more or less convinced that Roberta was his mistress. Alexis had told her a few days ago that Roberta's husband, the old Earl, was dying. If Roberta was widowed, it might not be so long before she was looking for another husband—and she was still a remarkably beautiful woman.

She now said to Willow.

"Could a man divorce his wife for something she had done before her marriage?"

Willow regarded her daughter with astonishment.

"What an extraordinary question, Lucy. No, of course not! Have you forgotten your marriage vows? A man takes his wife 'for better, for worse' and that is when the marriage begins. If she was having a liaison with another man before then, she would not have been committing adultery since she had no husband at that time. But why do you ask such a question?"

But with her customary reticence, Lucy would say no more and Willow was left pondering the matter.

Alexis had told Lucy she might buy a new dress for her birthday and she had chosen a ruby-red velvet gown trimmed with tiny seed pearls. When she was dressing that evening, he came into her room and put a small parcel on her lap as Polly was pinning up her hair. With her usual excitement at receiving any present, Lucy tore off the wrapping. In the box lay a necklace of rubies and two drop earrings to match.

Lucy jumped up and flung her arms around him.

"They're beautiful, Alexis. You chose them just for my new dress didn't you? How did you guess?"

"A little bird told me what color it would be," Alexis said with a smile at the grinning Polly.

Delighted with her birthday presents, Lucy enjoyed her evening to the full. After the ballet they had a champagne supper at the Savoy and by mutual agreement the war was not mentioned. Lucy forgot her concern about Roberta Inman and it was not until they were back at Cadogan Gardens that her sense of misgiving returned.

After Polly had undressed her and left the bedroom she went for the first time during their marriage into Alexis' room. He was in his dressing gown sitting in a chair by the fire reading some papers he held on his lap. There was no sign of his valet who, like Polly, had retired to bed.

Alexis looked up in astonishment.

"What's the matter, Lucy?" he asked. "Is something wrong?"

Polly had tied Lucy's long hair so that it fell in two golden bunches either side of her shoulders. The pale blue ribbons matched the color of her soie de chine negligé.

It did not seem possible, Alexis thought, that today she had come of age. It would have been easier to believe that they had been celebrating her seventeenth birthday.

Lucy was regarding him thoughtfully.

"I don't think it's right that you should refuse to sleep with me, Alexis," she said bluntly. Her words shocked him.

He lowered his gaze so that she could not read his expression.

"Lucy, you know the reason why I don't."

She frowned, looking more than ever like a child.

"But you make love to Roberta!" she said accusingly. "I don't think it's fair."

It was a moment or two before Alexis replied.

"I am surprised to hear you object, Lucy. Why should you mind?" he asked, his voice very quiet.

Lucy's blue eyes flashed with indignation.

"Of course I mind. It isn't as if *I* am not willing. They would be bound to believe *you* in a divorce court."

"A divorce court? What are you talking about, Lucy?"

"You could divorce me if you told them I was denying you your conjugal rights. I read it in a book. And the servants all know we never share a bed."

"And what exactly has Roberta to do with that nonsense?" Alexis inquired, genuinely curious.

"Well, if you divorced me, you could marry her when old Angus Inman dies."

Alexis' mouth twitched but Lucy did not notice his smile.

"I haven't the slightest intention of divorcing you, Lucy, and even less intention of marrying Roberta. Does that satisfy you, my dear?"

Lucy regarded him speculatively, her eyes uneasy.

"But you *could*, Alexis . . ."

"Lucy, you should know me better than to think that even had I wanted to divorce you, which I don't, I would be so unfair as to do so on grounds that were totally untrue. You do not deny me 'my conjugal rights.' It is I who do not claim them."

"What about my past then?" Lucy persisted doggedly. "You might bring that up!"

Alexis put down his papers and when he stood up, his face was stern.

"That would be equally unjust, Lucy. I knew about that when I married you and there is nothing in this world that would ever, *ever* make me reveal it—and certainly not to gain my own ends." He walked away from her and drawing back the curtains, he stared down into the dimly lit street with unseeing eyes. "Does the memory still trouble you?" he asked, his voice now gentle.

"I don't think about it often," Lucy answered truthfully. "Sometimes I wonder what has happened to all the girls over there in France. But it's beginning to seem like another world, it's all so long ago."

"Then forget it, Lucy, as I have," Alexis said. "Off to bed with you now. It's been a long day and you must be tired."

Obediently, Lucy walked toward the door where she paused to look back at him.

"Do you still love me, Alexis?" she asked.

Alexis' expression was unfathomable as he said:

"Of course I do, Lucy. Does it matter to you? I thought you did not know what the word meant?"

Lucy sighed.

"Well, I don't really, but whatever it means, I want you to feel it more for me than for Roberta. Do you, Alexis?"

For a long moment, Alexis stared at his young wife. For a brief second hope flashed into his mind. But it was gone as swiftly. He picked up his papers and sat down again in his chair.

"Whatever it means, I feel a lot more of it for you than I do for Roberta," he said. "Now go to bed, Lucy. I've work to do!"

As she closed the communicating door between them, her scent still lingered in the air. Alexis' body as he stared after her was motionless. Slowly his head dropped and he covered his face with his hands.

"Oh, Lucy, Lucy, Lucy!" he murmured, his heart aching with an unbearable pain. "Whatever 'it' is, I feel 'it' more for you than for anyone else in the world. Roberta could never be more than a pale, insignificant substitute for you. I feel 'it' more deeply than I ever imagined possible."

Today his Lucy had come of age. The world would call her a woman and childhood lay behind her. But what could the world know of the strange confusion of emotions that stood between his Lucy and womanhood? What did he, her husband, really know or understand? Perhaps like the hollow porcelain shepherdess, Lucy too, would prove to have no heart, no substance.

"'Do you still love me?' she had asked. 'Do you feel 'it' more for me than for Roberta?'"

Perhaps he should take hope from the fact that there could be no doubt now that she herself wanted to be loved. But the doubt remained whether Lucy would ever discover the capacity to give him her love in return.

With difficulty, Alexis turned his thoughts once more to his work. The new secretary was proving efficient and reasonably intelligent, he thought. She was quick and accurate and Lucy seemed to like her. Nevertheless, Alexis did not. He could not justify his feelings even to himself. He tried not to be prejudiced by the portrait Willow had given him of Madeleine Villier at the time Francis Rochford had been in love with her. His mother-in-law had described her as a hard, mercenary young girl, heartless and egotistical.

"I never trusted her!" Willow had reflected. And now Alexis felt the same mistrust. But he could not fault her as a secretary and despite the fact that she had obviously known better days, her manner was respectful and she never tried to ingratiate herself. From what Lucy had told him, she was enjoying a late romance and hoped eventually to marry the man who was courting her. It was difficult to picture his secretary head over heels in love. With her graying hair scraped back in a bun at the nape of her neck and with her high-collared blouses and neat, black serge skirts, she looked a born spinster.

Alexis might not have thought so if he could have seen Madeleine off duty. It had become habitual now for her to go back to Anthony's somewhat dingy little flat in Shepherds Bush to cook their evening meal—a far cheaper way to eat than dining out. When the meal was over, Madeleine would go into the bedroom and let down her hair, literally and metaphorically. Touching her sallow cheeks with rouge and reddening her lips, she would return to sit on Anthony's lap by the fireside.

She now permitted him to undo the buttons of her blouse and fondle her full breasts. Their relationship had become deeply passionate and Madeleine's dormant desires were even more ardent than her companion's. It was he who kept their embraces within conventional bounds; Madeleine who could hardly bring herself to keep her hands off him. She was far more in love than he. It was usually Anthony who disentangled himself from her arms saying that he respected her far too much to take advantage of her. Certainly he could have done so, as slowly Madeleine's love turned to an all-consuming passion.

Most of their evenings were spent in talk. Anthony seemed tirelessly interested in Madeleine's past and most especially in the days when she had known Francis. He expressed his concern at the cruel way life had treated her.

"I would not be surprised if you told me you hated all the Rochfords," he said. "They have titles and wealth while you, my poor sweet, have to work for your living. It surprises me that you do not envy the young Countess her position in that house. From what you tell me, Count Zemski spoils her utterly and she has everything in the world she wants."

"I suppose I do envy her," Madeleine admitted. "She's always quite nice to me but it's true, I hate her family." It was unquestionably Lady Rochford, she thought, who had put a stop to Francis seeing her after he had stolen one of the family's art treasures to buy her presents! Francis had been mad with love for her in those days—and but for Lady Rochford, who knew but that Madeleine might have married him.

But she did not really care. She wanted nobody now but Anthony—her romantic, elusive author cum poet who treated her as no one else had ever done.

"I reckon that family owe you some sort of recompense," Anthony said. "I've never thought it fair the way these titled families can inherit wealth without ever having to work for it. If only *we* were rich, my beautiful girl, we could be married by now and we'd be free to love each other properly."

Madeleine no longer wanted money for herself but she now resumed her former interest in it—for them, for Anthony and herself. It was obvious that he was not going to indulge in the final intimacies until they were respectably married and she dared not reveal her own eagerness to ignore convention lest he should lose his respect for her. Respect, he so often said, was essential in a relationship such as theirs.

She was growing increasingly afraid of losing him. At any time on any day, he might so easily meet a younger, more attractive woman than herself. After all, had they not met quite accidentally in a picture palace? Waitresses always smiled at him, liking him for his friendliness and good manners. With so many men going off to war, there were far too many women around looking for husbands like Anthony. He had had rheumatic fever as a boy, he told her, so he could not do his bit for his country like other men. A woman marrying Anthony need not fear she would soon be widowed.

His book seemed to be progressing very slowly. He could not even present her with one or two chapters that she could type for him.

"I shall have to think of some other way to earn money for us," he said, half humorously when he had helped a disheveled Madeleine off his lap after a particularly passionate series of embraces. "We can't go on for ever like this, my darling. I want you so much. Does that shock you, my dearest girl?"

Madeleine straightened her skirt and for a moment she looked almost angry. His purity was infuriating—a barrier to everything she wanted and needed now as a desert needed water. There were moments like this when his precious respect for her was so utterly frustrating that she wanted to strike him. But the moment he put his arms around her, her bitterness vanished.

"I love you! I love you, my darling!" she whispered. "I'd do anything in the world for you, Anthony—anything."

"Who knows but one day I may ask for proof of that beautiful declaration of love," he said as he kissed her tenderly.

"Then ask me now!" Madeleine cried. "I meant what I said, Anthony. I'll do *anything*."

For a moment she could not read the expression in his eyes. They were so often unfathomable. Her heart was beating furiously with hope. Could it mean that at last he, too, was ready to take their relationship to its ultimate conclusion?

"We'll talk about it next time you come here," he said softly, kissing her again. "I have to go to Cornwall this week-end to see a cousin of mine, so we won't be able to meet again until Monday. If only we were married, my love, I could have taken you with me! But my cousin is old and . . . well, I wouldn't want to put you in such an undignified position. One last kiss, my beautiful girl, and then I shall drive you home."

Next Monday, Madeleine thought as they drove back to her house in his shabby two-seater Ford, next Monday she would go out in her lunch hour and buy a really beautiful dress. She would wash her hair on Sunday night and then . . . then . . .

She looked up at Anthony's handsome, manly profile and wondered how she would ever survive the next few days without seeing him.

Their goodnight kiss on her doorstep was frustratingly perfunctory.

"Your neighbors might be watching," Anthony said, his arm accidentally brushing against her breasts. With a little cry that was almost despairing, Madeleine turned the key in her front door and let herself into the empty house.

She stood with her back to the door waiting until she could no longer hear the sound of Anthony's car engine as he drove away. Then she sat down in a chair in the darkness and tried to will her loneliness away.

Chapter 17

❦

April—June 1915

On 23rd April, 1915, an advertisement appeared in the New York papers. It advised travelers intending to embark on an Atlantic voyage that a state of war existed between Germany and Great Britain and her Allies; that vessels flying the flag of Great Britain or that of any of her Allies were liable to destruction in the zone of war including the waters adjacent to the British Isles. Passengers traveled in the *Lusitania* at their own risk.

The advertisement went unnoticed by Mark Grey who embarked on the Cunard liner with little thought in his head other than that he would soon be home again and hopefully could offer his services to his country before the war ended. He was as ignorant as were all the other passengers of the fact that the liner he was sailing in was carrying huge quantities of explosives, wrapped as parcels of cheese or furs to conceal their true identity.

The British and American Governments were fully aware of this dangerous cargo but neither country believed the Germans would sink a ship with so many neutral American passengers on board. As a precaution, her name was painted out on the bows and stern but to very little effect since she was easily recognizable by her shape and size.

As an economy it was decided to run the *Lusitania* on only three-quarters of her boilers in order to save coal. Her speed therefore was severely curtailed and for once she could not outrun a German U-boat.

On 7th May, to the horror of the entire world she was sunk by one single torpedo fired from a German U-boat. Despite her size, she sank almost instantly after the explosion. She was within sight of the Irish coast.

Stunned but only slightly cut by flying splinters, Mark was one of the all too few survivors. Picked up by a passing trawler,

246

he had been landed in Ireland from where he sent a telegram to Rochford Manor, announcing his escape and his intention to take the next boat to England.

Willow and Toby drove up to Liverpool to meet him at the docks. He had a bandage around his arm and another covering a gash on his forehead. There was no smile on his face as Willow clasped him in her arms and hugged him.

"Bit of a wounded soldier, aren't you?" Toby said smiling. "Glad you made it back, young fellow. I've cabled T.R.T.C. in New York as they were bound to be worried about you. Terrible business! Cunard say there could be over a thousand lives lost."

As Mark walked between them to the car, he said gravely:

"Bodies were being washed up all along the coast of Ireland. It all happened so quickly, you see. Otherwise many more might have been saved. There was no question of an orderly evacuation in the lifeboats. The crew did their best but the ship's bow went down so quickly and the stern went right up in the air which made it impossible to get more than a few boats away. It was obvious we were sinking and I jumped overboard." His voice quavered and Toby guessed that he was still suffering from shock.

"It was horrible!" Mark continued with a shudder. "I saw a small child no bigger than Zandra in the sea and I wanted to save her but I couldn't reach her in time. Her head disappeared before I got to her. They said there were nearly a hundred children on board and I don't think many of them could have survived. I saw a trawler coming toward me and I made for that. They picked up as many as they could but..." he broke off, his young face tense with the horror of his memories.

"You must try not to think about it," Toby said gently.

"I'm afraid I have nothing but these clothes," Mark said. "My steamer trunk and my suitcase were on board."

"That is not the least important," Toby said. "We will soon get you kitted out again and meanwhile we are bound to find something of Oliver's to fit you." He opened the car door. "In you get, young man. Your sister Jane is dying of impatience to see you. It was her sixteenth birthday yesterday and the poor child didn't enjoy one minute of it. She was distraught until we got your telegram telling us you were all right. Glad you sent it off so quickly."

Neither Willow nor Toby brought up the subject, during

the drive back, of Mark's reasons for returning to England.
Toby had thought it best to wait a while before talking the
matter over with him in the light of his terrible experience
on the *Lusitania*. Willow was even more determined to try
and persuade Mark at least to delay his participation in the
war for a while longer. He was still so young and she had
been deeply affected by the news of the latest German atrocity.
The enemy had broken their promise made at the Hague
Convention eight years previously, never to use poison gas.
In the battle at Ypres which had erupted on 22nd April, they
had made use of the wind blowing in the direction of the
Allied trenches to carry to the enemy the lethal greenish-
yellow clouds of chlorine gas.

The French and Algerian soldiers in the forward positions
had been first affected. They had tried to run back to warn
the British troops but so powerful was the gas that their eyes
were blinded by tears and they were choking and coughing,
almost unable to draw breath or to speak. Those who could
not run from the poisonous clouds and had inhaled too deeply,
were first paralyzed and then died slow and painful deaths.

For a brief while it seemed as if nothing would halt the
consequent German advance. But the Canadians, backed by
the British and Indian troops, put handkerchiefs over their
mouths and noses and fought back fiercely.

The day after Mark's return home, Willow asked Peter Rose
to take a look at the boy. The doctor promptly diagnosed
delayed concussion and ordered Mark to remain in bed for at
least a week.

"Absolutely no question of you being fit for war service
yet, young man," he told the disappointed Mark.

But Mark's youth and natural resilience enabled him to
recover sufficiently from his ordeal for the doctor to allow
him downstairs before the week was up. But first Mark had
to give his word he would consider himself an invalid and
take no violent exercise or tire himself unduly.

Mark's concern with the war remained paramount and he
plied Toby with questions.

When the news filtered through in mid-May of the halt to
the enemy advance, Toby spoke of the gallantry of the Canadian, British and Indian troops who had disregarded the
horrors of the poison gas and counterattacked.

"Had they not done so," he said, "the Germans might have
captured Calais, after which they could have attempted to

sweep the British Fleet from the Channel and then the way would have been open to London. The Germans have not yet captured Ypres," he added. "But our casualties are huge—some from the fighting and others victims of this foul gas. I believe the casualties could number sixty to seventy thousand and that is an appalling loss of life."

Oliver was the only one who shared Mark's longing to go to war.

"If you hang on a bit longer, Mark, I'll be old enough to join up with you," he said at a secret conference on the subject they were holding in the schoolroom—far away from his mother's ears. He had had his sixteenth birthday in February and Henry Barratt was already seventeen. "I look older than both of you anyway," he said grinning. "So no rushing off without me when I go back to school next term, Mark."

Owing to the fact that little Eleanor Barratt and Henry had mumps, the Easter holiday had been extended for both Oliver and Henry. Much to their delight, their housemasters had insisted they remain at home until they were out of quarantine.

Jane listened in silence to the interminable discussions about the war among the three boys. Oliver permitted her to sit in although she took little part in the conversation. She kept to herself her fears for their safety should they ever get into uniform. Yet she understood their desire to take part in the war.

"I shall become a nursing aid as soon as I'm old enough," she vowed. "If I were Lucy's age, I'd be working in a hospital now!"

Oliver and the other boys approved Jane's patriotic outlook. They equally deplored Lucy's seeming indifference to the war.

"I just don't understand it!" Oliver said unhappily. But he felt even more concerned about Alexis' disinclination to join up. The boys at school had fathers and uncles who were already in uniform and Uncle Toby had tried to get into the army. It was not his fault that he had been turned down on account of his bad eyesight.

Jane understood Oliver's disquiet. Everyone who was physically able wanted to help their country in some way, and even Willow understood this patriotic necessity. Whenever any of the servants came to announce that they wished to hand in their notice, she accepted it sadly but without question. At least eight of the indoor servants and a dozen outdoor had volunteered, and almost all the able-bodied men in Havorhurst village.

"Thank goodness you're a girl, Jane!" Oliver said on the last day of the holidays as they rode their bicycles through the quiet country lanes. "I wouldn't want to think of you being shot to pieces in the trenches or choking to death with that foul gas!"

"I hope the war is over before you have to go, Oliver," Jane confessed and wished the words unsaid when she saw Oliver's affectionate smile turn to a scowl. They were usually such very good friends that it was rare for them not to find themselves in accord. Jane was aware that Oliver's manner toward her had changed almost indefinably of late and now he seldom teased her or found fault with her. Although their relationship was still very much that of brother and sister, they had nevertheless become aware of each other in a new way.

Oliver in his turn had noticed that the quiet, shy child had grown into a singularly pretty young girl. Jane had come out of her shell in the four years since she had lived at Rochford and was now a lively conversationalist with a quick, ready sense of humor that brought a smile to her eyes and a gentle beauty to her otherwise unremarkable features.

Oliver, too, had changed. The untidy, rough and tumble schoolboy had become an exceedingly elegant young man. Enormously self-assured, yet without any inclination to brag or swagger, he dominated any group of his contemporaries and attracted the glances of the opposite sex. Jane had seen the younger housemaids blush and giggle when he bade them good morning or passed them in the passageway.

What Jane liked most about Oliver was that for all his fads about his clothes, he was not the least bit vain and never boastful. He seemed quite unaware of his good looks or his popularity.

Oliver had not yet returned to school when news reached Rochford that the head gardener, Purkiss, and the undergroom, Pilcher, had fallen at Ypres. Both men had joined the West Kents only recently and the suddenness of their deaths affected not only the remaining members of the staff but the family too.

There were others from Havorhurst village who had died or been wounded in the attack at Ypres, and in church on Sunday, the vicar offered special prayers for them and for the safety of all the fighting men. Jane felt particular sympathy for poor Lady Barratt who had still received no definite news about her son George. On the most recent Knitting for the Troops day at Glenfield Hall, the proud, imperious woman had for the first time lowered her guard, so carefully preserved against displaying fear, and had confessed to Willow that if George really was dead, she would prefer to know it than to continue the present uncertainty. It was, however, a further nine weeks before information finally came. It was a bright sunny June morning when the telephone rang at Rochford Manor and Willow was summoned to take an urgent call from Lady Barratt.

"I've had news, my dear," Lady Barratt's voice was shrill with excitement. "*Good news!* I can still hardly believe it, Willow. Our George is home!"

George, so she went on to relate, had been severely wounded on the battlefield at Mons. He had been found by a Belgian farmer whose wife had nursed him back to health while concealing him in an attic in their farmhouse.

"And now I come to stirring news for you, Willow," Lady Barratt continued. "George stayed with the farmer for two months before he was considered well enough to be transported in a cart to Brussels. The cart was covered with straw to appear no more innocuous than a load of turnips. George was taken to a clinic in the suburbs run by an extraordinary English woman whose name I forget."

She paused long enough to draw breath before she went on in a calmer tone.

"Under the very noses of the Germans, this nurse is concealing men like George, dressing their wounds and then arranging for them to make their way to the Dutch border disguised as Belgian citizens. I intend to write to her through the Red Cross to thank her for saving George's life. Without her, he would probably be languishing now in a prisoner of war camp."

"I am so happy for you," Willow said. "By the sound of it, he has been very lucky. But you said you have news that concerns me personally?"

"Indeed I have, Willow. George met your brother-in-law in Brussels. He wants to drive over to Rochford this afternoon so that he can tell you in person about Rupert. I won't spoil the surprise for you, but you and Toby are going to be very gratified."

"I'm gratified already to know that Rupert is alive and well,"

Willow said. "We have had no word from him since the Germans walked into Brussels and we were deeply concerned lest he had been interned."

She and Toby waited impatiently for George to arrive which he did very promptly after luncheon. He looked pale and thin but although he had a slight limp, he assured them that his wounds were healed and that the M.O. had said he could rejoin his regiment after a month's convalescent leave.

Once settled in the library, he proceeded to relate that Rupert and Max had taken part in effecting his escape.

"Nurse Cavell had guides to conduct us to the border," he said. "Some of them are young girls who risk their lives in undertaking such a task. But first we required civilian clothes and then identity cards befitting the Belgian citizens we were purported to be. For these cards, photographs were necessary and that was how I came to meet Mr. Rochford." He smiled at Toby's and Willow's look of astonishment.

"I had no idea when I was told to report to the bookshop to have my photograph taken that I should meet Mr. Rochford and Count von Kruege there," he continued. "We recognized each other instantly of course, and I was able to give him fairly recent news of you all. I dared not bring you a letter from him lest I was caught by the Germans on my way to the border and it was found on me. But Mr. Rochford did beg me to give you his fond love and to tell you not to worry about him. Count von Kruege has made it his business to be very friendly and obliging to Count von Bissing, the German Commander in Belgium, who they both knew before the war. Von Bissing is aware that Rupert is English and has no right to be in Brussels; but he believed him and his friend, von Kruege, to pose no threat. Mr. Rochford has made himself out to be terrified of war and with no inclination whatever for fighting."

Willow's glance met Toby's. The thought lay in both their minds that if the German Commander knew of Rupert's relationship with Max, he might well believe them harmless.

"Unfortunately, it is not so certain that Miss Cavell is free from suspicion," George said with a frown. "You may not be aware that she nurses everyone who requires her care, even German soldiers, and those of us who know of her activities assumed the authorities would believe her innocent of any subversion despite her nationality. But word must have got around of her assistance to the Allied soldiers whose number has been constantly increasing. The convalescents were not always as discreet as they should be, some going about the town quite openly."

George's frown deepened as he went on to say:

"Shortly before I left, there was a Polish soldier at the clinic who left behind a letter written in German when he departed. One or two of the nurses suspected he might be a German spy although Miss Cavell did not appear very concerned. But there was another fellow calling himself Jacobs whom we all suspected. He said he had escaped from a German labor camp but he would not tell anyone who had sent him to Miss Cavell's clinic."

"What will happen to her if her activities have been discovered?" Willow asked anxiously.

"Nothing too serious, I hope," George said uncertainly. "After all, she is a woman and she has nursed quite as many Germans as Allied soldiers. But I dare say she would be imprisoned. She is a singularly brave woman. Sometimes she herself conducts potential escapers to the rendezvous with their guides."

Willow was left with mixed feelings when, after taking tea with them, George returned home. She was relieved to know that Rupert was alive, although the conditions in Brussels which George described sounded bad. The civilian population was near to starvation, he had admitted. Rupert and Max were receiving occasional extra rations through von Bissing but most of this food they passed on to Miss Cavell who needed it for the men she was hiding in her clinic and in various houses in the town. There was no ignoring the risks Rupert and Max were taking.

"If a middle-aged Englishwoman can act so patriotically," Toby said gently, "then I don't think we have any right to wish Rupert were less willing. To tell you the truth, George's news gives me nothing but pleasure—unless it is pride. I just wish there were something that I personally could do."

Willow went to his side and put her hand around his shoulders.

"You did your best to join up, Toby," she reminded him, knowing that he had written twice appealing against his rejection on medical grounds. Privately she thanked God that it was to no effect. Other women might be anxious for their menfolk to be heroes but Willow had no such desire. She had lived too many long years without her beloved Toby by her side, and the thought of him becoming a war casualty was not one she could bear to contemplate, however unhappy he might be at the prospect of remaining out of uniform.

If she needed anything to reinforce her feelings, news of the death of young Richard Bartholomew during the Gallipoli Peninsula landings was sufficient.

"That poor boy!" said Willow to Toby. "He was so young, too. I know you will think me disgracefully ignorant, Toby, but where is the Gallipoli Peninsula? I've never heard of it."

"If you will come with me to the library, I will show you on the globe," Toby replied. He pointed to a small narrow piece of land shaped not unlike Italy which jutted out in the Aegean Sea. The east coast was bordered by the Dardanelles Straits, on the far side of which lay the main land mass of Turkey.

"The Aegean Sea leads to the Sea of Marmara, and then northwards through the Bosporous to the Black Sea," Toby explained. "If we could capture the Dardanelles and the Bosporous, we would have an unhindered sea route to Russia. I imagine the idea would then be to outflank the central powers and help to relieve Serbia. They would be in an excellent position to attack Austro-Hungary."

They were interrupted by Zandra who came in through the French windows with a basket of rose petals on her arm. She informed them brightly that her white rabbit was dead.

"Higgs has made a little coffin for Bernie and I'm going to read the service from the prayerbook and give him a proper funeral," she said cheerfully.

"Aren't you just a little bit sad about Bernie dying?" Willow asked as the child conducted her through the French windows into the sunlit garden.

Zandra's eyes regarded her with surprise.

"Oh, no, there's no need to be sad. Jesus will look after him now. If he'd stayed alive, the devil might have got him— or that's what Chesson said. When Bernie got out last week and ate his lettuces, Chesson said 'Devil take 'ee.'" Her voice was a perfect imitation of the old gardener who had replaced Purkiss. "Now Bernie's dead so he's safe from the devil!" Zandra added with satisfaction.

Willow sighed. Perhaps this small girl had the right attitude to death and one should not fear it, she thought. If one could truly believe in God then one could believe in Heaven too, where the hundreds and thousands of men who had been killed since the war started were now as happy and at peace as Zandra considered her rabbit to be.

Zandra, her small face bright with happiness, stood over the hole the gardener had dug for her, her voice that of the vicar's as she intoned solemnly:

"*'We therefore commit Bernie's body to the ground; earth to earth, ashes to ashes, dust to dust; in sure and certain hope of the...'* I can't read the next word...*'to eternal life...'*"

She broke off, staring down at the tiny coffin, the excitement suddenly gone from her eyes. Quietly, she slipped one hand into Willow's.

"All the same," she murmured, following her own silent train of thought: "I did love Bernie very much and I wish he *wasn't* dead."

Chapter 18

❦

June — July 1915

Lucy STARED ACROSS THE BREAKFAST TABLE AT HER HUSBAND'S white face, her expression bewildered. Alexis was holding in his hand an empty envelope and one single white feather.

"But what does it mean?" she asked innocently. "Aren't you well, Alexis?"

Alexis let go his breath and with it, some of his anger and bitterness evaporated.

"A white feather, my dear, is a symbol of cowardice. People have taken to sending them anonymously to any able-bodied man they feel should have offered his services to his country but has been too cowardly to do so!"

Lucy considered this explanation in silence. It was true that Alexis was perfectly healthy and he was only thirty-four years old...young enough to be a soldier, or as Oliver had decided for himself, a pilot. Even Uncle Toby who was nearly forty-eight, had tried to get into the army. But surely no one could possibly suppose Alexis was a coward.

"Isn't the work you are doing a kind of war work?" she inquired.

"Yes, it is!" Alexis replied curtly. He stood up and crossing the room, threw the offending envelope and its contents into the wastepaper basket. "But I suppose not everyone knows that. Moreover, my surname is foreign and therefore I am considered suspect by a number of ignoramuses!"

"But that's silly," Lucy argued. "Just because your name sounds strange doesn't alter the fact that you are as British as any other Englishman."

Alexis' smile was full of irony.

"Stupid or not, people are persecuting perfectly innocent men whose surnames sound foreign. There have been several shopkeepers beaten up, you know, for no better reason. House pets unfortunate enough to belong to the German-sounding

256

breeds like Dachshunds and Alsatians are suffering the same persecution. Their owners are either having them put down or abandoning them. Fear can bring out the worst as well as the best in human nature."

Since he could not discuss confidential Foreign Office documents with his wife, Alexis did not add that he had seen a suggestion that the King be advised to request his Battenberg relations to change their historic surname, or at least to alter it to the direct English translation using 'mount' in place of 'berg.' Alexis doubted if the Battenberg peers would care for this idea.

"I'll have to leave you, my dear Lucy," he said. "I do wish you would go down to Rochford," he added inconsequently. Ever since the zeppelin raid on London last month he had been frightened for her safety. Although only one bomb was dropped, five people had been killed and twenty-four injured. There had also been forty-one fires started as a result of the air raid. But Lucy seemed fearless and would not even countenance Nanny Meredith taking Teo to the country.

"How do you know they would be any safer there?" she argued logically. "Most of the raids so far have been in the country, not over London! I'll go down in August when Oliver is home."

In the meanwhile, Lucy was still enjoying herself despite the fact that there was no longer a London Season. She loved shopping in Bond Street and mingling with the crowds of young khaki-uniformed soldiers window shopping with their girls hanging on their arms. She liked the feeling of excitement everywhere. She went with her friends to see the popular comedy, *A Little Bit of Fluff*, at the Criterion and to admire the new heartthrob, Owen Nares, in *The Christian*. She danced the afternoons away feeling delightfully emancipated in her new dresses with their raised hemlines reaching only to her black, silk-stockinged calves.

The one person missing from this group was Hilda Sharples. She had suddenly abandoned her London life for her parents' home in Kent when George Barratt returned from Brussels, and it now seemed very much as if George and Hilda might become engaged before he returned to the Front. Hilda had told Lucy quite openly that if she was invited to become the future Lady Barratt she would accept.

"George may be dull," Hilda said bluntly, "but he's good and kind. Moreover, he can give me the sort of background Daddy has always longed for. You take for granted your *entrée* into the best circles, Lucy, but there are still many occasions when I am not invited because Daddy is in trade. I like a good time, Lucy, and after the war is over, George can give it to me. He is very lovable in lots of ways and there's no one else I care about."

Lucy missed her. Hilda had always been able to generate an atmosphere of fun no matter what activity the group engaged in. Now they all looked to her, Lucy, to invent amusements that were new or daring or exciting. Last week they had taken a picnic luncheon and driven down to see the remains of the airship which had been shot down after attempting to raid London. It was something different for them all to do, somewhere new to go.

Lucy was aware that Alexis felt she should be taking the war a great deal more seriously. But there seemed little point in doing so. To read the war news in the daily papers only made her depressed and she wanted her life to remain unchanged. It was, after all, only for the past three years that she had been able to enjoy herself without restraint of any kind. The marriage she had once thought of as a bondage had in fact turned out to be a gateway to freedom; freedom from work, poverty, responsibility, anxiety, fear. Her housekeeper took total control of the domestic running of her home; Nanny Meredith took care of little Teo; Alexis took care of himself—possibly with Roberta in the background of his life, Lucy thought with a twinge of uneasiness. And Madeleine Villier took care of a great many of her former worries such as answering the telephone, ordering fresh flowers for the house, declining unwanted invitations. She had become almost as indispensable to Lucy as to Alexis.

"The Countess trusts me absolutely and relies on me a great deal," Madeleine informed her lover truthfully. It was a state of affairs Anthony Black had requested she should try to achieve. He had now managed to persuade Madeleine that people like Lucy had no right to the frivolous, extravagant life they led while others, like Madeleine, had to make do on a few pounds a week. The Zemskis, he reiterated again and again, had more money than they deserved. If there was any true justice in life, some of that wealth should be given to Madeleine and himself. If they could acquire even a small amount of money, they could be married . . .

Slowly, he won Madeleine over to the idea that the misfortunes attending her own life were partly attributable to the Rochford family, of which Lucy was by birth very much a part. To take what was due from the Zemskis was her right, he insisted.

"But I don't keep the accounts," Madeleine protested. "I don't have access to their money, Anthony."

"You could gain access to the Count's papers, couldn't you?" Anthony persisted, stroking Madeleine's hand as he spoke.

Much as Madeleine wished to please him, she was forced to admit that there was no possible way she could get into Alexis' study. He now retained the key when he went off to his office, not even trusting his wife with it. The housemaids were only permitted to go in there to clean when he was present, she told Anthony.

He was bitterly disappointed. But gradually he resumed his insistence that there must be some method of obtaining one or two of Alexis' files. They must have a value—at least to the Count, he commented.

"We'll have to think of another way to get hold of them if *you* can't," he said half jokingly. "For instance, we might take the child just for a day or two; then we could offer to return her in exchange for the files."

Madeleine's expression revealed her shock.

"You can't really mean we should *kidnap* little Teo!" she gasped.

Anthony laughed, ruffling her hair affectionately.

"I wasn't serious, my dear, but now that you mention it, why should we not do exactly that? The child knows you. She would not be particularly frightened and we would not harm her. We could leave a note for the Count telling him he can have her back provided he hands over the papers we want."

"Papers? What papers?" Madeleine asked, now totally confused.

Anthony paused long enough to kiss the inside of her arm. The hot color flared in Madeleine's cheeks.

"Don't you see, Madeleine," he said, "if the Count keeps all those papers locked away so securely, they must be very important and very secret. Once we have those in our possession, we can photograph them and keep the negatives when we return the originals to him. We can then threaten to expose him for carelessness with his country's secrets in wartime unless he pays us whatever we demand."

"But that's blackmail!" Madeleine whispered.

Anthony pulled her onto his lap and kissed her. Momentarily the ugly word was forgotten.

"I cannot wait much longer for you, my dearest one," he murmured. "I want us to be married, my darling, to be together always. We could go away together—to your homeland, perhaps. In a country like New Zealand no one would ever find us. Imagine how it would be, my beautiful girl—the two of us without a worry in the world! But we must have money to realize such a dream."

The picture he painted was dangerously tempting. Nevertheless Madeleine could not seriously contemplate so outrageous a plan. Anthony became indefinably less ardent when she raised objections to his idea. To her dismay, each night they met subsequently, he had worked out further details. They would hire a little seaside chalet somewhere not too far away—Worthing, perhaps, or Brighton on the south coast. No one would think it odd for a couple to take their small child on a seaside holiday in summer. Madeleine must wait for Nanny Meredith's day off and then smuggle the child out of the house into the car where Anthony would be waiting. No one would suspect them and if it were done on a Friday evening, no one would notice Madeleine's absence until she failed to arrive for work on the Monday morning. They would post the letter demanding the papers before leaving London. His plan was foolproof, he insisted.

Relieved to have a genuine reason for refuting it, Madeleine told Anthony that the Countess was planning to take little Teo down to Rochford for the month of August—a date not more than a few weeks away.

"Then it must be before August," Anthony said ignoring her look of dismay. "I'll rent the cottage as from next week, Madeleine. You pack a suitcase for yourself and I'll collect it from your house. Every Friday afternoon from now on, I'll wait in the car at the corner of the gardens. You aren't going to let me down at the last minute, are you, my darling? Remember, the whole reason behind my idea is so that we can be married. You do still want to marry me, don't you?"

"You know I do, Anthony," Madeleine murmured unhappily, "but is there no other way?"

"Now don't be a silly girl. That isn't like you at all," Anthony replied sharply. "If there were any alternative, don't you think I would have found it by now? I'm beginning to think you don't love me as much as I love you."

"I do, I do, Anthony!" Madeleine cried.

"Then now is your chance to prove it," he said, taking her in his arms. "You will, won't you, my darling."

Madeleine nodded, her thoughts already elsewhere as Anthony's hands began skillfully to undo the buttons of her blouse and she raised her face eagerly to receive his kiss. But her ardor could not quite erase the bitter reflection that there was a far simpler, pleasanter way to prove her love if only Anthony wanted her more than he wanted those papers.

It was not until the last Friday in the month, when to postpone the plan further meant inevitably to cancel it, that Madeleine plucked up the courage to carry out Anthony's wishes. The night before, he had added the further persuasion that they would be virtually alone together in the little seaside house.

"I shall not be able to live so close to you, my beautiful, exciting witch, without giving way to temptation," he had warned her. Her heart had almost turned over with joy and relief that at long last the pure idealism of her lover was being overwhelmed by the force of his passion.

"I love you so much, I would die for you!" she whispered, and she had meant it.

But when Friday came, Madeleine was no longer the intrepid, daring accomplice her lover wished her to be. She was trembling violently as she made her way up the two flights of stairs to the day nursery. By a stroke of good fortune, the Countess was out—a rare occurrence on Nanny's day off. It was the nursemaid, Rosie, who was taking care of the little girl. And Rosie was being courted by the butcher's delivery boy who, when he finished work, as often as not dropped into the kitchen for a cup of tea. He had ingratiated himself with Cook by making sure that she always had the best cuts and was never short of a nice piece of suet and never had too much fat with the joint.

"I heard your young man's bicycle bell just now, Rosie," Madeleine told the girl as she went into the nursery. "If you want to nip down for a moment or two, I'll keep an eye on Teo for you."

"Oh, Miss, would you?" Rosie gasped blushing. "That's ever so kind of you, I'm sure. Be a good girl now, Miss Teo and do as Miss Villier tells you!" She could hardly believe her good fortune as she raced down the back stairs.

As soon as Rosie had gone, Madeleine turned to the child who was happily putting one of her many dolls to bed.

"Would you like a ride in a motor car?" she asked nervously. "If you'd like it, we can go to the Zoo and see all the animals!"

The child stared back at Madeleine from solemn blue eyes.

"Will Mummy and Daddy go too?" she asked.

"Daddy is waiting there for us!" Madeleine said hurriedly,

knowing of the three-year-old's devotion to her father. Immediately Teo jumped to her feet.

"It's quite warm outside," Madeleine said, grabbing the child's hand. "We won't need coats. Hurry now! Be as quiet as a mouse. If Rosie hears us, she might try to stop us going to the Zoo."

It took but a moment to reach the hall. The servants were all down below having their tea. Unless the bell rang Madeleine knew no one was likely to come upstairs. She opened the front door and leaving it ajar, ran with the child down to the corner of the street. There, to her relief, Anthony was waiting in his car.

"I'll have to go back," she shouted as she pushed the little girl into the front seat. "I won't be long."

Breathless, her heart pounding with fear, Madeleine ran back to the house. The door had not blown shut and the hall was deserted. Breathing deeply, Madeleine gathered up her coat, hat and handbag and went through the baize door down to the kitchen.

The staff were seated round the scrubbed wooden tables enjoying one of Cook's currant cakes.

"It's time I was leaving, Rosie," she called across to the nursemaid. "Miss Teo is quite happy with her dolls. I left her playing quietly. Don't be too long, though. Goodnight everybody!"

Cook shrugged as Madeleine retreated through the baize door.

"Not such a bad lot after all!" she commented. "Always thought her a bit stuck up but I'll say nought against someone as can have a thought for others once in a while. Now drink up your tea, Rosie, and be off. You've no right to be down here as well you know."

It was a further five minutes before Rosie bade a lingering farewell to her delivery boy on the back area doorstep; ten minutes before she was back in the day nursery. At first she thought Teo was hiding—a game the child loved to play. But Rosie's quick search of the day and night nurseries established her charge was not there. She raced back to the kitchen.

"She must be *somewhere* in the house," she said tearfully. "Help me find her, quickly. If the Countess gets back and discovers I don't know where she is, it'll be the sack, as sure as ducks is ducks."

"Off you go then, Doris, Myrtle—and you, Beryl!" Cook instructed the three youngest maids. "And when you find the child, take her straight to the nursery. I'll not have her down here!"

Rosie was in tears when a quarter of an hour later, the four of them confessed their failure to find the missing child.

"But she just *has* to be *somewhere*!" Rosie wailed. "Miss Villier saw her safe and sound in the day nursery not long since."

"That's a half hour ago at least!" Doris said dourly. "You didn't ought to have left Miss Teo that long, Rosie!"

Rosie needed no such admonition. The fact that the Countess had not yet come home was a merciful reprieve—but it could only be temporary. She had never known the child's mother not be back before Miss Teo's bedtime.

"Let's look again," she said despairingly. "One of you try the attics—she may be up there. Doris, you go and see if she didn't creep down to the kitchens unnoticed. Maybe she's in the butler's pantry, or in the laundry room. I'll do this floor again and then all the bedrooms."

It was nearing six o'clock when the butler decided after a consultation with Cook that he must telephone his Master.

"He may want me to call the police!" he said portentously.

Cook looked worried.

"If you do that, Mr. Bulford, it'll not be only Rosie as will get the sack," she said. "We all of us knew Miss Teo was alone up there. We'll all be for it! There's only Mrs. Taylor wasn't having tea with us. Trust her to be lying down with a headache when she should have been making sure Rosie was doing her job!"

"Mrs. Taylor is entitled to her afternoon nap," the butler said firmly. "No point arguing the rights and wrongs now. It's my duty to let the Master know what's happened and that's what I'm going to do."

But before he could reach the telephone in the cloakroom on the ground floor, the front door bell rang. He opened it to Lucy who was laden with parcels.

Squaring his shoulders, Bulford said:

"Beg pardon, Madam, but I was just about to telephone the Master. I'm afraid something quite unpleasant has occurred, Madam. It's Miss Teodora. She's missing."

Lucy's parcels fell in a heap at her feet. Regardless of etiquette she grabbed the butler's arm.

"What do you mean, *missing*?" she cried. "What's happened, Bulford?"

"Miss Teodora can't be found, Madam—not in the house.

They've been searching this past hour. She's not in any of the rooms. She's just vanished—gone!"

Lucy raced for the telephone. It seemed an eternity before the girl on the switchboard at the Foreign Office was able to locate Alexis. When he came on the line, he sounded impatient.

"What is it, Lucy? I was in conference and . . ."

"Alexis, will you listen to me. Teo's gone—vanished. Shall I call the police? Alexis, for pity's sake, what am I to do?"

Alexis' voice was perfectly calm as he said:

"You must not call the police, Lucy. That is a direct order. Now tell me—who is in the house?"

"Only me—and the servants. It's Nanny's afternoon off. Miss Villier went ages ago. I have just arrived home. They've been searching for over an hour. Alexis, I'm so frightened!"

She was trembling violently and the palms of her hands were making damp marks on the telephone.

"Listen to me, Lucy," Alexis said. "I am quite certain that there is no need whatever to call in the police. Teo is obviously hiding somewhere in the house. She may be accidentally locked in a cupboard or have climbed into the blanket chest—something of that sort. You know what the servants are like—they probably panicked and went dashing all over the house without searching anywhere thoroughly. I'll return at once. In the meanwhile, tell Bulford every single member of the staff is to stop what they are doing and be responsible for searching one room thoroughly. We'll find her, Lucy. Don't worry!"

A dozen questions rose to Lucy's lips but Alexis' voice, calm and emphatic had quieted her rising hysteria. She replaced the receiver on its hook and with an attempt to emulate Alexis' calmness, she gave Bulford his instructions.

Alexis arrived home twenty minutes later. By now Teo had been missing for nearly two hours and Lucy's terror was mounting as one by one the servants reported they had not found the child. She flung herself into Alexis' arms.

"Thank God you are back!" she cried. *"Alexis, we can't find her!"*

Alexis looked over the top of her head at the butler.

"Find Mrs. Taylor and Rosie and bring them to the library," he said. "Quickly now, Bulford!"

With his arm still around Lucy, he led her past his locked study door and into the library. Two square cut-glass decanters stood on a table with a soda water syphon and glasses. Releasing his hold upon Lucy, Alexis poured two whiskies and insisted she drink hers. He gave no outward sign of his own growing apprehension. He had been reasonably convinced when he left the office that someone would have found little Teo before he reached home.

Bulford came in with Mrs. Taylor and a sobbing Rosie.

Alexis addressed the white-faced housekeeper.

"I understand Rosie was looking after Miss Teo. Is that right?" Mrs. Taylor nodded.

"Rosie took over in the nursery as soon as Nanny left the house," she said nervously, "just as she always does, Sir. Doris took nursery tea up at four o'clock and Miss Teo was safe and sound then."

"You did not see her yourself, Mrs. Taylor?"

"No, Sir. I was not feeling very well and I had retired to my bed. First thing I knew that something was wrong was when Mr. Bulford knocked on my door—about six o'clock I think it was—and told me Miss Teo was lost."

Alexis now turned his attention to Rosie who was weeping into her apron, her hair disheveled and her eyes swollen with crying.

"Stop that noise, Rosie. It won't find Miss Teo and that's what we're trying to do. Now I want to know *exactly* what happened."

Rosie was by now aware that there was no way in which she could conceal the truth. Cook had already advised her to make a clean breast of it and there seemed no alternative. Still weeping, she stammered out the admission of her guilt.

"Honest to God, Sir, I didn't mean no harm . . . Miss Villier said as how she would keep an eye on Miss Teo and I was only gone a moment or two . . . and then she came down to the kitchen to say she had to be off and it truly weren't more'n a few minutes later as I went back up to the nursery . . ."

"Wait a minute!" Alexis' voice cut across Rosie's like a knife. "What business had Miss Villier in the nursery in the first place? Is she in the habit of going there?"

"No, Sir, she hasn't never been up there before not as I know of. She just came to tell me she heard . . ." Rosie faltered but Mrs. Taylor prodded her sharply in the back ". . . Ted, Sir, the butcher's boy. He and I are walking out. Miss Villier said as how she'd keep an eye on Miss Teo . . ."

"Yes, yes, you told me," Alexis interrupted, his mind working furiously. Something did not make sense and it had to do with Madeleine. But for the moment, he couldn't put his finger on the reason for his suspicions.

He sent the servants away and Lucy watched, as wordlessly, he paced up and down the room. She was shivering with cold despite the warmth of the evening and her hands and feet were like lumps of ice, her head burning hot.

"If Madeleine offered to keep an eye on Teo for Rosie, why didn't she wait till Rosie got back?"

Alexis' question startled Lucy from her nervous torpor.

"How should I know, Alexis! I expect she was meeting that man friend of hers, Anthony Black. She meets him most evenings after work. I think he drives her home."

Alexis was no longer listening. He was searching his brain to catch an elusive memory. *Anthony Black*. He had heard that name recently . . . but where? Why? It was nothing to do with Madeleine Villier. It was at the office . . .

"Oh, my God!" he cried, hitting his forehead with his hand. "Now I know. Anthony Black!"

As clearly as if the page were in front of him, he could see the circular that had reached his desk last week together with a dozen others. On it was the name Anthony Black. And each of those circulars gave the few details available of men suspected by Intelligence of being enemy agents working in England under an alias.

Lucy saw the deathly pallor of Alexis' face and her own fears increased. Without a word, he went out into the hall to the telephone. She forced herself to her feet and followed him. She was in time to hear him ask to speak to Intelligence when the front door bell rang. It was Nanny returning from her afternoon off. Seeing Lucy standing in the hall staring at her, she beamed.

"Good evening, Madam!" she said brightly. "I'm sure I don't need to ask you if our Teo has been a good girl. Never causes me a moment's worry, the pet, and I said as much today to my mother. No trouble to anyone, the little angel."

"No trouble, Nanny!" Lucy echoed foolishly. "No trouble at all!"

Behind her, Alexis put down the telephone just as Lucy's self-control snapped and she burst into tears.

Happily ignorant of the events that were taking place at Cadogan Gardens, Willow was enjoying a family tea on the lawn at Rochford. James, Dodie's husband, had returned home for the school summer holidays and Oliver was home from Eton.

The noise of a motor car coming up the drive, the tires sending up clouds of dust behind it, caught their attention. Willow shaded her eyes against the setting sun.

"Why, *it's Philip*!" she cried as Jane ran past her with a glad cry.

Philip, looking very smart in his naval uniform, climbed out of the taxicab smiling. He hugged his sister and kissed Willow's cheek.

Mark and Oliver came to join them, everyone trying to talk at once.

It was some minutes before Willow was able to ascertain that Philip had shore leave and would be with them for three weeks before he rejoined his ship, the battle cruiser, *H.M.S. Invincible.* He was now a Sub-Lieutenant and proudly displayed the gold ring round the cuff of his navy blue jacket.

He had traveled down from Scapa Flow and had spent an hour or two in London before catching a train home, he told them.

"I wanted to buy you all presents," he said shyly, "as I couldn't do so last Christmas. I'm afraid I'm not much good at choosing gifts so I made it easy for myself and got the latest books at Hatchards for everyone."

There was a novel each for Oliver and Mark by their favorite author, P. G. Wodehouse; the recently published *Of Human Bondage* by Somerset Maugham for Toby; a new edition of *The Wind in the Willows* for Alice. Perhaps most interesting of his presents was a copy of *1914*, a collection of poems by the new young poet, Rupert Brooke, for Jane.

"I met Brooke quite by chance in Egypt last March," Philip told his sister. "He was on his way to the Dardanelles in *Grantully Castle* which berthed at Port Said. We were both on leave and staying at the Casino Hotel. He was extraordinarily interesting to talk to, despite the fact that he wasn't feeling too well— he had a touch of sunstroke, I think. We found we shared a birthday on August 3rd although he's seven years my senior."

Willow bit her lip and then sighed.

"I'm sorry to have to tell you, Philip, but it was reported in the *Times* a short while ago that the poor young man died of blood poisoning on a Greek island called Scyros."

Philip looked shocked.

"Dead? Then he must have died soon after I met him. I *am* sorry! I liked him—and his poems."

It was, however, the only sad note as they celebrated Philip's return. That evening at dinner, Toby opened a bottle of vintage champagne and the atmosphere was entirely joyous. It would not have been so had they realized that not forty miles away in London, Alexis was sitting by Lucy's side staring anxiously at her white, stricken face, wondering whether she would be able to withstand the terrible pressures the next few days would bring.

Chapter 19

∽

July 1915

BY THE TIME THE STRANGE MAN IN THE BOWLER HAT LEFT CADOGAN Gardens Lucy had regained her composure. Although she now managed to contain her fear it lay not far from the surface, waiting like some hidden prey to spring out and engulf her.

It was nearly midnight and Teo had been missing for seven hours. Alexis sent all the servants to bed. He looked deathly tired but Lucy resisted his suggestion that they too went to bed.

"I cannot possibly sleep until you tell me what is happening," she said quietly. "Who was that man, Alexis? If he's not a policeman, then who is he?"

Alexis sat down on the sofa beside her and took her hand in his.

"I can't tell you his name, Lucy, but that isn't important. What matters is that he can help us recover Teo. You'll just have to go on trusting me to know what is best."

Lucy passed her hand wearily over her forehead.

"All those questions he asked me about Madeleine Villier!" she murmured. "He obviously suspects her, Alexis, but why?"

"Because we are now reasonably certain that this is a kidnapping and that it is related to the work I do, Lucy. It is very secret work—war work. I am not permitted to tell you about it but the relevant fact is that I have access to certain documents that could be of enormous use to the enemy. We have established that Anthony Black is a German agent—a spy, if you understand that word better. His real name is Anton Schwartz and we think he came to England about a year ago. Intelligence didn't know what he looked like—only his name, so they couldn't keep an eye on him. Now, thanks to you, we have a good description—and of course, if we can find Madeleine Villier, we can be reasonably certain of finding him."

Lucy digested this astonishing news in silence. Then she said thoughtfully:

"But we aren't even sure Madeleine Villier is involved. She may just turn up for work as usual on Monday and we'll be no nearer finding Teo!"

"Intelligence has already sent a man round to Madeleine's home, Lucy. She isn't there! I'm afraid there is little doubt she took Teo with her when she left this house. Although no one realized it at the time, in retrospect we know she was behaving strangely this afternoon. According to Rosie she had never been up to the nurseries before—except on one occasion when you had asked her to give Nanny a message. Cook said Madeleine had never before been down to the kitchen; nor was she in the habit of talking to the servants. And why *should* she offer to keep an eye on Teo for Rosie? It was not her job and Rosie was not someone for whom she might wish to do a kindness. So you see, we have to assume Madeleine took the child—probably on Anthony Black's instructions."

Lucy drew a deep breath.

"Madeleine would do whatever that man asked her," she admitted. "She was utterly under his spell. She wanted to marry him."

"A state of affairs I have little doubt that he purposefully engineered," Alexis said bitterly. "Madeleine was hardly much of a 'catch' and no beauty. I always felt it strange that any man could be as much in love with her as you described. The wretched woman probably believed everything he said. I am curious to know if she is aware he's a German."

"But what is to happen now?" Lucy asked. "Surely we are not just going to wait in the hope that they will bring Teo back?"

"We have no alternative, Lucy. My guess is that in the morning post there will be a ransom demand—not for money but for a number of vital documents to be delivered to some secret rendezvous in exchange for Teo."

"You'll let the man have the papers, won't you, Alexis?"

Alexis looked at Lucy's pale face and said gently:

"You know I can't do that, Lucy. If they fell into German hands, hundreds if not thousands of Allied soldiers might lose their lives because of it. We cannot trade Teo's life for theirs!" Lucy sprang off the sofa and confronted Alexis, her eyes brilliant.

"You'd let them harm—maybe kill Teo—rather than give them some stupid documents..."

"Lucy, calm yourself and consider the matter," Alexis interrupted. He tried to take hold of her arm but she twisted from him, crying:

"You don't care about Teo the way I do. It's because she is not really your child, isn't it? You pretend to love her but when it comes to proving it, you don't really care at all!"

Now Alexis was on his feet. His eyes were as angry as hers.

"That was not only cruel, Lucy, but a lie! I never think of Teo as only yours. Ever since she was born, I have felt she was *our* child. I love her and I am as terrified as you are to think of her in danger. I would willingly give my life if it would save hers. But they don't want *me*, Lucy. Can't you understand?"

Lucy was already regretting her outburst. No father could have been more devoted than Alexis. Nevertheless...

"You're going to let them kill her?" she asked, her voice trembling.

"Not if there is any possible way of avoiding so ghastly an eventuality," Alexis replied quietly. "And we think there is, Lucy. If we are right and they want certain specific documents, I will meet them wherever they suggest and offer them my portfolio—but containing fake documents. Intelligence are making up a set of false papers now—using officially headed paper and details that sound similar to the kind of things we believe they want to know. That way we have a chance—a breathing space in which to recover Teo."

Security forbade him to tell her the extraordinarily clever solution Intelligence had come up with. It was not officially known that the British were developing a long-range bomber. The construction of the prototype had been started early last year and the plane was almost ready for testing. This was the Handley Page 0/100. But a far more sophisticated version was in the pipe-line, the 0/400, and it was these details Anton Schwartz presumably was after. An expert forger was altering every figure 'one' to a figure 'four,' and by changing the dates on the plans, it was hoped that Schwartz would not realize the technical differences between the two sets of plans. It was a gamble based on the assumption that Schwartz was unlikely to be a highly qualified technician, and in his case the little knowledge he had on aircraft design would act to his disadvantage.

Alexis wished desperately that he could pass on this information to Lucy to relieve at least some of her agony. He reached out and this time Lucy did not resist him as he put his arms round her. The tension easing from her body, she laid her head against his chest.

"I'm so frightened for her!" she said. "Suppose there is no ransom note tomorrow, Alexis?"

"We're doing everything to make it easy for them to get in touch with me," Alexis said gently. "That's why we cannot involve the police. We don't want uniformed bobbies all over the place; or any kind of publicity; and for the same reason I have confined all the servants to the house for the time being. A careless word from any one of them..."

Lucy nodded. Alexis had called in Mrs. Taylor, Bulford, Nanny and Cook and spoken to them after the bowler-hatted man had departed.

"Miss Teo's life may depend on your loyalty and your obedience," he had told them gravely. "I cannot tell you why but for the present, no single member of the staff must leave the house; no one must write a letter or use the telephone without my permission. No one must gossip with any person who delivers goods to the house. If necessary, Cook, you yourself must deal with the butcher's boy, the baker's boy and so on. Bulford, you will take all messages at the front door, not any of the footmen. You are to pass on these instructions to all the junior servants and the day-to-day affairs of the house are to continue as if nothing whatever was wrong. Nanny, if there should be any inquiries about Miss Teo, she is confined to bed with a cold. I'm sure I don't need to tell you all that I am relying on you absolutely to obey these orders and that any single lapse, *however minor*, will result in instant dismissal without pay and without character. But I know that will not be necessary."

The servants would close ranks around them, Alexis told Lucy. Whatever their grumbles and dissatisfactions within the household, he had no fear that they would betray him in this present emergency. He remembered his father once telling him never to undervalue the British servant class.

"They may grumble amongst themselves and they may even on occasions steal your liquor and your food. But if you treat them fairly, they'll take as much care of your family good name as you would yourself. There's no one more loyal if they respect the master they serve."

Now his household would be put to the test, Alexis thought as he took Lucy's arm and led her upstairs to bed. He was not in the least surprised to find Polly and Simpson still up, waiting to see if their services were needed.

"Is Nanny all right, Polly?" Lucy asked as she gratefully accepted Polly's help.

"Cook sent her up a cup of hot milk not an hour ago," Polly said. "To help her sleep like, she being a bit upset, of course. I looked in ten minutes ago and she was dozing, so don't you worry none, Ma'am. It's you as needs the sleep."

"We all do," Alexis remarked as he came through in his dressing gown to say goodnight.

Downstairs in the hall, Bulford alone had not retired to bed. He had settled himself in a chair by the front door where he nodded fitfully. Sometimes the morning post came five minutes early and he wanted to be quite sure the letter his Master was waiting for was got to him without a moment's delay. No one had said much to him but he'd kept his eyes and ears open and he guessed poor little Miss Teo had been kidnapped. By the sound of it, it was a German behind the abduction.

"Filthy Hun!" he muttered as he stretched his aching legs. If it wasn't for his age, he'd have joined the B.E.F. long ago. As for that stuck-up secretary, Miss Villier, he'd never liked her. Let her come near the house again and he'd wring her neck. Meanwhile, he thought, a little nip of the master's whiskey would help to keep him awake. The decanter was like as not still on the table in the drawing room.

He poured himself a generous measure and took it back to his self-appointed sentry post by the front door. The Master's study door was locked as usual, he noticed. He'd often wondered what all the secrecy was about and now he reckoned he knew.

As he settled himself comfortably once more, there was a satisfied smile on his face. Just let that uppity butler at number thirty-two make another snide remark like '*my* Master has joined the Navy and he's doing his bit!' Not that he Bulford would be able to say exactly what the Count was doing but he knew now it was war work of some kind—secret, too. That fellow with the bowler hat he'd opened the door to an hour or so back was no ordinary detective. From Intelligence, like as not, Bulford guessed. He gave a satisfied yawn. No white feathers for his Master! The Count's work had to be important...wouldn't take the risk of kidnapping the child otherwise...penalty was fourteen years penal servitude ...perhaps even death...

The effects of the whiskey had reached Bulford's brain and he stopped thinking as his head fell forward and the hall echoed with the rumble of his snores.

In a small, two-bedroomed cottage by the sea at Hove, whimsically called 'Cockleshells,' Madeleine Villier paced the floor of the room she was sharing with the child.

"Daren't let her out of our sight!" Anthony said regretfully when Madeleine made as if to follow him into the room where he had put his own suitcase. "Hard on both of us, my dear, but we don't want to take any chances now, do we?"

Madeleine was barely able to conceal her dismay. She was certain that Anthony had intended for them to be together at last. Now it seemed she had been mistaken. Yet she could see no real necessity to remain with the little girl who had fallen asleep.

There was no way Madeleine could see that Teo could get out of the house even had she awoken and wanted to go out alone in the dark. The windows were closed and the front door was locked. But Anthony remained adamant.

"Never know who might have followed us...breaking in when we were asleep..." he argued unconvincingly.

Now Madeleine's frustration was giving way to fear. It had suddenly registered with her that she and Anthony had comittted a terrible crime. Kidnapping was a very serious offense, almost if not as bad as murder! Suppose it all went wrong and they were caught? It was all very well for Anthony to be so calm but it wasn't he who had actually abducted the child. No one would have reason to blame him. If she was not already a suspect, she would be on Monday and then every policeman in the country would be looking not for Anthony but for her!

Through the thin walls of the cheap little house, Madeleine could hear Anthony snoring. It was not a very romantic sound to say the least. She had heard him lock his door, otherwise she might have gone into his bedroom in order to hear his affectionate, reassuring voice. But since they had arrived at 'Cockleshells,' he had spoken unusually curtly to her and this had added to her misgivings.

Keeping to the letter of his plan, Anthony had pushed a ransom note into a letter box before they drove out of London.

The Count would receive it by first post in the morning, Madeleine reflected. Then what would he do? Would he meet Anthony at the end of the West Pier as he was asked, bringing the papers with him? It seemed suddenly such a silly plan. It would have been so much easier if he was asked to bring money. Then there would have been no need to sell the papers back to him, involving them in yet another crime—blackmail! It was true that they could go on blackmailing him for more and more money but that wouldn't be so easy all the way from New Zealand. Anthony had promised again and again that they would emigrate as soon as they could pay for their tickets. He had disregarded the fact that they were in the middle of a war and it might not be possible to get passages on a ship going to New Zealand.

"Of course we can!" he had argued. "There are ships going out there all the time to bring chaps home who want to join up."

Madeleine worried that she might be traced through her passport. This, too, Anthony swept aside. They would get married first by special license. Then she'd be on his passport as Mrs. Madeleine Black.

But as far as she could see, there was no special license ready and days could go by before she was safely out of the country.

In the morning Anthony looked at her white face, blotched with sleeplessness and crying and his voice softened:

"I never told you last night how brave I thought you'd been," he said putting an arm round her shoulders. She clung to him with a violence that was beyond caution.

"I don't feel brave. I wish we hadn't done it, Anthony. Can't we forget all about this scheme? Can't we just take the child out and leave her on the Promenade. Someone would find her and take her back home and..."

"Don't be silly!" his voice was sharp once again. "You're forgetting the ransom note. They'll have got it by now." He grinned. "Bet they're all in an uproar at Cadogan Gardens. Serve 'em right!"

The child was crying from the bedroom.

"Better go up and see to her," Anthony said. He gave her a quick kiss which did nothing to restore Madeleine's equilibrium. "Go on, there's a good girl. Don't want the neighbors coming round to see what's wrong!"

Not without difficulty Madeleine helped the little girl to

wash her hands and face and put on her dress. She had never had anything to do with children and Teo could do nothing for herself.

"Nanny always dresses me!" she said tearfully.

Madeleine abandoned the attempt to brush the child's fine, silky hair which had become a mass of tangles in the night. She took her downstairs and sat her at the table in the kitchen. Anthony, meanwhile, had been out to purchase the necessities. He put a large cottage loaf, butter, marmalade, eggs and a jug of milk on the wooden dresser.

"Quite a decent day!" he observed cheerfully. "Let's have something to eat, my dear. We'll all feel better when we've food inside us!"

But Madeleine could only drink a cup of strong tea. Teo had spilled egg and milk down the front of her dress and her hair was now sticky with marmalade. She bore no resemblance to the dainty little Madam in the nursery at Cadogan Gardens. A pool gathered beneath her chair.

"Oh, God!" Madeleine whispered. "I suppose I should have sent her to the bathroom. Anthony, how long is this going on? I'm no good at this sort of thing!"

Hearing the latent hysteria in her voice, the man stood up.

"I'll look after her!" he said. "Came from a large family myself so I know a bit about it—a bit more than you anyway!"

He removed Teo to the bathroom and Madeleine poured herself another cup of tea. Tears were threatening as she stared out of the window. Already there were families making their way down to the beach. On the sands men had their trouser legs rolled up and handkerchiefs knotted at the corners over their heads. The women wore sun bonnets and had taken off their stockings to go paddling with their children. Some were already swimming, their bathing caps bright in the sunlight and their excited voices shrill enough to reach Madeleine's ears. They all looked so happy. A young man went past with a girl on his arm and stopped by the cockle stall. He was staring down at her admiringly like any lover. If only she and Anthony were here by the seaside on their own...a happily married couple...

Anthony returned with the child riding pick-a-back on his shoulders. Both looked perfectly content.

"Good as gold, she was!" he said cheerfully. "No need for us to mooch around here all morning. Assignation isn't till three o'clock. We'll all go down to the beach for the morning, shall we? Do you know I haven't dug sand castles since I was a kid?"

He looked at Madeleine's sulky face—plainer than ever now she was so clearly frightened—and breathed a sigh of relief that his ordeal was nearly over. If ever a man had done his bit for his country, he had, he reflected, thinking of the interminable evenings in Madeleine's company when he had tried to keep the amorous woman at arm's length.

But his patience had proved worthwhile. Hopefully by three o'clock this afternoon, Count Zemski would be on the pier with the documents—the specific documents Madeleine knew nothing about, relating to the new airplane design. If his country were able to produce any kind of defense against the new bomber then they had to know its potential. It had been made perfectly clear to him how important his mission was— and urgent, too. But even his bosses had understood that he could not push Madeleine too far too quickly. It had been a clever move of his getting to know her in the first place—a plan he had conceived as soon as he had been given Zemski's name as someone involved in aeronautics. His foresight had already earned him considerable praise.

But it had become harder and harder of late to keep up the pretense of being an ardent suitor. The wretched woman was head over heels in love with him and if the amorous glances and words were not enough, he had to endure her even more amorous embraces. He was reminded suddenly of a poem he had read recently. Surely the poet must have had Madeleine in mind when he wrote: "*Oh, fat white woman whom nobody loves...*" he thought cruelly.

He glanced at his wristwatch. Still only ten o'clock. He would take them to the beach. Madeleine could not get at him there and it would pass the time.

Lucy was at the same moment putting on her car coat. Alexis had tried every persuasion to prevent her going with him to Brighton but Lucy was quietly and rigidly adamant.

"If you refuse to take me with you, I shall follow in a taxicab!" she said. Realizing she meant it, Alexis capitulated.

On the drive down, he warned her once more of the dangers.

"You, Teo, I—any one of us—or even all of us—could be killed!" he told her as he drove over Clapham Common to pick up the London to Brighton road. "I understand your compulsion to come with me, Lucy, but now I have agreed, you must give me your word to obey any instructions I give you—at once and without argument. All our lives could depend on it and so too will our chances of getting Teo back unharmed. Will you give me your word?"

Lucy nodded. She was feeling better now that the ransom note had actually come and they were actively doing something. She glanced at Alexis. He looked composed and slightly strange in his leather helmet and goggles.

"Isn't the pier a somewhat risky place for a meeting?" she asked thoughtfully. "Suppose you brought the police with you. He'd be trapped at the end of the pier!"

Alexis smiled.

"An intelligent question!" he said. "But you are forgetting Black has no idea we can recognize him. He said in his letter that *he* would approach *me*. He'll probably wait until he is absolutely certain I am alone before he makes a move. It's really quite a good choice of venue from his point of view. The pier will be crowded with trippers on a fine summer's day and he can merge with them!"

"But Madeleine, Teo . . . we'd know them at once!"

"He won't have them with him, Lucy," Alexis said quietly. "He'll take us wherever they are only when he is certain I have the papers he wants. I, of course, shan't hand them over until I see Teo is all right."

An uneasy silence followed his words. They were now passing through the suburbs. Soon they would be in Purley. They had plenty of time. Alexis was covering himself against the possibility of a mechanical breakdown or a puncture.

He was trying to behave as if this were an ordinary Saturday outing, Lucy realized. But she could feel his tenseness. It echoed her own as she endeavored not to think what they would do if the man failed to keep the rendezvous, or far worse, if Teo had been harmed. They might even take her away somewhere and Lucy might never see her child again . . .

Quite suddenly, Lucy thought of her own mother and how Willow must have felt when she knew *her* child had been spirited away; that there was no hope of ever finding her. What a miracle it must have seemed when Lucy had reappeared after all those years! No wonder her mother had been so overcome when they met at Rochford after her father's death! No wonder she had been so doting, continuing to seek

Lucy's devotion even though Lucy herself had shown no affection.

Lucy drew a deep breath. It had never been her intention to hurt her mother. She had simply not understood the bond that must have been forged when she, Lucy, was born. Now she felt a deep regret that she had never made any attempt to imagine how hurt Willow must have felt at her indifference. As soon as this terrible ordeal over Teo was behind them, she would go down to Rochford and do her utmost to show her mother she did really wish to be on affectionate terms with her.

Soon they were at the top of Reigate Hill and coasting down into the little market town. They were not far from Brighton and it was still only midday.

"We'll have a quick luncheon in the George Hotel at Crawley," Alexis said. "At most it will take us an hour from there and if we leave at one o'clock, we shall still have an hour in hand against possible mishaps. I am as impatient as you, Lucy, but the waiting would only be the harder if we were in Brighton."

Lucy realized he was right when they reached the outskirts of the town. Immediately her eyes began to search amongst the pedestrians for a glimpse of Madeleine and Teo—an absurd hope since they would obviously both be concealed somewhere where they could not be recognized. Nevertheless, she could not stop herself glancing continually from side to side.

Avoiding the east end of town, Alexis drove down into Hove, round the beautiful Georgian houses of Adelaide Crescent and out on to the sea front. To their right, the West Pier stretched out to sea. The sun was sparkling on the water and the beaches on either side were crowded. It was perfect holiday weather and people were making the most of it, some swimming, some lolling in deck chairs, others gathered along the side rails of the pier, fishing.

Alexis drew the car to a halt at the entrance to the pier.

"I want you to wait here, Lucy," he said quietly.

She nodded, her thoughts still uneasy. Although Alexis made light of it, she was convinced this meeting could be dangerous for him. But she had given her word not to interfere and Alexis was holding her to it.

Alexis paid his gate money and forced himself to stroll casually onto the pier. It was ten minutes to three. He had plenty of time to walk to the far end where Black had said he would be. In his hand, he held a portfolio. He was very far from being as confident as he had led Lucy to believe, that his enemy would be duped by the contents. Intelligence had had insufficient time to get hold of convincing alternatives to the real plans. The drawings had been easy enough—drawings made and scrapped two years earlier and long since out of date. It was the written data that had been almost impossible to assemble for all the papers were dated. It had taken a master forger every minute of the night to alter the dates of several old documents. The man had done a good job and the changes might pass the notice of a casual observer. But if Anthony Black—or Anton Schwartz—knew much about aviation, he would see within minutes that the plans referred to an airplane already flying.

There were a dozen or more people at the end of the pier— a family party with mother, father and three children; an elderly woman pushing an invalid in a wheelchair; two young soldiers in khaki with their girls; a man in a white coat and cap collecting payment for the use of deck chairs.

From years of Secret Service work, Alexis knew that he was being watched despite the fact that he could see no sign of his observer. He leaned with his back to the rail and waited.

It was several minutes before Anthony Black approached him, his eyes darting to and fro as if still not convinced that Alexis was alone.

"I am by myself!" Alexis said calmly.

His companion grinned.

"Thought you might be—just wanted to be sure!" He peered more closely at Alexis and at the portfolio in his hand. "I recognized you, of course," he said sneering, "apart from *that*! Seen you coming out of Cadogan Gardens when I've been waiting for your secretary."

Alexis' mouth tightened.

"Let's not waste time, Black. I want my daughter. Where is she?"

"Safe and sound, safe and sound! But first I want to see you have something worth trading. I reckon your little girl's worth quite a bit—to both of us, eh?"

Alexis longed to hit out at the dapper little man smiling at him so confidently. But he was far too well trained to betray any emotion. He said:

"Obviously I think so—or I wouldn't be here, would I? But you're a bit lucky, Black, although you may not have realized it. Had I been a real Englishman born and bred, I might have considered it my patriotic duty to sacrifice my child rather than my country. Fortunately for you, I'm a Serbo-Croat by birth and so I don't have the same degree of allegiance."

First round to me, Alexis thought as he saw his words bring a little glint of triumph into his companion's eyes. Black had taken the bait!

"That's the trouble with the British," Anthony said sourly. "Too trusting by half. Show us, then, what have you got? Plans for the new Handley Page bomber?"

"They're what you wanted, aren't they?" Alexis said quietly.

Anthony Black's face revealed his satisfaction.

"Yes," he admitted, "but I couldn't be sure."

He led the way to two empty chairs and motioned Alexis to be seated. Alexis put the portfolio on his knee and opened it. Black went to grab the papers from him but he kept a firm hold on them.

"Not until I have my daughter back!" he said in a low, vibrant tone. "You can see all you need from there."

As Alexis withdrew further papers and prints, Anthony cast a quick eye over them. As far as he could see, they looked perfectly genuine. Across the top of one was printed in large letters 'HANDLEY PAGE' and underneath the figures, '0/400.' These were exactly what his masters had asked him to try for, although they had doubted his ability to get them. They'd be very agreeably surprised—very agreeably. It would be a big feather in his cap. Promotion probably and with luck he'd never have to come back to England—or have to see the miserable Madeleine again.

Alexis was pulling the papers gently away from him and putting them back in his portfolio.

"Shall we go?" he suggested calmly.

"Self-confident bastard, aren't you?" Anthony said. He'd have preferred it if this aristocratic man had cringed a little, begged a little, or at least shown some apprehension.

"Has it occurred to you I might have a gun?" he asked. "I could just take those papers from you and scarper!"

"I too, might have a gun!" Alexis said with a faint smile. "But we'd both be very silly to use firearms, wouldn't we? It would create a lot of noise whichever of us shot first and that would involve the police which neither of us wants. So I suggest we keep to our arrangement. You hand over my daughter and these are yours."

His expression sulky but resigned, Anthony followed as Alexis began to walk back along the pier. He was still behaving with caution. Alexis might have a posse of policemen waiting at the exit—a likely trap!

"You go first," he said. "And wait where I can see you. I'll follow when I'm satisfied it's safe."

Alexis shrugged.

"As you wish—but I assure you it isn't necessary. I want my child back and if the police were to get their hands on you, you might never tell me where she is!"

Lucy saw Alexis come out—alone. Her heart jolted. She was about to get out of the car and run to his side when deliberately, he turned his back on her. He had told her to remain in the car, she recalled. He must be waiting for the German to join him.

Anthony appeared almost at once, reassured by the logic of Alexis' remarks. His anxiety returned, however, when Alexis drew his attention to the Lanchester with Lucy sitting in the front seat.

"I told you to come alone . . ." he began, but Alexis interrupted him.

"Someone has got to look after the child on the way home, Black. My wife won't bother us. Are we walking or driving?"

"Driving!" Anthony said shortly. "In your car. Mine's at the cottage."

Alexis did not attempt to introduce him to Lucy but opened the back door for Anthony to get in. His glance at Lucy forbade conversation.

"Drive west!" Anthony directed from the back seat. "Out toward Worthing!"

As Alexis started the engine and put the car into gear, Anthony turned to stare behind them.

"There's no one following us. You have my word!" Alexis said from the front seat.

He wished it were not the truth. But as he had told Intelligence, he dared not risk his child's life.

"It's not so much to ask," he had said bitterly. "You'll get Black later. He can't leave the country now you know him. I'll stop at the very first place I can and telephone you his address as soon as I'm clear of the house. If you have the local force alerted, they should be able to catch him before he gets out of Brighton!"

At first, they had refused to keep out of it. It wasn't until after he'd threatened Fanshaw that he'd resign if he didn't back his request, that Fanshaw pulled a few strings and it was agreed he would not be followed. Now, having met and talked to the German, Alexis felt a deep surge of repulsion and hatred for him. He wanted him caught; wanted him dead. Any man who could stoop to kidnapping a little child not yet three years old deserved death for that alone. As a spy, he doubly deserved to die.

Not half a mile from Hove, Anthony instructed Alexis to draw up outside the cottage—the only one in a row of seaside bungalows strung along the coast.

"It's called 'Cockleshells.' Got a double row of 'em up the pathway," he said with a grin.

Lucy felt sick in the pit of her stomach. She longed to cry out:

"What have you done with my baby? Have you harmed her? Is she all right?" But obedient to Alexis' command, she remained silent. As the car stopped, she glanced up and saw a curtain move in an upstairs window. She glimpsed a face— but not Teo's.

Anthony Black went ahead up the garden path and knocked impatiently on the front door. It opened almost immediately and Madeleine stood there.

Now Lucy's self-control gave way and opening the car door, she ran past Alexis and grabbed Madeleine by the arms.

"Where is she? Where's Teo?" she gasped.

"Upstairs!" Madeleine answered shortly. "Locked in her room and I have the key!" She looked over Lucy's shoulder to Anthony who grinned at her.

"It's all right," he said. "You can fetch her down—but don't hand her over until I say so."

They went indoors. Lucy's eyes darted round the dirty, disordered sitting room and her glance fell on one of Teo's little shoes. She looked appealingly at Madeleine.

"Please, oh please fetch her quickly!" she pleaded.

Madeleine shrugged and went slowly out of the room. She returned within minutes, the child half asleep in her arms.

"She isn't drugged, if that's what you think! She is just tired after a morning on the beach," Madeleine said, seeing Lucy's horrified gaze. Alexis caught hold of Lucy's arm, aware that she was about to hurry across the room to Teo.

"It's a matter of how we do the exchange!" he said dryly to the German. "I suggest you put the child in the car. My wife can go too, and then I'll give you the portfolio. That way neither of us can end up with nothing. My wife can't drive," he added.

"That sounds a good idea to me," Madeleine said with a fond glance at Anthony. "I think it's a sensible way to make the exchange."

The look he gave her was scathing, his voice even more so as he said:

"You keep out of this, you stupid woman! D'you think I care for your ridiculous opinions? Just shut up and do what you are told!"

Unable to believe her eyes and ears, Madeleine gasped. Still holding Teo, she moved a step closer to Anthony.

"But I don't understand. What's wrong? What have I done? Why are you so angry?" she cried, her voice trembling with shock.

"I'll explain, shall I?" Alexis said quietly. "There's no point in keeping the truth from her any longer, is there, Black? That's not his real name, Madeleine. He's really Anton Schwartz and he's a German spy. He set this whole plan up months ago and you were necessary to him as a means of getting into my house. The suggestion that you should become my secretary was very plausible and we both fell for it. I should have known better but you . . . you had no way of knowing that he was using you."

Madeleine's face turned so white that Lucy took a step forward believing she was about to faint. But Madeleine's mind was crystal clear. Count Zemski's words made sense of every past confusion. She could see it all as if it were happening in front of her eyes at one of the picture palaces. Anthony spilling his box of chocolates over her; getting to know her; pretending to care for her; pretending he wanted to marry her . . . refusing ever to commit himself in the act of love. He had never loved her. That was what mattered far more than that he was a German spy.

Very slowly she walked across the room, two bright spots of color giving a clownlike appearance to her white face as she set the wide-eyed girl on the table in front of her. It was still littered with the remnants of their breakfast—a sordid, untidy sight which she did not notice.

"I loved you, Anthony!" she said in a small voice. "I really did love you. I wouldn't have walked out on you even if I'd discovered for myself that you were a German and a spy. I wouldn't have cared if you'd been the worst animal in the world. What I can't live with is the thought that you don't love me—that you never did."

"I've heard enough of this drivel!" Anthony cried, cruelly indifferent to the terrible hurt he had inflicted on her. "Give the child to me!"

He took a step toward her but as he moved, Madeleine released hold of the little girl and grabbed the bread knife. Anthony lurched forward to grab Teo. As he did so Madeleine's arm lifted and lunged toward his chest.

It happened with such speed that Alexis was powerless to prevent the blow. Perhaps, he told himself later, he had not really wanted to and his reactions had subconsciously been the slower for it. But by the time he reached the table, Anthony Black was lying over it motionless. The knife had slipped fatally between two ribs and pierced his heart, killing him instantly.

"Oh, my God!" Lucy cried as she ran round the table to lift Teo safely into her arms. The child remained unaware of what was happening and smiled at her mother.

"I made a sand castle!" she said brightly. "Daddy, come and see my castle? Mummy, make another one!"

"Take her out to the car, Lucy!" Alexis said sharply. "I'll deal with Madeleine!"

As Lucy went out of the room, Teo chattering contentedly in her mother's arms, Alexis turned to the woman still standing unmoving as she looked at the blood seeping over the checkered tablecloth.

"He's dead, isn't he?" Madeleine said flatly. "He'll never take me in his arms again. He'll never hold me, kiss me! I love him, you know."

Despite the fact that she had betrayed him, cheated him, kidnapped his child, Alexis at that moment could only feel pity for her. She looked a disheveled, helpless, pathetic, middle-aged woman bereft of the only person in the world she cared about. And she had killed him.

"You'd better sit down," he said authoritatively.

Madeleine remained standing.

"I loved him, you see," she said. "That's why I had to kill him. It wasn't right what he did to me. I loved him . . ."

She was staring at Alexis but her eyes were glazed. She seemed unaware of his presence or even that of the dead man as she swayed to and fro moaning softly. This was more than a simple case of shock, Alexis thought as he put her in a chair. She was totally unresisting and apparently indifferent to everything but her own confused thoughts. Was it safe to leave her while he went in search of a police station, he wondered.

A strange smile now crossed the woman's blotched face.

"Can we go to the Empire on Saturday, Anthony?" she rambled. "I like it there. I wish I could remember where I put my gloves..."

She began once more her soft keening and Alexis was no longer in any doubt that her reason had deserted her. She was in no fit state to travel in the car with Lucy and the child. He would have to lock her up somewhere safe—in the bathroom perhaps. He would stop at the nearest telephone and get through to Fanshaw. He could deal with it all—and with the minimum of publicity.

There was a seafront hotel nearby where Alexis was able to make his telephone call. Reassured that Fanshaw had everything in hand, he returned to the car where an anxious Lucy sat cradling the sleeping Teo.

"What will happen to the wretched woman?" Lucy asked as they drove back to London. "Will they hang her for murder?"

"I honestly don't know, Lucy," Alexis replied. "They won't want to bring me into it. They'll try and hush it up somehow. They may put her in an asylum."

"*Is* she mad?" Lucy asked.

Alexis sighed.

"I don't know that either, Lucy. It's obvious she really did love Black and I suppose a woman of her age... Maybe she'll get over it in time and they'll send her back to her own country. We'll have to wait and see."

For a few miles they drove in silence, the only sound Lucy's gentle crooning over the child.

> "*I sowed the seeds of love;*
> *I sowed them in the spring...*"

Then she broke off and said thoughtfully:

"Love is a strange thing, isn't it, Alexis? I mean, if it can hurt enough to make you want to kill someone?"

"It shouldn't be like that," Alexis replied quietly. "It should be a happy, giving thing if two people love each other!"

"In a way..." Lucy said, more to herself than to him, "I can understand how Madeleine felt! A long time ago, when I was very young and probably very silly too, I cared very much for a man who didn't love me. When I found out that he didn't love me at all and never had, I hated him so much I suppose I could have killed him if I'd thought about it. Anyway," she added with a wry smile, "there wasn't a knife handy!"

Alexis felt his heart jolt with sudden understanding. Lucy had never before told him so much about her past, but now he knew she was talking about Teo's natural father—the man she had hated. But instead of killing the man who had hurt her, she had killed love instead. By denying its existence or any understanding of it, she had been protecting herself from a repetition of pain.

But she could not protect herself forever, Alexis thought, as in her clear, soft voice she began once more to sing. There could be no more hiding her fiercely protective, maternal love for Teo. She understood very well what it was to care so deeply for another human being. Perhaps before too long, he told himself, Lucy would learn to care as much for him.

Chapter 20

∽

August 1915—June 1916

PHILIP GREY WAS WORRIED. IT WAS THE FIRST WEEK OF AUGUST AND in two days' time he was returning to his ship. On previous occasions, he had never had the slightest concern about his sister, Jane. Since she had come to Rochford to live four years ago, she had never had a day's unhappiness that he knew of. Lady Rochford showed her no less affection than she did her own children and Jane looked on her as a mother. As a result of her happiness, she had blossomed from a shy, nervous, skinny twelve-year-old child into a really pretty girl. Although physically very different from Lady Rochford, Jane's nature was surprisingly similar: gentle, kindly, thoughtful and sensitive. Her sunny disposition endeared her to everyone—and there lay the cause for his worry, Philip thought, as he stood at his bedroom window staring down into the garden below.

Oliver and Jane were sitting side by side in the hammock that was slung between two branches of the big lime tree. They were holding hands and were deep in conversation, their young faces turned toward each other in rapt attention.

Throughout his leave, Philip had tried to ignore what he hoped was just a silly notion—that Oliver and Jane's relationship had changed from that of brother and sister. He had always known that his sister regarded Oliver with an undisguised hero worship and that young Oliver had tolerated Jane in an affectionate but dispassionate way. But now he was forced to admit to himself that his notion might not, after all, be so silly. Oliver was quite old enough to be taking an interest in girls and Jane was pretty enough these days to turn a chap's thoughts to matters other than cricket and war!

For a moment Philip's face looked far older than his years. None of this would have mattered—indeed, it would have been a cause for delight, he thought, had it not been for his sister's true relationship to Oliver. Neither of them had the slightest knowledge that they shared the same father. His great-aunt had told Jane when they went to live with her that her father, Edwin Grey, had been in the navy and died at sea. Jane had never questioned it and was ignorant of the fact that her mother had been the mistress of Lord Rowell Rochford and that all three of the Grey children were his.

Philip's hatred for his real father now rose like gall in his throat. If ever a man deserved to die, he did. The man had treated not only his mother but dear, kind Lady Rochford with utter callousness and brought no happiness to either. Over the years Philip had tried to forget him and recently he had attempted to model himself on his two uncles, Toby and Pelham, both of whom he admired and believed to be worthy of their illustrious surname. But his father's ghost would not, after all, be laid so easily.

Philip's dismay increased as he saw Oliver's hand reach out and touch Jane's shining, waist-length hair. Quite naturally, her head nestled into his shoulder as they swung gently to and fro, the sunlight filtering through the leafy branches and dappling their clothes.

He was reminded suddenly of a few lines from one of Rupert Brooke's poems in the book he had given Jane a few weeks ago:

> *"Sunlight in the boughs above,*
> *Sunlight in your hair and dress,*
> *The hands too proud for all but love,*
> *The lips of utter kindliness...."*

He turned abruptly from the window. His imagination was running away with him, he thought. Clearly, neither Lady Rochford nor his uncle had any such stupid suspicions or they would surely have mentioned them to him. It would not be many weeks before Oliver was back at Eton and Jane forgotten—or remembered only as a sister left behind in the schoolroom at home. They were both very young—far too young probably even to be thinking about love. Next time he, Philip, was home on leave, he could deal with the problem—if there really was one.

Oliver, too, was thinking about returning to school.

"I wish I need never go back!" he said vehemently. "I wish I was Mark's age and could join the army and *do* something!

This war is never going to last long enough for me to get into it."

He looked at Jane's anxious face and laughed—but with a hint of tenderness in his voice as he added:

"Now don't get all feminine and concerned for me like Mother," he said. "I'm counting on you to support me, Jane, when the time comes—*if* it comes. You will, won't you?"

Jane sighed.

"I suppose I'll have to—but I am a female like your mother and I couldn't bear it if you were wounded ... or ..."

"I won't be, silly!" Oliver said, squeezing her hand. "I suppose I do want you to mind really—I mean, it shows you do care about me."

"I've always cared about you, Oliver!" Jane said in a low intense voice. "I can't remember a time since I met you when you didn't mean every bit as much to me as Philip or Mark—and you know how much I love them."

Oliver's young face was a comic mixture of pleasure and anxiety.

"Yes, but they're your brothers!" he said earnestly. "You more or less have to love them. It's strange, isn't it? I always used to think of you as a sister and then I suddenly woke up to the fact that we weren't related at all and we could even get married if we wanted ..."

He broke off, his face coloring with embarrassment as he realized how easily he had betrayed his secret thoughts. Waiting for Jane to reply, he was on tenterhooks lest she thought he was being ridiculously soppy. But she seemed—as Jane always did—to understand exactly what he was trying to say.

"I've thought about it, too," she said softly. "If I had to share my life with someone, then I'd want it to be with you."

"I know!" Oliver said eagerly. "We get along so splendidly, don't we? Gosh, Jane, you will write to me, won't you—when I go back to school, I mean. It'll seem an absolute age till the Christmas hols."

He broke off as he saw Philip coming toward them across the lawn, followed by two middle-aged housemaids bringing tea. They had replaced the two pretty young maids who usually saw to afternoon tea, but who had now left for work in a munitions factory.

Jane jumped up and ran to her brother, linking her arm in his.

"I shall hate you leaving tomorrow, Phil," she said sighing.

"Your leave seems to have gone so quickly! Why *does* time always seem to fly past when you're happy and drag when you are doing something you don't enjoy!"

Willow came hurrying out of the house to join them. Her face looked pale.

"Toby has just had a telephone call from Alexis!" she blurted out. "He didn't say a great deal but apparently something awful happened to little Teo. Everything's all right now and he's driving Lucy and Teo down this afternoon to stay for a while—but Toby thought he said Teo had been lost! The line was very bad and he couldn't hear too clearly."

Oliver rose to pull up a deck chair for his mother.

"Lost! With Nanny Meredith in charge?" he commented.

"It was her day off!" Willow said, sinking into the chair. "My poor Lucy—she must have been worried out of her wits!"

"Then don't you do her worrying for her now," Oliver said gently. "I gather the flap is over and all is well, so have some tea, Mater. We'll hear all about it when they arrive."

But Alexis had forbidden Lucy to tell anyone the real story.

"It would involve too many questions I cannot answer," he explained. "I know it's family, Lucy, but my work is very secret and the least said about it the better. Let's just say Teo wandered out of the front door which Madeleine had left open and it wasn't until the early hours of the next day that we found her in the gardens."

Lucy had no wish to relive the memory of that dreadful day at Brighton. The sooner she could forget the horrible sight of Anthony Black's body slumped over the dirty kitchen table, the better pleased she would be. She was still numbed by the horror of it and was conscious of little else but relief in having Teo safe once more in Nanny's charge and gratitude to Alexis for managing to recover her so quickly—and without any sign of injury. The child appeared to have suffered no distress whatever—in fact, she had talked happily to Nanny of her morning building sand castles on the beach. It was mainly she, Lucy and Alexis who had suffered, Lucy thought— and the tearful Rosie who blamed herself, not without good reason. She had been demoted to the position of housemaid, Nanny having stated that she would go without her day off in future rather than have 'that flighty girl' back in the nursery.

Although Lucy had maintained a calm exterior throughout the whole affair, the terrible tension she had undergone was merely submerged. When Willow greeted her with tears in her eyes, Lucy's control suddenly vanished. As her mother's arms went round her, she burst into tears.

Willow led her up to her bedroom and dismissing the attentive Polly, sat on the side of the bed with her arm around her weeping daughter.

"I know how you must have felt, my darling," she said tenderly as she wiped Lucy's falling tears with her handkerchief as if she had been a little girl. "There is nothing more agonizing for a mother than to lose a child."

Lucy gulped as she fought for words.

"I don't think I realized how much I loved Teo until I thought I'd never see her again," she said. "Oh, Mama, I kept thinking of you—of how you must have felt when you realized I had been taken away from you."

Now it was Willow who was weeping openly as she hugged Lucy. But they were tears of joy. It was the first time they had ever embraced with real warmth and Willow could hardly believe that at long last a bond had been forged between them.

"Really, darling, we are a pair of sillies!" she said huskily. "Sitting here weeping our eyes out when we should be rejoicing. Teo is perfectly all right, isn't she? Nanny said she'd come to no harm."

Lucy attempted a watery smile.

"No, she's right as rain. I think I am the one who is suffering from delayed shock. All the time it was happening, I felt I was in a horrible kind of nightmare—that it wasn't really happening at all. Alexis was calm and wonderful. The servants were, too."

Willow nodded and then sighed.

"It's sad so many of the family retainers are leaving," she said. "I don't blame them, of course, and Toby will not allow me to attempt to dissuade any of them when they come to say they want to do war work. We're down to fifteen now. Toby says we don't need a chauffeur and he drives me into Tunbridge Wells if I want to go shopping. I shall really have to learn to drive myself. After all, other women do nowadays."

Lucy smiled.

"Alexis keeps telling me I should learn, too," she said. "But I don't think I'm very mechanically minded."

"Nor am I," Willow said happily. "We're quite alike, aren't we, darling?"

Lucy nodded.

"I suppose we are—in some ways. But you're a nicer person

than I am, Mama. You seem to like doing things for other people for instance, whereas I only like doing things for myself!"

"What nonsense!" Willow replied. "I only enjoy looking after the people I love."

"Yes, but I don't love anybody!" Lucy said.

"And that is an even greater piece of nonsense!" Willow laughed as she linked her arm through Lucy's and led her toward the door.

But it was not nonsense, Lucy thought, although she no longer felt the desire to disillusion her mother. Her feelings about Teo were the natural instincts of any mother, her affection for her family equally natural. As for Alexis, she had always admired him and she was fond of him and had never felt any desire to be married to anyone else, but love was not part of her repertoire of emotions.

Alexis referred once more to the word that night when they went to bed.

"I know you love Teo," he said, "and if you insist upon returning to London with me, at least concede the fact that she will be far safer here at Rochford than in London. The Germans are stepping up their airship attacks and although I have not seen the most recent figures, I know that there were twenty-four people killed and forty homes destroyed in one single raid on Hull in June. They are certain to go for London again soon and brave as our pilots are, they can't stop all the raiders."

Lucy was reluctant to be parted from her child and yet she had no wish to remain at Rochford when there was still so much fun to be had in London. There were no tea dances to be enjoyed in Havorhurst, she pointed out to an unamused Alexis. However, she agreed that Teo should remain with Nanny Meredith at Rochford.

On the last day of Oliver's summer holiday, an American war correspondent arrived at Rochford Manor, bringing with him a letter from Pelham. Ed Baines was a short, dark-haired, bespectacled fellow. Willow and Toby received him in the drawing room where Willow welcomed her fellow countryman with genuine warmth. Not only was he a San Franciscan like herself but he had come from Épernay with first-hand news of Silvie and Pelham and a letter especially for Oliver.

The American accepted an invitation to stay for luncheon

and was given a dry martini before Willow would allow him to relate his adventures. Oliver meanwhile was reading his uncle's letter with the utmost excitement.

"Uncle Pelham has actually met one of the Royal Flying Corps pilots!" he told his mother. "The chap was on a reconnaissance flight over the German lines and one of his airplane wings was damaged. He came down way off course, not far from Épernay and Uncle Pelham picked him up."

His cheeks flushed, he read aloud:

"Young fellow not much older than you, Oliver, and every bit as keen as you about flying. He joined the British Expeditionary Force aviators last month and he told me Brigadier-General Trenchard had just come out from England to command No. 1 Wing. I recall Alexis telling me Trenchard was quite a personality at the Central Flying School at Upavon. Most of the Upavon pilots are out here now, of course, doing a wonderful job—or jobs, I should say—reconnaissance, observation for both the army and the navy, directing artillery and they've even got a photographic section."

Oliver looked up to see his mother's disapproving glance and realized she would not be as excited as he by the possible prospects awaiting him. But the American journalist looked interested.

"You hoping to be an aviator, young man?" he asked in his slow drawl.

"As soon as I leave school, Sir!" Oliver replied.

"Your uncle thought as much," the American said. He turned to look at Willow. "Your brother and sister-in-law are doing a mighty fine job at Épernay. The Germans all but ruined their beautiful Château last year, but Mr. and Mrs. Rochford have had the place tidied up so that it could be used as a convalescent hospital. It's jam-packed now with doctors and nurses supplied by the Red Cross."

"That's splendid news," remarked Toby. "Although I can't see my brother as a Florence Nightingale," he added with a grin.

"No, Mrs. Rochford takes that rôle," Ed Baines said. "Your brother is much more actively occupied. He dashes around the countryside in that ramshackle old Sunbeam of his, bringing in the walking wounded who are straggling back from the front lines. It's pretty chaotic at times. The casualties following attacks by either side are appalling and what you or I would term a stretcher case may well have to slog his own way back to safety. A convalescent hospital is scarcely descriptive of what is going on there."

He did not go into any detail concerning some of the worst sights he had seen, aware that his hostess could have no conception of the brutalities of war. He was saved the necessity as the young Lord Oliver Rochford stood up with unconscious grace and came toward him.

"Let me get you another one, Sir," he said as he collected his guest's glass and walked over to the sofa table where Dutton had placed the drinks.

Ed Baines regarded his host and hostess thoughtfully. These past six months he had come to see the English aristocracy through totally different eyes from those of his colleagues in the States. There he had heard them called 'snobbish,' 'pig-headed,' 'lazy,' 'self-indulgent' and 'old-fashioned.' He had not expected to like them, far less to respect and admire them. But now at long last he was beginning to understand what it was that made an English gentleman different—and this huge historic mansion, its traditions, its servants, its way of life were part of the reason for that distinction.

During his travels in Europe, Ed Baines had not spoken to one man, from high-ranking officer down to the lowest ranked soldier, who was not prepared to lay down his life for his country. There were no two ways with an Englishman, he decided. Right was right and wrong was wrong and he'd die quite willingly for what he believed in. His loyalty and his courage were unshakeable—the example set by families like these Rochfords. Men trusted their officers absolutely in the conviction that they would not let them down...not even the weaker ones, the journalist thought, remembering the other Rochford he had met in Brussels.

He glanced at the pale, intense face of the beautiful woman sitting opposite him and wondered how she would take the news he could no longer put off telling her. The Honorable Rupert Rochford was only her brother-in-law, he reminded himself. Hopefully, she would not be too worried by his situation.

"I was in Brussels a week ago," he said quietly. "Mr. Pelham Rochford knew I was going on there from France and asked me if I would look up his brother. I did and I have news for you concerning him."

Willow's face lit up with a surprised smile which faded when she saw the serious expression on the journalist's face.

"He's quite well?" she asked tentatively.

Ed Baines nodded.

"Both he and his friend, Count von Kruege, are in good health. They are, however, somewhat anxious regarding their safety. Do you by any chance know of their friendship with an English nurse called Edith Cavell?"

Toby looked over the top of his spectacles. There seemed no reason not to admit the truth to this American since obviously *he* knew of her.

"We do and we know of my brother's activities in connection with her," he replied.

Ed Baines drew a sigh of relief.

"Then you must already be aware of the danger they are in," he said, "which makes it easier for me to continue. When I called to see them, your brother and his friend were deeply concerned because Miss Cavell had been arrested by the Germans on August 5th." He heard Willow's small gasp but continued nonetheless. "Although Miss Cavell's nurses were aware of her arrest, no one had been able to discover where she had been taken. Count von Kruege wrote to a German contact called von Bissing who, so he told me, was pretty high up in the hierarchy in Brussels. But he received no reply, so I offered to go to the American Legation in Brussels to see if I could find out what was happening."

"That was most kind of you, Mr. Baines," Willow said warmly.

"It seemed the least I could do, Mrs. Rochford. I met the American Minister, Brand Whitlock, and he was very helpful. He told me that Miss Cavell had been put in a cell in the men's quarters in St. Gilles prison—that's where the Germans are keeping the political prisoners in Brussels. She is not being ill-treated but everyone is worried because the authorities will not allow visits of any kind, despite the fact that the Legation have applied at the highest levels to see her. I understand that Miss Cavell has confessed to harboring French and English soldiers and providing them with clothes and funds to reach the frontier. She also helped a number of Belgian civilians of military age. A Belgian lawyer, Maître Thomas Braun, has been engaged to represent her, but nobody could tell me when she is to be tried—in fact the Minister is greatly concerned because there is no information of any kind regarding the Englishwoman."

"And Miss Cavell's confederates?" Willow asked anxiously. "What news of them?"

"I'm afraid many of them are also now in St. Gilles. But not, as yet, your brother or the Count, I'm glad to say. One evening we discussed the possibility of trying to effect their escape from Brussels; but the Count felt that they stood a good chance of not being implicated and your brother-in-law was hoping that when the present panic eventually dies down, they might be able to reopen the lines of escape. In the meanwhile, they are still harboring two Allied soldiers—a Frenchman and an Englishman. Mr. Rochford, your brother pointed out that were he and the Count to leave Brussels now, it would mean abandoning these two soldiers."

Toby nodded. He could not entirely conceal his anxiety.

"I understand their feelings," he said. "I also appreciate the danger they are in. It was good of you to advise us of the situation, Mr. Baines."

It was typical of the English character, Ed Baines thought as the butler came in to announce that luncheon was served, to show no overt sign of emotion. Nor, as the meal progressed, did Mr. Rochford or his beautiful wife harry him with further questions but proceeded to inquire politely how he had found Europe and in particular, the big German cities. Good manners were *de riguer* and he was secretly amused when Willow apologized for the lack of staff due to the numbers of maids and footmen who had left to do war work of one kind or another. There already seemed quite as many servants in attendance as anyone could want, he thought. The same apology was made when after luncheon, they walked round the gardens. They had only three old men and two young boys to do the work of eight, Toby told him.

Coming as Baines had from the holocaust in Europe, the contrast of this quiet, beautiful house and the traditional, unhurried life of its occupants was remarkable, he thought. He himself could observe no real sign that the country was engaged in one of the bloodiest wars in history. Only Toby Rochford's map in the hall indicated these people were even aware of the war. How strange it must feel to any member of the household returning home on leave from the Front, the journalist thought wryly. How to relate the large, beautiful rooms with their huge vases of freshly cut summer flowers and the curtains blowing softly at windows looking onto sunlit lawns, with the dust and heat and filth and noise of battle;

with the starkness of a countryside that had been devastated by shelling; with the endless streams of cars and horses and wagons and uniformed soldiers straggling in exhausted columns down unfamiliar lanes and country roads! Small wonder that both Pelham and Rupert Rochford in their separate turns had said to him:

"You must call in at Rochford—it's not too far from London. You'll see a corner of the real England there, the way it has always been!"

But not everyone here was immune from war fever, Baines decided when the time came for him to leave. Young Lord Rochford and his friend, Mark, came out onto the terrace to say good-bye. On each fresh, unlined face was an expression of eagerness and excitement.

"You will tell the Americans in your reports that we're going to win this war, won't you, Sir?" Oliver said. "We're not in the least afraid of old Fritz, are we, Mark? And tell your people the Huns can't possibly have pilots to match ours even if they do have more airships!"

Ed Baines smiled and nodded but as he drove away, he could not prevent the uneasy thought that courage might not in the long run be enough. The Germans not only had more airships, they had a fully trained, highly efficient army and a wealth of two hundred and ten millimeter howitzers pitted against the Allied seventy-fives. Outnumbered, out-gunned, the British Expeditionary Force largely comprised inexperienced peacetime clerks, solicitors, shopkeepers and men who, only a few months ago, had been mowing the lawn at Rochford Manor or serving drinks on a silver salver to its residents. There might be no lack of courage or determination and certainly no lack of patriotism, he thought, recalling the two boys' desperate anxiety to become involved—but what good were emotions against shells and armory; against poison gas; against the whole might of the Kaiser's army?

He could imagine young Lord Rochford's perfectly modulated voice as he argued the point:

"We held them back at Ypres, didn't we, and that was mostly due to guts! We're defending freedom, you see, so God's on our side!"

"Oh, hell!" Ed Baines said aloud as he drove through a sleepy Havorhurst village out into the countryside. War was a rotten business and a beautiful country like this should not be caught up fighting other people's battles. To his left, two men and a farm girl were stacking up sheathes of golden corn; to his right, a flock of black and white sheep were grazing near the banks of a small stream winding its way across a green field bright with buttercups. A dappled shire horse ambled toward him down the dusty road pulling a wagon that had seen better days. It reminded him of a Constable painting of a typical English pastoral scene.

His thoughts returned to the English nurse languishing in a German jail. Miss Cavell would make quite a good story, he reckoned—the kind of daring escape adventure that would catch the imagination of his newspaper's readers. The only trouble was that he could not as yet supply the ending. He'd have to wait for her trial before he could do a piece on her. Judging by the way he'd heard her spoken of in Brussels, she was a kind of legend already. It couldn't be long before the Germans brought the unfortunate woman to trial. The *Daily Post* in New York would doubtless hear the result and he'd sell his story then.

Ed Baines did not learn the dreadful and final conclusion until mid-October. By then the whole civilized world knew that Edith Cavell had been shot—and from all accounts with unseemly haste following a court martial which had taken place between the 7th and the 9th of the month.

Toby was horrified when he opened his *Times* on the morning of October 23rd and saw the headlines: 'HORROR AND DISGUST.' According to the Foreign Secretary, Sir Edward Grey, Miss Cavell had not been charged with espionage, yet the appeals for leniency had been ignored despite all the care and attention she had given to the German wounded.

In November Toby received a letter from Ed Baines reflecting the shock and dismay felt keenly in his country, too. He added that he had now discovered that although the execution of Miss Cavell had been ordered to take place on October 12th, it had been summarily brought forward and she had been hastened to her death within a few hours of the court's sentence being passed on her.

"It is a scandal and an iniquity," Baines wrote, *"and when these facts become better known, they cannot fail but arouse a great deal of anti-German feeling out here. Meanwhile, I am doing my utmost to obtain information about your brother..."*

But no further news was forthcoming. At Christmas when the family forgathered at Rochford Manor, the fate of Edith

Cavell was the main topic of conversation. Her bravery and dedication were frequently referred to and Alexis spoke admiringly of the rôle women were playing in this war.

"And not only in nursing," he reflected. "Do you realize there are now well over a million women employed in industry and commerce who would never have gone out to work before the war."

Jane looked up with interest from the muffler she was knitting.

"What kind of jobs are they doing, Uncle Alexis?" she asked curiously.

He smiled at the young girl.

"Just about everything you could imagine," he said. "If you were old enough, you could get a job in a munitions factory, a builders' yard, a jute mill; or if you were clever enough you could run a solicitor's office or work in a bank." With a twinkle in his eye, he added, "If you ate a little more and put on some weight you could join the women doing heavy work in the paper mills, the shipyards, gas works, collieries, flour mills and so on."

"I'd rather be a postman," Zandra piped up. "Mrs. Cooper brings the letters now instead of Mr. Cooper who's gone to fight the Germans."

"Wouldn't you like to be a train driver? Or why not a policewoman?" Alexis teased.

A log fell out of the fire sending a shower of glowing embers across the hearth. Lucy, who was curled up in front with a labrador dozing on either side of her, reached forward to pick up the fire tongs. Carefully, she replaced the embers in the grate, her cheeks flaming. It was not just the heat from the fire that had brought the color into them. When she turned to Alexis, her eyes were stormy with resentment.

"I hope you are not inferring that *I* should work in a flour mill or in a dirty brickyard," she said in a hard cold voice.

Oliver looked at his sister speculatively.

"Surely you want to do something, Lucy?" he asked. "Jane's going to train to be a Queen Alexandra nurse as soon as she's old enough. I should have thought you'd want to do *something* ..."

"Well, I don't!" Lucy replied shortly. "I think war's stupid and anyway, there seem to be plenty of women who *want* to work, so let them do the jobs if that's what they enjoy. As for nursing, Jane, if you want to scrub floors and wash dishes, that's your affair. I call it a skivvy's work!"

She had vowed when she left the modiste in Paris never to undertake such back-breaking tasks again, and no silly war was going to reduce her once more to the level of a servant. She was the Countess Zemski and she did not need employment.

Alexis made no comment but Lucy was well aware that silently he agreed with Oliver. In January, the newspapers were full of the evacuation of the Gallipoli Peninsula. Although much was said about the success of the evacuation as such, it was nonetheless an admission of defeat in achieving the original objectives.

"As First Lord of the Admiralty, it was Winston Churchill who carried the responsibility at the time of the Gallipoli landings," Toby said thoughtfully. "The Government had no alternative but to remove him from office last summer."

"Come now, Rochford, you know as well as I do that he was merely the scapegoat," Alexis replied. "Personally I think he should have been taken back into the War Cabinet and I admire him for resigning when he was overlooked in November."

"I'll grant you the chap has spirit," Toby said smiling. "I hear he's commanding the 6th Royal Scots and he's now at the Front."

The papers continued to highlight the evacuation of the Gallipoli troops.

"It's something of a miracle that not one single life was lost," Alexis remarked to Lucy a few days later as he laid down his evening paper. "The Navy got off the whole army with their entire accumulation of stores under cover of darkness. When the Turks woke up, they were gone!"

Lucy, who had just returned home after a tea dance at the Café Royal, was in no mood for Alexis' analysis of the Dardenelles campaign.

"It's always the war—war, war, war!" she cried. "I want to forget it!"

Alexis looked at his young wife over the top of his paper. She was wearing a peach silk gown and she was twisting the ends of its chiffon sash through her fingers. Her cheeks were pink, her mouth rouged, her blue eyes flashing.

"You might not find it quite so easy to forget if you had been with me a half hour ago," he said quietly. "I was walking

down the Strand and the road outside Charing Cross station
was packed solid with ambulances. A train load of wounded
had just arrived from Southampton and it was not a pretty
sight, Lucy. Whether you like it or not, the fact is our young
men are being killed, maimed, blinded in their thousands
every day. I dare say there were many of those lying on the
stretchers who might have whiled away the afternoon dancing
with you at the Café Royal had they not believed it was more
important to try to defend their Allies against the German
invasion. Has it ever occurred to you that if we don't beat
them, they could invade England, too? Where would you and
your smart friends be then, Lucy?"

For a moment, Lucy looked taken aback. Then she said
coldly:

"If you feel it's that important, Alexis, why aren't *you* in
uniform getting yourself 'killed' or 'maimed' or 'blinded.'"

She flounced out of the drawing room, calling for Polly.

Alexis sighed. Lucy's attitude was born of fear, he thought.
She did not want her nice, comfortable, luxurious life dis-
rupted. By pretending to herself that the war was stupid and
unnecessary, she was perhaps able to convince herself that if
people stopped behaving heroically or patriotically, the war
would end. Whereas the way things were going, Alexis could
see no end in sight. The reversal in the Dardenelles was but
another example of strategic inefficiency. The idea itself might
have been a brilliant one but there were not the men or the
ships to back up the initial landings. It had been a very costly
disaster.

If Lucy was totally resistant to doing any kind of war work,
Oliver was obsessed with the desire to do his bit. During the
Easter holidays, he talked of little else—although he was careful not to do so in his mother's presence. Philip was home
again on a brief leave and it was to him Oliver confided his
determination to leave school the moment he was eighteen.
He had had his seventeenth birthday in February and, as he
told Philip bitterly, he was physically as fit and strong as many
of the eighteen-year-olds who were already in the thick of the
war.

Mark had been turned down on medical grounds on the
first two applications he made to join the Royal Flying Corps.
Although it was nearly ten months since he had survived the
sinking of the *Lusitania*, the injury he had sustained to his
head had been greater than Peter Rose supposed. Minor dam-

age to his brain had resulted in a slight slowness of his speech and reactions, and he had been told by the medical officer that he must wait a further six months before renewing his application. It was he who inadvertently forced Philip to take seriously the developing relationship between Oliver and his sister.

"I think it's ripping!" he said to Philip. "Oliver's such a jolly, decent chap and I can't think of anyone I'd rather Jane married."

"Jane is not yet seventeen," Philip said sharply. "It's ridiculous to think of her marrying anyone for ages yet."

Mark looked surprised.

"Well, of course not yet, you chump. But they could be engaged."

"I'm not even going to discuss it, Mark," Philip interrupted. "And I hope they haven't been doing so. Oliver's still at school, for heaven's sake!"

Philip could see the bewilderment in his young brother's eyes but there was nothing he could do about it. Not for anything in the world would he let Mark or Jane know who their real father was. It was difficult enough for him to accept the shame of his illegitimacy—and he had known of it for years. He'd been lucky when he had had to submit his birth certificate to the Navy before he'd been admitted. They had not questioned the false statement his mother had made when his birth was registered. Otherwise they would very quickly have discovered that his so-called father, Viscount Grey, had died several years before he was born. He was counting on the fact that in the middle of the war, Mark's birth certificate would not be looked into too closely either.

For two days he kept an uneasy, surreptitious watch upon Oliver and Jane. Unless they were in the company of the adults, they were nearly always hand in hand. Or they were sitting side by side on the window seat in the old schoolroom reading aloud from the book of Rupert Brooke's poems he had given Jane on his last leave. Or they were taking long solitary walks over the fields, arms entwined, with the labradors bounding on ahead of them.

Sick at heart, Philip was left in no doubt that Oliver must be told the truth. Since there seemed little point in putting off the evil moment, he managed to persuade Oliver to take a walk with him down to Havorhurst village to buy a fresh supply of Abdullah cigarettes. Oliver suggested Jane should accompany them but Philip said bluntly that he did not want his sister to go with them.

"Want a private chat with you, old man," he muttered as he and Oliver walked down the drive side by side. It was a cold but sunny March day and the wind was ruffling Oliver's uncovered head. He did not look all that unlike Rupert Brooke, Philip thought irrelevantly. He could well understand why a girl might consider him a romantic figure. There was an air of distinction in the way Oliver walked—but it was unconscious, unassumed.

"It's a devilish awkward subject, as a matter of fact," Philip said, glad that he did not have to look at Oliver directly as they reached the end of the drive and turned into the lane. Oliver was grinning somewhat sheepishly.

"It's about Jane, isn't it?" he asked. "You want to know whether my intentions are honorable, eh Phil?" His words were half humorous as he gave Philip a friendly slap across the shoulders. "I suppose I was a bit naïve to imagine no one knew how I felt—well, how we both feel about each other. Thought we'd best keep it a secret a while longer as we're a bit on the young side. But I can tell you this, Phil, I love your sister very much indeed and one day I want:.."

"Oliver!" Philip's voice was like a gunshot. Both young men halted in their tracks and stared at one another. "It can't ever happen—*you and Jane, I mean*. Oh, God!" He passed his hand over his forehead and then scratched his chin. He had not felt so badly since that first time he'd plucked up courage to go and ask Lady Rochford for assistance. But there was no going back on this now. "Look, Oliver," he said in a small desperate voice. "It isn't that I've any objections. I like you a hell of a lot and...well, in other circumstances, I'd have welcomed you as a brother-in-law. But...the fact is, damn it, we're already half-brothers. I mean, we are related."

It was the best he could do in the circumstances but not enough for Oliver who was regarding him as if he'd gone crazy.

"Whatever it is you're trying to say, Philip, you'd better make it a lot clearer than you have so far. What do you mean, we're related?"

Philip cleared his throat.

"Your mother would have had no reason to tell you, Oliver, and nor would I if I hadn't seen with my own eyes how you felt about Jane. You see, you and I share the same father. That is to say, Mark, Jane and I are all you father's children."

"You mean he was married to someone else before he married Mater?"

"No, no, not exactly. Our mother was his mistress. We're his illegitimate children! So you see, you and Jane are half-brother and sister."

It was said at last. Oliver's face turned deathly pale.

"I simply don't believe it!" he muttered. "If it were true, what are you all doing under our roof? I've never heard anything so insane. I just don't believe it!"

Philip drew a long breath. The palms of his hands were sweating.

"I'm afraid it *is* the truth, Oliver. As for our living here at Rochford—well, your mother must be one in a million since it was she who offered to give Mark and Jane a home when our great-aunt died. I think she felt compelled to shoulder our father's responsibilities. We were, after all, his children and his association with my mother was not a casual relationship—it was long-standing."

"And my mother knew of it?" Oliver asked bitterly.

"I'm afraid she did. After our father tired of my mother, there were others. I suppose your mother gradually accepted the status quo. There really wasn't much she could do about it—until finally she left him, of course. It was a pretty rotten life for her. Personally, I look on her as a kind of saint."

Oliver had begun to walk again—striding forward with long, quick steps which betrayed his inner tensions. Only now was he beginning to realize what this news meant to him—and to Jane. No wonder they were so close in so many of their ideas and feelings! No wonder they felt as if they belonged to one another! They did! He was her half-brother—she was his half-sister.

"Christ, Philip, I wish you hadn't told me!" he cried out. But before Philip could speak, he added in a quieter tone: "Of course, I do see why you had to do so."

"I'm damned sorry, old chap!" Philip said miserably. "I didn't want to say anything to Jane. I felt...well, it's up to you really whether you think she should know the real reason why...why nothing can ever come of your affection for each other. She isn't aware she's illegitimate. My great-aunt naturally never spoke of it...and my father—that is to say, our father, had left home when Jane was little more than a baby. I doubt she even remembers his face."

It was a face that he too had tried very hard to forget, Oliver thought with a cold, hard bitterness welling up inside him. He realized now that from the moment his mother had told him of his father's death, he had deliberately shut his mind to those childhood memories which had so often disturbed his dreams. He had never spoken to anyone about them. He must have been about eleven years old, he thought now, and still prone to the tiresome sleepwalking episodes which had plagued him as a child, when he had woken one night to find himself in his mother's bedroom and had seen his parents struggling on the bed. His mother's terrified face had imprinted itself on his mind. Young as he was, he had sensed her fear and revulsion as she lay half naked, her arms pinioned by the man lying on top of her. He could remember his desperate desire to rescue her; and how ineffectually he had confronted his father as he stammered out the words '*let her go.*'

He had thought his father was going to strike him as he staggered drunkenly off the bed, his arm raised as he came toward his son. But his mother had come to his rescue, preventing that blow being struck as she begged him to leave the room. All night long he had lain awake worried for her safety. The next day, they had left Rochford to go to live in America, and his relief had been profound. He had never wanted to see his father again.

I hated him then, Oliver thought, and I hate him even more now. He was old enough now to appreciate the humiliation his mother must have felt all those years, knowing her husband had not only a mistress but children by that other woman. He glanced at Philip's pale face and just for a moment, he hated him, too. But then he realized that Philip, Jane and Mark were as much victims of their father's debauchery as was he himself. They had been no more able than he to choose their father. But at least Philip had known the truth.

"*You* knew, Phil," he said violently. "Why didn't my mother tell *me*?" He kicked angrily at a stone and watched it fly into the hedge, aware of the knot in his stomach tightening as the full import of Philip's revelation sank in.

"Your mother is one of the most compassionate of people, Oliver," Philip said quietly. "She always did her utmost to protect us from the stigma of illegitimacy and I've no doubt she was trying to protect you too from feeling ashamed of your father."

"He's certainly no one to be proud of, is he, Phil?" Oliver said bitterly. "No wonder my mother left him. But if only I'd known the truth, I would never have thought of Jane other than as a sister, and she would have thought of me only as a brother. Now she will have to be told the truth."

How else could he explain his sudden withdrawal from all physical contact with her? There could be no more holding hands, caresses, stolen kisses. The word love could never be spoken between them again. But then he realized that there *was* another way. He could let Jane believe that his emotions had suddenly changed—another girl, perhaps. They'd talked of faithfulness in love and each had expressed the feeling that nothing could ever change how they felt now. How hurt and bitter she would be! Yet would that not be kinder than to reveal to a young girl that she was illegitimate? That would be shock enough for her without knowing that they were so closely related.

"Philip, what do you think? I'm finding this all rather hard to cope with. I truly love Jane, you see. And I know she loves me. I don't want to hurt her!"

"I know that. I don't want her to be hurt either. But I don't see any way to avoid it. Perhaps if you were to go away for a while—or she could, you could just let it be thought you'd grown apart. But frankly, in Jane's shoes I'd feel entitled to some sort of explanation. I really don't know."

Oliver drew a long, shuddering sigh. Although the spring sunshine was bright and golden, it was as if the whole sky had darkened and his world was collapsing around him. Whatever happened Jane had to be hurt, just as he was tormented by a terrible, irrevocable sense of loss. Only yesterday they had walked with their arms around one another expressing the view that their happiness was almost too good to be true—that in a world at war, they had no right to be so happy. They'd felt guilty because at luncheon, Mama had told them that Higgins, the under footman and his young brother, the bootboy, had both lost their lives at Gallipoli. Although he and Jane were saddened by their deaths, it had not touched on their personal joy in each other.

The thought of the war hit Oliver now with a sudden jolt. Philip had suggested that he or Jane should go away. He'd been wanting for months and months to join up. If he joined the R.F.C. now and went abroad, he and Jane would have time to forget one another. No, not forget. But with luck Jane might find some other young man to divert her affections elsewhere. Their separation would be natural...

He outlined his thoughts aloud to Philip, who at first disapproved of the idea.

"You're still too young, Oliver—and anyway, imagine how your mother would feel... Jane, too, probably. You don't want to dash off and get yourself killed."

"You haven't tried to stop Mark... and you'll be in the thick of it when you go back to sea next week," Oliver argued. "It's the obvious way out, Phil, if we are to avoid hurting Jane too much. Meanwhile, I go back to school next week and between now and then, I'll make some excuse to go over to Glenfield Hall for a few nights. I want to talk to Henry anyway. I know he's on the point of applying to join the R.F.C. He's been waiting for Mark so we could all go together."

"So we say nothing to your mother?" Philip asked. "I don't want her to be upset if it can be avoided. She would be unhappy for you, I know—and for Jane."

For the first time since the conversation had begun, Oliver gave a half smile.

"It's obvious you're pretty fond of her, Phil. It's strange, isn't it, but I feel you and I ought not to be—well, friendly. Yet we are! I think I ought to mind that your mother made mine so unhappy—and yet I don't really believe that it was her fault. I think in my heart of hearts it was our father who behaved so badly. I never much liked him, did you?"

Philip grinned.

"Hardly! But I suppose he can't have been all bad—otherwise he wouldn't have had such jolly decent children—you, Mark, Jane, little Alice."

Oliver nodded.

"It's quite strange when I go round the estate with Uncle Toby—nobody ever seems to have a good word for our father. They don't speak against him, of course, but they just don't talk of him. Yet they never fail to ask after Uncle Pelham!"

They both smiled at the thought of this jolly, happy-go-lucky uncle who, Oliver now realized, was as much Philip's uncle as his.

"I've just realized..." he said sheepishly. "I always wanted a brother and now suddenly I've acquired two—you and Mark. It's hard to take in!"

"I wish for yours and Jane's sake it could be otherwise," Philip said quietly. "Though naturally for myself, I'm happy enough to have a second brother. If you do join up, you may be gone before my next leave, Oliver. If I don't see you before then, I wish you the very best of luck. I myself reckon that it is all a matter of luck whether one survives this war or not."

"Well, here's hoping yours holds good for a long while yet," Oliver commented as without embarrassment, he shook Philip's hand.

But Philip Grey's luck had run out and Oliver was deeply shocked to learn in a letter from his mother sent to Eton that on May 31st, Philip had gone down with his battleship *Invincible*, in a sea engagement off the Jutland Peninsula.

"As far as Uncle Toby has been able to ascertain, Invincible *sank with all her crew—over a thousand officers and men";* Willow wrote, *"and of course, Admiral Hood went with her. I am finding it impossible to grasp the fact that our dear Philip was one of so very many to lose their lives and I cannot take comfort from the fact (as I know I should) that the British Fleet emerged victorious from their encounter with the enemy.*

"Jane is inconsolable and you must write to her, my dearest boy. Mark is being very brave. We shall hold a memorial service at St. Stephen's for Philip—but I do not feel I could face it yet awhile. I will notify your housemaster when a date has been set..."

Although Philip was not officially a relative, Oliver now joined so many of his schoolfellows in wearing a black arm band. He suffered alone—the more so for not being able to go home to comfort Jane and his mother. The letter of condolence he finally sent to Jane was stilted and guarded, and he feared it would be of little comfort to her. She had not understood why he should have chosen to spend the last few days of the Easter holiday with Henry at Glenfield and when he returned home hurriedly to pack his trunk and tuckbox, her face had been white and her eyes red-rimmed as if she had been crying. Even to his own ears, his excuse that he and Henry had enjoyed some excellent fishing together, sounded ridiculous, for Rochford was no further away from their favorite trout rivers than Glenfield. Pretending to notice nothing, Oliver had laughed and joked his way onto the train to London. Now he could imagine all too easily how bereft she must be feeling—without the reassurance of his love to comfort her a little for the loss of her beloved elder brother.

News of Lord Kitchener's death followed almost immediately upon that of Philip's, the whole school being called into Assembly to hear how the Secretary of War, the first soldier to hold such an appointment, had gone down with *Hampshire*—the ship that was taking him to Russia to see the Tsar. The *Hampshire* had struck a mine just off the most northern island of the Orkneys and sunk with nearly all hands. It was in the nature of a national calamity to lose so great a man so unnecessarily. But Oliver could mourn only for his half-brother.

He watched every post, awaiting the letter from his mother calling him home for the memorial service for Philip. The moment that was over, Oliver intended to be off. He had already talked to Henry and Mark and they had secretly planned to join up at the beginning of the summer holidays. Oliver had little doubt that now Mark would be as keen as he to advance the plan.

The letter finally came on the last day of June. By mid-July all three boys were enrolled in the Royal Flying Corps and Willow realized that her days and nights of fear had finally begun.

Part Three

1916–1918

And if the spirit be not there,
Why is fragrance in the hair?

RUPERT BROOKE, *Doubts*

Chapter 21

✑

August—September 1916

"Y OU ARE LOOKING EXHAUSTED. MY LOVE!" TOBY SAID AS WILLOW sank into one of the armchairs in the morning room. "I'll ring the bell for some tea!"

Willow smiled up at her husband.

"I may be tired but I am more than satisfied," she commented. "In some ways, Toby, I prefer this room to the drawing room. It's not so vast for one thing and I like the french windows opening onto the garden."

Toby nodded. When first he had put forward to Willow the idea of turning Rochford Manor into a convalescent home for war casualties, he had been worried lest the sight of the wounded would heighten Willow's fears for the three boys—Oliver in particular. But to his gratification, his plan had had the opposite to a depressing effect upon her. With unexpected enthusiasm, she applauded the idea in principle and then, when the Red Cross arrived to formulate the proposal, Willow had been in the forefront of the discussions.

He realized now on reflection how passive Willow had been these past few years. It was as if life with Rowell and all its unhappiness had taken so great a toll upon her inner reserves that she had felt it necessary to hand over to him the responsibility for her life and family. Those long years of battling first for Dodie, then for Oliver and finally for herself had left her emotionally drained. It had required something revolutionary to galvanize her out of her lethargy into a renewal of mental and physical energy.

There had been much to do. They had surrendered all but the morning room and library, six bedrooms and the servants' quarters. It had required a major reorganization. The big, sunny, south-facing reception rooms, such as the drawing room and ballroom, had been cleared of furniture which was now stored partly in the clockhouse and partly in the cricket pavilion, and had been turned into wards.

Eight large bedrooms had been converted into smaller wards and three of the dressing rooms into bathrooms. The billiard room had remained untouched as Toby expected that some of the patients would be well enough to enjoy its usage.

Some of the comfortable armchairs and sofas had been arranged in the big hall with writing tables and card tables to form a pleasant sitting room for those who were not confined to bed.

A further conversion had taken place when the Havorhurst builders had hastily turned the old stables into pleasant bedrooms for the nursing staff. These were all V.A.D. volunteers whom Willow and Marjorie Sharples had recruited. They were for the most part school friends of Marjorie's daughter, Hilda.

"I don't think we would ever have achieved this state of preparedness so quickly without Marjorie," Willow said, as Dutton brought in the tea. "She has been something of a surprise one way and another, hasn't she, Toby?"

"A tower of strength!" Toby said grinning, as a picture of Sam Sharples' buxom wife came to mind. Although Lady Barratt had become quite well-acquainted with the Yorkshire-born woman following upon Hilda's engagement to George, Willow had known her only casually. When the Red Cross had told them that they had to have a trained nurse as a Commandant in charge of the V.A.D.s, Willow had been hard put to think of a suitable candidate. It was then that Lady Barratt told her of Marjorie Sharples' qualifications and Willow had discovered that the woman's direct, forceful, highly capable nature was exactly what was needed. With enormous energy and a jolly sense of humor, Marjorie had set about directing her troops and Toby had sometimes found himself co-opted into tasks to which he was quite unaccustomed, such as checking the Red Cross supplies of bed linen. Normally he would have assumed this to be woman's work, but Marjorie paid no regard to such niceties and commandeered the nearest pair of hands.

The only two parts of Rochford the good lady accepted as outside her province were the servants' quarters and the nurseries which remained Patience's territory. The nursery floor was untouched. Stella's twins, Katherine and Lawrence, had come to join Alice, Zandra, Teo and Jamie. Stella's husband, Dr. Peter Rose, had volunteered and been accepted for service in the Royal Medical Corps, an elderly doctor taking over his practice in Havorhurst village. Stella was moving in next week to become the children's governess when her husband left for the Front.

James McGill, like Toby, had failed to pass the fitness test and after a long discussion with his in-laws, had decided to give up teaching for the duration of the war and join his wife, Dodie, at Rochford where he would be responsible for administering the convalescent home. Toby was helping Fellows, the bailiff, to run the estate.

Toby smiled as he glanced at Willow's satisfied face. She seemed to have taken on a new lease of life ever since the discussions with Lady Barratt concerning the conversion of their two houses into Auxiliary Home Hospitals had first taken place. Lady Barratt was adamant that Glenfield should be a place of refuge for officers and was not a little shocked when Willow stated that she would offer Rochford as a haven for other ranks.

But Willow had laughed aside her warnings of a home 'ruined by the uncaring, unappreciative lower classes!'

"Judging by the way our children totally disregard the value and beauty of their surroundings, I imagine the soldiers will have a far greater, not a lesser, respect for our home," she said practically. "Besides," she had added to Toby later, "there are proportionally so very many more of them, and their need is far greater."

Already in Havorhurst village, eight men had returned from active service with wounds of a severe nature or, far worse, suffering the aftereffects of gas. There were four men who had once been Rochford estate workers, not to mention Jim Walker, their own under-groom who had been gassed in Flanders.

The Red Cross had been appreciative of the Rochfords' generosity. The conversion of the Manor into an Auxiliary Home Hospital had been an expensive operation and the administration of it would be a continued financial liability for the family, who would pay the running costs.

With George Barratt back at the Front, Howard somewhere in France and Henry in the Middle East in the R.F.C., Lady Barratt felt that Glenfield Hall was too bereft of children for it to be a satisfactory place for her fourteen-year-old daughter,

Eleanor, to spend the war. Not wishing her to go to a boarding school, she asked Willow if she would incorporate Eleanor into her own large family of youngsters, especially since Stella was going to live there. As a consequence, including the seventeen-year-old Jane Grey, there were now seven children at Rochford and Eleanor would be the eighth.

Willow welcomed the child who was Alice's dearest friend and constant companion, as readily as she welcomed Stella's twins. Little Lawrence and Katherine were only six months older than Teo and company for her. An only child, the four-year-old Teo had been somewhat spoiled by Nanny Meredith and she was having to learn to share not only Nanny's attention but her toys, too, with the other children.

Patience and Nanny Meredith were in their element in the nursery, running affairs like two generals with the aid of Violet and a young girl from the village acting as nurserymaid. Stella planned to begin regular lessons in September and Dodie's husband, James, had promised to tutor the two older girls, Alice and Eleanor, in the more advanced subjects of Latin and Geometry. Jane meanwhile, had enrolled for classes in Tunbridge Wells so that she could become a fully fledged nursing aid. She and Willow went twice a week to be given instruction on first aid, hospital bed-making and other relevant subjects which would enable them to be useful in the wards whenever the V.A.D.s were understaffed.

Tomorrow, on the 2nd August, the first ambulances of convalescents were expected to arrive. A dozen V.A.D.s were already installed in their quarters in the stable block.

Willow had written a lengthy letter to Oliver describing all these renovations. She had little doubt that he would thoroughly approve their family involvement in the war effort. She had suggested that Jane, too, should write, but somewhat to her surprise, Jane declined to do so on the grounds that she had quite enough letter writing to do keeping Mark informed of the activities at Rochford.

Willow was concerned about Jane who had taken Philip's death very badly indeed.

"She will get over it in time," Toby remarked hopefully. But for the present, the young girl showed no signs of recovering from the shock of her brother's death. There were many mornings when she came down to breakfast with red-rimmed eyes betraying a night of tears. She was quiet and uncommunicative, although she worked alongside Willow with a furious and excessive energy that often left her exhausted.

Willow had no inkling of the full reason for Jane's distress. Her brother's death coming so suddenly upon the mysterious rift between her and Oliver had taken their toll upon her nerves. Her nature did not harbor bitterness but life seemed unbelievably cruel to her that within a month, the perfect happiness she had known so briefly could be reversed to such despair. The brief note she had received from Oliver from Eton regarding Philip's death had been stilted and formal. When he had attended the memorial service at St. Stephen's, he had avoided her quite noticeably and when he and Mark and Henry had received their notice to report for training, he had not even kissed her good-bye.

Only Mark had noticed Oliver's sudden coolness toward her. He had tried to explain it to Jane by telling her that Oliver was totally committed to doing his bit in the war, this being the only logical reason he could think of for Oliver's sudden change of heart.

"He can't think of anything else. It's all he talks about," he had said to Jane uneasily. "I dare say he feels he'll make a better job of things if he hasn't any emotional involvements to worry about. It'll be different when the war is over, Jane. He'll need you again then. I know he's really fond of you, old girl."

But Jane believed matters went deeper than Mark's facile explanation. For one thing, Oliver himself could have explained such sentiments to her. If he had asked her to set her love for him aside for the time being, she would have understood. Equally, she would have understood had he told her that he felt any deep relationship between them was unfair to her in the light of the fact that he could be killed. But he had said nothing—*nothing at all*—and she could only assume that his fondness for her had been a transient emotion he now regretted.

Unfortunately, it was no transient emotion for her. She loved him totally with all her being and young though she was, she knew with perfect certainty that no one could ever replace Oliver in her heart. Meanwhile she welcomed the sudden surge of activity at Rochford, welcomed the claims on her time which would otherwise have been spent grieving. Work, she discovered, was the only antidote to her pain.

By mid-August Rochford Manor Auxiliary Home hospital

was a hive of activity. The battles on the Somme which had been raging since the beginning of July had resulted in quite appallingly high numbers of casualties. While the French and German armies were locked in conflict at Verdun, a British offensive along the River Somme had been launched in an attempt to divert some of the enemy troops away from the French whom the Germans greatly outnumbered. But the enemy positions on the Somme were well organized with deep trench systems. Despite the optimism of the British who had fifteen divisions with an additional three French divisions with which to encounter the enemy, some sixty thousand men fell on one day alone.

With four hundred thousand men and one hundred thousand horses involved, the British had expected an easy and early victory. But the battles continued and Toby's flags positioning the armies moved only a mile or two as the Allies tried to force a way toward Bapaume.

The wards were full. There were the shell-shocked, the gassed, those who were struggling to adjust to their new artificial limbs, those whose wounds refused to heal. Willow, Jane, and Stella were at first appalled by these mutilated men who could not hide their relief at being 'back in Blighty' and away from the shocking horror of trench warfare. But gradually they became more accustomed to the sights and sounds they encountered as they went about the wards, reading and writing letters for the blinded and for those who had lost a limb, soothing those who relived again and again in their nightmares the unbearable shelling that had broken their nerve; supporting those who tried ceaselessly to rid their lungs of the gas that had crippled them.

Occasionally there were moments of joy—a letter from one or other of the boys describing their lives as fighter or reconnaissance pilots. For Mark, Henry Barratt and Oliver, war in the air was an adventure, an excitement that the soldiers in their trenches did not experience. There was little doubt that despite the dangers inherent in flying over enemy lines or in aerial combat, all three young men were fired with enthusiasm for their tasks. It helped to counteract Willow's constant fears for their safety.

There was also an unexpected letter from Ed Baines, enclosing a missive from Rupert which he had smuggled out of Belgium through the kind offices of Brand Whitlock.

"Brussels is a silent shell—a parody of its former self," he wrote. *"No one talks to each other or gossips on street corners as was their wont. The shop fronts, including our own are boarded up, windows shuttered.*

"Not only has Nurse Cavell's death stunned us all, but so, too, has the news of the fate of those others known to have been involved. Branded as traitors, five more have been condemned to death, five sentenced to ten years hard labor and seventeen to imprisonment and lesser spells of hard labor.

"It may be some time before Max and I are able to renew our former 'book' trade. But we agree absolutely that we shall do so at the earliest opportunity. Wish us well..."

"He intends to carry on Nurse Cavell's work," Toby said quietly as he put down the letter. "No wonder Ed Baines writes as he does."

He handed Willow the journalist's covering screed.

"If you interpret your brother's last paragraph as I do, then he and his friend are very brave men," Baines had written. *"It was very courageous of Nurse Cavell to act as she did but I do not imagine she ever envisaged the penalty she might have to pay. Your brother, however, is now well aware of the consequences and being so, deserves the very highest praise, if you will allow me to say so. I sure am impressed..."*

Willow regarded Toby's expressive face with anxiety. No one knew better than she how frustrated he was by his inability to 'enjoy' active service. He had, she knew, deeply envied the three boys when they had joined the R.F.C. He had looked enviously at Peter Rose—a man not all that younger than himself—when he had joined the R.M.C. And as one by one, the able-bodied estate workers had been called up, his frustration had mounted. It was only a very minor comfort to him that he could at least contribute something to the war effort by ploughing up acres of Rochford parkland to grow vegetables. He had himself supplied the farmers with funds to increase their dairy herds or to increase the acreage put down to wheat. The nation was short of food, a lot of which had to be imported. German U-boats were hunting down the merchant ships plying the Atlantic and the Government was concerned about the terrible losses at sea and the growing need for some kind of control over the nation's consumption of food.

Toby's task was far from easy now that the Compulsory Service Act passed in January was claiming so many of the estate workers.

It affected Willow, too, for although none of the old Rochford retainers considered deserting the family, some of the younger maids had realized that jobs in factories not only brought in better money but allowed more free time than they could hope for in 'service.'

Up in London Lucy had also lost many of her staff, including the unfortunate Rosie who had given in her notice soon after the episode of Teo's disappearance.

Alexis was sent abroad on one of his many secret missions for two weeks during the month of August. Lucy went down to Rochford and Willow was delighted to have her there. Although she kept a tight rein on her outward behavior, there were few hours in the day when her thoughts were not with her son, and try as she might, she could not prevent herself imagining the dangers Oliver could be in. Despite his uniform and his undoubted qualifications as a pilot, he remained her child—only seventeen years of age—and she lived in constant fear of a telegram that could bring the news she dreaded. It had been heartbreaking enough to be so informed of Philip's death and she had but to walk down the wards to see, all too clearly, how terrible was the damage inflicted on those who fought in the war.

Although never as close to Lucy as she was to Jane, Willow nevertheless enjoyed her daughter's companionship and quite often, they shared such tasks as refurbishing the flower vases Willow liked to have all over Rochford and in the wards. One hot August afternoon Lucy was in the garden with the flower basket and secateurs cutting roses while Willow was in the conservatory preparing fresh vases to receive them.

At first Willow thought it was Lucy returning when she heard someone come into the room. But it was Dutton. Now seventy-five years old, the elderly butler should long since have been retired, Willow thought momentarily, as it struck her how bent and weary he looked. But then her eyes caught sight of the orange envelope lying on the silver salver he was holding and her heart jolted in icy fear. Her eyes met those of her old family servant and with yet another wave of fear she saw pity in them. The telegraph boy would have told Dutton what news the telegram contained, she thought, as Dutton said gently:

"Would you like to sit down, Milady?"

In all the years Dutton had been in her employ, he had never before touched her, she thought irrelevantly as he put an arm beneath her elbow and helped her to one of the wicker chairs. Her legs were trembling and but for the old servant she might have fallen. She looked up at him in mute appeal.

"You open it, Dutton," she said. "I can't."

The old man's hands were shaking as without haste, he took the telegram from its envelope and peered short-sightedly at the writing.

"It's Master Oliver," he mumbled, adding quickly "but not to say he's killed, Milady—only that he's been shot down..." Looking anxiously at Willow's ashen face, he said: "I'll see if I can find Mr. Toby or Miss Lucy..."

For a moment, his hand rested on her shoulder in a gesture of sympathy and Willow understood that her sense of horror was his also. Dutton had known and loved Oliver for as many years as she had, and the Rochfords were, in a sense, his family too.

But it was Lucy not Toby who came to comfort Willow. She had met Dutton outside the conservatory door, and hearing the news, she ran to kneel beside her mother's chair.

"Don't look so frightened, Mama!" she said urgently, as she took Willow's hands in hers: "I'm absolutely sure Oliver's all right. You know what he's like—you said yourself once long ago, when he was a little boy and he had that terrible accident when he fell from his pony, that anyone who could survive when they were so close to death must have the stamina to recover from anything."

Willow's eyes regarded Lucy's desperately.

"It's true, he did almost die—the doctors thought he would. But I was there to look after him, Lucy. God knows where he is at this moment, or how badly he is hurt. I can't bear it..."

Lucy understood very well her mother's agony of mind. Had she herself not felt the same when Teo had been missing? She recalled now how calm and reassuring Alexis had been, and how she had drawn comfort from his quiet conviction that all would be well. She must try now to emulate him.

"You have to believe me, Mama. I am quite convinced

that Oliver is all right. Uncle Toby will be able to get news of him soon, and if he can't, I know Alexis can find a way to discover what is happening when he returns from abroad. In the meanwhile, you must stop worrying. You know very well that Oliver would expect you to be brave. Why, even now he may be safe and sound, probably enjoying a drink with his friends."

"Do you really believe that, Lucy?" Willow asked, for the first time aware of a glimmer of hope. Lucy was quite right—the telegram said only that Oliver had been shot down. It was madness to presume he had been killed—or even necessarily injured. He could have made his way back to the safety of his own lines and, as Lucy said, even now be enjoying a drink with his fellow officers.

Lucy stood up as her uncle came into the room. He went at once to Willow's side and put his arm around her shoulder.

"Dutton told me," he said quietly. "I have rung up the War Office but I am afraid it is too soon yet for them to have any news for us. But they have promised to telephone me immediately they receive any further information, however insignificant."

"Lucy says she is convinced Oliver is alive," Willow said despairingly. Toby gave Lucy an approving nod.

"And quite right too!" he replied. "We have no reason to suppose otherwise. Now how about a nice cup of tea for us all, Lucy?" he suggested.

Lucy went out of the room, closing the door gently behind her. As she went slowly through the hall to the green baize door leading to the kitchens, she realized for the first time how frightened she was. Until now she had thought only of her mother's fear, but *she* loved Oliver too. She had never meant to do so. When first she had learned of her young brother's existence, she had felt a deep resentment at his right to claim everything she believed to be her own. But during that first miraculous summer they had spent together at Rochford, she had been charmed, amused, and delighted by him. He was the first boy she had ever known and without realizing it, he had given her a completely new attitude toward the opposite sex. She had enjoyed his masculine company and discovered with astonishment that she thoroughly enjoyed sharing his pastimes too. Of necessity, since her marriage, she had seen less of Oliver these past few years, but her affection for him had been in no way diminished—in fact, knowing that she would be in his company once again had been her main reason for spending as much time as she did at Rochford.

Rochford was not the same happy place without him. She had missed him greatly these past ten days—his laughter, his teasing, his jokes, his wonderful sense of fun and adventure.

Suddenly, fear clutched at Lucy's heart. Suppose Mama's worst fears were realized? That Oliver *was* dead? That he would never come back again? Once—so long ago that she could hardly recall it—she had wished her unknown brother dead so that *she* could inherit Rochford as her father had promised. Suppose that the cruel God of her convent days were to answer her prayer and destroy one of the few people in the world she really loved! Was it possible she could *ever* have wanted Rochford at such a price?

"Please God, I didn't mean it. Let Oliver be all right. Let him be alive!" she prayed silently. The alternative was too awful to dwell on. She must believe—as she had cautioned her mother—that the Oliver they both loved was coming back to them.

It was all very well for Alexis to talk so glibly about the importance of love, she thought bitterly. But perhaps he would not be quite so sure of himself if he could feel what she and Mama were now feeling. *He* had no beloved brother at the Front who might be lying crushed to pieces in an airplane, or bleeding to death with no one to help him, in a remote field in France.

The housekeeper came out of the butler's pantry and looked at Lucy in surprise.

"Did you want something, Madam?" she asked, her eyes directed meaningfully at the bell indicator above her head. War or no war, Mrs. Upton thought, she was not having the 'upstairs' lot 'downstairs' when there was a perfectly good bell to be rung if something was wanted.

"Yes I did, Mrs. Upton," Lucy said, her tone far sharper than usual. "Please send tea upstairs to the conservatory immediately."

Doesn't know her place, that one, Mrs. Upton thought, as she went in search of one of the maids. Cold as cucumber...not like her mother...got no heart.

She could not see the tears Lucy had only just managed to control, now pouring down her cheeks as she made her way up to the sanctuary of her own room.

It was a whole agonizing week before further news of Oliver reached them in the form of a letter from the War Office.

"Your son's Commanding Officer has informed us that Pilot Officer Lord Rochford was shot down while escorting one of our reconnaissance airplanes over enemy territory. He had attacked a German Fokker which was harassing the reconnaissance aircraft, successfully' diverting the enemy from his purpose. His own airplane, however, was severely damaged and he was forced to land behind enemy lines.

"Flight Lieutenant Bryant, pilot of the reconnaissance plane, reported that Lord Rochford's Sopwith went into a steep dive, the Fokker firing at him as he descended. He was making for a patch of clear ground but was unable to avoid some telegraph poles into which he crashed and nose-dived into the ground. However, Flight Lieut. Bryant was adamant that Lord Rochford was thrown clear of the wreckage and that he saw him up on his feet before the Germans surrounded him.

"It is hoped, therefore, that your son is now a prisoner of war and we await confirmation of this fact..."

"Thank God, *thank God!*" Willow whispered as Toby put down the letter.

Lucy smiled happily.

"There you are, Mama. I told you Oliver was a survivor. Now he'll be out of danger for the rest of the war so you need have no further worry about him."

A few days later, the news that Oliver was indeed a prisoner of war was received from the War Office. The Red Cross had confirmed that he was in Gütersloh Camp in Westphalia, a quarantine center in Germany where captured officers were received before being sent on to other prisoner of war camps.

Word of Oliver's safety spread like wildfire through Rochford. Not only the family and servants rejoiced but even in the wards, patients and staff were smiling, happy to hear that the young Lord of the Manor had survived.

In the schoolroom Stella announced a holiday from lessons and Cook immediately started to bake one of Oliver's favorite cinnamon cakes which, so Marjorie Sharples had told her, could be sent out to him via the Red Cross.

Jane spent the afternoon in the wards, her rejoicing private and her relief revealed only by the increased color in her cheeks as she wrote letters to the men's relatives and loved ones. Sometimes the less articulate found it difficult to express their emotions verbally, and gently she would suggest a word to them. It was not difficult, she thought, for love was universal and the longing to be within sight and sound of your beloved was no different for Private Humphries or Sergeant McMaster than for her. Her relief in knowing that Oliver was safe was overwhelming.

Lucy, too, was delighted. She returned to London to coincide her arrival with Alexis' return, longing to be the first to impart the good news. But he was out when she arrived at Cadogan Gardens. Disappointed and impatient to share her joy with Alexis, she inquired of Bulford when his master had returned home.

"Yesterday evening, Madam," Bulford replied as he took Lucy's suitcase from the taxicab driver. "He was at the office today, came home soon after four o'clock and then went out again shortly afterwards. I think he mentioned that he would be calling upon Lady Inman."

As Lucy followed Polly upstairs to change from her traveling clothes, her eyes were thoughtful. Old Angus Inman had died last winter and Alexis had made no secret of the fact that he called regularly at Eaton Terrace to offer what assistance he could to Roberta in straightening out the old Earl's complicated affairs. Busy with her own entertainment, Lucy had voiced no objection. But now, suddenly, she felt uneasy. It was true that Alexis had not known when exactly she would return from Rochford but equally she had been uncertain when he would return from his trip to Europe. That he had been home a whole day without troubling to telephone her to say that he was back was surprising; and now she asked herself if this was an oversight or whether it had been intentional.

Polly's cheerful voice interrupted her thoughts.

"Your evening gown, Madam?" the maid was inquiring as she began to unpack the first of Lucy's suitcases.

"No!" Lucy replied sharply. "It's too early to change for dinner. I'm going out. Tell Bulford to have my car brought round at once. I'll wear the blue cocktail dress, no hat, but the matching fillet."

She ignored the look of surprise on her maid's face and waited impatiently for Polly to find the gown and headband she required. Glancing at the small bedside clock, she noted that it was a little after six. If Alexis was still with Roberta she would surprise them there, she decided. As the minutes ticked past, Lucy's impatience grew as did her worst suspicions. While at Rochford she had spent an afternoon in the company of Hilda Sharples, who had told Lucy bluntly that her father had seen Alexis and Roberta dining together at the Savoy.

"Not clandestinely, of course," Hilda admitted. "But there's no smoke without fire, Lucy, and whether you like Roberta or not, she is a very handsome woman. I wouldn't blame her one bit if she set her cap at Alexis. After all, she knew him years before you did and everyone knew she was his mistress before Alexis married you."

Lucy had disregarded the warning, even laughed at it. But now Hilda's words were suddenly of import. There was no denying that her marriage to Alexis had become very much one of laissez-faire.

Alexis had long since given up any overt sign of the physical passion he had once felt for her. She in turn had ceased her offers to be a 'real' wife to him. They met only at mealtimes and now that Teo was at Rochford, they did not even share the child's evening playtime. Except that they shared house and servants, it was scarcely a marriage at all, Lucy reflected. She had taken for granted the fact that it would continue indefinitely on such terms, but now she realized it could be threatened—by Roberta.

Some months ago, when the old Earl was known to be dying, Alexis had sworn to Lucy that he had no intention of divorcing her even if Roberta were to become a widow. But Alexis could have had a change of heart in seven months, Lucy thought, especially if Roberta was, as Hilda implied, setting her cap at him. Were she, Lucy, in Roberta's shoes, she would do just that—unless there were some other man waiting in the wings. But according to Hilda, there was no other man in Roberta's life.

While Lucy was surmising, Roberta Inman was putting into effect a decision regarding Alexis which she had reached a week earlier. Immediately following her husband's death in November she had been too distressed and preoccupied with replying to letters of condolence to give thought to her own future. Although she had never loved Angus, she had been genuinely fond of him and while expected, his death was nonetheless a shock when it occurred. Inevitably it was to her closest friend, Alexis, she turned for support during the ensuing months. That support was readily forthcoming and without fully realizing it, Roberta had begun to lean on Alexis in a way she had never done in the past.

This dependence, added to the intense love she had always felt for him, had heightened his importance to her and she realized that before much longer she would be powerless to make a new life for herself which did not include him. It was no longer sufficient to be his mistress—available on those few occasions when his need for her company and physical solace overrode his desire to be faithful to Lucy. Those occasions were far too few and now that she had no sick husband to nurse, the rest of her life was entirely purposeless. At forty, she was too old to consider a career for herself as many women were now doing, and although she gave voluntary service to the Red Cross and the Women's Legion, there were still far too many days and nights which were lonely and meaningless.

Roberta was mature enough to appreciate that if she did not break with Alexis now she never would. She knew herself hopelessly vulnerable in their present relationship. At any time, *Alexis* might decide to break with *her*. He still loved Lucy and never spent a night with her, Roberta, without obvious signs of guilt when he left her afterwards. It was not in Alexis' nature to be unfaithful and Roberta knew it.

Deep down in her subconscious Roberta now realized, had lain the hope that Alexis might one day discover that his need for her was greater than his need for his young wife. That hope, minuscule though it was, nevertheless existed. It was now a contributory factor to her decision to tell Alexis their affair must end. If Alexis accepted her decision, then she had no justification for continuing to hope for the impossible. She had left a message with Bulford asking him to tell Alexis she wished him to call as soon as he returned to London.

As she had known he would, Alexis came immediately he could. He kissed her warmly and complimented her upon her gown—an especially becoming one she had chosen for this final meeting with him.

Now as he listened to the plans she had outlined for herself, he sat regarding her with an almost comical look of dismay on his handsome face.

"Going abroad, Roberta!" he repeated her last words. "But why? What has brought about such a decision? You said nothing of it when we last met..."

Roberta fitted a Turkish cigarette into a long ebony holder and lit it with studied care. Her voice was husky with ill-concealed emotion as she said quietly:

"I want to get away, Alexis—occupy my life with something quite new. My sister owns a large house in Alexandria. She wrote to me last month telling me that there was a desperate need for suitable accommodation for the wounded. She asked me if I would go out to help her to convert her home in much the same way as your in-laws have converted Rochford Manor. It's a perfect opportunity for me to make a clean break, Alexis, and anyway, it's high time I did something for my country."

"I applaud your patriotic sentiments," Alexis said dryly, "but there is plenty of voluntary work for women like yourself in London, Roberta. You don't have to go to the Middle East to do worthwhile war work. You must give me a better reason than that if I am to understand you."

Roberta bit her lip.

"London is where *you* live, Alexis," she said flatly. "I could have gone up to Angus' estate in Scotland had I wanted but even that is too near *you*. If I thought you needed me, I could be down from Fifeshire within a few hours by train. Do you understand me now?"

As her voice trailed into silence, Alexis' face flushed. Roberta was forcing him to acknowledge the fact that she loved him. That being the case, he had no right to try to detain her. He could not state selfishly that he needed her as well as Lucy—although there were many times that he did so. Roberta was no longer a young woman but still beautiful enough to find a second husband. But so long as she was involved with him, Alexis, she was unlikely to find a new companion for her later years. For her sake, he must conceal from her his reluctance to lose her.

"It's come as a bit of a shock," he admitted. "Egotist that I am, I had not given much thought to your future, Roberta.

Our relationship—well, it worked so well for me I never questioned it. But you are right, of course. There is no future in it for you."

There were tears in Roberta's eyes which she did not want him to see. She walked away from him, crossing the room to the window where she stood staring down into the street. It was a beautiful summer evening and despite the war and its somber news, people looked happy and pleased to be enjoying such lovely weather as they strolled unhurriedly along the pavement below.

Sensing something of the pain she was suffering, Alexis got to his feet and went to stand behind her. His arms encircled her waist and she leaned back against him, her eyes closed against the threatening tears.

"I'm so very sorry," he said. "I hate to think of you unhappy, Roberta, most especially that I should be the cause of it. You know how important you are to me. You always have been. I respect and care for you immensely."

"I know, Alexis!" Roberta said. "But you have never loved me. It will be best for you, too, you know. While you have me to turn to, you are not making any demands on Lucy and were you to begin a normal married life with her, your marriage could be the better for it."

Alexis made no reply. Roberta still believed that it was Lucy's frigidity that kept him from his wife's bed. Even now when it seemed as if he might not be seeing Roberta again for many years—and never again as his mistress—he still could not betray his promise to Lucy to keep her past a secret. Roberta would never understand how he could continue to deny himself the right to Lucy's body; nor indeed his obsessional need to win Lucy's love. Perhaps had he never met Lucy, he might even now be contemplating marriage to this beautiful woman. They suited one another remarkably well and she would have graced his house as completely as she had the old Earl's homes. Had he never experienced the phenomenon of 'falling in love' with Lucy, he would probably have settled contentedly to the kind of relationship he enjoyed with Roberta. The same thought must have occurred to her, he realized, and he admired her self-restraint that she had never once sought to malign Lucy or criticize her to him.

"When will you be leaving, Roberta?" he asked unhappily.

"As soon as possible," she told him, her tears now under

control. She turned to put her arms around him. "That's why I asked you here tonight, Alexis. It's good-bye, you see. I couldn't leave without an explanation, could I?"

The moment was tense with emotion, predominantly of sadness. Alexis buried his face in her dark hair.

"I shall miss you!" he said huskily.

He could feel the swift thudding of her heart through the thin silk blouse she was wearing and for a moment, desire for her eradicated all other feeling. Her beauty was undeniable and he was too much of a man to be immune to it. In other circumstances he would have lifted her into his arms and carried her immediately and without question into the bedroom. But now he looked down into her eyes uncertainly.

Knowing him as intimately as she did, Roberta was well aware of his feelings.

"If it is to be one last time," she murmured, "then you must promise to leave me afterward without a word, Alexis. No lingering good-byes, no last kisses. Love me—and then go!"

It was at that moment the doorbell rang. Roberta's butler answered it and was confronted by Lucy.

"Her Ladyship is not at home, Madam!" he said firmly, well aware that Lucy's husband was with his mistress.

Ignoring him, Lucy pushed past him into the hall. She had already seen Alexis' hat and gloves on the hall stand and her cheeks were bright with color as she threw open the drawing room door. As if in slow motion, without haste, Alexis and Roberta drew apart.

"I thought you'd be here—together!" Lucy said confronting them furiously. "You think I don't know you're having an affair. You don't care if I'm humiliated in front of my friends—and the servants!" She turned slightly so that she faced Alexis. "You once said you expected *me* to be faithful to *you*—and I have been, always, yet you think it right that you can cheat me with... with *her*!"

As Lucy's eyes searched Roberta's, a little of her self-confidence waned. Roberta did not look in the least guilty nor even dismayed. Her calm, beautiful face looked only sad, almost pitying.

"You think you can take my husband from me, don't you?" Lucy stormed. "Well you can't! I shan't divorce him if that's what you are hoping—and he can't divorce me—not without betraying me. He's *my* husband, Roberta Inman, whether you like it or not and..."

Alexis stepped forward and took Lucy's arm in a fierce grip.

"I suggest you refrain from insulting Roberta," he said quietly. "She is going away—to the Middle East, if that's of any interest to you. We were saying a final good-bye to one another as we won't be meeting again. Now, I think, it is time we both left."

He released Lucy's arm only long enough to lift Roberta's hand and raise it to his lips.

"Good-bye, my dear," he said with undisguised tenderness. "I hope you find happiness."

Renewing his grasp upon the now silent Lucy, he led her from the room. His wife's car was outside, the chauffeur waiting patiently beside it. White faced, wordless, Alexis helped her into the back seat and directed the chauffeur to drive them home.

Lucy's anger had evaporated with the news that Roberta was leaving England. It meant she had really nothing to fear. Alexis was not intending to divorce her and marry his mistress—nor would friends like Hilda be able to imply that she, Lucy, was unable to keep her husband's attentions to herself.

Alexis, however, was furiously angry. Not only was he losing Roberta but Lucy's outburst had made him feel cheap—humiliated. He knew that basically it was he who had transgressed and yet equally he would not have renewed his relationship with Roberta had his marriage been as he had hoped.

He waited only until they were alone in the drawing room at Cadogan Gardens before he rounded on Lucy.

"You may feel you have just cause for treating me to such a scene," he said quietly but with an underlying anger that was not lost upon her. "But it is time someone told you a few home truths, Lucy. You gained a great number of advantages when I married you and most important of all, you gained the freedom to do as you wished. When granting you that freedom, I did not imagine that you would feel justified in contributing so little to our marriage. I know you will consider this accusation unfair—that you supposed the offer of your body would 'even the score.' But that is not how I see marriage, Lucy. There are such things as companionship, sympathy, understanding, sharing. You give me none of those and if I seek them elsewhere, then you have no just cause to complain."

He turned away from her so that she could not see the despair in his eyes. His voice continued quietly but remorselessly as his bitterness flowed beyond his power of restraint.

"You are selfish, Lucy, seeing nothing beyond your own stupid childish desire for clothes, for amusement. When are you going to grow up—to face the fact that the whole world is at war and what you want is of utter unimportance? Men are dying in their millions, and you don't even care! I thought that when your own brother went to fight, you would feel as if you, too, must do something—*anything*, to aid his contribution. But not even when Oliver was shot down—perhaps killed—did it turn you from your egotistical, silly, meaningless quest for pleasure. Are you really so heartless, so devoid of purpose, of even a modicum of self-sacrifice, self-respect? I will tell you one more unpalatable truth, and that is that you are not worth one tiny part of Roberta Inman and that were it you who was about to leave for the Middle East, I would not shed one tear of regret as I do at her going. Your country would not miss you, your family would not and quite frankly, I see no reason why I might do so. But you won't go, will you, Lucy? War service would put an end to your tangoes and your shopping and disarrange that pretty coiffure of yours or maybe dirty those tiny white hands! So go away and play, little girl. You have nothing to offer your country—and nothing of worth to offer me!"

He walked into his study without looking at her and locked the door between them. Lucy's face was a mask of fury and astonishment as she gazed at the closed door. She ran to it and beat on the panels with clenched fists.

"You're cruel and horrible!" she shouted. "You're angry because you've lost your precious mistress and you want to blame me for it. You're trying to make me out to be no use to anyone because I don't fawn on you the way Roberta did. You want me to love you and I don't, I don't. I hate you. Do you hear me, Alexis? *I hate you.* You think I don't care about Oliver but I did care dreadfully when he was shot down. I worry about Mark—and Henry, too. And I minded very much when Philip was killed. I'm not heartless.

I'm not useless. You'll see, Alexis. I'll show you what I can do if I have to. It'll be better than anything Roberta Inman does. I'll go to France. I'm not afraid of danger—if that's what you think. I'm not afraid of anyone and I'm *certainly* not afraid of you!"

As her voice trailed away, there was no reply from Alexis' study. Lucy was not even certain that he had heard her. But she was too angry to care. Mouth tightly clenched, her cheeks burning, she ran upstairs and told Polly to pack her traveling clothes. She would not stay another night in this house, she told herself. By morning when he found her gone, Alexis would be sorry for all the hateful things he had said. Loving her as he did—or had once professed to do—he would be terrified for her safety. He would come after her; stop her going to France where she might so easily be killed.

The same thought occurred to Alexis who was already regretting his outburst. But he made no move to follow Lucy upstairs. No one knew better than he how next to impossible it was for a civilian to cross the Channel. Even for him in his essential war work, a passage to France was far from easy to come by and only intervention at the highest level made his visits to Europe possible. Lucy would never obtain permission to go—of that he was happily certain.

But Alexis had underrated her. Lucy had not forgotten Madame Lou-Lou's adage that a pretty girl could get anything she wanted provided she went about it the right way. Her pride was at stake and she was determined to carry out her threat.

She took the next train to Dover, and spent the night in a sea-front hotel. The following morning she did her best to transform herself into a French *poule de luxe*, before presenting herself at the docks where she made herself known to a Canadian major who was returning to his unit in France. It took her less than half an hour to persuade him to smuggle her on board. It was of small consequence to her that the price she had to pay for her passage consisted of a half hour alone with the major in his private cabin. The fact that she was finally being unfaithful to Alexis was in itself a pleasure. It was his fault, after all, that she was forced to offer herself in exchange for that Channel crossing. She knew that she might have to do so again if she were to find her way safely back to Aunt Silvie's Château in Épernay. That was where she intended to go. By what method Lucy quite simply did not care. Nothing mattered any longer but the need to prove Alexis wrong.

Chapter 22

September 1916

"*MON DIEUX, PELHAM, IT IS LUCIENNE!*" SILVIE CRIED IN UTTER astonishment as she watched from their sitting room window the slim, fair-haired girl descending from the French army officer's Peugeot. "*Ce n'est pas possible!*" she added, doubting the evidence of her own eyes.

Pelham came to stand beside her.

"Great Scott, you're right, my dear!" he commented as Lucy strutted toward the Château on inappropriately high heels, one hand clasping a large straw picture hat, the other tucked through the arm of her escort.

Silvie was no longer listening. She was already on her way downstairs to greet her niece. But her words of welcome died on her lips as she came face to face with Lucy and took in her heavily painted face and theatrical attire. She looked more like an actress off the stage of La Scala than a lady of quality.

"What on earth brings you here, Lucienne?" she murmured, glancing at the amused French officer as he clicked his heels and bowed over her hand.

"This is Capitaine le Fevre!" Lucy said quietly. "He was kind enough to drive me here from the station at Épernay! Capitaine le Fevre, this is my aunt, Madame Rochford."

The Frenchman bowed again and sensing Silvie's embarrassment, excused himself and went out to his car. With his departure, the proud tilt of Lucy's head slackened and she swayed slightly on her feet, betraying her utter exhaustion.

"Come, child!" Silvie said sharply. "Upstairs to my rooms. Your Uncle Pelham is there. You look as if you could do with a Cognac!"

"Most of all, I would like a bath!" Lucy said as she followed her aunt up the curving staircase.

It was seven in the evening and orderlies were serving supper in the wards. Lucy's brief glance took in the uniforms of the men and of the occasional nurse and nursing aid who went hurriedly about their business without paying her or her aunt any attention. There was a strong smell of antiseptic in the air and the hall was bare of any carpets or furniture, its once beautiful walls lined with wooden benches. Notice boards were affixed to a blackboard and two empty Bath chairs and a stretcher were drawn tidily to one side.

Upstairs in Silvie's and Pelham's suite, the comfort and elegance Lucy remembered in her aunt's house in the Rue d'Artois in Paris were immediately in contrast to the stark hospital atmosphere down below. She sank gratefully into an armchair, attempting a smile as Pelham took her suitcase from her. She had not realized until this moment how totally exhausted she was. The journey had seemed interminable— a nightmare of experiences that stretched over the past two days into a confused kaleidoscopic jumble of events that she preferred not to dwell on. Throughout the long journey there had been a series of different men to assist her with the problems she encountered—the absence of passport, French money, tickets for the steamer, the taxi across Paris, the train, the hotel where she had spent the first night in France. Always she had had to pay for that assistance in the only way she could.

When she had left London dressed in the manner that she had known would attract men's interest, she had forgotten that it was six long years since she had left *Le Ciel Rouge* and given no thought to the fact that she herself might have changed so markedly that she could not so easily return to her former way of life. She had not found it possible to reacquire the indifference with which she had once accepted men's passions. She had been painfully conscious throughout each interlude that she was betraying Alexis; and although she wanted to hurt him as he had hurt her, she was aware all the time of his undoubted revulsion were he to know how she was behaving. She had been tormented by such thoughts each time she paid for the privileges she needed to get her to Épernay.

The memory brought sudden tears to her eyes. It was silly to care about Alexis' respect when she had lost it even before she left London. That was why she was here—in answer to his accusations that she was a useless, egotistical butterfly, not worth a hair of Roberta Inman's head.

Pelham pushed a glass of Cognac into Lucy's hand and

manlike, waited for his wife to cope with this unexpected situation. He could see tears rolling down Lucy's rouged cheeks and hoped Silvie would soon be able to restore the girl's equilibrium. Despite Lucy's makeup and clothes, she looked extraordinarily young and vulnerable, he thought—like a child dressed for a stage appearance. What could Alexis be thinking of allowing her to travel to France alone in wartime? And in such attire? Did Willow know of this? And where was Lucy's child?

It was not until an hour later when Lucy had bathed and was safely tucked up in her bed, that Silvie learned some of the answers to Pelham's unspoken questions. Lucy was remarkably frank with her aunt and Silvie had sense enough not to offer any criticism as the girl's story was unfolded. Nor did she allow herself to reveal the extent of her shock when Lucy confessed that little Teo was Maurice Dubois' child.

"I have insisted Willow be told that Lucy is safe here with us," Silvie told Pelham after she had enlightened him as to the facts. She sat down beside him in the comfortable sofa. "Lucy will not allow me to tell Alexis. But I don't doubt Willow will do so. There is a batch of amputees leaving here tomorrow for repatriation to England. The Red Cross can deliver a letter for us to Rochford."

"So Lucy is staying here with us?" Pelham inquired curiously.

Silvie nodded.

"It's what she wants. She says she will help in the wards. I am not sure if she realizes how horrific it can be at times— but we can certainly always do with another pair of hands."

"It sounds as if the girl is trying to prove to Alexis she's worth more than he thinks!" Pelham commented shrewdly. "Not such a bad motive. Shows Lucy really cares about his opinion of her."

"It had better remain our secret how Lucy managed to get to Épernay," she said dryly. "If Alexis knew she had reverted to her old tricks to bribe her way here, he would be appalled. Fortunately she was wise enough not to reveal her true identity to any of the men involved. She adopted her old name, Perle. Hopefully the officers to whom she gave her favors would not recognize her if they met her on some future occasion," she added uneasily.

"I doubt if they would," Pelham said with a grin. "It was some moments before *I* realized that the girl on *le capitaine*'s arm was really our niece! I would not have believed Lucy could look so vulgar!"

There was a knock on the door and Marie announced that their supper was ready. The old cook had taken a tray of food into Lucy's room but the girl was asleep and she had not woken her, she told Silvie.

Wearily Silvie got to her feet. She had been walking or standing all day, going about her duties in the wards where there seemed never to be an end to all the tasks that needed to be done. Although Silvie lacked any formal training, this past year she had learned a great deal by practical experience and now she could assist nurses when they would dress wounds, blanket bath the patients, feed them, make their beds, and even on occasions carry bedpans when there was no young nurse or V.A.D. to perform the task.

Pelham said she worked too hard but although Silvie had lost a considerable amount of weight, she was happy to have something concrete to contribute to the war. Pelham's hours were quite as long as hers, she reminded him. He was the man to whom everyone turned when something was needed; when a piece of machinery had broken down; an invalid chair required mending, supplies awaited collection from the railway station. Despite the fact that the hospital had been in operation for a full year, there were still endless shortages and failures of equipment and it was Pelham who invariably found a way round the problems. His cheerful good nature and sense of humor were such that people wanted to help him if it was possible and he could acquire necessities when even the Médecin de chef or Matron failed to do so.

The Château d'Orbais had been originally conceived by Silvie and Pelham as a center for convalescence and rehabilitation. They had not at first envisaged their home becoming a Red Cross hospital. But the terrible casualties suffered by the French north of Rheims had resulted in an influx of wounded from the field dressing stations and without warning, the Château had become a Clearing Hospital. Field ambulances and horse-drawn ambulance wagons painted with the Red Cross symbol brought back from the Front an endless stream of wounded, their injuries hastily patched at the dressing stations. Wooden barracks had been erected in the once lovely gardens of the Château to accommodate these casualties; even the stables and coach house had been turned into wards or living quarters for the nurses, so desperate was the need for space.

For the most part the wounded were Frenchmen although occasionally a British soldier was brought in. Some came on foot and Pelham went out in his car every day to pick up the straggling remnants trying to find their way back to a sane world where their wounds and their needs could be dealt with. Most were pathetically grateful but others were too shocked or weary even to raise a smile of relief when Pelham's Sunbeam stopped to give them a lift.

There were times when Silvie found the torrent of broken, injured men so heartbreaking that she longed to hide away from the sight. She tried not to think about the ethics of war or to question whether any country could be justified in sending the flower of its manhood to endure such hell in the name of freedom. The carnage was sickening and there seemed to be no end to it. She would watch the untidy lines of French infantry, the officers of the once-proud Dragoons, shuffling blindly into the reception area, their red trousers chalky with dust, their blue wool greatcoats torn and bloodstained, their heads or limbs covered with filthy white bandages and their faces blank with the shock of their experiences. At such times she felt a deep, consuming hatred for the Germans until she remembered that they, too, were suffering with as many if not more casualties than the Allies; that their hospitals, like d'Orbais, were filled with the same shreds of broken humanity.

That night, as Silvie sank into bed beside Pelham, she pondered the question of whether Lucy would be able to accept what lay in store for her if she really did intend to remain at the Château and make herself useful. It was not unusual for girls to be sent home—very young V.A.D.s who had volunteered their services believing they would be doing no more taxing work than soothing fevered brows, reading to and writing letters for patients as was customary in English hospitals. But here, where at any time a string of ambulances could arrive with wounded not long off the actual battlefield or carried from trenches still under shell fire, nurses were required of necessity to remove blood-soaked bandages, wash gaping wounds, carry out bedpan duties, clean the patients' filthy, mud-encaked, bodies.

Knowing something of the deprivation of her niece's life at the Convent, Silvie did not doubt that Lucy could adapt to hard work. She had undertaken in her young life the most menial of tasks. But hard work of that nature bore no comparison to some of the more revolting aspects of a nurse's duties in a war-time hospital. In one emergency Silvie had seen a man's intestines fall onto the floor when his bandages were removed. In another she had found herself staring into a leg wound crawling with thick white maggots. She had seen men with eyeless sockets, without noses, with shell splinters sticking out of their skulls. She had listened to men screaming like tortured animals, watched them coughing up their lungs as they gasped for air. And she had seen men dying as their stretchers were laid at the feet of a doctor who might have saved them had they arrived a few minutes earlier. Perhaps worst of all, she had discovered one man half out of his mind, clutching to himself his own severed hand from which he had refused to be parted for two days, hiding it on his person.

None of this would be easy for the pretty Countess Zemski, Silvie thought, and Alexis who must know her better than anyone, clearly doubted if his young wife had anything worthwhile to contribute; or was he deliberately challenging Lucy to prove him wrong?

The question remained unanswered as she fell into a deep sleep.

The following morning Silvie found a spare V.A.D. uniform for Lucy before taking her downstairs to be introduced to the Matron of the hospital. The girl looked remarkably pretty in her white skirt, with a white veil covering her fair hair and held in place by a headband with red crosses on either side. The uniform was in strange contrast to the clothes she had arrived in the previous day! Silvie decided she looked exactly what she said she intended to be—an angel of mercy.

Matron, a gray-haired buxom woman of enormous efficiency, took one look at Lucy's white hands and sighed. What she needed were the strong arms of a working girl—not this pretty young Countess. But out of deference to Madame Rochford she kept her misgivings to herself and sent Lucy off with a nurse to Admissions. There were ambulances due in at any moment, she told Silvie, and every pair of hands would be needed this morning. The casualties were once again from the Verdun area. There would be no time to familiarize Lucy with her surroundings. She would have to assist as best she could.

Perhaps Lucy would not have been so deeply shocked had she first been able to spend a few days in the wards. She might then have accustomed herself to the maimed and wounded whose bandages and dressings were clean, whose amputated limbs had been neatly stitched, whose broken bones had been set and splinted.

But now, even before she had been introduced to the doctors and nurses in Admissions, the first ambulances arrived and the orderlies were carrying in their dreadful burdens. A wad of cotton wool, a sponge, a bottle of antiseptic were pushed into her hands; a bucket of hot water was set down beside her by an orderly, and the nurse in whose charge Matron had put her ordered her to set about cleaning up as many patients as she could in preparation for the doctors' examination.

There were two doctors in white coats, both French, standing by the door as the stretchers were carried in. They were indicating to the nursing Sisters beside them which were the most urgent cases they would deal with first. Another uniformed nurse began administering morphine injections on the doctors' orders, to those who would have to wait before they could be operated on.

Lucy knelt down beside the stretcher nearest to her. On it lay a young French *poilu* whose left foot had been torn off by a shell. There was a tourniquet around his leg with a label attached stating in French that it must be loosened before ten o'clock. It was already ten-thirty and frantically Lucy tried to gain the attention of a passing nurse. But the woman was too busy to heed Lucy's desperate pleas for help.

Two male Red Cross orderlies dumping yet another stretcher next to Lucy's patient, paused long enough to listen to her question. They looked at her as if she was a mental case.

"If the label says so, then loosen it," one of them said none too politely as he hurried off with his companion. Lucy's protest that she did not know how to loosen a tourniquet died on her lips. She could do nothing but pray that a doctor would soon be along to attend to the man.

The young soldier was moaning.

"Mon pied me fait mal!" he kept repeating. He seemed unaware that his foot was gone as he reiterated over and over again how much it hurt him. Lucy wiped the sweat from his face and flinched at the deep cut revealed beneath the mud cake on his cheek.

A nurse stopped to stare down at Lucy.

"For heaven's sake, girl," she said sharply. "Never mind

that. See to his foot. The doctor will be round in a minute!"
Aware of Lucy's horrified gaze and realizing that she must be
a new girl since she did not recognize her, the nurse said in
gentler tones: "Remove the bandage; wash the stump as best
you can and cover it with some clean lint. You'll find some
over there on that table."

She was gone before Lucy could voice her horrified protest.
Biting her lip, she walked over to the table and found a huge
roll of white lint. Cutting off a square section, she returned
to her patient. He seemed to have relapsed into unconscious-
ness or else he had been given morphine. But he had stopped
moaning. If she must remove the bandage from his wound,
she thought, then better it should be now while he could feel
no pain.

Her heart beating furiously, her stomach heaving, Lucy
unwrapped the bandages. As she neared the flesh, the cloth
became increasingly stiff with dried blood. She knew that it
would have adhered to the wound. Closing her eyes, she tugged
as gently as she could and at that moment, the man screamed.

When Lucy came to, she was lying on a hard oak settle in
Matron's office. Silvie was sitting by her side. She patted
Lucy's hand.

"Feeling better, *chérie?*" she asked gently. "You fainted,
you know!"

As the memory of her failure slowly returned to Lucy, tears
of mortification flowed down her cheeks. Silvie helped her
into a sitting position and gave her a handkerchief.

"There's nothing to be ashamed of," she said firmly. "I
understand exactly how you must have felt. You were pushed
in at the deep end, I'm afraid. What you have to do now,
Lucy, is make up your mind whether or not you want to go
back down there. It's a question of mind over matter, you
see. If you really want to help, then you'll force yourself to
cope somehow. Most of the time you'll succeed. It gets easier
with time. But you've got to *want* to do it. You are needed,
as you've doubtless realized. We're always short of staff. But
the service is voluntary. No one is going to make you help if
you don't wish to."

For a long moment, Lucy was silent.

"I won't go home," she said finally in a small determined
voice.

Silvie shot her a quick glance. The color was returning to
Lucy's cheeks.

"Then if you mean that, Lucy, you'll have to do something worthwhile if you want to stay here with us. We can't afford to keep you as a guest! Think of the effect it might have on those other girls—the nurses and V.A.D.s who are run off their feet. If they were to see you lolling around leading the life of a lady of leisure, it could have the most upsetting effect upon their morale. Think about it, *chérie*. Your Uncle Pelham has a very apt saying for this situation—if you fall off a horse, you must get back in the saddle immediately if you want to ride again. Now I must go. I hate to leave you alone but I've wasted enough valuable time here already! I'll see you later. Meanwhile you can stay here quietly and make up your mind."

I can't go back, I can't, Lucy thought, struggling into an upright position as her aunt left the room. Her head was swimming and she felt nauseated. But most of all she felt deeply ashamed. It dug into her pride to think of those other girls, some no older than herself, coping down there in what could only be called a hell, without a word of complaint or a sign of distress.

Never in her life had Lucy considered herself a lesser being than others. She had not felt ashamed because of the life she had led at *Le Ciel Rouge* although Mama and Uncle Toby had made it obvious enough by their refusal to talk of those days that *they* considered it shameful.

Nor, Lucy thought now, had she felt shamed when she learned she was pregnant. She believed herself justified in seeking revenge upon Maurice Dubois and considered it a cruel stroke of bad luck that she had fallen into the oldest trap in the world. Despite all the setbacks in her life, she believed she had successfully overcome them. But now that conviction was absent. Alexis had told her she should be ashamed of herself. Had she not come out to France to prove him wrong? Yet it seemed as if he could have been right after all—when put to the test, she had lacked the courage to face such horrors.

There must be something else I can do, other than nursing, she thought as her mind twisted in circles like a squirrel caught in a cage. Even if I have to become a ward orderly and scrub floors! Anything, she thought, rather than have to witness a second time such pain, such mutilation, such a nightmare as she had just lived through.

Slowly she stood up and felt her head swimming. Gradually it cleared and looking down at her hands, she realized that they had ceased to tremble. She remembered suddenly the young *poilu* she had deserted so ignobly and her sense of shame deepened. What had become of him now? Some other girl must have finished her task for her and hopefully, dealt with the tourniquet. Had help reached him too late? Had the soldier died because of her ignorance? Lucy realized that she could never rest until she knew. He had been her first patient—and probably was her last, and she felt inextricably bound to him. Fate had made him her responsibility, and she had now to return to that dreadful room to satisfy herself as to his well-being.

Clenching her fists, Lucy went out of Matron's room and down the hall. She had to ask a passing orderly wheeling a stretcher where she should go to find the door to Admissions.

"Down the corridor, first on the left, Miss!" he directed her. "Proper slaughterhouse in there," he added with a warning shrug. He disappeared with his trolley through a door marked *Ward 2, Fractures.* Lucy was once more alone.

A V.A.D. came hurrying toward her from the direction the orderly had indicated for Admissions. In either hand, the young woman carried a bucket filled with bloodstained dressings. A foul stench rose to Lucy's nostrils as the nurse passed by her with a friendly nod. Once again nausea rose in Lucy's throat.

It's no good, she thought despairingly, I could never get used to it!

Nevertheless, she continued her slow walk down the hall. Her hand poised on the handle of the door to 'Admissions.' With a superhuman effort, she forced herself to open it and go inside.

Her eyes went automatically to the floor beneath the window where her patient had lain. He had gone. In his place, a gray-haired man sat hunched, his back against the wall, his arms encircling himself, his bandaged head buried in them. He was rocking to and fro. The front of his uniform was covered with dried blood but his limbs appeared intact. She looked around her but the doctors and nurses all appeared engrossed with more serious cases. The room looked no different since she had left it fifteen minutes before. Slowly, Lucy walked toward the man. He seemed unaware of her approach and continued a soft keening. She knelt down beside him.

"*Vous avez mal?*" she inquired needlessly. As she spoke,

his head lifted and turned toward her. He reached out groping helplessly in her direction and she realized he was blind.

"Aidez-moi! Aidez-moi!" he pleaded, his hands clawing at her until they fastened on her veil.

For one long moment Lucy was unable to move. Then slowly she stood up, the back of her hand pressed against her mouth to stifle her scream. Her veil remained in the blind man's grasp as she backed away from him. She must have been out of her mind, quite deranged, to have come back here, she thought. She bumped into a doctor who swore at her softly in French. A nurse jogged her elbow. A walking patient asked her the way to Ward 5.

Step by step, Lucy backed toward the door. She was terrified now lest one of the doctors or nurses took hold of her arm and forced her back into the room. Her one thought was of escape. This room could only be hell, she thought. Beyond it there was sanity, a life she understood and which was real.

She had reached the door when two English orderlies came hurrying into the room. They were carrying a stretcher. Their cockney voices were audible to Lucy.

"English pilot by the look of 'im, Sir!" one of them was saying to the doctor.

"Don't look too good, Doc. Came down just beyond the river. A farmer brought him in on a cart," said the other.

"Put him on the table—gently!" the doctor ordered in heavily accented English. Turning his head, he saw Lucy standing by the door and called across the room to her. "You, Mademoiselle, *venez ici!* Come here. You speak English? Don't just stand there, I need your assistance."

Lucy walked toward him as if in a trance.

"I may need you to translate for me. Stand by his head."

Afterward Lucy was uncertain at which moment she had looked down and recognized Mark.

"I think it was when he opened his eyes and smiled at me," Lucy later told Silvie. "He didn't seem in the least surprised to see me but of course, he was very shocked—in shock, the doctor called it. I'm afraid I was too. I wasn't much use. I just stood beside Mark and held his hand." Lucy's face took on a haunted look. "The doctor couldn't save his left leg. Thank God I was not needed in the operating theater when they amputated what was left of it. A nurse told me they've patched up his right leg and they're hoping he won't lose that too."

It was now nearly twenty-four hours since Lucy had first arrived at Épernay. As Pelham poured a second Cognac for Silvie and herself, Lucy reflected that it might be three weeks since she had stepped out of the French soldier's Peugeot, so long ago did it seem; a month since she had left Cadogan Gardens.

Silvie looked at her niece's white, exhausted face and said gently:

"It was courageous of you to stay at Mark's side in the light of what you have just told me about your return to Admissions, Lucy."

Lucy took a sip of her brandy and gave a wry smile.

"I wasn't particularly brave, Aunt Silvie. Mark kept saying, 'Don't leave me, Lucy. I'll be all right if only you'll stay with me.' I couldn't exactly desert him in the circumstances, could I?"

"Yes, you could have done!" Silvie said bluntly. "Have you made up your mind what you want to do now, Lucy? You said earlier that you had decided to go home. Do you still want me to try to arrange that?"

Lucy drew a long shuddering sigh.

"I said I realized I'd have to accept defeat—but that was before I saw Mark. I can't go just yet, Aunt Silvie. I gave him my word before he went into the operating theater that I'd be around after he had his operation. I don't think he realized he was going to lose a leg. Someone will have to tell him, won't they? He'll need someone to comfort him."

Lucy was staring down into her brandy glass and did not see the swift exchange of looks between her aunt and uncle. Silvie's voice gave no inkling of her satisfaction as she said lightly:

"Yes, I suppose Mark is going to need you. He'll be put in Ward 3, I expect—that's where the amputation cases go. You can go and see him in the morning. I'll ask Matron if you can go on duty there. After all, Mark is almost a brother, isn't he? Your half-brother, in point of fact!"

The look of bewilderment on Lucy's face brought home to Silvie the fact that she had inadvertently revealed something of which the girl was ignorant. She looked at Pelham anxiously, horrified that fatigue could have led her to make such a gaffe. But Pelham nodded reassuringly.

"Lucy is quite old enough to know the truth, my dear," he said. "I understand that Willow may not have wanted to reveal the facts. But there is no harm in Lucy knowing about the past provided she is discreet in her use of such knowledge. You must realize, Lucy, that what I am about to tell you could be a hurtful subject for your mother. I know you can be trusted not to discuss it with her unless she herself wishes it."

Lucy nodded. Her eyes widened in astonishment as she listened to her uncle's voice describing the years before she was born, when a woman called Georgina Grey had been her father's mistress and later, given him three children. Lucy's overriding thought was one of pity for her mother. She could imagine how she herself would have felt had Alexis had three children by Roberta Inman!

"As it happened, the three Grey children inherited only the best from both their parents," Pelham said finally. "You couldn't ask for three nicer characters and I know your mother had a very special affection for Philip. Nevertheless, I think you will agree that it is indicative of her generosity of spirit, that she could adopt your father's by-blows with such impartiality. Philip worshiped her, of course, and Mark and Jane look on her as their real mother, as you are doubtless aware."

"So Mark really *is* my half-brother!" Lucy murmured. "Does Oliver know the truth?"

"No, Lucy, no one knows but you, us and your Uncle Toby," Silvie said. "Philip, of course, was aware of the facts. But you must not tell Mark. It is for your mother to do so when and if she wishes. I'm afraid I am so tired, I did not guard my tongue just now as I should have done and kept the secret from you."

"I'm glad you told me!" Lucy cried.

She could not voice to her aunt the extraordinary wealth of emotion she now felt as she considered her mother in this new light. It seemed impossible that she, Lucy, could ever have thought of her as a weak, ineffectual woman lacking any real depth of character. When Willow had returned from America and Lucy had met her for the first time, she had not even liked her mother very much and she had certainly despised her for all those sentimental appeals to 'her lost baby.' How cruel she had been to this selfless, loving woman! She wished she had given her more thought when she rushed off to France without explanation, doubtless causing her untold worry. She was grateful that Aunt Silvie had insisted her mother be informed of her whereabouts. The last thing she wanted was to cause her further distress after a life that had been so full of unwarranted tribulation.

The following morning Lucy reported to work in Ward 3. Mark's face was deathly pale as she approached his bed, but his brown eyes lit up with relief when he recognized her.

"Lucy!" he whispered. "So I didn't imagine you! It's like a miracle finding you here in France! I didn't know you were out here nursing."

Lucy sat down by his bedside and took his hand in hers. Her eyes avoided the cradle beneath the blanket covering his single leg. The Sister in charge of the ward had told her Mark was still unaware that the other had been amputated.

"It was quite a shock seeing you come in on a stretcher yesterday," Lucy said with an attempted smile. "What were you up to, Mark, getting yourself shot down! You're no better than Oliver!"

Mark grinned weakly.

"Actually I wasn't shot down," he said with a wry smile. "I got myself lost after a bit of a shindig with a Jerry pilot. I'd been doing some aerobatics and lost my bearings. I followed what I thought was the River Somme and it turned out to be the Aisne—at least, I think that's what happened. Anyway, I finally ran out of fuel and tried to land in a field but I hit some trees first. Oliver and Henry aren't half going to rag me for it!"

He grimaced suddenly and gave a little gasp of pain.

"It's my left leg," he explained to Lucy. "Hurts like the very devil. I got it jammed in the rudder pedals, I think."

Lucy bit her lip in an effort to control the tears that had sprung so suddenly to her eyes. It was Mark's left leg that was missing. Aunt Silvie had warned her that patients who had had limbs amputated often suffered pain in them—a kind of miscarriage of the messages of the nerves to the brain. She recalled suddenly the French *poilu* of yesterday telling her that his foot hurt. She shuddered and turned her attention back to Mark. His eyes were closed as if the effort of talking had been too much for him.

"Try and sleep for a bit, Mark," she said. "I'm on duty now in this Ward so I'll be around if you need me."

Sister came over to the bedside. She beckoned Lucy to the further side of the room.

"He's heavily drugged," Sister told her. "But don't worry about him—he's young and healthy and he'll survive. Take my word for it," she added seeing Lucy's look of apprehension. "Come now, my dear, there's lots to do. Will you take Lieutenant Hope's wash things to him. He's lost an arm and you'll have to hold the basin of water for him while he shaves, and the mirror. He's in the bed by the window over there!"

Grateful that she had no more horrors to look at, Lucy obeyed the Sister's orders. Lieutenant Hope was a stocky, middle-aged man with red hair and freckles and a lively sense of humor. He reminded Lucy a little of Howard Barratt as he might be in a few years' time. The infantry officer greeted her with a welcoming grin.

"I say, they aren't half raising the standards for V.A.D.s, what?" he joked with his next door neighbor—a French major in the Artillery who, like Mark, had lost a leg. "Guess the M.O. thinks we can do with a morale booster, eh? May I ask your name, you beautiful creature? You're new here, aren't you?"

"I'll be getting sick leave one of zeeze days soon," the major said with an admiring glance at Lucy's trim figure. "Will you have dinner wiz me in Maxim's, Mademoiselle? To imagine such pleasure will make me the more quickly well."

"My name is Lucienne Zemski," Lucy replied with a smile. "And I'm a married woman and would ask you both to remember it!"

The two men gave exaggerated groans of disappointment but continued their flirtatious but harmless badinage as Lucy did what she could to assist them. The morning passed swiftly. There were four officers in the ward, three of whom were French and delighted to discover that Lucy could converse with them in their own language. One, a Dragoon officer who had lost his right arm, told Lucy that now at least he could send an intelligible letter to his wife. The English V.A.D. who had offered to write his letters for him had been unable to cope with the foreign words.

At midday the doctor made his rounds. Lucy turned her face aside as he drew the covers away from Mark's leg. He glanced at her averted face with a look of disapproval until Sister said:

"The young man is a member of her family, *Monsieur le Docteur!*"

"Then you shall be the one to tell him he has lost a leg," the doctor said quietly to Lucy as he moved over to another bed. "Not yet, I think. He is still very shocked. But soon! You will know when the time is right!"

Could there ever be a right time to tell a young man he would be crippled for the rest of his life, Lucy asked Silvie that evening. Pictures came with painful clarity into her mind—Mark on the tennis court chasing after a backhand shot of Oliver's; Mark standing up in the punt, poling them across the lake to the island; Mark with his strong, young legs astride Longhurst's motorcycle; Mark jumping down the last three stairs at Rochford Manor as he hurried to greet Philip home on leave.

"You must train yourself not to think of what is lost," Silvie said gently. "Think only of what is saved, Lucy. Mark will not have to fight again in this war. He'll be sent home when he is well enough, so his life has been spared. The loss of a limb is not really so bad when you consider the future for those who have been blinded; those who have lost their manhood; those with spinal injuries who will never leave their beds again. And remember those thousands no older than Mark who will never be more than a memory now in their loved ones' hearts. Do not grieve for Mark, Lucy. He's one of the lucky ones!"

It was several more days before Lucy had to break the terrible news to Mark. The thoughtful major, Louis Bucquet, aware of her intention, arranged a game of cards with the other two officers in the ward. As Lieutenant Hope was not yet permitted to leave his bed at the far end of the room, this diversion took them far enough away for Lucy's conversation not to be overheard.

She sat down beside Mark and held his hand.

"It's good to see you looking so much better," she said softly. "The *Médecin de Chef* told me this morning that although you may need another operation on your right leg, you will not lose it as had been feared."

Mark's eyes narrowed as he said with a slight frown:

"You mean it *might* have had to be amputated?" he asked incredulously.

Lucy nodded.

"You were pretty badly smashed up when they brought you in, Mark. You've been lucky."

"But it's my left leg which is hurting me so damnably," he reminded her. "What did the surgeon say about that one?"

Lucy glanced at the cradle covering the lower half of his

body. Had the cradle not been there, she realized, Mark would already be aware that his left leg had gone.

"I'm afraid that it, too, was very badly damaged," she said hesitantly, "too badly for the surgeon to be able to save it, Mark."

All vestige of color drained from his face. The grip of his hand tightened on Lucy's.

"What do you mean? What are you trying to say, Lucy? Are you trying to tell me I'm going to lose it?"

His eyes went involuntarily to Major Bucquet's bed. He'd been so damned thankful when he had first seen the chap with his empty pajama leg pinned up that nothing so dreadful had happened to him. He'd pitied the unfortunate lieutenant, too, who'd lost an arm; and the French captain, all amputees... everyone in the ward had lost a limb, he thought with a sudden, terrible understanding. His eyes went back to Lucy's face. The sight of tears glistening in her eyes increased his growing horror.

"For God's sake, Lucy, out with it! Am I going to lose my leg?"

Lucy fought against the threatening tears. This was no time for weakness. She must try to convince Mark that the truth was not so unbearable as he might suppose. She drew a deep breath.

"Listen to me, Mark," she said calmly but firmly. *"You have no left leg now.* It is quite normal for you to feel pain in an amputated limb. It will wear off. You will feel it less and less, and when you get back to England they will give you a new leg and you will be able to get around without crutches..."

She broke off, aware that Mark was no longer listening. He had removed his hand from her clasp, and was reaching down beneath the bedclothes in a frantic attempt to prove her wrong. His leg must be there—it must, he thought frantically!

Lucy spoke more firmly.

"I know this is an awful shock, Mark, but when you are better, I will take you around some of the other wards where you will see for yourself how much more cruel Fate might have been to you. You're going to be all right. You'll be able to lead a more or less normal life."

Mark lay perfectly still, not looking at her, his young face filled with bitterness as he said:

"Normal? I'm nothing but a cripple. I wish to God I'd been like Philip and knocked out altogether."

Color flared into Lucy's cheeks.

"You've no right to say that, Mark. How do you suppose Jane would have felt if she'd lost both her brothers? How do you suppose I, or Uncle Toby or Mother would have felt, or Oliver? You may not value your life but *we* all do—and so will you in time."

His face was turned away from her, buried in the pillow. His shoulders were shaking and she knew instinctively that she had said enough. Moreoever she seemed to be suffering not only for him but with him. His pain, his fear, his horror were there deep inside her and momentarily she wished Mark were the whole person and she the crippled. Her compassion was absolute.

The kindly Major Bucquet had been keeping an eye on the two young people. As Lucy stood up, he propelled himself across the room on his crutches.

"Do not be anxious," he said softly to Lucy in his accented English. "I will take care of him now."

Lucy nodded mutely. As she went out of the ward she turned her head and saw that the sympathetic Frenchman was sitting in the chair she had vacated, not speaking, but with his hand lying lightly on Mark's shoulder as if to reassure him that he was not alone.

Gradually Mark picked up strength and with it, his natural resilience of spirit. He talked ceaselessly of his admiration for Lucy and *her* courage, shaming her each time she thought of her plan to return to England as soon as he was well again. She had not dared reveal to him this secret intention; nor had she talked to him of the horror of her first day on duty. She knew she did not deserve his adulation and as her shame grew, she tried to alleviate it by inviting the Ward Sister to increase the scope of her duties.

Lucy was unaware of the private conversation that had taken place between the Ward Sister and her aunt. She was equally unaware that they had jointly decided that, given time, Lucy would make an excellent nurse.

"One thing my niece has never lacked is courage!" Silvie said with conviction, and shorthanded as she was, Sister was prepared to wait for the young Countess to prove her worth—as Madame Rochford herself had done when she had first come to work on the wards.

It was Pelham who brought matters to a head exactly three weeks after Lucy's arrival at Épernay. As they were enjoying their quiet evening drink at the end of the day, he said casually:

"I think I can arrange a passage home for you, Lucy, next week. There's a batch of wounded being repatriated and the *Médicin de Chef* said he would be willing for you to accompany them. He is anxious not to spare one of his trained nurses and I convinced him you could cope."

Lucy's blue eyes regarded her uncle in dismay.

"But Mark isn't well enough to go home yet," she said. "I can't leave until he does."

"Oh, I don't think he'll mind too much, Lucy," Pelham replied with a surreptitious glance at his wife. "He's well enough to stand on his own foot now."

"That's a horrible thing to say!" Lucy protested but Pelham seemed unmoved by her reproach.

"Much best make a joke of these things," he said vaguely. "Mark would be the first to laugh at it, you know. So how about it, Lucy? Shall I tell the *Médicin de Chef* you've volunteered?"

Lucy made no answer. She looked at Silvie but her aunt was apparently engrossed in the view from the living room window.

"But it isn't just Mark," she said in a rush. "I promised Lieutenant Hope I would teach him to play chess. And Captain Trevise depends upon me to write his letters to his wife. Sister said she's going to show me how to do their dressings tomorrow and teach me how to tie a tourniquet in case of an emergency..."

"Oh, well, in that case, I suppose Sister *could* let another of the V.A.D.s go..." Pelham said, shrugging with assumed indifference. "Quite a few of them haven't had leave for ages so I suppose it's only fair, really."

Lucy's face brightened.

"Yes, it would be much fairer. I don't want to do anyone out of their leave, Uncle Pelham. I'll stay on a bit longer, shall I? Just a week or two, or a month, perhaps?"

Silvie made no comment. But that night when she went into Lucy's bedroom to say goodnight to her, she sat down on the edge of the bed and without any preamble, she invited Lucy to tell her about her relationship with Alexis.

It was not a subject Lucy had ever discussed with anyone—

other than Alexis himself. She had not thought of her relationship with him as being of much interest to anyone but themselves. Even she herself, one of the participants, had never wasted any time in self-analysis. Yet now, under her aunt's sympathetic questioning, she discovered for the first time the delight of confiding in someone who could be trusted; someone old enough and wise enough to understand; someone without any reason for bias.

"It's so strange the way Alexis always ended any talks we had with this insistence upon love," she said to Silvie. "I have never understood why it should be so important to him. I know I have not a great deal of experience of life as you have, Aunt Silvie. Nevertheless from the little I *have* seen of love, it does not seem to me to bring people much happiness. Consider poor Mama and the life she led! Consider even my enemy, Roberta Inman. Her love for Alexis does not make either of them happy! And Howard tried to kill himself—stupid boy!—because he fancied himself in love with me. Why could it not be enough for Alexis that I liked and respected him and was willing to give myself to him? He professed to want me and I know there were many times when he desired to make love to me. Yet he refused. Always he refused. Had he not been so stubborn, we could have been quite happy together!"

Silvie studied Lucy's innocent face and understood for the first time what Alexis was up against. He and the girl he had chosen to marry might have come from two opposing planets, so different were their values. Alexis, of course, was conventional. It was Lucy who was hopelessly confused, and yet Silvie did not believe it was really hopeless. From Lucy's story of the events that had led to her arrival in Épernay, it was clear that she was far from indifferent to her husband. Only a woman who cared—and cared deeply—could react as Lucy had done, first with angry jealousy of Roberta; then with so violent a determination to prove Alexis' judgment of her wrong. Silvie was convinced that in her own way, Lucy loved Alexis—but Lucy herself had yet to discover it.

"I can't tell you what love is, *chérie*!" she said gently. "It is a composite of so many emotions and in each of us, I dare say, it varies. But you are not as devoid of the ability to love as you seem to wish me to believe. You love your little girl; you are discovering a filial love for your mother; you love

Oliver and Mark. I think you loved Maurice Dubois too, long ago."

It had been difficult for Silvie not to reveal her deep shock when Lucy had spoken so casually of that visit to Maurice's studio leading to her pregnancy. She had not wanted to halt Lucy in her confession, if such it was, lest her desire to confide should dry up as unexpectedly as it had begun. But now she realized how little they had all known and understood the real Lucy; how skilfully the young girl had hidden her feelings from them all—even, perhaps, from herself.

"Have you considered how Alexis might be feeling at this very moment?" she asked. "Do you not think he will be worried?"

Lucy's cheeks flushed and her eyes looked stormy.

"I dare say Mama will have told him where I am; she has always liked Alexis and he can do no wrong in her eyes. But as to his feelings, Aunt Silvie, why should I care? He didn't take much care of my feelings, did he? He said the cruelest things to me. As far as I am concerned, he can divorce me if he wishes and marry his precious Roberta. I don't need him. I don't need anyone. I can look after myself. I did so for sixteen years and if necessary I can do so again."

Silvie sighed. There was little doubt that whatever the future held for Lucy, she *would* survive. She seemed to have little conception of how beautiful she was and how devastatingly attractive to men. Sister had told her there wasn't a patient well enough to feel any emotion who had not been affected by the sight of the young V.A.D. walking through the hospital.

"Your niece has made each and every one of them long to be well again," Sister had said smiling, "and that's half the battle won for their recovery. Mind you, I think their temperatures go up along with their blood pressure but even our crusty old *Médicin de Chef* is at Lucy's feet. Not that she realizes it!"

Lucy had been far too busy trying to come to terms with her own feelings to bother about those of anyone else. Her horror and disgust at the ugly wounds were at variance with the deep pity and compassion she felt for those who were suffering. She wanted to be able to help them yet she knew herself lacking the strength of will to overcome her revulsion. Each time she helped Sister dress a wound, she had to force herself to perform the relatively simple tasks required of her.

It infuriated her that she could not control the nausea; the flinching, the trembling of her hands. She would have preferred it if Sister had criticized her yet the older woman seemed totally unaware of her emotions. But the men were not, she was convinced. She did not want them to know that the sight of them offended her in any way. She tried to keep her eyes centered on theirs so that they would see only a smile and never the grimace she feared must be there.

"I'll never make a good nurse, will I, Aunt Silvie!" she said following her own train of thought. "Alexis was right, I suppose. I'm not much good to anybody unless it's to partner someone in a tango!"

Despite the gravity of Lucy's voice, Silvie laughed as she stood up.

"I dare say there isn't a male patient in this hospital who wouldn't prefer to see you dance the tango for them than have you empty their bedpans!" she commented, and was pleased to see Lucy smile.

"I suppose that horrible job is no worse than having to wipe the little ones' *derrières* at the Convent!" she said dryly. "I want to go back there one day, Aunt Silvie. I want to tell Mother Superior to her face just how wicked I think she is."

Silvie sighed.

"Vengeance may seem sweet at times, Lucy, but so often at the end of the day, you discover that it is you, yourself, who suffers the consequences. For your own sake, try to forgive those who have hurt you—most of all Alexis. I think in your heart you know he does not want Roberta Inman—nor ever did. He married you, and there are not so many men who would have done so knowing your past; knowing you were pregnant by another man. Yet you have told me he has never once reproached you and that he has been a marvelous father to little Teo. He could not have behaved so had he not loved you very much."

"Not enough, it would seem, for him to come out to France to fetch me home," Lucy said in a hard, cold voice. "He could get here if he wanted, Aunt Silvie. He often goes to Europe, you know—on affairs to do with his job. If he had really worried about me, he'd have been here long before now and forced me to go home with him. He may have loved me once, but he doesn't love me now."

"Perhaps not, *chérie*!" Silvie said quietly as she turned out the light. "Time will tell, I dare say. Sleep well, *ma petite*!"

But as she walked into her own bedroom, her eyes were thoughtful as she looked at Pelham.

"Lucy believes Alexis has stopped loving her," she said. "But from all she has told me, I am convinced that no man could love her more."

Pelham smiled.

"One of these days, when there's time, you can explain all that to me in detail," he said. "But right now, my dear, you are going to get undressed and come to bed. Otherwise there will be one man who has never loved you less!"

He was rewarded by Silvie's gentle laugh, the look of concern leaving her eyes and her frown disappearing as she obeyed the command and began to prepare for bed.

Chapter 23

❦

September—December 1916

"GRANDMA, ZANDRA WON'T PLAY WITH ME!"

Willow looked down at Teo's woebegone little face and patted the fair curls lovingly. This child of Lucy's was so like her, it was as if Lucy herself had been reincarnated and was now living the childhood she had missed at Rochford.

"Perhaps Zandra has more important things to do!" Willow pleaded comfortingly. But the four-year-old child shook her head.

"No, she don't have nuffink to do. She's just sitting all by her ownself!"

Willow took Teo's hand and invited her to take her to see Zandra.

Dodie's daughter was in fact sitting all alone under the big lime tree on the lawn, her arms clasped around her hunched knees, her head tilted upward toward the blue sky.

"What are you doing here all by yourself, darling?" Willow asked.

Zandra put a hand to her lips.

"Please don't talk to me, Aunt Willow!" she said solemnly. "You see, I'm listening."

"May I ask what you are listening to?" Willow inquired, hiding a smile.

"For a call!" Zandra told her. Her small face creased into a frown. "The trouble is, I may already have missed it. I've forgotten to listen all summer and then suddenly I remembered. Do you think I'm too late?"

Willow was used to these enigmatic conversations with Zandra. Taking little Teo onto her lap, she sat down in the wicker chaise longue and turned to the intense-faced child under the tree.

"Could you begin at the beginning, Zandra?" she asked. "Then I can give you a proper opinion."

Not only did Zandra adore her aunt but she sensed that Willow understood her better than did her Mama. Dodie quite naturally had been very involved recently with her new baby son, Jamie, with the result that Zandra had adopted Willow as a recipient for her many childish problems. Willow never laughed at her or considered her ideas and thoughts stupid, so Zandra trusted her.

She drew a deep breath.

"Aunt Lucy didn't have a governess when she was my age," she said in her precise, high-pitched tones. "She went to a convent and she was taught her lessons by nuns. Aunt Lucy told me that nuns never get married to ordinary people because they get married to Jesus Christ instead. He's allowed to choose as many brides as He wants and they all wear the same kind of clothes and veils so people know they're special."

"That's more or less right, Zandra," Willow agreed as the child paused.

"Yes, well, I asked Aunt Lucy how the nuns knew Jesus wanted to marry them 'cos He isn't around to propose to them. And Aunt Lucy told me that nuns hear voices calling them to Holy Orders."

"And what has all this to do with you, Zandra?" Willow inquired.

The child leaned forward, putting her elbows on her knees and propping up her chin with her hands as she replied:

"On my birthday I asked God in my prayers at bedtime to make me into a boy so I could be like Oliver and Mark and become an airplane pilot. But He didn't do anything and Patience said it was probably because He wanted me to be a girl for some special purpose of His own. So I thought about it and I thought it might be because He wanted to marry me and for me to be a nun. That's why I'm listening. But Teo and the twins keep talking all the time or Patience is telling me to go and wash my hands or Aunt Stella wants to hear my times tables or something. No one seems to understand I might MISS hearing just the very moment the voices are calling."

Willow was careful to control her amusement. In a voice as solemn as Zandra's she said:

"I don't think I'd worry about it too much, darling. You are a bit too young to marry anybody just yet and I don't think you'll hear those voices until you are very much older. Besides, you can be sure Jesus would know if you couldn't hear Him and He'd wait for a time when no one was talking to you."

Zandra's face brightened.

"I never thought of that!" she admitted. But almost at once, her face fell again.

"Something else worrying you?" Willow asked gently.

Zandra nodded.

"The Limbo babies!" she said slowly.

"Who are they?" Willow inquired with genuine curiosity.

"Aunt Lucy said the nuns told her that all the babies who die before they are baptized are sent to a place called Limbo. That's a sort of halfway house between Heaven and earth. And it doesn't matter how much the babies cry, they can't ever get to Heaven—not unless someone here on earth says the three Holy names—'Jesus, Mary and Joseph.' Each time anyone says them, one of the babies can get out of that horrid place and go to Heaven. Aunt Lucy said she didn't believe it but sometimes I wonder whether I ought to say 'Jesus, Mary and Joseph' more often—just in case! I've worked out if I say them very very quickly, I can do fifty-eight every minute. That's an awful lot of babies I could save if I tried!"

"Oh, Zandra, I agree absolutely with Aunt Lucy. God is a good kind person. He'd never punish innocent babies in such a cruel way. So there's really no need at all for you to bother your head about it. Just say your prayers every night and that will be quite sufficient."

Zandra's look of concern gave way to a beaming smile. Happily reassured, she jumped to her feet and took Teo's little hand in hers. Quite unconsciously, she adopted Patience's tone exactly as she said:

"Come along then, Teo dear. I'll play with you now if you're going to be a good girl. What's it to be then? Hide and seek?"

As the two little girls ran off hand in hand, Willow stared after them, a smile still lifting the corners of her mouth. Although Lucy's child was by far the prettier of the two, it was Zandra whose personality drew everyone's attention. Both Stella and James had pronounced her intelligence as way beyond that of her contemporaries; and with that quick little mind went a lively imagination. These, combined with her extrovert nature and remarkable ability to imitate, guaranteed Zandra a future that could never be mediocre. She was a loving but highly emotional child and at times, her tantrums had caused trouble in the nursery. But Stella believed these passionate outbursts to be caused for the most part by frustration. Her brain was developing quicker than her actual years and emotionally she was sometimes unbalanced. But for the most part, she was a laughing, happy child and her curiosity knew no limits.

Teo was almost Zandra's opposite—a quiet, placid little girl who adapted quickly to her surroundings without question. She had settled in to life at Rochford without any sign of disturbance and seemed not to miss her mother at all. Alexis had been down twice to see her since they had had word from Silvie that Lucy intended remaining in France. When told by Alexis that 'Mummy is nursing wounded soldiers in another country called France,' Teo had given no sign of anxiety. With Stella's twins for company, Nanny Meredith to watch over her well-being and Zandra to play with her when she wanted special attention, Teo's small world revolved smoothly and happily.

Willow's smile faded as she allowed her thoughts to dwell briefly on Lucy's extraordinary departure to France. Although Alexis had made light of it, loyally refusing to criticize his wife's precipitate behavior, Willow had seen the look of concern in his eyes and noted the lines of tension round the mouth when he inquired whether they had received any further news.

"You must miss her terribly, all alone in London, Alexis," Dodie had remarked not altogether wisely.

"Well of course I do miss her," Alexis had replied quietly. "But as you know, Dodie, I am so very busy most of the while that I only go home to eat and sleep. Lucy must have been very bored with me away so often. I fully understand her need to do something positive for the war effort."

Willow had no doubt that the marriage was far from satisfactory and that it could only have been discord between Alexis and Lucy that had prompted her to disappear without even telling her, Willow, of her intention. This last year, ever since Teo's disappearance, she and Lucy had grown very close in a way she had once feared impossible.

It was strange, she reflected now, how at one time it was Jane who had most needed her as a mother, a confidante. Now Jane had grown suddenly remote, distant, keeping Willow at arm's length whenever the conversation became in the slightest degree intimate. She did not understand Jane these days. Before Oliver and the two boys had gone into the R.F.C. they had all had such a jolly, happy summer together at Rochford. Willow could only suppose that Jane was missing the boys' company and perhaps resented the fact that she could not go to war with them.

Fortunately the girl was kept fully occupied with her V.A.D. work in the wards. Matron had told Willow that Jane was a born nurse and one of the most dedicated of her assistants.

Rochford Manor, now that it had become a fully fledged convalescent home, was quite literally bursting at the seams. Toby said that if they could be certain that the war would continue, they should perhaps consider enlarging the big Lodge at the end of the drive and moving the family in there so that their own rooms could be put to use for nurses and patients. There seemed no end to the constant influx of soldiers needing a place to recuperate. The battles on the Somme, which had been raging since July, continued throughout September with no conclusion in sight. On the fifteenth of the month, eighteen huge steel monsters called 'tanks,' were used by the British in an effort to force a decisive victory. But as Alexis had explained to Willow and Toby on his last visit, the eighteen had not been sufficient, despite the fact that they sported six-pounder guns which could fire from either side and four machine guns which could be fired simultaneously from the hull.

Forty-nine of these new inventions had been intended for use, he told them. But each of them weighed twenty-eight tons and many had been bogged down on the way to the battlefield while others had broken down.

"We shall use them again, make no mistake," he forecast. But meanwhile, the battles along the Somme continued. Violet's husband, Bill, was taken prisoner and now the family awaited news from him as well as from Oliver. They had had only one postcard from Oliver telling them he was shortly to be moved.

Up in London the population were reeling from the effects of a raid by fourteen zeppelins made on September 26th when they dropped bombs on the southern part of the capital. There had been forty casualties. Although London was better defended in that it now had efficient searchlights and guns capable of hitting the marauding zeppelins and setting them on fire, nevertheless the raids were frightening and brought home the imminence of war which had once seemed so far away from British soil.

At the beginning of October, news reached Rochford of the deaths on the Somme of Frank Watson, the under-footman, and one of the young gardeners. Violet was human enough to cease regretting that her Bill had been taken prisoner. He was no longer in the firing line, she told Willow, who felt exactly the same sense of relief about Oliver. She felt less easy about Mark who, although he would never fly his airplane again, equally would never be whole again. To lose a leg at the age of twenty seemed a ghastly tragedy and Willow found it only small comfort to know that Lucy and Silvie were taking care of him.

Henry was still flying. He had written two long, cheerful letters from the Middle East where he was operating under the command of General Allenby. In one of these, he referred to "*an extraordinary English officer by the name of Lawrence*" who was an intelligence officer. He had organized and set up the Arab Bureau.

"*Rumor says this chap has amazing influence with the Arabs,*" Henry wrote, "*and has stirred them up to revolt against the Turks. His exploits remind me for some reason of dear Uncle Pelham. Is he still doing his 'Scarlet Pimpernel' act . . . ?*"

"At least Sir John and Lady Barratt still have two sons left to them," Willow said sadly to Toby when in December, a telegram was delivered at Glenfield Hall announcing the death of Howard at Verdun. He had been killed by a sniper while delivering urgent dispatches to the French Commander in the area—a sad blow of Fate since his own regiment was stationed with the Fourth Army much further north at Bray on the Somme.

Fearing it might heighten the Barratts' sense of loss, she did not tell them of the second letter she had received from a prisoner of war camp 'somewhere in Germany' from Oliver. The first letter had come from the transit camp where he had stayed only six weeks. It had been brief and obviously written hurriedly to reassure her of his well-being. But this one was far more informative. Not only was he well, but content with his living conditions. This filled her with joy and she had felt like telephoning every friend they had to impart her good news.

"*I hope you have received my last letter by now and know that I suffered only very minor injuries when I was shot down,"* he had written, his letter obviously censored. *"This place is a former barracks and it isn't at all bad. I have been playing tennis and fives and I am learning fencing. Our C.O. does his best to insure we have lots to occupy us and the latest innovation is language classes. I have enrolled for Spanish and German.*

"The food isn't too bad, thanks to the Red Cross parcels the chaps receive. They make all the difference. I hope therefore to receive one from home quite soon. Food is shared out by the Mess so I'm a bit in debt at present. Our quarters are really quite comfortable. We have managed to get an old piano which one of the orderlies found in a store above the loose boxes where the men are housed, so we are having some fun. We are planning to have a Christmas concert, if we aren't moved on, which God forbid! It is something to look forward to. Some of the chaps have got really good voices so it should be amusing if not exactly professional.

"The girls might be interested to hear that a mongrel stray has adopted our room, and we've called him 'Kaiser.' He follows us about everywhere, and we've trained him to wag his tail when he sees a khaki uniform.

"We are allowed out on parole for walks. Last week our guards took us on a tram ride into the country and we must have walked for nearly ten miles that day. It was good to get out and the weather was just like an English summer and made me think of all of you at home...

"The Germans treat us very well and we can go about the town quite freely provided we take out a parole card which we surrender on our return..."

It was over a month since Oliver had written that letter and much had happened since then which he did not intend to tell his mother. He was in fact planning to escape.

There were only two people who were aware of this—Oliver's friend, an army officer by the name of Will Butler with whom he shared his sleeping quarters; and his batman, Albert Foster.

Foster had been only too pleased to apply for the job as Oliver's batman. Life in the nearby prisoner of war camp for other ranks was shocking. They were treated like animals, sleeping on straw and unable to stay clean of vermin. Unlike the officers, they received no food parcels from home and were confined to eating only the German beggarly ration of black bread, known as *pumpernickel*, watery soup, erzatz coffee, and a pathetic portion of meat once a week. Most of the men were bordering on starvation. Despite this, they were forced to work ten hours a day and were beaten for the most minor offense, such as failing to salute a German officer. One man had been killed with a bayonet for having accidentally broken a pane of glass. Punishments could mean being tied to a post in the compound for hours. Once the Germans had let loose a watchdog to attack a man so secured.

Oliver and his room companion, Will, were shocked by Foster's stories, and Oliver had taken it upon himself to report them to the C.O. But he was already well aware of the facts and had put in a report to the Red Cross—so far without result.

It was in the course of one of these conversations that Foster told Oliver about the working party at the Schloss Grünhügel. Situated between Krefeld and Düsseldorf, about two miles from the camp, the old castle had been appropriated by Germans when its Belgian owner, a Baron Vanzype had vacated it on the outbreak of war. The British prisoners were being employed to convert the place into a hospital—the patriotic Baron having done his best to demolish the interior before he had departed.

Down in one of the cellars, Foster's fellow prisoners had found what at first they had taken to be a huge parachute. A knowledgeable German guard had identified it as a *luftschiff* and on looking the word up in the dictionary, they had learned this was a gas balloon. Knowing of Oliver's interest in flying, Foster described it to him.

That night, Oliver and Will sat up until the early hours of the morning discussing the possibility of using the gas balloon as a means of escape. Krefeld was only twenty-six miles from the Dutch border. If the wind was in the right direction, it might just be possible to reach neutral territory, Oliver agreed, but they were ignorant of the balloon's condition. The Baron might have had it put in the cellar years ago because the fabric had become porous and the balloon unusable. Where would they find a gas supply to fill the balloon if it *was* usable? Was there a basket to attach to it? How could they cross enemy territory without being seen and subsequently shot down by guns or an airplane?

Oliver took Foster into his confidence. Far from decrying the idea, the middle-aged batman was enthusiastic. As an

officer, Oliver could get a parole card entitling him to go out
of the camp, Foster suggested. He and Lieutenant Butler could
go to the Schloss and inspect the balloon. It would not be
easy as the working party lived there in the charge of resident
German guards, but with luck, Oliver might be able to make
direct contact with the Tommies and enlist volunteers. Someone would have to be found who knew about the gas supply
to the Schloss. As far as Foster could recall from his own
working days at the castle, there was no electricity and there
had been gas fires in the bedrooms and old-fashioned gas
mantels hanging from the ceilings.

What at first seemed like a crazy idea slowly began to
appear less so. They started to believe in a genuine possibility
of escape. But before anything else, the condition of the balloon must be verified.

Two days later, a party of six British Officers including
Oliver and Will went on a 'sightseeing' trip to the Schloss
Grünhügel. They had told their German Camp Commandant
that they were particularly interested in architecture and that
this magnificent German castle was a perfect example of the
period they were studying in their class.

Since the Schloss was being turned into a hospital which
had no military significance, the Commandant had no objections to his somewhat unusual request and as the young
English lord had so far proved an exemplary prisoner, he was
not averse to granting his wishes.

The Schloss Grünhügel was an early eighteenth-century
Baroque edifice of great stature, situated a few miles outside
Krefeld on a gently rising green slope covered in pine trees.
The Baron Vanzype had loved his home too much to damage
the stonework of the exterior but the inside had been gutted.
As Foster had outlined, French and British soldiers were re-
plastering walls, repairing the plumbing, fitting new panes of
glass in the windows and clearing away the heaps of dirt and
rubble that lay everywhere.

The weather was now bitterly cold with sharp November
winds biting through every glassless window, whistling along
the high-ceilinged stone passageways, sending little eddies of
dust scudding along the flagged stone floors. Oliver was
appalled to see the condition of the men—their clothes filthy,
ragged and inadequate to combat such weather; their faces
pinched with cold and gaunt from long hours of hard labor
and insufficient food. Nevertheless, they raised a salute and

a friendly grin as Oliver and his fellow officers passed by and one cheeky Australian lad, eyeing the plump, tail-wagging 'Kaiser,' warned Oliver to keep an eye on him lest the friendly little dog found his way into the cooking pot!

Their German guard was happy enough to let them go down to the cellars alone while he chatted to his fellows who were guarding the soldiers. There, near the wine vault, still untouched, lay the gas balloon Foster had described so graphically.

"Think it's all right, Rochford?" Will inquired as Oliver felt through the string netting cover to the thin silk material beneath.

Oliver gave a wry smile.

"The truth is, Will, I don't know all that much about ballooning. My brother-in-law took me up to Ranelagh twice and told me how they operate but I've never actually flown in one!"

There was a loud groan of derision from his companions but Oliver refused to be daunted.

"There's not a lot to it—not like flying an airplane," he told them. "It's just a matter of filling the thing up with gas, which because it is lighter than air rises upward. Then off you go in the direction of the wind. Of course, in time some of the gas leaks out and down you come, but so long as you pick a nice soft place to land, you don't break too many bones!"

Another loud laugh greeted this sally but Oliver continued his examination. When the others wandered back upstairs, he said to Will:

"There are a couple of holes which need patching but the rest of it seems fine. I'd say it was fairly new—or at least that the Baron hasn't had a great deal of use out of it. We can get some green oilsilk from the M.O. to make waterproof patches. Our main problem is going to be the gas."

Will grinned.

"Leave that to me," he said. "I'm going to ask the German guards if I can give the Tommies a little pep talk—and I don't want you interrupting."

In return for a packet of English cigarettes, the guards readily agreed to giving the men a five-minute break while the officer addressed them. Will faced the row of curious faces, his own expressionless as he said:

"I know you chaps all want to do your utmost to make your officers proud of you. Leading the life you do in the perfectly splendid prisoner of war camps your captors have provided for you, you will appreciate my meaning when I say it is only fair that you should reward them for housing you, feeding you and giving you worthwhile work to do..."

His sarcasm was not lost upon them and grins had begun to appear on the men's faces. They leaned forward with interest as he continued:

"Many of you, I know, learned trades before you became soldiers and I would like each of you to stand up and tell me what job you had before the war. Who knows but the day might come—soon even—when I or another of your officers might have need for the services you are now giving the German nation."

One by one, each of the men stood up as requested and announced his peacetime trade. Two had been farm laborers, one a docker, another a plumber; there was an Australian bricklayer and—as Will had hoped—a gas fitter.

Now Oliver understood the reason for Will's speech. He noted the name of the gas fitter and went over to the German guard.

"That soldier with the fair hair and hooked nose," he said. "He comes from my home village. Have I your permission to speak to him?" Casually he produced another packet of cigarettes which the guard pocketed with a nod.

To the astonishment of the Tommy, Oliver went up to him and gave him a friendly slap over the shoulders.

"Fancy running into you, Roberts," he said brightly. "How's your family? Come over here where we can have a quiet talk!"

Once apart from the main working party, Oliver dropped his voice.

"You gave your trade as a gas fitter, Roberts. I need a man like you to help me make my escape. Are you willing to help?"

"If I can, Sir!" the man said instantly.

As quickly as he could, Oliver outlined his idea. At first the soldier looked dubious.

"Ain't no gas connected to the Schloss, Sir," he said. "Pipes is all busted. It's my job to fix 'em up—that's how I got on this working party."

"But there must have been a mains supply at one time," Oliver persisted. "Would you know where that is, Roberts? I'd need quite a bit of pressure—otherwise it would take too long to inflate the balloon."

Roberts' grubby face broke into a grin.

"There'd be enough pressure all right if we tap the mains. I know where the stopcock is. I could tell Fritz I need to test the supply. I'm not sure if it's been cut off down in the town—though I doubt it. But even supposing I could do that, Sir, it would have to be piped to where you wanted to launch that balloon of yours."

"Yes, of course!" Oliver agreed. "Any ideas?"

Roberts scratched his head.

"Be about a four-inch bore, I imagine," he said knowledgeably. "How far away would you want to be, Sir?"

Oliver had already noted a large treeless area of overgrown grass that must once have been a lawn. Although surrounded by woods on three sides and the Schloss itself on the fourth, the clearance was more than sufficient for his purpose. But at the same time, he could see the difficulty of laying a gas pipeline across the grass field in full view of the German guards.

"Reckon as how those cast-iron drainpipes might do the job," Roberts was saying more to himself than to Oliver. "Couldn't hide 'em of course. Dare say we would loosen 'em when the guards wasn't paying attention. Stupid lot they are! We could pretend as how they needed tightening! Then when you were ready to go, we could lift 'em off easy and lay 'em down in line..."

"We'd have to do it at night!" Oliver broke in. "I'd never get across German territory in daylight. What chance of you chaps being able to help at nighttime?"

Roberts grimaced.

"Not much, Sir. We're locked in. Of course, if the guards were to be given a few drinks—enough to befuzzle them. But how to get hold of the liquor, Sir?"

"That's no problem," Oliver said quickly. "The officers can buy what they want in the town. I can see to that side of things."

"Then I reckon it might work out!" Roberts said with a broad grin. "I'd do my best, Sir, if you decide to make a run for it. The lads will all help if they can. Not one of us wouldn't welcome the chance to do Fritz a bad turn. Rotten lot of bastards they are, Sir, pardon the language. Beat one of my mates half to death last week!" He spat on the floor with a venom that momentarily surprised Oliver until he recalled Foster's stories.

"Any of you able to sew?" he inquired anxiously. "There

are two places in the balloon need patching and I can't be sure I can get here again myself. I'll need some sort of basket too. If the previous owner had one, it's been lost. I looked around and couldn't find it."

"No problem there, Sir. There's a couple of old laundry baskets in the attics. We was talking of using them for fires. I'll get one of the lads to check one over and make certain it's in good enough shape for what you want."

Oliver's excitement began to wane as the inherent dangers of this madcap plan suddenly hit him. He was not afraid for himself should they be caught—which was a likely possibility. But he did not want these men to suffer. By the look of it, they were having a bad enough time as it was. But Roberts swept aside such misgivings.

"We can lock ourselves in again after you've gone, Sir, Joe's a locksmith and he can make a copy key easy as pie. Then it won't be none of our fault what you officers got up to in the night. Don't you worry none about us."

But Oliver continued to worry when they all returned to the camp and sat enjoying an evening drink in the Mess discussing his escape plan. Will Butler made light of Oliver's concern for the other ranks who must, it was now clear, be involved.

"Dash it all, Rochford, the decision is up to them and by the sound of it, they'll welcome any chance to get one up on the Boche. Roberts sounds a sensible sort of chap and if he says it can be done, then I'll leave that side of it to him."

Oliver sighed.

"But it's not as if I can offer them a chance to get out," he said. "Doesn't seem right, Will, that I should escape and leave those poor devils behind."

"Can't you take one of them with you?" one of the other officers asked. "You could hold a lottery—you know, chap with the winning number goes."

Oliver bit his lip.

"I'll have to find out if the balloon can carry the weight of two," he said doubtfully. "The trouble is, I don't really know too much about the technicalities. Maybe the whole idea is crazy!"

But that night as he lay in bed unable to sleep, he knew that he would have to make the attempt now that the thought had been put in his mind. He had no wish to spend the rest of the war in a prison camp. He'd waited long enough to get into the R.F.C. and then only enjoyed five weeks' action before busting up his airplane and getting himself captured. If he could get back to England, he could fly again; contribute something to the war after all.

He was able to make one more visit to the Schloss Grün-hügel, continuing with the myth of architectural interest and enlisting Will and others of his friends to support him. He took with him several large pieces of green oilsilk he had begged from the M.O., needles, and reels of silk thread he'd purloined from the Entertainments Officer who was responsible for theatrical costumes.

He also took as much food as he could scrounge from the Mess Officer which he and his friends hid as best they could in the pockets of their heavy greatcoats. Down in the cellar, Roberts, the one-time gas fitter, surveyed the cold meats, sugar, tea and cakes incredulously.

"Don't know how to thank you, Sir! Ain't seen anything like it since I got nicked. Can't hardly believe me own eyes, Sir!"

Oliver grinned ruefully.

"I'm afraid it's not as much as I'd have liked to bring," he said. "We were afraid we might be searched if we looked to bulky! Lieutenant Butler is making himself responsible for getting the booze for the guards the night the balloon goes up," he added with a smile. "From what our guards tell us, the local population are almost as short of food as you lot, and Mr. Butler is pretty certain he can swap food or cigarettes for some Schnapps when the time comes."

Roberts returned his smile.

"By the look of this," he said staring hungrily at the food, "officers like yourself, Sir, don't need to escape!"

Oliver nodded.

"You're right about our living conditions," he admitted. "But it's a question of duty, Roberts. If I can get home, I can become operational again and maybe help shorten this grim war just a little."

Roberts stared with mixed feelings at the handsome young man. This officer was little more than a lad, still in his teens by the look of him. One of the chaps had told him he was titled and owned a huge estate in Kent. What did he want to go and get himself killed for, silly young devil! Yet at the same time, Roberts felt proud of him. It was good to know that the nobs who'd be ruling the country after the war were doing their patriotic duty, same as those like himself who'd been drafted into the army. He'd do what he could to help this boy escape. They'd need his sort in England when things got back to normal.

"We've had a look at the drainpipes since you were last here, Sir," he said. "No trouble to prize them loose—the stonework's pretty old and the brackets rusty. Our corporal told the guards they needed attention afore they fell off this winter and killed one of 'em! So Jones has been detailed to see to 'em. He's going to loosen 'em so that on the night, it'll take only a minute to pull 'em off!"

Roberts returned to his working party and Oliver went out into the grounds to inspect the proposed launching site. It was once again a cold blustery day. He looked up at the clouds racing across the blue sky and made a mental note of his bearings. It was vital now to keep track of the wind directions. He needed a gentle easterly wind to carry him toward the Dutch border. One of the chaps had lent him a map and he'd worked out that his route from Krefeld would require to be west-north-west to the Dutch border town of Venloo. Too far north and the length of his journey would increase considerably where the border curved west toward Arnhem. Too far south and he'd end up in Belgium.

Fortunately the undulating hills he could now see stretching beyond the grounds of the Schloss were not very high. With luck, he'd be passing hundreds of feet above them. Beyond, when he began to lose height, the terrain became flatter.

Everything depended upon two factors, he told Will Butler as they walked the two miles back to camp. First, that Roberts would be able to provide the gas supply. Second, that the balloon proved to be nonporous. He would have no chance to insure the latter until they bagan to inflate it.

For the next few days, Oliver set about planning the details on paper. Assuming a wind speed of between fifteen and twenty-five knots, he would need to be airborne for an hour to an hour and a half.

His excitement mounted. Given just a little luck, it could be done! At worst, he'd land somewhere short of the border and even then, he might make it on foot under cover of darkness if the distance were not too great. The biggest danger lay in being spotted by a German gunpost or searchlight. It was a danger that would increase rapidly as he lost height and became visible to anyone on the ground. The only other danger lay in the landing itself. He would have to open the valve at the top of the balloon to let out the gas, otherwise the semibuoyant balloon would be dragged along the ground by the wind, pulling the basket after it. Traveling through the air at twenty-five knots would be a very different matter to bumping along the ground at twenty-five miles an hour in an old laundry basket. Not knowing from experience how long his ballast would last, he would be forced to land regardless of the terrain below.

Oliver's preparations were made easier by the fact that he had been nominated as officer in charge of the architecture classes. If the German Commandant thought it surprising so many Britishers seemed interested in this course of study, he must have assumed this no stranger than a lot of other British oddities of behavior. Their jokes and humor were quite beyond his understanding and when reprimanding an officer for imitating the German goose step, he accepted that officer's explanation that he had been born with a stiff hip which required him to walk in such a fashion. Provided there was no trouble and no escapes, he was prepared to allow a certain amount of laxity and if the young Lord Rochford wished to take regular parties of his men to see the Schloss, he had no objections.

It was therefore made easy for Oliver to establish moderately friendly relations with the guards in charge of the working party. He always took them cigarettes and occasionally food, although most of what he could get from his own meager resources he gave Roberts to distribute among the men who were assisting his escape.

After three weeks Roberts announced that as far as his responsibilities lay, everything was ready for Oliver's attempt. The ropes on the balloon had been inspected and found to be sound. Sacks had been filled with sand and hidden down by Oliver's chosen launching site. So too, had buckets of wet clay ready for Roberts to link the lengths of drainpipe. The stopcock for the main gas supply had been located and there was adequate pressure. The biggest problem had been making a connection to link the smaller bore drainpipe into the four-inch mains. The resourceful gas fitter had improvised with the use of clay and a pair of puttees wrapped in alternate layers and packed tight to make a near perfect joint.

Several strong ropes had been stolen from the German building stores. These would provide tethering ropes for the balloon and were necessary, Oliver had been told by one of his fellow officers who was a physicist, if he was to get his balloon inflated to its maximum before it lifted off the ground. Although the sandbags would provide weight to resist the natural lift, this extra holding capacity might be vital to gain those extra hundred feet or so that would enable him to reach the border undetected.

There was by now not an officer in the camp who was unaware of this proposed novel escape and who failed to offer his enthusiastic support. One provided a compass, another an invaluable altimeter. A Belgian officer gave Oliver some Dutch guilders he had been hoarding against his own escape, and there was a combined whip round for food with which to barter for the Schnapps Will Butler needed to get the Schloss camp guards drunk on the night.

Reports flowed in on wind directions and wind speeds, and there was no lack of offers to assist on the launch itself. But for three more days, the wind was northerly and on the fourth it rained, an undesirable condition since it would add to the weight of the balloon fabric and serve to lessen the height. The physicist warned Oliver that he would almost certainly find changes of wind directions at different heights. It was bound, therefore, to be an extremely hazardous journey and only Will was agog to go with Oliver. He understood, however, Oliver's feeling that he must take one of the other ranks with him. An officer, when all was said and done, did not run off to freedom leaving his men in captivity, he agreed.

There was a further whip round for warm clothing for the would-be balloonists. The temperatures at the heights they hoped to reach would be well below zero and Oliver would need the mobility of his hands to operate the valve at the top of the balloon which allowed the gas to escape. This, the physicist had explained, might be necessary if they rose too high and the gas expanded at these lower pressures, causing the balloon to burst.

On December 3rd, Oliver woke to bright blue skies. What little wind there was seemed to be blowing westward across the chilly compound of the camp as he went out for roll call. He whispered to Will:

"Can you organize an architectural group to go to the Schloss today and alert Roberts. Unless the wind gets up or changes direction, we'll try it tonight!"

Foster, together with the camp orderlies, had made himself responsible for cutting a hole in the wire through which Oliver must get out of camp and four of his fellow officers would follow him out and then get back in again. The orderlies planned to wear officers' uniforms and take the places in their quarters to cover their absence on nightly roll call. Another group of officers organized by the Adjutant were going to create a diversion so that the escapees stood a better chance of getting out of the camp unnoticed.

Security around the compound was fairly slack at night— in that the German guards had become more apprehensive about the local population getting in than the inmates getting out. There had been several angry demonstrations by the town's residents who were resentful of the fact that they were short of food while the commissioned prisoners of war, thanks to the Red Cross parcels, were eating like Kings.

All day long men stopped by Oliver's room to shake his hand and wish him good luck. Some gave him letters to take back to England. Others, more skeptical, asked him to put calls through to their families if he got back.

At five o'clock it was pitch dark—almost too dark, Oliver thought as he gazed out of the window. He wanted moonlight, not so much that the balloon would be silhouetted against its bright light, but enough for him to be able to pick up some of the landmarks below—always supposing he succeeded in getting airborne!

At seven o'clock, as the bulk of the officers went down to the Mess to dine, a commotion began in the regions of the camp kitchen. The word 'fire' followed by its German equivalent '*feuer*,' spread as rapidly as the flames which the prisoners were wildly fanning while pretending to put them out. It was the diversion Oliver and his friends needed. As the sentries' heads turned toward the blaze, they sprinted to the gap Foster had cut in the wire and within minutes were running in the direction of the Schloss.

The moon Oliver had wanted so badly rose slowly in the east. It disappeared occasionally behind a racing cloud, its beams intermittent as it reappeared again a few minutes later. It was very cold. Their breath issued like steam from their mouths as they panted from their exertions. They slowed their pace as the ground began to rise. Down to their right, they could see the dimmed lights of Krefeld and a solitary church spire glinting in the moonlight. Above and in front of them loomed the trees surrounding the Schloss. They were now picking their way forward as the heavy pine branches obscured most of the light there was. Their nostrils were filled with the scent of pine needles which formed a soft carpet beneath their feet.

Quarter of an hour after leaving the camp the six officers were standing on the edge of the estate. As far as Oliver could see, there were no sentries patrolling the grounds. Roberts had told him there were usually only two men on duty, circling the perimeter of the Schloss, walking in opposite directions and stopping for a chat as they passed one another. The remaining guards were inside where they huddled over a big log fire in the hall, playing cards, sleeping or brewing cups of camp coffee.

The prisoners were housed in what had once been the banqueting hall and was now one large dormitory quarter for the twenty or so men who comprised the working party. The windows were shuttered and secured from outside by iron bars. There was little possibility of their escape and for the most part, the men were too weakened by the long hours of hard work and poor diet to be fit to make a run for freedom.

Oliver caught Will's eye. This next step in their plan was his. Will had been a student for two years in Heidleberg before the war and spoke excellent German. It was his intention to pass himself off to the sentires as a Swedish manufacturer who had been visiting Krefeld on business and become so drunk that he had lost his way. Krefeld, which before the war had exported over three million pounds worth of silks and velvets which it manufactured, had also a huge dye works, as well as railway repair shops and iron foundries. Lieutenant Will Butler in the guise of a salesman called Sven Joergessen, was to have been doing business at one of the foundries. Beneath Will's uniform he wore a dark blue suit appropriate for the part he had to play. Over his shoulder was a knapsack containing six bottles of Schnapps. He held a half empty one in his hand as, ready for action, he went staggering across the lawn, singing and hiccuping alternately.

"Grüss Gott!" he shouted a loud greeting as the first of the two sentries caught sight of him and called on him to halt. He stumbled to attention and wobbling on his feet, he gave the German a parody of a salute. The second sentry came running toward him, his rifle at the ready.

"Ein trunkenbold!" said the first grinning.

"Nein, nein, mein freund!" shouted Butler, vociferously

denying he was a drunk and insisting that he was a Swede, in Krefeld on business.

It was an excellent performance and Oliver and his companions were hard put not to laugh as they observed Will putting an arm round each of the sentries' shoulders in drunken bonhomie. Within minutes the rifles had been lowered and the Schnapps was being passed round. Will pointed to his knapsack.

"Lesh all have a party," he suggested in a slurred voice. "Lesh all go inside. Too damn cold out here. Have another drink, my friends. Here's to the Kaiser!"

Amused by rather than suspicious of this unexpected diversion, the sentries laughed and half dragging Will between them, made their way to the front door. A beam of light shot across the lawn as the door opened. A few minutes later, it closed, leaving the men outside in darkness again.

It was not only dark but extremely cold. Oliver shivered as they waited for the next stage of the plan to come into effect. They were to allow half an hour for Will's Schnapps to take the edge off the guard's senses. Then one of them was to remove the iron bolt fastening the shutters of the men's dormitory. Oliver glanced at his watch. Quarter of an hour to go. The minutes seemed to crawl past. It was a relief to them all to see that the sentries who had been on outdoor duty did not reappear. They edged closer to the walls of the Schloss and now they could hear singing—"*Trink, trink, trink, bruder, trink!*" It sounded as if Will had got a good party going!

The enforced inactivity was getting on Oliver's nerves as he stamped his feet on the frosty grass trying, as were the others, to keep warm.

At last it was time to remove the iron bars securing the P.O.W.s' dormitory windows. One of the officers crept round to the back of the castle. Quite suddenly, the grounds were alive with dark shapes. Someone—his face blackened with soot—appeared at Oliver's elbow.

"All set, Sir!" It was Roberts.

Four P.O.W.s were man-handling the balloon up the stone steps from the cellar where once the wine had gone down for storage.

"Careful, for God's sake!" Oliver whispered as the men pushed the cumbersome bundle through the wooden trapdoor. "If it rips, we're done for!"

Roberts disappeared round to the front of the house. Half a dozen men began dismantling drainpipes. The clink of the cast-iron metal against the stonework of the walls sounded alarmingly loud in the stillness of the night. Two more men passed Oliver as they carried the prepared buckets of clay round to the east wall where Roberts would seal the first section of pipe to the mains gas supply. Four of the officers went to stand guard by the front door. If the sentries appeared, it was their task to silence them before they could give a warning to those inside.

His excitement mounting, Oliver accompanied the men carrying the balloon down to the site where he hoped to launch it.

"Lay it out flat!" he ordered. "Keep the holding lines untangled."

It wasn't an easy task in the fitful moonlight. And not a man among them was unaware that at any moment they might hear the sound of a shot if the Germans caught even so much as a glimpse of them.

As the folds of fabric were spread out, Oliver knelt down on the grass, anxiously inspecting the panels. There was simply no way of telling whether the material would contain the gas. If it did not, then all these officers and men were risking their lives for nothing. The responsibility lay heavily on his young shoulders and for a moment, he wished he had never thought of such a wild, improbable scheme.

But now he could see the line of drainpipes being laid nearer and nearer, Roberts and his two mates crouching over the joints as methodically they plastered three or four inches of clay around them. A leak would mean a drop in pressure. Moreover, if someone struck a match near it, it could ignite. If that happened, they might as well put a searchlight on their operation for the flame would be visible to the German garrison in Krefeld.

A dark shape bent down beside Oliver.

"I'm Able Seaman Pengelly, Sir. I won the lottery to go with you!"

Oliver found himself looking into the face of a young man not much older than he was. Fair-haired, blue-eyed, the boy could not yet be twenty, he surmised.

"Glad to have you along, Pengelly. Where are you from?"

"West Country, Sir, Cornwall."

"You realize I've never flown one of these before, Pengelly?"

Oliver said quietly. "I can handle a Sopwith but I've no guarantees to give you with this thing." He refrained from adding that the physicist had given only a tentative assurance that the balloon would carry two men. "If we don't reach the border we could both be shot if we were caught."

The lad's expression did not change.

"I'll take the chance, Sir. Roberts told me it could be dicey. Begging your pardon, Sir, anything's better'n that hellhole I've been living in. It's one of the reasons I volunteered to work at the Schloss. I'm a fisherman by trade, Sir. Can't stand to be locked in."

Oliver smiled.

"Then if you're a fisherman, Pengelly, you'll know something about the stars. I may need you for navigation."

"Yes Sir! I'll help anyways I can!"

By now Roberts had only to link one more section of drainpipe to reach the mouth of the balloon. With nothing more to do, the men had gathered around in a silent circle watching his deft hands at work with the clay. There was still no sign of the guards, and the P.O.W.s had the moonlit lawn to themselves. The shadows of the big pine trees surrounding them made an outer circle of sentries seeming to guard them from intruders, a silent audience as the men performed their tasks like actors on a stage.

Oliver went over to Roberts as he stood up with a sigh of satisfaction.

"Job completed, Sir!" he announced.

"Whether this works or not, I'm more than grateful for all your help, Roberts!" Oliver said. "I'm really sorry you won't be coming along with me—you deserve a break! But perhaps the lottery was the fair way to decide. Anyway, I want you to have this, Roberts—as a sort of memento. Don't feel you've got to hang on to it, though. If you need to sell it or anything, I'd understand."

He handed over a silver cigarette case engraved with his initials and the Rochford crest—a present from his mother on his seventeenth birthday. Roberts stared at it open-mouthed.

"Can't take that, Sir, it's yourn!" he said.

"Nonsense!" Oliver replied. "I haven't anything else to give you and I'd be pleased if you'd accept it. I've put some cigarettes inside. I expect they're a damn sight more use to you than the case, eh?"

They both smiled and then without embarrassment, the two men shook hands.

"Off we go then!" Oliver said turning back to the big wicker basket. He detailed six of the men to hold tight to the sides.

"Your job is to keep us down as long as possible," he told them. "Don't let go till you have to."

The four officers who were to hold the thick guy ropes as an additional tether moved back to wind the ends round the trunks of trees.

Oliver called out to them:

"When you hear me shout, you chaps, let go those guy ropes—and all together or Pengelly and I may turn turtle!" he added with a grin.

There was a whistle from the man stationed by the stopcock on the far side of the Schloss. Roberts gave a grunt of satisfaction as an evil-smelling stream of gas poured from the pipe into the neck of the balloon. The two men supporting it, gasped at the fumes but retained their hold.

For a moment, it seemed as if nothing further was happening; then slowly there was an undulation of the balloon fabric as if a giant sea monster were swimming inside it. It grew until it lost its uneven shape and became hemispherical. As the minutes passed, the gas poured in, filling out the contours of the balloon.

Oliver turned to the Cornish lad.

"In you get, Pengelly, unless you've changed your mind?"

A soft laugh greeted his sally as he joined Pengelly in the basket. The balloon began to rise inch by inch from the ground.

"Cor, it's working!" one man said, causing the others to laugh in a general release of tension. "Who'd have believed it!"

"That's quite enough from you, Forbes!" It was Roberts' voice, sharp but with a strong undertone of satisfaction. It was a matter of personal pride that he never did a job by halves. This might be the first time he'd attempted *this* job but that didn't mean he would excuse himself any mistakes. Gas was gas and had to be treated right—with the proper respect. He noted with a professional eye that the pressure was good. Provided it did not drop, there was no fear of failure.

The whole balloon was now lifting off the ground, although it was not yet straining on the ropes attaching it to the basket.

Oliver watched it with an anxious stare.

"Doesn't seem to be leaking!" he remarked. "Hard to tell

really. We'll know for sure once we are airborne!" he added with a reassuring grin at Pengelly.

The balloon was now almost upright, bent slightly as the light breeze caught the upper half. It looked enormous and several pairs of eyes turned anxiously in the direction of the Schloss. If a Jerry were to look out of one of the windows...

But by the sound of the raised voices and laughter carrying across the night air from inside the castle, the party Will Butler had instigated was now in full swing. With luck all the Germans were well and truly drunk and oblivious to everything but their own enjoyment.

Despite the fact that there were six men to hold down the basket, it was straining to lift off the ground. The officers holding the guy ropes slung round the tree trunks tightened their hold. The outer strands of the hemp began to snap and fray as the gas continued to pour into the balloon.

"She'll go up like a champagne cork!" the physicist muttered nervously. The six men were no longer able to retain their hold. The guy ropes tautened like violin strings. Oliver shouted, the balloon was released and with alarming momentum it shot upward, the basket swaying perilously beneath.

Despite the warnings that had been passed around to make as little noise as possible, the excitement of the moment as the balloon sailed upward into the sky was overwhelming. A wild cheer rose from twenty throats and every man's upturned face was bright with joy. Just for a brief moment or two, each man was up there with Oliver and Pengelly, sailing away into the night—to freedom. Every man's thoughts were on home and England.

It was Roberts who brought them down to earth.

"Get that stopcock turned off, Forbes," he ordered. "You lot on pipe duty, get them separated and cleaned off. The rest of you carry them up to the Schloss and bracket them back in place. And keep your voices down. This ain't no Saturday night at the local!"

There was one last pause while eyes strained upward to the balloon, now little more than a dot high above the woods, floating silently in the direction of the hills, silhouetted against the sky.

"Get a move on, lads," Roberts said quietly. Then it was all hands on deck.

By the time the men had completed their tasks, there was

little to show for the extraordinary night's activity. All that remained as evidence were the patches of trampled grass and the marks on the four trees where the pull of the ropes had scored the bark.

"Must have been a herd of bullocks what done that!" one man remarked seeing Roberts' eyes on the lawn. Those near enough to hear laughed.

"Dreadful stampede we heard in the night!" another said. "Reckon them Jerries will take our word for it. By the sound of it, they won't know no better!"

Down in Krefeld, the church clock struck nine. The whole operation had taken two and a half hours. One by one, the P.O.W.s clambered back through the window into their dormitory. With an apologetic grin an officer replaced the iron bars bolting them in. Before he did so, he threw in after the last man a knapsack full of cigarettes and food. Not much to be shared among them all—but no one grumbled. As Roberts said a short while later:

"It's the thought what counts and say what you like about some officers, I'll not hear a word against this lot, and that's a fact."

They were sitting in a circle round the light of a single candle. Slowly, Roberts withdrew the cigarette case Oliver had given him. His companions gasped as it gleamed in the candlelight.

"Reckon we can bribe someone with this to get us some food," he said. "Worth quite a bit, I'd say."

As it was handed round from man to man, some staring curiously at the Rochford crest, Roberts lit a cigarette and drew the smoke deep into his lungs. No point in keeping a luxury toy like that, he told himself. Couldn't never use it. Like as not get stolen if he kept it. Decent, though, of the young gentleman to give it to him personally. In different circumstances he might've kept it as a souvenir. But now...well it could help to keep the wolf from the door a bit longer. Give 'em all that much better chance of holding on until they could make it back to Blighty.

He pulled again on his cigarette and let the smoke expel slowly through his lips. Be nice if the officer made it safely home—Pengelly, too! He wouldn't like to think of them facing a Jerry rifle if they failed to reach the border. Kids—that's all they were, the both of 'em. Crazy, mad idea, ballooning over to Holland. Folks at home wouldn't never believe it. He wouldn't—not if he hadn't seen it with his own eyes.

"God be with 'em both!" he said, not realizing that he had voiced his prayer out loud until the men on either side of him nodded their heads and muttered a soft "Amen."

Chapter 24

⟨⟨⟩⟩

December 1916

Silvie was concerned about Lucy. It was not the girl's ability as a V.A.D. which was any longer in question. With every day that passed Lucy had become more efficient, less averse to the unpleasant side of her duties in the ward, more determined to remain at the hospital. Silvie suspected that she was beginning to enjoy her work. She was even talking of "my patients," referring to those she had now come to know; grieving over those who died; delighting when one or other took a step nearer recovery. In particular, of course, she rejoiced at Mark's slow but steady improvement and Silvie had noted the look of pride when the Ward Sister had remarked that this was in part due to Lucy's dedication.

Nevertheless, Silvie knew Lucy was far from happy. When the girl was unaware she was being observed, her face looked withdrawn and sad.

"You aren't worrying about Teo, are you?" Silvie asked innocently on one occasion as Christmas drew near. "We could always arrange for you to go home on leave, Lucy."

Lucy denied any concern for her little daughter, although she agreed that she missed her greatly and would have loved to see her, especially as Teo was quite old enough now really to enjoy Christmas and all that it meant. But under no circumstances whatever—short of being physically forced to do so—would Lucy go home, she told her aunt in a cold, hard voice.

"I shall never give Alexis the satisfaction of saying that I proved inadequate; that I lacked the courage to see this through. If we ever see each other again—which I am beginning to doubt—then he will be obliged to apologize to me for his cruel, unwarranted accusations."

Alexis, therefore, was the reason for Lucy's secret depressions, Silvie realized. Had she not given Alexis her word not

384

to tell Lucy that they were regularly exchanging letters about her, it would have been but a minute's task to put Lucy's mind—and heart—at rest.

"Alexis knows what he's doing," Pelham said when Silvie asked him one night if he did not think she would be justified in hinting to Lucy that Alexis had not allowed her to disappear from his life without a comment! "Lucy is his wife—and it is his marriage," Pelham added thoughtfully. "We have no right to interfere, my dear. Besides, he has shown concern only for Lucy's physical welfare. We have no idea whether he still loves her or not. We don't even know if that mistress of his Lucy told us about has left England. Alexis may be enjoying *her* favors for all we know and now *want* Lucy home!"

As Christmas approached, Lucy's depression deepened and Silvie suggested that a period away from the hospital might be good for her. The humorous French major, Louis Bucquet, had been given leave by the M.O. and planned to go to Paris, taking with him Lieutenant Hope and another Ward 3 convalescent, Jacques Trevise, a French captain from the Dragoons. All three had been begging and pleading in their jocular way that Lucy should be detailed to go with them.

"Even if I wanted to go, I wouldn't leave Mark all alone," Lucy said when Silvie asked her why she did not welcome the invitation.

"Your uncle and I will have Mark upstairs with us," Silvie said at once. "Although I fancy he might prefer to be moved into Ward 2 for the holiday. There are two exceptionally pretty V.A.D.'s in there and judging by the number of times they both find excuses to go to Ward 3, I suspect they have their eye on young Mark. He's a good-looking boy, you know."

Lucy refused to commit herself. She was not in the least worried about her reputation for although the three officers all professed to be head over heels in love with her, she knew it was all fun. How could she not when she wrote their love letters and watched the joy light up their faces when their wives or fiancées wrote to them? The young Captain Trevise, in particular, wrote in the most romantic vein to his fiancée, expressing in extravagant but heartfelt French volubility, his idealistic adoration of the young girl he hoped to marry as soon as the war was over. The English lieutenant Edward Hope, was more tongue-tied when he dictated his letters but nevertheless they still managed to convey the same adoration, in this case for his wife.

At night, when she was alone, Lucy thought about the phrases she had written so laboriously, and pondered the closeness of the bond between lovers. The men's longing to be reunited with their loved ones had nothing to do with their physical desires. That, she could more readily have understood. But their desires were for the simplest of things—to be able to walk through the beech woods hand in hand; to be able to sit with arms around each other by the fireside; to look at one another across the candle-lit table of their favorite restaurant; to wake up in the morning and smile at one another, sharing the joy of a new day.

Lucy had experienced none of these things. She realized, of course, that the writers of the letters were expressing that favorite word of Alexis'—love.

It seemed to Lucy as if she were the only person in the world who had not experienced such an emotion. Yet she was not without a heart. More and more often since she had come to Épernay, she had felt a deep, gnawing pain at Alexis' silence. Even if he had not cared enough about her safety to come to France to take her home, he could at least have written to her, she thought unhappily. But unlike the men in her ward, he could not be bothered to put pen to paper.

The truth was that never a day went by when she did not miss him. Although she had Sister Dickenson, her aunt and uncle to turn to if she were faced with a problem, since her marriage it had become a habit to consult Alexis; to be reassured by him; encouraged by him. He had always been there beside her in his quiet way, supporting her; when Teo was kidnapped; when they went to the memorial service for Philip; when Oliver was reported missing. She had believed herself totally independent and yet she had relied on him, taking him for granted, taking her marriage for granted. Finding him that day with Roberta had been a shock. She had never really believed that Alexis loved his former mistress. Now she was obliged to consider that one of the reasons for Alexis' present disinterest in her was that he welcomed her absence so that he could spend more time with Roberta. She feared Roberta had never carried out her intention to go to Egypt; that she had remained in London to be near Alexis.

Once or twice when Lucy had been in one of her deepest depressions, she had considered returning to England to fight Roberta. But her pride would not allow this. She could imagine Alexis' indifferent shrug as he said: 'I always knew you'd never stand the strain!' Well, she could and she was not going to give up now. She had learned to overcome the worst of her revulsion and had even managed to survive a whole day in Admissions when a new influx of wounded had arrived. She would never like this side of the work she had to do, but at least she no longer fainted at the sight of a gaping wound or felt sick when a man screamed in pain. According to Sister Dickenson, she was becoming an excellent nurse.

The longer Lucy considered matters, the less valid reasons could she give her aunt for not going to Paris on leave. Uncle Pelham had offered to lend his precious Sunbeam to transport them all; Aunt Silvie had long ago suggested they should all stay at the house in the *Rue d'Artois*. A *gardien* and his wife were living there, keeping the house aired and clean. They would be able to provide what services were needed for the anticipated three-day visit. This was the maximum length of time the M.O. would allow his patients from under his wing. A driver and a hospital orderly would go with them—the maximum number of passengers that could be fitted into the Sunbeam.

Unfortunately both the major's wife and the captain's fiancée lived too far away to be able to get to Paris—the one living in Bayonne in the extreme southwest; the other on the island of Corsica. Lieutenant Hope's wife was, of course, back in England. Lucy, the officers told her, would therefore have three escorts. With a sudden surge of excitement, Lucy packed her suitcase with the few civilian clothes Aunt Silvie had found for her. They were probably quite unfashionable, she said, but Lucy could doubtless adapt them for her use. At least she would be out of uniform and wearing pretty dresses again.

All those who were well enough to walk came out onto the hospital steps to see the party off. The large Red Cross painted on each side of the Sunbeam should ensure their safety from an aerial attack, Pelham told them with a grin as they all climbed into the car. Major Bucquet had to be lifted, the orderly carrying his crutches.

"Have a good time, *chérie!*" Silvie said as she blew kisses to Lucy, delighted to see the girl smiling as she waved a cheerful good-bye.

"We must be getting old!" she said to Pelham as they turned away from the departing car. "A year or two ago we would have wanted to go with them. Consider how long it is, my love, since we went to the Comédie Française or ate a delicious meal in Maxim's!"

"You really don't mind staying here?" Pelham inquired taking her arm and assisting her indoors.

Silvie smiled.

"You know very well I wouldn't leave here for a dozen nights in Paris. It's up to us to make Christmas in the wards as happy as possible for all our soldiers. Who would lead the carol singing if you could not, Pelham? And who would play *Papa Noël* and distribute presents and parcels and letters? You cannot have forgotten how appreciative the patients were last year—or what fun we had!"

Pelham grinned.

"I just wanted to be sure you felt the same way as I do," he said. "In a way, I'm sorry Lucy won't be here to enjoy it all, too. But I agree with you it will do her good to get away for a few days—the men, too. Let's hope the same Christmas spirit prevails with our enemy as it did last year. It would be very sad if the barbarities of war destroyed that universal Christian acknowledgment of the birth of Christ. There's still hope for the world if Allied soldiers can play a friendly football match in the middle of hostilities. No one, if seems—not even the Germans—have the heart to kill on Christmas Day."

By Christmas Eve all the wards with the exception of those containing men too ill to be concerned about Christmas, were bright with holly and chains made out of colored paper. In each ward was a small, decorated fir tree beneath which were grouped the men's presents for the Sisters and nurses. These were touching little gifts, for the most part handmade—a carved wooden ornament painstakingly sculpted with a pen-knife; a bracelet beaten out of the metal of a shell case and polished until it shone like silver; a handwoven basket; a bunch of paper roses. The patients had been making them for days, hiding them from the V.A.D. or nurse for whom the presents were intended.

Those intended for the soldiers had been given to Pelham to add to the growing pile on the trolleys which he would take round the wards after the Army chaplain had served Mass. Most of the gifts were food from Red Cross parcels although some of the nurses had found time to knit mufflers or mittens or balaclava helmets. Silvie and Pelham had had sent by friends in Paris parcels of cigarettes and tobacco which she was hoarding for this occasion. But the big surprise this Christmas was to be a gramophone and a collection of records to be put in the recreation room for the convalescents to enjoy.

In anticipation of the long day to come, they decided to retire early on Christmas Eve. They dined at eight and were about to go to bed when a little after nine o'clock, Marie proclaimed to their astonishment that they had a visitor from England.

Before the old cook could announce him, Alexis walked into the room.

"Obviously you were not expecting me," he said with an apologetic smile as he kissed Silvie's hand. "I did send you a telegram from Paris but I suppose it has not reached you."

As Pelham hurried forward to take Alexis' heavy coat and fur hat and gloves, Alexis glanced round the room. He looked at Silvie expectantly.

"Lucy is still on duty in the wards, I suppose?" he asked.

"Oh, dear!" Silvie cried unhappily as suddenly she realized the reason for Alexis' visit—he had intended to surprise Lucy. "I'm really very sorry to have to tell you, Alexis, but she isn't here. She's on three days' leave. She has gone to Paris!"

Only then did she notice how tired Alexis looked; and as she spoke, how terribly disappointed. Pelham produced a large brandy and Alexis sank wearily into the chair which Silvie pushed nearer the fire for him.

"You must be cold—and exhausted," she said. "If only we had known a few days earlier, Alexis, Lucy would be here to greet you. I know she would have wanted to see you."

Alexis seemed not to be listening as he stared down into his brandy glass.

"Why Paris?" he asked shortly. "Is she alone?"

Pelham came to Silvie's rescue.

"No, not exactly, old man. She's in charge of three patients—officers in her ward. Amputation cases, actually. You know she looks after young Mark, don't you? He wasn't well enough to go with them of course. She's due back the day after tomorrow, Alexis. You can stay until then, I hope?"

Alexis' mouth tightened.

"Unfortunately not! I have to be in Vienna tomorrow."

"Vienna!" Pelham repeated. "But that's..."

"I know—enemy territory!" Alexis broke in with a half-smile. "I have ways and means of getting there and if it interests you, Rochford, the passport I'm currently using will show you that I'm an American war correspondent by the unlikely name of Wilbur Messinger. Don't you think I look the part?"

Pelham returned his smile.

"As a matter of fact, you do! That racoon fur looks distinctly New World. But your accent's somewhat British."

Silvie listened to this exchange uneasily. She sensed Alexis' bitter disappointment at Lucy's absence. Equally, she realized that he was far from pleased to hear that she had gone off to Paris with three men.

She launched into an account of Lucy's surprising efficiency as a V.A.D. and with genuine warmth, praised her untiring efforts in the wards.

"She never spares herself, Alexis," she ended. "I felt she needed a break. If she has any faults as a nurse one is that she becomes too emotionally involved. Some of our patients do die and there are others who will never fully recover. Lucy takes it very badly if she has been involved with them. She has been very concerned about Mark too. After four months, a little lighthearted frivolity in Paris seemed a good idea."

Alexis gave no indication of his reactions to this speech although he had listened attentively. As if unwilling to discuss Lucy further, he turned to Pelham and said:

"Did you manage to buy those paintings by Dubois, Rochford? If so, I must owe you quite a lot of money."

"The answer to both those questions is 'yes'!" Pelham said. "Silvie, can Marie rustle up something for Alexis to eat? I'm sure he must be starving. You don't mind a tray in here, old fellow? We don't stand on formality any more—not like the good old days at the Manor. We only have Marie and a daily maid to look after us and a chap who does boots and such like."

"Anything will do me," Alexis said. "Food has never been one of my priorities!"

While Silvie went to arrange some supper for him, Pelham poured Alexis a second brandy and went to sit beside him. It was now nearly two months since he had received Alexis' brief letter stating:

"Buy every relevant painting or drawing that you can, regardless of price!"

It was a tall order, Pelham had thought at the time. It necessitated a trip to Paris to see an art dealer and to arrange for him to buy what he could and have the stuff delivered to the *Rue d'Artois*. It was not safe to store anything at Épernay. Pelham had also left instructions for each canvas and drawing to be photographed and the copies sent to him.

"Silvie wrote and told you half the story, so perhaps you should know the other half before I show you copies of what you asked for," he said to Alexis.

Alexis nodded, hiding his impatience to see the results of his request to Lucy's uncle. He did not know Pelham well but he liked the frank, open nature of the man, his sense of humor and his determination to make the most fun out of life that was possible. What Pelham Rochford lacked in intellect, he made up for in boyish enthusiasm for anything he undertook.

"Please go ahead," he said quietly. "I'd appreciate the whole story."

"My wife in the days before her marriage to me, was friendly with a number of artists," Pelham began obediently. "They were mostly young students who had not yet made their mark on the world. One of the chaps—a fellow called Pierre—was a close friend of Maurice Dubois."

He heard Alexis' short intake of breath as he mentioned the name but continued talking.

"Silvie did not meet Dubois until Lucy's mother went to Paris to stay with her, in 1905, I think it was. Dubois fell madly in love with my sister-in-law and painted a magnificent portrait of her which he called 'Juliet.' Willow was about thirty years old at the time and very beautiful. My wife saw the portrait and bought it. She never met Dubois again but Pierre visited my wife from time to time and saw his friend's portrait of 'Juliet.' He did not know who she was, of course. Then one day he noticed a young waitress who worked in a brothel in Paris called *Le Ciel Rouge*...you know of this already, Zemski, else I would never have spoken of it."

Alexis nodded, his green eyes narrowed in thought.

"Pierre noticed that the girl bore the most extraordinary likeness to 'Juliet.' He told Dubois about her and he began to use her as a model. He too, was struck by the astonishing likeness between the twelve-year-old girl and the woman with whom he had fallen in love. He did some superb drawings, Zemski, which I'll show you in a minute. But the last one Dubois did...it's quite different from all the others. Where he had been depicting his model as a *gamine*—a street child with that half-starved, wistful, innocent look some of them have—he suddenly switched styles and painted a magnificent but in some ways horrifying picture of the woman he thought the child would become. The look of innocence was gone. The expression, the pose, the harsh colors—all portrayed her inevitable future. He called it *La Perle* and it made Dubois' name. He never painted Lucy again."

Alexis nodded.

"I think I understand what happened. The man was half in love with her, until the moment he saw her without her innocence. That last painting was his rebellion. He wanted to keep her as she was..."

He looked up at Pelham, his eyes sad.

"Lucy would not have understood the reason behind Dubois' sudden rejection of her," Alexis went on thoughtfully. But she had been deeply hurt by it, he told himself—sufficiently so to want to be revenged upon him. And her chance had come many years later.

"Anyway, the fellow became quite well known," Pelham continued his story. "When the war broke out, he was invited to become an official war artist. He was given a commission and sent off to a unit at the Front. He was killed at Verdun three months ago, poor devil! But Silvie wrote and told you that, didn't she?"

Alexis nodded.

"I'm more than grateful to her. I'd no way of knowing who he was, you see. Lucy never told me his name."

Pelham scratched his chin, feeling the awkwardness of the moment. He and Silvie had debated for a long time whether or not to pass on to Alexis the news of Maurice Dubois' death. It was Silvie who had overruled his doubts. Her woman's instinct proved sound when she said Alexis would welcome such information. Now that the unfortunate man was dead, he could present no threat to Alexis or Lucy, Silvie had argued. She had foreseen that his paintings of Lucy might—if he became posthumously famous and universally acclaimed— betray a period of her past that neither she nor Alexis would want revealed. "*Buy them all,*" Alexis had ordered by return of post. Silvie had warned him he might have to pay a high price—especially for the one called *La Perle*. But Zemski had given no thought to the cost.

Silvie returned with a tray on which sat a bowl of onion soup topped with a square of toasted Gruyère cheese. There was a plate of cold chicken, a generous cut off Marie's home-

made bread and an assortment of cheeses. Beside this appe-
tizing meal sat a bottle of chilled white wine.

"The Germans didn't get their hands on all of it!" Pelham
said with a grin. "Our gardener buried as many bottles as he
could in his chicken run!"

When Alexis had finished eating, Pelham went to the tallboy and pulled open the bottom drawer. From it he withdrew
a portfolio of photographs, some of oil paintings, others of
crayon or pencil sketches.

Pelham hoped he had prepared Alexis for what he was about
to see. Nevertheless, Alexis gasped as he looked for the first
time at Maurice Dubois' portrait of *La Perle*.

Despite the henna'd hair, despite the pouting, heavily rouged
mouth, despite the streetwalker's pose, the artist had caught
an aspect of Lucy he himself recognized, Alexis thought. He
had seen her with that inviting look in her eyes; with that
self-confident, feline half-smile as if she were saying: 'I'm
beautiful, am I not? You desire me and I'm willing to give
myself to you—but for a price!'

Oh, Lucy, Lucy! he thought. What did they do to you in
that place! Was it your 'motherly' Madame Lou-Lou you so
admired who corrupted you? Can you really have been happy
there?

She looked so very, very young, yet at the same time,
Dubois had given her the age-old wisdom of her kind.

If only he had found her sooner, Alexis told himself silently
as he put aside *La Perle* and looked instead at the charming
sketches of the bedraggled child the unknown Frenchman
had found so fascinating. Lucy must have been about twelve
years old then with a purity of the convent schoolgirl still
shining in her eyes. It was almost impossible to remember
now that she had still been only just eighteen when he had
married her and that he had met her when she was seventeen.
Maybe he had expected too much, too soon. He had tried so
hard to be patient—yet in the end he had failed, resenting
the frivolity of her existence, her choice of friends, her way
of life. Had it not been for the child she was carrying, it might
have been better not to have married her so soon; to have
allowed her to live with her mother at Rochford and assimilate
the values of her real background. It was easy to lose sight
of the fact that she had been under her mother's care only
thirteen months before Fate had overtaken her and Alexis had
provided yet another change of background for her.

His disappointment at her absence from Épernay struck him with renewed pain. He had hoped that at least they could have spent Christmas Day together and healed the rift brought about the last time he had seen her. He had wanted to apologize—not so much for what he had said because at the time he believed himself justified—but for the manner in which he had berated her. She had had every right to be angry and resentful about poor Roberta. It wasn't enough simply to tell her that Roberta was going away—Lucy had had only his word for it and it could so easily have been his way out of his predicament. Nor should he have compared Lucy with Roberta—a woman eighteen years her senior whose life had been relatively stable. At heart, Lucy remained a child—irresponsible, it was true; selfish, it was undeniable, but never without true worth, as he had implied.

He had thought of writing to her many times; but in the end he believed he must tell her how proud he had been to hear of her exploits at Épernay. He still did not know how she had managed even to get to France without a passport or papers and Silvie had not enlightened him. But Lucy had had the courage of her convictions and from all accounts had settled down to the hard, taxing life of a V.A.D. in France without complaint or grumbles and never giving way to the childish impulse to run home.

"Are we to tell Lucy you were here?" Silvie asked as if aware of the trend of his thoughts.

Alexis nodded.

"I have a small gift for her. Will you please give it to her with my love?"

He reached in the traveling bag he had placed by his chair and withdrew a beautifully wrapped parcel which he handed to Silvie.

"Just tell her I'll come to see her again. I don't know when it will be—but I'll come as soon as I can."

"And these?" Pelham asked, indicating Maurice's work.

"I'd rather Lucy didn't see them. Can you keep them for me, Rochford? As for the originals—well, if they too can remain where they are, I'll make a decision about them after the war. If by any chance anything should happen to me, then I'll leave it to you both to decide what's best for Lucy. You may feel they should be destroyed—I'm not sure. If Lucy doesn't already know, tell her Dubois is dead, will you? I think she ought to know. In one way it seems terrible that so talented a man should die so needlessly. But I'm human enough to be relieved. It's the end of an unfortunate period of Lucy's life. Now there is no fear that she—or Teo—will ever meet him by chance."

At last they all three retired to bed—Alexis being given Lucy's blue and white bedroom for the night. There were small signs of her everywhere—her uniform draped untidily over a chair; hairpins scattered on her dressing table; stockings, underwear, nightdress stuffed into a drawer. Her untidiness was typical and although he did not approve of it, it made him smile. Lucy was always in such a hurry—as if, were she to tarry for long, the tide of life might leave her in its wake. Without Polly to follow after her, Lucy left a trail of herself wherever she went.

In the morning Alexis went to see Mark. The boy had been moved into Ward 4 where he was playing poker with four French officers, all with head wounds. Mark greeted him shyly but with pleasure. They talked for a half an hour, Alexis giving him the latest news from Rochford and also what little information he had about Oliver. Then Alexis left, slipping Mark a ten-pound note as a Christmas present with the caution not to lose the lot playing poker with strangers! Neither mentioned Mark's missing leg, Alexis taking his cue from the boy.

Willow was experiencing the best Christmas she had ever known. On Christmas Eve, Oliver walked into the house.

"I suppose I should have warned you," he said apologetically as he saw the stunned expression on his mother's face, "but I wanted it to be a surprise!"

The next moment, Oliver was in Willow's arms. For the remainder of the evening she held fast to his hand while he sat with the family grouped around him, telling them the story of his escape. Zandra sat determinedly on his lap, Jane a short distance away, pale but smiling, her eyes never leaving his face.

"I suppose I was just lucky," Oliver told them as he neared the end of the story of his escape. "I never really quite believed that I *could* get out in that old balloon. I don't think Pengelly really believed it either..." he added with a self-deprecating smile. "The only person who didn't seem to have any doubts was Roberts—he's the chap who fixed up the gas supply for us. I want to get a Red Cross parcel off to him as soon as possible, Mater. And to Foster—he was my batman and I'll tell you about him in a minute."

"We want to hear about the balloon," Zandra demanded, kicking her legs impatiently. "What happened after it went up in the air like a champagne cork?"

Oliver laughed.

"Well, we chucked out some of the sandbags—so as to make us rise a bit higher. I wanted to get out of range of the German searchlights and guns. But no one seemed to notice us and we sailed off to the west, drifting silently in the wind. It was a bit stronger high up than it had been on the ground, but it's not easy to judge your speed up there because you're traveling *with* the wind so there's no resistance."

"What's resistance?" Zandra asked, but was promply hushed as Oliver continued:

"I can't tell you how beautiful and peaceful it was up there in the moonlight. There's not a sound to be heard. Pengelly— he's a sailor—said it was a bit like sailing on the ocean all by yourself—but quieter as there's no water rushing past the hull. Down below we could see woods, fields and hills, and then some lights which I think was a town called Kempen. I estimated that to be about five miles from the Schloss and I was a bit worried about a leakage of gas as we seemed to be losing height. We chucked out some more ballast and then we crossed a river—a tributary of the Meuse called the Niers. Next thing we saw were the lights of Wachtendout. And then, over a ridge of hills, the River Meuse—a silver ribbon in the moonlight running from north to south. By now I was beginning to get worried. There was no longer any doubt that we were losing height rapidly. We chucked out the rest of the sandbags and that gave us enough lift to take us over the top of a farmhouse."

Zandra was wriggling with excitement as he continued:

"We were down to a few hundred feet and I knew we were going to have to land whether we wanted to or not. I told Pengelly to look out for a field without trees and preferably with a bit of grass or stubble to cushion us. That was when Pengelly said 'Reckon as how we do be over the border, Sir!'" Oliver imitated Pengelly's Cornish accent. "Idiot that I was, I'd forgotten in my excitement that the Meuse was in Holland. Next thing we were sailing over a hedge, the bottom of the basket scraping on the twigs and then we hit the ground with a fearful bump. The basket turned over and both of us were flung out. We were a bit bruised and winded but with no broken bones. Meanwhile, without our weight the balloon shot up in the air and goodness knows where it might have ended up if the rigging hadn't got tangled in the farmer's Dutch barn."

"And were you really safe and sound in Holland?" Willow asked.

"Yes, but not near Venloo as I imagined. We'd flown further north to Horst. The farmer in whose field we'd landed came out to see what the commotion was—his dogs had set up a furious barking when we went over his roof. When we told him we were English, he beamed all over his face and took us indoors where his wife gave us a perfectly ripping meal. The food wasn't too bad at our camp, but poor Pengelly had been half-starved in his and I've never in my life seen any man put away so much!"

"Did he get hiccups afterwards?" Zandra inquired gravely.

"No, he was just fine!" Oliver told the child laughing. "The farmer showed us the way to the nearest Dutch guard post and we stayed there until a military car came to take us across Holland to Rotterdam. There was a certain amount of confusion when we arrived but eventually we were taken to the British Consulate. The Consul turned out to be a jolly decent fellow and insisted I should stay with him and his wife until I could be got home to England." He shifted Zandra's weight onto his other knee and continued:

"They wanted to send poor old Pengelly off to the quarantine camp at Enschede but eventually they allowed me to keep him with me as acting batman—not that Pengelly had the vaguest idea what to do. But I couldn't see the poor chap being shoved into another camp when he had only just got out of the one he was in. It took about ten days for our papers to come through, and we left Rotterdam on Monday night and docked at Harwich yesterday. We traveled down to London by train this morning where we reported to our headquarters. I had to make them promise not to ring you!" Oliver laughed. "I was determined just to walk in and surprise you all."

"It's the most wonderful surprise I ever had!" Willow cried. "I'll never forget this Christmas as long as I live. Thank God you are safe, my darling. You might so easily have been killed!"

"That's what all the journalists said," Oliver told her smiling. "We were besieged by the fellows in Rotterdam once the story got out. I don't think they believed me at first but then one of the more enterprising chaps drove down to Horst and took a photograph of the balloon. He gave me a copy as a souvenir—Pengelly has one, too. I'll show it to you!" He reached in his tattered uniform pocket and handed it to his mother.

"Look at that!" he said pointing to a dark shadow hovering over the barn roof. Just beyond the barn was a duck pond. "We'd have been in a right old mess if we'd landed in that," he laughed. "It's a big pond but we never even saw it that night!"

"Where's the Cornish fellow now?" Toby asked.

"He got a leave pass and went home to his family!" Oliver said. "He's pretty certain none of them will believe his story about the balloon!"

"*I'm* still finding it difficult to believe!" Willow said, as she sent the reluctant Zandra off to bed and then conducted Oliver to his own room.

Oliver, of course, had seen nothing of the conversion of his home into a hospital. On Christmas morning he toured the Manor with Toby and his mother before going to church and was thoroughly approving of everything he saw. He did not at first recognize Jane in her V.A.D. uniform as they came to one of the wards where she was on duty. Impulsively he complimented her and saw the blush rise to her cheeks. It was the first moment of unhappiness for him since he had left Krefeld. It was so difficult to remember that this pretty young girl was his half-sister, he thought, or that it was now entirely his responsibility to try to reestablish some kind of relationship between them that was purely fraternal. There must be no more such compliments, he told himself.

A huge Christmas luncheon was served in the main hall and Oliver following Toby's and James' example, donned an apron and waited on the men. Zandra seemed to know each man by name and was constantly introducing the patients to him.

"This is Sergeant McMasters. He's only got one eye. This is Private Humphries. He's only got one leg like our Mark and he's got a great big wound in the other leg, haven't you, Humphries? And this is Private Gilmore. He keeps on coughing 'cos he got gassed . . ."

Oliver was interested to see that none of the soldiers seemed to object to the little girl's graphic descriptions of their incapacities but grinned cheerfully when she spoke to them.

"We can't keep her out of the wards," Willow told him. "The Commandant—that's Hilda's mother, Marjorie Sharples—has given up trying to confine Zandra to our part of the Manor. The truth is, Oliver, she does more good than harm. You see, it never occurs to her to pity them, no matter how serious their disabilities. When new patients arrive, she trots up and asks them what is wrong. Some don't like to talk about their wounds but she nags them until they do. Then she'll say something like: 'Oh, is *that* all! You'll soon get well here.'"

"Aunt Dodie doesn't mind her mixing with the men?" Oliver asked curiously.

"Dodie doesn't see her coming to any harm. The men all adore Zandra and do their best to mind their language when she's around. She has a quite remarkable ability to cheer them up. Humphries, for instance, was pretty unmanageable when he first arrived. He was rude to the nurses and totally unco-operative. Then Zandra took him in hand!"

"What did she do?" Oliver asked curiously.

"Gave him a severe talking to!" Willow told him. "The Ward Sister overheard her one evening telling him he was grumpy and horrible and that it would be his own fault if Father Christmas didn't bring him any presents."

"From then on, Humphries began to improve," Toby added with a laugh. "He's become Zandra's special pet."

Willow had made for the child a miniature V.A.D. uniform for her Christmas present and Zandra was beside herself with excitement as she went from ward to ward to show herself to 'her patients.'

Oliver noted that throughout the Christmas excitement Jane was very quiet. He tried to convince himself that it was because her two brothers were absent. All the family had put flowers beneath the plaque put up in St. Stephen's for Philip when the memorial service for him had been held there.

He had seen her tears and longed to put his arms around her and comfort her. He understood, too, her grief for poor old Mark. It had been quite a shock to hear from his mother that Mark had lost a leg. From the letter Aunt Silvie had sent, it seemed he'd been pretty fortunate not to lose both.

The other shock had been the news of Howard Barratt's death at Verdun at the beginning of December. The day after Boxing Day Oliver went over to Glenfield Hall to offer his condolences to Sir John and Lady Barratt. His visit coincided with the arrival from France of Howard's personal effects. His unhappy parents were sitting on a sofa, Lady Barratt holding Howard's mud-stained uniform on her lap, Sir John with his son's peaked cap, staring at the bullet hole which had killed him.

"No, don't go, Oliver!" Lady Barratt said as Oliver suggested he had arrived at a most inopportune moment and would leave at once. "Sit here by me and let me derive comfort from the fact that you are a warm, living person who has survived." She took his hand and held it tightly in her own. Oliver could feel her trembling as she said: "There's part of a letter Howard must have been writing to us before he was sent on that...that final mission. I haven't been able to bring myself to read it yet. Will you read it to us, Oliver?"

Oliver hesitated. This voice from the dead seemed somehow macabre, as did the sight of Howard's uniform. He found himself questioning whether this was really a humane action on the part of the authorities. But he caught Sir John's eye and realizing that they both wanted him to read Howard's letter to them, he steeled himself to pick up the mud-stained sheets.

"Dear Family, things are fairly quiet and there is only an occasional skirmish to bother about. I think our biggest concern is MUD. It's proving more inconvenient than the enemy!

"It's quite lonely sometimes walking along these trenches especially at night. You seem to go for miles and almost forget there's a world out there above your head. Occasionally one passes a dug-out—a deep hole like a badger's sett with steps leading down into the earth. As you go by, you can pick up the smell that always seems to come from them—a mixture of fumes from the coke braziers and candle grease and frying bacon, and even from the chaps' clothes which have been slept in too long! More than anything in the world, I think I'd like a big, deep hot bath if you are wondering what to send me for Christmas!

"As I am writing this in my own dug-out, I can hear a chap walking down the trench outside. He's humming a favorite ditty out here: 'Oh, my! I don't wanter die, I wanter go 'ome...' It's not as morbid as you may be thinking as the chaps sing it quite cheerfully. They're a fine lot and..."

There the letter came to an abrupt end. Lady Barratt was weeping softly; Sir John had taken off his glasses and was wiping his eyes with a big handkerchief. Neither seemed able to speak. Oliver said:

"It may be difficult for you both to understand but when I was taken prisoner what concerned me most was what Mater and Uncle Toby would be feeling when they heard about it. I think most of us find war quite an adventure and we're all prepared to die if we have to. What worries us is how our families would take it if the worst happened. Howard really wouldn't want you to feel sad or bitter. He'd want you to be proud."

"The boy's right!" Sir John said huskily. "Come now, my dear. We must count ourselves fortunate that Henry and George are spared to us. George is in France too, Oliver. We had a letter last week. He's hoping to get leave soon if the Front stays quiet this winter. If he manages it, he and Hilda may get married."

Oliver set off for home with a sense of relief. Rochford with its crowd of excited youngsters seemed bursting with life. Glenfield Hall had of necessity been a house of mourning. He did not want to think about death or the painful fact that he would never see Howard again. As soon as he could, he wanted to be back in France with his squadron. He did not particularly want to kill his German counterparts for there was a certain camaraderie among pilots of all nationalities—the Jerry who'd shot him down had not flown off until he'd been assured Oliver's rescuers were on their way—but he'd shoot at any German soldier and be glad if he killed him. One for Philip, one for Howard, one for Mark and others for Bartholomew, Purkiss, Watson, Pilcher, Higgins and his brother.

As he drove through Havorhurst village, the lights of St. Stephen's were glowing. Evensong was in progress and the congregation were singing: *"Peace, perfect peace, death shadowing us and ours..."*

It would take a great deal more than prayers to bring peace to the world, Oliver thought as he turned into the lane leading to Rochford Manor. Victory, if such was to be theirs, was still a very long way off and before it could be claimed, there would be many more lives lost. He'd been lucky so far; lucky to cheat death when his airplane had crashed; lucky to survive the balloon escape. Could he be lucky again next time?

Despite what he had said to the Barratts, Oliver was only seventeen years old and he did not want to die.

Chapter 25

❧

January—July 1917

WILLOW SPOKE TO MARJORIE SHARPLES ABOUT JANE. IT WAS her intention to arrange for Jane to have three weeks free from ward duties during Oliver's leave.

"He needs companionship of his own age," Willow said to the older woman. "I suggested he should go up to London to see some of the shows and enjoy himself, but his answer was that he preferred to be here with us at Rochford. Now if Jane were free to go with him..."

"But of course it can be arranged, my dear," the Commandant said. "I'll rearrange the rota with Sister this afternoon. I'm sure Hilda will fill in for her if necessary."

But to everyone's surprise, with the exception of Oliver who understood Jane's reasons, she steadfastly refused the offer of a respite from work.

"I'm really quite angry with her," Willow said to Toby. "You would have thought she would have more consideration for Oliver. After all, they were such good friends a year ago. She simply reiterates in that quiet, stubborn way of hers that she'd feel guilty abandoning her duties merely to have a good time. Anyone would think she believed herself indispensable—in fact, I told her she was not and she burst into tears which made me feel most uncomfortable."

Toby sighed.

"I understand your wish to arrange matters entirely for Oliver's enjoyment," he said with the hint of a smile. "Nevertheless, my dear, they are both quite old enough to make these decisions for themselves."

But neither Jane nor Oliver felt in the least capable of coping with their relevant situations. Even with Jane preoccupied in the wards it was not possible to avoid each other's company. They met at family mealtimes and every evening when Jane was not on duty.

Tongue-tied in Oliver's presence, Jane made a point of including the thirteen-year-old Alice who was apt to dog her footsteps, preferring as she did Jane's company to that of the little ones in the nursery. Alice was now a plump, pink-cheeked schoolgirl with an easygoing, uncomplicated nature and a willingness to fall in with everyone's suggestions. Even the seven-year-old Zandra could cajole her into aiding and abetting her childish pursuits. But it was Jane with whom Alice most preferred to be, looking on her as an older sister whom she admired and tried to emulate.

Jane had always tolerated good-naturedly the younger girl's adoration and now she actively encouraged it, inviting her to sit beside her at mealtimes, in the drawing room, or to walk with her to church on a cold Sunday morning in preference to driving in the car. As a result, Oliver seldom saw one without the other.

It was a relief to him too, and he covered any awkward moments between himself and Jane by teasing his younger sister in a kindly way. He was genuinely fond of Alice and when he was required to go up to London for a medical, he decided to take her with him by way of a treat. It was Jane, of course, with whom he would have liked to enjoy the day— lunch at Wheelers, a matinee and finally a tea-dance at the Dorchester, the first one Alice had ever seen. She observed the dancers round-eyed and thrilled, but was too shy to accept Oliver's kindly invitation to tango.

"I can't, Olly. I don't know how. Anyway, I'd look silly in these clothes. You should have brought Jane instead of me. It's such a shame she had to be on duty today of all days! But I'm glad really. I've never had such a topping time. It's jolly decent of you to invite me!"

They spent the night by arrangement at Cadogan Gardens. Alexis made them both welcome and after Alice had gone to bed, he sat up until the early hours discussing airplanes with Oliver. Oliver had always liked Lucy's husband and now, suddenly, he knew that this was the one person in whom he could confide; who was to be trusted absolutely yet who was sufficiently "outside" the family to be unbiased.

Alexis listened quietly while Oliver confessed his love for the girl he had discovered too late was his half-sister. Although his account of his father's infidelities was news to Alexis, it was not the shock it might have been had Roberta not told him long ago about Georgina Grey. He had often wondered whether the Grey children Willow and Toby had adopted might be her offspring. But it had not seemed to him to be any of his business and he had never discussed the subject with Lucy. The idea had in any case struck him as a bit farfetched since it seemed most unlikely that any woman would take under her wing the children of her husband's mistress!

"You see what a hopeless mess it all is!" Oliver said unhappily. "I know the truth but Jane doesn't. And I can't tell her. I promised Phil I wouldn't and anyway, how could I be the one to humiliate her by telling her she is illegitimate!"

"Your mother doesn't know how you feel about Jane?" Alexis asked gently. It disturbed him to see Oliver looking so unhappy. He was usually such a cheerful chap.

Oliver shook his head.

"I don't think Mater has the slightest inkling—and anyway, what could *she* do? And I *know* Jane is just as wretched as I am...she really was fond of me, Alexis—I know she was. We'd talked about love and all that and how we were really well-suited to each other...before I knew the truth, of course. But I think it's possibly worse for her, not knowing why I've cooled off, I mean. I'd hoped when I joined the R. F. C. and went off to France that she'd find someone else. She's so pretty she's bound to have other fellows after her. But Alice tells me Jane isn't interested in boys or love or marriage and that she was going to dedicate her whole life to nursing!"

Alexis sighed.

"She is very young still, Oliver. Perhaps given a little more time, she *will* find someone else. You must, too. After all, old chap, you'll have to get married one day, won't you. It'll be up to you to produce an heir for Rochford!"

Oliver did not return his brother-in-law's smile.

"I just can't see myself happily married to anyone else," he said miserably. "Don't you see, Alexis—we were ideal for each other. As for producing an heir for Rochford—well, by the time this war is over, I doubt if things will ever get back to normal. Mother said it was going to be terribly difficult to get staff when that time comes. Too many women have found themselves better jobs not 'in service.' There wasn't much else for girls to do before the war, was there? Now they're even working in factories! I don't see how we could run Rochford the way it used to be without the servants."

"We'll have to see when the time comes," Alexis said, deliberately vague. He did not want Oliver to know how heartily he agreed that nothing could ever be quite the same again after the war. Even the wealthy who enjoyed the luxuries, were beginning to realize the injustice of such a vast division between rich and poor. Now that they were having to dispense with their chauffeurs and drive their own cars, to dress and undress themselves, to do their own shopping, they were beginning to understand a little of the drudgery of domestic service.

"In many ways, I shan't be sorry to get back on duty," Oliver said sighing. "It isn't easy for me at Rochford when I know that at any moment I might turn a corner and come face to face with Jane. What disturbs me so much, is that I still love her, even though I know I shouldn't, she being my sister, I mean. I still want to take her in my arms and kiss her. Does that sound as shocking to you as it does to me?"

"No, it doesn't!" Alexis said very firmly. "It merely means you have not yet got it fixed in your head that Jane is your sister. After all, you thought otherwise for a long time and habits are hard to change overnight. Fortunately you did discover the truth before it was too late and now you have no choice but to look to the future, Oliver. Find yourself a pretty French girl in Paris if you can manage to get there on leave. Enjoy yourself the way other young men of your age are doing when they get the chance. Sow a few wild oats! When you come home again, I'll see what I can do to introduce you to some pretty girls—there are lots about, you know."

He was rewarded by Oliver's grin and the boy attempted to talk more cheerfully over a nightcap before they finally retired. Two weeks later, Oliver was back with his squadron and Alexis' private concerns had once again to be put on one side. With his ability to speak Russian, it was inevitable that he should be drawn into the discussions arranged by Fanshaw on the trouble brewing in Russia.

"The unrest is escalating," he told Toby on a weekend visit to see little Teo. "The Russian armies have suffered a series of military disasters and have lost quite literally millions of men. In the cities they are not far from starvation and those who have any idea of what is going on mistrust the Tzarina. They think *she* controls the Tzar's opinions and that the crazy monk, Rasputin, who had charge of her sick child, controlled her!"

"And did he?" Toby asked with interest.

"Undoubtedly," Alexis said. "Which is why he was shot—

and none too soon, it would seem. Another cause for unrest—perhaps well-justified, is the oppressive regime of the Tzar's official adviser, Protopopoff. He's feared and hated."

He did not tell Toby that he was to leave on the Monday for a visit to St. Petersburg for an unofficial look into the situation. He was away for three weeks and on his return, he reported to Fanshaw that he could see no way in which the Russian government could avoid a serious political upheaval in the near future. Whilst in Court circles there had seemed little awareness of the degree of antipathy to the regime, Alexis had mingled with the man in the street. He had been shocked by the extent of the bitterness and mistrust he had uncovered—too deep-seated, he believed, ever again to be suppressed.

It was not widely known in England by the general public that the Russian Tzar was a first cousin to their own King George. But when the Russian people finally forced the Tzar's abdication on the 15th March and the Royal family were imprisoned in the palace, the whole world was deeply shocked. Despite this revolutionary uprising, the Allies continued to press the Russians to start a new offensive on the Eastern Front.

But the war news from distant Russia could not preoccupy those at home to the same degree as did the war news from the Western Front. The battle for the French town of Arras had begun on Easter morning in an attempt by the Allies to reach the Hindenburg Line in the north. The fighting began on a rugged hill called Vimy Ridge. Not only George Barratt was involved but Oliver, too. In all there were twelve British divisions in the assault supported by four hundred and eighty airplanes and forty-eight tanks.

Despite the fact that the Germans had their most renowned air ace, Oberleutnant von Richthofen, pitted against them, the Royal Flying Corps, emerged victorious in aerial combat. Although slightly wounded by a bullet grazing his left arm, Oliver survived. But the Barratts were to lose their second son.

It was undoubtedly due to the bravery of the Canadian soldiers that Vimy Ridge was captured. The battle for Arras continued for almost three weeks and George Barratt was amongst the eighty-four thousand British casualties. It was a grievous blow to his parents, perhaps the more so for the fact that the victory, if such it could be called, was only partial.

At the end of the day, the Allies had advanced between two and five miles along a twenty-mile stretch of the Front.

"Will it never end!" Willow said tearfully to Toby. "Poor dear George will never come home now to marry Hilda. I feel so sad for her, and most of all for his parents. Thank God Oliver is safe!"

They received a cheerful letter from him not long after the fighting ceased. He had been given a short leave pass and had made his way to Épernay where he had seen Lucy, Pelham and Silvie and been reunited with Mark.

He's in good heart! Oliver had written. *I ragged him about the peg-leg he'll get when he comes home and he took it all with a grin. He hopes to be home before long—but I dare say you know from Aunt Silvie that his other leg is taking a long while to heal.*

"Lucy looks rather thin and tired but she is positively dedicated to her work. I must say I never thought she would turn out to be a Florence Nightingale. Alexis would be proud of her, as indeed I am. Mark and I think she works too hard.

"Back to the squadron tomorrow. Poor Mark is very envious but tried not to let on...

"We're all tremendously bucked by the news that the Yanks are in the war at last. I dare say you are pleased, Mater. I think that journalist fellow, Ed Baines, might be too...."

Willow had insisted that Toby should now pin the Stars and Stripes beside the Union Jack over the maps in the hall.

"It's flying over Westminster and so it should here!" she said.

"The Germans asked for it!" Toby said dourly as he carried out Willow's request. "Goodness only knows how many American merchant ships have been sunk by the U-boats. That's hardly been conducive to a state of neutrality. I'd call it a challenge and clearly President Wilson has had enough!"

As Oliver had foreseen, Ed Baines was delighted that his country had finally joined the Allies. He considered the American participation long overdue. He arrived one May day at Rochford with the glad news that his paper had made him their war correspondent.

"It's just what I wanted," he told Willow and Toby as he followed them into the morning room which he surveyed with interest. On his last visit, Rochford Manor was still a large private mansion and he found this transformation to hospital of great interest.

"I'll know where to ask them to send me if I get wounded!" he said jocularly as old Dutton carried in the tea.

Willow brought the friendly American up to date with Oliver's news and then asked him if he had heard anything recently about Rupert and Max.

"We always hope to get another letter from him one of these days," she said smiling. "Perhaps via an English soldier they have helped escape. We did receive a telephone call from a Lieutenant Bradley about six months ago, saying how grateful he was for Rupert's and Max's assistance and that they were both well. But we have heard nothing since..."

She broke off, aware that something must be wrong for there was an expression of acute discomfort on the journalist's rugged face. She regarded him anxiously, waiting for him to speak, but he refused to meet her eyes.

"You have some sort of news, Baines?" Toby asked quietly.

The American nodded. He looked very embarrassed.

"I assumed you knew... that someone would have advised you. I wrote myself to say how sorry I was but... the letter must have gone adrift," he stammered. "I sure am sorry to be the one to have to tell you—it's the worst news possible, I'm afraid. Their house was searched and they had an Englishman and two Frenchmen on the premises. They knew what would happen to them, of course, and they must have resisted an attempt to arrest them. They were both shot in their own front room."

Toby hurried to Willow's side and put his arm around her shoulders.

"We must try and console ourselves with the fact that they can't have suffered any pain under the circumstances. Poor old Rupert! Poor Max." He looked up at Ed Baines. "Thank you for letting us know, Baines. I take it you are certain of the facts?"

The journalist nodded.

"I had a letter from Whitlock just over a month ago. I immediately wrote you—but there seems no guarantee that mail will reach its destination these days. I really am very sorry."

He declined an invitation to stay to dinner and they did not press him to prolong his visit. He left, promising to get in touch with them if he was able to discover any further details. He was leaving in the morning for Liverpool at which port the Americans were expected to arrive. Later, he would accompany the troops to France where he thought it possible that he might be able to track down more facts about Rupert and Max. His main task, of course, was to cover the arrival of an American division commanded by Major General Pershing—the first troops to set foot on French soil.

"We can thank German stupidity for the fact that we now have the Americans on our side," Toby commented to Willow in an attempt to keep her mind off Rupert's death. "President Wilson was not in the least anxious to plunge your country into war, a fact the Germans must have been aware of. Yet still they encouraged their U-boats to sink American shipping—even though some of those ships were supplying *them*. It's unbelievable—and encouraging, too. If they can make these kinds of mistakes, we should surely be able to win this war before much longer."

The war was now beginning to affect the day-to-day lives of the civilians. There were long food queues everywhere since imports were restricted, and it was obvious controls were necessary. In June, Lord Rhonda, a big industrialist from South Wales, was put in charge of the Ministry of Food. He elected Sam Sharples as one of his right-hand men to assist him in establishing complete control over the country's food supplies. Sam's organizing ability was given free rein and Marjorie Sharples told Willow that they could expect compulsory rationing by the New Year.

"I gather from Sam that the Government are now buying everything we eat, whether it is imported or home grown. They are going to fix the prices and organize distribution with local Food Committees to implement the Board's decisions," Marjorie continued in her bright, cheerful voice. "I suppose it will mean a lot more work for all of us running this place, but Sam says it had to be done. It will be carried out in a totally democratic manner. Even the King will have to make do on the same rations as the poorest man in the street."

At the beginning of July, both the King and Queen went to France. It was the King's fourth visit but the first time Oliver had seen him out there. He wrote home expressing his admiration for the far from fit fifty-two-year-old monarch whose physical presence amongst his troops at the Front was having an enormously stimulating effect upon them all.

In mid-July, Toby's *Times* gave considerable space to the proclamation that henceforth the Royal House of Great Britain and Ireland would be known, not as the House of Saxe-

Coburg-Gotha, or as it was popularly called the House of Hanover or Brunswick, but as the House of Windsor.

"Long overdue!" was Toby's terse comment. "The people don't want to remember our Royal Family's relationships with the enemy's Royals. It must have proved highly embarrassing for them to possess such German sounding surnames. The House of Windsor is a far more acceptable name as is the change from Battenburg to Mountbatten."

"At least no one doubts the total devotion of the King and Queen—or their dedication," Willow commented. "In the circumstances it's as well for them both that they are so beloved."

News of the King's visit to France filtered through to the Château d'Orbais.

"I wish President Poincaré would pay a visit to us here!" Silvie said with a smile as she helped Mark pack his few possessions in readiness for his return to England. He was departing on the following day and although he was genuinely excited at the thought of going home, he was sad to be leaving so many friends at the Château.

"I shall miss you all dreadfully," he said with his slow, boyish smile. "You, Uncle Pelham and Lucy, of course, not to mention Susan..." he added with a grin. He and the youngest of the two V.A.D.s in Ward 2 were now referred to by all the patients as "The Sweethearts" for it was quite plain to everyone that they had fallen in love. Mark could not wait to take the girl to Rochford to introduce her to his family. He was convinced his sister Jane would love Susan quite as much as he did—and Susan had put in for a home posting so that she could at least be within reach while Mark was continuing his convalescence at Roehampton House—the lovely old Elizabethan mansion where men like himself were fitted with artificial limbs.

"Any letters to take home, Lucy?" he asked her. Silvie had given him a long epistle to hand to Willow and another for Alexis as Mark was to be allowed two weeks' leave at Rochford before going to Roehampton.

Lucy withdrew an envelope from her apron pocket. It was for Teo, written in large block capitals which she hoped the child would be able, with Stella's help, to read. But there was no letter for Alexis as Mark had assumed there would be.

Lucy had abandoned her many attempts to put her feelings into words. It had been a bitter disappointment when she had returned from leave in Paris to learn that Alexis had been at

Épernay and left before her return. She would have been so happy to see him, especially as Aunt Silvie had said he was quite as disappointed as herself at the abortive rendezvous. According to her aunt, Alexis had been tremendously impressed by her account of the work Lucy was doing, but Lucy would like to have heard his praise at first hand. He had left her a Christmas gift for which she had not yet thanked him.

The present itself was one that gave Lucy great joy—and a moment or two of sorrow. It was a charming, hand-painted miniature of Teo set in a gold filigree frame. The child was dressed in a white organdie frock with a wide sash the identical blue of her eyes. She was smiling at the brightly colored golliwog she was clutching in her small chubby arms.

Whenever Lucy looked at the miniature—which was usually every night before she went to sleep—she felt a deep surge of longing to be able to lift the little girl into her arms and cover the small, happy face with kisses. At such moments she felt a deep homesickness and found herself wondering yet again why Alexis had called for her on his return from Vienna and then taken her home with him. Had he given her the miniature as a reminder of what she had left behind? Was he trying to tempt her back? Did he *want* her home with him? The questions remained unanswered.

It would have been easy enough to pose them in a letter. With Mark carrying mail personally to England, she could be sure that a letter would reach Alexis' hands safely. But when she attempted to write to him to express her feelings she was overcome by a renewed sense of pride. She would never let Alexis know she needed him; wanted to be friends with him again, she thought unhappily. She had declared her independence and she would only go back if he begged her. It was now nearly a year since she had stormed out of his house. It seemed obvious that he had not greatly missed her.

In all the many talks Mark had had with Lucy, they had neither one of them mentioned Alexis. It was Silvie who had warned him that there had been what she called 'a slight rift' and it was best he should keep off the subject. Mark was sad—not just for Lucy who he adored; but for the interesting, good-looking Count Zemski who, like Oliver, he hero-worshiped. He thought it cruel of Lucy not to write to him.

Risking her rebuff, he took his courage in both hands and said tentatively:

"If I see Count Zemski, shall I tell him you sent your love?"

The color rushed into Lucy's cheeks. Her eyes flashed angrily as she said:

"If I had wanted you to give Alexis any message, I would have said so, Mark!"

With which she turned on her heel and left the ward. She had intended to go to her own room but Sister accosted her in the hall.

"You speak fluent French, don't you, dear. I wonder if you would go and see *Caporal* Lyon—Ward 6. He has refused to eat for the past four days and I'm reasonably certain it's a deliberate attempt at suicide. We've all tried to cheer him up but I'm afraid without any success at all. He won't even speak to us. Ward 6 contains the blind, you know."

For the most part, Lucy had been on duty either in "Amputations" or in "Head Wounds." Both had contained officers. Ward 6 was for the other ranks and Lucy now made her way there, glad of the opportunity to take her mind off Alexis. She was already regretting the sharp voice she had used to young Mark.

The big, sunny room contained twenty-five patients, all of whom had lost their sight during a battle or whose head wounds had been such that infection had spread to the optic nerve and they had become blind.

"Would someone tell me which is *Caporal* Lyon?" Lucy inquired. All heads turned in her direction. The men had recognized a new voice. A dozen hands pointed vaguely toward the far end of the room. As she walked toward the occupied bed, she tried to quell her feelings of pity for these blind patients groping their way about the ward.

Lucy approached the French soldier's bedside. The man was lying with his face turned to the wall, his eyes invisible behind a clean white bandage.

"*Caporal* Lyon? I am one of the V.A.D.s from Ward 3. My name is Nurse Zemski. As I speak French, Sister asked me to come and have a chat with you."

There was no acknowledgment of her self-introduction. Lucy sat down on a chair by the bedside.

"Sister told me you were refusing to eat, and of course, that is a state of affairs that cannot be permitted," Lucy continued in a low tone. "You are not ill, *Caporal* Lyon. There is no reason why you should not enjoy your food. Besides, if you won't eat of your own accord, they'll only force-feed you— and that is a horrible business you would certainly not enjoy."

The head turned slightly—sufficiently for Lucy to see a rugged countenance, close-cropped dark, wiry hair above the bandage and a wide, sensitive mouth beneath. His lips were trembling.

In a strong, country patois, the soldier said:

"No one can force me to eat if I don't want to!"

"But that's just it—they can!" Lucy told him truthfully.

Obviously her tone held a ring of truth for he turned fully toward her now and said:

"Then I'll find some other way. I'm never going home like this!"

Lucy steeled herself to speak unemotionally.

"That's really very silly. I can't keep calling you *Caporal* Lyon. Will you tell me your name?"

After a short pause, the man muttered his name—Gaston.

"Are you married, Gaston?" Lucy asked.

The bandaged head nodded.

"Then you must realize how selfish you are being. Besides, you are a Catholic, I presume, and know that to kill yourself is a mortal sin. And it isn't just *your* life, Gaston—it's your wife's too. What has she done to deserve widowhood?"

She could feel the man's anger and see the bitter lines tighten around his mouth as he said violently:

"It's her I'm a-thinking of. She's still young, beautiful. She'll find another man who wouldn't be a burden to her. If I were to go home like this..." he pointed to his eyes, "she'd have to support me for the rest of my life, doing all the heavy work, getting worn out before her time. I'll not allow that, *mon Dieu!*"

Lucy waited for a moment until the man seemed calmer. Then she said:

"You haven't told me what your trade is, Gaston."

"I'm a baker—the best there was in our village," he added proudly.

"And who is running your bakery now, while you are away?" Lucy inquired.

"Bernadette, my wife; my father's come out of retirement to give her a hand for the duration of the war."

"You have children?"

"Four—three girls and a boy. Jean, my son, will be eight next month."

"So!" said Lucy thoughtfully. "There is no reason why your father should not continue to help Bernadette for a few years longer—until your boy is fifteen or sixteen. Then he'll be old enough to help your wife in the bakery, won't he?"

For a long moment Gaston did not speak. Lucy was uncertain whether he had instantly rejected her suggestion or whether he was considering it. When next he spoke, it was on a different subject.

"When I'd come back of an evening from the mill carrying flour for the next week, in a sack on my back, I'd open the door of the kitchen and see her there. She'd be in a chair by the fire, if it were wintertime; or by the open window if it were summer. She'd be feeding our youngest before her bedtime and like as not she wouldn't hear me if the bigger ones were making a din. Then she'd feel the draught and look up at me and smile. Silly as it may sound, I'd walk to Armentières and back to see that smile, so full of love it was. No, I'm telling you. *My Bernadette deserves better than a blind man.* There's plenty of fellows in our town who would give their right arm to be wed to her."

Lucy heard the bitterness in his tone and said quietly:

"Have you thought that she might not want any of those others? It's you she loves, Gaston—you just said you knew it from the look in her eyes, so you can't deny it. I think you're feeling sorry for yourself because you won't be able to see her face again; because you're afraid there would be pity in her eyes instead of love!"

"Ce n'est pas vraie!" The man's voice was angry but with an underlying uncertainty nevertheless there.

"If you were my husband," Lucy said, deliberately cruel, "I'd tell you to get rid of yourself as quick as you could. A man who's as sorry for himself as you are wouldn't be much use to me. I should think your youngest has got more courage than you have!" She gave a derisive laugh adding, "I'd not want a husband so filled with self-pity he couldn't think of me!"

He rose at once to her taunt.

"You've no right to make fun of me!" he said furiously. "It's no laughing matter as you'd well know if it was you who could see nothing but darkness!"

"I wasn't laughing at you!" Lucy replied evenly.

"Yes you were!" he retorted.

"I don't know what makes you think so, Gaston."

"I'm not that stupid!" he said. "Being blind doesn't make me daft, *quand même*. I could feel it—hear it in your voice."

Lucy felt a swift stab of pleasure. Keeping her excitement subdued she said:

"Do you realize what you have just said to me, Gaston? You could hear me laughing at you. You could *feel* it. That's what you said."

"And what if I did? It was no lie!"

"Exactly!" Lucy said with deepest satisfaction. "Don't you understand, losing your sight isn't the end of the world? It isn't an end to everything you value. You spoke just now of seeing your wife's smile. It's true you won't ever do that again, but you'll hear it in her voice; feel it, just the way you heard and felt the emotion in *my* voice. And you and I are strangers. You're going to be all right, Gaston, I promise you. You'll be happy again with your Bernadette and this will all seem an impossible nightmare, believe me."

She reached out and laid her hand against his cheek. He caught hold of it and clung to it fiercely.

"Who are you?" he asked hoarsely. "How come you know these things? I want to believe you..."

"I'm only a nurse," Lucy said softly as she withdrew her hand. "But I'm also a woman, Gaston, so perhaps I know better than you how much your wife wants you back. Now you must get well for her—and quickly. To have you home tomorrow would not be soon enough for her."

When she reached the privacy of her own bedroom, Lucy removed her uniform and, putting on a dressing gown, lay down on her bed. She felt unbelievably tired—far more so than usual—and was conscious of a deep depression. Despite the warmth of the room, she was shivering. Her head ached unbearably and the various objects in the room seemed to be shaking as she tried to focus her eyes on them.

She hoped she was not about to fall ill. Whatever happened, she wanted to be downstairs tomorrow to see Mark off. She must tell him she regretted speaking to him so sharply. It was natural he would expect her to write a letter to her own husband. I am Alexis' wife, she thought, and I *should* be writing to him just as he should be writing to me. All these wounded men she nursed lived for the letters they received from their loved ones.

Lucy closed her eyes. She seemed unable to control the jumbled passage of her thoughts. Her forehead felt burning hot and yet she was shivering. It was quiet and lonely up here in her room. If she were to die now, this minute, no one would know. It might be hours before Aunt Silvie came to look for her. It would be comforting to have someone come into the room; someone to fuss over her, wipe her forehead, hold her hand the way Alexis had done after Teo's birth.

Why doesn't Alexis come up to see me? she thought. She was so tired and her head hurt so much! It would be so nice if the door opened and he was standing there, smiling at her.

"I always like it when you smile at me, Alexis!" she murmured.

"Lucy, are you all right, *chérie*? *What* did you say?"

It was her Aunt Silvie, staring down at her with a look of concern in her eyes.

"They should be green . . ." Lucy whispered vaguely. "Alexis' eyes are green. Why isn't he here? I'd feel so much better if he would only come to see me . . ."

Silvie hurried back downstairs to find Pelham. He was on his way up to her and they all but collided in the hall.

"It's Lucy!" Silvie said. "She's ill. Very ill, I think. She's delirious. Can you find the *Médecin de Chef* for me? I don't want to leave her alone."

Pelham did not waste time asking questions. The look of anxiety on Silvie's face was enough to warn him that this was no trifling matter.

Back in Lucy's room, Silvie covered her with a duvet and began wiping the perspiration from the girl's forehead. Lucy was tossing from side to side, moaning softly, her words no longer distinguishable. Her skin was burning hot to Silvie's touch. With difficulty she slipped a thermometer under Lucy's armpit. When she withdrew it and looked at the mercury, she could not withhold a gasp of horror. The reading was not far short of one hundred and five degrees.

Chapter 26

July—August 1917

NEWS HAD REACHED THE CHÂTEAU D'ORBAIS OF RENEWED fighting in the Ypres area. The C.-in-C., Sir Douglas Haig, had ordered yet another offensive in an effort to push back the Front. But Silvie had no emotional resources to spare for such concerns. Lucy was dangerously ill with pneumonia and the French doctor who had taken her under his wing for the past three days was unwilling to commit himself as to whether she would recover.

A telegram had been sent to Alexis two days previously. His housekeeper, Mrs. Taylor, had sensibly opened it and telephoned Willow who had replied at once stating that Alexis was "somewhere in Europe" and not expected back for several weeks. Willow herself was trying to get the necessary permits to come to Épernay.

Silvie discussed the possibility with Pelham. They jointly decided that such a decision was unwise. There was nothing whatever Willow could do for Lucy that was not already being done. The girl was far too ill to recognize her mother and it could only be distressing for Willow to see Lucy struggling for breath.

"Besides," Silvie said finally, "it is Alexis Lucy wants. Even in her delirium she calls for him—never for her mother."

As a consequence Willow was telegraphed to remain at Rochford and given the assurance that she would be notified if the situation worsened. Meanwhile Silvie had appropriated for Lucy her own private physician.

In the peaceful years before the war, Silvie and Pelham had been on excellent social terms with the Vicomte Edouard de Valle, a young doctor who lived in a château some fifty miles away near the town of Compiègne. Although a Frenchman by birth, de Valle had English ancestors and the past four generations of males had all been educated at Eton.

Although Edouard de Valle was fifteen or so years younger than Pelham, they had run into each other by chance in Paris and found that apart from their public school, they had much in common. Both had a passion for motor cars and both were keen shots. At least twice a year, Pelham went to shoot in the beautiful forest surrounding the Château Boulancourt and the Vicomte had been a summer guest at the Château d'Orbais on many occasions. Silvie thought him both charming and intelligent and he was a welcome visitor.

Since the outbreak of war Pelham had from time to time voiced concern about the young Vicomte's safety. The fighting in the autumn of 1914 had reached Compiègne. They had no word from de Valle until a year later when they had received a postcard from him saying that he had joined *le Service Santé* as a Medical Officer and was at the Front. They had no further news until a few days after Lucy fell ill when he had turned up on the doorstep in his favorite Bugatti, asking if he might stay a few days with his old friends.

"I heard you had converted the Château into a hospital," he explained, "and I hoped there might be some way I could lend a hand here."

As Pelham led him upstairs to their private rooms, de Valle had pointed to his heavily bandaged left foot and explained that he'd lost half of it when the first aid post where he was operating had received a direct hit.

"I know I shouldn't grumble—I'm lucky to be one of the few survivors," he had said in his perfect English. "But grumble I'm afraid I do. You see, Rochford, they've given me the push. Not fit for active service . . . all that rubbish. I can't even work in a civilian hospital because I can't stand up for long without a stick. Damn silly, really! There's plenty I can do sitting down!"

Could Pelham and Silvie not find *something* for him to do? he asked them.

"Bien sûr!" Silvie exclaimed smiling. With their hospital *Médecin de Chef* and his assistant already working to capacity, Lucy's illness was proving an added burden to them. Edouard, she told him, could with the greatest pleasure take over her niece's full-time care. His presence was heaven-sent as Lucy's condition seemed critical.

But for Edouard, Silvie thought, Lucy might very easily have died. She did not have the robust constitution of someone whose childhood had included the very best of nourishment in a protected environment. For the first twelve years of Lucy's life at the Convent, she had not been all that far from starvation and she had no inner resources of strength to call on.

The young doctor sat now in Silvie's drawing room enjoying an evening aperitif with his host and hostess. He had just returned from Lucy's room. His brown eyes had deep shadows under them and he looked tired.

"I think your niece may be just a little better this evening," he said in his soft, attractive voice. He smiled—his dark eyebrows lifting slightly but the smile not quite touching his mouth. He was a singularly handsome, aristocratic-looking man, Silvie thought, as she put a stool beneath his foot which was obviously paining him. She remembered an occasion when she had seen him on horseback, highly polished riding boots dug firmly into the silver stirrups. What a shame it would be if this man could never ride again.

She was still unsure how severely his foot had been damaged but Pelham believed it must be serious else he would not have been discharged from the army at a time when doctors were so badly needed.

"I am interested in this husband, Alexis," Edouard said as he accepted with a grateful nod the glass Pelham handed him. "He is not in the Services, I believe you told me? Why then can't he come to see his wife? I feel her progress would be much more rapid if he were here to encourage her."

Silvie sighed.

"No one seems to know just exactly what Alexis does," she said. "It's Secret Service work of some kind—that's really all we know. He disappears into Europe, sometimes for weeks on end. He's 'away somewhere' at the moment and he does not even know Lucy is ill."

Edouard de Valle was silent as he drew out a silver cigarette case and lit a cigarette, his long sensitive fingers moving deftly and with a natural grace. His thoughts were on the beautiful young woman struggling for life in the room above. If she were *his* wife, he thought, he'd abandon everything to be with her. But he quickly set aside the notion. The last thing in the world a doctor should do was become emotional about his patient!

Nevertheless, he thought with a sigh, no one could blame him for admiring Lucienne Zemski's beauty. That extraordinary pale silky hair, the almost violet-blue of her eyes and pale, porcelain skin—he would not have been human had he been unaware of her fascination. He'd seen quite a number of pretty nurses since he'd been wounded, not to mention the many society beauties he'd squired in Paris before the war; yet he had never seen any girl whose looks appealed to him as Lucy's did. It did not help him to know she was married. Her face had begun to haunt his dreams and his fight for her survival had become almost a battle not just for the Rochfords' sake but for his own.

"If Lucy is really turning the corner at last," Silvie remarked, lost in her own thoughts, "then it will be entirely due to you, Edouard. You have scarcely left the sickroom for the past four days."

The man sighed.

"If we only had an antidote that would attack the pneumonia virus!" he said. "There is really so little I can do for her, Silvie. At such times it's often a question of how hard the patient fights as to whether he or she will pull through."

Lucy was indeed battling for life. In between bouts of her delirium, her aunt had told her that Alexis would be coming to see her soon, *very soon*. She was determined to see him to tell him that she really had intended to be a good wife; that she was sorry that she had disappointed him in the past; that she wanted to prove herself a useful member of society as a nurse, that even if she had failed to love him the way he wanted, it mattered very much that he loved her. If only Alexis would smile that gentle, tender smile so that she could be certain he did still love her, she wouldn't particularly mind dying. But until then...

Seven days after she had fallen ill, Lucy once more became aware of her surroundings. Her chest hurt too much to encourage conversation but she smiled and nodded as Aunt Silvie busied herself around the sickroom.

"Now you know what it's like to be a patient yourself!" Aunt Silvie teased gently. Lucy also became aware of the French doctor who came to see her several times a day. Somewhere in the recesses of her mind, she thought she remembered one night when he had sat until morning by her bedside. But it was not until her senses had fully returned that he introduced himself.

"Your temperature is down at last," he said, his dark eyes smiling as he sat by the bedside holding her wrist to feel her pulse. "You're going to get better, Madame Zemski—or may

I call you Lucy? Your aunt and uncle refer to you so often by your Christian name, it is difficult for me to think of you other than as 'Lucy,'" he added, his smile broadening.

"I'm afraid I've been an awful nuisance to everyone," Lucy replied.

"Not to me!" declared Edouard sincerely. He related briefly the reasons why he was so pleased to have a job to do once more. Lucy smiled.

"So that is why you sit by my bed rather than stand!"

Edouard nodded, glancing ruefully at his foot.

"How long before I can go back on duty?" Lucy asked the question that was uppermost in her mind.

"A long time, I'm afraid. You will be very weak at first. You may not realize it, but you have lost a great deal of weight this past week. We have to take great care of you for some time to come. Your fever may be gone but you are not yet well again."

The effort of conversation had tired Lucy and she closed her eyes. The doctor's voice was confident and reassuring. She felt instinctively that she could trust him.

"Thank you for everything you've done," she murmured. "You're very kind!"

From then on Lucy's recovery was quicker even than Edouard had thought possible. Each day she became a little stronger; her cough became only a wheeze; the color returned to her cheeks; the alertness to her eyes. It became Edouard's custom to sit with her in the afternoons when she awoke from her rest. Although ostensibly it was to relieve Silvie to return to her duties downstairs in the wards, in reality he could not keep away from his patient. Lucy fascinated him. He asked interminable questions about her home in England, about her little girl; about Rochford Manor and her relations. She was reticent only about her husband and he suspected that all was far from well with the marriage, but he could not understand why. Alexis Zemksi sounded a reasonable enough fellow and there was little doubt that Lucy cared about him or his name would not have been so continually on her lips when she was delirious. But he was far too new an acquaintance to be able to ask her the personal questions he was continually asking himself.

Three weeks after her illness had begun, Lucy asked if she might be permitted to go out into the garden. It was mid-August and many of the convalescents were either sitting or

lying in wicker invalid chairs in the shade of the trellised vine
on the south side of the Château. Despite the fact that the
once beautiful garden no longer existed, the perennials had
continued to push their way up through the long grass and
where once there had been an immaculate herbaceous border,
there was now a haphazard blaze of colors. The overgrown
rose garden too, was bright with fragrant blooms which had
managed to fight their way through the tangle of weeds and
brambles.

"I don't see why Lucy should not go out, do you, Silvie?"
Edouard said. "It's certainly warm enough—well into the
eighties, I'd say! Pelham can carry her downstairs if you prepare an invalid bedchair for her!"

Lucy felt a thrill of excitement as her uncle carried her
into the soft, scented air and tucking her warmly into her
chair, pushed her down to the rose garden. It was lovely to
be out of her room with its smell of antiseptic and all the
paraphernalia of a sickroom.

Edouard seated himself beside her on a stone bench, watching the pleasure in her face and thinking yet again how fascinated he was by her fragile beauty. Pelham and Silvie returned
to the house, and patient and doctor were left alone.

"Tell me about yourself!" Lucy demanded, now quite at
ease in the familiar presence of the young Vicomte. "I know
your home is in Compiègne. I have never been there. Is it
attractive?"

"Compiègne itself is a beautiful town with a magnificent
palace," Edouard told her. "My château, which is called Boulancourt, is some miles outside the town. You must travel
through a great forest of oak and beech trees to reach it. It
is bigger than the Château d'Orbais—too big for my solitary
usage. My parents are dead and my only brother went to live
in America before the war. Boulancourt has a moat surrounding it and a drawbridge and several towers. It is, of course,
very old."

Lucy's interest was aroused.

"Weren't you overrun by the Germans at the start of the
war?" she asked.

Edouard nodded.

"Yes, the Boches were in Boulancourt, but not for long.
There was no one there at the time—I was at the Front and
the servants had hidden in the forest. The Germans, as is
their custom, behaved like pigs—even the officers; but I think

they may all have been too drunk to distinguish between the real antiquities and those of little worth. They took what they could carry but at least they did not wreck the place beyond repair—probably because it would have been too long an operation. It's not the first time Boulancourt has been ravaged. It was burned down in the French Revolution. My great grandfather rebuilt it in 1813."

"My aunt was telling me that the de Valles are a very old family," Lucy said. "And partly English?"

Edouard nodded. "The English element did not appear until the middle of the last century," he replied, "when my great grandfather, Gerard de Valle, married an Englishwoman by the strange name of Mavreen.★ Family documents relate she was quite a character—she had had two husbands before she married into the de Valle family and after my great grandfather died, she was married again—on that occasion to a onetime highwayman. There is one letter in our family archives which shows her as having shared in his exploits and then rescued him from the gallows!"

Lucy laughed. "She sounds quite fascinating. Tell me more. Edouard!"

"Well, perhaps more fascinating still are the stories surrounding my grandfather, John de Valle. My great grandfather had an illegitimate son called Antoine who was a thoroughly black sheep. He married a rich widow and then locked her in the east tower at Boulancourt while he tried to get his hands on her money. She went mad and killed herself. He meanwhile, had restored the ruins of the amphitheater which I'll show you one day, and held Roman games there in great secrecy because the fights that took place were to the death! He bought criminals from the Paris prisons and fed them up for the purpose. One of them went mad in his dungeon, then escaped and killed the infamous Antoine. Then John de Valle took over."

"I don't believe it!" Lucy laughed. "You're making it all up!"

"Indeed I am not!" Edouard replied, enjoying the sound of her laughter. "My grandfather, John, was also quite a character. He fell in love with the highwayman's daughter—a very beautiful girl, half-Neapolitan, called Chantal. She was ship-

★The de Valle family feature in the trilogy *Mavreen*, *Tamarisk* and *Chantal* as central characters.

wrecked somewhere in the Indian Ocean and was marooned with a Portuguese pirate and a black slave girl on a desert island in the Seychelles archipelago. My grandfather set off in a sailing ship to look for her and eventually he found her. By then she had gone native. My father always maintained that she was in love with the pirate and that although she left the island, she never forgot him. Her marriage to John de Valle seems to have been happy enough nevertheless. My father remembers quite distinctly meeting this pirate when he himself was very, very young. The man had turned up one night out of the blue, dressed as a Portuguese nobleman. My grandmother—that's the one called Chantal—had taken him up to the night nursery to see her children—there were five of them, all girls but for my father. He remembers watching this flamboyant, somewhat frightening character pick up one of his little sisters from her cot and saying to my grandmother: 'This one is just like you, my Koosh-Koosh!' and my grandmother, so father said, began crying—something so remarkable that my father never forgot it."

"I think that's rather sad!" Lucy said.

Edouard smiled.

"I prefer to think it romantic ..." He broke off, aware that Lucy was no longer listening. She was staring at a tall figure walking across the grass toward them. The color raced into her cheeks.

"It's my husband, Alexis!" she said weakly to Edouard.

He looked up at the man curiously and was immediately filled with a wave of jealousy. The husband, Alexis, who had been only a name for so long, was tall, slim, handsome and walked with a smooth, graceful stride. Edouard was painfully conscious of his maimed foot as he stood up clumsily.

"I must go and have a word with your aunt and uncle, Lucy. If you will excuse me?" he murmured tactfully.

She turned to him with sudden shyness.

"Oh, no Edouard. Please stay and meet Alexis!" she cried. "He'll want to thank you for taking such good care of me ..."

Alexis was now beside them. Edouard gave a stiff bow.

"Alexis, this is the Vicomte de Valle, my doctor. Edouard, this is my husband, Alexis."

The two men shook hands before Edouard, with a brief nod to Lucy, hurried away leaning heavily on his walking stick.

Alexis sat down on the bench and took Lucy's hand, raising it to his lips. His green eyes searched her face anxiously.

"I have been so worried about you," he said huskily. "I arrived back in England two days ago and telephoned your mother. She said you had been very ill...I came as quickly as I could, Lucy."

Lucy felt her whole body fill with a warm, happy glow. There could be no cause for doubting that Alexis did love her. It showed in his voice, in his eyes.

"I'm so glad you're here," she said simply. She did not let go of Alexis' hand. "I was very sorry when we missed each other last Christmas."

Alexis smiled gravely.

"I was too. Did you have a good time in Paris?" he added, gently teasing.

Suddenly, they were both smiling. With a little of her former spirit, Lucy said:

"I suppose the truthful answer is 'yes'! My three escorts were so nice, Alexis—you'd have liked them all. They were like boys on an outing from school—in fact they ragged all the time just the way Oliver and Mark and Henry carry on. It was such a relief for them, you see, being away from the war and all its horrible memories. For me, too, though I had far less to forget than they did."

Alexis nodded.

"Your aunt told me how greatly you have been missed in the wards since you became ill, Lucy. I hear you have become a very fine nurse!"

Lucy drew a deep breath.

"If I have, Alexis, it's because I wanted you to know I *could* do it. At first I was trying to prove to you that I wasn't useless as you had said. Then suddenly the work I had to do came to mean a great deal more than just proving you wrong. It's strange, isn't it? When I first saw a wounded man, I ran away! I was not nearly so brave as I had believed myself to be."

"The living wounded can be much more frightening than the dead!" Alexis said with understanding. "I am very proud of you, Lucy. I hope you can forgive me for all those unkind criticisms I made..."

"But they were justified then!" Lucy broke in. "And I'm glad you spoke out as you did. You were quite right—I was being appallingly selfish and I only wish you had told me so much sooner."

"I'm not altogether sure about that!" Alexis said thoughtfully. "Maybe I was the one being selfish—I didn't want to do or say anything that would drive you away, Lucy. Besides, my work keeps me from home so much I understood why you were bored." He gave her a charming smile. "I've missed you terribly since you went away!" he added softly.

Quite unbidden, tears sprang to Lucy's eyes. She wiped them away angrily with the back of her hand.

"I never cry! It must be my illness!" she said crossly.

Alexis recaptured her hand and said tenderly:

"When your mother told me you were so ill, I kept asking myself what I would do if you died!" he said. "It's just as well I did not know about it sooner, my darling. I don't think even my work would have kept me from you. But you are better—really better?"

Lucy nodded, not trusting her voice. She attempted to smile.

"Now that you are here, Alexis, I shall be well in no time at all. You don't have to hurry away again, do you?"

"No, my love! I have three whole weeks' leave. I told Fanshaw before I left London that I'd resign if he didn't sign my pass!"

Lucy leant back against her pillow, smiling happily.

"I shall be up and about before then, Alexis. Edouard says I can soon begin to take a little exercise each day. My legs feel so weak. Perhaps," she added shyly, "we could have a few days in Paris together before you go, Alexis? Aunt Silvie would lend us the house and..."

Alexis was regarding her strangely.

"I'm not going home to England without you, Lucy. You're to return home with me as soon as you are fit. I'm here to fetch you. Your mother wants you back at Rochford so that you can get really well and strong again. And I want you safe and sound, far away from the Front and not too far away from me!"

Lucy looked at him doubtfully.

"But Alexis, I wouldn't want to stay at Rochford. I want to be with you in London."

Alexis bit his lip.

"But I won't be home, my darling. Immediately this leave is over, I have to go to Russia. I probably shouldn't be telling you that, but I want you to understand. I could be away for as long as six weeks."

Lucy tried to hide her disappointment.

"Then I would prefer to remain here at Épernay until you come back, Alexis," she said. "I have work to do here. Aunt Silvie says that with the new offensive on the Somme, fighting could escalate in the south and we might soon be very busy. I would be needed here if that happened."

Alex regarded her doubtfully.

"But you are not well enough to nurse others, Lucy. You will need a long convalescence."

Lucy smiled.

"I shall get well quickly now. Edouard says I am recovering very quickly. Please, Alexis, I would really prefer to stay here. I'm not needed at Rochford."

Alexis did not argue the point although he wanted her away from any possibility of danger. It was all too easy sitting here beside Lucy in the beautiful garden, to forget the fighting still doggedly continuing to the north and west. The soft drowsy heat of the afternoon, the heady perfume of the roses, the shrill calling of the cicadas gave an illusion of endless peace. But he had only to turn his head toward the scarred walls of the Château to see the blue and the white uniforms of the patients and their nurses moving about on the terrace, to be brought back to reality. The war could well return to this area and he could not bear to think of Lucy, his Lucy, caught up in it.

He turned to look at his young wife, concerned anew at her pallor. How delicate she looked, but how appealing! This was a new Lucy—the person he had always suspected lay hidden deep within her; the woman he had glimpsed singing lullabies to her child. The brittleness, the defensiveness were gone. He could still not be certain, but he was almost convinced that she loved him. The tenderness in her eyes, her obvious desire to please him, her disappointment that he was going away again—all seemed to indicate someone who cared deeply.

"You know that I love you—very very much," he said. He watched with delight the color rush into her pale cheeks.

"Perhaps I needed this year apart from you to discover how much you mean to me, Alexis," she replied thoughtfully. "I have learned a great deal about people's feelings, working here on the wards. I think I know now what love really is— the kind of love you used to talk about, Alexis, which seemed so strange to me. It's in here, isn't it?" she added shyly pointing to her heart.

Unable to hide his joy, Alexis nodded, speechless with happiness.

"I was very jealous of Roberta!" Lucy said, a smile touching the corners of her mouth. "I was afraid you loved her more than you loved me!"

"I never loved her!" Alexis said quietly. "Except, of course as a friend. But she was very kind to me, Lucy. You and I seemed to be growing apart, and I was often very lonely. But that's all over and done with now. Roberta left for Egypt soon after you left for France, and I haven't seen her since."

"I'm glad," Lucy said simply. "I don't like to think of you needing her. You won't ever need her again, will you, Alexis—not now you have me!"

"No!" Alexis replied, his heart beating swiftly as he pressed a kiss to the back of her hand. "And while we are talking of feeling jealous, my lovely Lucy, what of that French doctor you call 'Edouard'? I hope there is no cause for rivalry there?"

Although his voice was light, Lucy heard the hint of anxiety in it. She smiled reassuringly.

"Of course not, Alexis. He's charming and nice looking and I like him very much but now you are here, I wouldn't care if I never saw him again."

"Nevertheless, I saw the way he looked at you just now—and at me. I fancy the fellow is half in love with you, Lucy—not that I blame him!"

"Honestly, you can forget him," Lucy said, "except that I do owe my life to him, Alexis—or so Aunt Silvie says."

"Then I shall be duly grateful to the fellow," Alexis said.

In the ensuing three weeks, however, he and the Vicomte never really became friendly other than on the most superficial of levels. Edouard, as Lucy's doctor, forbade Alexis to share his patient's bedroom on the grounds that Lucy was far from well enough to respond to a husband's demands. Sitting on the side of Lucy's bed before she fell asleep, Alexis said furiously:

"Does that stupid fellow think I intend forcing myself upon you, Lucy? I know he is your doctor and can be forgiven for instructing me on how I should behave. Obviously he believes it his duty to protect you. But equally obviously, he can't know me very well if he thinks I would risk hindering your recovery in any way!"

Lucy regarded Alexis uneasily. She longed to draw him into her arms and kiss away the angry lines around his eyes and mouth. More than anything in the world, she wanted him to be happy. Ever since the day he had arrived, the tension between them had grown stronger. Most of the time they had sat holding hands talking about Teo, Rochford, Oliver, the boys, the Barratts. Lucy had told Alexis about her patients; Alexis had told her about the unhappy Madeleine Villier, now shut away in a secure mental hospital with little hope that she would ever recover her sanity. Lucy had described to Alexis her life as a little girl at the Convent which, although much of it he found disturbing, nevertheless gave him a far better understanding of her, so he said. He did not talk at all of his war work; and she did not speak of her life at *Le Ciel Rouge*.

But more and more often as Lucy's health and strength returned, they found themselves falling silent, hands and eyes interlocked as their physical awareness of each other increased.

Lucy was now well enough to go for short walks and it became their habit to wander away from the grounds of the Château, strolling arm in arm through the vineyards, looking toward the fields of ripening corn, the gold bright with scarlet poppies. On such occasions they would pause and Alexis would take Lucy into his arms and kiss her soft mouth with hungry passion. Lucy no longer objected to kissing although, she told Alexis smiling, it seemed to have the strangest effect upon her, causing her legs to tremble and her body to be filled with a yearning that was both sad and exciting.

"Is it because I love you, Alexis?" she asked.

"It is because we love each other," he told her. "Love is so many different things, Lucy. Wanting to be a part of each other is one aspect of it."

The day before Alexis was due to depart, they took a last walk together in the bright August sunshine. Lucy was strangely silent. Edouard had not lifted his embargo upon their continued separation at night, insisting that Lucy needed as much rest as possible and that her sleep would be better for being undisturbed. But Lucy, as she walked with her hand tightly clasped in Alexis', made up her mind that this one night they would be together. It was not just that she was so aware of Alexis' need for her. She was equally aware of the need within herself. She had to prove to herself that in this way, too, she could be the kind of wife Alexis wanted.

When he came into her room to say goodnight, she reached up her arms and drew him down to her with an urgency that she had not previously shown.

"I want you to stay with me, Alexis!" she whispered. "I don't care what the doctor says. I want us to be together. I want to go to sleep in your arms!"

She was wearing a shell-pink satin nightgown, cut very low, the creamy white lace only just covering the curves of her breasts. Her hair was newly washed and it gleamed a silky gold cloud in the soft glow of the bedside lamp. Alexis buried his face in it, his mind and body in conflict. He had never desired her more intensely, more urgently, more passionately. Yet he could not bear the thought that he might harm her in any way. Sensing his hesitancy, Lucy said:

"Please, Alexis, don't leave me. If you will not come to my bed, then I shall get up and come to yours!" she added with a half-smile.

With a sigh of acceptance, Alexis removed his dressing gown and pajamas and climbed into bed beside her. Lucy, suddenly shy, reached out and switched off the bedside lamp. He heard her voice, trembling slightly as she said:

"I expect you think I am being very silly, Alexis, but it's almost as if we'd never done this before...I mean, it's different, isn't it? I'm not quite sure what to do. I want to be what *you* want, Alexis. I want to make you happy."

Alexis drew her into his arms and very gently, he kissed her.

"I want you to be yourself, Lucy—nothing more. What we do together isn't important provided we do it with love in our hearts. For a man to satisfy his needs with a woman is not the same as making love. The act may be the same but the emotions are quite different. Do you understand, my darling?"

"I'm not sure!" Lucy said nervously. "I'm frightened!"

"Not of me, surely!" Alexis protested.

"Of losing you again!" Lucy replied, her voice almost inaudible.

"My love, my only love!" Alexis cried. "You never lost me. Since that first day I looked across the Barratts' drawing room and saw you, I have loved you. I have never stopped loving you. Don't you understand, Lucy—I don't care about the past, if that is what is worrying you. It is the future—our future that matters. Nothing more!"

Very gently he began to stroke Lucy's hair, his hands moving to the soft curve of her cheeks and then to her shoulders. He could feel her slim body trembling but rigid in his grasp, and felt her fear. It enhanced his intense feeling of joy for now, added to his familiar longing for her, was the need to protect her; guide her; initiate her into the true delights of lovemaking.

It was indeed an initiation for Lucy. Alexis' hands moved to her breasts and she felt a mounting excitement as her nipples suddenly hardened beneath his touch. Unconsciously, she drew his head down to her so that she could experience the touch of his lips where his hands had been. For a moment, she was overcome by a swift maternal urge to nurse him as if he had been her child.

But the feeling was quickly replaced by a new sensation as his hands moved downwards to her thighs. Her nerves seemed to leap at his touch and a strange shivering longing began to spread from her loins into the very pit of her abdomen. She could feel his body, burning, rigid, hard in its manhood against her soft, yielding flesh. Her body lifted, arching against him, seeming of its own accord to demand his touch. But he would not come into her yet, although her legs had widened involuntarily to receive him.

All the time Lucy could hear the soft murmur of his voice, almost inaudible, speaking her name. She closed her eyes and surrendered her body to him. She felt the butterfly touch of his hands between her legs and the ache in her loins became a burning sweetness that seemed to increase until she felt such an agony of longing that her arms reached out and her fingers dug into Alexis' back as she tried to draw him down into her. As she looked up into his face searching for the reason for his denial of her need, she found him staring into her eyes.

"I love you, Lucy!" he said. "With all my heart, I love you!"

Her own words of love died on her lips as he lowered himself into her, filling the great empty cave that her body seemed to have become. She gasped with pleasure as he began to move, slowly at first and then with an urgency that answered her unconscious need. Her body began to move in harmony until they seemed to become one being. As if from another world Lucy heard herself crying out Alexis' name. She was aware of an agony of longing without understanding what it was she desired. Then suddenly, she felt Alexis plunge even deeper into her and the unbearable tension of her body was transformed into waves of indescribable pleasure pulsing through her.

She heard Alexis calling her name and was briefly aware that he too, was experiencing the same release, the same wonderful joy as herself. His breathing, like her own was coming in swift short gasps which gradually slowed with the beat of their hearts. Lucy managed to find her voice:

"I never knew it could be like this," she murmured as her hands reached upwards to his face. "Oh, Alexis," she added on an afterthought, "you should have told me...think how many years we have wasted..."

Alexis smiled in the darkness, perfectly content as he kissed her with deepest tenderness.

"It wouldn't have been like this, my darling. You didn't love me before!"

"I did, *I did!*!" Lucy cried, covering his face with kisses. "I just didn't know it, Alexis. I must have loved you. I can't believe that I didn't!"

"Perhaps you did!" Alexis conceded. "But it isn't important, my dearest one. We have our whole lives ahead of us. Let's hope this horrible war is over soon and then we can be together all the time."

He felt Lucy tremble suddenly beside him.

"I had forgotten you were leaving tomorrow. Alexis, I can't bear it. *Must* you go? Do you really have to go? Can't you stay just a *little longer?*"

His silence was her answer although he kissed her to comfort her.

"Now you must try to sleep," he said gently. "I don't want that doctor of yours blaming me tomorrow for the dark shadows under your eyes."

Lucy clung to him fiercely.

"Don't leave me now, Alexis. I promise I'll sleep if you stay here with me. I'll sleep in your arms. Oh, I *wish* you weren't going. What time do you leave?"

"Very early, I'm afraid," Alexis said regretfully. "There's a train to Paris at six o'clock and a driver will bring a car to take me to the station about twenty minutes to the hour. I'll stay with you until five when I shall have to get up."

Tears sprang to Lucy's eyes but she brushed them quickly away, not wishing Alexis to be upset by her unhappiness. Like a child she snuggled down beneath the bedclothes, laying her head in the curve of his shoulder. She knew it must be nearly midnight and that Alexis would have only five hours' rest before he left.

Although her mind was teeming with things she would like to have said to him she remained silent, allowing her thoughts to roam. She was still filled with wonder at the astonishing and totally unexpected miracle that had taken place between her and Alexis. It seemed unbelievable that she had known so much about the desires of men and yet never once supposed that women might feel the same passions; the same pleasures. Nicole had been the only girl at *Le Ciel Rouge* who had ever spoken of enjoying her work; of getting some personal satisfaction from it. For Lucy, what she had once done in those long-ago days bore no possible relationship to the lovemaking she had just shared with Alexis. Most of the time she had trained herself to think of other things—whether there would be ripe apricots in the market next day; what she would buy Yvette for her birthday; whether Madame would have her room repapered in the spring. There had been no intimacy; no kisses, for Lucy had always hated kissing. She had remained totally detached.

Smiling, she leant over and kissed Alexis' mouth. He was asleep, she knew, but the gesture was for her pleasure, not his. Her happiness was total but for the fact that she would be parted from him tomorrow. But six weeks would go quickly, she thought. It would give her time to get really well so that when he returned to her, she could go home with him no longer a convalescent but brimming with energy. Now suddenly she was very tired. Although she wanted to stay awake so that she would not waste one minute of the time left to her with Alexis, her eyes would not remain open. Despite her will, Lucy fell asleep.

She awoke to find Alexis already washed and shaved and about to get dressed. The dawn sunshine was streaming in the window and his naked body gleamed in the light filtering through the half-open curtains. Lucy felt her heart pounding as she recalled the previous night.

"Alexis!" she called softly.

He turned his head and saw she was awake, her arms held out in invitation. He hurried to the bedside and kissed her.

"I was trying so hard not to wake you," he said.

"That was unkind!" Lucy cried, clinging fiercely to him.

"I can't bear it if you go now," she added. "Alexis, I love you. I want..." she broke off, burying her burning face against his bare chest.

Alexis glanced at his watch. It was getting late...but he understood only too well what Lucy wanted of him and it matched his own urgent desire for her. Marie would be up and in the kitchen cooking his breakfast, but he could forego that easily enough. The scent of Lucy's sleep-warm body was a temptation beyond rejection.

They made love with a quick, desperate urgency. It was no less pleasurable for either of them but tinged nonetheless with the awareness of imminent parting. Afterwards, as he dressed hurriedly, Alexis tried to persuade Lucy to remain in bed. But she would not hear of it, insisting that she would go down to see him off.

"I'll go back to bed afterwards, I promise!" she said, handing Alexis his coat and tying his tie between kisses.

There were still a few minutes to spare as Alexis hurried down to the sitting room to drink a quick cup of Marie's freshly made coffee while Lucy went to the bathroom. She heard the soft hoot of a car horn and realizing that his driver was already awaiting him, she ran to the sitting room. Her bare feet made no sound as she went in through the half-open door. Alexis was kneeling on the floor by her uncle's tallboy, the bottom drawer open as he leaned over it. His coffee, untouched, was steaming on a tray on the table.

"Alexis?" Lucy said, only half-conscious of the strangeness of his behavior. Surely he too, had heard the car horn?

Alexis' head turned toward her sharply, as if he had been caught in an unworthy action. The expression in his eyes was equally strange as he regarded her almost with dismay.

"I never heard you coming!" he said abruptly as hurriedly, he closed the drawer and stood up.

"I think the car has come for you," Lucy said.

The expression on Alexis' face returned to normal as he smiled. He went across the room and took her in his arms.

"Promise me you will take care of yourself, Lucy," he said as he kissed her. She nodded, tears choking in her throat as she said huskily:

"You too, Alexis!"

And then with a last hurried kiss, he was gone.

Lucy waited until the sound of the car wheels crunching the gravel of the drive had died away before she went slowly back to her bedroom. The hospital was already waking up below. The familiar sounds reached her ears as she climbed back into bed. The pillow still held the indent of Alexis' head and Lucy buried her face in it as she allowed the tears to flow.

It was silly to cry, she thought. Everything between her and Alexis was perfect now; their marriage was all it should be. They were going to be happy for ever more. She loved Alexis with all her heart. There was no longer any doubt in her mind what love was. Its beauty, its perfection, its wonder were understandable to her at long last. But what Alexis had not warned her about was that, without the person who mattered so much, love was not only joy—it was also loneliness and pain.

Chapter 27

❧

October 1917 — July 1918

By October the weather was abominable and the soldiers' letters home spoke of the No Man's Land between the Allied and German lines being a quagmire of sticky mud, punctuated with deep, water-logged shell holes in which wounded men often drowned. Movement by troops, guns or tanks was almost impossible. The water increased the deadliness of the mustard gas released by the Germans. It soaked into the mud and its fumes continued to poison men long after it had been released. All soldiers now carried respirators but the gas saturated their uniforms and burnt their skins.

Toward the end of October, the weather improved slightly and Toby was able to move the Allied Front line flags forward very slightly on his map, only to find he must move them back again soon afterward as the guns became bogged down in the mud.

But on November 6th the Canadian divisions stormed the Passchendale Ridge and the town was finally captured. It was during this battle that the first aid post in which Major Peter Rose was operating, received a direct hit from a Howitzer shell. Peter Rose was one of the few survivors. But there could be no future for him in his profession. Within two days of the attack, he was in a hospital ship heading for Dover, blinded in both eyes.

Stella remained courageously calm as she prepared herself to go up to London to see him in Moorfield Hospital. Although she knew it would be some while before he was released from hospital to convalesce at Rochford, she refused to think beyond the time when she would have him safely home.

"I shall not allow him to despair," she told Willow as she put on her coat and hat and picked up her gloves. "Peter always said he intended one day to write a book. When he comes home he shall dictate it to me. And there is always Sir

436

Arthur Pearson's hostel, St. Dunstan's, where Peter can learn the blind alphabet. He was talking to me with great enthusiasm about the developments there since it opened two years ago..."

"With Stella behind him, Rose will be all right," Toby said after she had gone. He could not grieve too much for this one casualty when he had read that very morning that over three hundred thousand men had been wounded or had fallen during the capture of Passchendale. There was news of another sort to worry over, too. The Bolsheviks with their doctrine of communism had taken over the government of Russia and were arranging armistices with Germany, Austria and Turkey. Russia could no longer be counted upon as an Ally. In all, there seemed little to cheer anyone's spirits as winter approached.

It was a further month before England had cause for rejoicing. In November, four hundred and seventy-six tanks burst through the Hindenburg Line at Cambrai and the Front at last moved forward four precious miles. But that minor victory was to be short-lived. By the end of the first week in December, the Germans had counterattacked and the British were left occupying only the rear positions of the original Hindenburg Line.

"I fear I'm in danger of becoming hardened to all these horrors," Willow remarked to Toby following a telephone call from Lady Barratt in which the poor woman had announced that her only remaining son, Henry, was in hospital.

"I very nearly said 'thank goodness!'" Lady Barratt had added ruefully, "for at least my dear Henry is only ill and not dead. It seems he crashed his airplane following an observation sortie over the Turkish lines in the hill country northeast of Jerusalem. He managed to evade capture by the Turks but it took him three days to walk back to the British lines. By that time his feet were very badly blistered and had become gangrenous. Goodness only knows when the boy will be home."

"At least General Allenby has secured Jerusalem without a shell or bullet touching the Holy City's walls," Toby said sighing. "Lloyd George's faith in Allenby has proved well-justified. The *Times* says the Turkish garrison was in flight when he was handed the keys."

But Willow was no longer listening. The postmistress had arrived that morning with a letter from Silvie and its contents concerned her far more deeply than the war in the Middle East.

"Alexis has now been gone over sixteen weeks," Silvie had written, *"I have been trying to assure poor Lucy that there is nothing for her to worry about but the truth is, dearest Willow, I myself am very worried. Alexis was so adamant that he would be back in six weeks at the latest.*

"Lucy becomes more silent every day. She is working much too hard—often quite unnecessarily, and Edouard de Valle, her doctor, is as anxious as I am. Lucy will not listen to either of us and insists she is perfectly well.

"Can you ask Toby to make further inquiries at the Foreign Office once more? I know when I requested this last month, he came up against a blank wall but maybe by now they have news of Alexis. Someone surely must know where he is..."

Lucy was using the selfsame words to herself as she sat restlessly beside Silvie, watching her uncle and Edouard playing chess by the fireside. She had ceased to talk to anyone about Alexis' continued absence. There seemed to her to be only two alternatives—that he had met some dreadful fate; or that he was intentionally staying away from her, using the war as an excuse until he could find a better reason to make a final break with her.

Several weeks had now passed since this possibility first crossed her mind. One late November day, desperate for some clues to Alexis' whereabouts, she decided to see if he had by chance put some private documents in the drawer of the tallboy. If she could only write to him, she thought, it would ease the anxiety and the longing in her heart. When her uncle and aunt were both absent from the room, she had gone to the tallboy and pulled open the bottom drawer.

It was the first time Lucy had seen Maurice Dubois' painting of her which he had called *La Perle*. When she had run away from his studio the day he had completed it, she knew nothing of the portrait's implications. She now felt sick with horror as she stared down at it with adult eyes, understanding its meaning. This then was how Maurice had seen her. This was how Alexis must have seen her when he had put the pictures in the drawer! How he had come by them she had no idea. Her aunt had told her before she fell ill that Maurice had died and she had quickly forgotten about him—been happy to do so. It had not crossed her mind to consider what had become of his paintings. This particular one she had long since forgotten. Where, she wondered, was the original? Did Alexis know? Had he been as horrified as herself to see it?

It occurred to Lucy that she could ask her aunt and uncle to tell her of Alexis' reactions. But the memory of those last few minutes shared with him before he left for Russia had prevented her doing so. She recalled now that he had looked somewhat guilty—as if he had only just discovered the paintings himself.

The more Lucy stared at the picture, the more frightened she became. The expression was so true to life, one could not doubt its genuine portraiture. Although she was certain she had never looked like that, she could believe that had she stayed at *Le Ciel Rouge*, she could very easily have become the girl in Maurice's painting. Had the same horrifying thought struck Alexis too? He knew only the bare facts about her past. He had never seen *Le Ciel Rouge* or the girls who lived and worked there. How depraved, how vulgar he must think her as he looked at *La Perle*. Did Uncle Pelham think her so now? If, in the middle of the game of chess, Lucy were to bring out that photograph and put it before Edouard, she could imagine how quickly that admiring, interested look would disappear from *his* eyes; how quickly his respect for her would vanish! Her own self-respect was gone; and for the first time in Lucy's life—she hated her past.

But despite all her fears of Alexis' change of heart, she continued to go about her duties, hoping against hope that he would suddenly arrive, as he had last time, to surprise her for Christmas; that he had not turned against her; that he would take her in his arms and everything would be as it was the night before he left.

But still no word came from or about Alexis and as the year 1918 started, Lucy began to doubt if she would ever see him again. She began to spend more of her brief hours of leisure in Edouard's company—not because she found him attractive but because he afforded her a measure of distraction from her painful thoughts. He seemed intent upon jollying her along, bringing a smile to her lips, a spark of interest to her eyes.

Although Silvie was well aware of Lucy's suffering, she said nothing to her, sensitive to her reticence. She had seen the burgeoning of love between her and Alexis during his summer visit and she feared for Lucy's sanity were something terrible to have happened to him. With this in mind, she encouraged Lucy's companionship with Edouard de Valle, grateful to the young doctor for being there to provide the friendship and diversion she needed.

"Who knows but Lucy may one day need more than Edouard's friendship!" she said gloomily to Pelham. "He would not make at all a bad husband for the poor girl and obviously he adores her." She ignored Pelham's reproachful comment that Lucy was by no means widowed nor particularly in need of consolation as yet.

But Silvie's words were uncannily prophetic, except that it was not news of Alexis' death Lucy was to receive, but the totally unexpected, tragic news of the death of her child.

At Rochford Manor the whole family were still trying to come to terms with the horrifying accident that occurred one late January afternoon. Heavy snowfalls had kept the children indoors for several days prior to the event and they were becoming restless. Suddenly the weather changed, the temperatures dropped and everything froze. Although it was bitterly cold, the sky was a brilliant blue and the white snow covering the countryside sparkled in the winter sunshine.

It continued to freeze for several more days and an invitation arrived for the children to go skating on the lake at Glenfield Hall. It was young Eleanor Barratt's sixteenth birthday and her mother was giving a small party to celebrate the occasion. The older children brought their skating boots down from the attic, and, as the roads were considered too icy for the motor car, the big sleigh was brought out of the stables. Harnessed to one of the remaining greys, it would be an added excitement to their ride in it to Glenfield.

Patience was confined to bed with influenza, which seemed fortuitous in that it was only just possible for Stella and Nanny Meredith to squeeze into the sleigh with the six children.

Eleanor, who was spending the Christmas holiday with her parents greeted the family excitedly as they reached the Hall with glowing cheeks and laughing faces.

"Father went down to the lake this morning with the gardener," she told them, linking her arm in Alice's affectionately. "He says it's perfectly safe providing we keep to the east end of the lake. The ice is not quite so thick at the other end because of the trees. Come on, everyone. Don't let's waste any time. Let's go straight down there. I can open my presents later."

Down by the lakeside, Stella helped the older girls and her twins fasten their skates, while Nanny Meredith kept a watchful eye on Teo and Jamie who were already contentedly sliding about on the ice. For half an hour, the crisp bright air was filled with the sound of their shouts and laughter, but suddenly the seven-year-old Lawrence took a nasty tumble and cut one of his knees as he fell against Eleanor's sharp-edged skates. The bleeding would not be staunched with a handkerchief and Stella realized she must take the child to the house to have the leg properly bandaged. Nanny Meredith was left to comfort Lawrence's tearful twin, Katherine, who, unable to bear the sight of her brother's discomfort, was weeping in sympathy. As Stella disappeared with Lawrence between the tall, snow-clad rhododendrons lining the drive up to the Hall, Nanny Meredith comforted the little girl and tried to encourage her back onto the ice. It was while her attention was thus distracted that the five-year-old Teo espied a moorhen on the far side of the lake and forgetful of the warning she had been given, ran across the ice to get a closer look at the little bird.

Light as the child was, her weight was too much for the thin covering of ice beneath the overhanging branches. A series of fissures spread outwards from the bank. The noise of the cracking ice was sufficient to warn Teo of the danger, but as she turned to go back across the lake, there was another ominous crack as a large section of the ice gave way beneath her.

From the far side of the lake, Nanny Meredith had heard the noise and stood watching with horror as the tiny figure of the child disappeared slowly in front of her eyes. With a terrified scream, she started toward the spot. But the ice impeded her progress and she slipped and slid and fell like an ungainly clown in her dark brown uniform. Her bonnet flew off and her gray hair, dislodged from its pins, blinded her vision.

Unaware of what had happened to Teo, the older children had nevertheless stopped skating in order to watch Nanny Meredith's clumsy progress across the ice. Their mouths gaping, their eyes followed her in utter astonishment.

Eleanor found her voice and shouted a warning.

"You're not supposed to go over there, Nanny!"

Beside her, little Jamie tugged at her arm.

"Where's Teo gone?" he asked in his small, piping voice. "Me and her were playing. Where's she gone, El'nor? Where's Nanny going?"

Only then did the girls realize why Nanny Meredith had screamed in so shocking a manner; why she had raced away across the ice. Aghast, they watched as she threw herself down and stretched out full-length on the cold wet surface. Eleanor took charge, grabbing Alice's arm as she spoke.

"You little ones are to stay here," she said sharply to Zandra, Jamie and the weeping Katherine. "And don't you *dare* move. Come on, Alice. We must help Nanny."

Silently, the two girls skated swiftly across the lake. They could now see Teo's red woolen hat floating in the dark circle of water where the ice had broken away. Nanny Meredith was trying frantically to reach it, the front of her cape inches deep in the water that had overflowed onto the ice.

"Lie down—not too near me—and get hold of my feet," she shouted to Eleanor and Alice. Both girls obeyed her instantly, and thus anchored, Nanny Meredith reached further forward. But for the third time the air was rent with a loud report and the top half of her body slipped downwards as the ice beneath her gave way. Eleanor and Alice pulled frantically on her legs and bit by bit eased her back to safety. The poor woman was now crying hysterically as the water poured from her drenched hair and clothes. Too shocked to speak, the girls turned their heads to stare at the gaping hole where Teo had been. There was no sign of the little red hat.

"I'm going to get Mother," Eleanor said, wondering how her voice could remain so calm when inside she was shaking with horror. Alice was crying quietly. "You'd better stay here with Nanny, Alice," she muttered. "I'll try not to be long."

Then she caught sight of Stella on the far side of the lake, returning with a bandaged Lawrence. At that moment, her self-control snapped and she began screaming, the sound of her voice drowning the unbearable truth of which Stella Rose was still blissfully unaware.

The horror of Teo's death affected them all. But for Willow and Toby there was the additional distress of deciding how Lucy should be informed of this dreadful event.

"If only Alexis were here!" Willow said, over and over again. But no one knew where Alexis was, and Toby felt that in his absence, it must be Silvie and Pelham who broke the news to Lucy.

"To send a telegram would be cruel in the circumstances," he said to Willow. "It is not as if she could come home in time for the child's funeral—and even if we were able to get her home with the help of the Red Cross, I see no point in putting her through such an ordeal."

Teo's body had been recovered when, two days after the accident, the ice had melted sufficiently for a team of estate workers from Rochford and Glenfield to wade out in line until they had come upon her little body caught in a tangle of weeds.

"Lucy must be spared such terrible details," Willow agreed tearfully. In all the circumstances, it seemed best to write to Silvie and leave it to her to tell Lucy as best she could.

"I wish I did not have to ask you to undertake such a tragic task, dearest Silvie," Willow wrote. *"I don't know how you will find a way to tell her. You will understand that I can hardly bear to write about it; but I expect Lucy will want to know the facts. Try to make her understand that really no one was at fault. It was a series of mishaps. Lady Barratt feels there is a jinx upon their house but thank God, Henry should be home soon and Gillian is coming down from Scotland to be with her parents as Lady Barratt is so distraught.*

"Toby is still trying to get news of Alexis. Wherever he may be, if he knew of this terrible tragedy, he would come home to comfort Lucy. We would like to have Lucy here with us but maybe she is better at a distance from the scene of the accident. I thank God in my prayers that it did not happen at Rochford as I do not think I could bear to live here were that the case.

"Everyone is deeply shocked and most touchingly every soldier contributed to a beautiful wreath for Teo. She has been buried in St. Stephen's and Toby has ordered a marble angel chosen by Zandra to put over Teo's grave. Zandra is perhaps our only comfort for she tells us with the utmost gravity that Teo is quite safe now with God since luckily she was not 'one of the Limbo babies.' Lucy will know what that means. I just wish I had Zandra's faith.

"Oh, Silvie, when will all the suffering end..."

"I wish I could delegate this task to you, Pelham," Silvie said as she handed Willow's letter to him across the breakfast table. "But I am being cowardly, I know. I just wish that men could sometimes cope with the tragedies of life."

With a sinking heart, she called Lucy into her own bedroom, and with her arm around the girl's thin shoulders, she did her best to break the news gently, trying to eliminate the more gruesome details. But Lucy demanded fact after fact. Her eyes were cold and, Silvie thought uneasily, condemning as she looked unwaveringly into her aunt's face.

"Your mother is quite right, Lucy dear," she said quickly. "No one was to blame. If Lawrence hadn't fallen..."

"I'm not blaming anyone else, Aunt Silvie, I am blaming myself," Lucy interrupted. "I should have been there to look after Teo. After all, she was *my* child."

Silvie looked shocked.

"But *chérie*, that is nonsense," she cried. "You know very well that your Nanny was totally devoted to little Teo, and you have told me many times how sensible and responsible she is. Besides, a woman in your position is not expected to look after her own child. How could you possibly have done so, even had you stayed in England?"

Lucy's face remained impassive.

"Other women take care of their own children," she said stonily. "It is only the rich who abrogate their responsibilities. If I'd really loved her, her safety would have meant more to me than anything else in the world. I shall never forgive myself. *Never!*"

"Lucy, surely you can see that even had it been you who was there on the lake instead of Nanny, exactly the same set of circumstances could have prevailed. Don't you understand that it might have happened anyway?"

For a long moment Lucy seemed lost in her own thoughts. When she spoke, it was in a tone that Silvie could not understand.

"Yes, I know that perfectly well—and I think you are right. As you say, it *had* to happen." Gently, she detached herself from Silvie's embrace and stood up. "You mustn't worry about me, Aunt Silvie, I am not going to have hysterics or throw myself out of the window." She walked over to the door. "I appreciate that it can't have been very nice for you having to tell me about it. Thank you for being so kind. If you are writing to Mother, will you tell her she was perfectly right, I wouldn't have wanted to go to Teo's funeral. This way, I don't have to think of her as dead, do I?"

As Lucy left the room, her head erect, her movements as unhurried and graceful as always, Silvie stared after her departing niece with a look of bewilderment. She had expected an emotional outburst of some kind—tears, most certainly. For a moment, the uncomfortable thought struck her that maybe Lucy had not really loved her child as much as Willow supposed. But Silvie had not worked here in the hospital for the past two and a half years without having learned that grief could affect people differently. It was always easier for those who could give in to their suffering. Others concealed their emotions, finding this the only way they could cope with their grief. Lucy, she thought, must come to terms with her tragedy in her own way, and there was nothing she could do to help.

From that morning onwards Lucy refused to talk of her child in the same stubborn way that she refused to talk about Alexis.

Lucy's suffering was internal. She was convinced that her child's death was God's retribution. Her thoughts had returned to her Convent days when the Mother Superior had threatened them continually with ultimate punishment for their undiscovered sins. Sooner or later God would be avenged upon them for the evil ways they hoped to conceal, she said. And Lucy now accepted that she had behaved very wickedly. Not only had her life at *Le Ciel Rouge* been terribly wrong, but so too had been her secret vengeance upon Maurice Dubois. Teo had been his child. What more fitting punishment could God inflict than that she should be taken from her. The German, Anton Schwartz, had made one attempt to take Teo away—and failed. Now God had done it.

Lucy told herself she must try somehow to accept the fact that she was never meant to be happy—or not for long. She ceased to hope that she would ever see Alexis again.

Only too well aware of Lucy's growing depression, both Silvie and Pelham tried to reassure her. With Russia in such disarray, caught in the grips of the internal revolt against the old order, there were a hundred reasons why Alexis might not have been able to leave the country or send word of his whereabouts, they both told her, trying to give her some hope for the future.

Edouard de Valle shared Lucy's belief that Alexis was dead. Her silent suffering aroused all his most chivalrous instincts and he no longer made secret of the fact that he was hopelessly in love with her.

"I want to marry Lucy," he admitted openly to Silvie and Pelham. "I realize that it could be some time before she gets over her husband's death—if indeed he is dead. Even then, she may not turn to me for comfort. But I wanted you both to know my intentions—in case you feel I am monopolizing too much of her time!"

"My dear fellow," Pelham said, "Silvie and I are grateful for your attentions to Lucy. We are naturally terribly concerned for her—first Alexis' disappearance and now the child ... The more distractions we can find for her the better."

"If only we knew whether the worst had happened or not!" Silvie said sighing. "It's the uncertainty that is so trying—and it must be agonizing for Lucy. She was very much in love with her husband, Edouard. And he with her."

"I do have several influential contacts in Paris," Edouard said thoughtfully. "If it would help, I might be able to obtain news for you through a friend of mine who is fairly high up in our Intelligence Service. If you think it worth a try, I can go to Paris and at least make a few inquiries."

They accepted his offer gratefully and Pelham insisted on driving Edouard to the city himself. The Vicomte was still unable to walk without the aid of a stick and Pelham's assistance would greatly ease the physical effort his plan involved.

Lucy was unaware of the true reason for their visit to Paris. Edouard muttered something vaguely about seeing a bone specialist—and she did not inquire further. Although she appreciated his company and liked him as a friend, she was indifferent to him as a man. Her emotions were frozen somewhere deep inside her. She doubted whether she would ever feel deeply about anything again. Certainly she knew she would never love again. It had taken her six long years to discover her love for Alexis and in as many weeks, she had lost him. She did not want another love—or another child. The only reference she ever made to Teo's death was to tell Silvie that she could never forgive herself for leaving her.

"I should have been there to look after her!" she reiterated in a cold, self-condemnatory voice.

Edouard and Pelham were gone for three days. When they returned, it was to bring the worst possible news. Edouard's contact in French Intelligence had finally managed to speak directly to Fanshaw in London. Although Fanshaw had no proof of the facts he had received, he had learned from sources in Russia that Alexis Zemski had been shot by the Red Army, probably some time during November of the previous year. Fanshaw had decided to withhold this information from Alexis' wife until the facts were verified. This was proving difficult. Alexis had had a servant-cum-bodyguard with him at the time he had been shot, and the man had been arrested. As far as Fanshaw knew the man had been accused of 'aiding and abetting a Royalist' and was now in a labor gang working in one of the Baltic ports. Fanshaw might not be able to obtain positive proof of the death of Count Zemski until the fellow was released.

"I suppose we do have to tell Lucy?" Silvie asked, knowing even as she posed the question to the two men on their return that it would have to be done. "Coming so soon on top of Teo's death, it seems very cruel!" she added unhappily. "I'm afraid she will break down completely. She has been living on her nerves for months!"

But Lucy listened to the news with the same lack of any outward sign of emotion as she had received Willow's account of her child's death. Only her extreme pallor and the tight clenching of her fists as Silvie was speaking, gave any indication of her silent horror.

Lucy had tried to prepare herself for news of Alexis' death. But now when it came, she could not accept it. She *had* to see him again—if only once, she thought agonizingly. She had to know whether he had stopped loving her after he had seen *La Perle*. If she was to live the rest of her life without him, she must know that nothing—not even the painting—had turned him against her. She could not forget how strangely he had regarded her that morning when she had surprised him at the drawer of the tallboy! Had his eyes been condemning or forgiving? Would she ever know?

Silvie wrote a long letter to Willow about her daughter.

"It is so hard to know how Lucy really feels," she said. *"She refuses to discuss anything of a personal nature with me and we talk only trivialities. Edouard—her doctor who I wrote and told you about—is convinced that it is only a matter of time before her control breaks. We are all keeping a close watch on her without appearing to do so.*

"Pelham and I read in our newspaper (three weeks out of date!) that you now have ration books and can only obtain sugar, meat and butter in limited quantities. We do not suffer too badly here with the Red Cross supplies. But what concerns us more is to read of the air raids by those horrifying Gotha

bombers—far more terrifying I imagine, than the old Zeppelins. Was it true that over forty people in London were killed by a bomb while hiding in an air raid shelter? Thank goodness you and the family do not live there in these times!

"Have you news of Mark for me to give Lucy? And how is Oliver?"

Willow sighed as she read Silvie's letter. Mark was fine—making excellent progress at Roehampton and hoping very soon to be fitted with his new, artificial leg. But Oliver—although he was safe and sound and home on leave—was causing her deep concern. She tried to tell herself that it was only natural he should look tired and strained considering the constant danger to his life each time he went up in his airplane. Yet although he had just celebrated his nineteenth birthday he looked nearly ten years older than his true age.

It was Toby who pointed out to her that there could be a very different reason behind Oliver's quietness and depression.

"I think the boy's in love!" he said, as he lay in the darkness of their bedroom with Willow's head cradled on his shoulder. "And although you are not going to be in the least happy to hear it, my love, I fear young Jane is at the root of all this."

"Jane!" Willow cried, startled into a sitting position. She switched on the bedside lamp and looked into Toby's sympathetic face uneasily.

He nodded.

"I was watching the two of them in the sitting room this evening and suddenly I realized why their behavior seemed so strange. They were both studiously avoiding one another the way you and I once tried to conceal our love."

"You don't think they may have quarreled?" Willow asked.

"No, I don't think that!" Toby replied honestly. "I think they are in love, Willow!"

Willow frowned.

"But that's nonsense. They're like brother and sister."

"But they're not! You and I both know that," said Toby quietly.

Willow's face paled and her hand went up to cover her mouth.

"But, Toby, neither of them know Rowell was Jane's father. So even if they are in love, why should they hide their feelings?"

"You are forgetting that Philip knew the truth," Toby reminded her gently. "And I think he may have told Oliver when he was home on that last leave before he was killed. I suspect Philip may have guessed how the two youngsters felt about each other—he was very close to Jane—and wanted to warn Oliver before it went too far."

Willow was silent, her expression profoundly unhappy as she searched her mind for reasons to refute this unwelcome suspicion. But each remembered incident served only to confirm Toby's suspicions—Jane's sudden reticence, Oliver's last leave when he had taken Alice, not Jane, with him to London; Oliver's failure to write to Jane.

Toby drew her back into his arms, stroking the fair hair that was now slightly touched with threads of silver.

"The past can never quite be buried, can it?" he asked rhetorically. "Do you think the time has come to tell Oliver the whole truth?"

Willow's eyes widened with sudden understanding—and concern. If Toby was right, and Oliver knew Rowell was Jane's father, Oliver would believe himself to be the girl's half-brother. No wonder he was aghast at the thought of being in love with Jane. He had no possible way of knowing the true facts about his own parentage, unless she were to act on Toby's suggestion and tell her son the *whole* truth.

"But I couldn't do that, Toby," she said slowly and with difficulty.

How could she tell Oliver that she had been unfaithful to his father, and that he was not Rowell's son? How could she hope that he would ever again look on her with love and respect? He was far too young to understand her desperate loneliness during those years when Rowell had spent so much time away from home with his mistress; how tormented she had been by her secret love for Toby; how tempted she had been by the transitory moment of pleasure with Pelham which afterward she was to regret so deeply.

"*I can't tell him*, Toby," she repeated.

"It has to be your decision, my dear," Toby replied quietly. "Oliver is your son and it is for you, his mother, to tell him the truth if you feel it best for him."

Willow's face was now chalk white. Her hands were trembling.

"Toby, I can't! You cannot expect me to reveal something so shameful! It would be a terrible blow to him!"

It was a moment or two before Toby spoke again. When

he did so, there was no hesitation in his voice as he said very carefully:

"I think what you must do, Willow, is ask yourself what matters most to you—your son's happiness or your own. That may sound cruel but in the last resort, if Oliver did lose his respect for you—which I doubt *very* much—would it matter if he were to gain true happiness?"

"You think I should tell him!" Willow said miserably.

"If not you, Willow, then me, perhaps? Maybe it would be better if I were to tell him. But I think one of us should. Not with emotion but as a statement of fact followed by a quiet explanation."

Toby was right, Willow thought. It would be selfish to withhold the truth. But she, not Toby, must be the one to tell Oliver in the right way. But there seemed to her to be no right way to tell her son that his father was not really his father at all; that he was his uncle's child . . .

"Don't look so horrified," Toby said, taking her back into his arms, "Oliver is no longer a child. And he has always loved and admired Pelham. As a matter of fact, the boy is far more like him to look at and in character than ever he was like Rowell. It's my belief Oliver had little affection for my eldest brother and still less respect. He might even welcome the news, for that reason only. And if he does love Jane, he'll know he can eventually marry her if that's what he wants. They are only cousins, you realize. There's no close blood tie to stand in their way."

Willow was still far from reassured.

"Don't you think the stigma of illegitimacy will horrify him, Toby?"

Toby sighed.

"I doubt it, my darling. We are in the twentieth century now and in the middle of an horrific war. The social niceties are of little concern to any of us any more—we are all too busy fighting for survival—and I am sure that will be Oliver's attitude if it is not actually that of our modern society. Besides, it is not as if anyone knows or will ever know other than Oliver himself. We are not going to put an announcement in the *Times*! Philip, Mark and Jane all have the surname 'Grey' on their birth certificates—I know that is so because Philip told me. And Oliver is a Rochford, born in wedlock. As you know, my love, had the truth been told when Rowell died, it would have been I who inherited the title and estate. But I never wanted either, and so everything is all right, Willow, and Oliver will realize it. He's an intelligent, understanding chap."

Oliver had two more days of his leave left. Before Toby and Willow settled to sleep, they decided that Willow would tell him the true facts on the following afternoon when she would be free from her duties on the wards.

But fate decreed otherwise. During luncheon, Dutton brought a telegram for Oliver, ordering him to return immediately to his squadron.

"That means there is something brewing," Oliver said with a glint of returning excitement. "They warned me I could be recalled. I'll have to rush off and pack. With luck, I'll get the two-fifteen to London!"

Toby shot a warning glance at Willow who was regarding him across the table with a look of anxiety.

"Confessions should not be made in a hurry, my dear," he said after she had bidden Oliver a tearful farewell at the station. "It can wait until his next leave. Better he should have nothing on his mind if he's going back to war, especially if he is right and something big is brewing across the Channel."

American troops were now pouring into France at the rate of fifty thousand men a month. The day after Oliver's departure, Willow and Toby received a letter from Ed Baines who commented on the fact that many of the newly arrived troops had not completed their training.

"They're a brave bunch of boys and your Tommies think highly of them for coming to their assistance," he wrote. *"There's little doubt that the sight of them has put fresh heart into everyone, me too! You may already have heard the new song: 'The Yanks are coming, it'll soon be over, over there!'"*

But if the sight of American uniforms cheered the Allies, it had a far less desirable effect upon the enemy who promptly counteracted by launching a major offensive, concentrated in the province of Picardy. The disintegration of the Russian army had increased Germany's confidence that she could now win the war. That confidence received a bitter blow when despite all efforts, their armies failed to reach Amiens. They failed again early in April to capture the vital railway center of Hazebrouck further north; and yet again when they tried once more to capture Amiens.

The Allied resistance was only short-lived comfort to the French who deeply resented the shelling of Paris by a huge

German cannon some seventy miles away. By the end of May, the Germans were pressing hard toward the capital and at the Château d'Orbais, the sound of gunfire had become louder and was almost continuous.

Edouard de Valle had at last reached an understanding with the hospital's *Médecin de Chef*. The fact that he was no longer fit for active service did not detract from his medical qualifications, he had pointed out repeatedly, and he was now a fully fledged member of the Voluntary Aid Detachment working under the senior French doctor. A lot of the time Edouard worked from a wheelchair in which he could make his rounds more quickly and less tiringly for himself. As the sounds of warfare drew closer, it was obvious to everyone that his presence at the hospital could prove essential if they were suddenly to become a casualty clearing station. Those patients who it was at all possible to move, were packed off by train to Paris to make place for the expected influx of wounded.

Silvie tried her utmost to persuade Lucy to leave with the wounded for the comparative safety of Paris. But Lucy would not even listen to her aunt's pleading.

"You know very well you will need every pair of hands available," she said with quiet stubbornness.

"But you could be killed, Lucy. Worse even. I beg you..."

"No!" Lucy broke in fiercely. "If you are afraid, Aunt Silvie, *you* go. *I'm* staying here!"

"Let her be, Silvie!" Pelham said wearily. "She's a Rochford when all is said and done and they don't believe in running away!"

But Silvie was uncertain if it was courage dictating Lucy's decision or a subconscious desire to put an end to her life and with it her inner suffering. If Lucy was not afraid to die, it could only be because she did not want to live.

"Willow will never forgive me if Lucy comes to any harm!" she said unhappily to Pelham.

But Willow was still ignorant of the extent of the German advances and had been greatly heartened by the cutting from the April 24th edition of the *Times* Toby had pinned up on the board in the hall. Headed "DARING FEAT AT SEA," it gave an account of British naval forces carrying out a raid on the Belgian coastal town of Zeebrugge. Under cover of darkness, *Thetis*, *Intrepid* and *Iphigenia*, filled with concrete, had been deliberately sunk to blockade the mouth of the canal, preventing the exit of the German U-boats which had been caus-

ing such havoc to the merchant shipping. Over two thousand
ships had been sunk the previous year, and the raid had been
daring and successfully accomplished.

For as long as he could, Toby kept from Willow the news
of the situation on the Western Front. But soon enough word
spread through Rochford that the Germans were only thirty-
five miles northwest of Rheims and the men in the wards
were telling each other gloomily that they were back almost
where they had started in 1914. By the end of May, the enemy
was within three to four miles of Rheims and the Château
d'Orbais was receiving the expected casualties direct from the
battle areas.

For Lucy it was as if time had retrogressed and she was
experiencing once again her first day at the hospital. But this
time the Germans were not retreating but advancing and the
noise of the gunfire was frighteningly close. And this time,
she told herself, she could face without flinching the more
terrible sights brought in on stretchers; she could deal with
them at least capably until one of the doctors could take over.

Her life was now lived in the big reception room called
'Admissions.' Time ceased to have any meaning. Every now
and again she would look up and see Edouard calmly attending
to each emergency as if it were an ordinary day in the hospital.
Yet there was barely a spare inch of floor space for another
stretcher. As the orderlies carried out the dead, the spaces
were quickly filled by other wounded men. Lucy lost count
of the number who died before she could do anything to help
them. Death became too commonplace to matter. It meant
no more than room for another patient.

Every now and again, another V.A.D. would appear at her
elbow to relieve her while she went wearily to the emergency
canteen set up by Silvie in the main hall. Twice she nearly
fell asleep before someone told her to go and lie down for an
hour or two. On her return nothing seemed to have changed.
Edouard was still there in his chair, leaning forward over a
mutilated body. The wounded were still being carried in or
were staggering in on foot; the nurses and V.A.D.s were still
washing, bandaging, giving injections of morphine, wheeling
men away to the now overflowing wards. The only difference
seemed to be that the piles of bloody bandages and field dressings had grown larger.

For three long, exhausting days Lucy existed, doing what
was necessary in a kind of mental vacuum, snatching a little

food, a little sleep before returning yet again to Hell. For that is what 'Admissions' had to be, she thought, hearing with a detached objection the groans, the screams, the strange-sounding wails of men whose pain had reduced them to little more than animals. The smell of blood and sickness and antiseptic she no longer noticed.

Someone told her that the Germans had crossed the Marne and the railway line and that no trains were running from Épernay. Someone else said that the road to Château-Thierry lying between them and Paris had been taken by the enemy, and that anyone trying to reach Epernay with supplies from the city must travel to the south via Châlons-sur-Marne. But Lucy had no energy left to concern herself with such matters, although a small part of her tired brain registered the fact that they might soon be surrounded.

She was not quite certain when first she became aware that the sense of urgency had left the room; that there were now several empty spaces on the floor and that the noise and confusion had almost died away.

Edouard came over to her.

"That's enough, Lucy," he said gently. "You can go to bed now. The emergency is over. That's an order, Lucy. Off you go!"

She nodded, too tired even to talk. Somehow she made her way upstairs and without undressing, fell onto the bed. For the first time since she had learned of Alexis' death, she slept without dreaming, without waking. When consciousness returned twelve hours later, it was daylight. Memories of the previous days and nights flooded her mind and immediately she jumped out of bed and donning a clean uniform, hurried downstairs. Silvie was in the kitchen talking to Marie. Somewhere close at hand, guns were firing and the crockery on Marie's kitchen dresser was rattling with every shell burst.

"The French and Italian troops are counterattacking," Silvie said quietly. "Edouard gave orders you were not to be woken. We are more than likely going to be busy again very soon. He wanted you to have some rest before you went back on duty! Your uncle meanwhile has driven to your old Convent, Lucy. He's hoping to arrange for some of the wounded to be nursed there by the nuns."

Lucy nodded as she sat down on one of the rush-seated kitchen chairs and accepted a cup of steaming café-au-lait from Marie. Her whole body seemed to be aching, in particular her back and across her shoulders. But despite the pain, she quickly made her way down to the wards.

For most of that day and the following one, Lucy was instructed to assist Edouard. Under his calm direction, she had frequently to perform tasks that were normally confined to trained nurses.

"Just do exactly as I tell you," he said. "I want this man anesthetized. Now bring that machine over here..."

She became an automation, following his instructions minutely and becoming slowly more efficient. Edouard himself seemed tireless and she refused to give in to her own exhaustion. Outside the hospital the battles continued to rage, the German lines slowly but surely being forced back. They judged the situation by the slowly decreasing numbers of wounded coming straight from the battlefields. As the day wore on, the stretchers arriving contained men who had been hastily patched up in Field Dressing Stations. Gradually the hospital staff were able to return to a less hectic routine until finally even the sound of gunfire died away.

"It is like the ebb tide," Edouard said when after a whole day's sleep, he presented himself for the evening meal in Silvie's and Pelham's private rooms. "The waves are no longer pounding on our shore but with their departure, we are left with the driftwood, the flotsam and jetsam that were once whole men! Death has greater nobility, I think!"

Lucy regarded the man's pale, handsome face with sudden interest.

"I hadn't thought of war in such terms," she said. "Perhaps death itself *is* noble but like you, I see little nobility in the mutilation of a human being for whatever cause."

"At the same time, suffering can bring out the noblest of instincts," Edouard replied smiling. "You were magnificent, Lucy. I have not before had an opportunity to tell you how much I admire the courage and determination you showed. You were responsible for my being able to save many lives!"

Lucy's moment of pleasure at his compliment was short-lived. If only Alexis were alive to hear Edouard's words, she thought with a sudden aching sense of loss. Everything she had endured since she had come to Épernay had been in order to prove to him her worth as a person. But if her Uncle Pelham was right when he said the war really would be over soon, what purpose was left to her for the future? She would no longer be needed here. At Rochford she had never been needed and now that Teo was gone, she had no child to give her life meaning. Her future seemed at this moment to be a black, empty void.

But Edouard de Valle, now that he had time to think once more, was even more determined about Lucy's future than he had been before she had worked so devotedly beside him. A whole week passed before he was able to persuade her out of the hospital to drive to Compiègne with him on the pretext that he was anxious to see if the Germans had assaulted his home. But the Château Boulancourt was untouched and might have belonged in a fairy-tale world as they sat in the quiet gardens where everything seemed to be sleeping in the afternoon sunshine.

"It is very beautiful here," Lucy said as she stared at the white, pink and yellow water lilies on the sparkling water of the moat. House martins were flying in and out of their nests in the crevices of the stone walls and it seemed as if the war had never touched this corner of the world. There was no bird song at the Château d'Orbais; no trees heavy with green leaves—only broken stumps left after the shelling.

Watching the changing expressions on Lucy's face, Edouard said:

"Could you be happy living here, Lucy? After the war, I mean? You don't have to go back to England, do you?"

Lucy shook her head, her eyes suddenly filling with tears.

"No, I don't *have* to go back, Edouard."

He leant forward and took her hand, his dark eyes searching her face.

"Then stay here, Lucy—with me. You know that I love you. I fell in love with you the first day that I saw you when you were so ill. Do you remember? Since then I have grown to admire and respect you. I could make you happy, Lucy. Perhaps it does not seem possible for you to be happy just yet. But given time..."

"Edouard, don't continue, please," Lucy broke in. "I like you very much, but I could never love you. I shall never love anyone but Alexis. I know I am never going to see him again...but that can't alter the way I feel."

Edouard had been prepared for such a declaration. He did not try to argue with her but said gently:

"I accept that, Lucy. I am not asking you to love me—only to allow me to love you. I want to marry you—to make you my wife. If you did not want to live here, we could go to

Paris; or to the South, if you wished. My one objective would be to make you happy. At least say you will consider it, Lucy!"

"I don't know that I want to get married again—ever!" Lucy answered truthfully. Edouard might believe he could be happy even if she did not love him, but Lucy herself knew now that marriage meant a sharing of oneself and without love, it was empty and pointless.

Her thoughts went back to the last precious weeks she had spent with Alexis and in particular to their night of shared lovemaking. She tried to envisage Eduoard in Alexis' place, Edouard's hands on her naked body; Edouard's mouth kissing her; Edouard's head beside hers on the pillow. But she could only see Alexis' face, his green eyes smiling down at her.

Momentarily her sense of loss was unbearable and once again tears filled her eyes. Perhaps, she thought, she had never until now permitted herself to accept that the loss was final; that she never would see Alexis again. On the other hand, were he to come back, would she see love in his eyes and hear it in his voice, or remembering *La Perle*, would he look at her with sadness, even loathing?

She became aware once more of Edouard beside her, his dark attractive face anxious, uncertain. She felt a wave of pity for him for he, too, was caught in the painful grip of doubt. She had grown too fond of him to be indifferent to his unhappiness.

"I am so sorry, Edouard!" she said huskily. "I cannot give you any worthwhile answer. It would be unfair to pretend I cared—enough to consider marriage to you, I mean. I'm very honored...you know that. But I'm hopelessly confused. Too much has happened to me too quickly and it would be wrong were I to reach any decisions at the moment."

"But at least you are not saying that there is *no* hope for me," Edouard said. "And that is enough for the present, my beautiful Lucy. Now I suppose we must set the future aside and return to the present. The war is not over yet and in a few hours, we must both be back in the wards!"

But Edouard's proposal had awakened in Lucy a new restlessness. For the first time she had allowed herself to think deeply about Alexis' death and she became more uncertain as to his feelings that last morning. Her doubts tormented her. However distressing, she thought, she had to know the truth.

Awaiting her opportunity, she found a moment to be alone with her uncle in the sitting room. She was genuinely fond of this tall, kindly man and knew that he and Alexis had liked one another.

"You have some photographs in the bottom drawer of the tallboy," she said, coming straight to the point. "Alexis was looking at them the morning he left. Was that the first time he had seen them, Uncle Pelham?"

Watching her uncle's face, Lucy imagined that he looked embarrassed. But he replied without hesitation:

"I first showed them to Alexis last Christmas. It was not long after Dubois' death and Alexis had asked me to buy the originals for him. They are at the house in Paris. As a matter of fact, Lucy, he left them in my charge, in a manner of speaking. He said I was to decide what to do with them should anything happen to him. I suppose a decision will now have to be made."

The first wave of relief that had swept through Lucy gave way to a new anxiety.

"Then Alexis did not say what *he* intended doing with them if he came back?"

Silvie had warned Pelham not to talk of Alexis to Lucy unless the girl herself raised the subject. But now that Lucy had not only spoken of Alexis but of the pictures too, Pelham felt freed from the obligation for silence.

"Alexis was very uncertain, my dear. We discussed the matter the day before he left, on his last visit. I think he was afraid that they might harm you were you ever to be recognized—and for that reason, he felt it best to destroy them. But he could not bring himself to do so. He told me he felt the artist had been able to portray your early life in such a way that it had helped him to understand you better. I recall his words, as a matter of fact—they struck me at the time as very revealing of the way he felt about you, Lucy. He said: 'Now I can love all of Lucy and not just the part of her I know.' Quite a remarkable chap, really. I'd like to have known him better."

He saw the tears in Lucy's eyes and fearing he had said more than was wise, he patted her hand in an avuncular manner.

"You must try not to grieve too much for him. One thing I am sure of—he wanted your happiness above everything. You have to think of the future now. You are only twenty-four years old—a child almost. Your whole life lies ahead of you."

Lucy fought back her tears.

"It feels as if my whole life lies behind me," she said wearily. "I'm very far from sure I want any more of it, Uncle Pelham."

"But you will, my dear, you will!" Pelham said. "Consider your mother, Lucy. When she was your age, she must have felt much as you do. But now—now she's married to dear old Toby and they're both as happy as your Aunt Silvie and I are. You're going to be happy, too. I dare say you'll end up married to young Edouard and with a brood of children to fuss over. You'll look back on all this and wonder why you let yourself suffer so much. Life has to go on, you see."

But now that Lucy was reassured that Alexis had never stopped loving her, she had no wish to move forward into the future. She wanted to stay as she was, clinging to the memory of those few precious weeks with him when they had been so marvelously happy together. She busied herself in the wards as a means of escape from reality. She began to allow herself a tiny glimmer of hope. No one had ever been able to prove Alexis was dead. She had even had a letter from Fanshaw in which he had said that with the upheaval in Russia, it was just conceivably possible that the report he had received was wrong. But he did not think so and in all the circumstances, he must *presume* Alexis' death.

The word "presume" became more and more important.

"Don't you see, Edouard, there is hope—however slender," she said on more than one occasion when he tried yet again to interest her in a future they could share. He was painfully aware that she scanned every newspaper item that concerned Russia. It was in fact Lucy who was to read first of the reported executions of the entire Russian Royal Family, including their young children. The White Russian army, comprising counter-revolutionists, had fought their way into Ekaterinburg in the hope of rescuing the Tzar and his family who they believed to be imprisoned there. But their efforts had been in vain. No trace of the Royal prisoners, alive or dead, was found and the grim assumption by the world was that they had been secretly removed and murdered. In England, the King and Queen attended a memorial service for their relatives, and it now had to be accepted that the Red Army had been victorious and the old Russia no longer existed.

It was only a week after the memorial service for the Tzar and his family that Lucy received a second letter from Fanshaw. One of his Secret Service agents had returned from

Russia with part of a coded letter from Alexis intended for Fanshaw himself.

"Obviously, I cannot reveal all the details of that message," Fanshaw wrote. *"But I attach herewith a small part of it. I am deeply sorry to say that following the information I have received, I must now confirm the fact that your husband was shot and killed by the Red Army in November last year.*

"I have been in touch with the Home Office and your late husband's lawyers will be notified. This will enable them to settle his estate..."

Other than his condolences there was little more than a postscript saying that the "Rogers" referred to by Alexis in his letter to Fanshaw was his servant and bodyguard. Her hands trembling uncontrollably, Lucy detached the sheet of paper pinned to Fanshaw's letter.

"Rogers and I have been holed up here for three days. We are surrounded and unless we can get out tonight under cover of darkness, I think the Reds will force their way in tomorrow. Rogers has offered to try to get this message out by way of the roof but burly though he is, he has no head for heights. Besides, there's a sniper on the top floor of the building opposite. This waiting isn't easy but I still feel they might go off and leave us if something unexpected comes along to distract them. We have no food but some water, so we can hold on for a bit longer if they don't force a way in. Fortunately, for us, they don't know there are only two of us in here. I feel badly about Rogers as I don't think it is his blood they are after. It's 'à bas les aristos' all over again.

"If you should ever get this unusually long epistle, my dear Fanshaw (I have little else to do with my time but juggle with our coding complexities!) I fear you must assume the worst as I shall certainly not bore you with this account of my last remaining hours if I do get away. The real purpose of this is to ask you to do whatever possible for my wife. Please let her know that she is never out of my thoughts and that if I die, then I do so without bitterness for she has made me a very happy man. (If that sounds maudlin, put it down to a lack of food—we're very hungry!)

"If Rogers makes it home and I don't, please see that he is well rewarded for..."

For a few moments Lucy's eyes were too blinded by tears to see the other letters still unopened which had arrived together with Fanshaw's. When she could bring herself to read them, they had no power to move her. One was from her mother telling her that at long last, the family firm in America had completed the legalities concerning her inclusion in her grandfather's will. Lucy now had a share in the vast capital of T.R.T.C. and, now that the Corporation had fully recovered from the slump in 1907, its resources were such that Lucy could consider herself an extremely wealthy young woman.

The other letter was from Alexis' firm of solicitors in London. It was too soon yet to be able to give her details, they said, but Alexis' estate was very substantial. Lucy was his sole beneficiary. If she was in need of anything at all, she had but to write to them.

Slowly, Lucy walked over to her dressing table and sat down. For a long time, she stared at her reflection.

"You..." she said to the pale girl with the haunted eyes who was looking back at her "...you are Lucienne Zemski, widow of the late Count Zemski. You, who began life as the orphaned Sophie Miller and became *La Perle* and then Sophia Rochford, you have just been given what you thought was your heart's desire. You have been given your independence. You are rich, wealthy beyond your wildest dreams. Why then do you cry, you silly girl! Have you forgotten that you never believed in love? That your marriage to Alexis was only a way out of the mess you had so stupidly got yourself into? You are rich, rich, rich, and the world is yours for the taking!"

But the eyes of the girl in the mirror told Lucy the truth. Without Alexis, without love, she had never been so poor.

Chapter 28

✀

July—October 1918

WHEN OLIVER RETURNED HOME ON LEAVE ONE HOT JULY DAY, IT was to see the front terrace crowded with convalescents enjoying the fresh air and sunshine. Some lay in Bath chairs, others were sitting, but all were watching the group of children gathered on the lawn beneath. Zandra, as was to be expected Oliver thought with a smile, was directing operations. Dressed in an overlong white nightgown with a silver paper crown on her head, she was reenacting for her captive but appreciative audience, the recent Thanksgiving Service held at St. Paul's Cathedral in honor of King George's and Queen Mary's silver wedding. Stella's six-year-old Lawrence was King to Zandra's Queen, and diminutive Jamie and Lawrence's twin, Katherine, were the King and Queen of the Belgians. Alice, by the look of her, was the Archbishop, a cardboard mitre on her head.

The look of weariness on Oliver's face momentarily vanished as he surveyed this remarkably peaceful scene. Not twelve hours since, he had driven away from an airfield west of Montdidier after nearly two weeks of constant reconnaissance over the retreating enemy lines. An exceedingly bad landing watched by his C.O., had resulted in him being sent home on compulsory sick leave.

Oliver had not wanted to leave—not only because at long last the Jerries were on the run, but because he had no real desire to go home to Rochford. Much as he longed to see his family, he dreaded the inevitable encounters with Jane. Alexis' advice to Oliver to 'find himself a pretty girl' had been to little avail. Like most of the unattached young officers in his unit, Oliver had discovered the brief delights offered by the French girls whenever they had had a few days' leave. But such encounters—more often than not when he had drunk far too much wine—had somehow only served to increase his longing

462

to be with Jane. Action in the air, danger, were the only real antidotes. But he had been refused permission to fly again until after he had had a good long rest.

He had directed his taxicab to drop him at the end of the drive up to the house. It was, he now realized, only a futile delaying tactic that could do no more than postpone the moment he dreaded when he must come face to face with Jane and pretend that she was not of any special importance to him.

Zandra was the first to recognize him. Hitching up her long skirt with one hand and clasping her crown to her head with the other, she abandoned her theatrical cast and flew to meet him. Oliver lifted her into his arms and hugged her. She was his favorite amongst all the children. The death of poor little Teo had shocked him deeply but in his heart, he had been glad that it was not Zandra. That would have been a far harder blow to bear.

Chattering like a magpie, Zandra dragged him past the rows of patients into the house, her small face scarlet with excitement.

"You've got another pip on your shoulder. Have you been promoted, Olly? Did you know Henry was home? And that Mark will be here at the weekend?"

Without waiting for a reply to the questions that poured from her, she tore off to find her mother, Aunt Willow, and any other grown-up who might want to welcome her adored Oliver home.

Oliver went into the library, removed his Sam Browne and undid the buttons of his tunic. Then he sank wearily into one of the comfortable leather chairs. He had not realized quite how tired he was. Living as he had been under great tension, it was only now when he finally relaxed, that he was aware that he had reached the limit of his reserves. The room was cool and, with its book-lined walls, somewhat dark. Upstairs he could hear the sound of Zandra's voice but far away now. She must have gone up to the nurseries, he thought. His eyes closed and without warning, he drifted into sleep.

When he woke, the room was really dark. Someone had covered his legs with a rug. There was no sound of gunfire. The fighting must have stopped for a bit...He sat up, suddenly aware of his real surroundings. A shadow moved in the chair opposite him and a moment later, there was a soft glow from a table lamp and he saw his mother smiling down at him.

"You've been asleep, darling," she said. "For almost six hours! Zandra is nearly going off her head with impatience."

They smiled at one another as Oliver stretched and yawned and then sighed:

"Don't think I've ever done that before," he said. "I *must* have been tired. It's good to see you, Mother. You're looking very pretty as always!"

It was no idle compliment, he thought. Her nurse's uniform was feminine and becoming. She had removed her cap and her greying hair made a soft frame for her still youthful face. Just for a moment, she reminded him of Lucy. But her eyes were unsmiling as she walked over to stand behind Oliver's chair.

"No, don't turn around," she said sharply as he made to do so. "I have something to tell you, Oliver, and it isn't going to be easy for me. Or for you to hear, I'm afraid. But I have to say it and I would have talked about it on your last leave had you not had to rush off so unexpectedly."

The seriousness of his mother's tone forced the last vestiges of sleep from Oliver's brain. Her anxiety communicated itself to him and he tried to find a way to help her say whatever it was she felt obliged to tell him.

"Is it someone I care about who has been killed?" he asked. It was the only possibility which occurred to him.

"Oh, no, Oliver—no one we know has died since poor Alexis, thank God! No, it is a confession I have to make. It concerns you very deeply. The fact is, I transgressed very badly some years ago—many years ago, I should say."

Despite himself, Oliver smiled.

"Dearest Mother, whatever your transgression is, it cannot be so bad that you are afraid to tell me about it—if tell me you must," he said gently.

"But you don't know...understand...you think because I'm your mother that I am beyond reproach," Willow cried. "Oliver, I am not the woman you think me. All children put their parents on a pedestal and in a way, it is right that they should, but in many cases it is undeserved..."

With a maturity which Willow had not recognized before in her son, Oliver stood up and went round his chair to confront her. He stood looking down at her—as if *she* were the child, she thought irrelevantly.

"Parents are also human beings," he said. "It would be unrealistic to expect them always to be perfect. As far as I am concerned, I never put my father on a pedestal. I'm not sure if I disliked him or only feared him—but I never admired him. I'm sorry if that upsets you, Mother, but it's the truth. If I put *you* on a pedestal, then it is because you deserve to be there."

"Oliver, I don't!" Willow cried. "That is what I am trying to tell you. You're old enough to know...to understand ...that your father and I were not...not exactly happily married. The fact was, he...he did not love me and..."

Oliver interrupted, his voice gentle as he said:

"I know he had a mistress, Mother, if that is what you want to tell me. As a matter of fact, I've known for some time that Jane, Mark and poor old Phil were all my father's children. But I cannot see that it was in any way *your* fault—or theirs!"

So Toby was right, Willow thought. Oliver did believe himself to be Jane's half-brother. Now there remained no doubt— she must make a full confession.

"Oliver," she said, biting her lip, "that is only half the story. There is the question of *your* parentage—I was lonely, unhappy. It was terribly wrong of me, but..."

She looked up at his handsome young face and thought how even as a small boy he had resembled his Uncle Pelham far more than the austere dispassionate man she had married. That resemblance had grown even more marked with manhood as the lines of laughter had begun to etch themselves around Oliver's mouth and eyes. The young chin had become more square-set, the jawline stronger. Her son bore no sign of Rowell's weaknesses, his cold indifference, his self-indulgence. He had all Pelham's charm and, in addition, the clear, logical, intelligent way of thinking that Toby had instilled in him.

Now that the moment had come to admit the truth, she found herself gladdened by the fact that Oliver was not Rowell's son. Shameful, immoral though it might be, she could rejoice in the knowledge that his real father was charming, kind, affectionate and immensely attractive. She could even find it in her heart to excuse herself that lapse one sunny afternoon so long ago when Pelham had taken her for a picnic, enticing her for a little while away from the bleak dreariness of the long, lonely days at Rochford Manor. How easy it had been to succumb to his flirtation that had begun so innocently and ended so naturally in each other's arms! The sun, the champagne, the fun had been a heady mixture, the regrets only coming later when they both realized that the easy camaraderie they had shared in the past could never be recaptured. She had missed Pelham terribly when he had gone abroad soon afterwards, while she had tried once again ineffectually to make her marriage work.

"Oliver, I was unfaithful to your father—*or to the man you think was your father.*"

The words came out in a rush.

Oliver caught hold of her arms, unaware of the strength of his grip as he said urgently:

"Are you trying to tell me that I am not Rowell Rochford's son? That there is a chance I am not after all related to Jane?" His tone brooked no prevarication and Willow nodded.

"You are Pelham Rochford's son!" It was said at last. "He doesn't know—although your Uncle Toby does. We never meant to tell you, Oliver. But Toby felt you should know that you and Jane are not brother and sister. You are cousins— first cousins! Do you want me to tell you more, Oliver? You have the right to know all the facts."

Oliver's face was transformed into a smile of pure joy.

"Mother, I don't care how or why it happened. Nothing matters but me and Jane. I love her, don't you see? I've loved her for ages and I thought . . . and all the time . . . oh, *Mother!*"

He swept her up in his arms and hugged her.

"You may think yourself the most wicked woman who ever lived but to me, you're the most perfect, wonderful mother I could possibly have. May I go and tell Jane I love her? You don't mind, do you? About Jane and me, I mean?"

Willow wiped away her tears and attempted to smile.

"No, I don't mind, darling. I love Jane—she's already a daughter to me, you know that. I'm just so relieved *you* are not too upset."

Oliver paused in the doorway, his eyes suddenly glinting with mischief—the very replica of his father's, Willow thought.

"One day I may ask you to tell me more, Mother. But I honestly don't care even if it means I'm illegitimate. So is Jane, isn't she? And I love her. And I love you. And I'm going to ask Jane if she will marry me when the war is over. If she says 'yes,' I'll be the happiest man in the world!"

It was true what Oliver said, Willow thought as she hurried out of the room. Her son *was* a man now—and Toby had once again been right in his conviction that not even this skeleton from her past could destroy Oliver's love for her. She must go and find Toby—tell him that all was well. He'd be so happy for her.

Jane was on duty when Oliver burst into the ward and grabbed her unceremoniously by the arm.

"Tell Sister you're taking half an hour off," he said. "C.O.'s orders!"

"What C.O.?" Jane asked when a few minutes later Oliver led her upstairs to the old schoolroom. She was not only startled but totally perplexed by his extraordinary behavior. He had seldom been into the wards when he knew she was on duty.

The schoolroom was empty. The children were being put to bed and as Oliver had hoped, they had the place to themselves. By force of habit, they both went over to the window seat and sat down side by side. Oliver was grinning as he replied to Jane's question.

"I'm your Commanding Officer!" he told her. "At least, that's what I'm hoping to be..." He took one of her hands and held it tightly, the smile leaving his face as he saw the color rush into her cheeks. "You may not think so, the way I've been behaving on my last few leaves," he went on quietly, "but the fact is, Jane, I'm very much in love with you. I've just been speaking to Mother and she knows and approves of what I'm about to ask you. Jane, when this ghastly war is over, will you marry me?"

It was a moment Jane had never allowed herself to think about since the heartbreaking leave when Oliver had suddenly seemed to lose interest in her. Only pride had sustained her, for she had been determined never to let Oliver see how deeply she suffered. Her bewilderment at his sudden change of heart had tormented her as she asked herself over and over again whether she had only imagined their closeness, their growing love, why, if Oliver had been fond of her, had he suddenly begun to avoid her? Why had he lacked the courage to give her the explanation that was surely owing to her in the circumstances? But now it no longer mattered. Oliver loved her. He wanted to marry her!

Oliver was regarding her anxiously.

"Jane, *darling* Jane, you *do* love me, don't you?" he demanded.

She flung her arms round him, speechless with happiness. With a long sigh of content, Oliver hugged her and then very tenderly, he kissed her. It was the first lover's kiss they had ever exchanged. It lasted but a few seconds but left them both breathless and happy beyond words. Oliver was about to kiss her for the second time when the schoolroom door burst open and they were confronted by a scarlet-faced Zandra dressed in her long white nightgown. She looked like an avenging angel as she stood in the doorway shifting impatiently from one bare foot to the other.

"Aunt Willow said you weren't to be disturbed but Patience says it's long past my bedtime and I haven't even *seen* you yet, Olly. It just isn't fair!"

Oliver released Jane's hand and held out his arms. Zandra rushed into them and buried her face against his neck.

"Jane and I have a secret to tell you, Zandra," he said. "No one else knows yet—not even Mother! We're engaged to be married!"

Zandra's expression clearly revealed her disappointment.

"Olly, you can't. I don't want you to be engaged. *I* want to marry you..." she broke off, biting her lip as a thought suddenly occurred to her. "Though maybe I won't have time to get married now I come to think about it. You see, I've decided to be a great important actress like Sarah Bernhardt or Ellen Terry; or maybe I'll be a film actress like Mary Pickford."

Oliver pulled gently at one of the wayward strands of fair hair.

"And what do you know about her, may I ask?"

Zandra snuggled closer to him.

"She's 'The World's Sweetheart'!" she announced. "Lots of the soldiers have got postcard pictures of her and they say that sometimes I'm better'n what she is when I act for them. Humphries' favorite is 'A Lesson with the Fan' and it makes them all laugh. I'll show you a bit of it, Olly, shall I?"

She jumped down from his knee and picking up a piece of paper to use as a fan, she struck a coy pose. Her small clear voice filled the room.

> *Then you flutter it and fidget with it so!*
> *And you hide your little nose behind it low,*
> *And when he tries to speak*
> *Just lay it on your cheek*
> *And fix him with a fascinating glow!"*

Clearly Zandra would have continued with a second verse had Patience not come into the room waving an admonishing finger. But for once the child was not reproved and was allowed to remain up as the family gathered in the library to celebrate the occasion with champagne. Even the servants were called in to toast the newly engaged pair. By morning, word had spread round the hospital and everywhere Jane or Oliver went, they were offered congratulations.

"It's done us all a power of good!" Marjorie announced in her Commandant's imperious voice. "Just the kind of news we need to cheer us all up."

"You'd almost think we had engineered it as a morale booster for Lady Sharples' patients!" Oliver laughed as he went up to London with Jane next day to choose an engagement ring. Marjorie's husband had been given a knighthood in the last Honors List and the tribute to Sam Sharples had done much to compensate him for the sad fact that he would not now have a future baronet, George Barratt, as a son-in-law.

Willow felt as if she had been given a new lease of life. Oliver's and Jane's happiness was a radiance encompassing them all.

"I must write to Lucy and tell her all the good news," Willow said happily. "I do hope she is feeling a little better now!"

"I doubt very much if Lucy has any time to spare to think about herself," Marjorie Sharples told her, not altogether wisely. "There's been a great deal of fighting not very far from Épernay. I imagine they have been pretty busy at that hospital of theirs!"

But by September, the Front was far enough away for Edouard to take Lucy for another day away from the wards to his home in Compiègne. She was well aware that she must expect another proposal and she was therefore not in the least surprised when Edouard took her out onto the terrace of the Château Boulancourt and brought up the subject of marriage.

"It is a year now since your husband died, Lucy!" he said in his gentlest tone. "You cannot grieve forever . . . and although many people find great comfort in their memories—as I am sure you do, you cannot *live* in the past!"

Lucy sighed.

She had refused adamantly ever to talk to Edouard about Teo's death although he had on several occasions tried to express his sympathy. He could not know how often she thought of the little girl, not in the unbearable surroundings that had brought about her death, but when she had been sitting on Alexis' knee, laughing contentedly, in the drawing room in Cadogan Gardens. Lucy had clung to such memories of Teo—Alexis stooping over her pretty primrose cot to kiss the child goodnight; Alexis carrying her up to bed riding on his shoulders, her small face pink with excitement; Alexis rocking her gently in his arms when she had been cutting her first teeth. His love for their daughter had been paramount since the day of her birth and Lucy could not now forget how often Alexis had reiterated the words: "How could I help but love her when she looks like a tiny image of you!"

What could Edouard—or even Uncle Pelham—know of such memories and the mixture of happiness and heartache they brought. Yet it was an inescapable fact that life went on, whether one wished it or not, and somehow each day had to be lived through without the two people who had been dearest of all to her. Could Edouard and her uncle be right in that her future lay in Edouard's hands? At least here in France there were only memories to torment her. But did she really want to live in this magnificent château with Edouard? Did she want to share her life with him? Could she bear to share her life with anyone but Alexis?

She glanced at Edouard's strong, serious profile and her mood softened. He had proved himself such a good friend—understanding, patient and sensitive to her moods. It was not fair to compare him with Alexis. As a man, Edouard had a great many assets to offer his future wife. Good looks, immense charm, a beautiful home, one of the oldest French titles. She would become the Vicomtesse de Valle. Why then did her heart not stir even slightly at the prospect?

"I love you so very much, Lucy," Edouard said beside her. "You are the most important person in my life, you know."

Lucy bit her lip. Could Edouard—could any man—love her as Alexis had done, forgiving her past; accepting the very worst of her? He had accepted Teo; if anything, loving Maurice's child even more than she herself had loved the little girl. How saddened he would have been to learn of her tragic death! At least he had been spared that grief. Now she must ask herself if Edouard would have accepted as readily another man's child? And would he still want to marry her if he knew she had once sold herself for gain at *Le Ciel Rouge*? She doubted it very much.

"Edouard!" she said on a sudden impulse. "I want to ask you something. It has to do with love and I would be interested to hear your point of view. It concerns the depth of love—as an emotion, I mean. Do you think it should be all forgiving or could there be some things a man could not overlook?"

"That's a very broad question, Lucy," Edouard replied, smiling. "Can you be more specific?" he asked curiously.

Lucy nodded.

"It concerns a girl I once knew. Her name was Louise. In one single moment of weakness, she allowed herself to become pregnant by someone she did not love. Then the man she did love asked her to marry him and she confessed her condition. If *you* had been in love with her, Edouard, would you still have married her?"

Edouard gave no sign that he was surprised by Lucy's question. He gave it a moment of serious consideration before he replied:

"I suppose it is possible—if unlikely. It would depend how deeply I loved her in the first place. I don't know how I would feel about the child. I would, of course, want to be absolutely certain in my own mind that my future wife would not transgress again after our marriage. I suppose I would lose some of the respect I had for her. On the other hand, I might feel she was a victim of circumstances, a very human person, subject as most of us are to a moment of weakness. Is that a good enough answer, Lucy? And please tell me, did your friend get married in the end?"

"Yes, and very happily," Lucy replied. "That husband's behavior has always seemed to me to be a symbol of real love, Edouard. Do you agree?"

He nodded.

"The trouble is, Lucy, men tend to idealize the women they adore and expect them to be perfect! Fortunately, being a doctor, I am far more of a realist. Nevertheless, I would not want to marry a girl who I knew to be unworthy of my respect. You would know nothing of such people, Lucy, coming as you do from your background, but there are women of a certain type who, however attractive to enjoy as companions, one would never consider marrying."

He glanced briefly at her face, thinking how pure and innocent she looked.

"It might shock you to hear of it but there are some who go around with no regard whatever for their reputations," he continued. "Perhaps unfairly, men enjoy their company and what they offer, but they do not ask such girls to marry them. I myself would not do so. I would be afraid of running into one of my friends who had known my wife intimately before I married her; and I would never feel able to trust her after we were married. If she had so little respect for her body that she could offer it where she willed, how could I expect her to remain faithful to me!"

Lucy made no reply. She had invited Edouard's honest opinion deliberately and knew she had no right now to feel aggrieved by it. Moreover, he was perfectly justified in his attitude, she thought bitterly. Most men and women would agree with him. It was only Alexis who had loved her enough to accept her without one single proviso.

Edouard regarded her attentively. He took her hands in his and said with renewed urgency:

"Must we talk in hypotheses, dearest Lucy? I am on tenterhooks to hear your answer. Will you marry me? I swear I will do everything I can to make you happy!"

Sudden, unexpected tears stung Lucy's eyelids. Her sadness seemed to be dragging its way up from deep inside her. It encompassed her with an unbearable sense of loneliness as her heart ached for the man she loved—the man who had truly loved her.

"Forgive me, Edouard, but I have to refuse!" she said huskily. "If it were possible for me to believe in a second marriage, then I would choose to marry you. I am very, very fond of you. I really wish I could say 'yes.' But I do not want to marry again."

For a long time, Edouard did not speak. He looked bitterly disappointed. Something in the finality of Lucy's tone told him there was no cause for hope for the future.

Nevertheless he said:

"If you should ever change your mind, Lucy, you'll tell me?"

"Of course! But I don't think I will, Edouard. I'm so very sorry."

For a little while she had escaped from her unfortunate past, Lucy thought. Alexis had given her her chance to get away from it. But now he was gone and her past was back with her once more, awaiting the opportunity to catch up with her.

Now that matters had come to a head with Edouard, Lucy felt awkward working beside him in the hospital. But he was dedicated to his job and there seemed no likelihood he would leave. She was uneasily conscious of his eyes following her when he believed she did not know he was looking; of the awkwardness between them when he came up to her aunt's and uncle's private rooms for a drink or a meal or simply to play a game of chess. The easy camaraderie was gone and Lucy was lonelier than ever.

As September gave way to October, Silvie began once again to try to persuade Lucy to go home to Rochford.

"Do you realize, *chérie*, that you have been here for two years! Your uncle is convinced the end of the war is not far off. He says your English General Allenby will without doubt soon force the surrender of the Turks. The Germans are in retreat and the British, French and Americans have begun an offensive against Italy. Much as I love you, *chérie*, your presence here in the hospital is no longer essential, and you must know as well as I how much your dear Mama longs to have you home! Besides, you are far too thin, child, and you need to recuperate your strength."

The suggestion, though meant for Lucy's benefit, only served to increase her belief that her life lacked any worthwhile purpose. She knew with certainty that she could not be happy at Rochford without Alexis, without little Teo. The house would be too full of memories.

I am like a ship without a harbor, she thought wearily.

One night, not long after her aunt's talk, Lucy dreamed that she was back at *Le Ciel Rouge*. She was sitting with Yvette and Nicole in the empty salon before the house opened for the evening. Nicole was telling a funny story about one of her clients and Yvette and Lucy were laughing. Madame Lou-Lou came into the room and began laughing, too. Presently, more girls arrived and they started to sing as they had done in reality on the night before Yvette had left to get married. In the middle of this song, Madame Lou-Lou decided to give Lucy a dancing lesson. And then Lucy woke up.

The laughter of her dream turned abruptly to tears as she realized that her happiness was a myth. There was no fat, jolly Madame Lou-Lou to give her instructions about life; about dancing; about men and the way of the world. There were no close, loyal friends like Yvette and Nicole with whom to laugh away the day. There was no laughter any more.

It was at that moment that Lucy decided she would cease trying to find her way forward into an unbearable future. She would go back—back to the place which had once been her home; where life had been so simple. For that was what she now craved—a way of life that was without complications or responsibilities. Perhaps Madame would be able to tell her where— if it existed at all—she might find it. Madame had always held all the answers to the world's problems. Was it not she who, when Lucy had spoken of her dream of being rich and famous, had told her: "Happiness, my child, is to be found only in what one has and never in what might have been."

For a few years, she had sampled a different life; a taste of the cruel world outside the narrow confines of *Le Ciel Rouge*. She had been transplanted into a very different soil where she had flourished briefly and then, when the conditions hardened, she had wilted. Madame Lou-Lou had so often warned them all that the price of independence was high; that even marriage was often not the bed of roses the girls imagined it to be. As for love— Madame had always vouchsafed that it brought only heartache. And she had been right . . .

Lucy knew she was not being entirely honest when she allowed her aunt and uncle to believe she intended to spend only a few days in Paris at the *Rue d'Artois* before she went home to Rochford. She had no clear idea in her head of what she wanted to do with her life. She was certain of only one thing—that she must go back to *Le Ciel Rouge* and talk to Madame Lou-Lou. Madame had never been at a loss when one of her girls had needed advice. Lucy could not envisage the kind of frank discussions Madame encouraged, taking place with her mother. However much her mother loved her, the fact remained that she preferred to forget her daughter's past; that any mention of it disturbed her greatly. And not even Aunt Silvie, outspoken and modern in her attitude to life, had ever encouraged Lucy to speak of those days before she had gone to live at Rochford.

"I shall be perfectly all right in Paris by myself," Lucy insisted when Silvie offered to accompnay her. "I shall be very busy shopping since I cannot go home in these unfashionable clothes, can I?" She had felt guilty when her aunt had nodded sympathetically and accepted the lie without question.

"You will come back and see us when the war is over, won't you, *chérie*?" Silvie said tearfully when at last Lucy's few belongings were packed and she was ready to go. "You have become like a daughter to me. To your uncle, too. He meant it when he said you will always have a second home here."

Just for a moment Lucy wondered whether she should stay here with her kindly aunt and uncle. But then Silvie said sadly:

"We are both so sorry you do not feel inclined to marry poor dear Edouard. I know he loves you, Lucy. I still believe you could have been happy with him. He is quite heartbroken!"

Lucy gave a wry smile.

"He will find someone else to love," she said gently. "I know he is hurt and disappointed but I don't think his heart is so entirely broken that it will not mend!"

Edouard had gone to Compiègne for a few days—to avoid seeing Lucy depart, Pelham said. He believed, like Lucy, that it was more the young man's pride which was suffering than his heart. Lucy was grateful that she did not have to face a farewell scene with him. She was genuinely fond of him and it gave her no pleasure to see the disappointment and unhappiness in his eyes.

The train to Paris was full. Silvie had insisted Lucy should travel in her uniform as a means of self-protection. No one, she said, would molest a young V.A.D. Recalling her journey two years ago to Épernay, Lucy smiled bitterly as she considered the hypocrisy of her life. Had Edouard known the truth, he would have seen her with different eyes. He would have known Lucy was "one of those women whose company men enjoyed—but did not marry!"

Paris had changed little, she thought on her arrival, since her three-day visit with the jolly Major Bucquet and his two companions. Perhaps the only marked difference was the number of American servicemen obviously on leave and with money to spend. Lucy had to compete with one for a taxicab at the station, the driver obviously preferring to take the foreigner. Petrol was short, he grumbled to Lucy as he finally drove her to the *Rue d'Artois*, and the Americans gave lavish tips!

Although it had not been her intention to do so, Lucy decided to go shopping after all. She did not want to appear in uniform at *Le Ciel Rouge*. Nor did she wish Madame to see her in her own civilian outfit which was so hopelessly dated.

Without any real enthusiasm but with a detached determination, Lucy spent the afternoon in the *Rue St. Honoré*. Her uncle had given her a large sum of money, which, Lucy thought with a sigh, she could now afford to spend as lavishly as she wished. She was rich enough to buy whatever took her fancy.

She barely recognized herself when on the following morning, she told the admiring *gardienne* to find her a taxicab. She had returned from her shopping expedition the previous afternoon still wearing her old outfit and the caretaker obviously failed to recognize her when she took in Lucy's *café complet* at breakfast time.

"*Ah, Madame la Comtesse!*" she cried. "*Que vous êtes chic— et si belle!*"

Lucy surveyed herself in the tall looking glass with a critical eye. The grey, loose-fitting, velvet coat-frock with its three-quarter-length sleeves was very smart. She approved the silky softness of the high sable collar and wide cuffs. The skirt, falling to her calves, was shorter than her uniform had been and revealed her new pale gray silk stockings. She wore a black sable cloche, gray kid gloves and gray suede shoes with Louis heels. Her face was very pale, her eyes troubled. With a sigh, she turned away from her reflection and went downstairs.

If the taxi driver was surprised when Lucy directed him to the side street in Montmartre, he gave no sign as he accepted her large tip with a satisfied grin.

"Shall I wait, Madame?" he inquired hopefully. Lucy shook her head.

The front door of *Le Ciel Rouge* was locked. It was several minutes after she had rung the bell before an untidy little maid opened the door to her. The girl's mouth dropped open in surprise as she gawped at the elegant woman standing there.

"I wish to see Madame Lou-Lou!" Lucy said, strangely affected by the sight of the child. She was so young—no older than Lucy had been the first time she had come through the door. "See if you can find her for me," she added gently with a smile.

The little maid scuttled off without a word, her dark hair escaping in strands from beneath her white mob cap, leaving Lucy standing in the hall beside the forgotten bucket and mop.

The familiar smell of cheap scent and cigar smoke, filled Lucy's nostrils. Her eyes went to the wall above Madame's private office. It still supported the huge, gilt-framed oil painting of "The Storming of the Bastille." On the office window, the same notice still hung: "*Clients are Permitted to Smoke in the Salon but not in the Bedrooms.*" Lucy smiled, remembering Yvette's and Nicole's endless Turkish cigarettes.

Then suddenly, the double doors beside the office swung open and Madame's enormous bulk came through.

"*Oui, Madame?* What can I do for you?" she asked, too professional to reveal as the maid had done, her surprise at the sight of this elegant female visitor. Lucy smiled.

"You do not recognize me, Madame Lou-Lou?"

Madame removed the tiny gold-rimmed spectacles perched on her nose and, leaning forward with difficulty, peered into Lucy's face. Slowly, a smile widened still further the folds of flesh beneath her eyes.

"Mais ce n'est pas possible! Perle! Ma petite Perle!"

Tears rushed into Lucy's eyes as she was enveloped by Madame's trunklike arms. She was crushed against the lace jabot covering the upper half of the huge, soft bosom.

When Madame released her, it was to send the little skivvy, who was still gawping with curiosity and excitement, about her business. Her voice was sharp but Lucy knew that the child was not really frightened by it. There was no need to fear Madame, provided one did as one was told.

Madame ushered Lucy into her private sitting room behind the office. Normally, none of the girls and only the most privileged of clients were allowed in here. Madame waddled over to the sideboard and withdrew two glasses and a bottle of port.

"It should be champagne to celebrate, *non?*" she said. "But *hélas*, at this time of the morning it will not yet be chilled!"

She handed Lucy a brimming glass of port and then lowered herself carefully onto a pink brocade sofa. She patted the seat.

"Here, next to me!" she said drawing Lucy down beside her.

The crimson satin curtains with their gold pelmets and tassels were still drawn across the windows from the previous night, but a rosy glow from two fringed table lamps lit the room. A canary in a hanging wicker cage was hopping from perch to perch. Madame's black cat—could it possibly be the same one?—was curled up asleep on the dark green chenille tablecloth, impervious to the bird's activities.

"Now, tell me all that has been happening to you, *chérie!*" Madame said. "I can see that you have prospered. Yet you do not look very happy."

Her sharp eyes went to Lucy's ungloved hand. "You are married—but not happily. It is another man?" she asked cynically.

Lucy attempted to smile but instead, the tears began pouring down her cheeks. Madame patted her hand and made soothing noises while she waited for Lucy's sobbing to quieten to an occasional gulp.

"Now you will tell me the whole story!" Madame ordered. "I received your letter, you know, asking for my help when you feared you were pregnant."

"But you were too angry with me for leaving you without warning, to reply to me," Lucy said, her tone both sad and reproachful.

"Mais non!" Madame said emphatically. "You should know me better than that. I would never refuse help to any of my girls if I could assist them. But what could I do for you, there in England? I did not dare to send you by post the ergot which would almost certainly have put an end to your troubles. It is a poison, *enfin*, and how was I to know who would open my letter to you? You had written that you were now a member of the English aristocracy. Consider the repercussions were your mother to have found such a letter from me and learned of the contents! It would have meant certain imprisonment for me and the end of *Le Ciel Rouge!*"

Lucy sighed.

"I suppose it would have been dangerous," she admitted. "At the time, I wrongly assumed you did not want to help me."

"Then you underrated my affection for you, *ma petite!*" Madame said. "Now begin at the beginning—from the time you left here!"

At first, Lucy found it difficult to talk with fluency. But soon the words were tumbling from her, sometimes accompanied by tears when she spoke of Alexis and Teo, but for the most part with a growing sense of relief. With Madame Lou-Lou there was no need to be careful what she said; to be afraid of shocking her; surprising her; offending her. Madame was the one woman in the world who had heard it all before. Life held no mysteries for her.

"I want you to tell me what I should do with my life now!" Lucy cried as she reached the end of her story. "I can't go home. I don't belong there. I never really did. This is more home to me, Madame Lou-Lou. I was happy here. Could I not stay here with you for a little while? I could help you run the place. I would not need a salary—or be a burden to you."

Madame sighed.

"On the contrary, *mon enfant*, you would be a huge asset!" she said with a sideways glance at Lucy's perfect profile and slim, elegant figure. She sighed again—this time with regret for what she must now forgo.

"You do not belong here, child!" she said firmly. "Look at me! Look with your heart, my dear. You spoke just now of me being so content, so jolly, so settled in my chosen way of life. But the truth is quite different, as I will now tell you. Once, long ago, when I was your age, I was almost as beautiful as you are now, although you may not believe it," she added patting her enormous body.

"Like you, I went to work for a Madame, and I had no doubt that one day I should find a husband, or a patron, perhaps, and become a great courtesan. But instead, I grew older and older until I was forced to realize that soon I would have no looks, no figure and that I might well end my days in the street. I had saved for the dowry I never needed. With that money, I bought this house and after years of hard work and effort, I managed to open *Le Ciel Rouge*. A success maybe— but still it remains a house of ill repute—a brothel." Her eyes bored into Lucy's as if willing her to listen.

"I have made a great deal of money—enough to retire if I so wish. But what would retirement mean to me in my old age? I would give all my money to be married to a good, kind, respectable man and to be able to sit back now in my chair with children, grandchildren, to fuss over and spoil me. I am nearly seventy years old and I am tired. Beneath this mask of white powder, I am wrinkled and ugly. I shall never know a man's love or the love of children. The girls I employ are the only children I shall ever have. But you, Perle, have the world before you. You can marry again; you can have more little ones to ensure your contentment when you are my age. *This is no place for you, child.* If you would allow yourself to open your eyes, you would know it."

"I do not want another husband, other children!" Lucy whispered. "Once long ago, you told me that the only thing worth having in life was money—gold, preferably. Now you tell me it is love..."

Madame smiled.

"Once, long ago, *ma petite*, I told you that money was the only *security*—and gold the most secure currency of all. That will always be true!"

"You said then that love only brought heartache!" Lucy's voice was childishly accusing. But Madame remained calm.

"And who should know the truth of that better than you,

child?" she said with a hint of irony. "But we should not fear pain—life itself begins with the pain of childbirth, and the rewards God gives us so often go hand in hand with suffering. It is a risk we have to take if we want what is worth having. Come now, I want to take you upstairs to your old room. It is empty at the moment and we shall disturb no one."

Climbing the stairs behind Madame, Lucy was fully aware for the first time how truly old Madame was. When she, Lucy, had lived and worked here, she had thought of her as timeless, unchanging. But now she was stiff with arthritis and her movements, always slow because of her huge weight, were even slower. The black velvet band around her throat was almost lost amongst her many chins and the scarlet bow of her lips had had to be painted into shape where her mouth had fallen inwards over her pink gummed, false teeth. She resembled an enormous, shapeless female clown.

Pity momentarily stirred Lucy's heart. Then Madame opened the door of her old bedroom and Lucy forgot her thoughts as she stood facing her past.

Her sense of shock was twofold. What struck her first was the room's size—its smallness. She had become used over the years to the big sunny bedrooms of Rochford and the Château d'Orbais. Yet when she had first come here she had been charmed and delighted by the room's contrast to the tiny attic she had slept in at the *modiste*'s and to the long, dark, chilly dormitories of the Convent.

Her second impression was one of horror at the shabby sordidness, the vulgarity of the furnishings. The brass bedstead was tarnished, the red carpet patchy with stains where wine, perhaps, had been spilt. The dark gray wallpaper with its red, blue and silver design was grubby and garish. The marble of the washstand was cracked and the purple and green jug did not match the bowl of the china Toilet Set.

This room, Lucy thought, had once been her haven. Here on this very bed she had so often sat talking to Yvette, dreaming her improbable dreams of the rich, titled family who would one day claim her while Yvette, with a cigarette dangling from the corner of her mouth, would listen with only half an ear as she stitched up the hem of her beloved kimono.

There were many times when she had thought of this room—but always kindly, without any sense of the revulsion she now felt as she recalled the nights and the nameless, faceless clients who had paid Madame's price to be here.

"*Ça suffit.* It is enough, *ma petite!*" Madame broke into Lucy's thoughts, her sharp eyes seeing very well Lucy's reactions. She led the way downstairs and when they were once more seated on her pink sofa, she said gently:

"Sometimes in life it is good to close your eyes to the truth, but not on occasions of importance such as this, my dear. You are no longer my little Perle. You have grown up and my cygnet has become a very beautiful, very elegant swan. You are not a harlot who once tried to become an aristocrat; you are an aristocrat who once had the misfortune to be a harlot—and that is a very different thing. We all saw it—even the girls used to call you '*la Duchesse,*' do you remember, *ma petite*? You belong in a different class—a different world— and you have no choice but to return to it."

"You are telling me to go home—home to my mother?" Lucy asked, her voice husky with threatening tears.

Madame Lou-Lou nodded.

"I am sure she longs for your return. She was without you for so many years, was she not? Forget your own unhappiness for a little while. Give your attention to making *her* happy. It is only children who are permitted to consider themselves all the time, you know, and you are no longer a child." Madame took Lucy's hand and held it in her own as she added gently: "You may wish to argue with me, to deny that you have been the *egoiste.* You will tell me that you have spent two years devoting yourself to the care of others. But ask yourself, *mon efant*, if that also was not for your self-glorification? If it was not to impress your husband? To win his admiration? To give yourself the importance you felt you deserved?"

Lucy's cheeks were pink with distress.

"But I continued nursing, Madame Lou-Lou, long after I knew Alexis would never come back!"

"Huh!" was Madame's caustic exclamation. "You are now telling yourself another fib, are you not? You hoped in your heart that the reports of his death were wrong. But once you were certain they were true, you gave up, did you not? First you saw an easy way of escape with that young Vicomte; and when he disappointed you by falling short of your husband's standard of love, you came running here to me for help! But I can do nothing for you. You cannot always have everything you want. You must face up to life, child, and try not to be so selfish."

"That is cruel!" Lucy cried. Yet even as she did so, she knew that everything Madame had said was true. Her life had been one of complete selfishness. It was *her* happiness which had always mattered most. She drew a long, shuddering sigh.

"I suppose I am being selfish now, am I not!" she said ruefully as she rose slowly to her feet. "You must have been up late last night, Madame, and you need rest. I should not keep you here trying to knock a little sense into me."

She helped the old woman to her feet and put her arms around her.

"I wish there was something I could give you," she said. "You have always been so kind to me. As I told you earlier, I am an exceedingly rich woman now. I would like to have made you a gift but I do not wish to offend you. Perhaps you have no need of money now?"

Madame's eyes were unfathomable as she moved backwards from Lucy's embrace and said sharply:

"My dear child, in this life one can never have too much money. Naturally, I would have done my best to advise and help you as I would any of my girls who came to me in trouble. But that is not to say that I would refuse a little 'thank you' if you feel so inclined. You mentioned that you have funds in the United States. Dollars are an excellent currency. I shall be very happy to accept your offer."

"I will send you a check as soon as I can," Lucy said. "I am sure it can be arranged without difficulty once I get back to England. Thank you again, Madame, for *everything*. I may never see you again but I will remember you always."

Long after the little maid had closed the door behind Lucy, Madame sat on in her empty room, permitting herself one of her very rare moments of self-pity. The black cat came to sit on her lap and she stroked it absentmindedly as she thought of the girl who had once waited on her and her clients. The Countess Zemski, she mused, was quite possibly one of the most beautiful young women in Paris. And she, Madame Lou-Lou, could have kept her here—at *Le Ciel Rouge*—as a receptionist! It would have taken so little to persuade the girl to remain. Had she stayed, in no time at all the whole of Paris would have been at her door. She, Madame Lou-Lou, even at this late stage of her life, could have become one of the most respected and admired Madames in the capital—maybe in the whole of *la France*!

The girl would never know how great was the sacrifice she

had just made, she thought. Lucy had offered money as a means of showing her gratitude 'for your advice, Madame'! As if money could compensate her! Nor had she any need of it. Allowing Lucy to believe she had settled her debts was to allow her to go without regrets. *La petite Perle* had looked on her as a mother—but mothers were not paid to be kind, and when Lucy had time to realize that, she would cease to feel sentimentally about the past. This was Lucy's gateway to freedom.

But Lucy had always been the favorite of all her girls and the freedom Lucy had now gained was Madame Lou-Lou's loss.

Chapter 29

∽

November 1918

"I'M AFRAID THERE'S NO REPLY, SIR!"

Fanshaw looked up at his secretary impatiently.

"There must be. You're sure you got the message right when you rang Rochford Manor?"

The bespectacled young male secretary nodded.

"Absolutely sure, Sir. I spoke to the butler—fellow called Dutton. The whole family is in London. They've gone up for the purpose of giving a party to celebrate the engagement of young Lord Rochford. They're all at Cadogan Gardens for the night."

"Well, try again then!" Fanshaw ordered irritably. "If they're giving a party, someone must be there to answer the telephone!"

Everyone was busy at Cadogan Gardens. Mrs. Taylor heard the telephone ring as she went through to the dining room with another tray of glasses.

"Drat that blinking machine!" she said to the maid following behind her with a second tray. "It can just wait till I've time to answer!"

It rang a third time half an hour later, but by then the first of the eighty guests was arriving and the housekeeper was kept busy running up and downstairs showing the ladies where to put their coats and tidy their hair.

Jane, too, heard the telephone but could not leave to answer it as she stood in the doorway of the drawing room beside Oliver, welcoming their friends and receiving their congratulations. It was her first formal reception and she was nervous, although she knew she would have to get used to such formalities if she was one day going to become Lady Rochford. Oliver was being very considerate and had not moved from her side. For the most part, their guests were his friends from the Royal Flying Corps and many were still in uniform. Although the war had ended a week ago, it would be some time before they were all demobilized and wearing civilian clothes again. Oliver was due back at his squadron H.Q. next week but at least he would not be engaged in aerial combat, she thought thankfully, glancing for the hundredth time at his laughing, happy face.

The mood of guests and hosts alike this evening was really only a continuation of the same euphoria that had gripped the whole country when on 11th November at eleven o'clock in the morning, the Armistice had been signed. The Germans had surrendered and England was at peace once more. The family had been at Rochford where all day long they could hear the bell of St. Stephen's ringing out its joyful news. They had read in the *Times* of a London with the streets lit up and people dancing and waving flags; of the King and Queen going out onto the balcony at Buckingham Palace to receive the cheers of their people. Victory was a heady draught to swallow and at Rochford there had been a whole day of celebration in the hospital, the Commandant for once turning a blind eye to discipline and even allowing alcohol to be drunk in the wards. Toby and Sam Sharples had supplied it!

It seemed to Jane that she had been happy for weeks on end—ever since Oliver had proposed to her. If there were anything at all to mar her joy this night, it was her pity for Lucy who was trying so hard to enter into the spirit of the occasion. Lucy had lost both her husband and her child, Jane reminded herself, and it was unreasonable to expect her to rejoice quite as enthusiastically as the rest of the family. But she was making a brave attempt not to show her sorrow as she sat chatting to Annabel Barratt. She had cause for mourning too, Jane thought, with two brothers killed and poor Henry still unable to put his feet to the ground. Not that he seemed to mind his handicap. He was here tonight, laughing and joking with Mark, and watching the couples dancing without any obvious sign of envy.

Her eyes returned to Lucy, looking so ethereal but very beautiful in a creamy white brocade dress embroidered with silver thread. The ruby necklace around her throat had been one of Alexis' presents. Jane felt a fresh wave of sympathy for her—and momentarily a little guilty at her own happiness.

Lucy was listening politely, but without any real interest, to Annabel's ardent voice discussing women's rights now that the war had ended. Her thoughts were elsewhere. Madame Lou-Lou was right when she said I had changed, she was telling herself. And Madame had been right about many other things—most of all in pointing out that her mother wanted her home. Since Lucy's return to Rochford a month ago, they had grown very close. The change in their relationship had begun one rainy afternoon when they had passed the time together looking through the old family photograph albums. Her mother had suddenly begun to speak of her early married life at Rochford and how she had had to deny so many years her deep love for Uncle Toby. To her consternation, Willow had without warning burst into tears and it was only with the greatest difficulty that Lucy had persuaded her mother to reveal what she termed her 'guilty secret.'

"You must think me such a terrible hypocrite, Lucy, preaching morality to you when I myself was guilty of such an unforgivable lapse. Perhaps I was secretly afraid you had inherited my weaknesses and that you would suffer the consequences as I did."

With calm sympathy and logic, Lucy had pointed out that one transgression did not justify the label "immoral"; that her mother had owed her husband no allegiance and that never, ever, must she regret the existence of Oliver. She had praised her mother's courage in confessing the truth to Oliver in order that he and Jane could find happiness.

It seemed that day as if their rôles were temporarily reversed and Lucy was the mother reassuring her wayward daughter. She had brought a smile back to Willow's face when she admitted how relieved she was to know that her mother too had a few guilty secrets.

"You always seemed to me so unapproachable because of your perfection," Lucy explained smiling. "Now I know I can come to you for understanding."

These intimate confidences had encouraged Lucy to speak of her love for Alexis, so newly discovered before he was killed. They talked of the child Lucy might have given him had he lived, and comforted each other when they went together to put flowers on little Teo's grave.

Perhaps most of all, Lucy appreciated Madame Lou-Lou's assessment of her. At the time it was given, she had resented being told she was selfish. The criticism had hurt deeply and for some while afterwards, she had tried to justify her behavior to herself. But now she accepted that Madame had been right and that she, Lucy, had always demanded life on *her* terms. Since the memorial service for Alexis soon after she had arrived home, she had genuinely tried to set aside her own grief and do what little she could to make herself useful and to consider the happiness of others. It was her idea to offer Cadogan Gardens as a place where Oliver and Jane could have a party, Rochford itself being far too full of patients for a private celebration.

The gesture was an unselfish one. It had not been easy for Lucy to face going to her own home which had been closed up for almost a year now. Mrs. Taylor and a few servants had remained to air the rooms and give an occasional polish to the furniture beneath the dust sheets and to clean the silver. The remainder of the staff had gone to help out at Rochford. Lucy had wanted to take her lawyer's suggestion and sell the house; but her mother had thought it might come in useful after the war. "With the new generation growing up so fast, we may all be glad of a *pied-à-terre*," Willow had said, "especially as it could be some time before all our patients have left Rochford." She had bemoaned the fact that there was no room there for her to indulge her wish to give a big celebration party for Oliver and Jane. Dreading the thought of being there without Alexis, Lucy had nevertheless offered to open Cadogan Gardens for tonight's party.

For the past two weeks, she, Jane and her mother had been supervising the reopening of the big London house. Invitations had gone out following an announcement of the engagement in the *Times* and although many of the family friends had not yet returned from their bases abroad, there was still a sufficient number of acceptances to make this a gala evening for the young couple.

Lucy steeled herself against the memories that seemed to haunt every room. She avoided going up to the nurseries which she had ordered to be locked after Nanny Meredith had removed her belongings. Teo's nurse was now in a new post in London and Lucy had invited her to tea on her day off; but the poor woman felt as Lucy did about the past and wrote to say she could not bear ever again to set foot in Cadogan Gardens. One day, Lucy thought, she would go and see poor Nanny Meredith at her new home where the memories would be less poignant for them both.

Lucy now forced a smile to her lips as Oliver and Jane approached her. Jane looked radiant in a long, floating georgette dance frock, primrose-colored, with tiny gold straps over her bare shoulders. Oliver looked immensely smart in his tails, a white carnation in his buttonhole.

"The party's going well, don't you think, Lucy?" he asked smiling. "Aren't you and Annabel dancing? Shall I try finding you partners? I'm afraid we seem to be rather short of chaps—it's the war, I suppose!"

The four-piece band were playing a Hesitation Waltz and Lucy could see that Jane was longing to dance.

"Annabel and I have lots to talk about, so why don't you two show us how good you are?" she said unselfishly.

As a very special treat, young Alice had been allowed to attend the party, although it was understood that she would remain quietly in the background. She sat perfectly content between Mark and Henry, occasionally going to the buffet table to bring them back some of the cold delicacies laid out for the guests to enjoy when they felt hungry. The informality of the evening seemed to please everyone, especially the younger generation. Willow had reluctantly agreed to it because of the shortage of staff. As the evening wore on, she had to admit everyone seemed to be having an especially good time.

It was nearly two o'clock before the older guests began to leave. By three, all but a few of Oliver's closest friends had departed. Alice had long since been dispatched to bed and now Mark and Henry also rose to say their goodnights. Oliver went over to his mother and Toby.

"It's been a ripping party!" he said, kissing Willow warmly on the cheek. "The happiest in my life, I think. Jane thinks so, too. We are both very grateful." He grinned at Toby affectionately. "It didn't seem to matter one whit that we weren't at Rochford, which goes to show it's not the place but the people that are important."

Willow hugged him, her heart filling with gratitude to a God who had spared her this beloved son. The war was over at last and she could look forward now to the future. When Oliver and Jane were a little older, they would marry and she would have a grandchild again to fill the gap left by little Teo.

Her eyes followed her son's tall figure as he went out to the hall, to stand in the open doorway and watch the last of his friends drive off into the night.

I must be one of the luckiest chaps in the world, Oliver thought as the last car roared away and their 'Good-byes' faded into silence. He had everything in the world he wanted, the war was over *and* he had the best family and the best girl in the world.

The street lamps were still on, their glow slightly diffused as the November fog swirled softly around them. It was getting cold as well as damp, he thought. He was about to go indoors when he saw the headlights of a car rounding the corner of Cadogan Gardens. He paused, wondering whether one of his guests was returning for a forgotten possession. A tall, disreputable looking, bearded fellow emerged from the taxi and fumbled in his shabby coat pocket for money to pay off the driver.

Oliver frowned. Something was not quite right, he thought. The bearded man was not wearing the kind of clothes usually associated with people who could afford to hire cabs. The coat was crumpled and shabby and the hat pulled down over the man's head looked somehow sinister. The man turned toward him and involuntarily, Oliver's hand went to his hip where his service revolver would normally have been. As the taxicab drove off into the darkness, with a furtive hesitancy, the man stumbled up the steps toward the house. The hall lights were streaming through the front door, but Oliver's body cast a shadow over the oncomer whose bearded face looked almost black as he confronted Oliver.

"It *is* you, Oliver, isn't it?"

Oliver peered at his visitor suspiciously. He had no intention of allowing so unsavory a character into the house.

"My name *is* Rochford, Sir, but I certainly don't recognize you," he said, standing his ground.

The man gave a soft, amused laugh.

"That's hardly surprising, old chap! I hardly know myself!"

The voice was educated, familiar. Oliver was trying to place it when Jane called to him from inside the house.

"Oliver, do come in and shut the door. It's absolutely freezing!"

"That's not Lucy, is it?" the man said. "Is Lucy there? If she is, I think perhaps you ought to warn her..."

Oliver gasped. For the first time since his childhood, he broke into a nervous stammer.

"G...g...good G...god, it's y...you! For Heaven's s...sake, d...don't s...stand there in the c...cold. Come on in!"

He gave a last long look at the man and charged back into the house. Ignoring Jane who was waiting for him in the hall, he burst into the drawing room, then pulled himself up short as he confronted a bewildered Lucy.

"There's someone here, Lucy...someone you...Don't be frightened. He looks a bit rough but..." He broke off, suddenly at a complete loss for words.

Lucy gazed at him in astonishment.

"What are you talking about, Oliver? Who's here? Why should I be frightened?"

"Because...because...Lucy, it's better you should go out to the hall and see for yourself. I don't believe it. I just don't believe it!"

Lucy lay back against the cushions of her chair and yawned.

"I'm too tired for jokes, Oliver, and I'm certainly too tired to go anywhere!" she said. "And don't expect me to stay up talking to one of your old friends because I'm going to bed as soon as I can drag myself out of this chair. Mother and Uncle Toby went up half an hour ago. The party's over now, little brother!"

Regaining some of his lost composure, Oliver knelt down beside Lucy's chair and took both her hands in his.

"I want you to think, Lucy," he said earnestly. "What would make you the happiest woman in the whole world? If I could give you anything you wanted—*anything*—what would you ask for?"

Lucy ruffled his hair affectionately.

"You're talking in riddles again, Oliver. Anyway—what *do* I want—other than my bed? A sable muff—to match my Paris coat? A new crystal vase to replace the one your squadron commander broke tonight?"

Oliver's face remained unsmiling as he interrupted her.

"Lucy, I'm talking about something you really want *with your whole heart.*"

He saw her face pale, her eyes fill with unmistakable sadness.

Oliver was being cruel, Lucy thought, reminding her of Alexis at such a moment. He must know very well that what she wanted most, she could never have. Her heart gave a sudden jolt as she stared into Oliver's eyes. What had he said? Someone here? Someone she should go and see...?

She looked at him mutely, not daring to believe in such a possibility.

"You'd want Alexis back safe and sound—if it were possible, wouldn't you?" Oliver said doggedly. "If a miracle could happen, you'd want it to be Alexis. Lucy, miracles can happen...do happen and..."

Lucy sprang up and ran past him. Her feet seemed to move unbearably slowly as she raced to the hall. Her heart was pounding so fiercely, her breath was coming in gasps. Then she saw him. There with his back to the front door, stood Alexis.

But for Oliver's warning, Lucy thought, as she flung herself into his open arms, she might not have known him. At first, only the green eyes searching her face were recognizable, and then his voice as he said huskily:

"Lucy, my own sweet Lucy!"

Tears of joy rolled down Lucy's face as she hugged and kissed him and then hugged him again.

"Alexis, it's you! It's really you!" she cried. "You're home! And I love you and, oh, darling, your beard. You look so fierce! You look..."

She broke off, suddenly aware how thin and pale and exhausted he looked despite the smile on his face. His clothes were shabby and he wore a high-collared seaman's jersey beneath the threadbare overcoat. His tall, Russian-style boots were covered with dust and so scuffed Lucy could not be sure of the color. Her eyes returned to his face which she covered once more with kisses.

"I thought you were dead!" she cried. "We all thought so. Alexis, *where have you been?*"

"Didn't Fanshaw notify you?" Alexis asked. "I telephoned him from Newcastle when I docked and he promised he'd find a way to break the news that I was back. I came down on the night train. I hadn't dared to hope you'd be here in London. I expected you might still be in Epernay—or at best at Rochford."

"Fate must have made me come here to meet you!" Lucy cried as she hugged and kissed him yet again. "We all came up to celebrate Oliver's engagement to Jane, Alexis—and I didn't really want to come because you wouldn't be here. Oh, I can't believe it, I can't!"

Alexis was regarding her in astonishment.

"Oliver's engagement to Jane?" he echoed. "But I thought..."

"It's all right, Alexis. They are only cousins. I will explain it all to you some other time. But for the moment I can't think of anything but how wonderful it is that you have come back. Is it really true?"

Alexis looked down into her starry eyes, his own glowing with happiness.

"The thought of you, Lucy, helped me to survive," he said quietly. "Whenever I felt low—when things were a bit rough— I told myself that I must get back to look after you. I did promise to come back to you and I was determined not to break that promise."

He was shocked to see the look of happiness in Lucy's eyes suddenly give way to one of suffering. As she gazed up at him, her eyes were filled with a profound sadness.

"I needed you so much," she murmured brokenly, dreading the thought of the terrible news she must now give him about Teo's death. "Something awful happened in January...so awful that I can hardly bear to tell you about it. I would give anything in the world not to have to spoil your homecoming...and yet..."

Very gently, Alexis put two fingers across her lips.

"It's all right, my darling. Fanshaw told me on the telephone. I know already that our little Teo was drowned. Later, we will talk about it, and you shall tell me how it happened. I only wish to God I had been near you to help you bear such an ordeal. You mustn't cry, my love. We must both try to remember the happy years that she enjoyed."

Lucy's eyes were full of tears.

"When Mama and I visited Teo's grave, she said I must try to believe God had a purpose of His own—that He lent Teo to us for a little while in order to bring us together—and that then He reclaimed her."

She drew a long sigh.

"It seemed such a cruel thing for Him to do and I couldn't think of God as someone kind," she said thoughtfully. "But perhaps I was wrong, Alexis. He has sent you back to me." She smiled tremulously.

"It is the future that matters now, Lucy," Alexis said. "In a way, it will be like a new start to our marriage. I would like it if we had children. I always wanted a son, you know."

Lucy pulled his head down to hers and kissed him fiercely. She could feel his heart pounding against her own and it was only with reluctance that she broke away.

"You must be cold and hungry, and we can't stay here, Alexis. Shall we go and tell the others—if Oliver hasn't already done so? There's lots of food—and champagne."

"Sounds like the party is just beginning—anyway for me!"

Alexis said smiling again as with his arm around her waist, they walked into the drawing room.

Just for a moment, Lucy was jealous as her family surrounded Alexis and she had to stand apart from him. But as soon as they had all given him a hug, his arm reached out to encircle her shoulders. They sat down side by side on the sofa as Oliver and Jane hurried off to find food and drink for them. Alice came downstairs to see what all the commotion was about and ran up again to fetch Willow and Toby. Soon, there was a large, smiling circle grouped around Alexis as he told them his story.

It was not he who had been shot a year ago, he related, but his bodyguard, Rogers. Rogers had been picked off by a sniper at one of the windows of the house where they were hiding. Alexis knew that his own chances of survival would be far greater if he were thought by his captors to be from their working-class background; that as an aristocrat, he stood no chance at all. He had exchanged clothes and papers with the dead man, switching every clue to their identities. Two days later, when he was finally caught, he had been questioned for almost a week before his captors were satisfied that he posed no threat to their communist regime. But as a punishment for serving a Royalist, he was sentenced to three years hard labor in the Baltic port of Memel.

"I worked there for six months in the coal yards," he told his spellbound audience. "Most of the time I was nearly starving, and all of the time I was so weary I was almost immune to the conditions I worked in or the squalor I lived in. I realized that if I did not escape I would soon be physically too weak ever to be able to do so. So I made my plans and about a month ago, I just walked away. No one stopped me. I stole money to buy food. I hung about the railway yards and jumped a freight train to Danzig. It was bitterly cold, hiding as I was under a tarpaulin in an open wagon. Several times we were shunted into a siding and I thought I would freeze to death as night fell."

"It must be pretty bad so far up north at this time of year," Oliver commented. Alexis nodded.

"A lot of those Baltic ports just freeze solid and have to be closed," he said. "But I managed somehow to survive and traveled another two hundred and fifty miles or so in a carriage, to Rostock. Being able to speak the language, I was able to bluff my way through a ticket barrier. But I wasn't so lucky at Rostock. I had to walk or beg a lift from there to Esbjerg—that's in Denmark. There I was more fortunate for I found a cattle boat leaving that night for Liverpool. The captain was pro-British and having told him part of my story, he agreed at once to take me on board. We arrived in Newcastle this afternoon."

"But why didn't you let us know, old chap?" Toby asked. "We'd have come to meet you..."

Alexis smiled.

"I hoped you had been warned!" he said. "Fanshaw did promise me he would telephone. I think I gave him quite a shock, poor fellow. He'd been convinced I was dead!"

"Oh, dear, I think I may have heard the telephone—and I was too busy to answer it just then," Jane confessed. "I am sorry, Alexis. I thought it was just someone else offering congratulations. Our engagement was announced in the *Times* recently and the telephone was ringing all day!"

Alexis gave her a kindly pat on the hand.

"Maybe it was more of a surprise this way!"

"You certainly surprised me!" Oliver laughed. "Do you know, Alexis, I actually reached for my revolver when you started to walk toward me? Shades of life at the Front, I suppose. I shall have to get used to the fact that doubtful-looking characters are no longer the enemy!"

Between sentences, Alexis had been eating ravenously and Lucy was shocked by the hollows in his cheeks, only partially concealed by his beard. His high cheekbones seemed more prominent than ever and the dark shadows beneath his eyes gave them an added depth and luminosity.

"Alexis," she said anxiously, "you look exhausted."

He nodded.

"What I would like most, I think, is a hot bath. I seem to have been traveling for weeks and weeks. The Danish captain was good enough to give me these clothes—the ones I had were little more than rags—but although I was very grateful, I doubt if they are particularly acceptable!"

Willow stood up and said firmly:

"It's nearly four o'clock and I think it's high time we brought this day to an end and retired for the night." She kissed Alexis and smiled at Lucy. "I'm so very happy for you both," she said. "Tomorrow, when Alexis has had a good rest, we'll hear more about his adventures."

Only Lucy was unaware of any tiredness as she waited upon

Alexis, running a bath for him, finding a pair of pajamas and warming them in front of the gas fire she had turned on in her bedroom. Alexis wanted to shave off his beard but Lucy would not hear of it and in any event, she could not find his razor, she told him. When finally he came out of the bathroom, he looked more like his former self. Lucy flung herself into his arms.

"Oh, darling!" she said ruefully. "When last we were together, it was I who was the convalescent. Now I am going to have to feed you up. You're so thin!"

His arm around her waist, he sat down in the chair in front of the fire and drew her onto his lap.

"I was so lonely without you, Alexis!" Lucy murmured. "I could not believe at first that you were really never coming back. But Fanshaw finally wrote last July sending me your letter to him, in which you told him he would only receive it if you were dead..."

Alexis' arm tightened around her.

"I was afraid of that!" he murmured. "But I knew I had to convince the Reds that I wasn't Count Zemski—and leaving that letter on poor Rogers' body was, as it happened, a deciding factor when they were trying to make up their minds who we both were. During the time they were questioning me, they asked for a sample of my handwriting. I knew they suspected that I might have switched identities with Rogers and I disguised my writing—made one or two spelling mistakes; used some bad grammar. That seemed to convince them. I am so very sorry, my dearest, that you suffered because of it!"

Lucy leaned over and kissed him.

"I don't care now I know it saved your life. Alexis..." She paused as she tried to find the right words to say what needed to be said: "I think what worried me almost as much as your safety was my fear that you might have stopped loving me."

His voice was gentle but indignant as he replied:

"But how could you have imagined such nonsense, Lucy? When I left you after that night we spent in each other's arms...and next morning...how could you possibly have doubted me?"

Lucy drew a deep breath. She stood up and looked down at him white-faced.

"Those photographs...of Maurice Dubois' paintings of me...in Uncle Pelham's tallboy..." she said hesitantly.

"Oh, those!" Alexis replied immediately. "But Lucy, why should I stop loving you because of them?" He sounded genuinely astonished.

Lucy bit her lip nervously and said in a small desperate voice:

"The one called '*La Perle*,' Alexis. I kept thinking how shocked you must have been, seeing me like—like a harlot. I wouldn't have blamed you if you'd turned against me; if you'd wondered how on earth you could ever have married me..."

Alexis stood up and gently covered her mouth with his hand to prevent her saying more.

"Lucy, we will be starting a new life together now the war is over," he said quietly. "It's very important, I think, that we should understand each other so that we can have the kind of marriage we both want. So I shall be as honest with you as I hope you will be with me. Yes, the first time I saw that picture I was shocked. Then I was sad. Then I realized that it was only Dubois' projection of the future and that he was really trying to illustrate what could happen to a child of the streets—that charming, innocent child in his other sketches and paintings of you. He was a clever artist and it is a matter of regret that I cannot allow those paintings to be shown publicly—*not because I am ashamed of them, Lucy*—but because of the danger it could present to your reputation. But I shall keep them all—and treasure them. They are as much part of you, the woman I love so much, as the Lucy I know. I am a very fortunate man because I have married three women in one, have I not? Little innocent Sophie, bewildered and vulnerable on the threshold of a new life so different from her Convent days; La Perle—that young, immensely provocative, exciting woman who understands men's needs and desires and promises fulfillment; and Lucy—my Lucy—tender, adorable, fascinating—and above all loving. I love all three of you, my darling, and I would not change any single part of you!"

It was a long speech, but for Lucy it was the final answer to all her fears; the vindication of her guilt; the expiation of the wrongs done to her at birth. If she had spent her childhood at Rochford where she belonged, she might never have met and married Alexis—and she regretted no single one of the hardships, no moment of suffering since it had all led to this understanding of love between them.

Alexis smiled as he looked at her radiant face.

"You cannot imagine how often I have dreamed of us here, in this very room, alone together," he said softly. "Come to bed, my love, I want to show you how much I love you."

The color spread quickly into Lucy's cheeks. Shyly, she began to remove her clothes, aware that Alexis' eyes were on her as she undressed. He climbed into bed and lay back against the pillows waiting for her to come to him.

"No, don't put on a nightgown!" he said as she stood naked beside the bed. "You are so beautiful, Lucy. I don't think I could ever tire of looking at you." He held out his arms and Lucy went to him.

Their passion was mutual and overwhelming. They made love with a desperate urgency as if each was afraid it might be for the last time. The shyness and uncertainty Lucy had known was suddenly gone as she responded to the man she loved with total abandon. When finally she lay beside him, her arm across his waist, she drew a long, shuddering sigh of happiness.

"Zandra is convinced that the war ended because she willed it so," she murmured as she settled her head in the crook of his shoulder. "Miracles are her latest passion, Alexis, but I'm afraid I told her I didn't believe in them. Now I do."

In the darkness, Alexis smiled.

"I knew miracles could happen when I came to see you in France," he said softly. "That moment when I looked at you and knew that you loved me. I had almost given up hope! And then you smiled that special smile—and I just knew it would all come right."

"I understand!" Lucy said drowsily. Love, she thought, was such a boundless emotion, and yet as her blind *poilu* had taught her, it did not necessarily need words or actions or even deeds to express its enormity. It could be revealed in as simple a thing as a woman's smile.

She reached up to touch his face. But Alexis was asleep. Lucy lay quietly beside him in perfect contentment, listening to the steady comforting beat of his heart.

Chapter 30

December 1918

Two days before Christmas, Toby received a letter in his morning post which Willow realized immediately must contain news of importance for he ignored the crisp new morning edition of the *Times*, took off his spectacles, cleaned them without a word and then read the letter through a second time.

It was from the Commanding Officer of his grandfather's old regiment. Written on regimental note paper, it read:

"It has come to my knowledge that your brother, the Hon. Rupert Rochford was shot by the Germans in April last year. His bravery was brought to my attention by one of the many officers whose lives he saved.

"I have now had time to look into your brother's activities during the war and feel you might like to know that Lt. Bradley was but one of many of the officers and men whom your brother assisted in escaping from Brussels, thus enabling them to return to their own countries and eventually to fight again.

"The name of Rochford is, of course, already a prominent one in this regiment's rôle of valor. As you will know, your grandfather, General Lord Cedric Rochford, distinguished himself both in the Crimea and in India.

"Although your brother was not a member of the armed forces, he acted with the courage and total disregard for personal safety that one normally attributes to a soldier. Had he been a member of my regiment I would have recommended him for the Military Cross.

"Since this is not possible, I would like you to consider this letter to be one of recognition by me and my regiment of your brother's gallantry.

"I am, Sir, Your obedient servant

"Major General Sir John Cornwall-Clyne, Commanding Officer."

Silently Toby handed the letter to Willow. When Willow had read it, she looked up with tears in her eyes.

"The irony of this, Toby," she said bitterly, "is that Grand-mère is not alive to see the grandson she despised for his weakness now honored in such glowing terms."

Toby nodded.

"It goes to prove, does it not, the fallibility of making judgments prematurely. Grandmère failed to appreciate that the Rochford blood ran in Rupert's veins as surely as it did in my grandfather's."

"I know it's silly of me," Willow said as she dried her eyes. "Rupert can't know of this, yet I am so happy for him. He'd have been very proud. We must have the letter framed, Toby. Oliver may want to show it one day to his children."

Oliver's squadron had now returned from France and he had been given Christmas leave. Mark was likewise on leave from Roehampton and Henry was making good progress at Glenfield. He and Eleanor and their parents were spending Christmas Day at Rochford—a suggestion made by the thoughtful Jane who felt the bereaved parents might notice less at Rochford the absence of their two soldier sons.

Willow was more and more convinced that Jane was going to prove that ideal wife for Oliver. Her quiet sensitivity was a perfect complement to her son's more extrovert, adventurous nature. Although he had not yet left the R.F.C. he was already engaged in serious talks with Sam Sharples concerning the development of a commercial airline that would carry passengers across the Channel to Europe "just as if they were in coach—only miles quicker!" he had told his mother and Toby. It sounded to her like a madcap scheme but Alexis was encouraging him. It was Oliver's hope that he would be able to create worthwhile occupations for both Henry and Mark in "his new airline." Sam Sharples had offered to fund the idea.

"I dare say nothing will ever come of it," Willow said to Toby, but in her heart she was not quite so certain.

All "the children," as she called the younger generation, were busy decorating the big Christmas tree in the hall. She could hear their voices as she sat with Toby in the library. She could not hear Zandra's piping tones and a little of her joy in the letter about Rupert evaporated. The child had been deeply affected by the death of her favorite patient, Private Humphries. The poor man had been taken back to hospital in Tunbridge Wells. He had had to have an emergency operation, which, sadly, had failed to save his life. The little girl had been heartbroken.

"He was getting better, I just *know* he was!" Zandra wept. "He stopped altogether being cross and now I'll *never* be able to finish reading him the story about Florence Nightingale."

"She's really grieving, Toby," Willow had remarked. "I've never known her so quiet and mopey!"

"Don't concern yourself too much, my dear," Toby had advised her. "Our Zandra is made of cork—she'll bob up again given a little time!"

That time had now come, Willow realized as Zandra burst into the library, her pigtail flying, her cheeks pink with happiness. She subsided onto the floor in front of Willow's chair, her blue eyes staring solemnly into Willow's as she said:

"I've just worked it out, Aunt Willow—about Humphries, I mean. I've been very worried ever since he died. I was afraid God might not let him into Heaven because he used to say he didn't believe in God." She gave a deep sigh. "But I thought and thought and then I remembered the day before they took him away in the ambulance. He asked me to read him that nice Psalm Twenty-Three—the one that goes: *'Yea, though I walk through the valley of the shadow of death.'* Well, at the end Humphries said 'Amen' and that's a sort of a bit of a prayer, isn't it? So you see, Aunt Willow, he *must* have believed, mustn't he. I think he's in Heaven now and God has given him a new leg and made him Captain of the football team—Humphries was a Manchester United supporter, you see, and he always used to say that the nearest thing to Heaven he could imagine was to play for them. I know a Heavenly XI wouldn't be *quite* the same as Manchester United but I still think he'd like it—don't you, Aunt Willow?"

Toby was hard put to hide his smile until Zandra left the room. He went over to Willow and still grinning broadly, he said:

"I told you Zandra would sort it all out to her satisfaction. One day, Willow, that child will be sorting the world out for us—mark my words!"

Christmas morning was bright and sunny. The little church of St. Stephen's was full, although with so many gaps in the family pews, it was perhaps inevitable that the vicar's sermon could not be as entirely joyful as befitted the day. He, too, had lost an only son and there were tears in his eyes as he referred to those who had given up their lives for their country.

Nevertheless, he told them, the great sacrifice had not been in vain. This first Christmas after the war must be a celebration not only of the birth of Christ but of the rebirth of a Peace so dearly won. Those absent loved ones were with their families in spirit, he finished his sermon, and would not be forgotten.

Zandra tugged at Willow's arm.

"I think Humphries is here in spirit too!" she whispered. "Just for Christmas Day, I mean."

Willow nodded, her eyes full of tears as the service came to an end with the vicar's blessing and his quiet intonation of Laurence Bynion's poem:

"... *at the going down of the sun and in the morning, we will remember them.*"

"So many who will never return, Toby," she murmured as he tucked his arm through hers and led her out into the bright December sunshine. "Philip, Rupert, George, Howard, Richard, Max..."

Toby nodded.

"The servants, too—Watson, the Higgins brothers, Purkiss, Pilcher, Walker..."

"But thank God, not Violet's Bill," Willow said with a sigh. He had been repatriated three weeks after the Armistice and Dodie and James had lent them the little house in Cornwall for a second honeymoon. James had decided to sell the house after Christmas and he and Dodie would make their home permanently at Rochford—a decision that had brought Willow great happiness for she had dreaded the departure of Zandra, of all the children the one to whom she was closest.

Her eyes wandered to young Mark struggling so bravely to walk with his artificial leg; to Henry limping beside him on crutches.

"We must be grateful for those who have been spared," Toby reminded her gently.

Willow's glance followed Toby's eyes as they lingered on the figures of Lucy and Alexis walking in front of them. The tears dried on her lashes and she smiled.

"You are right, as always," she said. "It's wonderful to see

Lucy so happy—and so much in love with her Alexis. Do you know, Toby, I have found a word that exactly describes our Lucy—she is a Wilderling. It is the name given to a cultivated flower that has managed to survive in the wild—just as Lucy has done. Despite that terrible childhood, she has grown into a beautiful, mature, contented woman as capable as you or I of love."

Toby nodded.

"We have much to rejoice about," he said quietly. "Most important of all, my darling, we can rejoice that this horrible war has ended. Those lives have not been lost in vain since we can be assured now that the new generation will grow up at peace with the rest of the world."

He watched as little Zandra and Alice, with young Jamie between them, ran down the church path to the lyche-gate, their laughter as bright as the winter sunshine.

"That was a war to end all further wars," he said solemnly. "There'll never, ever be another one, Willow—not in our lifetime and not in theirs. Such madness cannot happen again."

Willow smiled as she gazed into Toby's comforting eyes.

"No!" she said with complete conviction. "It will never happen again."

ABOUT THE AUTHOR:

Claire Lorrimer was born in Sussex, England. She has travelled extensively around the world, but has made her home in the lovely Kent Weald where she lives in a four hundred-year-old, oak-beamed cottage. She enjoys such outdoor activities as gardening, tennis, skiing, and golf, and loves to travel and entertain, but her life is centered mainly around her three children, her work, and her lovely home.

Miss Lorrimer comes from an artistic family that includes several authors, artists, and musicians. She, herself, is a prolific writer with many novels to her credit, including the phenomenally bestselling MAVREEN and THE CHATELAINE, to which THE WILDERLING is the sequel. She believes that once started, a story writes itself.

Ballantine's World of Historical Romance...

"Are you going to stay with me tonight?" she asked curiously. "I'm not in the least tired, Alexis."

"I love you!" he said. "With my body, I thee worship. I meant those words, Lucy. I want you—only you."

Lucy made no protest as he lifted the night-gown over her head and let it drop to the floor. The curve of her waist and hips, the silky texture of her skin, the beauty of her breasts were both strange and yet astonishingly familiar.

He kissed her passionately with a desperate hunger as her legs parted and her body arched to receive him. But as he was about to lower himself into her, he felt her face twist aside as she freed her mouth.

"I love you, Lucy!" he murmured. "Don't turn away from me. You do love me a little, don't you?"

He felt a slight stiffening of Lucy's body beneath his own.

"I'm trying to do what you want, Alexis. I mean to be a good wife to you, I really do." She reached out her hand and touched his cheek. "I want you to be as happy as I am. I'll do anything you want."

Also by Claire Lorrimer
Published by Ballantine Books:

THE CHATELAINE